Split Infinities

Split Infinities

BY

Bill Bailey

SPLIT INFINITIES - *Blurb*

About the Book

In this potent and compelling tale, sexual depravity, corruption and violence splatter the pages as people and ideas are irrevocably locked in a battle that may mean the life or death of the earth itself. The global power of transnational corporations continues to grow as it spawns political and paramilitary heads to its gargantuan body. Pockets of resistance form in Europe and America. A small band in England are nearly overwhelmed as an ex-patriot American anchors the group which is led by a distinguished government permanent secretary of state. Kidnappings, rescues and assassinations raise the stakes when a media tycoon finally meets his match in a dangerous struggle with a beautiful Texan blonde.

SPLIT INFINITIES

by Bill Bailey

CHAPTER ONE

The sun hung low in the sky, drawing the mosquitoes from the stagnant pools in dense clouds. You could see them, airborne and floating, when you looked east just above the trees, against the dark blue sky. There must have been millions, like locusts in plague years. But these feathery insects came every evening, all searching for warm bodies and warm blood. They were big, too, but not big enough to feel before they bit you.

Etymologists are said to be able to trace the origins of language through the varieties of root words. Some languages are found to contain many basic references to water, and researchers suppose these languages must have developed near the sea or chains of lakes and rivers. In Panama there were at least sixteen different words for mosquito, if you included local slang. It was a low, swampy country, and when the United States dug the canal many died from Yellow Fever. Of course the United States did not actually dig the canal. They provided the *management* and machinery and finance to dig it. Any actual digging was done cheaply by local and imported Indian and black labour.

J C Ritter's ranch was not that near the Canal Zone. It was as prime a piece of land as you could find in Panama, just over 20,000 acres, most of it excellent pasture for grazing a fine herd. Ritter bought the ranch fifteen years ago for twenty five cents an acre. Plus $50,000 cash to the President of Panama, a Cadillac to a fat generalissimo, and two Buicks and a pickup truck to local chieftains. Ritter sold his Texas ranch for nine and a half million before the oil market crashed. His timing had been perfect, and his profit was phenomenal. Five million had been wisely and safely invested and the rest used as working capital

1

for the Panama ranch, which he had sentimentally named The Rose of Texas. Perhaps it was the only rose growing in Panama. His herd was more a hobby than a money earner, and Ritter reckoned himself a scientific breeder. Basically they were Friesians crossbred with native Texan Longhorns, and they were now throwing true.

J C Ritter was tall and rangy and was nearly fifty-eight. He stood six feet three inches without his cowboy boots but had never acquired the overhanging gut so many lean men develop in middle age. And he was never a loud Texan. He was one of the quiet, dry ones. He had light blue eyes, a tanned and tough hide and black hair trimmed short. His Stetson was pulled down to his eyebrows and he was watching the pilot reading through the navigation instructions in the little flight office built on Ritter's private airport. It wasn't that big an airport, but the runway was long enough for his Lear Jet. And it was certainly long enough for the light plane this pilot was going to fly.

Ritter was sitting behind the old oak desk which had various names and oaths carved in several places. The pilot, Buck Colby, was sitting in a battered chrome tube armchair studying the papers. Another man had his back to them and stared out the window. This was Enrico Gomez, a man J C Ritter knew well and trusted.

Gomez was a small, tense man in his early forties. He, too, had short black hair, but it was thicker than Ritter's and had to be smacked down with pomade. He wore an open white shortsleeve shirt and carried a windbreaker under his arm. And from the back you could see he was wearing a shoulder holster harness. In fact Enrico Gomez was a killer, a very good one. Ritter kept him on retainer, then paid him good money for special jobs like this one. Gomez was going along on the flight to make sure the pilot behaved himself and to deal with any unexpected incidents. Gomez could do this. Gomez was a real professional and never, ever opened his mouth when he should keep it closed.

Buck Colby stretched back in the chair, thumbed up the bill of his dozer cap and wiped the sweat from his exposed forehead. The office was air conditioned, but it had only been turned on about forty minutes ago when they first entered. Colby was a little nervous, because he knew the cargo was drugs. Either cocaine or heroin or possibly both. This was the first time he had done anything this illegal, and he was well aware what would happen if he was caught. But it was damn good money, and he needed money. The man who recruited him in Houston, Sam Jasper, assured him it was a no-fail situation. The man he would be working for had high government contacts, and it was a special assignment. It sounded OK so far, but Colby knew he was low man on the totem pole here. He would only be told what he had to know, and the things he didn't know worried him.

Colby had been in Vietnam, arriving during the final two weeks to help pull out US personnel from the collapsing country. He told friends and relatives he saw fierce combat, but in fact his helicopter wasn't even fired upon. His story sounded much better the way he told it now to anyone who was interested enough to listen. Colby was, however, a good pilot. He had worked the oil rigs in the Gulf, done some crop dusting and was a regular employee for a while in a small Louisiana airline before it went bankrupt a year ago. But now times were hard for pilots, and there seemed to be six or seven for every job on offer. This little number might be just enough to set him up. If. If everything went smoothly. If there was no doublecross. If, if, if. He shifted again in the chair. The longer he was unemployed, the more he worried. The more he worried, the more he ate. And most of the extra weight settled around his hips and underneath his chin. Soon he was going to be too fat to pass the medical anymore.

Colby tidied the papers and stuck them back under the clip. He looked up at the Texan staring patiently at him and shrugged. "Seems easy enough, Mr Ritter. Fly it with my eyes closed."

"Keep your eyes open, son," Ritter said. "You drift outta that twenty mile corridor once you cross into US territory, you gonna find the boys in blue all over your ass. And I'm gonna lose a lot of money. And," he nodded toward Gomez, "my good friend Enrico is gonna be awful upset if that happens."

Buck Colby laughed nervously. "Ah, no chance of that, Mr Ritter. I know my job."

3

Ritter's eyes were cold. "Do you?"

"Well, you can ask old Sam Jasper. He knows what I can do. Got a good record. Never done anything like this, though."

"Yeah," Ritter said. "That's one of the thangs worryin' me. 'Pears to me you're kind of a weak man."

Colby laughed again without conviction. "Well...no, I mean, hell, I was in Vietnam, you know. Saw a lot of action. *That* doesn't worry me. It's just...you know, the cargo. Hell, if they catch me doing something like that...god, it's not worth thinking about..."

"Then don't think about it."

"And the gentleman over at the window..."

"That's Enrico Gomez," Ritter drawled. "He ain't Messkin, incidentally. He's Cuban. One of the good Cubans who got the hell outta Castro's fuckhole."

"I mean, does he have to go along? Why can't I just..."

"Aw, Enrico's only hitchin' a ride, boy. You gonna drop him off with the plane in Miami after you finish your business in Texas."

Enrico Gomez turned around, aware he was being talked about. He had a face like a rat, except for the eyes. His nose was large, and the chin was small. But his eyes were nearly black and had no expression at all. He never seemed to blink.

He stared blankly at Buck Colby, who shifted nervously and crossed one leg over the other, lowering his gaze. "Yeah, I was wondering why the flight plan included Miami..."

Ritter leaned over the desk and stared from under the brim of his Stetson. "You don't have to do any wonderin' in this job, son. It's not a wonderin' job. Think of yourself as just a taxi driver goin' from one place to another. All you need to know is how to get there."

Colby laughed again, trying to relax. "Yeah, yeah, that's the safest, isn't it? The safest way. For me. Yeah. You're right, Mr Ritter..."

Ritter nodded his head toward the papers in Colby's hand. "Now hand that clipboard to Enrico. He'll keep it from now on. The last thang I want is for that flight plan to work its way outta that plane and into somebody's pocket."

4

Colby leaned forward and handed the board to Gomez with a smile. Gomez took it but did not return the smile. He put it under his arm with the windbreaker.

"When you get to Miami," Ritter continued, "Enrico will show you where to park the plane and get your money for you. You go along to the bank with him, and he'll get a cashier's check for you. Now, I recommend you pay that check into an account right there, 'cause carryin' anythang of value on the streets of Miami is like dressin' up in feathers at a turkey shoot."

Colby stood up, hitching his belt over his bulging stomach. He looked at his watch. "Well, I better warm up the engine. It's already getting dark, and I've got to at least be able to see the tops of the trees for the takeoff."

Ritter wordlessly shoved a can of aerosol across the desk.

"What's that for?" asked Colby.

"Unless you spray some of that all over you, I estimate you would lose about a quart and a half of blood before you reached the cockpit."

"Blood?" Colby's expression changed from false bonhomie to concern.

Ritter leaned back in the swivel chair, and it squeaked. "We got bigger mosquitoes here than they got in East Texas, son, and the ones in East Texas are the size of buzzards."

Colby took the can and sprayed his hands, face and neck.

"Spray your clothes, too," said Ritter. "These are sabre-tooth mosquitoes. I've had 'em bite right through my boots."

When Buck Colby had finished with the aerosol, Gomez picked it up and sprayed directly into his own face, then soaked his clothes with it before putting on the windbreaker.

"Enrico's been here before," observed Ritter. "He went outside the screen door to throw a cigar out once, and five minutes after he got back in his face looked like a pineapple."

Colby held out his hand and Ritter grabbed it almost reluctantly. "Well, sir, I hope we can do business again soon."

Ritter held on to the pilot's hand. "You do this one without trippin' over your dick, and we'll see." He turned away toward the water cooler as the two men left for the plane.

5

Once the plane was in the air Buck Colby felt a lot better. Gomez was sitting behind him with the clipboard, and Colby realised conversation was out of the question. But that was alright. He loved flying, and flying at night could be very peaceful despite the roar of the engine. The stars were bright, the air was fresh and the sense of freedom was invigorating. He had slept in a huge bedroom of the big ranch house until well after noon. A maid had served him breakfast in bed, more than half of which he left on the plate. It was a huge steak with a half dozen fried eggs on the top and what looked like a pound of prime bacon encircling it. There were two jugs, one of coffee and one of fresh orange juice, and he drank most of both. Because he had been hung over. He recalled drinking most of a bottle of Benchmark with a groan. It always seemed like a good idea at the time, and he felt more comfortable around strangers after a few drinks. He relaxed and wasn't so awkward anymore. Men seemed to take him more seriously, and women were more attracted. Thinking of women made him involuntarily suck in his gut. He had to do something about his weight soon.

The ranch house - what was the name? Rose of Texas, that was it - was a huge, sprawling structure. It was all built on one floor, but you could hardly call it a bungalow. It circled a courtyard where there was a gigantic swimming pool carved in the shape of the state of Texas. Ritter had a wife - or was it his woman? - a gorgeous dark haired girl of Spanish origin. She couldn't have been more than 25 and had breasts the size and colour of coconuts, but smooth and soft-looking. The girl lurked around the pool without her top on, wearing some kind of thong. It was the first thing he saw after he finished his breakfast and opened the French doors onto the courtyard, and he very nearly collapsed with a combination of embarrassment and desire. But she had ignored him and didn't seem to care whether he looked or not.

Ritter seemed to treat the girl only a little better than the servants, and there were plenty of those. Cooks, gardeners, maids and handymen. For Ritter it must be like living in paradise, he thought wistfully. Ritter sat back like a god and gave orders to be carried out by these or those people and fired

6

anybody who gave him trouble, hiring another from the long queue the next day. He wondered if the girl was like that. If he fired her, would he hold auditions for the next household sexual ornament?

Colby looked up at the stars, so much brighter than they were on the ground, and shrugged. He was not much more than a servant, somebody with a skill to do dirty work for the boss who had the money. If he did it well, there would be another job. If not, there were plenty more where Colby came from. How he yearned to be like Skinner some day when he wouldn't have to worry about having to make impressions or charm people into liking him. Then you could say, fuck 'em, do what you want. Hire a piece of ass, and if she doesn't give what you want, fire her. Same thing with drivers, cooks, maids, fuckin' pilots...

He turned half around and asked Gomez about the next bearing quadrant.

* * *

Deputy Sheriff Bilge Butler was very pleased with himself as he drove his cruiser slowly down the dirt track to his favourite spot of all. At one time this had been a nice little ranch run by a local family out of Franklin, but that family had died out and the land had been bought by some big shot out of town who never used it. The brush had grown up, the fences hadn't been repaired and the two old hunting lodges were falling apart. It was a damn shame, thought Bilge Butler in a brief moment of civic concern. On the other hand, it provided one of the most private shagging grounds he had ever found in his life. He could cruise in, close the gate, drive way out of sight behind one of the rundown hunting lodges and have himself a fine time.

The Deputy could smell Ruby Faye Pyle's perfume, and it smelled real sweet. This was his goddamned lucky night. Now that was a fact. Ruby Faye had been a Franklin High School beauty queen about eight or nine years ago, and Butler very well remembered seeing her dressed in a white gown, sitting up on that float just like an angel with no wings. She had been Ruby

7

Faye Shaw then. That was before she married Hoyt Pyle, the young lawyer out at the Harrington Ranch. Then about four years ago Ruby Faye had started going a bit wild, and rumour had it she was sleeping first with the football coach, then the Lucas boy who taught art at Franklin High and then Nicky Porter, who sold medical books out of Fort Worth. Hoyt Pyle either didn't know about all this or didn't care. He was probably too busy himself with the daughter out at the Ranch.

Bilge Butler had pulled her over about 2.30am on the old Paris road. She had been doing over 70 miles an hour in a 45 zone. When she blew in the breathalyser she damned near melted the thing. And on a hunch Butler had asked for her handbag. When he looked inside, sure enough, there was about half an ounce of marijuana rolled up alongside some of those fancy long cigarette papers. She had the top down on her new Mercedes convertible, and he leaned on the door and shook his head sadly. She was looking up at him with those big brown eyes of hers. She was wearing a light blue summer dress cut low enough to give a hint of her tits, but it was the creamy, wonderful looking skin he was gazing at as he shook his head.

"There's nothin' I can do, Ruby Faye. Now, you know I'd like to. I know your maw, knowed her for years." In fact Bilge Butler had been two grades behind her mother. He was fifty three years old this year. He pushed his uniform hat up from his forehead. "But you got three thangs here. And all of 'em are bad. Nearly thirty miles over the speed limit. You're drunk. And, worst of all, you got a bunch of illegal drugs on you. Now one of those thangs, hell, since I know your maw and know you're a good girl gone a little off track, I might have been able to ignore." He shook his head again. "But all three, I just cain't do it."

"Aw, come on, Bilge," she drawled, pouting her lips slightly. "I wasn't hurtin' nobody. Had a couple of drinks, drivin' a little too fast, OK..."

The Deputy held up the grass. "And what about this, young miss?"

8

She shook her head impatiently and used a finger to hitch her shoulder length hair over one ear. It was beautiful hair, he thought, coloured just like new straw.

"Oh, you know everybody smokes that stuff now. It's old hat in today's world. Judge Carmichael, he smokes it, you know that!"

Butler shook his head again. "No, I don't know that, Miss Ruby Faye. I've only heard tell. I've never seen him once. And in the book, you know it's a hard drug. You know what it leads to. And you know it's illegal. 'Gainst the law, just like drinkin' and drivin'. So...I'm afraid I'm gonna have to take you in now. I don't wanna do it, but I got a conscience, and I got my duty as a peace officer to look to. And I wanna warn you, Ruby Faye, that this is bound to cost you a little time in jail. I'm gonna do my best, but I just don't think Judge Carmichael is gonna like it one little bit." He was being very fatherly, his voice full of kind concern.

Ruby Faye Pyle looked down and bit her lip. It had been a lousy night, a fuck-up right from the beginning. One way or the other she was *not* going to go back to that lousy jail and have to call Hoyt in Texarcana. He would start screaming about his career and how could she do such a thing to him. Then there was her mother. She could just hear that whining, sanctimonious woman now. No. It was going to just have to be the other way. She knew about Deputy Sheriff Bilge Butler, and she knew what he was really saying as he leaned his fat hands on her beautiful white car. It was going to cost her, but it was not going to cost her as much as the other way. True, she was a little drunk. That was because she had been sitting with Henrietta waiting for Nicky to turn up. They only had four Tequila Sunrises, her favourite cocktail. But Nicky didn't show, so she and Henrietta drank and talked in front of the television until two in the morning. Damn Nicky! That was the last chance he was going to get. There were other flowers on the vine for a frisky young woman in Franklin, Texas.

Ruby Faye Pyle looked up at the Deputy, her big eyes wide. With two fingers of her right hand she lifted the hem of her blue dress just far enough so the cop could see the top of her stocking.

She had even dressed in her fancy underwear, anticipating a steamy session in the back of Nicky's Lincoln.

"Do ya'll really have to go to all that trouble of arrestin' me, Bilge?" Her voice was as sweet as honeysuckle dew.

Deputy Butler looked at the leg under the dress held by two fingers with bright pink polish on the nails for a full thirty seconds before pushing himself away from the Mercedes, taking off his regulation wide brim hat, pulling out a handkerchief and wiping his forehead with it. He was balding, but the hair on one side had been pulled over to cover some of the bare space. He cleared his throat. "Well, now, Ruby Faye..."

She was still smiling sweetly. "I've heard all about you, honey. Remember, us girls talk together real frank. I've seen you trailin' behind my car for near ten years now. And it looks like you finally hit the jackpot. Because I *ain't* goin' into that jail. But you better enjoy it, Bilge Butler, because tonight is the only time you're gettin' into *this* pussy." She dropped the hem of her dress with a flourish.

Butler licked his lips. "Now, Ruby Faye, I just don't like a woman to use that kind of language."

She checked her make-up in the rear view mirror. "So. What's it gonna be? Your car or mine?"

Deputy Sheriff Bilge Butler pulled in behind the old hunting lodge and killed the lights. His heart was beating like a washtub bass, and his hands felt sweaty. He turned to Ruby Faye, who was smoking a cigarette now and staring out the windshield. "I been wantin' to touch you ever since I saw you in the Homecomin' Parade, sittin' up on that float like a livin' doll."

She sighed heavily. "Come on, Bilge, let's get it over with so I can go on home, now. I'm tired."

The Deputy turned on the ignition angrily and snapped on the lights.

Ruby Faye looked around at him. "What in hell are you doin'?"

He tried to look stern and shook his finger at her. "Now, Ruby Faye, if you're gonna be like that, I'm gonna turn right around and take you into that jailhouse like I shoulda done in the first place."

She was puzzled. "Be like what? I said I would *do* it!"

He leaned over toward her, still stern. "You're either gonna do it like you wanna do it, or it ain't gonna be no good, I might as well just turn around and take you on back and let my conscience be clear."

"Oh, for god's sake, Bilge Butler!"

"Like you *really* wanna do it!" He was emphatic.

Ruby Faye Pyle laughed and swung her legs around toward the Deputy. She had on little silver sandals with low heels, and she placed one foot at the bottom of his seat and the other one on the top of the steering wheel column, knocking off a black plastic covered warrant book full of notes which fell on the floor. She pulled up her dress and gently covered her crotch with her hand. "For your information, Mr Deputy Sheriff, this is the finest pussy in East Texas, and what you are gonna get tonight is an experience you just gonna dream about for the rest of your fuckin' life and never, ever, have again!"

Butler's eyes must have been as big as duck eggs because he felt them bulge from their sockets. His chest was tight, too, and it was hard to breathe. "I don't like you talkin' like that, Miss Ruby Faye. It ain't nice." His voice was strained, and it didn't sound right.

She licked her lips. "You don't like women talkin' dirty? Then maybe you never had a real woman before, honey." She was gently stroking herself through the material of her panties.

The Deputy gulped. It was dark inside the cruiser, and he couldn't see very well, but what he could see was driving him crazy. Her panties were light coloured and very high cut. Between the tops of her stockings and the underwear was the smoothest looking flesh he could ever remember seeing. He placed one tentative, trembling hand on the inner thigh above her knee and slowly moved it up. As it moved off the material of the stocking onto the flesh, he was surprised how warm it was to his touch. "Goddamn," he said. "Goddamn."

"Language, Deputy Sheriff. Language," she taunted. "So...you gonna fuck me or just sit around like an ole dog with his tongue hangin' out? Huh?"

He had touched the material on her crotch and began to rub it with the fingers of his hand. He was lurching with his body, trying to get a better angle. And he could feel an erection in his trousers, one that was harder than any he could remember having for years. His sight was blurring, and he felt feverish. No woman had ever been like this before.

Suddenly she swung her legs away from him and opened the car door. The engine was still running, and the lights were shining on the side of the old shack. Ruby Faye went around to the front of the car so she was standing in the light and lifted up her dress, pulling it over her head. She could just see the shadow of the Deputy gawping through the windshield. She threw the dress on the hood of the car and shook her hair like a mane, lowering her eyes as she leaned forward slightly to unhook her bra. When she stood up it was in profile, and she moved her shoulders rhythmically so her breasts trembled. They weren't huge, but she liked to think they were perfectly formed. The bra followed the dress onto the hood. Then, with both thumbs hooked into the tops of her panties, she lowered them to her ankles, stepped out with one foot and kicked them high in the air with the other foot. She turned full frontal to the cruiser, her feet apart, and pointed through the windshield. She curled her finger, once, twice, three times. It was quiet and cool, and she heard the car door open. She could then hear his rasping breath.

He came into the light a little like a zombie and reached for her, but Ruby Faye slipped to one side and grabbed the Deputy's tie, pulling down on it so his head lowered to her height. She put her face close to his, and he puckered up his lips, thinking she was going to kiss him.

"I want you to beg for it, Bilge. Like a dog. On your hands and knees. With your tongue hangin' out."

"Huh?" His eyes had glazed over, giving his face a look of comical bovine stupidity.

"You heard me, Mr Deputy Sheriff. I'm gonna show you just who's in charge here. Get your ass down on the ground.

Hands and knees." She jerked on the tie, and Butler went down clumsily. "Now pant like a houn' dog, and hang your tongue out, like I said."

The hair the Deputy combed over his bald pate fell forward making him look more pathetic. Ruby Faye had moved right in front of him, and he was staring at a dark brown triangle of hair, the tip of which disappeared between her legs. He hung his tongue out and panted.

She pushed the triangle into his face. "Now lick it and beg for it, you dirty old son of a bitch!

"I want it, I want it, please, please, Ruby Faye, please, please..."

She yanked on the tie and pushed him on his back. The Deputy was like a baby now, whimpering, and all she could hear was "please" being muttered endlessly. She stepped over him, standing with one foot each side of his head. He reached up with his hands to stroke her legs.

"Put your hands down, you ugly pile of dogshit, and tell me what you are!"

"Huh?" he muttered. His head was in darkness, and she stood above him bathed in light. His erection was driving him crazy, and he wanted that beautiful dark patch above him. It was the most beautiful thing he'd ever seen in his life. "Huh?"

She leaned forward and shouted. "You're a dirty old son of a bitch! Say it!"

He didn't know what he was doing any more, didn't care. The two beautiful legs, the swinging breasts, that wonderful triangle. "I'm a dirty old son of a bitch."

"Louder!"

"I'm a dirty old son of a bitch!" he shouted, almost crying.

She squatted down and sat on his face. "Now give me some head, you old bastard." She reached around and unbuckled his belt, zipped down his flies and pushed his underpants away from the mound of his stomach. His penis popped out like a lewd novelty in a joke shop. She ground her pelvis back and forth on the Deputy's face, not bothering to be gentle.

Suddenly she raised herself up onto her knees and moved her bottom back towards his penis which she grabbed hard in her

13

right hand, digging her nails into the shaft. The head she used like a toy to lubricate herself before she sat on it brutally. The Deputy groaned and lurched from side to side.

She grabbed his tie again and pulled. "I'm doin' the ridin' this time, cowboy. You an' me are gonna remember this fuck, and ever time I look at you in the street, I'm just gonna smile so you know what I'm thinkin'. Me ridin' your fat ass in the headlights of your car and you beggin' me like a dog, pantin' and droolin'..."

She froze suddenly. It wasn't silent anymore. Someone was clapping. She looked around but couldn't see anything for the glare of the headlights.

"Wonderful show, little lady. Wonderful show," said a voice from the darkness. It came from the old shack.

The Deputy hadn't noticed or heard anything and continued to moan and thrust his hips. Ruby Faye slapped him on the stomach. "Bilge. Bilge. Somebody's out there." She stood up, putting one arm across her breasts and a hand over her pubis. Slowly she backed toward the darkness.

"Stay right where you are, little lady. And get that fat Deputy off the ground. Slow."

Terrified, she moved over and gave Butler a kick. He rolled over and got to his hands and knees, staring around with a confused look on his face.

"OK, Big Dick," said the voice. "Take your gun out with two fingers, real slow, and throw it over here."

"Who the hell is that?" Bilge Butler asked.

There was a sharp *thuk* of a silenced pistol, and the earth in front of Butler exploded.

The Deputy grabbed his face. "I'm hit! I'm hit! Cain't see!"

"You're OK, fatso," the voice said. "Now the gun."

Butler reached slowly to his waist, then fumbled around until he found the holster. Unsnapping the strap, he pulled it out with two fingers and threw it toward the house.

The sound of an airplane was growing louder in the distance. A short heavy-set man with a moustache stepped into the light.

14

He held an automatic with a silencer. His eyebrows were bushy and his hair thick and black.

Ruby Faye gestured towards her clothes on the hood of the car. "Uh, can I...?"

The man stared at her. "I like you just like you are, sweetheart. Stay that way."

The Deputy was slowly getting to his feet, zipping up his trousers, and his eyes showed disoriented fright. The man reached over and grabbed the two pairs of handcuffs from his belt. With a deft movement he snapped one on the Deputy's wrist and pulled it behind his back. Butler understood and put his other hand behind, and the other cuff snapped in place. Without saying anything the man moved to the girl and made a motion with his gun. She held out one hand tentatively, biting her lip and looking toward the ground. He pulled it behind her, and when she didn't immediately comply like the Deputy, the man cracked her sharply on the head with the silencer. Ruby Faye screamed but put her other arm behind her.

The man walked back in front of the girl and tucked his pistol in his belt. With hardly any effort he lifted her up and sat her on the hood of the cruiser, stepped back and unzipped himself.

"Open up, baby," he said. "I'm going to give you something to scream about."

"We ain't got time for that, Zoot," said another voice from the darkness. "The plane's coming in."

The car door of the cruiser opened and someone got in. "I'll use the lights from this one," the voice said. You can bring the sex maniacs on down to the air strip, and we'll decide what to do with them then."

* * *

Buck Colby was upset and very nervous. Before he landed in Texas he was nervous, but now he was definitely upset as well. It was a great relief to have the drugs out of the plane, but now he had two extra passengers as well. A nude woman and a hick deputy sheriff. They had apparently been caught fucking near the landing strip by the two men who met them. The men had wanted to shoot the sheriff and keep the girl, but Gomez overruled them in his little high-pitched voice. They couldn't waste time like that, he told them. They had to get on the move. The whole idea of the operation was speed, and it was going to take the men long enough to dump the sheriff's car and burn it somewhere off the little ranch. There was an argument, but the two strange men backed off from Gomez. Gomez was a frightening little man, Colby thought with an involuntary shiver. The eyes were big and black, but they were also cold and held no emotion.

The deputy was sitting on the bench seat at the rear, his hair dangling down on one side. There was a deep gash where Gomez had struck him with his pistol when he objected to getting into the plane. The blood was drying, making a mess of the hair. Since then the deputy had been silent, except for the occasional whimper.

The girl - a pretty, wholesome-looking girl - sat beside Gomez and looked completely miserable. Buck Colby wished he could do something for her. But what? He could see them both from the corner of his eye, and now they were aloft Gomez had turned his attention to her. He had grabbed one of her breasts and was rubbing it, and Colby could just hear snatches of conversation over the roar of the engine.

"You like this, sweetie?" asked Gomez.

"No, I don't," said Ruby Faye glumly.

"Sure you do. This is Gomez. He is a great lover. Nice tits, sweetie."

Ruby Faye Pyle was petrified. Since that strange man - Zoot? - walked into the lights back at the ranch she had been in a kind of hypnotic trance. She observed what was going on, but from a distance. Deep inside she was cowering behind the last ramparts of sanity. The awful man beside her had now put his arm around her neck and was kissing her. The other hand he forced between her legs before shoving a finger in her vagina.

"Hmmm," Gomez murmured, his face inches from hers now. "I bet you like theese, huh?" Then he opened his mouth and stuck his tongue out, waggling it. "In the mouth. In the

16

cunt." He waggled his tongue again. "I am a wonderful lover. Cubano. The best in the world."

"Hey, lay off her, will you?" said Colby uncertainly from the pilot's seat.

Gomez turned and looked at the back of the pilot's head as if searching for the best spot to shoot him. "One more word, amigo, and I cut off your ear. She is now going to give me a blow job. You watch. You learn. I have never had a blow job from a Texan." He unzipped his pants and got out his manhood. He was very proud of it. Perhaps it was not so long, but it was very wide. "They say Texans have very big mouths. That is good." He grabbed a handful of hair at the back of her head and pushed her face down on him.

Ruby Faye fell off the seat and onto her knees as she tried to pull back. The little man was wiry and strong. Inches away from the dark red penis she caught the smell. He was one of those men who didn't wash his genitals - if he washed at all - and she felt herself gagging. The stench was appalling. Desperately she tried to retreat further behind her barricade, but the smell was too real. Instinctively she clenched her teeth and refused him.

She heard a snick, then felt the point of a blade on her neck.

"Open and suck, Texan," said the Cuban. "And swallow," he added with a high pitched laugh.

Her mouth went over his organ, and only fear prevented her from throwing up as he rammed his penis in and out of her mouth. She closed her eyes and felt her guts churning as he came a few short strokes later. He pulled her head up and pushed her away, and Ruby Faye turned and spat on the floor of the plane.

"Hey, amigo," said Gomez to Colby as he zipped up his trousers. "Are we over the Gulf yet?"

"Been over it for an hour," the pilot answered sullenly.

"Good. Then slow down the plane a little bit. I want some fresh air."

"What?" Colby half turned toward the little man.

"You heard what I said, amigo. Slow the plane down. I am going to open the door."

"Are you crazy? What for?"

17

Gomez's right hand struck like a snake. The knife blade scored the flesh along the join between the pilot's head and ear. Beads of blood oozed from the wound.

"Hey, goddamn it, that hurt!" screamed Buck Colby, grabbing his wounded ear.

"Slow the plane down, amigo. Next time the ear goes off."

Colby brought down the airspeed low enough for the door to be pulled back. Somehow he knew what was going to happen, but he kept the deadly information trapped behind the sewer sluice of his mind, the place where he stored things he never wanted to know. The girl was screaming. He could hear her wail over the terrible rush of wind from the door.

Gomez dragged Ruby Faye across the seat. With her hands cuffed behind her she could only resist with her legs, and he easily kicked them away. The Cuban grabbed the top of the door and put his foot in the woman's chest. "Nice blow job, Texan. But I've had better." He kicked.

Colby turned in time to see the absolute terror in her eyes before the slipstream sucked her out and backwards. It was a sight which would live with him for the rest of his life. The mouth stretched open in a scream, the eyes wide with panic and fear, her hair blowing wildly in the wind. Then she was gone. Colby stared out in front of him, not seeing the morning sky anymore. He heard Gomez dragging the whining body of the deputy toward the door. There was some more screaming before he felt the plane lighten. Then the door closed, and the wind noise abated. Colby's mind was frozen. He couldn't even identify one single thought. But he heard the Cuban slip back into his seat behind him and rummage in his flight bag. Colby stared straight ahead and realised his knuckles on the wheel were white. He felt a tap on his shoulder and slowly looked around. Gomez was holding a jar of some sort in his hand.

"Want a chili, amigo? Very good. Mexican." He put one of them into his mouth and bit down on it.

A single thought slowly and finally floated to the surface of Buck Colby's mind. He could just manage to visualise the words:

What the fuck have I got myself into?

18

CHAPTER TWO

Joe Wayne Haug watched himself in the mirror as he carefully went down into a squat. When his thighs were parallel to the ground he reversed direction and pushed. As he pushed he thought he heard his tendons squeak. He could certainly see a few of them in the mirror, along with veins which stood out like rope on his neck and forehead and along his shoulders to his arms. And he could feel as well as see his head filling with blood. When he straightened up, he locked his knees briefly before going down once more for the second repetition. There were ten 20 kilo plates on the bar, five on each side, and the bar was bowing in the middle. That was nearly five hundred pounds, if you counted the weight of the bar, and he wanted seven more repetitions.

Keef Sams was standing behind him, shadowing his movements. Spotting, it was called. He went down as Haug went down, his arms ready to help if he slowed or staggered. You must have a spotter with heavy squats. It was dangerous not to. Haug remembered an incident years ago when he was 20. An experienced weightlifter, alone in the gym, was squatting with a little over 300 lbs when he lost his balance. Somehow, as the weight dropped, the man's neck was trapped between the bar and the floor with his body at an awkward angle. It broke his back like a matchstick. Haug had been in the dressing room at the time. He still remembered the sickening sight when he ran out after hearing the cry. The big young body was bent the wrong way just at the shoulders. One leg was splayed forward underneath the bar, and the other one was split behind. The gym manager panicked into catatonia as Haug ran to the telephone to call for an ambulance. When he returned he shouted at two other men who were about to move the victim, who had a spinal injury, and that may just have saved the man's life. He never walked again, but at least he lived.

Since that time Haug called for a spot for any weight he used over 250 lbs and helped anyone else he saw struggling alone in a gym.

19

The eighth rep was hard, and Keef had to help, pulling up under his armpits and across his chest. Then he dumped the bar on the rack with a sound like a lorry loaded with locomotive wheels going over a cattle guard. Haug backed from underneath the bar and staggered over to the bench where he sat down heavily. Keef took his turn under the bar, and One Time spotted.

Keef and One Time were like chalk and cheese, though both were West Indians. One Time was a tall, good looking, stylish man who punctuated his otherwise incomprehensible speech with body movements. Even his gym clothes were chosen with the same care most people used when invited to Buckingham Palace. Subtle colour matches were chosen, and thought was given to textures and the overall impact of an ensemble. Shoes were of course a vital feature, and though he didn't immediately adopt the latest street craze in shoelace embroidery, you could always see a lot of time and effort had been spent to achieve the right effect. One Time had an arcane interest in European designer labels, most of them unpronounceable by the bulk of gym personnel. And One Time always wore a hat. There were a range of berets, knitted pull-ons, trilbys, pirate scarves and even dozer caps worn at a streetwise tilt. It was surprising he didn't wear Ray Bans as well, but One Time always wanted the women to know he was looking at them. Because he *knew* they were looking at him.

Keef was shorter, with a heavy upper body and narrow waist. He was the one who most looked like a real bodybuilder, and in fact he had competed for years, once coming second in Mr UK. He had a deep gruff voice which gave him a certain gravitas. The fringe he wore as a goatee transmitted an element of menace. His choice of clothes was a source of constant irritation to One Time. If One Time was a musician of style, Keef was tone deaf. Colours were mismatched and so were socks. Once he even came in wearing a different brand of trainer on each foot.

The three friends had trained together at the Tufnell Park gym for years. They were fairly closely matched in strength, despite the variation in size. Haug liked to go at training hard.

The gym was one place he could express the dark pools of anger which sometimes bubbled deep inside like hot oil.

He wiped the Guinness bar towel over his bald head and grinned as he watched One Time take his turn under the squat bar. He went over behind him to spot. If One Time couldn't make the movement classy, he wouldn't do it at all. Simple brute strength was not for him. He moved under the bar like a heavy-limbed ballet dancer, easing the bar off the rack in one smooth movement. He went down and didn't seem to stop before he was starting up again, everything controlled. Four repetitions. Then he stepped forward to the rack on one foot, the bar perfectly balanced, and settled it noiselessly back in its place.

"One time," said One Time as he stepped back and raised a finger.

"Not much more than one time," Haug grunted. "You not trainin' today?"

"You don't understand," said One Time. "I'm coming back."

Haug grinned at Keef. "You've got to have been someplace before you come back to it."

Keef laughed as he added another two twenty kilo plates to the bar. "We're gonna get four out of *this* one, man, and you're gonna be left where we always find you. In the back."

One Time was adjusting his knee wraps. One of the windings was slightly out of place. "You forget who I am."

Haug got under the bar again. "That's easy, 'cause your personality's like a hole in the atmosphere."

"I don't have a hole in my socks," he replied, looking at Keef's feet.

Haug heaved the weight up. It felt fucking heavy, as if it was going to drive him slowly into the concrete floor. For one brief moment he felt as if he wouldn't do it. Then a tongue of anger licked upward from the pit. He set his teeth and went down. Keef was counting behind him. On the fourth rep he came up very slowly, pouring everything he had into the lift. When he reached the top something came over him. He had never done five with this weight before, and it was a little dangerous to try without additional spotters at each end. Keef could only help him so much if his legs went completely.

Fuck it, he said to himself and started down. In the mirror he caught a glimpse of One Time who moved swiftly off the bench to stand closer if things went wrong. The weight was nearly a quarter of a ton. Haug got to the bottom and stopped. He mustn't stop the movement, not at that weight. Visions and images flickered before his inner eye. Visions of his enemies, men who walked around like they owned the earth, stealing everything, even if it was nailed down, and then pocketing the nails. His head went back, looking toward the ceiling, and he drove with his legs. Everything went into it. Heart, mind and soul. Slowly the bar began to move upward again, inch by inch. He could hear Keef encouraging him, and he felt his hands in his armpits. Halfway up he felt collapse coming on. His body was screaming, telling him all his reserves were gone. The fuel was spent, the overdraft was being called in. But somewhere Haug found another pool, a deeper one stretching back to his youth in Vietnam. He was holding on there, too, that one terrible night. He had two partners on that night as well, though one of them was dead and the other wounded. But he continued fighting, holding down the trigger, moving, holding it down again, rolling and reloading, firing and firing as the bodies fell around him in mounds...

Haug opened his eyes and looked in the mirror. He was up, and he stood with the weight on his back, his face distorted with hatred, his teeth bared, eyes glowing insanely. Was it insanity? He staggered over to the rack and dropped the bar as the big plates clattered on the end.

"You're gonna kill yourself, man," Keef murmured as Haug groped for the bar towel and sat down gratefully.

"I gotta give you guys a real act to follow," Haug said, his chest heaving. He looked in the mirror again. There were mirrors everywhere, on three of the four walls. Was he getting too old to do this stuff anymore? Christ, he looked old today, and he felt every one of his forty four years. Grey was streaking the fringe of hair he had pulled back in a ponytail. The body was still awesome, but for how long? He was a shade under six feet and weighed 235 lbs - or 17 stone as the limeys would say. His shoulders were as broad and thick as they were when he played linebacker for the Green Bay Packers. A bit too much gut, but what the hell?

Haug turned and looked down at the other end of the gym while he fought to get his breath back. It was a long barn of a place ending in a hallway which led to the dressing rooms and the street. Directly across the hall was the women's gym. The women who were really serious always trained with the men, but it was good to have a place where beginners could avoid the gratuitous lecherous stares of some of the men. Sarah and Joanne were on the stepping machine. They were two young models and spent hours on aerobic exercises to sweat off what they considered to be excess weight. They always looked anorexic to Haug - skinny, no hips, no chest, just skin stretched on bone with enough muscle for locomotion. Nice girls, though.

One Time had taken off the two twenty kilo plates and was finishing his set. Haug had been too knackered to spot, and Keef was doing it. Again, when he finished, the bar went smoothly back on the rack in contrast to Keef and Haug who just let the thing smash down.

Haug asked Keef to call Chris, the manager, and reached for another twenty kilo plate. One Time put one on the other end.

"Right now," said One Time with a crooked smile. "The man. Feeling strong." He winked and moved sharply, sweeping off his red beret with one hand and wiping his forehead with the other one. He bent his knees to look in the mirror as he replaced his cap carefully, making sure it had just the right tilt, pulled down on one side. "Gonna go for it. Tryin' to make me look bad."

"I don't have to try very goddamn hard," said Haug. "Your mother must have been a disappointed woman when you were born."

"That's alright," said One Time as Keef returned with Chris, the manager.

Chris was a Greek with a nose that looked like a toasted pitta. Everybody liked him. Haug got under the bar again. Keef was behind him. Chris and One Time stood at each end for

23

safety. There were now fourteen 20 kilo plates on the bar, nearly 650 lbs. Everyone else in the gym stopped training to watch.

"I want two," said Haug.

"What am I supposed to do if you can't get up?" Chris asked with a smile.

"I'll get up," Haug muttered as he took the weight on his shoulders. He staggered backward away from the rack. Why was he doing this today? What did he have to prove? What was the point? There was no point. Something was bothering him, that was all, and he was trying to release it. It was certainly better than sitting on it and letting the gangrene spread. Haug went down with the weight, and it felt like he wanted to keep on going, straight on down to hell or whatever there was below the crust of the earth. He reached the bottom and started up again. Fuel, he needed fuel. The job he was working on now was the most important one in his life, and he knew he would probably fail. It was too big. There were too few of them. No, fuck it! Fight! Fight! He put his head right back again and pushed with his legs. This time he had to bend his back slightly, and that was a little dangerous. But he was up.

"Watch the back," he heard Keef say behind him.

One more time. It was important that he did it one more time. He started down and felt despair seeping into his consciousness like seawater seeps into a submarine under extreme pressure. There just didn't seem to be anything left in his body or his legs. He had to return to Vietnam. That was the only way. He had been hit, but not badly. The ammunition was gone, so he had used AK-47's. There were plenty of those lying around. Fire and move - and move hard. Fire toward the flashes. Suddenly he was among them in the woods, a whole squad - or what was left of a squad. Four or five men. He swept them with the rifle, two out, empty, rifle butt into the face of another, snatching the barrel of another as he fired, grabbing the last man by the feet and breaking his back against a tree. Then move again, don't stop. Speed. Speed is the only chance.

The images flashed through his head in split seconds as he poured the last resources of his body into the push upward and the bar moved slowly. The slower it moved, the more the images flickered, like an old film. Yes! He had enjoyed it! Loved it! Never had he been so close to life as when he was so near death. And Haug felt monumental anger toward those who tapped into that pleasure and used him to kill men he never even knew. The anger moved the bar all the way to the top, and Haug slowly stepped toward the rack. One. Two. Bang! A little cheer went up behind him. It wasn't all that much weight. Top power lifters could do almost twice that amount. But it wasn't bad for this gym.

"Take a plate off, man," he heard Keef say as he reached for his bar towel. "I'm not going for this today."

"Ah, anybody could do that," Chris said with a dismissive wave as he walked back toward reception.

"You wouldn't have a problem," said Haug to the retreating Greek, "if you could use your nose as a lever."

His two friends laughed as Keef got under the bar again. When he finished his set One Time said he had enough of squats, and they moved over to the leg press machine. Haug caught Chris' eye as he poked his head into the room and made the sign of the telephone with his little finger and thumb.

"Back in a minute," he said, glad for the break as he walked toward the hallway.

It was Mainwaring. He had given him the number of the gym in case of emergency.

"I'd like for you to attend the meeting tonight if you can," said Mainwaring.

"Hell, Jonathan, I'm only the dishwasher. Might not understand what y'all are talkin' about."

"Modesty is not always an attractive virtue," Sir Jonathan Mainwaring replied. "Why are you panting?"

"'Cause I just ran to the phone. Thought it was the broad I was takin' out tonight."

"Broad?"

"Woman. Works in a bar in Highgate, met her on Sunday night. I was lookin' forward to a sordid and depraved evenin', turnin' my bed into a pile of junk springs with the air fulla floatin' feathers."

25

"I'm terribly sorry if you had other plans. But this is important."

"I guessed that, ole bean, and therefore I've just kissed my piece of ass goodbye."

"Your way of expressing yourself falls short of the low watermark for human decency," Mainwaring replied.

"You're only jealous because of my better American education."

"American education, what a splendid idea. But enough of this banter, as I'm sure you find it an unequal struggle. The meeting is eight pm for half past."

"I'll be there at half seven," said Haug, "to check for mice."

"Right you are. Always a pleasure."

"See you later, alligator," Haug said as he hung up.

The address was in Great Smith Street in Westminster. Haug decided not to drive this time. Because of recent IRA attacks in the area, police were liable to tow away any vehicle without a resident's sticker even if you could find a legal parking place, and Haug's pickup truck had attracted too much attention. One Time carried his bag of electronic tricks in an immaculate holdall advertising the name of an Italian football club. He was dressed in one of his black outfits. Black sweatshirt, black jeans, black socks and trainers. On his head he wore a black beret snapped smartly down on one side.

They met before seven at Tufnell Park underground station, not far from the gym, and Haug looked at his friend and shook his head. "Goddamn, man. How did you get a crease in a pair of jeans?"

They moved toward the ticket office, and One Time made a fist and pressed it forward. "Steam heat."

"You iron your jeans?" Haug asked as he paid for the tickets. "You *iron* 'em?"

One Time held up a finger. "Right now." A young woman with a short, tight dress was walking toward them, and she locked eyes with the black man. When she passed, One Time slid into the lift. "Steam heat," he said again, a big grin on his face.

He turned to Haug when the doors closed and looked him up and down. "Look at you, man. No dress sense. Motorcycle boots, old wrinkled blue jeans...what's this, a check shirt? Hey? And an old leather waistcoat." He grabbed Haug's dozer cap from his head and smirked. "Harley Davidson. No style. I'll get you one, man. I'll get you a hat."

Haug grabbed his hat back. "Don't bother. One of us lookin' like a pimp is enough." The lift door opened, and they walked onto the southbound platform.

They decided to change trains at Camden Town for the Charing Cross line. The electronic board there told them the next train was on Platform 2, so they climbed the steps and crossed over. The platform was a little crowded with late commuters on their way home, but one section was nearly vacant. As Haug and One Time moved along, they could see why. Four skinheads, one holding a half empty bottle of wine, leaned against the wall. The one with the bottle took a swig and passed it to the next man. They were staring at Haug and One Time with a menace they must have practiced in front of a mirror. They all wore Doc Martens, battle camouflage trousers and torn T-shirts. Swastikas were prominent on their tattooed arms, some of them obviously DIY jobs.

Haug returned their stares as they approached. It was one segment of subculture he hated most. He knew their swaggering savagery was a result of social violence, but this particular expression of revolt was nothing but pus from the wound. As they started to pass by the four thugs, the one who had handed on the bottle stepped toward them.

"No coons down at this end," he said with a sneer.

One Time was on the inside. Without seeming to look, his free hand struck like a python. He grabbed the man's throat, then pumped him back into the wall with such force his head smacked on the tiles. Haug stepped over and swept his feet out from under him on the rebound. The skinhead sat down so heavily there was a sharp report as his coccyx cracked on the concrete floor, and he slumped sideways unconscious.

The entire platform seemed to have gone quiet, as if the crowd were all holding their breath. It was certainly quiet enough to hear two sounds. One was the breaking of the wine bottle, the other was the chilling *snick* of a flick knife. Haug was closest to the one with the knife.

"You've done the wrong thang, bo," he said. "You pulled a knife on me."

Before he finished his warning, the skinhead lunged at him, the knife held well out in front. Haug was a big man and looked slow. But he wasn't, not when he felt the sap beginning to rise. He dropped one foot back so the knife passed harmlessly, like a bull's horn past a good matador. His left hand shot out and clamped on the wrist. Then he pulled hard. As the skinhead came off his feet, Haug's right hand joined his left on the man's wrist, and he swung the body out over the tracks in a semicircle back onto the platform and into the tiled wall. The knifeman actually hit the wall upside down at a bonecrushing speed and literally slid down in a heap. His broken tibia stuck out through a tear in his camouflage trousers. Haug heard running footsteps down the platform as he turned to see a head bouncing off One Time's knee like a soccer ball. The last skinhead was disappearing into the crowd as if he were being chased by devils. They could hear a train in the tunnel, the sound getting louder.

Haug looked at the unconscious man at One Time's feet. He was puzzled and cocked his head first one way and then the other. The skinhead's face was a collage of blood and exposed bone, but the man's right arm was bent into what looked like a "Z". Or half a swastika. "How the hell'd you do that?" he asked, turning to One Time.

One Time picked up the bag he had carefully put to one side. With his other hand in a fist, he moved it forward. "Steam heat."

Haug chuckled. "You *ironed* him?" The train was slowing as it roared by them.

"One time," said One Time.

The doors of the train opened, and Haug was still laughing. As they got in, he thought he heard one of the bodies behind them gurgling. The passengers in the carriage stared out at the misshapen tangle of bodies as the two friends sat side by side.

One Time crossed his legs, then frowned. There was something that looked like a small piece of red tooth stuck to his

28

black jeans. Fastidiously he flicked it off with his finger then drew out a large red bandana with black polka dots and wiped his finger carefully.

Haug observed this. "You never know what kinda disease you can get when you step in shit."

The doors closed, and the train lurched before moving off. Two passengers sitting nearby got up and moved to the other end of the carriage.

They got off at St James's Park station, and it was about a ten minute walk to Great Smith Street where Mainwaring had the use of a large room on the second floor of one of those large buildings with no name. One Time always came with him to "sweep" the room with what he called his ghetto blaster. The machine was about the size of one but had intricate looking dials and plugs for various probes. Electronic surveillance was becoming so sophisticated it was difficult to make absolutely certain there were no eavesdroppers, but One Time assured him his ghetto blaster would make a room 99 percent pure. The Barbadian had been trained by the British Army, spending most of his service years in Northern Ireland attached to the SAS. He told Haug he couldn't guarantee a room he swept would be completely clean because every year several dozen new products would appear at the top of a market made greedier for information. And the long range stuff was getting better and better. At each meeting One Time fixed a fine metal mesh to the four windows in the room which was difficult to see unless you were close to the window. He had some kind of transformer which he linked to the mesh which he said oscillated at random frequencies. Or something like that. Haug had never been good at technical stuff. Math. Engineering. Electricity. Electricity? Hell, as far as he was concerned, electricity worked by magic or religious spells. But One Time was a real whiz. He was quick, and he was silent, moving from one point to another, testing, probing and listening. As usual with him, every movement was stylish and economical. His eyes moved first, then he moved. And he could never resist a little flair. While Haug watched, One Time turned after he finished sweeping one wall to find a chair in his way. Without breaking stride, the black man hurtled the chair easily, landing silently on the other side. He was like a big cat.

Haug had never attended a meeting before. Previously, after One Time swept the place clean, he would position himself on the second floor landing so he could see who came up the stairs and who entered the room. Meanwhile One Time was downstairs watching the front door from the shadows. One Time suggested they not use telephones - for security reasons - so they used buzzers instead. One buzz: someone coming up, recognised. Two buzzes: party unrecognised. Three buzzes: trouble. They never had to use three buzzes yet, but if they did, the plan was for One Time to follow up well behind, and the two of them would deal with the problem on the landing after Haug had warned those already arrived. The meeting room door would then be locked from the inside, and when the meeting was over people left by the fire exit on the other side. It wasn't foolproof, but at least it was organised. Ideally he should cover the fire exit as well, but that was a heavy door locked by an iron bar. It was far better to keep security as simple as possible. That way there were few misunderstandings.

Sir Jonathan Mainwaring arrived at about ten to eight. Mainwaring was very tall and looked even taller because he was so remarkably lean. He had an angular body. There seemed to be too many knees or elbows. His head was skull-like with large, nearly imploring, eyes. Receding and slightly greying hair was pulled straight back and looked as if it had been sprayed on the skull. And of course he wore his immaculate suit with the regulation pinstripes. Haug wondered if he wore a suit to bed. He had never seen him out of it, even when they attended the Ashes test at Lord's together last summer. His idea of informality was to leave his briefcase at home. Sir Jonathan Mainwaring was Permanent Secretary at the Department of Trade and Industry.

Mainwaring nodded to Haug and One Time as he entered. One Time was replacing his ghetto blaster in the spotless holdall. He picked up the holdall and held up one finger. "One time," he said, moving smoothly out the door.

"Extraordinary man," said Mainwaring. "What does he mean by that? One time?"

"It's his name," Haug replied.

"Yes, I know that," Mainwaring said testily. "But I actually asked you what it meant."

"Well, the story goes that it refers to his reputation. He warns you one time, and then he hits you one time."

"I see."

"And some say women only need to try him one time, and they'll never want anythang else."

"I don't think I want to know that." Mainwaring had placed his briefcase on the long oak table which had a number of chairs around it. The table was positioned at the end of the room near the entrance. Other chairs were placed in rows beyond the table. It wasn't a particularly well-appointed meeting place. The carpet was industrial strength grey, the table and chairs functional rather than comfortable.

"It is a committee evening," Mainwaring continued. "We've had some rather interesting information which may well involve you. Besides, it's time you met those you have been protecting so efficiently."

The buzzer went once and then again at intervals over the next thirty minutes as the seven committee heads arrived. Mainwaring had not introduced them, preferring to wait until all had gathered. Everyone knew who Haug was and what he did. Several had spoken to him individually or chatted before a meeting was convened. The American was especially fond of Stuart Easton, who was the first to arrive.

Easton was a Labour MP for Sheffield, a left wing gadfly of Parliament who constantly raised embarrassing questions in the Commons. He had been ejected from the House a record number of times. Eschewing his parliamentary salary, he took as his wage the average take home pay of the miners who sponsored him. The rest of the money went to the National Union of Mineworkers. Love him or hate him, there was not a Member who wouldn't instantly agree his integrity was of the highest quality. He was, in fact, the first man Mainwaring approached when they were forming the United Opposition.

The United Opposition was the unofficial name of this group, and it had nothing to do with the party in opposition at the House.

After the last man arrived, Mainwaring looked at his watch and asked them all to take a seat at the table, including Haug. The Permanent Secretary indicated a seat beside him for the American. Finally Mainwaring sat down himself and opened his briefcase, extracted two files then closed it.

"To begin with, I'll make the introductions," he said. "I'm sure you all recognise Mr Joe Wayne Haug, who has been providing security for our meetings here. He is an American resident in this country and fully sympathises with our aims. Indeed he has been so vital with his assistance in the past I can assure you we would never have progressed to this stage without him. He is the proprietor of a small and obscure detective agency in North London but now, since he spends most of his time on our projects, somehow manages to subsist principally on what we are able to pay him from rather meagre resources. I would finally like to add that it is his eccentric preference to simply be called "Haug"."

Mainwaring then turned to the seven people sitting at the table. "From my left. General Sir Timothy Portland, now retired but formerly commander of the British Army of the Rhine. Justin Lyndhurst, an eminent Queen's Counsel and former advisor to the Cabinet Secretary. Stuart Easton you already know and admire. Louise Templer, Labour MP for Islington. Matthew Tillson, Conservative MP for Hampshire..."

"Just a minute, Jonathan," Haug interrupted. "This is the first time in my life I can remember knowingly sharin' a table with a Tory. I wouldn't trust one of 'em to sign his real name on a note to his mother."

Stuart Easton threw his head back and laughed out loud, and Louise Templer chuckled. Surprisingly, Matthew Tillson joined in.

Mainwaring was unamused. "I forgot to warn the company of Haug's social inadequacies..."

Tillson held up his hand. He was a portly middle-aged man with a pleasant face topped by what appeared to be a halo of white spun sugar. "No, no, I have to say that, on the whole, I might be quite inclined to agree with Mr Haug. Particularly in recent years the party has undergone a transformation which makes it unrecognisable from the party I joined many years ago."

"Yes," said Mainwaring tersely as he squared up the two files in front of him. "Now, if I may continue, this is Kenneth Cranshaw, who is the only other civil servant performing as head of committee. He attends these meetings at some risk because of his position as programmer and analyst at GCHQ and is therefore somewhat limited by what he can say to us by restrictions under the Official Secrets Act. And finally this is Professor Ewan Thomas who held the chair of history at Cambridge for a number of years, the author of many distinguished books and lectures.

Haug was impressed. Most of their names were familiar from newspapers or television. He still was not sure about the Tory, but his eyes returned to Louise Templer, the Labour MP. In her mid-thirties, she had dark brown hair with a bit of red in it. It was pulled back into a ponytail revealing a long neck and two dangling silver earrings. Her face was a near oval with wide dark eyes and a nice chin. Her mouth, though, had a natural downward turn, and he wondered if she had a sense of humour. She was a small woman, maybe a little over five feet tall, and slightly built. She wore a pair of jeans and sweatshirt showing the collar of a blouse underneath. Haug always looked at women very frankly and openly, and when she looked up from her hands she caught his eye. At first she frowned slightly, but Haug always enjoyed this moment because this was where a lot of initial information was passed between man and woman. She held his gaze longer than he thought she would before looking away at Mainwaring who had just begun to speak.

"Now, Haug, you will notice quite a range across the political spectrum here. Yet we all agree that is how it should be. There are only two criteria for membership. Honour and loyalty to the Crown. If 'loyalty to the Crown' sounds too monarchistic for you, then please feel free to substitute loyalty to the parliamentary ideals of this country. As, indeed, many of our members do. Honour is more difficult to define, so I won't bother. You either know what it is or you don't. We intentionally keep party politics out of our plans and discussions - with difficulty, I might add. We collate information, we deal with specifics after consultation and voting, we decide on future gambits.

"We call ourselves the United Opposition and have been in existence for just over a year. Prior to our formation, I - and others - had been increasingly concerned about the growing shift of real power out of the hands of Parliament towards extra-national interests. Parliament in general, and the Government in particular, were being lobbied and pressurised and, yes, blackmailed, to provide easements for these extra-national interests. In my position as a senior civil servant I was privy to the passage of documents across my own desk and across the desks of some of my colleagues which filled me with growing alarm. Because these outside interests are not simply anonymous ebbs and flows of economic or greedy elements. In fact they are orchestrated and work in collusion with parties in many countries around the world.

"Who are they? We have yet to discover the identity of the head which controls the body, but we have inescapable evidence the body is there, alive and active. This creature developed in a rather natural sort of evolution. The internationalisation of business was an important tap root. One very large corporation would grow well beyond the borders where it was given birth. A very normal development, you may say. Indeed. But as they grew and multiplied, large corporations found they had more in common with other large corporations than they had with the governments of parent countries. The media - including motion pictures, television, radio, video, newspapers and magazines - were a legitimate diversification. *And* they found they could bring much weight to bear with advertising, giving to those who cooperate, withholding from those who do not.

"All relatively normal so far. Suspect morally perhaps, but normal. We cannot pinpoint the time or place so far, but between the 1950's and 1980's there developed a more sinister linkage with paramilitary groups which operate within the infected countries. These groups have a strong fascist flavour, and members are often drawn from and operated by cadres of trained militarist personnel. Some of you may not know, incidentally, that Haug has direct experience of these groups. He single-handedly destroyed several of them..."

"Not single-handed. I had plenty of help," Haug interrupted. "And most of 'em were a bunch of beanpickers. An idea woulda busted their heads open."

"So," said Louise Templer, "you are a man of violence."

"That was a pretty aggressive thang to say," Haug replied calmly as he looked into the Labour MP's eyes again.

She dropped her eyes to her hands. "It was, and I apologise. I simply have no patience with violent men."

"Well, lady, the reason I got involved with those assholes was because they tortured and raped a good friend of mine. They were about to kill her, and I somehow don't think they woulda responded very well to reason. In any case it's best not to judge a man by what you *think* he is. Better to wait and see what he's really like." He smiled at her, and he could see she was a bit agitated.

"These meetings do tend to drift a bit," said Mainwaring, tapping a bony forefinger on the top file which he then opened. "We have a specific reason for inviting you to attend this evening. This coming weekend - we believe Saturday - someone is expected to arrive at Heathrow from the United States, a man called..." He paused a moment to adjust his reading glasses. "...Hercules DeLoop. The extraordinary name was unknown to me, but I am told he is a Texan of immense wealth who is a contributor to the finances of the Livermore Institute, one of the organisations which may be involved in coordinating the strategy behind some of these illegal extra-national activities. He will be involved in a series of meetings here in London and elsewhere with, among others, Jeremy Evans who is Deputy Head of MI6, Michael Regis who is an arms dealer and lobbyist..."

Haug snorted. "An asshole.."

"Just a moment, Haug. Alexander Hinkley, who is a professor of philosophy, freelance now, I believe. Sir Samuel Goodman, the Cabinet Secretary. And, last but not least, our imported Australian media tycoon, Harvey Gillmore." Haug snorted again and was about to interrupt. "Please let me finish. We are unsure whether they will meet separately or together on various occasions. But," he continued, turning finally to face Haug, "we need to know as much as we can about these meetings. What is said, if at all possible. Or...anything. I admit my ignorance on matters like these."

"Jesus," muttered Haug. "Michael Regis. Harvey Gillmore. Be tough to keep my hands off 'em."

Sir Jonathan Mainwaring frowned. "I'm afraid this is an operation requiring absolute discretion."

"Well," Haug shrugged. "We can try. But you know as well as I do that if they want to make these thangs really secret, they can do it. You're talkin' State and State resources. I'm a two bit North London private eye, and I sometimes got trouble fillin' up the Harley."

Mainwaring smiled a rare smile. "Perhaps we are a little short of resources, but I have confidence that your head...how did you put it?...your head does not burst open from the presence of ideas."

"Somethin' like that," Haug muttered.

Mainwaring handed the American the top file. "These are the details we have gathered so far, including proposed locations of the meetings, arrival time at Heathrow, some rather fuzzy photocopied photographs. Mr Cranshaw here may be able to advise you on what to expect in the way of electronic countermeasures for security. He is really quite good. Now," he continued as he rose from his chair, "I suggest we boil up the kettle and have some tea and digestives. Perhaps you will be able to chat to our committee heads more informally. Get to know each other."

The others immediately began discussing the problems in the operation. Stuart Easton went to plug in the kettle. Louise Templer remained in her seat for a moment and finally looked over at Haug.

Haug had the file open. He was studying an old newspaper photograph of Hercules DeLoop, frowning.

CHAPTER THREE

Corky DeLoop kicked the covers off and looked up at the mirrored ceiling. For as long as she could remember she liked looking at herself. Even before her adolescence she was always a sensation with all the adults making over her. After adolescence the eyes of the men changed, but they were *all* turned in her direction. All the time. She smiled to herself and was pleased with the body she saw naked and spread-eagled on the seven foot bed. A tangle of platinum blonde hair haloed her head, nearly the same colour as the silk sheets.

Suddenly she put her hand to her mouth and laughed out loud. She remembered the day before in the airport after arriving on the plane from Dallas after a week's visit with her mother. She had been wearing a pair of tight white shorts, a little polka dot top that stretched over her boobs and stopped just short of her navel, a pair of high heeled gold sandals and her favourite heart-shaped sunglasses. Corky DeLoop was a shade under six feet tall, and the heels put her well over. She strode across the concourse like an empress and could feel her whole body in motion. Her shoulders moved rhythmically, her breasts jiggled and bounced, her bottom swung from side to side and her long legs flexed with each great stride. A porter struggled behind pushing a trolley piled high with expensive luggage. But in front of her there was chaos, and as she passed the chaos intensified, folding in on itself like computer fractals. When she entered the concourse it was just a typical crowded, bored throng of people waiting for flights or arrivals. The rattle of her heels on the tiles announced her arrival like a snare drum. She had to walk the whole length of the huge room to get to the exit where Herk would be waiting with the Rolls. One man, a briefcase in his hand, his jaw slack, his eyes wide, walked straight into a support column. Suitcases were dropped, and some of them sprung open to form lethal traps for other gawkers who fell or skidded into waiting queues. A porter, his mind obviously numb with disbelief and desire, ran down an old lady on crutches. A passenger on the down escalator was oblivious to the fact he had reached the bottom, and a howling pile-up ensued with the men fighting others simply to get them out of the way so they wouldn't miss one quiver of her flesh. The crowd itself parted like the Red Sea as she marched forth, a pink frosted smile showing her perfect white teeth. A fat man with a large frozen yoghurt stepped into a newspaper rack and bellowed like a lunatic as he became entangled in the wire mesh and crashed to the floor. The scattered newspapers and frozen yoghurt provided a skid pan for an elderly couple who momentarily looked like ice skaters before landing heavily and screaming for help. Another man in the newspaper kiosk itself had been receiving change for a hundred dollar bill. The crisp bills remained on his flat hand as his eyes followed Corky DeLoop in her triumphal parade, then slowly dipped forward as his brain slipped out of gear and whirred in neutral. As the bills wafted to the floor they were quickly snatched up by a young female student who then shot off into the crowd looking for more males turned to pillars of salt with their wallets open. Most of the women, instead of exhibiting jealousy, simply watched in amazement dipped in envy. One woman chewing a stick of gum turned to her friend and shook her head. "Well," she said. "If she's got it - and She Has Got It - best to flaunt it while she can."

When she reached the other side, the electronic glass doors parted just like the crowd with the puffing porter still behind her, his eyes glued to the stretched dancing white material covering most of her buttocks. If she had kept on going, he would probably have followed her all the way into Houston and across it and out of it and as far along to Galveston as he could go before he dropped dead in his tracks from exhaustion. Behind her the chaos was complete as men snarled at each other like dogs. Fist fights began in spontaneous combustion. She had wound the spring as tight as it would go, and when the stored energy was released it was an electrical storm. Corky DeLoop would have dearly loved to turn around and watch every detail as chaos resolved itself through the laws of nature, but she knew that would spoil the whole effect. She consoled herself just listening to the incredible noise. As the doors were closing behind her she thought she heard a gunshot. When she was on form, Corky DeLoop was a one woman theatrical event.

The gold Rolls Royce was right there, and Herk was behind the wheel, a Stetson clamped on his huge head. Hercules DeLoop was sixty years old. Corky was thirty two, and she knew what she was doing when she married him. She always knew what she was doing. The world and how it worked was crystal clear to her from the moment she hit her teens. DeLoop was bigtime wealthy, no piddling little millionaire with a few cows and a few thousand acres. Like his good buddy in Panama, J C Ritter, he sold his immense oil holdings at just the right point before it all started to crash and other wealthy men nose-dived into relative poverty. And when land values fell, he started gobbling property. When the stock market crashed, he gobbled up blue chip stock at a fraction of its value. "Buy low, sell high," he had roared many times. "Any goddamn Jew can tell you that." Hercules DeLoop already had a wife when Corky met him just after winning the Miss Fort Worth Rodeo title, but wives were no problem to Corky. She just dangled the bait, and he rose up out of the water like a blue marlin to take the line. The wife was paid off and sent back to California, and Corky moved into a lifestyle she knew was custom made for her.

When she got into the Rolls, she leaned over and planted a kiss on Herk's cheek. The big man didn't move. He stared out at the longhorns which replaced the silver lady ornament on the hood.

"Wearin' clothes like that on a goddamn airplane, it's a wonder you ain't been gang raped all the way from Dallas to Houston,' he growled finally.

She looked at him innocently. "Why, it's summer Herk, and I didn't want to get too hot."

"Hot? Ever since I've knowed you, you've been hotter'n a nanny goat in a pepper patch. You just wanted to show your ass," he said as he started the car.

She laughed again as she stared at her image in the ceiling mirrors. Well, she said to herself, if god gave me an ass to show, it might be sacrilegious to hide it. She woke up in a very good mood. Herk was away in New Orleans on business, and today was the first visit of her new trainer, the one she had interviewed last month. Duane Roscoe. He was one good-looking boy. A bleach blonde himself, she figured, his body was tanned and smooth. His muscles were big but not too big. Edible. Yes, that's the word. Edible. She had very nearly devoured him right then and there, but Herk had been in the house somewhere, prowling around. She had taken a little risk in asking the young man to drop his trousers for her. Herk certainly wouldn't have liked that, if he had walked in. But she just had a hunch this young man was carrying a full-sized snake coiled up in those trousers. Duane Roscoe had sat in the leather armchair for a full two minutes before he made up his mind, but he finally dropped them with a charming blush, and yes, she had been right. It looked like a hoe handle, and it wasn't even inflated.

She shook her breasts and watched them wobble. Still good at 32. When they fell out, men's eyes followed them, right out of their sockets. 38D's and no sag. Well, not much anyway. Hell, she didn't know what some women were on about. When she saw something she wanted, she grabbed it. She had grabbed Hercules and was able to wake up in a bedroom the size of a bus garage with mirrors on the ceiling and real gold leaf on the mouldings. There was French furniture from the court of Louis the Fourteenth. There was even a grand piano in her bedroom. Which she couldn't play. But Chopin did, whoever he was. At the side of the huge bed was a bell for the maid and a kitchen bell. She rolled over and pushed the kitchen bell, so her breakfast would be ready for her when she finished her shower.

Duane Roscoe was waiting patiently in the gym built in the basement when Corky DeLoop entered. She was wearing a red lycra one piece with high-cut legs over diaphanous tights, deciding against a bra because she felt the effect of the one piece would be spoiled. She wore pure white low quarter training shoes with shoe top socks which had fuzzy balls at the back. Her hair was pulled back into a ponytail and held with a pink ribbon, perfectly matching her lipstick. Duane Roscoe blushed when she walked in and looked for someplace to rest his eyes. Corky's look was, of course, direct as she walked straight up to him, very close, her breasts nearly touching his chest.

"Hello, Duane," she said gaily with her biggest smile. "Time to break a little sweat, huh?"

"Yes, ma'am," he said, still trying to find something non-sexual to look at. He was himself wearing lycra mid-thigh training pants, very tight. They were silver, topped by a matching vest trimmed in blue which displayed his wide shoulders and narrow waist to good advantage.

"I cain't wait to get started, can you?" She was glad he was only an inch or so taller than she was, as she hated looking up to a man.

"No, ma'am," he replied, blushing again.

"Well," she said, moving a shade closer, "what do you suggest we do first?"

"Well, ma'am, I think we oughta warm up..."

"I'm already warm."

"Uh, first of all, maybe we could do the exercise bike?"

She was still smiling at him. "Do you like ridin'?"

Roscoe backed up a step. "Oh, yes, ma'am, I think it's real good for you."

"You do, do you? Then we better get on our bikes, Duane."

They spent ten minutes on the bicycles, then did sit-ups and leg raises. Then Duane put her through a general body development programme which took about thirty minutes. Corky remained bubbly and full of double entendres, and the stronger the meaning, the more confused Duane became. She would move close to him after an exercise and pretend to misunderstand "back exercise" for "exercise on your back". Duane did his best to try and regain the high ground with neutering technical information, but not once during the session did he manage to regain the initiative, if he ever had it in the first place. They finished off the session with ten minutes on the Life Steps.

"Well," Duane said, looking around for his bag, "you did real good, ma'am."

Corky sat down on a padded bench and patted the space beside her. "What do you do, Duane?"

He sat as far away on the bench as he could, to be polite. "I'm a student. Junior. Majorin' in physical education."

41

"Oh, I just *love* physical education. Started mine years ago. Oughta have a PhD by now." She leaned so her breast touched his arm and used her hand to stroke his pectorals. "Nice chest you have, feller."

Duane was bright red. "Why, thanks, ma'am. Now, look, I gotta be goin' soon, and..."

Her hand moved down to his tight, muscular stomach. "Oh, I don't think you're gonna go yet, honey chile. I got a coupla exercises I still want to do."

They were both aware of Duane's growing erection which was impossible to hide in tight lycra.

The boy must not have been more than twenty and was not used to handling sex at this octane rating. This woman had taken charge at the very beginning. He had always thought that was the man's job. This had unsettled him, and he was staggering from inner crisis to inner crisis. "Uh, I think I better tell you, ma'am, that I got a steady girlfriend, and I live with her, and..."

"I don't give a shit how many girlfriends you got, honey. They ain't here, and I am."

For less than three seconds Duane's fingernails dragged on the cliff face, and then he was gone. Her face and lips were close, and he could smell her body and perfume. He had been longing to touch her ever since he first saw her. She was so...abundant. He leaned forward, and they kissed. Those incredible tits pressed into him, and her tongue explored his mouth aggressively. Clouds of colour hissed through his brain, and everything but the touch of the woman was covered by the mist. His hand was drawn inevitably, inexorably to her breast, and when he touched it electric fire jumped through his body. It felt even better than it looked. Then he felt her hand on his dick, and the electric fire became a roaring furnace. All Duane Roscoe wanted then was to fuck. With a guarantee that one wish would come true, he would take the fuck over everything else the world had to offer at that moment.

Corky pulled away from the kiss and looked into the young man's eyes. They were completely glazed over. He was gone. He was hers. No sweat. She put her immaculate pink fingernails underneath his pants on either side and started sliding them

42

down. He accommodated her completely, lifting his buttocks, holding his feet up. His chest was heaving, and his whole body was flushed.

Corky got to her feet. "Stand up for me, honey," she held her hands out to him, and he obligingly got up. For a moment she stared at his erection which was standing strong and straight, about thirty degrees from his abdomen. "Now *that* is what I call a blue steel hard-on." She grabbed his penis firmly in her hand. "Come with me, boy. I'm gonna show you what you do with one of those things."

Holding onto his dick, she led him out of the gym and up the stairs into her bedroom, pushed him down on the bed, kicked off her shoes, stripped off her one-piece and tights and dived on him. She licked and bit him on the body, as he fought for control. But she was much too much for him. She slapped him in the face with her breasts, and when he tried to get one in his mouth she slapped him hard with her hand. When one of his hands groped for her vagina, she knocked it away, spinning on top of him until her sex was over his face, then sat up and ground her groin back and forth over the moaning, demented head. Once Duane, in a final effort, simply tried to overpower the woman, but Corky immediately grabbed him by the balls and squeezed. He let go. He surrendered to the wild woman who was ravishing his body the way *she* wanted to. A fragment of rational thought drifted through the storm in his mind. What the hell, this is the most fantastic fuck of my life...why should I complain?

Good sex could drive Corky DeLoop into an atavistic spiral toward the jungle of her distant ancestors. The same wide eyes that could be liquid pools of innocence widened even further and flashed with danger. The large mouth ringed with frosted pink lipstick would draw back into a snarl, baring teeth which could draw blood and tear another animal into bite sized pieces. Nostrils flared dangerously, and the platinum hair became a tangled mane which she shook from time to time triumphantly.

And now was the moment she had been waiting for. The fire in her belly told her it was time, and Corky DeLoop literally sprung upon the young man's penis like a lioness. Holding it underneath her she worked her hips from side to side as she slowly enveloped it, yelling violently with her diaphragm as each inch disappeared, shaking her head and snorting. It was a beauty, she thought, a beauty! Must be a good eight or nine inches and as thick as her wrist. When she finally got him all inside, she moved her hips in a little rocking motion from side to side so she could feel the great blue steel hard thing inside of her. Volcanic emotions began erupting from her abdomen all the way to the tingling top of her head.

"Yeeeeeee Hawwwwwwww!" she bellowed in a voice that echoed around the huge bedroom. Then she started to ride. At first she stood on her knees, pounding up and down, then she beat her fists on his chest like a kettle drum. She scratched and clawed at the boy and ground her pelvis into him, around and around, up and down.

Duane had begun to buck like a mule. He had long ago given up trying to stem the mad woman's onslaught, only trying to protect his face and vitals from her clawing nails and pounding fists. The sounds coming from her were the sounds of the night in places near the equator. Duane was simply swept up in the hurricane, and he just let it carry him. But now he was coming, and nothing - from God to the kings of the earth - could stop him. He came deep from the bottom of his spine, and it felt as if the sperm was immediately sucked from him by the irresistible vacuum raging on top of his loins. The woman was bellowing like a wounded baboon, her hips pumping and completely out of control. She didn't stop, even as he began to wane, even as the blood began to drain from his penis and he felt himself going soft.

"No, no, no," she yelled. "More, more, I want more, you no good son of a bitch!" Like a wrestler from hell, she crawled up his body and grabbed his head between her legs, clamping it there and holding fast. "Give me some head, now, get me off again, you lousy bastard. Use your tongue! Yes! Yes! More! Yes!"

For a few seconds Duane was disgusted tasting his own fluids in her slippery overflowing vagina. He had never, ever done that before. But he was swept along by her animal sexuality. His hands massaged her bottom and hips which felt wonderful as they enveloped the top of his body. Several times he forced his face up for air, one time blowing bubbles, before she pushed him back with both hands. He felt his erection coming again, and with it came the same urgent emotions.

When Corky caught sight of the restored shaft of his penis, she yelled with delight and leapt on it again. Duane tried halfheartedly to flip her over on her back, but she was having none of it. This time it quickly disappeared inside her, and she windmilled her arms, letting out an explosive whoop. Then she grabbed him in an embrace, gnawing at his neck with her teeth. Incredibly, she was still coming. She hadn't stopped from the moment she began. It only receded slightly from time to time before returning with renewed force. She was pumping her hips up and down and around. Her nails dug furrows on his back, and blood spurted onto the silk sheets. Duane himself was screaming in pain and the anguish of mindless sexual ecstasy. At one point he looked into the mirror above and didn't recognise himself. Who was that, he wondered? It looked like a horror movie. His face was red, covered in bite marks and was slimy, like a newborn baby. It was just a flicker before he was swept again into the storm.

When the boy came again, it was another one from the base of his spine, though he didn't think anything at all could be left after the first one. But he was yelling with his eyes open, uncomprehending of the image he saw above of two primaeval bodies thrashing on the bed as if they were in final death throes.

It was her last rush, and she knew it. The end of her long climax. A great gong sounded somewhere, a huge gong as tall as a skyscraper, hit with great force by a giant redwood tree. The reverberations went through her again and again like sonic booms. She stretched up in one final wail, thrashing at the air, then fell off him completely exhausted.

The silence was palpable. Duane wondered where the hell he was and who he was. What had happened to him? Something had happened. What was it? He looked again up into the mirror and groaned. Bruises were forming, and he was bleeding. Guilt and worries started to flood into his consciousness. What about Gail? What would she say? Oh, my god, what have I done? His look transferred to the woman lying as if dead beside him. Her eyes were closed, and she had a look of supreme contentment on her face. Maybe, he thought hopefully, I can tell Gail I got caught in a combine harvester and only just managed to get out with my life.

Corky DeLoop raised herself languidly up onto one elbow and looked at the ruined body of her new trainer. "Well, feller, I give you eight outta ten for that one."

Duane Roscoe didn't move. "Eight? Eight?" he repeated incredulously.

"To get ten, honey, I woulda had to put you on the barbecue spit, roast you for four hours, eat every last bit of you and lick your bones clean. I have *never* had a ten."

Hercules DeLoop stood with his back to the huge roaring fireplace and cast a giant shadow across the vast room. It was the middle of summer, but DeLoop liked a fire from time to time, so the air conditioning was turned up to freezing so he could have one. He always said he had the money to change the seasons to suit his mood. So he got Pedro, one of the Mexican servants, to build a fire for him when he got back from New Orleans. A room like the one he stood in could only have been found in Texas. The size of a football field, the floor was polished wood from one end to the other. There were dead animal skins scattered here and there. Zebra, tiger, polar bear, grizzly, gazelle. On the wall opposite the fireplace hung a huge buffalo skin, which included the head. Above the fireplace and on either side were antlers, tusks and heads of numerous threatened species. There was an enormous leather sofa stretching for over twelve feet. At one end, DeLoop's favourite sitting spot, an elephant foot stood with the top open. He used it for a beer cooler, but the servants were airing it out before re-stocking it. At the other end of the room, the whole wall was glass incorporating an intricate system of sliding doors and screens. But these doors to the outside world were seldom, if ever, opened, as the atmosphere inside was centrally temperature controlled year round, including the humidity. Only in Texas could you find a crackling fire inside a house when the temperature outside was over 100°F in the shade.

DeLoop was six foot eight inches tall in his socks and about six ten with his cowboy boots on, and he weighed over 350lbs. He was dressed in light-coloured tapered trousers which stretched a bit over his gut, a black and white check shirt, string tie and leather fringed vest. He did not normally wear his Stetson indoors, but today he had it on. The side of his mouth held a long black Honduran cigar which was dwarfed by the size of his lantern jaw. Hercules DeLoop was a big man, and he was used to people being afraid of him. In earlier days he had used his fists, a pickaxe handle or a gun to get his way if any man or group of men opposed him. Now that he was sixty years old, his presence and reputation were usually enough. Except for that damn woman stretched out on the other end of the sofa, as comfortable and relaxed as a house cat.

Corky DeLoop wore a short pink skirt with a matching tight fitting top in stretch cotton. She was barefoot, and she had just heard her husband accuse her of fucking the new trainer.

"You got some kind of persecution complex, Herk," she said comfortably. "Ever time you go away, you think I get laid by the gardener, the garbage man, the clerk at the Seven Eleven..."

"Lissen here, woman!" he boomed, pointing his finger at her menacingly, "I paid good money for that piece of ass, and I don't want anybody else rootin' around in it but me!"

Corky laughed. "When was the last time *you* rooted in it?"

"Don't make no difference if I root in it once a day, once a week or once a year. So long as you're married to me an' stay in my house and run up accounts in ever goddamn store in Texas and get ever fuckin' thang you want with *my* money, then that fuckin' snatch belongs to *me!*"

She stretched herself again. "I'm right here, honey, anytime you want me, day or night. Like you say, you paid for it, and I never welch on a deal. Have I ever turned you down?"

DeLoop jerked his cigar out of his mouth and re-lit it. "You don't seem to unnerstand what I'm talkin' about, woman, and my patience is runnin' a little thin. Ever time I turn my back,

47

you got somebody else's dick in you, and that ain't right. That ain't Christian. It ain't decent. And I ain't havin' it!"

"It's just your 'magination, Herk," she yawned. "You just got no sense of trust in you."

"Whaddya mean trust! Ever time I come back here the young bucks are swarmin' like bluebottle flies around a fresh pile of cow shit."

"That's a real cultured thing to say about me."

"Fuck culture! Culture's for fairies! I wanna know, and I wanna know right now how come you fucked that goddamn meatball yesterday on a bed *I* paid for!"

She turned and looked at him with a sense of pity in her eyes. "Herk. I promise you I never touched that boy. Hell, he wasn't more'n twenty years old. What would I be wantin' someone like that for?"

"It's no good you lyin' through your teeth. It's me you're talkin' to, not some dumb ass mule skinner who don't know his ass from a hole in the ground. I *know* you did it. I got proof you did it. I even got a recordin' of some of the hell raisin' you were doin'."

Corky smiled sweetly. "Now, Herk, you haven't got your own servants spyin' on me now, have you?"

"What about those goddamn noises? I've lissened to 'em myself, and I wanna tell you, I was plain disgusted!"

"For chrissake, Herk, I was playin' the television loud yesterday, and your spy picked up somethin' outta a movie I was watchin'."

"I know you're fuckin' voice when I fuckin' hear it, woman! I ain't made my mind up yet, but I think I'm gonna take you outside and horsewhip you."

Corky DeLoop sat up slowly, staring at the big man in front of the fire. Then she raised her hand and pointed at him. "You do that, Hercules DeLoop, you make one mark on me, an' I tell you what I'll do. I'll wait til you go to sleep tonight, and I'll get a gun and put six holes in that big gut of yours, then I'll piss in your face while you're screamin' for help!"

He advanced two steps towards his wife. "Ain't a man or woman walks the face of this earth gets away with threatenin' me."

She stood up and took two steps towards him. "I ain't afraid of you, you big horse's ass!"

He swung at her with his huge right hand, and Corky easily dodged the blow. But she did not give ground. "One mark, you son of a bitch, one mark, and I swear on my father's grave and an ass high stack of Bibles that you're a dead man the next time you close your fuckin' eyes."

DeLoop glared at her for a full minute before taking off his Stetson and slamming it down on the floor. His wife stood glaring at him, arms akimbo. "I ain't never seen a woman like you in all my born days. The worst tempered jackass and mule I ever owned was sweet and accommodatin' compared to you."

"Well," she retorted, "you're not exactly the pick of the litter, either, you seven foot high stack of buffalo shit."

DeLoop drew himself up to his full height and pointed his finger at her like a gun. "I ain't havin' you fuckin' no other men, not while you married to me! I'm puttin' a stop to it!"

Corky dropped one arm and put the other behind her head, thrusting out her chest, and her eyes opened wide. "I'm not wearin' any panties. Wanna see?"

The hand he was pointing dropped as if drawn by magnets to one of her breasts, and she began moving rhythmically. "I'll be goddamned if you don't take the cake and the platter it was cooked on."

"When you get mad, it makes me horny," she said.

He massaged her breast. "Anythang makes you horny. Pourin' a glass of Seven-Up. Or swattin' flies. Or mowin' the lawn."

"So...you gonna do somethin' about it?"

"I ain't in the mood right now, 'cause I'm so pissed off."

She unzipped his trousers. "Then I'll get you in the mood. Now where's that ole pump handle of mine." She put her hand inside.

"You liable to get bit by a snake puttin' your hand in a dark place like that."

49

"Not by this snake. He ain't nothin' but skin."

"I tol' you I wasn't in the mood, and I ain't the kind to *lie*. Get out that big dick I bought you, and I'll watch."

She shrugged and crossed to a giant mahogany cabinet which supported a large oval mirror and opened a drawer. Pulling out a long box, she flicked off the lid and extracted a large dildo in the exact shape of a man's penis.

Hercules DeLoop stared at his wife as she lay back on the sofa and pulled up her skirt. Using her fingers first, she was soon moving and moaning. He felt his whole insides turning with regret. Regret that he wasn't young anymore, regret that he couldn't screw this magnificent woman three times a day and have her beg for more, regret that his body was sliding down a long slope and was nearly at the bottom. He had been to the doctor, who gave him injections. They helped. At least he could get it up and keep it up for a while. He looked wistfully as she started to insert the vibrator into her vagina. That could be me, he thought. That could be me. I want to, but I can't. The doctor warned him the injections were causing problems with his prostate, and pre-cancerous cells had been detected there. He was putting off the operation, but in the meanwhile he dared not have any more injections. Goddamn it, he thought, it's just a shame that this fine woman has to go to waste on whippersnappers too young to appreciate what they had got hold of. Corky was now moving the dildo in and out, up and down. She had turned on the electric vibrator, and her head was jerking from side to side. Her vagina was stretched tightly around the instrument. God, how that woman loved sex. He didn't mind her having her toys, but he was determined that was all she was going to have. He was not the kind of man to walk around his own house among his own servants with horns sticking out the top of his head. He could see. He could tell by their attitude. Jesus, the woman was screaming at the top of her lungs now, heaving her pelvis up in the air and working that rubber dick like a pump. How he would dearly love to be there, goddamn. Watching was better than nothing, though. He could feel little tingles in his organ and feel it trying to move. Then nothing. Nothing at all would happen. Corky was still going, yelling, throwing her head off the sofa, barking like a fucking dog. A bitch in heat, if he ever saw one. But she was *his* bitch. He was sure going to see to that, by god.

Corky was lying on the leather sofa breathing heavily. The old man liked to watch her sometimes, and she was willing to do it for him. A few years ago he wasn't too bad in the sack. No imagination and too fucking big for her to push and pull in the right direction. She thought it was absolutely amazing that so few men knew how to screw properly and fewer still knew how a woman was put together down there. Some of them poked and fumbled around with their fingers like they were looking for something they'd lost. So, years ago, before she was even twenty, she had just decided to take charge of things and make sure the dumb old boys gave her a proper good time. Mind, there were one or two who sure had the right idea. That calf roper - she forgot his name - from somewhere around Abilene was sure OK. She had just won the Miss Fort Worth Rodeo prize, and this guy was a lean, hard, Marlboro man type. Tall and stringy, put together with piano wire. Didn't say much. She had given him a blow job while they were driving out to the motel, and when they got inside the two of them damn near gutted the place. There wasn't a stick of furniture left in one piece. The manager had been banging on the door for thirty minutes because of all the noise and screaming, but the calf roper paid him off in crisp hundred dollar bills without saying a word. As a matter of fact, she couldn't remember anything he said that night except just before they parted. He turned to her as solemn as an undertaker, bit off a plug of his tobacco, worked it around inside his mouth and said, "I reckon that was the best piece of ass I ever had, honey." Then he drove her home without saying another word.

The sound of the telephone interrupted her reverie, and Herk crossed over to answer it.

"Yeah," he said into the receiver. Then he listened. "Uh-huh, yeah. Good." He listened again. "OK, OK. Yep. Good, good." Then he put the phone down and walked back to warm himself in front of the fire, taking a fresh cigar from a box on top of the mantelpiece. He unwrapped it, bit the end off, spat it into the fire, took a wooden match from a dish beside the cigar box and lit it.

"That was Gomez," he said after a few puffs to get his cigar going. "'Member Gomez?"

Corky came up on her elbow. "You mean that little Cuban creep came around here a couple of times with Ritter?"

"That's the feller," DeLoop replied. "Well, he called to tell me he's just finished cuttin' the balls off that boy you fucked yesterday."

Nothing happened for several beats, then Corky threw the dildo at DeLoop with all her strength. The big man ducked, and the rubber dick hit the wall, then bounced in an odd arc and hit the ceiling, came down on the mahogany cabinet, hit the wall once more and made a perfect landing in the open elephant's foot standing at the end of the sofa.

She was on her feet. Her eyes flashed dangerously. "You lousy son of a bitch! You motherfucker! You great, big bullyin' cocksucker! How could you *do* somethin' like that? What kinda man are you? No kind of man. Just 'cause you cain't get it up, you jealous of somebody who can, that's the problem, ain't it? Answer me, you fucker!"

DeLoop rolled the cigar to the side of his mouth. "Gomez is goin' to London with us. Takin' him along to look after you when my back's turned."

"You stinkin' ole turd! I'm not a piece of your property! And that poor fuckin' boy, it wasn't his fault. I grabbed him and pulled him in there, in the bedroom, he didn't even want to go!"

"Well, you right, you know. You're too purty to mark up, and the only reason for havin' you around here is your looks and the way your body feels. I could sure do without that goddamn mouth. Only time you ain't givin' me a hard time is when you got a dick in it."

Corky picked up a pillow and threw it back into the sofa. "Well, I'm tellin' you, you fuckin' dirty slob, this is the last time you pull one of these stunts..."

He took the cigar out of his mouth. "I hope it is. I hope you're right. But the next time I catch one, the balls come off. Up to you how many steers you want."

She moved toward him menacingly. "I told you a few minutes ago, Hercules DeLoop, that I would fill that big gut fulla lead if you fuck me around, and by god that's what I'm gonna do!"

He shook his head. "No you ain't. You ain't gonna kill the golden goose. You think I'm so stupid I ain't got somethin' in my will about an unnatural death? You kill me, woman, and you ain't gettin' a red cent. My lawyers'll kick your purty ass right out on the road without a stitch of clothes to stand up in, on account of the fact they all belong to me. In the meantime, it's a real pity I cain't think of anythang to do about that goddamn mouth."

"I'm not goin' to London! Not with you!"

"Oh, yes, you are. I got plans for you. I wanna dangle you in front of those limeys, those that ain't queer, to keep their minds off the fact I'm feedin' 'em a plate of shit. It's just a little backwater country, no more important than Bolivia, but those assholes still think they run the world."

Corky sat down, wanting to cry but not wanting to give him the satisfaction of seeing her weak. "You cain't make me go to London."

He moved toward the sofa and stood towering over his wife. "Oh, yes I can. In fact I can make you do anythang, 'cause I hold mosta the cards we playin' in this here game. I got the power, and I got the money. Money you'll get someday - maybe - if you do what you're told. There ain't no children, so you may as well have it all, as I never was the charitable sort. That's what you married me for, hell, I know that. But goddamn it, woman, it's like everthang else. You gotta *work* for it!" He paused for effect. "Now tell me again you ain't goin' to London."

Corky threw herself back into the sofa and crossed her arms angrily, staring straight ahead. She clamped her mouth tight shut, her full lips now a thin line. Alright, she thought to herself, you won that round, but that's not the end of the fight. I'm going to get your ass for that poor boy. It made her wonder what else had happened. It made her wonder about Darian, her hairdresser. They told her he moved away, but Darian was crazy about her. Would he go without saying something? Then there

53

was David. Where had he disappeared to? She did see Tom from time to time, but he acted real scared. A picture began to form in her mind. What had happened to these lovers? Had he killed them? Castrated them? She was well aware there was an evil and dangerous side to the huge man who loomed over her. All kinds of people came to the house. Some were politicians, in both the state and federal governments. There were money men as well. And military people. And lawyers. But also, yes, there were a lot she would call gangsters, some like Gomez, some even more dangerous looking.

She hadn't really taken an interest, but maybe now she should.

CHAPTER FOUR

Despite it being summer, the weather was cool and unsettled. But London had brightened up for the past two days, and Haug got a call from Stuart Easton who suggested they meet at a little Italian restaurant in Victoria for lunch. Against his better judgment, he drove the pickup and spent twenty minutes trying to find a parking space, so he was nearly ten minutes late.

He found Easton sitting inside, despite the warm day. Louise Templer was with him. It was an inexpensive little restaurant, more a combination cafe and cafeteria with serve-yourself food. The tables and seats were for function rather than display, but it was cheerful, if a little crowded. He greeted the two MP's and collected a tray. The queue wasn't long and moved swiftly. He grabbed a lasagne, a salad and some Italian bread. At the till he asked for a Coke and glass of ice. They brought him back a glass with two lumps in it, and he sent the fellow back for more. A glass of ice to Haug meant a glass *full* of ice. Britain as a country was extremely frugal with its ice, even when you were in an Italian restaurant. Easton arrived at the till and insisted on paying. When Haug started to argue, the Sheffield MP told him it was probably the only time in his life he would see a Yorkshireman put his hand in his pocket, so it was an experience to remember.

As he put his tray down on the table, Louise Templer smiled at him. In daylight he observed she was a very interesting looking lady, and the smile brightened her whole face. Her dark hair was down today, held back by a red velvet band. She was wearing a cream blouse with the top button open and a grey skirt which seemed to fall just above the knee. He could now see she had a touch of green in her light brown eyes.

"I'm sorry I was a little ratty the other evening," she said. "I'm afraid I was extremely tired and not at all in my best form."

Haug slipped into one of the fixed seats. "I'm glad you said what you thought. I like that a hell of a lot better than if you said I was wonderful, thinkin' all the time you couldn't wait to get to the other side of the room."

She smiled again warmly. "When Stuart mentioned he was having lunch with you, I bullied my way along so I could apologise. Hope you don't mind."

Haug poured out his can of Coke. "Absolutely delighted, ma'am. Gives me somethin' a lot nicer to look at than the face of Stuart Easton."

Easton pointed with his fork at the glass of Coke before winding more spaghetti onto it. "Some countries are famous for their beer, others for their wine. I think this says something about yours."

"Oh, I agree with you, Stuart. Tastes like horse sweat. That's why it has to be served nearly frozen with lots of ice. Same with American beer. Got to kill the taste somehow."

"The question is, why do you drink it?" asked Louise Templer.

"Same reason you folks eat marmite, which was a puzzle to me, or chip butties..."

"I'll not have a word said against chip butties," said Easton. "On a cold rainy night, you'll never taste anything better."

"That's the only kinda nights you got," Haug said, washing some lasagne down with the Coke.

They all laughed. Stuart Easton always looked the same. His sandy hair was going a little grey, but his slender, athletic build and sky blue eyes made him look younger than his 52 years. Haug had never seen him in anything but grey, off-the-peg suits, lightweight in the summer, and a red tie. Haug and Easton had met shortly after the group called the United Opposition was formed by Mainwaring over a year ago. He was a man Haug had always admired from what he knew and heard of him in the press. Easton was a fiery and unrepentant class warrior and a fine parliamentarian, though he had in fact been thrown out of the House over a dozen times over the years for his refusal to withdraw insults to Tory opponents. He was as relentless in his attack on the Conservatives as they were against the unions and the working class. He would, with equal ferocity, set upon the right wing of his own party when they offered political accommodation to the Tories, or, as he said once, tried to elbow their way to the trough at the expense of their

56

constituents. Easton considered his seat at Westminster as just a job, a job like any of his beloved miners had. So he attended every session - unless very ill - and fought in every session. In fact he had been a miner until his mid-twenties, and Haug could tell from his big hands that they had seen hard work earlier in his life. Easton heaped scorn on MP's of any party, but especially the Conservatives, who had other jobs or used their political position to feather their own nests. Which of course so many of them did. For them it was the whole purpose of being in Parliament.

After they finished eating Easton commented the place was too crowded to talk and suggested they go for a walk in St James's Park.

They entered the park at the southeastern end of Spur Road.

"This is where I first met Jonathan," Haug said. "He'd sit there and feed the damn ducks half his sandwiches. Over there on that bench that's empty. He probably just left."

"No," said Easton as they moved toward the bench. "He's very busy at the moment and asked me to pass on a few details you'll need to know."

"I like him in spite of myself," Haug said. "An absolute pillar of the English establishment, yet you should have seen him in his little sports car. Last summer he took me to an Ashes Test at Lord's in his Morgan. Had it ever since he bought it back in the sixties. Like a little boy."

They sat down with Easton in the middle. "Sir Jonathan and the senior civil servants run this country and always have," he said. "They are the intellectual elite. They know the answers to everything. Or think they do."

"It surprised me," said Louise Templer, "that he chose to do this, to bring people together into the United Opposition."

Easton folded his arms. "He represents a dying breed, a kind of dinosaur really. The world he believes in doesn't exist and never did. But he thinks it did and acts as if it did. It was a world where his class stood upright and strong against evil whilst taking care of the less fortunate. A patrician world where leaders are trained to bear any burden for their country without flinching. As for the inadequates, as they call them, they are to be fed, housed and looked after just like children."

Haug leaned forward, elbows on knees. "I think you're bein' a little hard on him, Stuart. He's got somethin' inside 'of him I kind of envy."

"Oh, I trust him as a *person*," Easton said quickly. "Which is unusual for me. But I don't trust him to choose the future for me or any working man in England."

"He's a good man," commented Louise, "through and through. But what he represents is an unrealistic dream, one that has been used by men who manipulate people like him as a moral base for a damaging system that doesn't have any morality."

"Well, I like ole Jonathan. He's a little stiff, though. I'd like to take him on a fishin' trip one day back in North Carolina. Just him and me and a quart jar of moonshine and a couple of cans of beans."

Easton laughed. "I can just picture that, Haug. For about a half a second." He suddenly became serious. "Apparently there is a problem. Sir Jonathan has acquired the information that an important meeting is to take place. Including this Texan, Hercules DeLoop. It's to be held aboard Harvey Gillmore's yacht called, I think, Matilda. Somewhere off Corfu. They will travel by air to Corfu, then board the yacht to sail around in little circles while they drink gin, take the sun and plot their nefarious deeds."

Haug stared out at the pond for a moment. "Now that *is* a problem. I got no idea how to get close to a goddamn yacht. I've never even been on a yacht in my life, and if you asked me what a yacht was, I'd have to say it was a big boat, probably white, that floats in the water. The extent of my knowledge."

"Well, that's more than I know about them," Easton replied. "Sir Jonathan seemed quite worried that it would set you impossible difficulties. He is, however, keen to find out something about the reasons for the meeting, why it's taking place and what might be said. What we lack at the moment is hard evidence of direct American involvement. Not the American government, of course. Obviously what's been happening here is also happening there as well. Or has already happened. A shadowy linkage has formed over the years between transnational organisations with global interests, wealthy individuals, the media and rightwing ideologues. Penetration has been made in the ranks of the military, secret services, the diplomatic corp, as well as domestic civil servants and government itself."

Easton stopped and looked up at the sky which was clouding over. "Hard to believe at first. But Sir Jonathan is nothing if not thorough, and the documentation, collected over the years, is impressive. It exists. It is there. We have got to know more, get a complete picture, just how it works, and bring the information right out before the people."

"Maybe it's because I know more about things now," Louise Templer commented, "but it seems they are becoming more open now. It's as if they don't care if anyone finds out. I've seen Michael Regis in the House having lunch, talking to Ministers. Right at home."

"Yes, I think you're right," Easton replied. "My own theory is they feel they have little to fear, now the great archenemy has virtually disappeared in the East. The USSR has disintegrated, along with their allies in Eastern Europe. The arrogant always start to swagger when they think they've won."

Haug crossed his leg and flicked a bit of dirt off his boot. "Hell, maybe they have."

"I'll be damned if they have," Easton said bitterly. "I'll be damned if they will. So I think we should be able to afford a return fare to Corfu for you, if you'd like a working holiday."

Haug shook his head. "Have to be for two. I'll want One Time with me. He's our electronics department, and he's damn near invisible when the sun goes down."

"I'll have to check," Easton said. "Two tickets may stretch our finances. That's how bad things are. Sir Jonathan mentioned he had a relative living in Corfu you could stay with, an eccentric musicologist. Or something like that."

"Well," said Haug, "havin' a place to stay is a help. That way we don't have to act like tourists. I'd like to get down there a coupla days before they arrive so we can pick 'em up at the

59

airport to see how many are in the party. If this thang's really important, they'll probably have some purty good security, even though they're on a boat."

"That's no problem," Easton shrugged.

Louise Templer looked at her watch. "I'm sorry, I'm going to have to make off now. I have to attend a constituency meeting at the Red Rose Club, just off the Holloway Road. The Underground is unpredictable."

"I'm goin' that way. I'll give you a lift. If we're finished here."

She smiled. "I wouldn't want you to go out of your way."

"No problem. I live just around the corner from Archway. Goin' right up Holloway Road."

"Well, if you don't mind," she said as they got up.

Stuart Easton waved goodbye and set off at a brisk pace towards Westminster, while Haug and Louise turned in the opposite direction to find the pickup. The sun had now gone behind the clouds, and it looked like it might rain. England probably has no more rain than many other countries. It is just so changeable. A day starts bright and sunny and ends cold, wet and miserable. The English are never really confident enough to leave the umbrella at home. And it was the weather Haug and Louise talked about until they got to the pickup.

Louise Templer shook her head. "I might have known."

Haug flashed at the central locking. "What?"

"An American truck."

"Consider yourself lucky, ma'am," Haug said as he slid under the wheel. "This is a livin' symbol of the dyin' South."

"Good lord," she said as she closed her door. "It's like a...a gin palace inside. It's huge."

"What kinda temperature would you like? 68, 70 degrees? The heater operates with the air conditioner to keep it steady." He started the engine, which had a growling, menacing roar, and pulled out into the traffic.

"I think I'll just lower the window, if I can find the right button. How many are there here?"

"Some are for the seats." He pointed at the one for the window, then reached into his pocket for his tobacco pouch. At the lights he opened it and bit off a piece from the plug inside. He offered the pouch to Louise. "I suppose you don't chew?"

"I'm sorry?"

"This here's chewin' tobacco." He put the pouch away as the lights changed and put the pickup in gear.

Louise Templer stared out the windscreen. "That sounds the most disgusting habit I've ever heard of."

"What about some music, then?" He picked up a cassette.

"What kind of music?" she asked dubiously.

"Scarlatti OK? Harpsichord sonatas? A Dutchman called Koopman is playin'."

"Yes," she said with a raised eyebrow. "Fine."

Haug laughed. "Yeah, I know, it completely spoils the image, doesn't it?"

"Do you really like classical music?"

"I fuckin' love it. Like literature, I only came across it later when I finally went to college. At first I didn't like it, but it's one of those thangs you kinda double take on. Wait a minute. What's happenin' here. Once I started lissenin' to it, I didn't wanna lissen to anythang else. OK, sometimes I lissen to a little hillbilly. Bluegrass, especially."

"I see."

Haug felt an uneasiness in the atmosphere he found difficult to define. The MP seemed to be making an effort to be nice, as if she had decided that was the right thing to do. Frankly he preferred her the way she was at the meeting. He remembered how their eyes had met. She had been interested, he was sure of that. At the meeting she protected herself with a ring of aggression, now it was a halo of niceness. Both were acts, and he wondered why. Sitting beside him in the pickup she was obviously nervous. She had put her window down, then halfway up and down again. She crossed her legs, then uncrossed them and crossed them again.

"You got somethin' on your mind?" he asked finally.

"What? No, no. I'm alright."

"I'm not goin' to take a chunk outta you, you know."

"What are you talking about?" She sounded a little cross.

"You seem kinda uptight since you got into the pickup."

"Well, if I am, it's no business of yours," she said sharply.

"Yeah, you're probably right there," he replied and decided to shut up.

He actually heard the little hatchback before he saw it in the side mirror. A sound system big enough to fill an auditorium was playing something with a heavy beat at maximum volume. The little car was trying to beat the queue by squeezing through on the inside, between the line of traffic and the curb which was marked as a cycle path, and he was going too fast. Haug could see a cyclist up ahead, and so, apparently, could the driver of the hatchback, but he thought he could force his way back into the queue and avoid the cyclist. He saved his braking until the last minute, and the queue closed up instead of opening for him. He caught the unsuspecting cyclist from behind. The bike sprung up on the pavement, while the cyclist hit his bonnet and bounced onto the windscreen before falling to the tarmac.

Haug pulled out of the queue quickly and braked to a stop behind the hatchback just as the driver angrily threw his door open and got out. The drumming music filled the atmosphere. Haug and Louise got out of the pickup and ran forward to the cyclist who was just trying to straighten herself from a crumpled position.

The car driver was young, about twenty-four or five, with a heavy gold bracelet on an arm which was pointing at his bonnet. His hair was cut short in a style that was heavy with "attitude". Haug could smell the cheap aftershave as he passed him.

"Look at what you fucking did to my car!" he shouted at the prone cyclist over the din coming from inside. "Look what you fucking did!"

Haug leaned over the figure and placed a reassuring hand on the back. He could see it was a young woman. "Don't move," he said. She was lying on her side.

"Are you alright?" Louise asked as she knelt beside the woman.

"I don't know," she muttered. "I think so."

"Move your head from side to side, if you can," Haug asked. That seemed to be alright, and he moved his hand down her spine with a professional touch. "Can you move your legs? One at a time, try and straighten them out."

"Are you a doctor?" she asked.

"I was a medic once. Your legs seem alright. Any pain anywhere?"

"My elbow. Side of my head."

He checked the head first. The skin wasn't broken, but a lump was beginning to form. "I think we better get you to a hospital. You're probably OK, but there's no harm in makin' sure."

Haug gently moved the woman so Louise Templer could cradle her head. As their hands touched he unexpectedly felt a little thrill and looked up. She was looking at him and held his eyes for just a moment before turning away and withdrawing her hand to hold the woman's head.

"What about my fucking car!" An angry face loomed over Haug.

Haug stood up. "You coulda killed this girl, feller."

His mouth pulled back into a sneer. "She pulled out right in front of me. It's her fault. And look at my fucking car! Look at it! She's got to pay for that!"

"Best thang you can do, bo, is go sit in that little car of yours, turn off that fuckin' racket and keep outta my way til I can get this lady into my pickup." The young man didn't move, so Haug went to the hatchback, leaned in and ejected the cassette. Finally it was quiet. He threw the cassette towards a row of bins and started back to the injured woman.

The young man blocked his way and punched at his chest with his finger. "'Ere, who the fuck do you think you are, mate? That was me best tape."

Without pausing Haug smacked the man with a huge backhand that sent him sprawling towards the bins. Haug followed him, picked him up by the belt, kicked off a lid and dumped him in headfirst. The bin was half full of rotting vegetable matter.

He returned to the injured woman and, taking great care, lifted her into his arms and carried her back to his truck. Another motorist had stopped, but Haug waved him on. Louise

63

helped get her on the seat. The woman was now protesting she was alright, but Louise insisted they take her to a hospital, which, she said, wasn't far. Haug had collected the bicycle and put it in the back of the pickup. He got in and restarted the engine. When he looked out his window he could see the young man sitting on the pavement, his head and shoulders covered with garbage. Louise directed him to the hospital where they helped the cyclist into Emergency. Louise, being an MP, was able to shake some life into the nursing staff. Then she demanded to use the telephone, called the police and reported the incident.

"Tell me something," Louise Templer said finally as they moved off toward Camden Town. "Is violence a solution to every problem for you?"

"Look," said Haug. "You better unnerstand somethin' right now, babe..."

"Don't call me 'babe'," she said sharply.

"Little events I approach in life, I take one by one. I react to what's *happenin'*, not what I *think* is happenin'. I don't go around beatin' up folks for fun. Now you've obviously heard some stories about me and got some ideas..."

"I only need my eyes. I saw what happened back there."

"Did you really?" he asked. "Or did you squeeze it into some kinda format you already had set up?"

"There was no reason to hit that idiot back there or tip him into a dustbin. You could easily have pushed him back into his little car..."

"Then he would have hit me."

"And *then* you could have hit him," she retorted.

"If I always gave the other man first lick, my face would be even uglier than it already is. Now lissen. I don't know a goddamn thang about gettin' a bill through the Commons. Which you do. But I do know about some thangs. The way I did it was about the best way I coulda done it."

"I hate violence," she said. "I loathe it."

"It might surprise you that I do too. I hate what it does to me inside. I hate the kinda person it makes me. Sometime, if you're really interested, I might try and tell you about it so you can unnerstand it. If you unnerstand somethin', it's a lot harder to grab the moral high ground and do a lotta preachin' when you don't know what you're talkin' about."

"I do know what I'm talking about," she said hotly. "I'm afraid you're the one who doesn't. Or doesn't seem to."

Haug shook his head. "There's somethin' kinda strange goin' on here, and I'm just tryin' to figger out what it is." They had stopped in another traffic queue for lights and he turned to look at her. She stared back at him, her arms folded across her chest. There was more than anger in her eyes. He looked back at the traffic, putting the pickup in gear and moving forward a few feet. "What time do you finish at the Red Rose Club?"

"What?"

"Let's have a drink together."

"That is a typical male response, Haug. If you can't win a rational argument, make a proposition."

"Goddang it," Haug said with a laugh. "You're as ornery as a jackass with a toothache. Now who said anythang about fuckin'?"

"I didn't. You just did."

"You said 'proposition', and the way I unnerstand proposition, is one person asks another person to go to bed. And once in the bed - or on the floor near it or on the table in the room or swingin' from the chandelier over it - they fuck. I did not proposition you, Louise Templer, MP. I asked you if you'd like to have a drink with me after you finish work, mainly so we could get to know each other a little better. Besides, I kinda like you. I got no fuckin' idea *why* I like you, on account of the fact you spend half the time with a darnin' needle up my ass. You're exasperatin' and get on my nerves, but I detect somethin' there I'd like to know a little bit better." He held up his hand to stop her interrupting. "And I wanna tell you somethin' while I'm talkin'. I am not the sort of guy to press myself on anyone. Besides, since *you* brought the question up, I don't even think I'd want to go to bed with you, 'cause on present evidence, it's liable to be the sourest experience of my life."

As Louise Templer listened, she was staring straight ahead. They drove in silence for a few moments. She could see the junction of Seven Sisters Road just ahead. Then, suddenly, she laughed and turned to him. "I don't know what it is with you, Haug," she said in a much softer voice. "There is something I find irritating about you. But I don't think it has much to do with you. If you see what I mean."

"Well, I already *know* that. It's one of the reasons I asked you out. Give us a chance to sort thangs through in a relaxed atmosphere, learn a little about each other."

"Alright, you're on. But not tonight. I'm meeting my husband later. I am married, you know."

"Yeah," he replied. "I keep forgettin' people still do that sorta thang. Never had much luck at it myself."

"I wonder why?" she asked with a twinkle in her eye. "But it does take a little self discipline sometimes, I do admit."

"Never any good at self discipline myself," he said, pulling up in front of the Red Rose. "Give me a ring when you've got some time."

"I will," she said, getting out of the pickup. "I promise. And thanks for the lift."

Haug watched her walk away with a puzzled expression on his face. Yes, she had an attractive movement. Not just her hips but the angle of the body, how it was held. It was natural, with a little roll, rhythmical, almost athletic. There was a lot of expression in body movement, and, yes, she was attractive. But in a way Haug had not encountered before. That's why he was puzzled. He put the pickup in gear and got back round to the Holloway Road.

His office was on Junction road, just above an Asian "supermarket". The family who ran the shop were extremely nice, and he had always liked them. He rented a flat above his office. On the second floor. He climbed the stairs and passed the office of the Greek solicitor who never seemed to be in and opened the door marked Phoenix Investigations. Lizzy was still there, sitting behind his desk in his chair, operating the word processor.

He threw his dozer cap over on the sofa and went to the side counter where there was an electric kettle and a small fridge. "I suppose you want one, too," he grumbled at Lizzy.

"Of course," she said without looking up.

"What are you doin' here, anyway? Thought you had to pick up the kids."

"It's a holiday, you bald-headed American git. Half term."

He filled the kettle and waited for it to boil. "Who you writin' to, some old Irish potato farmers, tryin' to find one to marry you?"

"I wouldn't marry another man if he had a pot of gold in one hand and a stack of titles in the other."

Lizzy McGuire was his secretary. She only worked part time because of her kids, but Haug loved her. She weighed about 15 stone, and he could only just beat her in arm wrestling. He found her years ago working at the Drum across the street where they became friendly. Now she was invaluable to him, particularly since he had been working for the United Opposition. Smaller jobs, mostly divorce cases, were divided up between him, Keef and One Time. She somehow managed to juggle their various times so enough money came in to cover the rent and her salary.

"Oh, by the way," Lizzy said. "There's someone waiting for you upstairs."

Haug turned to her. No one went to his flat upstairs. "Who, for god's sake?"

"Surprise." She smiled at him briefly before returning to her word processor.

"Aw, come on. Who is it? You shouldn't let folks into my flat. I don't even want you up there."

She raised her eyebrows. "I don't *want* to go up there." She continued typing.

"Oh, Jesus Christ," he said, walking over to the door. "Never can get shit outta you. Gonna fire you one of these days."

"Hey," she shouted. "What about my tea, you Yankee bastard?"

He climbed the stairs. His small flat was the only one on the second floor, with one bedroom, sitting room, kitchen and bath with a flat roof outside where he sometimes crawled out to lie in the sun. The door was open, and he pushed it cautiously, looking around carefully.

"Hello?" he said.

He saw an expensive looking red shoe with a high heel dangling in midair from the doorway of his sitting room. The shoe was attached to a tanned foot, and as he watched, the foot came up, showing first the knee, then most of the naked thigh. The leg then bent at the knee and kicked once, high in the air. A tanned hand crept sexily down the thigh, and the nails were painted the same colour as the shoes.

"Goddammit," he shouted, "I'd know that beautiful leg anywhere! Lemme see what it's attached to!"

He was moving into the sitting room as Jennifer Montgomery came out, her arms open. They embraced and kissed. Both of them only meant it to be a friendly, happy-to-see-you-again kiss, but it turned into something more than that. Their mouths opened, slightly at first, then enthusiastically, and they continued to kiss deeply. Jennifer finally pulled away.

"Hello, Hoggy," she said, her face radiant with a big smile. "Welcome home from work."

"If I had you to come back to all the time, I don't think I'd go in the first place."

"Don't hand me that," she said, laughing. "You don't want to live with a woman."

"In your case I might make an exception." She had on a long red dress split high up her thigh. The top revealed her cleavage and clung snugly to her breasts. Haug shook his head as he looked at her. "I sure do miss those tits."

"I thought it was my mind that attracted you."

"I cain't get your mind in my mouth," he replied.

"I don't see why not. It's plenty big enough."

He grabbed her and hugged her again, swinging her back and forth. Her blonde shoulder length hair seemed bleached by the sun, even more blonde than he remembered. "Where you been? Somewhere nice and sunny?"

"Corfu," she said. "Spent six lovely weeks there."

He released her from the hug. "Corfu? Hell, I'm just goin' there."

Disappointment flooded into her face. "Oh, no! You're joking! That can't be. It would have been marvellous if you had been there."

"It's work, I'm afraid," he said, dropping his hands. "I wouldn't have much time to do what I'd like to be doin' with you."

He met Jennifer Montgomery over a year ago and knew her by sight longer than that because she trained at his gym. Or used to. For the past six or eight months she had been on a tour with the Royal Shakespeare Company. He had received cards and short letters from Edinburgh, Liverpool, Birmingham and Dublin, but he hadn't seen her for a long time. They had a short affair after a terrifying attempt on her life. He had managed to save her life and find out why she had been targeted. Though she was a recent graduate from drama school at the time, she had been working for Michael Regis as a top drawer prostitute in order to pay off the mortgage on her Hampstead home. Abused as a child by her father, she had decided she was not going to be just another poor actress hopping from bedsit to bedsit in London. She wanted a nice house as a base and for security and decided to pay for it by being a top class London call girl. This, however, led her to Regis who basically used her as a political favour and inducement for his clients. And Michael Regis was a man the United Opposition was very interested in. Regis was a vital link in the suspected political and economic web stretching around the globe.

"When are you going to Corfu?" she asked.

"In a few days, I think. Probably early next week. I expect Michael will be there, too."

She looked down at her hands. "Oh. That's still going on, is it?"

"I'll get him one day. One way or the other. But you've been workin' a lot. Real work, instead of spendin' the time on your back."

"Yes," she replied. "And I'm going *broke*, too. Especially considering the amount of money I burned in Corfu."

"Think you'll go back to the old business?"

She threw her head up. "If I really need the money, sure, I'll do a bit of freelancing. Not for Michael, of course." She walked over to his window and looked out the back. The clouds had made the late afternoon very dark. "But there's something I've got to tell you..."

Haug shook his head and sat down on the edge of the bed. "Now, I know that tone of voice real well. You got a boyfriend."

She still had her back to him. "He's a nice fellow and a good actor. I met him on tour, of course. I've never had what you could call a 'relationship' before. Except what I had with you, and that was special. Really special. The thing is, Hoggy, I have lied to him. I haven't told him about last year. Nor the fact that I'm a whore."

Haug got up from the bed and went to her, enveloping her in his arms from behind. "You aren't a whore, Jenny. You're one of the greatest, nicest people I've ever met. Made my life a little richer. You're a woman and a good woman. And I've known a lotta women. Hell, lotsa women're Tories. That's a *lot* worse than bein' a whore."

"Damn it, you big old bear, you're so sweet." She turned around to him and touched his face with her hands, stroking his hair back to his ponytail. Her lips started to tremble a little. "But what about you? If I ever loved anybody on the face of the earth, it was you. Is you. You're certainly the only man I've ever trusted."

Haug had his arms around her. "What about the new feller?"

She paused for a moment. "That's something different. I can't explain it."

"Don't you trust him?"

"Well...yes. But I haven't had to trust him like you. With my life. My dignity, my self respect. Everything. You're the only one who knows everything about me. And you still like me."

Haug looked out the window into the distance. "I think the word's love with me, too. It's a word you gotta use sometimes to describe a point where a lotta thangs come together. Maybe we'll never stop lovin' each other."

70

She brought her head up and kissed him. This time their tongues gently played together, touching, withdrawing, touching again. She pulled away and looked into his eyes. "I want to make love to you now."

"I'm not gonna stop you," Haug said. "I don't have that kinda willpower."

She led him over to the bed by the hand and then kissed his hand. She pushed him back, tore open the snaps on his shirt and used both hands to caress his chest. "You're still big and ugly," she said.

"Just the way you left me," he replied as he stroked her hair, pulling it gently back from her face.

"I didn't leave you. I don't think I ever could, you know."

"I've been dreamin' about your tits."

"I can make your dreams come true," she said as she eased one of her breasts from the cleavage of her dress. "There you are."

"Fuck," he said caressing it with his hand from the side, where it joined under her arm, slowly around to the nipple which stood erect as he touched it tenderly, then he cradled it from underneath. "These thangs oughta be preserved somehow as a natural wonder of the universe. There oughta be a shrine built somewhere in the desert looked after by holy men so pilgrimages could be made from ever country over hundreds of years."

"Oh, dear," she said. "You do have a lyrical string to your bow. Don't you like the rest of me?"

"This is just a fine beginner, except here you sorta start with the dessert, then go on to the main feast."

She sat up and unzipped her dress. Haug stripped off his waistcoat, shirt, trousers and boots.

"Want me to keep the knickers on?" she asked. "They're silk. The French sort."

"Yeah, and the shoes as well. You never did give me treats like this before."

She crawled onto the bed beside him. "You never gave me time."

They made love to a slowly beating drum at first, but the rhythm quickened to a frenzy as they touched and moaned and shouted obscenities together before the climactic emotional and physical discharge. Then they collapsed into each other's arms, saying nothing, lying side by side, just holding on together as one person, holding tightly, both hoping the secret moment would last forever. As Jennifer Montgomery's thoughts began to re-form from the periphery of her mind, she realised it was the quickest lovemaking session ever. Yet she was convinced it was one of the best. She had her arms inside his, around his huge chest, and one of her legs was over his waist. She buried her face into his neck and kissed him with more love than she could even remember feeling before, and she felt his kisses on her head, on her ears. She was so happy she nearly wanted to cry. It was so safe, so warm, so wonderful to be in the strong arms of a man who wanted nothing from her except what she was able to give. And sometimes she just wanted to give him everything.

She thought of Adrian, and he seemed so far away. Adrian had been with her in Corfu for three of the six weeks. An intense, funny, ambitious, insouciant man of twenty six, so full of life and energy. He made her forget things with his impersonations and his lively chatter and took her out of herself. Their affair had begun two months before the end of the tour, and the lovemaking was good. But it wasn't volatile and shattering, and Adrian wasn't Haug. She didn't want to choose, didn't want to have to choose, between them. Couldn't she, she prayed to a god she didn't believe in, couldn't she somehow have them both? Instinctively she knew she couldn't live with Haug. The combination in close quarters would be too explosive, and she didn't want anything - ever - to separate them finally, forever. Could you have two different kinds of love? Was it possible?

In a rush of emotion, she held on to the man in her arms, overcome with a sudden desire to be part of his flesh and give birth to his child.

CHAPTER FIVE

Later that same day, in the evening, Michael Regis was having dinner in Le Bonheur with Jeremy Evans, who was Deputy Director of MI6, a man whom he did not completely admire. But, by virtue of his position in the Secret Intelligence Service, he was very important to Regis and to the Community of Association. Jeremy Evans had been selected eight years ago as ideologically suited to fast lane advancement in the Service. Words were whispered into the right ears. Other, more competent, men were elbowed firmly aside, and Jeremy Evans whipped round the circuit quite rapidly. He was only a year younger than Regis at forty two, but there the similarity between the two ended. Evans was still boyish-looking. His hair tended to fall forward, and he had a habit of raking it back with his left hand while he was talking. He also still maintained an adolescent enthusiasm with, unfortunately, an accompanying tendency to lack of discretion. It was this which turned down the corners of some mouths in the civil service as Jeremy Evans was continually promoted over wiser heads. However, Regis recognised, Evans was in place. He was a fact. And an asset. The final appointment as Deputy Director was a close run thing before the Committee.

Michael Regis suddenly remembered it was Jennifer Montgomery who was instrumental in persuading the key member of the Committee to change his vote. One of his "girls". His best one, really. She actually oozed sexuality, and they all fell for it. Then there was that wretched business last year when everything nearly came unravelled. So she was no longer available. A pity. And he rather enjoyed screwing her himself.

He put the thought out of his head and raised the drop of red wine the waiter had poured into his glass to his nose. He took a sip and nodded for him to pour.

"Do you know what it is that DeLoop wants?" Evans started to say before he broke off, warned by a look from Regis, who glanced at the wine waiter.

Evans waited until the waiter retired from the little whitewashed alcove where Regis had his permanently reserved table in the old converted wine cellar. He had been there several times and was quite envious of the restrained privacy inside the little known, but exclusive restaurant. He repeated his question.

"I believe the Texan wants to outline details of financial policy with a view to the setting up of fresh conduits, and the establishment of some sort of central accounting."

"Sounds very dreary," said Evans.

Regis stifled a sigh. "On the contrary, it's something which has needed doing for some time. In fact we have become a very long spine with no central control. At the moment we have largely uncoordinated efforts in a number of countries with a great deal of duplication. And consequent financial waste. Not to mention the waste of resources both physical and mental." He broke off as a waiter brought two bowls of bouillon and what smelled like freshly baked French bread.

Jeremy Evans envied Michael Regis, his confidence, his knowledge, the people he knew, his money, his ability to command a table at such a smart restaurant. He was certainly glad to be on the same team with such a man. His thick black hair had hardly a trace of grey, and the olive complexion made him almost exotic - though in fact he was very English indeed, from an old and respected family. He knew little of his background, except for the fact he had been a lieutenant colonel and liaison adjutant to the NATO commander a few years ago. From this position he had moved into arms brokerage and political lobbying. There were also stories of his fabulous women used as favours amongst those whom he did business with. Indeed he was surprised he did not have one on his arm this evening. He usually did. Evans was married and so far very faithful to his wife. Mostly because of fear. Women made him uncomfortable, and marriage to Alicia had well suited him. He had always found it very, very difficult to approach the opposite sex. Alicia had done all the work at the beginning and didn't seem at all displeased when she found he tended to avoid sexual encounter within the marriage. Jeremy Evans had other, darker, feelings which he largely forced himself to keep stuffed into a deep locker in the recesses of consciousness. But occasionally he would see the body of a young man, and something within him would sink and his knees felt weak. And long ago, bound hand and foot with weights swinging from his testicles, the sting of a leather whip... The thought was hurriedly swept out of sight again, back into the deep trunk. Only occasionally did he use the memory when he had sex with Alicia.

He took another sip from his spoon. The bouillon was absolutely delicious, as was the bread. And the wine. The wine was from Regis's own reserve, kept especially for him in the cellars. "I always look forward to coming here, Michael. As usual the food is exceptional."

"As I've already suggested," said Regis, "I believe we should travel separately to Corfu and separately be taken out to the Matilda. I do wish it could be anything *but* the Matilda, but that is the only yacht we have placed in the Med with sufficient accommodation area. Unfortunately, it belongs to Harvey Gillmore. Who, of course, will also be present. Perhaps his infernal rudeness will take the edge off the Texan."

"Is DeLoop rude, then?" Evans asked.

As if DeLoop's name was a cue, they were interrupted by the waiter with the entree, a speciality of the chef. Very, very thin slices of lamb which had been marinated for days, with a chestnut and drawn butter sauce. Before the waiter retired, he refilled their wine glasses.

"I gather he can be very rude, like many Texans," he said, finally answering the question. "I understand he is also bringing his wife, who he insists must accompany him on the yacht."

"I see," said Evans. "Does that interfere with plans of yours to provide..."

Regis held up his hand, a little annoyed Evans had been about to refer to women he sometimes made available for meetings. "I would rather have no female company on this particularly important date. But Gillmore has already twisted my arm, in his inimitable way, to supply him with one. She has, in fact, just flown out to join him. Perhaps it's best. Now the two women can keep each other amused while we talk." He transferred a morsel of flesh to his mouth, following it with a sip

75

of wine. "We shall all be arriving at staggered intervals, as the whole purpose of the yacht is for increased security," he continued.

"Surely that is no problem here," Evans replied. "Why go to all the extra trouble and expense of Corfu?"

"Oh, there's no problem in finding a secure address in London. But I don't want even the faintest flicker of a chance of our being seen together. Or even being seen leaving or arriving at the same address. It is simply a precaution, Jeremy. One with which I am sure you are familiar. We are doing nothing illegal of course, but in business and politics, as when you are playing a hand of cards, it is always wise to keep your own hand hidden until the final moment. We don't want some idiot left wing journalist falling upon us by accident, doing a doubletake, then adding two and two and making five."

Jeremy Evans thought the lamb delicious, wondering how it could be so tender and trying to identify the herbs and spices used in the marinade and sauce. He cut one asparagus tip in half, loaded it on his fork, then added a bite of lamb. Whilst chewing this with his eyes half closed, he remembered something. "Ah," he said. "I very nearly forgot. Gordon, at Special Branch, sent along a memo last week. I didn't know whether or not you would be interested." He reached for his inside coat pocket and found a copy of the memo. "Apparently he has noted something of an unusual group forming up at Westminster. Meetings in corridors, Whips' rooms, restaurants, St James's Park. Personally I think it looks completely innocent, and Gordon is always coming up with suspicious and strange groupings. I think he believes there's a spy behind every lamp post."

"Hmmm," Regis said without much interests as he unfolded the copy memo. However, as he read the names, his brow creased slightly, and he sucked discreetly at a piece of lamb stuck between two teeth. "Hmmm," he said again. "Odd. An odd bunch. Stuart Easton, General Portland, Matthew Tillson, Jonathan Mainwaring, Justin Lyndhurst... Doesn't appear to have a common denominator. Indivisible, like a prime number. Now, I wonder what interests they could possibly share?"

"Yes," Evans said, raking his wayward hair back with his hand. "Gordon also mentioned on the telephone that one of his men followed them to a meeting place one evening but couldn't gain access. He even tried using one of the new scanners - I don't know exactly how they work, but you point them at a window and you can sometimes pick up interior conversations. But apparently there was too much interference. Couldn't hear a thing."

"Meetings, eh?" Regis picked up the list again, and again he frowned. "I'm afraid I'm stumped. Wouldn't mind knowing more, though. Ask Gordon to monitor. As you say, he loves the cloak-and-dagger stuff. Give him something to do. If nothing else, it will satisfy my curiosity. Like an indecipherable crossword puzzle clue, isn't it?"

"Indeed," Evans agreed. "Very odd." He reluctantly put the last piece of lamb in his mouth, wishing so much there had been more of it.

* * *

At two o'clock in the morning Louise Templer sat in her kitchen with a cup of hot chocolate, staring out the garden window. She could not get to sleep and finally decided to get up and read for a while until she felt sleepy. The book lay open in front of her on the counter. She decided to come into the kitchen because she didn't want to wake Alan, who had an early day tomorrow. Alan. They had been married now for seven years, two years before she was selected for Islington. It was a fairly safe London Labour seat, so they had decided to move into the borough from Oxford, even though it meant Alan must commute. He was an economics lecturer at the University. Now they didn't see much of each other, except occasionally at the weekends and holidays. Louise was a conscientious MP, and between late sittings at the House and constituency work, she saw little of her husband. The question which that evening had begun ringing round her head was, did she still love him? Of course this was not the first time the question had floated to the surface of her mind, but tonight especially it had become obsessive.

Why? Why tonight? Louise Templer heaved a sigh and took a sip of chocolate. Somehow the American, Haug, had set things off. And that seriously irritated her. *Haug*? He was obviously a coarse and violent man and physically not her type at all. Never in her life had she been attracted to the heavyset powerful type. Powerful. That was a key word, wasn't it? Everything was in total contrast to Alan. Alan was studious, intelligent, kind, considerate...and distant. She couldn't fault him. Yet...it was more a brother and sister situation, really. In many ways it couldn't be more comfortable and cosy. They trusted each other. Perhaps Alan had an occasional affair, she didn't know. But he was certainly too thoughtful to leave any evidence on the doorstep. There were no odd telephone calls, no strange letters. Louise had been unfaithful once. It had been in Edinburgh at a Labour Party conference during one of the rare summers when the sun reaches as far as Scotland and warms it romantically. She met a student - he couldn't have been more than twenty one - at an art gallery. The next day they had a picnic at Arthur's Seat, finishing off with a bottle of wine. After the picnic they went to his tiny flat near the Grassmarket, laughing all the way. She still remembered his hands on her body wistfully. The student had red hair and an impish sense of humour. It had been one of the loveliest experiences of her life, and that had been the only time. As an MP, particularly' a woman Labour MP, it was imperative that her private life be as irreproachable as possible. This was her career, and she wanted to protect it. Not because she wanted a job for life, but because of her passionate belief in the community of human beings. Louise Templer was a socialist and had been a socialist all her life. There was no reasonable alternative. Inequality was manmade and implemented by men, enforced by them, so some could live their lives in comfort while others were forced to carry the economic load. Louise Templer wanted to fight for those inarticulate people twisted into marginal lives and somehow give hope to the hopeless so their sons and daughters and grandchildren would have better chances in a more equal world.

She was proud to be a Labour MP. Though she was on the left of a party which seemed to be moving unsqueamishly and rapidly to the right, she was well thought of by the shadow cabinet because of her quick-thinking commitment in debate.

When Stuart Easton first approached her about the United Opposition, she was very wary. Then, as the evidence unfolded before her eyes, she wondered why she had been invited to join and not so many others. At 36 she must be the youngest member. Only slowly did she begin to realise it was because of the respect others had for her. Particularly Easton. The realisation stunned her, really. As a woman she felt she always had to work twice as hard as a man for equal honours, but there were always some things she would not compromise. She seldom gossiped, and backbiting had never been to her taste - and that automatically set her apart at Westminster. Enemies she openly attacked or confronted, and friends she supported unconditionally. If something was right, it was worth defending with all your resources. If it was wrong, then it must be exposed for its evil. However, she had never imagined she had earned anything like gratuitous respect. For that is what it must be.

She realised her chocolate was going cold and swirled it around to mix the sediment. Then she swore to herself and took it over to the basin and threw it out. What she really, really wanted was a proper drink. That was about the only way she was going to get to sleep. The whiskey was in the top cabinet, and she poured two fingers into a tumbler, thought for a moment, then made it three. She tried to resist the puritanism she must have inherited from her father, but it was always there. No drinking, no irresponsible affairs, early to bed, early to rise, work, work, work. She suddenly realised she had never had the opportunity to enjoy her youth. While other girls went to dances, got drunk, took drugs, stayed out late and came home with their knickers around their ankles, she stayed home and studied. O levels, then A levels, then university. Time *must not be wasted*, her father had said.

Louise Templer took a big swallow of whiskey and enjoyed the burn in her mouth and throat. Turning to look again at the dark garden window, she caught sight of her reflection in the glass. Was she pretty? Did men really want her? Weren't those silly questions? She took another sip of whiskey and crossed her arms, holding the glass to warm the drink. The compression made her unexpectedly aware of her breasts, and she flushed slightly. Or was it the drink?

She returned to her stool and sat down again, supporting her chin on the palm of her hand. Was this all - incredibly - because of the American? It seemed so stupid if it were. She was 36 years old, not a teenager. Then, again, she had never been a teenager, never been allowed. Haug asked her out for a drink, that was all. Nothing more. She took another sip of whiskey. Under her dressing gown she wore a cotton nightie. What would it be like to wear something really provocative, little flimsy bits of this and that? Louise Templer had always been scornful about men's objectification of women, but she let her mind wander just this once. What on earth would it feel like to walk down the street in high heels and a mini and have all the yobs whistling at you? Or - better - to make an entrance to a party in a designer dress exposing an acreage of flesh while every man's eyes turned to look.

She broke off her fantasy and silently scolded herself for being ridiculous. She hated men's hooded eyes mentally undressing her, and her personal presentation was therefore of a no-nonsense professional woman - a woman, incidentally, whose tongue could flay the skin from any male who came too close.

Was that what she had been trying to do to Haug? Warn him off? He had looked at her, into her eyes. The first time was at the meeting, then again at the restaurant and in the truck. She took another big swallow of whiskey. Yes, damn it, he was fascinating. OK, now it was out. She had said it, at least to herself, openly. His weren't elevator eyes, looking her up and down, leering. He looked straight at her, openly, honestly. And she had held his eyes. Most men would break away, look down, because of the warning she had planted there. But there was something emotionally powerful in Haug. That word again, powerful.

And, damn it, he had also been right. He had dealt with that stupid boy as justly as anyone could under the circumstances.

The only thing damaged had been the boy's ego, and that was obviously long overdue. He didn't threaten, he just did it. What needed to be done. So...*why* had that frightened her?

She took another sip of whiskey and looked out the window. Then she saw "frightened" was the wrong word. "Interested" was the correct one. It had interested her. Alan wouldn't have acted like that. Neither would anyone else she knew. Yet it was the right thing at the right time.

Louise Templer also remembered something else. She remembered the flutter in her stomach when he asked her to join him for a drink. When had *that* ever happened before? Taking another sip, she realised she was a little tipsy and might now get to sleep. She looked through the glass, closing one eye so the room and garden window were distorted. Then she giggled and immediately finished the rest of her drink, got up, rinsed out the glass, turned off the light, climbed the stairs and went back to bed.

* * *

Harvey Gillmore sat in the compact dining room of the Matilda smearing low-fat spread onto a piece of dry toast. It was half past eight on Sunday morning, and he was having his breakfast while reading copies of his Sunday Sentinel, faxed from London, highlighting some passages in red to remind him when he called the editor later. He was a small man with sour, sagging facial features. It was a face that had never known a natural smile. The only time the corners of his mouth ever turned up were the occasional wolfish grins after besting someone in business or ruining an employee who crossed him. No one loved Harvey Gillmore, not even his wife. But they all feared him. His nickname among journalists working for him was the Prince of Darkness, and, though he was only five and a half feet tall, he always cast a long, long shadow when he entered a room.

He took another sip of hot black coffee, put the corner of dry toast in his mouth and bit it. He much preferred salted butter but had been put on a strict diet by his consultant after his heart attack the year before. He wore a purple dressing gown with his initials regally embroidered on the top pocket.

Gillmore looked up from the fax and stared out the window at the Mediterranean Sea, thinking Greece was more like Australia where he grew up. Except for the locals, of course, who were a bunch of workshy Greeks lazily sucking on the tit of tourism so they could buy the family Mercedes and drive from one end of the island to the other and back again. He had heard most of them were lefties, which was probably one reason they didn't like work. Get the state to do it all for them, from free birth in the hospital to a free funeral at the end. He picked up another piece of dry toast and spread some more crap on it, deciding to add a bit of marmalade so it would have some taste.

Underneath the table Sarah Courtney had Gillmore's cock in her mouth, and the back of her neck and jaws were becoming tired. She would much rather be out on the deck sunning herself or watching the cute steward as he bent over to serve drinks. However, she had resigned herself to seeing little of the sundeck. Gillmore obviously wanted more than sex from her. Even before she left for Corfu she knew he was a kinky one from what Glenda had told her. Glenda didn't want anything else to do with Gillmore, whatever the money. Afterwards she said she felt so dirty she had trouble sleeping at nights. But Sarah Courtney didn't mind the kinky ones so much - so long as they didn't actually damage her. That was the line she drew. No marks and not too much pain. Otherwise the little scenarios could actually make the time pass a lot quicker than straight sex maniacs.

But this, she thought, was dead boring. On hands and knees under the breakfast table while the arsehole ate his breakfast. He never even bothered to ask whether or not she had eaten, just get down and do it. A steward had been in to serve the table and must have seen her bare bottom sticking out the other side. She hoped it was not the cute one, as she would at some time like to run her fingers through that thick black hair. If Gillmore gave her the time. She had arrived the day before, her suitcase stuffed with little more than sexy underwear and a bikini. All her time was to be spent on the yacht, so she had brought only two dresses, one of which she had worn on the flight. A few pairs of shorts and tank tops, the usual cosmetics, condoms and pills. And of course tampons, just in case. Her cabin was tiny, and there was a buzzer beside the bed which Gillmore used to summon her.

She smiled at him when they first met in the lounge, extending her hand and introducing herself. He ignored the greeting and the hand, walking around her like a racing scrutineer until he came to a stop directly in front. Without saying a word he put his hand inside her dress and squeezed her breast, took it out and examined it carefully, felt her bottom, then her tummy. Finally he lifted the hem of her dress, looked at her knickers and put his hand inside, fidgeting around for a moment or two before grunting again. He left her to pull her own dress down and rearrange her breast in the bra while he poured himself a Diet Pepsi and sat down behind his desk to stare at her. Finally he invited her to strip off her knickers and sit in the sofa opposite him with her dress up and legs open. He told her he expected guests on Wednesday, and she was to act as girlfriend and not whore, reminding her he was paying her eight thousand pounds for ten days. For that he expected quality of the highest order. She was to wear what he wanted her to wear and behave as required. It was as simple as that. Furthermore she was not to fraternise with the crew or any of the staff, though she might herself be required occasionally to serve at table. She was not to argue with any of the guests, only to smile and be polite at all times. If at any time these regulations were broken, Gillmore would turn her off the yacht instantly without pay. Did she understand?

Yes, indeed, she understood very well and told him so. With a smile. Though the introduction had unsettled her and she actually felt quite embarrassed sitting in front of the man exposed like that, her middle class upbringing helped mask her discomposure. If that is what got the little man off and if he was paying that kind of money, well, Sarah Courtney would surely oblige. The odd stuff always paid more anyway, and it was a beautiful yacht. No one else aboard need know she was doing it for money, so there might be time to have a little fun as well. Sarah Courtney loved fun. Which is what eventually succeeded in estranging her from her parents. Twenty four years old, she had dropped out of university three years ago because she partied every night. For a year afterwards she lived with a Guards officer in Chelsea, and it was at a regimental do that she met the charming Michael Regis. Almost immediately she fell for him, and this led to the break-up of her affair with the Guards officer. And that, she thought, was how she came to be on a large yacht in the Mediterranean sitting before the famous Harvey Gillmore with her legs wide open. He asked her if she had brought any high heel shoes with her, wanted to know what colour they were and told her to wear them all the time. Then he ordered her to open her case and show all her underwear, which he spread out on his desk and examined like copy proofs. Obviously he was a stockings-and-suspenders man, and she was glad she had brought three belts and plenty of extra stockings. Finally he chose what he wanted, told her to put the rest in her case and keep them there and asked her to undress and put on his choice for the day. After she had taken her clothes off, he had her parade around as if on a catwalk while he made occasional sour comments on her figure. The only things she gathered he liked were her breasts, which she was quite proud of herself, and what he called her plummy pom accent. He didn't like her dark hair at all. It was short and cut in a bob. He told her she needed to lose weight, and she would stay on a diet while she was on board - yet he thought her hips were too narrow and her bottom a bit flat. After the parade, he told her to put on her "gear". When they were alone together, she was only to wear her "gear", but when moving about the boat, she could use a monogramed staff dressing gown.

Later that evening Gillmore summonsed her to his bedroom and again told her to sit with her legs open in a straight back chair just beside his bed while he watched television propped up on pillows. From time to time he reached over and pushed his fingers inside her vagina or squeezed her breast. Finally he pulled the covers off and pointed to his crotch. She went to the foot of the bed, gently pulled his pajama bottoms down and began manipulating his organ. It remained soft, so she knelt between his legs and began caressing it with her mouth and

84

tongue. Slowly it grew bigger. And bigger. Well, she thought, a surprising little man with a surprisingly large plaything. But it never got completely hard, and she had to work to get the thing up inside her. After the first flash, she realised he was taking pictures of her and shrugged inwardly. After about ten minutes, he ordered her off and told her to go sit back in her chair beside the bed. He took several more photographs, and she obliged him by posing lewdly. Twice she was sent to the little en suite kitchen to fetch another Diet Pepsi and ice, and finally he let her go to bed.

Harvey Gillmore put the scraps and remains of his breakfast underneath the table for the whore. There were crusts from three pieces of toast, a smear of marmalade on the knife and half a boiled egg, mostly the white. He also handed her down a half cup of cold coffee.

"Eat it there on the floor on your hands and knees," he said as he folded the fax to the editorial page.

Sarah Courtney was both angry and offended. "I don't see why I should!" she blurted. Again he had not come, and his penis hung like a window weight in front of her face. She had done her best, but eating scraps from the floor was going a bit far, really.

Gillmore reached down and grabbed her by the hair and pulled her head into his lap. "That's where my wife eats when I am at home. Do you think you're better than my wife?"

"You're hurting me. Please."

"And you're boring me and wasting my time. In ten minutes I'm going to throw you off this boat without a penny and send you right back to the third rate whorehouse you came from. And I can tell you one thing, sheila: you'll be lucky to turn a trick at King's Cross after I get through with you. You're off Regis's list, no more fancy clients, and I'll run a series of stories in The News. With pictures. About a middleclass nymphomaniac slut and how she lifts her skirt for anybody for five pounds. And if you think I'm joking, you don't know me. That's ten minutes, sheila. You've got exactly ten minutes to turn your arse around and do what you're told when you're told to do it."

He shoved her head back under the table, got up and went to a cabinet on the other side of the dining room. Opening it with a key from his dressing gown pocket, the pulled out a large box which he angrily searched until he found what he wanted. Then he returned and told her to come out from under the table.

As she backed out Sarah Courtney felt confused and frightened. She raised up on her knees. "I very sorry, but I'm afraid I simply don't understand what is required..."

"What is required is that you put this in your fucking mouth," he said. "It's an inflatable gag. I'm fed up listening to you, so put it in your mouth or get out now."

She looked at the gadget and couldn't remember seeing one before. There was a strap for the head with a limp rubber gag attached to the front. She reluctantly put it in her mouth, and Gillmore strapped it behind her head. A squeeze-bulb pump dangled from the front, and the Australian started pumping air into the gag, which slowly filled her mouth, forcing it open. He adjusted the air to his satisfaction, then detached the little pump.

"Now bend over the table," he said as he went back to his box. "First I'm going to put a lock on the gag so you can't take it off when I'm not looking, and then I'm going to give you twelve red stripes across that arse so you remember next time you think about crossing me." He returned with a cane and a little lock which he snapped onto the back of the gag strap.

When she saw the cane in his hand, she shook her head violently and pushed her palms toward him. Nothing to mark her, she wanted to say, and his looks told her the punishment would be heavy. She couldn't possibly let him use that thing on her bottom.

Harvey Gillmore again grabbed her by the hair and pulled her face close to his. His voice was always soft. He never raised it. "You don't believe I can destroy you, do you? You think I'm joking."

She shook her head to say, no, she believed him.

"You have two choices, you fucking pommy slut. You bend over that table right now or you go. And if you go, you'll be crawling in the gutter in three months. I swear that to you on the

Holy Bible. I'll break you, then ruin you - and enjoy every single minute." He pushed her away from him.

Sarah Courtney was trembling as she leaned reluctantly across the table, swept up by fear and the force of Gillmore's personality. Indeed she believed what he told her, and that is what frightened her most of all. Never had she dealt with a man like this whose venom was palpable. She was wearing only stockings and the high heel shoes, and she began wondering if she could throw up with the gag in her mouth. It might come out through her nose and suffocate her, and that, too, scared her.

The pain from the first stroke of the cane almost made her pass out. It landed directly across the middle of her buttocks, and the shock involuntarily straightened her spine. As she stood up, her hands went behind to protect herself.

"That's thirteen now," Gillmore said remorselessly. "Every time you stand up or put your hands back there adds a stroke."

Sarah Courtney laid her belly back on the table and began to sob. The second one landed, then the third. She screamed and screamed, but only a small sound came through her nose. Strangely, she later remembered the feel of the tears rolling down her cheeks as she grabbed the edge of the table with her hands. It seemed hours and hours before the newspaper publisher was finished. She was too overcome with pain to count and twice had to catch herself from arching back in reaction to the strokes. But finally he stopped. She held her breath, anticipating a trick, with more to come after a pause. For several minutes she waited, aware only of the unbearable throb of pain from her bottom and the tops of her thighs.

"Stand up, whore," Gillmore grunted. He was holding a square of cardboard on which he had written I DISOBEYED MR GILLMORE. A string was attached to the notice, and he hung it around her neck so the sign rested on her back. "Now go stand in that corner, feet together, nose in the crack. You're going to stand there all morning, and if you move out of that corner or fall down, you get twelve more of the best. I'll have staff come to check you are still there. From the look of your arse, I advise you not to cheat."

Gillmore returned to his table, picked up the fax and put his granny glasses back on. Over the top of the glasses he watched as the girl picked her way over to the corner and stood in it. "While you're standing there, I want you to think about your behaviour. You bitches with upper crust accents think you can come in here and walk all over me. Next time you look at me, you won't be so mocking, will you? That's right, I saw it in your eyes last night. But when you come out of that corner, you're going to be a changed whore." He turned back to his newspaper and ignored her.

Sarah Courtney stood for almost four hours in the corner. It was nearly one o'clock when Gillmore returned. Given the choice she would have taken another beating if it could all finally be over. After the first hour she no longer noticed the pain of her bottom, and soon afterwards she couldn't have cared less who came into the room. She heard the doors open and close a number of times and the tread of feet on the carpet, but she dared not look around in case it was Gillmore. He had succeeded in absolutely terrifying her beyond belief. She imagined those photographs he took the night before in The News, the most popular tabloid in Britain. Her family would finally disinherit her, of that she was certain. No longer would she be invited to smart parties. Friends would snigger and catty remarks would be passed behind her back. She would become a laughingstock. And her flat in Kensington was expensive. How would she pay for it? No, no, it was too much to risk. Somehow she would have to endure these ten days, take the money and run like crazy. She wished desperately she had listened to Glenda, but, no, instead she had succumbed to the lure of a big yacht, internationally famous people and the thrill of the unknown.

Halfway through the morning she imagined she was going to die. Her legs and particularly her feet were killing her. Her toes had long ago become numb as they were progressively pushed down into the points of her shoes, and she silently cursed herself for bringing such a high heel. Four or five times she risked squatting down to ease the strain and tension, but that only seemed to make things worse. She would then rub her thighs and her poor feet before standing again in agony. But there

88

seemed no alternative. If she hadn't been on a boat, perhaps she would have had the nerve to simply run out before he hit her, get on a plane and leave the island, come what may. Now, however, she was trapped. And in pain, pain, PAIN! By the end she ached in every joint and stopped even looking at her watch. Every muscle cried for relief. When she finally heard Gillmore's soft voice behind her, it was the most welcome sound she could ever remember hearing. He had unlocked the strap holding in the gag, let the air out and removed it.

"Turn around, sheila," she heard him say. When she turned she saw him standing by the table where he had his breakfast. He was dressed in an open neck white shirt and blue trousers, wearing plimsolls. "Now get down on your belly and crawl over here." The relief to bend her knees was overwhelming, and when she stretched on the carpet it was heaven. She wanted to lie there forever, but instead she crawled over to Gillmore's feet and waited for him to speak.

"Now lick my feet." He held up one plimsoll, the bottom at the top of her head. She raised up on her elbows and licked the sole. "Lick it like you mean it. Lick it clean. Keep your eyes open so you can see what you're doing." The soles weren't that dirty, but conscientiously she wet one dark area with spit to soak it before licking it over and over again. It had a strange, unpleasant taste. It didn't matter though. She licked and licked. It was so much better than standing in the corner. It was so much better to lie on the floor and lick his feet. He finally put his foot back on the floor and grabbed her by the hair, pulling her up to a kneeling position.

"Look at me," he said in a barely audible voice. "Look into my eyes."

She found it difficult to look at him directly. His eyes were staring hatred into her, boring through to the back of her skull. She was so desperately afraid he was going to hit her again that she started trembling, but his hand held her firm. As he put his face close to hers the tremors coursed through her whole body.

"Open your mouth," he said. "Wider. Wider."

It was as wide as she could get it, and her lips were stretched around her teeth. "Now, you're going to do as you're told from now on, aren't you?" She was nodding wildly even before he finished speaking. Suddenly he spat directly into her mouth, and some of the spray she felt on her face. But still she held her mouth open, still straining to make it wider, terrified. "Now close it," she heard him say, and she did, tasting his spit on her tongue and in the back of her throat. "And swallow," he said with utter contempt.

Still holding his eyes as best she could, Sarah Courtney swallowed.

The Australian let go her hair and brought his arm up, pointing a finger directly between the woman's eyes. "That's the first lesson you learn when you come to work for me, sheila. You don't fuck around with Harvey Gillmore."

CHAPTER SIX

The battered Mercedes taxi dropped them in front of the old house on top of the hill. Which was actually part of the address. Ralph Harrison, Old House On Top Of The Hill, near Kalami, Corfu. The taxi driver in Corfu Town knew right where it was. Haug paid the driver and stood with One Time at the gate which led into a small walled courtyard. It seemed to be an old house, not one of the newer concrete constructions, and looked almost Spanish. Whitewashed, it was built on two floors with lots of vines and arches.

"Looks like a goddamn postcard," Haug said. "Wonder how you get in the place."

Without saying a word, One Time reached over, opened the gate, walked inside and held it for Haug.

"Always have to be a smartass, don't you?" Haug walked through carrying his holdall. They crossed the courtyard and stopped in front of the big oak door. Haug knocked loudly on the door. "Hello? Anybody there?"

A few moments later the door was opened by a little man with thick glasses. His short white beard closely matched the hair he had left on his head.

"Ah," he smiled. "You must be my guests. Jonathan's friends from London. Ralph Harrison." He held out his hand.

Haug shook it. "Haug's my name, and this is One Time."

Harrison shook hands with One Time. "Very good. Excellent. Haug. One Time. Two ciphers - one impossible to spell, the other begging an impossible question. This way, please, and perhaps I can offer you a drink after a thirsty journey. Wine, ouzo, brandy, a beer called Mythos, mineral water or tea."

They had stepped down into a large comfortable-looking sitting room washed in light. Haug put his holdall down beside the sofa. "I think I'll have a big glass of mineral water, if you got any ice."

One Time held up a finger. "One tea. Right now."

91

Harrison smiled. "In a hurry are we?" Then One Time's body language connected. "Of course. Street slang. Very interesting. One tea, one mineral water. Right now."

Haug watched One Time slide into an armchair like an otter. "You gotta forgive my friend. He feels a little inadequate in a house with indoor plumbing."

The man who owned the house was chuckling as he left the room. Haug looked over at his friend who had just taken off his red beret. One Time was dressed immaculately in a white silk shirt, white linen trousers which still held their crease after the flight, thin white socks and white slip-ons with crepe soles. His eyes were hidden behind wrap around sunglasses which he hadn't taken off since they met at his office early that morning so Lizzy could drive them to Heathrow. Haug removed his Harley dozer cap and put it on the cane side table standing beside the sofa. He wore a black Harley T-shirt, jeans and boots.

When Harrison returned with the tray, he passed round the drinks and sat in the other armchair with a mineral water. "And how is Jonathan? Well, I hope."

"He's still standin' in the hedge to take up the gap," Haug replied.

"Wonderful," Harrison said good naturedly. "The two ciphers speak in ciphers as well. I am impressed. I was actually dreading playing host to two extremely boring civil servants with wooden faces. I gather you are American and like motorcycles."

"Yep. Ridden Harleys most of my life. Nice and comfortable, plenty of grunt."

"What's it say on your T-shirt?"

Haug pushed it out so he could read the lettering. There was a picture of a hog on a Harley, and above it was "Hawg University". He liked it because of the play on his name. "I wore it for One Time. Reminds him of his family."

One Time balanced his cup and saucer carefully on the arm of his chair. "That pig is white, man."

Harrison chuckled again. "It's a pity you haven't been introduced to proper motorcycles, Mr Haug. I have a Vincent Black Shadow and a Thruxton Velocette..."

Haug sat up with a jolt. "You got those bikes here?"

"In the back. They have their own little house..."

"Well," Haug interrupted, "you got two of the best motorsickles made in the history of the world. Goddamn. What kinda luck have I stumbled on here? Jonathan said you were a musicologist, and I thought I'd find somebody with a eyeshade sittin' over dusty manuscripts written in High German. Now you tell me you got a Black Shadow and a Thruxton Velo. Hell, how'm I gonna find any time to do this fuckin' job?"

Harrison frowned. "A musicologist. That's interesting. I'm only a second cousin, but it's my brother who is the musicologist."

Haug pointed his finger at him. "If you tell me you're a motorsickle engineer, I'll make you an honorary North Carolina colonel."

"I'm afraid I'll have to remain a civilian, Mr Haug. By training I am a mathematician, and I still maintain an interest in the subject. But now I'm a kind of tinkerer, I suppose you'd say. Years ago I fell in love with Corfu - or Kerkira, as the inhabitants call it - and retired here to tinker. That includes tinkering with the motorcycles, of course. I do make the odd part on the lathe when necessary." He took a sip of his mineral water. "However. You are not on holiday, I gather. You are doing some work? For Jonathan?"

"Did he say anythang to you about it?" Haug asked.

Harrison scratched the top of his head gently. "He was a little mysterious in his fax, a little vague. So my guess is that the information is a bit sensitive, and I won't ask any further questions. When you are ready I will show you to your rooms and the amenities. Please help yourself to food in the kitchen or anything else you might need while you are here. You are welcome to share a meal with me at any time or, alternatively, there are a number of tavernas open all hours, since it's still the tourist season. The sea is not far away, a twenty minute walk, but if you want to swim you'll have to go a little further. I have a housekeeper who comes in three times a week to tidy up after me. Otherwise, I live alone."

Haug smiled and got up. So did One Time. "Well, I wanna thank you a hell of a lot for puttin' us up on short notice and for

93

your hospitality. We wanna do a little nosin' around, but first thangs first. You mind if I go drool over those motorsickles?"

* * *

Ralph Harrison stood in the doorway of the large double bedroom where his two guests were staying and carefully put on a pair of surgical rubber gloves. Thirty minutes ago he had watched the taxi pick up the two men to take them back, they said, into Corfu Town. He had closed the big oak door with a worried expression on his face. They were big, they looked very much like trouble and one was an American. He had gone through all the alternatives and had decided on this one, more to confirm his suspicions than anything else.

He examined the three cases carefully. Two belonged to the black man, one to the American. All three were locked. From his pocket he drew out a small set of lock picks.

None of them gave him any problem. They were simple, small locks and came open easily. The search operation would be more difficult. Everything must be placed back exactly as it was, so he studied what lay on top in each case before disturbing the contents with his hands.

The black man had an interesting looking hard leather case which was rather heavy. The other two seemed mostly to contain clothes. He opened it slowly and peered inside.

Frowning, he stood up and sucked air through his teeth. It was what he had suspected. Electronics. He recognised various types of sending devices, tracers, a receiving unit and a micro recording machine. And dozens of empty tapes. There were also two pairs of infrared night binoculars

Harrison spent a long time replacing all the items he had disturbed before putting the cases back exactly as they had been before. Returning to the doorway, he studied the room in detail before closing the door and stripping off the surgical gloves. He walked quickly down to his workshop and picked up the telephone. After a moment's hesitation, he dialled.

* * *

The Matilda could be seen off the coast near Paleokastritsa, and the sea was blue and calm in the late afternoon. They were standing on the long finger of land which pointed out toward the yacht, and One Time had the binoculars to his eyes. To be exact, the binoculars were pressed to his sunglasses.

Haug looked at his friend. "You cain't see shit with those shades on, asshole."

One Time was shaking his head. "Man sitting on deck. Woman gives him drink from a tray." A white slice of smile opened up underneath the binoculars, and his head started moving to some inner rhythm. "Woman has no top on. Right now."

"Gimme those glasses."

One Time dodged away easily, keeping the binoculars pressed against his sunglasses. "I'll tell you, man, if there's anything you need to see."

Haug finally grabbed the binoculars and put them to his eyes.

"She's gone in now," said One Time.

"Yeah," muttered Haug. "That's the son of a bitch. Here comes the broad again..." He dodged away as One Time tried to get the glasses back. "Never seen her before, bringin' him somethin' else on a tray. Now she's standin' by his side. Looks like he's up to the same sorta crap again. Gettin' his kicks bein' served by a pretty woman..."

He handed the glasses back to One Time, walked over to the towel thrown on the rock and sat down. He looked up at his friend and saw the smile had returned to his face. The black man had on a pair of expensive looking swimming trunks. They were also white and tight and set off the washboard muscles of his abdomen. They had walked out onto the beach like tourists, and Haug guessed every woman there turned to look at One Time whose wrap-around sunglasses made his head look like a moving turret as he clocked each pretty face, bottom and bosom for two hundred yards. Haug sighed. He was going to have to keep the man away from women - or was it the other way around? - or they were going to quickly lose sight of their objective. And

95

waste time. And make themselves a higher profile than he wanted. The pair of them weren't exactly the type to fade into crowds unnoticed.

At first he was a bit worried about the binoculars, but when he looked around he was aware several other people were using them as well as cameras and camcorders around the beach. He checked again. One man was sitting with his family looking at something further up the beach. Someone with a camcorder was trying to direct his children. There was a woman taking a picture of her boyfriend with a camera. Then Haug frowned. About fifty yards away a small dark man was pointing his glasses out to sea. Out towards the Matilda, the only yacht on the horizon.

Leaning on his elbow, Haug picked up a Classic Bike magazine he brought with him and opened it, pretending to read. But over the top of the magazine he was watching through his sunglasses the dark man sitting by himself on the beach. He heard One Time still making little grunts of pleasure above him. Then, as he turned a page of the magazine, he saw the man move his binoculars slowly around. They stopped when they were pointing directly at Haug and One Time. Haug counted to ten before they moved on. Then the man took the glasses down and sat staring out at the sea.

"If you can tear your eyes from that broad for a minute, I want you to sit down facin' me." Haug pointed at a place on the big rock for his friend to sit so he could keep an eye on the dark man.

One Time sat down gracefully in a pose that would have been perfect for an ancient Greek sculptor.

Haug put his magazine down. "Like somebody once said, we don't walk alone."

One Time nodded his head silently. He understood.

"Down the beach behind you," Haug murmured. "Black man. Dark hair, neatly cut, and I would guess about five foot nine when he stands. I cain't think of that many friends we got, so he's gotta be foe. I didn't expect anybody to be runnin' interference until the bigwigs got here. Anyway, he's spotted us. I'm just waitin' to see if he's got any obvious buddies, but he seems to be sittin' on his own, weighin' up chances just like us.

If we come across him again, I reckon we're gonna have to take the son of a bitch out."

One Time nodded and eased himself up into a sitting position to scan the beach. "Right now," he said finally, and Haug knew he had spotted the man.

Haug put the new problem aside for the moment. After they had rented a small car, they found the position of the yacht by asking a few questions at the marina. There was, however, no way of knowing whether or not it would stay there. So, as soon as possible - tonight - they had to get a tracer on the hull somehow. Not a big problem, really. Rent an inflatable with a motor, some scuba gear for cover, talk loudly about doing some spear fishing at night, then push off for the Matilda. One Time swam like a seal, so they only needed to get within two hundred yards of the thing, maybe a little closer if there was plenty of traffic in the water. Then he thought of oars. Make sure the inflatable had oars. Then they could get even closer. The tracer could be attached below the waterline.

The really big problem would come later. Tomorrow. Or tomorrow evening. Before the main body of guests arrived. Somehow they had to get aboard the yacht, there was no other way. And again it was probably going to have to be One Time who did the dirty work. Which he hated. It was completely against his nature to send a friend to do a nasty, dangerous job. But Haug was honest enough with himself to admit he was no good at the stealthy stuff. He was athletic enough, but he *always* made the floorboards creak. The door hinges *always* squealed. Or he would step on the cat's tail. Or bump into the cabinet of crystal.

On the other hand, One Time was the quietest man he had ever known. He moved like a shadow, and in the dark he was invisible to the naked eye. How he did it puzzled Haug. The most famous Red Indian brave couldn't snake through the forest like One Time. Particularly unusual when you realised the black man weighed 230lbs.

Well, Haug thought, grinding his teeth, it would have to be One Time. He would stay with the inflatable and worry until his friend returned. Much worse than going yourself.

Haug got to his feet. So did One Time, but he did it with one sweeping movement that was as graceful as a gazelle. Then he carefully adjusted the rake of his white baseball cap, sweeping the brim with his finger.

Haug watched him. "I finally got you figgered out. You're all style and no content. Everthang's on the outside, nothin' on the inside."

One finger went up in the air. "Righteous."

The women's heads started turning again as they left the beach.

"We're about as inconspicuous as a massed Scottish pipe band," Haug grumbled. "Better get your mind off pussy and start thinkin' about tonight. We got to go rent a boat."

* * *

Hercules and Corky DeLoop arrived in Corfu the next day with two steamer trunks and a half dozen expensive suitcases. They were not expected until the following day, but the weather was awful in London on Saturday when they arrived from America and got worse on Sunday. Corky insisted on going immediately to Corfu. On Sunday evening, if possible, or Monday at the latest. After speaking at length with Regis, Herk finally gave in to his wife but couldn't book a flight until the Tuesday morning because of all the excess baggage they were carrying.

The news was not well received on the Matilda, and Gillmore did his best to be diplomatic in his refusal, saying he was quite busy clearing away important personal business before the gathering on Wednesday. He was rewarded for this unusual display of tact with a return fax telling him to expect his Texan guests on Tuesday, giving the time of arrival and flight number. The Australian was seething with anger, and the crew of the Matilda tried to melt away into the panelled woodwork to avoid him. For him, Monday was an exceedingly lousy day. Consequently everyone on the boat suffered.

The Captain, Alex Hagan, was humiliated with a tongue lashing in front of the cook and two stewards. Hagan, being a long-term Gillmore employee, knew what to expect in the course of his working life. But for the young steward, Ian Clark, it was a fresh and disgusting experience. The young man had been told what Gillmore was like, but witnessing his cruelty to the captain shocked him. The fact that Captain Hagan took the abuse without a murmur was astonishing. Then he made Hagan stand in the corner for three hours like a naughty child. Ian Clark decided to stay well away from Harvey Gillmore if he could. Young as he was at twenty two he could see his boss enjoyed abusing people. Even the woman Gillmore had with him was subdued and submissive, doing what she was told without complaint. The steward liked the woman, though. Very, very pretty with short dark hair and matching dark eyes, full lips and perfect teeth. And to Ian Clark her body looked perfect. Long legs, beautiful breasts - he had glimpsed them once when he was passing through the dining room. The woman - Sarah, he believed her name was - was standing topless beside Gillmore's table in her underwear. It never occurred to the steward that Sarah Courtney was being paid. He just assumed that a man as wealthy as Gillmore would attract beautiful women.

And Sarah Courtney had herself borne much of Gillmore's fury. She had had little time to herself since her arrival, and the beating he gave her on Sunday upset her so much she had little sleep that night. The next morning she made an attempt to talk with him about it to try and repair her battered confidence. She actually found herself stuttering, and he cut her off brusquely and ordered her to wear the gag again. This was before breakfast and she had not eaten anything, but by the end of the day it was her thirst which was all she could think of. Even when she was alone in the toilet she could not remove the thing because of the lock. As afternoon turned to evening she began to panic. What if Gillmore forgot and the gag stayed in all night? She was afraid to go near him after he heard about the early arrival of two guests, yet her thirst was slowly driving her insane. Standing beside his table, she watched him finish his dinner with greedy eyes, and she would have murdered for a drink of his Diet Pepsi. Finally, she could bear it no longer. She went down on her knees in front of him and clasped her hands in front of her, eyes misty with tears. For five minutes he simply ignored her, sipping his drink and reading his newspaper. Then suddenly he looked at her.

"What the fuck do you want now?"

She pointed at his drink.

"You want a drink, do you?," he asked as she nodded her head vigorously. "Well, maybe we can do a deal, eh? It's not going to kill you to leave that thing in your mouth all night, do you a world of good. But if I take it out now, I've got to be sure this shit is not going to happen again. I'm paying good money for you, and I'm getting no enthusiasm. What you've got to do is *like* it. You've got to *want* to fuck, *want* to suck my dick, *want* to lean over when I feel like squeezing your tits. And if you don't want to, you've got to *act* like you do." He leaned over towards her and slowly took a sip of Pepsi. "I'm paying top dollar, and I want top quality. Always."

Gillmore leaned over for a metal ashtray from the next table and poured it full of water from the pitcher. Then he placed it on the floor in front of her. "Employees are just like horses and dogs. They need to be broken. Especially women. That's the only way you get anything out of them. My father taught me that." He fetched a key from his pocket. "I'm going to take that thing off now, and if you don't convince me, I'm going to put it back on, and it's going to stay there until you do. Simple as that. I want to hear it in the tone of your voice, and when I touch you, I want something to happen." He grabbed her hair and pulled her forward to release the air and unlock the gag. "Now lap that up like a dog."

Sarah Courtney fell forward and lapped but couldn't get much water down her throat before he ordered her to stand.

"Now kiss me, whore. Like you mean it."

She leaned over, running her tongue erotically around her lips, slowly closing her eyes as she cradled Gillmore's face with both hands. As she began probing into his mouth with her tongue, his hand went down the front of her knickers. Ecstatically she moved her hips and made her legs tremble as he poked his fingers into her. Or she fervently hoped it was ecstatic - or rather that it felt like ecstasy to him.

100

"A little better," Gillmore said as he pulled away from the kiss. "Now tell me what you are."

"I am a slut," she said in a husky voice.

"What kind of a slut?"

"A *filthy* slut," she murmured, opening her mouth in mock passion as she felt for his penis. "And I only want to be fucked by you. I want you...I want you, Mr Gillmore. Please, oh, please give it to me."

"That's the kind of shit," Gillmore said as he pushed her away. "You knew how to do it all along. Now pull off those knickers and finish up your water with your arse turned this way and your legs open. From now on that is the kind of behaviour I'm going to get."

Sarah Courtney slipped off her knickers smiling seductively at Gillmore and tried to get her bottom as close to him as possible while she knelt down and drank greedily.

* * *

On Tuesday Captain Hagan summoned Ian Clark and told him he wanted him to drive to the airport near Corfu Town to pick up two guests, Mr and Mrs Hercules DeLoop, travelling from London. He was to use the hired Jaguar and wear his uniform, making sure his appearance was quite smart. The steward was grateful for the chore, as he found the Matilda more and more oppressive when Gillmore was aboard. And guests were bound to distract the boss from raking the staff over the coals when he was in a bad mood.

He made certain he got there well before the flight landed and waited patiently with a sign outside customs. However, in the event, he didn't really need the sign. He knew who they were the moment they stepped through the door. It simply couldn't be anyone else. The old guy must have been nearly seven feet tall, weighing twenty-odd stone. And the woman! The sight of the woman was just like taking a straight right from a good heavyweight into the solar plexus. It took the wind out of him. She was taller than the young steward in her high heels, wearing an extremely tight mini skirt - in fact very nearly as tight as the stretch cotton jersey singlet that clearly showed the outlines of her breasts which trembled with every step. Her hair looked like spun sugar, soft and shoulder length. Ian Clark suddenly felt like a boy, an adolescent - gawky, awkward, without a clue what to say or how to say it. DeLoop walked straight up to him, towering like a statue.

"I'm DeLoop, boy. Where's the car."

Ian Clark had forgotten he was holding a sign. "Uh, oh, this way, sir."

"Got a shitpot fulla luggage here, boy. Think we might need as taxi as well. Or a goddamn trailer truck."

"I'll take care of that, sir," he said efficiently, trying not to look at the woman, who was smiling and looking around the airport. He noticed a sinister looking man with a face like a rat lurking near the luggage trolley.

DeLoop jerked his thumb at the ratfaced man. "That's Gomez. He'll ride with the trunks on account of the fact my wife cain't stand the sight of him. He'll be stayin' at a hotel on shore most of the time. Don't worry about him. Gomez can look after himself."

Gomez and the luggage, pushed unsteadily out by a porter, seemed to completely fill a Mercedes which followed them on the twisting road out of Corfu Town and across to the west coast of the island. The two Texans settled in the back seat of the Jaguar. A conversation started, but for Ian Clark it ended abruptly. The lady had asked him his name. He told her.

"Do you work on the boat?" she asked.

"Yes, madam. I'm one of the stewards."

"Well," she said. "Maybe we'll be seein' a lot of each other."

There was a hint of something in her voice that made Clark a little unsteady. "I hope so, madam. I hope so." Then he felt a large, heavy hand on his shoulder.

"Boy," said DeLoop, "If you or any other son of a bitch touches this here woman durin' our stay, Gomez'll cut your balls off."

Ian Clark felt the blood drain immediately from his head to his stomach. "I...I..." He tried to say something that wouldn't come out.

"Lissen, you bastard," said Corky. "I want you to 'pologise to this young man right now."

"A bossy woman and a crowin' hen always come to a bad end," DeLoop grumbled.

"I am not gonna put up with you givin' ever man I meet a hard time. I've come out here to enjoy myself, and you are gonna start behavin', or you'll be chokin' on your *own* balls. 'Pologise!"

DeLoop sighed heavily. "Nothing personal, boy."

"That's not an apology!"

"It's all he's gonna get."

Well, thought Ian Clark, this little sideshow ought to be enough distraction for Gillmore.

* * *

There was more than a little truth in the young steward's thoughts. Gillmore had watched the motor launch returning to the Matilda, and the gravity of his acid thoughts had a downward pull on his features. The launch nearly capsized from the weight of a hillock of luggage in the stern. Hell's teeth, he thought, where do they think they're going? On an around-the-world tour in the Queen Mary? He had previously met Hercules DeLoop, but not his wife. So he assumed the mountain of cases belonged to her. Fucking women. There were probably ball gowns in there and certainly enough clothes for six changes a day. The DeLoops were assigned to the biggest guest bedroom, but you wouldn't be able to swing a cat with all those trunks piled on the floor.

When they came aboard, however, Gillmore was, for a moment, speechless for the first time in his life. Mrs DeLoop was wearing an inappropriately tight mini skirt and found she could not negotiate the steps on the ladder, so, without giving it a second thought, she pulled the skirt up around her waist, showing high cut white knickers, and stepped out like a sailor, got to the top, wiggled it back down and held out her hand to Gillmore.

Harvey Gillmore was still fruitlessly searching for words when her husband came aboard red-faced.

"Goddamn it, woman. We ain't even got on the boat, and you're already showin' your fuckin' ass!"

"Don't be stupid, Herk," she replied in good humour. "In ten minutes they're gonna see more'n that when I slap on my bikini." She turned to the Australian. "You must be Mr Gillmore. I've heard so much about you."

"Good day, Mrs DeLoop," Gillmore managed to stutter.

"Howdy, Harv," said DeLoop, sticking out a giant paw.

Gillmore's hand disappeared inside the Texan's. It seemed he was a small boy, looking up at an adult. Even Mrs DeLoop was tall. For the first time in a year he had felt his dick tingle as she came up the last three steps. It was the finest looking piece of pussy he could remember seeing in his life. There must be acres of flesh there. He could dive into it like a porpoise. Behind his sunglasses, as if behind a gunsight, his eyes found the crotch of her knickers tucking away between the classical white marble columns of her long gorgeous legs. This was, without a doubt, prime triple A Texas beef, and just at that minute he would have given away two newspapers and a TV station just for one fuck with her.

Gillmore gave them a brief tour of the Matilda then showed them to their room. Meanwhile the crew were struggling with the luggage like blacks with cotton bales on the Mississippi. If the sea had not been calm, half of it would have disappeared overboard. Corky DeLoop was as good as her word and appeared under a quarter of an hour later in a black thong bikini with a top that was basically two small triangles testing the stress limitations of the fabric. She spread first a towel and then herself on the deck and opened up a thick novel. She told Gillmore on the way to the deck that Herk was "tireder than a tobacco farm mule" and was taking a nap.

As he stood in the dining room, Harvey Gillmore realised his face was twitching involuntarily. He was looking out at Mrs DeLoop lying on the deck. He wanted that woman badly, and that is the first time for many months he felt so strong an urge inside him. And he knew why, too. It was because of that stupid woman whose name he couldn't seem to forget. Beth. An employee who had liked the taste of his dick. Liked the taste of the cane, come to that. She had been the wife of his chauffeur, and it had been amusing to torment the poor bastard by screwing his wife. The chauffeur lost his life because he stole an important tape from him. Then Beth threw herself into the Thames with his whole tape library. Every telephone conversation for years had been on those tapes, at least all of the ones made in London. Important ammunition in the jungle of business and politics. Beth had been screwy anyway, and he had been crazy to let her stay at his Fleet Street flat. He snorted. She had said she "loved" him. No, she hadn't. She was like all the rest. She *feared* him and used it as a sexual turn-on.

Subsequently Harvey Gillmore had a massive heart attack, and he was certain he saw the very doors of death open for him. Beth was already dead, but he had a vision of her returning to his deathbed to crow. Then she... Gillmore slapped his face, which was twitching again. She cut off his dick. It had been so real, so lifelike, and he could still remember the pain and the blood spurting from his crotch. But it couldn't have been Beth, and it couldn't have been real. Because Beth was *dead*. In the morgue. Identified. Yet the stupid fucking slut returned to haunt him, and since that time, for some mysterious reason, he had never been able to come in a woman. Or get it really hard. Like it used to get. Hell, he was only 53 years old. It couldn't be age. Doctors were useless, and he had sent three of them packing. He stared at Corky DeLoop. She was lying on her back, and he could see right down her cleavage...those two soft, huge, wonderful mounds...

Harvey Gillmore turned away from the window grinding his teeth, aware his dick had tingled again. Going below deck he followed the corridor to his bedroom which was situated just underneath the deck where Corky DeLoop was lying. He put the key in the lock and turned it.

She was still there, of course, as she had no other option. Sarah Courtney was spread-eagled on the large double bed, her hands and feet fastened to the four posts. She was on her back, blindfolded, and had nothing on but her stockings and shoes. He walked over and looked at her feet, wondering for a moment why he loved high heel shoes so much, even this tacky pair the whore was wearing. He traced his finger around the patent leather and fingered the stiletto heel before letting his hand drift up the nylon to the inside of her thighs. She had begun to moan at his touch, and her hips were moving. He sneered silently. It was so easy. Most people were just weak. That was why Gillmore was king of the media. He could break people. As easy as pulling the wings off flies.

His hand moved onto the warmth of her flesh, then upward to the damp hair of her vagina. Yes, he thought, already a bit of dew there. He pushed his thumb into her, and her hips began to thrust back and forth. It hadn't taken long with this one. Give them a little pain, show them what happens when they're disobedient, cut off their options and exits. Given time, he could break any woman. His eyes looked up at the ceiling, then back down again. Or any man. The National Union of Journalists was supposed to be an impregnable union, yet he had smashed it like a nut with a hammer. A former father of chapel had got down on his knees in his office at The News and begged him with tears in his eyes. He was fifty years old with a big mortgage and too much credit as well as a wife and family. He had crawled out of the office and down the corridor and into the news room as everybody watched. Just to keep his job. After that, the man belonged to Gillmore, just like the chairs and tables in the building. There was no more bullshit about unions. In fact the man became rabidly anti-union, and Gillmore had already promoted him twice. Carrot and stick. It was the only way.

He unzipped his trousers and climbed on the bed between her legs. Gillmore had the money and power to take sex when and where he wanted it, he always made sure of that. Women were toys to be handled and trained and fucked and cast aside like a used rubber. Men had become too soft in the last ten years, he thought as he looked down at the begging pussy in front of him. The woman was jerking her hips now and still moaning. He pulled out his prick and rubbed it with his right hand. It was becoming a little harder than normal. When he put the end of it into the opening of the vulva, he suddenly pushed hard. The shaft still bent a bit, but he loved the reaction of the woman when he did this. Pleasure for him, pain for her. He grabbed both her breasts in his hands and squeezed hard as he pushed again, violently, until he banged into her cervix. Then he pulled half way out and banged again. And again. And again. He tried thinking of the gorgeous woman lying on the deck upstairs, but it was no use. Slowly he was losing his erection. He could not come.

"You love it, don't you?" he asked her.

"Yes, Mr Gillmore. It was wonderful. I hope you enjoyed it as much as I did."

"I didn't," he snarled. "It was a lousy fuck. Your cunt's too loose. It's like fucking a cow. You're not worth eighty quid for ten days, nevermind eight thousand, maybe not even eight. I'd be overpaying you with a tenner."

His words were hurting Sarah Courtney, but she tried her best not to show it. She didn't want the gag back in her mouth, and she surely wanted no more of the cane. But his verbal abuse was nearly as bad as the physical. Because she couldn't defend herself. She couldn't fight back. Constantly she had to pretend. Every time he saw her he told her that her tits were beginning to sag, she was carrying too much fat on her waist, too little on her bum, her hair was wrong, her nose too big, her eyes too wide apart, her neck too short. She tried her best to ignore the torrent of criticism, but she realised she was beginning to loathe the image she saw in the mirror in the morning. A monster was growing there. A frog with its eyes set on the sides of its head. A no-neck, fat, unattractive...slut. Never before in her life had she felt like that. Sarah Courtney was a good time girl. Working for Michael Regis allowed her to have a fine flat at a nice address, sleep in late every morning, party at nights, roar out to nice country homes in fast cars, sport designer clothes and underwear, eat in fashionable restaurants and occasionally indulge in expensive drugs. When she was depressed she could always bounce back by going to a party to soak up the admiring

107

glances of the men around her. The yacht was slowly becoming her prison and her crucible. She was going down and down, and now she wondered if the mirror was really lying. She couldn't remember ever meeting anyone as grossly cruel as Gillmore, a man without pity. He had paid for her body the same way as he had paid for the boat, and he simply used it when and how he pleased. Now he told her that her vagina was "loose". Was it? Oh, my god, she thought, maybe it is, and no one ever told me before. Seven more days. Could she last?

"I'm sorry you don't like my cunt," she said, trying to smile and sound sexy. "I certainly *love* your beautiful prick..." She lurched about, hoping it was convincing.

Abruptly Gillmore pulled limply out of her and put himself back into his trousers. Zipping himself up as he opened the door, he didn't even bother to look back at the woman still moaning and thrusting her hips on the bed.

CHAPTER SEVEN

It was late on Tuesday afternoon when Haug and One Time directed the inflatable dinghy toward the Matilda. The previous evening One Time had no difficulty in attaching the tracer to the hull. For safety they had waited until midnight, and they had a great deal of trouble finding the yacht. Which was why they were going early this time. One Time wanted to get there well before dusk so he could try and reconnoitre the layout and guess which room or rooms to wire. Neither of them had ever been on a yacht before and had little idea of the scale of things. Mainwaring had arranged for them to view a model of a yacht very similar to the Matilda, and they had made copies of the plans to take with them. The dining room they thought was the likeliest meeting place, as it was the largest and converted to a small ballroom for parties. Haug knew, however, there was no substitute for viewing the real thing. What *seemed* to be could turn out to be something quite different in reality. In addition there were furnishings and alterations to be taken into consideration.

Whenever he was honest with himself Haug knew they had about a 50/50 chance. And even that might be optimistic. "Winging it," as the Brits said. Something the limeys were good at and one of the factors which made their engineering so interesting. Poor supply, unavailable materials, lack of funds - they all provoked the British ingenuity to create a machine which worked well or simply, despite the handicaps. In fact British engineers seemed to work better under vast handicaps. If you gave them everything they wanted or needed, they turned out the same boring product as everyone else, but much slower.

A strange and weird folk, Haug thought as he steered the little craft toward the horizon. Neither of them wore the wet suits they had rented. Haug wasn't anticipating going into the water, and he suspected One Time found the wet suit spoiled the line of his figure. He had argued without conviction that it was a lot easier to move about without one, to feel his way silently and avoid detection. But Haug knew it was a long swim, and the

Med could be cold at night this far out. Instead One Time had pulled a pair of black lycra shorts from his bag that looked absolutely obscene when he put them on. It left little to the imagination. Haug insisted he keep his trousers on at least until they had cleared the last woman on the beach. Haug had on the same cut off jeans he had worn the morning before at the beach. Last night he had worn jeans and trainers, but they had got soaking wet, so he thought he might as well go barefoot and wear his shorts. On top he wore a sweatshirt and carried a rolled up windbreaker. Hell, he didn't like wet suits either. Better to be cold and comfortable than a little warmer and uncomfortable.

The night before they discovered something interesting. There was a raft tethered near the yacht, about sixty or eighty yards out, presumably for the benefit of guests wanting a swim. Haug thought it too risky to tie up to it. It was too close. But if they pulled in about a hundred yards from the raft, One Time could have a rest if he needed it and get his breath before approaching the boat. Meanwhile Haug would try and maintain position using the oars.

They were getting closer and could just see the Matilda now, and Haug throttled the little engine back. One Time sat in the bow and was putting on a pouch which looked and fitted like a shoulder holster. The electronic bugs were inside, tightly wrapped in waterproof polythene. There was also one of Haug's buzzers. If One Time got into bad trouble, he would buzz. And the Haug private navy would attack and board. Somehow. He was glad the black man hadn't asked him his plans. There weren't any.

Haug judged the distance and let the dingy run in little figure eights. He had brought a rod and reel as a kind of cover, and cast a line over the stern. What the fuck, he might even catch something. One Time was looking at his watch and the sun, waiting about ten minutes before going over the side, giving Haug the thumbs-up sign. Haug knew there was no need for words in times like these. Signs were enough. And when you have been in a war for a long time, even the signs finally disappear. He thought again briefly of Vietnam before shoving the thought violently out of his mind. Instead he watched One

110

Time's head until it disappeared. The man was a truly magnificent swimmer.

Corky DeLoop was chasing the last bit of sun on the Matilda and had moved over to the starboard side. Herk was having his whiskey now, joined by that sourpuss creep, Gillmore. It had only been one day, but she had already developed a strong distaste for the man. And, dear heavens, the way he mistreated Sarah Courtney! Corky suspected the girl was paid for her efforts, but no kind of money would be enough to make her take that kind of shit. Courtney was not allowed to sit with them at meals. Instead she would stand beside Gillmore, fetching ice for him or pouring his fucking Diet Pepsi. And all the while the little Australian talked about her in the third person, like somebody would talk about their mule or pig. My mule was stubborn today and wouldn't come out of the barn, so I set fire to its tail. Or my pig was eating too much slops and getting fat, so I put her back in the shed for a while. Corky had tried to talk to Sarah, but as yet there was no way to pry her away from Gillmore. When she wasn't standing around looking at him like a god, he had her locked away in his bedroom. Well, she thought, there were ways and ways. She was sure that girl needed some support. Or at least a little time away from his pawing hands.

Yes, and Corky DeLoop had noticed the little slimeball looking at her. Maybe he thought she didn't know he stood and stared at her from the dining room window, his eyes going over every inch of her body with the intensity of Sherlock Holmes searching for clues. She shuddered involuntarily with disgust. She would rather have sex with a giant slug than let that slimy bastard on top of her. The thought of it made her stomach churn. Fornicating with Gillmore was the *only* thing, she mused, which would possibly put her off sex for life. It had occurred to her, however, that Herk wasn't really much different. Except he was a Texan. And bigger. Both men thought they owned people, just like they owned cars or TV sets. Ignorance and wealth were bad combinations. When Herk finally kicked the bucket - soon? - she hoped to use his money like a great artist would use paint or a famous poet used words. These stupid men had no idea, none at all. They used money to make other people miserable, mainly. If anything, money is for the exact opposite use. It's to make you *happy*. *If it's not for that, then why the fuck have it?* OK, maybe it wouldn't make her happy all the time, but she was damn well going to make sure it made her happy *most* of the time.

And, speaking of happiness, she reckoned this little trip was going to be kind of dull. With a capital "D". Word seemed to have got around with the crew of the yacht, and so far they avoided her like she had advanced syphilis. When she entered a room, any crew members there would flock to the exits like geese. She hadn't even seen the cute boy who drove them from the airport. That fucking Gomez. Herk had dragged him along from Houston, and she had insisted the little Cuban travel economy to keep him away from her. Once she went to Harrods in a taxi while she was in London, and the little rodent was right behind her the whole while. Several times she had tried shaking him by dodging quickly out of changing rooms, but he always reappeared. She wondered if the little animal sniffed the carpet and tracked her by smell. Something, she thought firmly to herself, was going to have to be done about Gomez.

Corky DeLoop stared at the orange ball of the sun which had just touched the sea in the west and sighed. Well, that was it, she thought. May as well put on her bikini top and go have a large gin and tonic. Grab some video tapes and disappear into the bedroom for a wank while the two men in the dining room bored each other to death.

She reached for the top and was just about to put her arms through the loops when something made her turn her head. At the very moment she turned, her arm poised, the top in the other hand, a black man's head appeared from below, no more than a foot in front of her face. It was the most beautiful black man's face she could remember seeing. Their eyes immediately made contact and locked solid, and the moment itself seemed to freeze in time, like a motion picture stopped on one frame. Neither moved a muscle. Corky still had her arm up and the bra in her other hand as she sat with her body half turned toward him. The black head was totally motionless and could have been carved from ebony. Slowly, though, his eyes widened until she could see all the white around the dark iris. Then, suddenly, the eyes flicked briefly to take in her breasts before returning to the locked embrace.

"Well," Corky said in a low husky drawl, "I'll be goddamned. Are you a merman?"

"One time," whispered One Time after a long pause.

She leaned a little closer to the face. "Play your cards right, honey, and we can do it as many times as you want." She rubbed her lips softly against his. "Now, why don't you back your black ass down that ladder you're hangin' onto, and I'll follow you down. But we cain't make any noise," she turned to point a finger with pink frosted nail toward the dining room, "because the bad men in there will hear us and come out and shoot off guns." She dropped the bra to the deck and smiled. "I don't think we're gonna be needin' this, do you?"

Corky DeLoop stood up and shouted in a voice that would have carried to Corfu. "Goin' for a swim, y'all. Back in a little while."

One Time was already in the water, still dazed. When he had carefully put his head over the side of the boat, he came to the immediate conclusion that someone must have shot him and he had gone straight to heaven. A large angel with breasts the size of Barbados melons sat in front of him. One Time had known a lot of women in his life, but this one was the most beautiful he had ever seen. He forgot everything else but the angel. He no longer knew what he was doing, where he was or why. A fragmentation grenade had exploded in his mind. Each fragment was a different colour, a different perfume, a new and thrilling sound, a taste he had never experienced. When she spoke to him, it was hard to sort the words around into the right order. Did she say what he thought she said? Could such things really happen?

He looked up from the water just in time to see a long leg swing over the side of the boat. Its foot found the first rung. His eyes followed the leg slowly to the top of the thigh where a silver bikini disappeared into soft folds. The other leg followed.

113

One look at the woman's bottom, at the thong disappearing between two round and beautiful cheeks, made One Time aware of three things all at once. His dick was getting hard very quickly. His heart was beating like a tom-tom. And The Most Beautiful Woman In The World was joining him in the water.

He held onto the ladder with one hand. He found the bottom rung and pulled himself up a bit, bringing his head and torso out of the water. When she reached his level she turned to him, and he pressed her to him with his free arm. Her hands were all over him, his back, his shoulders and arms, down the washboard of his abdomen, his thighs, his dick and his bottom.

"Right now," he said in her ear.

She pulled back and wagged a finger in front of his face, shaking her head. "No, not right now," she whispered. "We swim to the raft first." She pointed. "This way. Follow me."

When they reached the raft, it was gathering dusk. One Time helped Corky climb on. While her legs were still hanging over, he hooked his fingers into the top of the thong and eased it from her hips, pulled it off and threw it into the middle of the raft. Then, with a single easy movement, he hoisted himself out of the water. She was on him the moment his bottom touched the wet boards, swiftly ripping off his shorts and flinging them toward her thong as One Time shrugged out of his shoulder harness.

"Wow," she said as she stared at his prick, which throbbed at every beat of his heart. "So what they say about black men is really true? That is one goddamn work of art. I just cain't decide whether to eat it like a hot dog or ride it."

One Time moved sinuously, like a seal, toward the woman, his whole body in motion. "One, two," he said, holding up two fingers, before snaking the fingers toward her tummy and confidently touching the flesh above her pubic hair.

Corky understood somehow, when the man added the body language. There were two of them, not one. They were lying side by side, and she had no idea how they had got there. It was the strongest body she had ever felt next to her skin. Each individual muscle moved and rippled, in constant motion. It was taking her breath away. She had just been about to take charge of the whole event but was now being swept along in a current she couldn't control. Her breasts were being fondled like beautiful sculpture, then kissed and sucked. A pink tongue traced around them, then in the valley between and up to her neck and chin and then into her mouth. Another hand - how many hands did he have? - followed the curve of her hips, carefully weighed one buttock before disappearing between her thighs. Without realising it, she became aware she was on her back and her legs were wide open. A large finger had touched her lightly on the vulva. Involuntarily her hips left the raft as if a high voltage had discharged into her.

Neither was talking. They couldn't talk. Words were superfluous. Corky's own hands and mouth were touching and licking and kissing the powerful and beautiful man who had appeared suddenly from the sea. She wanted to fold around this sinuous and sleek flesh, envelop it, take it all into her womb and have the whole black man secretly in her belly, inside her, warm and safe and moving. She had no idea what she was doing anymore, but she felt her legs were in the air as the black man knelt for a moment between them. She realised she was caressing her own breasts, presenting them to him. And her belly was heaving. Her breath was rasping and heavy. She had never before felt like this with a man, and it was wonderful.

Then slowly, tantalizingly and perfectly he began to enter her. She opened her legs still wider and moaned, not really knowing where she was or who she was anymore. All she wanted was him, this man, this warm, wonderful half-fish from the sea who had appeared as if in a vision to her. A genie, maybe. Had she made a wish? She didn't remember. Must have. Was he completely inside her now, or was there more to come? Oh, god, she simply couldn't bear much more of this. It felt like she was going to the brink of death itself. Her body was juddering and trembling and swept all the questions away as she thrashed around impaled and helpless to the cascade of emotions crashing through her.

Opening her eyes, she realised it was now virtually dark, and she couldn't even see the man. She was being fucked by an invisible spirit on a raft in the middle of the sea. She began

115

coming in the same rhythm as the rise and fall of the raft, and it seemed a peal of thunder had reverberated in the heavens. Her orgasm was a firework that just went on and on and on and on. It didn't want to stop, and she thought it never would. It was only the pain of exhaustion which finally melted her body back to a time and place she remembered. She only had strength enough to hold the man to her with her arms and legs wrapped around him.

"One time," said the man she was holding. And she could only see the white teeth of a smile in front of her face.

"Holy shit," she murmured. "I think you're right. One time is about all I can manage, and I never thought I'd hear myself say that."

"Righteous."

"This is my first time with one of you fellers. I reckon I just didn't know what I was missin'."

"Right now."

"Not very talkative, either. Which has got to be a good thing." She slowly pulled away and brought her elbow up to cradle her head while she looked back at the lights of the Matilda. "But maybe you'll be able to tell me now why you were climbin' onto our little boat over there..."

Haug's bare feet were wet and freezing in the bilge water at the bottom of the dingy, and he was getting nervous. The previous night there had been no problem, and now he was worried that One Time wouldn't be able to find his way back. He used the oars constantly to keep the inflatable at right angles to the Matilda and a light on the shore, and he had hung the low wattage coloured lights on the side of the craft. But why was he worried? The buzzer hadn't sounded. Nothing seemed to be happening on the yacht, though he could see very little at this distance.

He tried to be a realist about the situation. The most likely outcome would be his friend returning to say it was impossible. The second most likely would be discovery while he was trying to plant the bugs. The man had a good chance, though, of making his escape. The crew would be surprised. One Time

116

was fast and strong and thought on his feet. Within five seconds of trouble starting, he would be back in the water. And once in the water, they would never see him again. The third most likely outcome would be success.

Haug frowned. Where was the son of a bitch? What the fuck was happening? There was nothing. No buzzer. No activity on the yacht. No shout from the water. He checked the glowing dial of his watch. Nearly nine o'clock. He would give it twenty minutes more, then risk going closer. Moving in a direct line, hoping he wouldn't miss the black swimmer. He rubbed his feet together and cursed out loud. He could just hear the sound of merriment from tavernas on the shore and pulled out a small flask he had filled with Greek brandy. He never liked to drink while on an operation, but goddammit, he was cold.

The brandy was thick and sweet to his throat, and he immediately felt the heat in his stomach, sloshing in motion with the dingy. Just the thing, he thought, taking another long pull from the flask before screwing the cap back on and stuffing it into his jacket pocket.

When he next checked his watch it was almost twenty five minutes past nine. He made a decision. He would check the raft first, then slowly approach the yacht, stopping to listen every few minutes or so.

He had only pulled on the oars five times when he felt a heavy thump on the bow. Looking around quickly, he saw One Time pulling himself into the inflatable, so he immediately counterbalanced on his side. Then he pulled against one oar to turn the little boat around in the opposite direction. One Time came over carefully, one finger waving in the air, a huge smile on his face. The finger was moving in time to the dipping shoulders. The black man grabbed the oars from him, sat down and heaved away mightily.

Haug let him row and squatted in the bow, staring at his friend suspiciously. He was silently telling him it was OK. It was successful. All was well. But there was something else. There was something triumphant in his manner. The smile

117

remained as he rowed away from the Matilda. If anything it grew in size to cover half his friend's face.

After a few minutes of thought, Haug took a deep breath. "You found a woman, you dirty bastard," he whispered loudly. The smile grew even bigger, and the dingy leapt forward from the increased power of the strokes. "You cain't be trusted, you goddamn pervert. I knew I shoulda left you at home and brought Keef..."

One Time broke the rhythm of his strokes just long enough to make a small dismissive circular movement with his open right hand, accompanied by a shake of the head and the word, "Keef." Missing only one stroke, he grabbed the oar, and they were moving again in the water.

Haug raised his voice a little as they moved away from the yacht. "While I'm sittin' out here freezin' my ass off, worried sick about your safety, you got your prong in somebody's ass havin' a party. I suppose it was that broad you were eyeballin' through the binoculars."

One Time shook his head. He could only see the head because of the permanent smile. "Guest. Arrived today, man."

"A guest? They're not supposed to come 'til tomorrow."

One Time shipped the oars. They were far enough away now to start the engine, and he grabbed the pull start rope. "Two Texans." He pointed to the boat. "And a Cuban." He pointed to the shore.

"So who the hell did you fuck? One of the Texans?"

The motor started, and One Time stood up, popping the fingers on one hand in rhythm. He held one finger up with the other hand.

"Fine, you had a great fuck, but, Jesus Christ, are you crazy? They're bound to know..."

One Time interrupted him wagging the finger. "She's doing it, man. *She's* doing it."

Haug was flabbergasted. "She's plantin' the bugs?"

The black man was nodding and popping his fingers, still grinning ear to ear. "Told her where. Showed her how. Said we were the good guys. Man, this woman...this woman...oh, *man*..." He popped his fingers.

118

"Goddammit, One Time, draggin' information outta you is like interrogatin' Harpo Marx overdosed on Spanish Fly." He watched his friend steer the inflatable through the dark waters "It's a pain in the ass bein' around you after you've had a little pussy. I hope you don't expect to get paid for tonight. I cain't see payin' you good money to fuck some Texan," he said tongue-in-cheek.

One Time was wagging his finger. "This ain't pussy, man. This is..." His fingers were snapping again.

"Aw, shit, you're not talkin' about *love*, are you?"

The black man pointed at him. "Viv Richards."

"I thought you said it was a woman," Haug said. "Richards was the captain of the West Indies cricket team..."

He wagged his finger, shaking his head. "*What* is Viv Richards?"

Haug turned his palms up and shrugged. "The best?"

The finger went up and the smile returned. "That's it. The best."

Haug laughed out loud. "And you're sure - I hope to hell I can take your word on this - that this broad will do all that for you?"

"Opposite of negative," One Time replied.

"You're positive," Haug confirmed. "OK. I gotta trust you, even when you're thinkin' with your dick. What's this Cuban got to do with it?"

"Bad medicine. Minder. For the old man. Anybody touch her, he cuts his balls off."

Haug laughed. "Hey, I'm not gonna help you on this one. I can just see it now, those two old black balls finally nailed over somebody's fireplace."

"Not me, man. Not One Time." He stared ahead at the approaching lights of the pier, guiding the little boat toward them.

It was after ten o'clock when they tied up the dingy and dumped the gear in the rented locker room at the end of the pier. Haug was glad to get his shoes and socks back on. He was going to stop in the first taverna he came to and buy a beer and something to eat. He realised he was starving. Glancing at One

119

Time, who had on what he called his Dress Whites, he saw the man still had the same smile on his face.

"You been grinnin' like a mule eatin' briars ever since you climbed back on the boat. You'd think it was the first time you ever scored a piece of ass," he grumbled as he walked out the door of the locker room with his holdall.

As they passed out of the lights into a dark area of the pier on the way back to the shore, Haug realised the hairs on the back of his neck were tingling. Glancing up, he had just noticed the string of lights which should have been on were out. Immediately after that, he heard the sound he would never forget. Because, of all other sounds, it was unmistakable. It was the sound of a safety catch being eased off an automatic. Nothing else he had ever heard sounded like that.

The instant he heard it, he dived to the left, realising One Time had simultaneously dived to the right. The moment he hit the wooden deck he rolled until his body was stopped by a spool of rope. Haug knew where the sound had come from. A little lean-to shed on the pier. But the darkness was intense, and he could see nothing. Glancing toward One Time, he realised his friend was exposed in his Dress Whites. He wagered the very next thing to happen would be a shot into the whites. Immediately Haug got to his knees, wrapped his fingers around the big roll of rope next to him, then, lifting with all his strength, he pulled the spool around in a hammer throw toward the lean-to.

Thuk. Thuk. The bullets hit the rope roll in quick succession before it hit the middle of the shadow in the lean-to. Haug knew the gun was silenced from the sound and probably had a flame suppressor, but he caught one little flicker of light. To the right. Ten feet away. Moving low, with his legs pumping like pistons, he drove into the lean-to. He expected to take at least one bullet and just hoped it wouldn't hit anything vital.

In half a second he was nearly there when he felt something hit his head, and for a moment his vision swam out of focus. Then a man's knee caught him in the chest as he hit the shed with his full weight, bringing down at least half of it. But now he had the stranger's leg, clamped between his arms. Swiftly he

120

placed one palm on the knee and gripped the ankle with his other hand, ready to break the leg. But he was stopped by a man's voice.

"Don't make me kill you, señor," said the voice from the floor of the smashed lean-to.

Haug stared at the automatic held by the wiry dark man lying on the floor. The man was calm, and the gun was steady. It was the man on the beach. And Haug knew he was Cuban. He was also a pro. Haug held the leg tightly. He would still have a chance if he broke it and moved at the same time. Not much of a chance, but enough to try. "Nobody pulls a gun on me, bo. You might get me, you might not. But I tell you one thang. You never gonna walk again, 'cause I'm gonna tear this leg right off. Unless you put that gun down real easy." He stared at the Cuban, his eyes level and threatening.

The Cuban didn't flinch. "I was trying not to kill you, señor. I want answers to questions only."

Haug stared at the man, waiting for the first flicker, the first lapse of concentration before he moved. "You want to ask me questions, you don't start by pullin' a gun. You tap me on the shoulder and ask nice. And if it's any of your business, I'll tell you."

"Who do you work for?" the Cuban asked calmly, his eyes never wavering.

"None of your fuckin' business."

"CIA?"

Haug very nearly laughed. "CIA? You must be a lot greener than you act. Those guys wear suits and stay in Holiday Inns and don't like to get their hands greasy."

"Then why are you guarding the Matilda?" asked the dark wiry man.

Haug was genuinely baffled for a moment. "I think we better get our roles right before I kill you. *You* are guardin' the yacht. We're not."

"Me, señor? Now I begin to be confused."

Haug had not broken eye contact with the man, not even to blink. "You're Cuban, right?"

"Yes. Then you *do* know."

"And you're guardin' the Texans, right? Makin' sure the woman doesn't get poked."

The man on the ground smiled thinly. "You are thinking of another Cuban, a man called Gomez, a criminal."

Haug thought for a moment. "So. What does that make you?"

"I, señor, am a *real* Cuban. My home is not in Miami or Texas but in Havana."

Haug sighed heavily. "Well, thangs are gettin' a little complex here, feller. This looks like bein' a long, drawn out kinda conversation which I think oughta continue until we sort all the pieces outta the puzzle box. I personally feel it could be the first taverna we come to. But lemme tell you somethin', bo. I am not gonna let go this leg til you put that fuckin' gun down. I just got this awful lifelong habit of smashin' people to pieces for pullin' those thangs on me. I will make an exception in your case for the first time in my life, if you just lay it down beside you, real careful."

They stared at each other for a full minute, and the atmosphere was tense, explosive. Haug could hear One Time moving over to his right, but he knew he wouldn't attack until the action began. He was moving to remind the Cuban that he had someone besides Haug to worry about.

The Cuban made up his mind finally and lay the pistol down beside him. As Haug reached for it, he held up his hand. "No," he said. "This is what you wanted, señor, for me to put it down. I have put it down. When you let go my leg, I will get up, bend over and recover my pistol and put it back in the holster."

Haug thought another few moments. "OK, bo. Remove the clip, and jack out the bullet in the chamber."

The Cuban shrugged with the corners of his mouth and followed the instructions. Haug let go the leg and extended his hand to help the man to his feet. The Cuban leaned over carefully, picked up the pistol with thumb and forefinger, replaced the clip and put the gun into a holster inside his coat. The extra bullet he dropped in his pocket.

"You are a very strong man, señor. I am impressed." He looked warily at One Time who emerged from the shadows. "Is he American also?"

"Barbados. Lives in London, like I do."

"Ah. London," said the wiry man. "A London connection."

"I sure hope you don't find that as strange as I find the *Cuban* connection," Haug said as he checked his head. He was bleeding from the blow of the pistol. Looking at his hand he said, "This is the first time I can remember walkin' away from a fight and I'm the only one bleedin'." He leaned over and opened the holdall to find the small first aid kit he had pushed in before they left the house. "One of you assholes put a Band-Aid on that so I can put my cap back on."

One Time moved him into the light to clean up the wound and cut a plaster to size before sticking it down. Then Haug clamped the dozer cap back on his head and grabbed the holdall again. "I'm hungry and thirsty and curious. In that order. Let's find a place to eat, drink and talk."

They had to walk quite a distance to find one of the more unpopular tavernas, one that wasn't so crowded but still had tables outside. When they walked into the light One Time started complaining.

"Hey, look at my threads," he said in an anguished voice.

"It'll wash out," Haug commented as he looked at the dirt on his friend's Dress Whites. "Still got the creases."

"You don't understand," One Time said as he went inside looking for a lavatory.

Haug went to the bar and asked the waiter for three beers and a menu, mostly by pointing his fingers. The waiter, however, spoke quite good English. Returning to the table he extended his hand. "My name's Haug, and my friend is called One Time."

The Cuban shook his hand. "I am Raul Dominguez, Mr Haug."

"Drop the 'mister' and call me Haug. Everbody else does."

Dominguez leaned back in his seat as the waiter brought the beer. He poured his into a glass. "So. Haug. We are now on more casual terms. Perhaps you can tell me now what interest you have in the Matilda."

Haug took a drink from the bottle, enjoying the ice cold lager as it tingled in his throat. "What we gotta do first, Raul, is find out if we're friends or foes. Or neither. In which case we might still have mutual interests. For reasons of confidentiality I cain't reveal who I'm workin' for. Or why. But anyway I'll put the first card on the table face up. The Matilda belongs to Harvey Gillmore, a man who owns newspapers and TV stations in England, Europe, Eastern Europe, America, Australia and the Far East. Oh, yeah. And South Africa. Recent purchase. Off hand I cain't think of an animal on the face of the earth or underneath it which would bear the insult of comparison. I would personally rather be up to my ass in snakes and polecats than be in the same room with the man. And if I do find myself in a room with the varmint again, I'll cut his ass too thick to fish with and too thin to fry. And if you're a friend of his, I reckon I might do the same to you."

Raul Dominguez had fine mixed racial features which pulled themselves back in a smile. "If these are your feelings, we cannot be enemies, Haug. I will ask you a question which you do not have to answer, of course. Do you work for the British government?"

Haug took another swallow of beer and signalled for the waiter to bring two more bottles. "I cain't answer that. But don't jump to conclusions. I don't work for MI6 or the domestic branches of MI5 or SB. Or anythang military or diplomatic. Now I got a strong feelin' you *are* official. I know goddamn well you're a pro."

Dominguez leaned forward and put his elbows on the table. "Perhaps I am official, perhaps I am not. Are you aware that there is to be a meeting aboard the Matilda?"

One Time returned following the waiter. There were damp patches on his trousers and elbows. He sat down and poured out his beer into his glass.

"What's the matter," growled Haug, "Couldn't you find an iron or blow dryer?"

One Time brushed at the damp patches. "You don't understand, man."

124

"I bet all the broads dropped dead from shock when they saw you weren't absolutely immaculate."

The black man shook his head, laughing. "That's all right. You'll see."

"I got the liability, Raul, of havin' to work with a fashion model. This man irons his *socks*." He finished off the remains of the first bottle and grabbed the fresh one. "The meetin' is what we're here for, and I don't think I'll be far wrong if I guess it's your reason for bein' here, too."

"Do you know who is going to attend?" asked the Cuban.

"Some. Not all. Hopin' to pick 'em up at the airport as they arrive."

"Two, you see, have arrived already. Today. Early. Hercules DeLoop and his wife. And of course the other Cuban, who is staying in a taverna here in Paleokastritsa. I am very interested in DeLoop. As you are American, I'm afraid I jumped to the conclusion you were somehow working with him. Or with the CIA. Or both. DeLoop and his associates are causing a great deal of trouble for my country. Not just in propaganda and lobbying pressure on the American government, but by drugs." He took a drink from his glass. "Drugs, Haug, heroin, cocaine. At the moment, Cuba is under great economic pressure, and it is even questionable whether we will survive. Drugs are being imported into Cuba, first in order to corrupt civilian and military officials, and second to export illegally to America. Which we are accused of masterminding by the American drug enforcement agencies. A great deal of money is involved in a country which is very, very poor at the moment. Human beings are human beings. We have executed a number of officials, including one distinguished army officer who fought in the Revolution." Dominguez held his hand in a horizontal plane as if it were on a fulcrum. "If it is only poverty we have to deal with, perhaps we shall survive. But with corruption on this scale..." He used the hand in a shrug.

"Being an American," he continued, "I know you may have little sympathy for Cuba. But I tell you one thing, señor, during the past twenty five years we have made many, many mistakes. But for the first time in our history we have had self respect.

125

Many people have had the opportunity to realise their potential. Instead of becoming prostitutes in Havana, women can now have careers as doctors or teachers. We don't want to return to becoming a country of prostitutes and peasants so poor they pull their own teeth with pliers."

Raul Dominguez stopped talking and had another drink, looking out at the sea. Haug and One Time were also silent. The sound of bazouki music came from within the taverna, and they could hear people shouting and laughing.

"I am interested in DeLoop," said Dominguez, "for these reasons. I believe you when you say you are not CIA or British Intelligence, but if you are, I assure you, señor, I have no other interests in these people. I am one person here. We cannot even afford a pair to work together. Or expensive electronics. I have only the one friend on the island."

"Who's that?" asked Haug.

"The man who kindly puts me up," said the Cuban. "Your host and mine. Ralph Harrison."

"Harrison!" Haug exploded in disbelief. "This thang gets more and more intricate, the more you dig at it. What fuckin' room are you stayin' in?"

"I was in your room until Monday. Now I stay out with the motorcycles." He held up his hands. "Please don't ask me any questions about Ralph. I will let him explain things for himself."

"Well," said Haug as he leaned back in his chair, "I started off hatin' Fidel Castro, just like we were taught to by the newspapers and TV. Over the years, as I found out a little more, most of it the hard way, I came to respect him and what your country has done for itself. I hope you will allow me to pay for supper as a first small instalment for years of shitty treatment by a country big enough to know better."

"Thank you, señor. I accept."

Haug waved the menu at the waiter, who was leaning against the doorway. "I'm so hungry I could eat a bull and it still bellerin'."

CHAPTER EIGHT

"First of all," said Ralph Harrison, "I'd like to apologise for going through your luggage. But I hope you'll understand. You two gave me a terrible fright, because I was certain you were CIA thugs. Particularly since Jonathan arranged for you to stay here."

The four men were sitting in the courtyard with the light from the doorway illuminating an area the size of a small thrust stage. Haug, Dominguez and Harrison drank ouzo. One Time stuck with beer. The inside of the house was still uncomfortable from the heat of the day, so they decided to move into the courtyard for a drink.

The wicker chair Haug sat in creaked with his weight. "Maybe you don't know Jonathan all that well, Ralph."

Harrison snorted. "I know he is a senior civil servant, knighted by the crown, a pillar of the establishment."

"Yeah, he's all those thangs, but he's got somethin' else, somethin' that seems fast disappearin' from the face of the earth. A sense of honour."

Harrison stroked his short white beard. "A bourgeois sense of honour perhaps, in defence of his class."

"Well," Haug said, taking a drink of ouzo, "you're wrong. I cain't go into *why* just yet, but he's smarter than a tree fulla owls. What's your story, though? How come you befriendin' this poverty stricken spic?"

"I think I could safely wager all that I have that you are not CIA. Or British Intelligence, come to that. I've never met anyone quite like you." Harrison was sitting on the steps and leaned back on his elbows. "I am a communist and have been in the Party since I was seventeen or eighteen. About fifteen years ago I visited Cuba as part of a delegation and had the pleasure of meeting Dr Castro. When I mentioned that I was a mathematician, he was delighted and asked if I would like to liaise with his education minister, have a look at the curriculum, meet some of my peers at the university. One thing led to another, and I stayed for eighteen months. Over the years I have kept in touch with friends I made while I was there. Indeed I have been aware of the worsening drug problem and am glad I could do something to help."

Haug stared off into the night. "I killed a lotta communists."

"I see," Harrison said softly. A long uncomfortable silence followed. "I find that very, very unpleasant information."

"I think I know what he means," said Raul quietly to Harrison as he turned to Haug. "You were in Vietnam?"

Haug didn't answer. Instead he stared off into the night, reached into his hip pocket and pulled out his tobacco pouch. Opening it, he bit off a piece of plug and pushed it around to his cheek with his tongue. "Outside football, killin' was the only thang I was any good at. I was a kid and thought the American flag stood for truth and justice and democracy. Communists were scum who wanted to enslave the world. So I killed as many as I could. When I did it, it was the 'right' thang to do, so I cain't be ashamed of it, 'cause I didn't know any better. After I got out, I found out different, went to college, got a degree in English on the GI Bill. But somehow, at forty four years old, I find myself in the same fuckin' business." He spat out into the darkness.

"And what side are you on now?" asked Raul, still quietly.

"The right one, as well as I can judge it."

"I'm sorry," Harrison said. "I didn't realise..."

"Naw, don't apologise, Ralph. I don't. What good does it do, apologisin'? I thought about it. Goin' back there to 'Nam, tryin' to look up a lotta families and say, look I'm sorry I shot your father/brother/mother/sister/son/daughter...uncle, aunt, grannie. I reckoned the best thang I could do would be to try and figger out what the hell is goin' on and why, and try to sit my ass on the back of the right pickup truck this time."

"Are you on the right one now?" asked the Cuban agent.

"Lot closer than I used to be." He spat again. "I had an idea of comin' to England to do some more study in literature and, I don't know, maybe teach. 'Stead of that, I wind up in the trenches again. Well, maybe I cain't go against the flow of life. Maybe that's what I was made for."

128

"You are very good. Very brave." Dominguez turned to One Time. "You don't say much, señor."

Haug nodded at One Time. "I'm in charge of the thinkin' and talkin' department, and he runs the style and fashion end of the business."

"One time," said One Time.

"He's also a goddamn first class eyes and ears," Haug added. "He *claims* to have got some ears on the boat tonight. I personally have my doubts, on account of his claims bein' passed through a woman's sex organs."

Harrison leaned forward. "Are you serious? You got some electronics aboard the Matilda?"

One Time checked his watch and held up a finger before sliding out of his chair to disappear silently into the house. When he returned he had his leather case with him. He sat down and opened the case, pulling out the receiver. Then he plugged a set of headphones into the side and turned it on. A telescopic aerial was extended upward. He took off his white beret and carefully laid it beside him on the table before putting on the headphones. For several minutes he sat scanning frequencies and turning dials. He checked his watch again.

"Too many miles, man," he said, holding one hand over his ear. Suddenly his eyes lit up. "Right now! One Time! Only static, but it's on!"

"I'll be a son of a bitch," Haug said, turning to Harrison and Raul. "He talked the Texan's wife into plantin' the bug."

One Time was snapping his fingers. "You forget who I am, man."

"I'd sure as hell like to sometimes. Trouble is, we're on the other side of the island from the yacht, and, because of the size of the receiver…"

"I have a bigger one," Harrison interrupted. "And a bigger aerial." He pointed to the roof of the house. "In fact I had cobbled together something for Raul. A directional pickup. But we would be restricted to conversations held outside, on the decks. And of course, like you, we would have to get close in. Perhaps we could combine resources in exchange for information."

129

Haug thought for a moment. "It's not my information to give, Ralph. I mean, let's face it, we just met tonight, and we've all told stories about who we are and what we're doin' and why, but ever one of us could be lyin' through his teeth. But," he held up his hand to stop Harrison's protest, "I don't see any harm in givin' you any information you want regardin' drugs. So I'll promote myself on the spot to an officer and make that decision. Later on, it might be possible to give you more. Is that enough for you?"

Harrison looked at Dominguez, who shrugged. "It is more than we could have hoped for, señor. I think also I will use the directional at night in case discussions take place outside."

Haug smiled. "You're welcome to our inflatable when we're not usin' it. Not much, but it'll get you there and back. And if you pick up anythang interestin', maybe we can have a tradin' session." He finished his ouzo and Harrison took his glass into the house for a refill. "Now what about this other Cuban? Have we got to worry about him?"

"I would think so," Dominguez replied, showing his teeth. "A very dirty man, very dangerous. A thug. A murderer. A drug runner. Hitman. Bandit. Often he is escort for contraband from Panama or Colombia to Texas, Miami, Cuba. And elsewhere. For this man DeLoop he often acts as bodyguard when he travels. He is armed and is very, very good with a knife. Watch yourself, señors. He is like the scorpion, to sting when least expected. When you pick up a broom or a hoe, he is stuck to the other side. Perhaps I will have a chance to deal with him myself. It is something I have been particularly looking forward to."

"Well," said Haug, "I'll do my best to save him for you. Tactically we gotta keep as low a profile as possible. Information increases in value a hundredfold if folks don't know you've got it."

One Time finally put his headphones down, wrapped them around the receiver, refolded the aerial and put them away in the case. He finished his beer just as Ralph Harrison returned with a fresh round. He pointed his finger aloft. "Tonight?"

Harrison turned to Haug with a quizzical look on his face as he handed him his ouzo.

"He wants to know," said Haug, "if you're gonna show him the gear tonight. Goddammit, it's like bein' a translation service. You see, if he cain't say it in the very latest street craze, he won't say it at all."

Harrison laughed and turned back to One Time. "Eight o'clock in the morning too early for you?"

"Righteous," One Time nodded.

* * *

"Did you catch this fish off the boat?" DeLoop asked through a mouthful of food. They were sitting around what was called the Captain's Table, though the Captain himself was seldom invited. It was half past eight.

"I don't know," Gillmore replied, picking at his salad. "Have to ask the chef. Probably bought it in Corfu."

"Wouldn't think you were far enough out to catch swordfish," DeLoop said as he put another enormous piece of fish in his mouth. He chewed on one side and talked out the other. "It don't taste frozen like some of the crap I get back home." Small morsels of food occasionally sprayed forward to drop around his plate.

DeLoop's eating habits were annoying Gillmore. The big Texan was shovelling in more food in one sitting than he ate in a month. He glanced at Sarah Courtney, who was standing a step back from his chair. "Fetch me some more ice and Pepsi, sheila."

"Of course, Mr Gillmore," she said with a smile and curtsied. She took his glass and put it on a small tray, then walked toward the door. She was wearing a tight mini skirt and vest without a bra.

"How come you treat that girl like that?" Corky DeLoop asked when she was gone.

"Women like it that way, that's why," Gillmore muttered as he found some boiled egg to spear on his fork with the lettuce.

"Bullshit," said Corky. "*You* like it that way."

131

The Australian wiped his mouth with a napkin. "I've had a lot of experience with women, Corky. I know what I'm talking about. If you don't keep 'em under control, you get hassles, trouble, backtalk. I haven't got time for that." He turned as Sarah returned with his Pepsi on the tray with a fresh glass and ice. "Don't you like it like this?" he asked her.

Sarah Courtney smiled broadly as she poured his Pepsi. "Like what, Mr Gillmore?"

"Doing what you're told. Fetching for me. Not talking back. Being punished for mistakes."

"Oh, yes, indeed," she replied. "I wouldn't have it any other way, sir."

"There. You see?" He reached over and stroked her bottom, then patted it proprietarily.

"I think he's right," said DeLoop as he used a piece of bread to sop up the butter from the swordfish. "I shoulda done the same thang with you, right from the beginnin'."

"Ha," said Corky. "I'd like to see you try."

Gillmore took a drink of his Pepsi. "I've never found one I couldn't break yet, Herk." He nodded toward Corky. "Give her to me for ten days, and she'll be eating out of your hand."

Corky laughed out loud, genuinely amused at the thought. "Listen here, shorty. You lay a finger on me, and I'll thrash your ass until it won't hold shucks."

"She would, too," DeLoop mumbled as he put four ounces of swordfish into his mouth. "She's meaner than a junkyard dog."

Harvey Gillmore stared at Corky malevolently. She stared back at him. He finally broke off eye contact and looked at the huge Texan, who was gathering another swordfish steak from the platter. "My father taught me how to handle women. Men, too. The whole principle is based on carrot and stick. I got married when I was thirty, and my wife is ten years younger. The marriage contract was drawn up by my lawyers, and she signed it. If I die first, she gets everything, either to sell or to run. If she divorces me, she gets nothing..."

"Aw, come on," said Corky. "You can't do that these days. Not even an Australian judge would go along with that."

Gillmore held up a finger. "I made her pose nude with another woman and sign passionate letters to a number of dykes dated over a period of years. The photos and letters are held by my solicitors in sealed envelopes. All they've got to do is lay that in front of a judge, and he won't give her a penny. Particularly since she renounced all claims in such a case before the marriage."

DeLoop laughed, spraying seafood.

Corky put down her fork. "Well, now, that is a dirty, rotten piece of blackmail if I ever heard it."

Gillmore shrugged. "It's the carrot. Then there's the stick. If she misbehaves, she gets the cane across her arse. Or stands in the corner. Or writes lines for me on a piece of paper. Or she goes to the doghouse. Literally. I take all her clothes away and chain her outside to the doghouse. Though that hasn't happened for a long time now. Because she knows how to behave. She knows what will happen if she doesn't."

"I don't rightly believe I'm hearin' this," Corky said. "*You* decide if *she's* misbehavin', right?"

"Of course. I'm the head of the household."

"You got some beer?" DeLoop interrupted.

Gillmore turned toward Sarah. "Go get Herk a glass of beer."

She picked up her tray. "Yes, Mr Gillmore."

"Well, mister," Corky said without smiling. "If my husband tried somethin' like that with me, I'd cut his fuckin' dick off while he was asleep."

Gillmore nearly choked on a piece of celery. She could have mentioned anything but that. He had a recurring nightmare since his heart attack, and it was so real. Every time. That stupid woman who killed herself last year would have a carving knife. Or a large pair of scissors. Or hedgetrimmers. Or a scalpel. He would be helpless, tied down to a bed or table, and she would approach him, laughing, waving the hedgetrimmers or the knife. Picking up his penis by the foreskin she would stretch it out as far as it would go before hacking at it - always hacking, never a clean cut. Gillmore would wake up in a sweat with his heart thumping like a rubber drum.

133

"Are you alright, feller?" DeLoop enquired.

"Something went down the wrong way," Gillmore said, as he drank some Pepsi, his hand trembling.

Sarah returned with a glass of beer for DeLoop who took it off the tray without thanking her and drank half of it.

Corky DeLoop watched the woman and felt sorry for her. She was attractive and sounded quite educated, and it was difficult to figure why she was here and why she took the kind of abuse the Australian gave her. Corky didn't believe for one minute she did it because she wanted to. She would just love to see the woman turn and dump a tray of food all over Gillmore's head when he snapped his fingers for this or that.

Gillmore was talking again, but she ignored him. The swordfish was good, but she ate only half of hers. The other half Herk forked into his plate and scoffed. The yacht was rolling a bit now as the sea moved, and that reminded her of the raft almost two hours ago. Of the mysterious black man with the fantastic body, the best lover she could remember having. Who was he, and why did he want the boat bugged? Or did she really care about the answer to that question? What difference did it make? These men at the table were slobs, and the ones coming tomorrow were probably just as bad. Men who thought they ran the world. Big deal. She looked around the dining room. This was bound to be where they would meet to talk and sound important and smoke cigars while she and Sarah were doing female things somewhere else. Female things, like getting hold of that black ass again and having a real good time. She looked up at the chandelier hanging over the table. The fellow had mentioned light fittings but cautioned not to put it where it could be seen if someone changed a bulb. Her eyes followed the chandelier to the ceiling where a coil of wires exited from a shank before disappearing into the ceiling fitting. The "bug" looked like a six inch nail, but with a more rounded head, and she should be able to push it into that space. Then the wires would hide it from view. And, she smiled to herself, even if they discovered the bug, who would imagine it was little ole Corky, the helpless female from Texas? One of the two bugs the black fellow gave her was lying at the bottom of her makeup case.

134

When these two assholes went to bed, she would just stand on the table and...

"...my father did the same to me. That's how I learned, Herk. When I did something wrong, it was pants down and a damn good hiding that I never forgot."

Herk was picking his teeth and leaning back in his chair to make room for his stomach. His forehead was sweaty, and his face was red. "Yeah. A few years back, I horsewhipped a couple of Messkins I caught stealin'. And I tell you somethin', Harv. That taught the rest of 'em a lesson. I never had any more trouble since."

Gillmore nodded sagely, only a little irritated at being called Harv. "That's right. Without fear, you've got no respect. Once they fear you, you've got their balls in your hand. All you have to do is squeeze a little bit, and they'll do anything you want. Every company I've got is run like that, from the top to the bottom. Get rid of the unions..."

"Unions!" DeLoop exploded as he wiped his forehead with his sleeve. "I break out in a rash when I hear the goddamn word! The fuckin' *employees* think they can run a company when *you* own it! If I own somethin', it's mine to do whatever I want with, whenever I wanna do it. I bought it. It's mine."

"This yacht belongs to me," said the Australian. "I paid for it with money I made, and I don't want some ex-deck scrubber sitting in London with a loud necktie telling me what I can do with those I got working on it. I can fire any one of these crew just like that." He snapped his fingers. "And they know it. And I tell you what: I can also damn well make sure they don't find another job, except maybe working on a tramp steamer in the South Seas for three rupees a day. You'll find these guys work. They give me twelve good hours a day. *Good* hours. And if anybody, from the Captain on down, gives me any crap, they're punished. Just like in the old days. Just the other day Captain Hagan forgot to give me the daily breakdown, and I had him stand in the corner." He pointed. "Over there, in the corner."

DeLoop guffawed. "You're jokin'!"

Gillmore jerked his thumb toward Sarah. "And her. She's been there, standin' naked for four hours."

135

DeLoop was still laughing as he drained his glass of beer. "I wouldn't mind if she stood there naked now."

Gillmore snapped his fingers. "Sheila..."

Corky pushed her chair back angrily and got up. "You men are all the same. You just wanna talk about it. Nobody ever wants to *do* it anymore." She grabbed Sarah by the arm and pulled her toward the door. "We're goin' outside for a little woman talk while you two compare the size of your dicks."

Gillmore slapped his hand on the table. "She stays here with me."

Corky placed herself between Gillmore and Courtney, then smiled charmingly and leaned over to enhance her cleavage. "You don't want to refuse a guest a little company, do you? I cain't just wander around on my own with all these good lookin' sailors on board."

"Aw, let 'em go," DeLoop said. "You can ring for the steward if you want another Pepsi, Harv."

Gillmore was staring balefully at Corky DeLoop. He raised his finger and pointed it toward her. "Don't cross me," he hissed.

"What are you gonna do, shortstuff? Spank me?" She jiggled her bosom at him, turned on her heel and pushed Sarah Courtney toward the door.

Hercules DeLoop leaned sideways and farted. It reverberated around the room like a sonic boom. Then he began to laugh.

Gillmore turned bright red and threw his napkin down. "Don't you know we are at the bloody dinner table?"

DeLoop was still laughing. "I ain't laid one like that in two years, not since the pig pickin' on Corky's birthday."

"Don't they teach you any manners in Texas?"

"It's OK, Harv," he laughed. "It don't stink."

"Well, don't fart at my fucking table on my fucking yacht any fucking more." He jabbed his finger at the Texan. "And you need to do something about that fucking woman of yours. While you sit there farting, she runs off with the help."

"She's a handful alright, Harv..."

"...and don't fucking call me Harv!"

136

"...but you gotta admit she's the best lookin' piece of ass you ever laid your eyes on."

"What I admit," said Gillmore, still angry, "is that you must have a spine made of India rubber to let her walk all over you like that."

"She walked all over you, not me, asshole."

"She's *your* woman, you Texan halfwit, which makes *you* responsible for her."

DeLoop leaned over the table, put his elbows in the middle of it and pointed one finger the size of a six shooter barrel. "You may've been born short, feller, and I'm about to slap you down flat. You ain't talkin' to the help any longer. I can buy you for dollar bills and sell you for nickels without even goin' to the bank. I reckon you got the right to say whether or not I can fart at your table, but puttin' on airs and makin' threats and tellin' me what I'm responsible for is shittin' on my foot. Best thang here is for you to back up and start all over again." He dropped the big hand on the bell at the side of the table and rang it three times. "It's time for a drink and a cigar." He pulled out a case from his pocket, selected a long black primero and bit the end off it.

Ian Clark stepped through the inner door. Seeing DeLoop with a unlit cigar in his mouth prompted him to step forward and light it for him.

"Thank you, son. What I want you to do is bring me a glass and a bottle of bourbon and a case fulla ice. Think you can manage that?"

Clark smiled. "Yes, sir." He turned to Gillmore. "Anything for you, sir?"

Harvey Gillmore was slumped in his chair, and his face was dark and ugly. He didn't speak for a moment. "Bring me a Pepsi and some lemon slices."

The night was cool, and the yacht rocked gently from side to side. Sarah Courtney sat in a reclining chair with her shoes off. Corky DeLoop was sitting on a cushion massaging the English girl's feet.

"That feels so good," Courtney said, "I could almost melt. They have been killing me."

"If you'd take your stockings off I could do a better job," said Corky.

"Ohh, couldn't do that. He's one of those. You know. Wants me to wear them all the time, even when I am sleeping."

"That's just stupid, honey. Spoils the fun if you wear 'em all the time. Any fool knows that. How long you here for?"

"One more week and one more day," Sarah sighed. "I won't lie to you. I'm doing it for money." She opened her eyes wide and spread her palms. "I mean, would I be doing it for *love*?"

"Well, don't blush, sugar. That's what I'm doin' it for, too. I'm beginnin' to wonder if it's not makin' a fortune the hard way."

"But...I thought you two were married."

"Oh, yeah, Herk and me, we're married alright. But I didn't marry him outta love. I mean, did you hear what he just did? Farted at the table? *Very* romantic. If he fell overboard, I'd throw him an anchor. Naw, I'm just a vulture, waitin' for the carcass to fall over so I can start havin' a good time."

Sarah Courtney was getting nervous. "I better go back inside..."

Corky pushed her back into the seat. "I can still hear 'em talkin' in there. So you just lay back and rest your ass for a while. Relax. Once Herk starts bullshittin' and braggin' and drinkin', he'll talk for hours."

Sarah shuddered. "Gillmore frightens me, really frightens me. I thought I could handle it, but I can't. I just collapsed inside. Now I do my best to give him what he wants."

"Yeah," said Corky. "Once you fear somethin', it's got a hold of you, and you can't be yourself anymore. It's like a bully at school, isn't it? One who's too big or too popular to do anything about. He starts controllin' your whole life, a good bully. You sit on the other side of the room, walk home in different directions, play a game you don't like on the playground just to keep away from him. Or her. I remember what it feels like, honey."

138

Sarah laughed shortly. "I can't imagine anyone bullying you!"

"Oh, it happened alright. I just found out how to deal with it, that's all."

"But what do I do? He's completely trapped me here. I can't get away, and even if I do, he says he will hound me, and I won't be able to work anymore. Unless I do what he tells me. *And* pretend I enjoy it! If I make the slightest mistake, he beats me..."

"He *what?*"

"Beats me with a cane. You ought to see my bottom!"

"I'd jam that goddamn cane up his ass, if it was me."

"And even worse is this inflatable gag that's locked on my head. I can't eat or drink water until he unlocks it..."

"It's the ultimate control, isn't it?" Corky said through her teeth. "They don't want women, they want robots with chains around their necks. Go fetch, come fuck, go cook, come clean, smile and be sweet all the time, look after me, tell me I'm the handsomest thing in the whole world and as wise as god, and kiss my ass any time I bend over. Jesus Christ! Men are so fuckin' stupid and infantile. If they played their cards right, hell, we could all have a good time. I bet that little son of a bitch doesn't even know how to fuck."

Sarah giggled. "Just pokes it in and pulls it out. Mostly he can't even get it up properly." She thought for a moment. "But I think he's different. Because he doesn't enjoy anything about sex unless he sees me in pain. Or suffering. Or doing something because he is forcing me to do it. Do you know what I mean? I don't mind playing games..."

"...oh, hell, no. Let's play all kindsa games, but let's *both* have fun!"

"But this isn't a game. It's deadly, and it's real. That feeds the fear because you know he means it." She was frowning, trying to put her feelings in words. "Your name is Corky, isn't it?"

"Uh huh."

"Well, Corky, I know I haven't lived an exemplary life. I should have done this, I should have done that. I like to party..."

139

"Who doesn't?"

"...have a good time. I've met a very few nice fellows, a lot of very average ones and a few bad ones. Never before have I met a really *evil* man, one who thrives on the pleasure of someone else's misfortunes. I suppose I never really believed in evil, really. Now I think I do. But..." She looked down at Corky who was now massaging her calves which were aching terribly and realised her eyes were full of tears. Wiping them carefully with the back of her hand, she leaned forward and rested on one elbow. "I'm glad you're here, Corky. God, I don't think I could bear another week of this."

Corky smiled. "When the rest of the bigwigs arrive, we'll have to get together while they're yakkin', get you into a bikini with a nice gin and tonic."

Sarah shook her head. "Oh, I don't think so somehow. The old devil thinks ahead. If he sees any little oasis of pleasure, he make certain it's only a mirage. He will probably keep me tied to the bed. Like he did today."

"You're jokin'! Hell, if he does that, I'll sneak in and untie you."

"They're leather cuffs with little locks on them. Can't get them off without a key. And he locks the bedroom door."

"The little pervert. Lissen, honey, I'll think of somethin' to get you outta there." She winked at the English woman. "We'll stick together."

Sarah smiled. "Thank you, Corky. It's such a relief just to sit here and talk to you for a little while..."

"Lissen!" Corky sat up and spun around to face Sarah Courtney. "Lissen, how much is he payin' you?"

Courtney bit her lip. "Eight thousand for ten days."

"Pounds or dollars?"

"Pounds."

Corky DeLoop thought for a minute. "Shit. I cain't get hold of that kinda money without goin' to Herk."

"What are you talking about?"

"Well. I just had the bright idea of payin' you myself, marchin' you off this boat tomorrow and seein' you get on a plane to London..."

"Oh, I couldn't possibly pay it back. But thanks for the lovely thought..."

"Pay it back? I was gonna give it to you, honey. You've already earned it."

Sarah turned her head away, feeling the tears again. "Christ, I can't bear it when someone's nice to me."

Corky reached for her beachbag which was still sitting on the table and found a tissue inside which she handed to her friend. "But my darlin' husband makes sure I don't have too much loose cash. A double deck of credit cards, yes. Cash, no. Well, it was an idea..."

The door to the dining room opened, and Gillmore stuck out his head. "Get in here. Now."

Sarah Courtney sat up, smiling and took the shoes Corky handed her. "Yes, Mr Gillmore." She quickly put on the shoes, got up and walked through the door.

Harvey Gillmore stood for a moment glowering down at Corky DeLoop. She stuck out her tongue at him, and he immediately slammed the door, rattling the glass.

* * *

Sir Jonathan Mainwaring sat at the head of the table with the United Opposition Heads of Committee. These smaller meetings were now becoming more common. The full membership was becoming too unwieldy, as the register of members continued to rise. The agenda had been committee reports, and the final one of the evening was a discussion of strategies for the Media Committee, headed by Louise Templer. Her committee included a number of newspaper and television journalists who were pressing to make the attack more open and more direct. They strongly felt it was time to increase the media pressure on the government and on selected figures of known enemies, particularly those in the UK. Louise Templer was presenting their arguments.

She tapped her pencil on the table. "We feel the need to highlight a cross section of the power structure, turn a brief spotlight on a representative cabinet minister, say, and high court

141

judge, financier, chief constable, newspaper proprietor, governor of the BBC..."

Justin Lyndhurst shook his head as he interrupted. "It's much too early for that, Louise. Besides giving the game away to our opponents, you must bear in mind the nature of libel laws in this country." Lyndhurst was a QC and head of the Judiciary, Legal and Constitutional Committee. He sat back in his chair, his face impassive.

Louise Templer held her ground. "In *general* terms, Justin. No libellous accusations - even though true. Just an atmospheric spotlight..."

"An atmospheric spotlight? What the devil is that?" General Sir Timothy Portland was a compact man with startlingly clear blue eyes.

"I think she means that journalism is a good creator of mood," said Stuart Easton. "After all, that's what *they* use it for. And her committee feels it is time to start bringing up the lights." He turned to Louise Temper, who nodded in agreement.

Professor Ewan Thomas leaned forward on his elbows. He was a very tall, gaunt man with unruly iron grey hair. He headed the History and Economics Committee. Scratching his lantern jaw with one large hand, he chuckled. "The problem here is a general one we all face, but with newspapers and television it becomes more focused. Journalists are employees. They do not own the newspaper nor direct its policy. One article in a newspaper - or one good documentary programme on TV - will have very little impact..."

"Precisely my point," said Louise Templer. "It is not enough to 'give the game away', but it *will* raise the temperature."

"But at what cost?" Thomas asked, smiling. "If they are specific enough to do any good, they may well alert the enemy to our existence at too early a date. I can understand that journalists are anxious to fire the first salvo. That is the nature of their trade."

"When *do* we make our existence known?" asked Stuart Easton. "I keep asking that question and only get waffle and fluff."

Sir Jonathan Mainwaring always took notes. It was a habit of his from early days, and he much preferred it to recordings because it reminded him of the "feel" of what had been said. He looked up from his notepad. "It may seem we are a large group of people, but in fact we are still very, very small and very, very impotent..."

"Pop guns facing cannon," added General Portland.

"Well," replied Louise Templer, "one of the ways of becoming a larger, more effective group is by growing exposure. Publicity."

"However well we plan it," said Professor Thomas, "it will probably be accidental and could happen at any time. My thoughts are that we must be prepared for this eventuality so that we all move forward together, rather than scattering in panic."

"So," Louise replied, "what do you propose I tell my committee?"

Sir Jonathan looked at the Labour MP. "Do you want a vote on your proposal?"

"I want a fair airing first, Sir Jonathan." She tapped her pencil on the table again.

Mainwaring looked at his watch. "We have a time problem this evening, and I don't want to be unfair to you, Louise. So I suggest we adjourn just this side of the hour and put this at the top of the agenda for our meeting next week. Meanwhile I think we should all consider the problem of opening shots or salvoes or whatever they're called. While we must remain deeply careful and as closely coordinated as is possible in the circumstances, I think Ms Templer does have a valid point here. Because I believe one danger we face is stagnation. When we become more a debating society instead of a wedge or vanguard for reform."

As the meeting broke up Mainwaring noticed Keef Sams in the doorway trying to catch his eye. He walked over to the black man who had a worried look on his face.

"What is it, Keef?" he asked.

"There's a car outside," Keef replied in his low bass, keeping his voice well down. "It showed up about twenty minutes after the meeting started and parked just across the road

143

on a double yellow. It's a new Grenada, and new cars nearly always mean police. Or bailiffs, right? Two men inside. I thought about going over and trying to move 'em on..."

"No," agreed Mainwaring. "Wrong thing to do."

"Yeah, so I just watched them, right? Definitely interested in this building. In this floor of the building. Couldn't see much because I couldn't get close, you know what I mean? But I'd say Old Bill. One department or the other."

"Thank you very much, Keef," Mainwaring smiled. "Would you care for a cup of tea? I'm sorry I forgot to offer you one earlier."

Keef held up his hand. "No, thanks, Sir Jonathan. Do you want me to follow them when they leave?"

"Now that's an idea, Keef, if you think you can do it without being noticed." Mainwaring stopped Justin Lyndhurst from leaving the room by the front door with his arm. "Just a moment, Justin. I think we should all..."

Keef leaned over and whispered to Mainwaring. "If they're listening, maybe you shouldn't tell them which way you are leaving, not too loud."

Mainwaring smiled and raised his thumb to the black man. Justin Lyndhurst overheard the whisper and moved toward the rear door, while the Secretary told the rest in a low voice what the problem was.

"Perhaps," said Professor Thomas, "this is our accidental eventuality." He gathered up his papers and stuffed them into a file which he put under his arm.

They all moved toward the rear fire exit and went carefully down the darkened stairs. Keef went in front with a torch showing them the way. He also made sure the lights were left on in the room after they left. He knew that if the Bill outside were listening, they would soon realise what had happened, so he wanted to get to Haug's old yellow van as quickly as he could. When they got to the bottom, the committee heads came out quickly and silently, dispersing mostly toward the underground station.

He switched off the torch and ran around to the corner, glancing to his right before turning. The van was parked in the same street as the Ford, about thirty yards behind. He was relieved to note the Bill were still there, but just as he slid silently into the van, he heard their engine start and saw the lights come on. He cranked the van twice before it fired and waited until the car pulled away before cautiously easing the van out of the parking space. When the big Ford turned the corner, he switched his lights on. The way the cops were moving it was going to be a big job keeping up with them. After all, they never gave themselves speeding tickets.

CHAPTER NINE

Corky DeLoop got up early the next morning because she had made up her mind. Herk was still snoring in his bed, sleeping off a bottle of bourbon. She washed and made up her face very carefully, then chose her briefest bikini. It was white and seemed to be almost transparent, and she adjusted the halter around her neck to reveal as much of her bosom as possible without being positively pornographic. Previously she had combed her hair, but now she carefully ran her fingers through it to make it seem she had just been rolling in bed. Turning right, then left, she checked everything in the mirror, then frowned. The frown turned to a smile as she spotted her high heeled sandals. Normally on the boat she wore rubber soled flats for stability. But this morning it had to be heels. Checking again in the mirror she gave herself two thumbs up and put on her silk beach robe, leaving the tie undone.

As she guessed, Gillmore was eating what he called breakfast in the dining room. Sarah stood beside him attentively. She was nude except for the inevitable stockings and suspender belt.

Gillmore looked up from his newspapers when Corky entered, and his face immediately clouded over. He stared at her over the top of his granny glasses. "Just passing through, I hope," he said with a sneer.

But Corky walked straight to his table, grabbing a chair on the way. "As a matter of fact, no. I'm glad I caught you this mornin', 'cause I wanted to have a little private talk." She beamed her most winning smile as she sat down opposite him, allowing the beach robe to fall open.

"What kind of talk?" he asked sourly.

"You won't know until we try it," she said brightly, crossing her legs.

He looked at his watch. "Go on, then. I'll give you two minutes."

Corky glanced at Sarah. "I said, *private*."

147

Gillmore waved his fork in Sarah's direction. "She doesn't matter. I'll get her to put in earplugs, if that'll make you feel better."

Corky leaned forward and noticed how his eyes widened involuntarily as he glanced at her breasts. "Please," she said, pouting her lips. "Five minutes. Sarah can wait in your bedroom. I'll go get her myself when we're finished. If you want some more coffee, I'll pour it for you." She leaned over further and took the carafe in her hand the way she would touch a penis, then topped up Gillmore's cup.

Gillmore put his knife down noisily and leaned back in his chair. "So you want something, do you?"

Corky nodded with a big pouting smile, her eyes wide.

Gillmore half turned to Sarah. "Beat it, sheila. Go to my bedroom and stay there. Sit up straight in a chair and don't lie down."

"Yes, Mr Gillmore," Sarah said as she curtsied before leaving the room.

Harvey Gillmore sighed heavily and looked across at the Texas woman. However much he loathed her, he had to admit she was absolutely gorgeous. A phenomenon of sexy flesh with the biggest tits and the longest legs he could ever remember seeing in his life. He drew his dressing gown closer around his small frame. "I'm waiting," he said testily.

"I want to do a deal with you, Harvey," Corky said as she leaned back with enough force to shake her bosom. "A good ole Texas deal. I want you to let Sarah keep me company for half a day every day."

Gillmore inflated his cheeks and blew out the air derisively. "Absolutely not. I need her twenty four hours a day. That's what I paid for, and I want my money's worth."

Corky uncrossed her legs then re-crossed them. "Think, Harvey. From what Herk says, you'll be in meetings most of every day. Or maybe on shore for meals or relaxation. All together, just you men. You won't want Sarah around then. The other guys will look at you like you're nuts, havin' this girl standing at attention by your side all the time..."

"I don't give a fuck what they think."

Corky held up her hand. "You'll have her in the mornings and all night. I'm just asking for a half day every day, say six hours."

"Six hours? Go fuck yourself."

Corky nodded. "OK, four hours. You're bound to be tied up in business for at least four hours every day. In meetings, Harvey."

Gillmore stared at her without blinking for almost a full minute. "What do I get in return?" he asked finally.

"On the final day aboard, I'll let you run your hands over me," she said coyly.

The Australian actually laughed, and it wasn't a pretty sound. The times Gillmore had laughed in his lifetime could be counted on the fingers of one hand.

"I know you'd like to," she said quietly, still smiling. "You've had your eyes over every inch."

Gillmore tilted his head forward. "Piss off. Get out of here."

Corky reached behind her head and untied the halter, and her top fell away. She pushed the beach robe to the side with her arms and leaned toward him. "Are you sure?"

Beads of sweat formed on Harvey Gillmore's brow. They were superb. Large and juicy, without a single flaw. Though heavy looking, they did not fall or sag - something he always hated. He actually bit his tongue to stop himself from agreeing right there and then. What stopped him was instinct. Business instinct. She wouldn't be sitting there with her tits out if she wasn't prepared to go further. When somebody else wants something you have, *squeeze 'em*! That's what his father taught him. *Squeeze 'em!* And as he looked at the tits, that's exactly what he wanted to do.

"Not interested," he said dismissively. "I can buy any kind of tits I want. No. Now piss off and let me finish my breakfast."

Corky rolled her halter top around her hand. She pulled the beach robe to cover her chest. "OK," she sighed finally. "OK, a quick fuck. What the hell. On the last day."

Gillmore leaned toward the Texan. "I'll tell you what I'll do, bitch. The whore can have two hours off every day, and on the last day you take her place. For the whole day."

This time Corky laughed. She threw her head right back and guffawed. "You must be outta your mind, you little Aussie pervert. A whole day with you would be a nightmare I wouldn't even dream of. I think you're right. I'll just piss off." She got up, letting the robe fall open once more as she turned.

Gillmore's head filled with blood. "A half day!" he growled aggressively. "Six hours."

Corky turned back to him slowly, biting her lip. "I'll give you one hour. Chained to your bed. But no marks, and I mean that. *And* no more marks on Sarah, not one more. No more cane. You have to promise."

He smashed his fist on the table. "Don't you tell me what to do with my whores!" he hissed. "Don't you ever tell me what to do! Nobody tells me what to do!"

Corky pulled the robe tight again and leaned forward from her hips. "I'm not tellin', Harvey. I'm askin'. As a part of a bargain. A deal. Somethin' you seem not to be interested in."

Gillmore sat back in his chair and forced himself to be calm, then took a sip of coffee. A thought suddenly occurred to him. His leverage here was the whore. He hadn't seen that before. "I won't beat the whore on one condition. For one half of one day, you do exactly as I tell you, whatever I tell you to do. Just like she does."

Corky turned away angrily toward the door leading to the deck. "Fuck you."

"If you don't agree, I'll beat her every day," Gillmore said quietly as she started to open the door. "Once in the morning, once at night."

Corky stood at the door for a full minute without moving. Then she turned and walked back to the table. She sat down. Then she leaned over the table and pointed her finger in Gillmore's face. "That is what we call dirty pool, asshole. That is not playin' fair."

"I've never been accused of fair play."

"If you do that," she said quietly and evilly, "it is steppin' outta the game." She turned her pointing finger into a palm to stop him interrupting her. "If we're gonna step outta the game, sunshine, well, I wanna tell you I can do a lotta real nasty things. You beat her like that, and you will fuckin' regret it."

"Do what you like, bitch."

She smashed her fist on the table. "I'll give you two hours on the last day."

He smacked his palm down alongside hers "Six hours, and you will obey me every minute. Not one whinge."

"Fuck you."

"Take it or leave it." He grinned nastily. "Hurry up, because I want to go beat my whore."

Corky DeLoop bared her teeth and snarled. "Harvey Gillmore, I'll give you four hours. That is the max. That is it. Final. For that, I want the following: no marks on me, no marks on her. In other words, no cane for either of us. Understood? No physical damage. If you turn that down and go whip that poor girl, I promise I'll hunt you like a stag til I bring you down. You hear me? I'll bite your fuckin' prick off and feed it to the pigs."

Gillmore blanched for a moment before he caught himself. "Four hours is nothing. It doesn't give me time. It'll take time to break a bitch like you."

She exhaled dismissively. "You are a fuckin' dreamer."

"Piss off."

Corky got up angrily. "OK, asshole, but you're gonna regret this for the rest of your life." She turned again to leave.

Gillmore let her get half way across the room and realised she really meant it. "OK," he sighed reluctantly. "Four hours with one condition."

Turning back to him, she put her fist on her hip. "And what might that be?" she asked sarcastically.

He stared at her and took off his granny glasses. "Four hours and a quick fuck right now."

"Oh, get lost, you dirty little turd!" she shouted.

He shrugged, trying not to look concerned. "OK, the deal's off." He got up from the table. "I'm going to beat that sheila until her arse falls off. Right now." He started for the door.

"You can have a quick feel," Corky said, her voice low and threatening.

Gillmore stopped and turned. "Five minutes."

"One fuckin' minute. Max."

The Australian walked toward her. "Tell me when to go."

Corky stopped him with her palm outward. "First, repeat after me: no beatings, no marks, no cane, not with me or with her. Four hours on the dot."

Gillmore stood in front of her. He was sweating again. "No beatings for the bitch or the whore, no cane, four hours only." He reached for her.

She pushed him away. "She spends four hours every day with me. At least."

"OK, done."

"Four hours continuous, not an hour here and there."

"OK. Four hours continuous. When I'm in meetings."

Corky stuck out her hand. "Shake first. On the deal. When you shake hands, it is sealed, right?" When he held out his hand, she shook it once and dropped her hand. Then she raised her left arm and looked at her watch. "One minute. From...now."

Gillmore opened her robe and instantly grabbed both tits, rubbing and squeezing. Then he let one hand drift down her belly to her bikini bottom. The other hand went behind to grab one of her buttocks.

Corky started whistling *The Yellow Rose of Texas* as she looked at the sweeping second hand of her wristwatch. The man knew nothing at all about how a woman wanted to be touched. "Do you really like it this way?" she asked sarcastically. "Touchin' up somebody who doesn't want your hands on her?"

Gillmore moved his face close to hers as he jammed his fingers under the bikini and clawed for her vulva, which was difficult because her legs were closed. "It's the only way it's any good," he whispered. "When you do it by force. When the woman hates it." He grabbed her tit again with the hand which

152

had been rubbing her bottom. He jiggled it up and down while trying unsuccessfully to force his fingers into her.

"Ding-dong, time's up," she said and pushed him away sharply, closing her robe. "Have to wait til next week for the rest." Turning, she started for the door.

Harvey Gillmore stood in the middle of the dining room and watched her walk away. "I can't wait to see you crawl."

She opened the door and looked back over her shoulder at the little man in the middle of the room. "Look in the mirror, Harvey, and you can see a creep."

* * *

They arrived at intervals between 10 am and 5 pm the following afternoon. Two of the flights were from London, one from Brussels and one from Frankfurt. Haug had bribed an attendant called Spiros to let him park his rental car right at the front of the lot near where the Jaguar from the Matilda stopped to pick up the arrivals. He chose a bay behind some greenery planted to break up the monotonous concrete and tarmac. Behind this he could risk using his big lens, a real telephoto mostly used in the past to snap portraits of errant husbands with girlfriends on their arms. It wasn't quite as big as those used by journalists on The News to snatch pictures of princesses swimming topless on private beaches, but it was a good one, a Nikon. Haug was not a natural photographer, so his camera was a high tech job that made all the settings automatically. Including the focus - unless he used the telephoto. Then he had to do it by hand.

Before he left the house that morning he coated his exposed head, neck and arms with sun screen, and Ralph Harrison gave him a big thermos full of iced mineral water. Harrison had also loaned them two mobile phones, which was very handy. One Time was on the beach at the other end and would phone Haug when the Jag left for the airport. That way it was not necessary to spend all his time out in the ever hotter sun. He could nip into the air conditioned airport lounge for a cold beer and a chat with Raul Dominguez.

Dominguez had his own camera but without a telephoto lens and had to work in a little closer to his subjects. Haug had to admit he was good at it. He never once saw the camera and even had trouble seeing Dominguez, who joined the crowds of incoming tourists from the flight who milled around the front waiting for coaches or taxis. The Cuban was a difficult man to see in a crowd. He kept on the move in an organised but plausible way. Haug would catch sight of him, and then he would be gone. A very experienced professional, he thought to himself. Haug was too noticeable to be a good shadow, and One Time was worse - except at night.

After the first flight from London he had sat with Dominguez in the lounge eating a sandwich for lunch. He had a shoulder bag which contained the camera and telephoto, along with the mobile telephone. He definitely was not going to leave that lens in the car. Two men had arrived together on the flight, and Haug knew one of them.

"Michael Regis," said Dominguez carefully and frowned. "Never heard of him."

"He could wear a top hat and walk under a snake's belly," Haug muttered darkly. "Crooked as a barrel of fish hooks."

The frown turned to puzzlement on the Cuban's face as he thought for a moment. "Top hat and snake's belly? Oh, I see." He placed his hand near the floor. "Very low, very sneaky? Not a nice man."

"What I call trash," said Haug. "Though he looks ever inch the fine English gentleman with a high class accent, his ethics would embarrass a meetin' of polecats. I had a chance to whup his ass once, and I wish now I had.' He took a bite of his sandwich and washed it down with Greek beer. "Regis knows everbody there is to know who've got hands on levers of power or stacks of money. He makes a fortune as a middle man. You know: he introduces somebody with a lotta somethin' to somebody who only has a little and takes a small slice for himself. Main source of income is arms dealin', though he's much too fine a gentleman to call it that. Also furnishes first class whores to top judges, cops, cabinet ministers and oil sheiks. Uses the girls like lollipops you hand out to little kids. A master

154

of blackmail and extortion. Though," Haug raised his hands in mock alarm. "Heaven forbid anybody usin' such language to describe his profession."

Dominguez nodded. "I am aware of the type. I am afraid they exist everywhere. It is like - what do you call it? - infested timber. Even the strongest, healthiest wood can crumble into dust?"

"Dry rot."

"Yes. It is sometimes difficult to resist a bribe when it is put into an irresistible package and called by some other name. But when the main timbers of a house have dry rot, the house falls down, even the biggest and grandest." He poured the remainder of his beer into his glass. "This Michael Regis, is he involved in drugs?"

Haug finished the last bite of his sandwich. "I don't honestly know that he is. Nothin' has ever come up along that line. Regis is kinda obsessed by keepin' his name clean - even if he's standin' up to his chin in pig shit. Now in my opinion, arms dealin' is a hell of a lot worse than drugs. Any drugs. But it hasn't got such a bad name. So long as you keep it at arm's length, you don't actually get your own hands dirty. Morally speakin' I doubt if he's got anythang against drugs. Or slavery, for that matter. Particularly if there's a buck in it. So. I don't know."

They both left the airport after seven o'clock when One Time told him they had garaged the Jaguar and the three crewmen had returned to the Matilda. Only five men had arrived. Regis and his friend from London. Another man came from London on the second flight, a peculiar looking fellow with teased ginger hair sporting a polka dot bow tie. Another arrived on a flight from Brussels and one from Frankfurt. After the call from One Time, Haug rewound the film, put it securely into a parcel clearly marked "film" and found a firm of couriers who would insure the parcel arrived at the address the next morning, delivered by hand. He sent it with a covering letter to Louise Templer, asking her to pass it on to Sir Jonathan - without of course using his name. Maybe it was safer that way, maybe not.

Then he gave Raul Dominguez a lift back to Ralph Harrison's house in Kalami.

Harrison had been monitoring the receiver and had managed to record some of the introductions which had taken place in the dining room of the Matilda. So, apparently, everyone did not already know everyone. Two men, Michael Regis and Jeremy Evans were not introduced by title, so he had no idea who they were. But there was a Dr Carlton Fine, an American with some connections to the Lawrence Livermore Institute, an English professor by the name of Alexander Hinkley and another American, Wren Olsen - he was not sure about the spelling of the first name - who was an executive director of the International Monetary Fund.

Ralph Harrison shook his head as he handed the list to Haug. "The only name familiar to me is Alexander Hinkley."

"That name rings a bell," said Haug. They were sitting in the courtyard again in the deep shade of the grape vines. Except for One Time, who was upstairs with the headphones on. He was very proprietorial about the sound equipment and seemed a little upset when Harrison actually seemed to know what he was doing.

"He's a pompous little git," said Harrison, pouring some iced mineral water into a glass. "A professor of philosophy, I believe, who, while he was at Cambridge, taught a number of students who rose rapidly during the Thatcher years. In my view his reasoning is as bogus as his reputed intelligence. But he is certainly the doyen of the right wingers, who practically worship him. I suppose it is understandable," he sighed. "After all the Right traditionally have great difficulties in attracting anyone intelligent to their banner. Most of his theories are pure bunkum - *Mein Kampf* with big words - and the Cambridge student body finally combined with their lecturers to chuck him out of the university, despite howls of protest from the Right. Now he has a seat at the table of the Adam Smith Institute, I understand, in addition to holding expensive weekend seminars for his acolytes."

Haug propped his feet up on the chair opposite him. "I'm surprised they don't have any real security, except for your friend, Cuban number two," he said to Dominguez.

The Cuban shrugged his shoulders dismissively. "He is not security. You would know real security. They would have spotted us today."

"I presume," said Harrison, "that they feel they are safe here. They do not know of our existence. Or if they know of it, they are not worried about it."

"Oh, I think they'd be very worried if they knew they were bugged," Haug said. He had a beer bottle in his hand and was enjoying the little breeze which had picked up when the sun went down.

"After all," Harrison replied. "It is a private yacht in the middle of the Ionian Sea. I suppose it just never occurred to them."

Haug nodded. "We assumed security was part of the reason they decided to meet here rather than London.

Dominguez suggested they go to a local taverna for dinner, but Harrison was worried about leaving One Time. He went up and offered to take over while the black man had something to eat, but One Time insisted he was fine. He asked for a takeaway. Harrison was beginning to understand the patois a little better, now he had got the hang of watching One Time as well as listening.

The taverna was set beside the sea, but there was no beach. Tables were placed outside on a patio of poured concrete which had been laid right up to the rocks. The owner apparently knew Harrison well, so they didn't have to wait for a table. And the first round of drinks was free. The taverna was quite full of tourists. They all were at this time of the year. Harrison told them the retsina was superb in Corfu and insisted both his guests try some. Haug said it tasted like pine needles soaked in owl piss, but the Cuban quite enjoyed the wine. Harrison told them he fell in love with Corfu when he was a child. His mother brought him and his brother every spring and once stayed for a whole year. He had made friends with the local children, some

157

of whom he still knew, and he had only idyllic memories of his childhood here on the island.

Though he was a Corfu resident now, he did not spend all his time there. At some point perhaps he would. He would accept temporary lectureships for year or half-year terms, sometimes in Paris, occasionally in Rome, but more often in the UK. And of course Athens. He had been invited to America, but his political views resulted in a visa being denied him. More and more of his time in Corfu was spent on his hobby, which he insisted was "tinkering". He worked on his beloved motorcycles, fashioning some of the parts by hand on a lathe. He toyed with computer programming, but also repaired any computer hardware which needed replacement. For Dominguez he had knocked together a personal directional listening device which would pick up conversations from about 100 yards. Two of the upstairs rooms in his house were packed with pieces of equipment in various stages of restoration. His tinkering gave him relaxation from maths. It was something completely different. They were problems which *had* solutions, which were real. And he could work with his hands.

He admitted he could not easily cope with marriage. On the one hand he regretted the loss of companionship. On the other, it was just more peaceful. He had more control. Probably, he stated frankly, it was simply selfish. He had married once but found the intrusion too severe. He couldn't think as well, nor could he work. His life at that time was even more peripatetic than it was now. Perhaps that was the problem. But above all else he valued his privacy and the peace it brought to his life.

Harrison was an articulate, soft-spoken man who could have a wry turn of wit. He was no longer active in the Party, though he occasionally attended local meetings in Corfu Town. There had been more splits and heresies than in the Christian church during a shorter period of time. This did not make him cynical, but it did make him wonder whether the Party was any longer the right instrument to carry on the battle. And if not the Party, then what? At the moment it seemed as if the barbarians had triumphed, and the left was in disarray. He felt the Party would re-emerge from the ashes as the historical pressure increased and the rich countries stepped up their plunder of the poor ones.

Haug had done more listening than talking. He found Ralph Harrison a very interesting man who spoke extraordinarily well. At one point the Englishman had asked him about Vietnam, but Haug insisted he never talked about those days, not to anyone.

Dominguez listened, too, rather than talked. At the end of the meal, while they were waiting for One Time's takeaway, he told them quietly that this was the last time he would be able to "be on holiday." Every other evening he must now be out on the dingy just after sunset.

When they returned to the house, all three men were in a mellow mood. A huge half moon was suspended in the sky, painting the courtyard a luminous silver. Except for faint, distant tourist shouts, it was profoundly quiet. The three of them stood there for a few moments enjoying the soft magic of the evening.

Haug broke the silence first. "I guess I'm gonna turn in. Tirin' day."

Harrison stepped toward the door with the takeaway. "Would you like a nightcap?"

"Maybe a little one. Some of that ouzo, maybe." When Harrison disappeared through the doorway, Haug turned to Raul Dominguez. "I don't wanna offend you or anythang, but...do you need any money? I mean, I haven't got a lot, but I could probably dig up a couple of hundred extra."

Dominguez was looking up at the moon, and he smiled. It pulled the tight skin on his face away from his teeth. "It is no offence, señor. True, I have few resources. 'I depend upon the kindness of strangers.'"

"Streetcar Named Desire."

"What a beautiful name for a play," murmured Dominguez. "What a wonderful dramatist."

"My favourite," said Haug. "Though I'm prejudiced, bein' a Southerner. Williams was our greatest poet."

Dominguez chuckled. "Here we are, danger men, violence our profession, talking of poetry in Greece."

"That's what I'd rather be," Haug muttered, almost to himself. He, too, was looking at the moon. "A playwright. A

159

poet. Somebody who could do somethin' beautiful and leave a little moment like this behind me for someone else to enjoy. Instead of a trail of broken bones. And dead men. Women and children..."

"You can't live in guilt, señor. It was as you said before. What's done is done, and when it was done, you thought it was right."

Haug continued as if he had not heard the Cuban speak. "I got a talent alright. But it's not a talent with words or notes of music - how *great* it would be to write music - or paint or be a sculptor. I cain't even add and subtract like Ralph. What I *can* do is destroy thangs. I don't think that's much of a talent in anybody's book."

"Some things need to be destroyed for poets to live," Dominguez replied quietly.

The two men turned together, ready to move, as something snapped behind them. It was One Time's fingers, and all that could be seen of him was his big smile, like the Cheshire Cat, as he stood in the shadow thrown by the house in the courtyard.

"You oughta wear a bell around your neck at night," Haug grumbled. "Or somethin' that glows in the dark like a lightenin' bug."

"One time," said the black man. The hand that wasn't rhythmically snapping was holding the takeaway. His whole body was moving to some inner music. From time to time the snapping hand would drop a piece of food between the white teeth. Then one finger would go up in the air and drop into a snapping rhythm again.

Haug shook his head. "I guess you wanna tell me somethin', since you don't have your hat on the ground for my loose change."

"Righteous." There was an accompanying laugh this time.

"Go on, then. Don't make me drag ever fuckin' word outta you."

"She wants to see me, man. Tomorrow."

Haug threw his Harley dozer cap on the ground. "Goddammit, I knew this was goin' to happen. Once you get your winkle into an oyster, you ain't worth gully dirt. I'm not

160

gonna spend my time doin' your job and mine while your hips are pushin' your brains up some goddamn broad."

One Time was still laughing. "She's the boss, man. She got our ears. I gotta do what she say. She wants One Time, One Time gotta go."

Haug picked up his cap and smacked it against his leg. "Now this is just one fine kettle of fish, I tell you..."

Some more food dropped between the teeth. Then he held up his finger again. "One for you, too, man. A friend is a friend. I say, I got a friend. She say, OK, *I* got a friend..."

Haug sounded pained. "What are you tryin' to tell me? That you got us a fuckin' double date right in the middle of an operation? I swear this is the last time I bring you to do an important job. Next time it's gotta be Keef. Never gives any trouble. Always does his job..."

Haug could tell One Time was shaking his head by the way the still smiling teeth moved from side to side. One Time was making that circular movement with his hand, palm down, toward the ground. "Keef, man. He's a has-been. *Has* been. Been there, but gone now. One time."

Haug looked around at Dominguez who seemed to be enjoying the show. "This is kinda embarrassin' in front of a professional."

"Not embarrassing," chuckled the Cuban. "It is warm. You are good friends."

"Not anymore," said Haug, turning to One Time. "OK, asshole, when is all this romance supposed to happen?"

"PM, man." The smile disappeared for the first time. "Got to take out the bad Cuban. He follows her with a knife."

"And I know who *that's* gonna be, right? The hell with the ouzo. I'm gonna hit the sack. You're probably too excited to sleep, but my advice is to get your ass upstairs as well."

"Right now," One Time said as he dumped the rest of the takeaway into his mouth and followed Haug up the steps, waving one finger to Raul Dominguez who remained standing in the middle of the courtyard.

* * *

161

Alex Hagan, the captain of the Matilda, joined the guests at dinner that evening wearing his white uniform with "HG" embroidered on each shoulder underneath the epaulettes. The stamp of Satan, he called it privately. Gillmore was obsessed with property and always considered the crew as part of the fixtures and fittings. Hagan loathed his employer and looked forward to the quiet days during the voyage back to England. That would be after Gillmore left next week.

Hagan was chained to the Matilda like a galley slave. That was how he thought of it sometimes. Or rather he was bound to Gillmore. When he was not acting as captain of the vessel, he worked as "defence advisor" to the Sunday Sentinel. This actually meant he did research and wrote some copy which was hacked about or dipped into by editors looking for interesting facts. When Gillmore's chauffeur died last year, Hagan even acted as his driver for two months. With a peaked cap. It certainly underlined his true worth to Gillmore. In other words, next to nothing.

His friends wondered why he stayed. The crew wondered, too. They were all casuals, hired for one journey. Alex Hagan was the only full time employee. He knew the crew laughed behind his back at the humiliations he received from Gillmore. Like standing in the corner with his nose to the wall. They didn't know he also received canings. Two of them so far. He had to drop his trousers and take six or twelve licks on his backside. But Hagan never said anything and never openly complained. He was forty eight years old now, and, as an employee of WORLDWIDE would receive his pension in another seven years. That was part of his contract.

He never complained or explained because he couldn't. As far as he could see, he had two choices. He could murder Gillmore or he could carry on. Alex Hagan sighed inwardly as he looked around at the dinner party. He was here as an ornament and nothing more. People were introduced and then spoke to him no more the whole evening. The two women seemed the nicest of the lot. He supposed they must be attractive, but Hagan had been gay since his adolescence.

162

Though he didn't "look" gay, he did keep his body in good condition for his age. He guessed Sarah Courtney was in fact a prostitute. Gillmore often hired them when he came aboard the Matilda, treating them even worse than he treated him. He had seen Courtney standing in the corner once, her bottom bare, and observed how his boss made her fawn upon him every minute of the day. Tonight, at least, she was fully dressed in a white sun dress as she stood at Gillmore's side and, as usual, fetched him his Diet Pepsis.

Mrs DeLoop certainly made his spirits rise, as she brought a feeling of anarchy with her. She was wearing a pink, low-cut silk dress which hugged her figure and rustled with every movement. But her husband was dreadful, a coarse, filthy rich bucolic peasant. He scratched his arse, spread food all around his plate and intimidated everyone with his size.

Professor Alexander Hinkley was sitting at the second table with the DeLoops picking at his food like a bird. He was small in stature, at least as short as Gillmore and would have looked like an exotic stick insect if it hadn't been for a ragged and thin goatee sported underneath his chin.

The man introduced as Jeremy Evans sat beside Hinkley. Another small man, though a little fleshier than Hinkley. He had a youthful appearance, though Hagan would guess he was nearly his age. Evans seemed quite excited and talked a great deal.

At the first table - the Captain's table - were two Americans, Michael Regis and Harvey Gillmore. Sarah Courtney stood behind her boss with a smile fixed to her face.

Dr Carlton Fine was a Team Leader and executive of the Lawrence Livermore Institute. He was a tall, heavyset man with small eyes and very large glasses hung on a humourless face. The remaining hair on his head was brushed straight back, so black it could be dyed. He had a deep voice and spoke in short dogmatic phrases as if what he was saying was bound to be true, and anyone who didn't know it was stupid.

The other new American was a shorter, fatter, quieter sort. He, too, was bald but only had a fringe left, and it was turning grey. Wren Olsen was an executive director of the International Monetary Fund.

163

Fine and Regis did most of the talking at the table. Gillmore dug unhappily at his inevitable salad and drank lots of Diet Pepsi. Alex Hagan liked Michael Regis and knew him from his other visits with his boss. Regis would stop and chat with him, showing great interest in details of the yacht, its speed and manoeuvrability. Once he even brought Hagan a little gift, a pair of gold cufflinks with his initials engraved on them. Regis sat next to the Captain and did make an effort to include him in the conversation. Such consideration was indeed welcome in such an atmosphere where he generally felt of little more value than the polished brass ship's clock hanging on the wall. Michael Regis was a fine gentleman, a man of his own class, someone he could talk to warmly and freely.

Yes, thought Captain Hagan as he finished off his entree of barbecued lamb, why indeed was he here? Simply because of an unhappy mistake in his past. He had been an ensign in the Royal Navy when it happened. Hagan and two other young officers had far too much to drink one evening ashore. On their way back to the destroyer they found a rating from the same ship too drunk to read his own watch. Instead of helping the poor sailor they began taunting him. It began as harmless fun and then drifted slowly toward danger. In the end, the rating was made to take his trousers down, and each young officer in turn entered him. Except Hagan. Hagan did not rape the young sailor, but he did hold him down for the other two. Actually he became disgusted with the whole thing half way through, but it was too late then to do anything because of the inevitable peer pressure. He did intervene when his two friends wanted to do it again, though. He stopped it and helped the rating back to the ship while the other two laughed and walked on. That is what saved him from court martial. Because the rating remembered what happened the next day and reported the matter. Alex Hagan received a severe reprimand while his two fellow officers lost their commissions and were dismissed from the RN.

He was later assured the reprimand was deeply buried in the files, but, no, it was not deep enough. Somehow Harvey Gillmore found it. And threatened to use it. It would, he was certain, break his mother's heart. She was not even aware he

164

was gay. He had never even brought himself to tell her that. Damn it, he thought, it would kill the poor woman.

He looked over at Gillmore, aware his own smile was as fixed and as plastic as the one on the face of the girl behind his boss. As he held his glass for more wine from the waiter, he wondered how natural justice had let the swine survive his heart attack last year. But then again, that was natural justice for you.

CHAPTER TEN

"Looking at the landscape in perspective," said Michael Regis, opening the meeting the next morning, "we can modestly congratulate ourselves." He was impeccably dressed in pressed white shorts and white T-shirt. Sunglasses hung from the only pocket of the shirt. The white suitably contrasted with his olive skin tone and dark hair. They were sitting comfortably around two tables which had been pushed together in the middle of the dining room. Two pitchers of iced mineral water and one of Diet Pepsi stood among seven glasses. Folders and papers were neatly stacked in front of every guest except Hercules DeLoop, and Wren Olsen had an expensive looking laptop computer on the table.

"The overall picture," he continued, "particularly with regard to Europe and America, is an optimistic one. Our organisation has grown through shared interests, circuits have been established - along with targets and objectives - and we have learned to work together in a more coherent way. With the spectacular collapse of the Soviet Union and Eastern Bloc satellites, some of our dreams have come true almost too easily, opening up further horizons. Directly due to our influence and lobbying, liberal and socialist legislation has been rolled back in virtually every European country. Taxation has fallen dramatically. And, not surprisingly, we find most of the people right behind these new ideas which we have helped introduce.

"However, we are failing in two principal respects. Having grown so large, we have also become cumbersome and ungainly - yet increasingly we operate without real coordination. We are in danger of becoming like a giant herbivorous dinosaur with a huge fat body and a small brain. At this point we have the European, the American and Far Eastern Directorates. Others, like the emerging African continent, will arise. What we don't have is a central governmental policy committee. Therefore our movements are sometimes uncoordinated and occasionally duplicated. Haphazard, in other words. We are meeting here partly to consider the foundation of such a committee and partly to iron out wrinkles resulting from the lack of direction.

"The second item is a corollary of the first. Some operations are beginning to go wrong, and there is some indication our existence has been suspected, if not detected, in several countries. We should therefore expect increasing opposition, and we need ideas on how to deal with this..."

"That's crap," said Dr Carlton Fine. "It's the same wishy-washy people we've always had honking at the sidelines. Liberals in sandals, folk singers, faggot writers, a few do-good lawyers. Harvey can tell you how to deal with them. Easily marginalised, if you've got the press and TV behind you."

"In America perhaps," Regis smiled charmingly. "But there is a much longer and infuriating leftwing tradition in Europe which, as you know, threatened to sweep Europe after the war. And there are still pockets of real power which we must attend to as a matter of urgency. We have reports from France, Italy, Germany and Holland that small groups are being formed, and our members are being identified and occasionally harassed. We have successfully dealt with the one in Holland, by the way, through the Direct Action units."

"Yeah?" asked Fine. "What about England?"

Regis stood up and walked to an open window. It was a brilliant and hot day, and he enjoyed for a moment the breeze blowing in from the sea. "To be honest, we are a little worried, but no one has as yet been identified. Some very important and highly classified tapes were lost last year..."

Harvey Gillmore slapped his hand on the table. "You know very well what happened to them, Michael. They are ruined. At the bottom of the bloody Thames."

Regis turned and held up a finger. "We *assume* they are destroyed. We do not *know*. Until we know for certain, we have to presume they could be in the hands of our enemies, whomever they might be."

"That's fucking rubbish," said Gillmore. He poured himself a glass of iced Pepsi. "You just want to use those fucking tapes as a guilt prod. I know you, Michael. Slippery as an eel. I didn't even know you were involved in this until all that happened last year. You came into my office pretending you didn't want to hear this or that when all the time you're into it up to your elbows."

"It was because we felt it wise to include you, Harvey, that you found out anything at all." Regis turned to the others. "Harvey had a bad habit of taping all his telephone conversations, including ones on a secure phone. And keeping the tapes. They were subsequently taken from his safe by an employee who threw herself from a bridge, presumably with the tapes clutched in her hands."

"Not presumably. Definitely."

Regis shrugged and smiled. "We do not have them, and they were not found. That is all we can say."

Gillmore jabbed his finger at Regis. "You're trying to thwart me, Michael!"

"Calm down, shorty," DeLoop growled, scratching the side of his face.

"My height is genetic," Gillmore snarled. "Just like your intelligence."

DeLoop laughed at him. "If you're so smart, how come you lost all them tapes?"

Harvey Gillmore grabbed some papers in front of him. "Why the devil are we talking about tapes? I don't see anything about tapes here on the agenda. Where is it? Show it to me?"

DeLoop ignored him. "Well, you boys all know what I'm here for, don't you?" Unlike Regis, DeLoop was not dressed expensively or well. He had on a vest and a pair of Bermuda shorts, and the vest was the kind usually worn underneath a shirt. It stretched over his massive belly and revealed his shoulders were covered in hair. He wore his reflective sunglasses, even though they were indoors. "I don't know anythang about dinosaurs, but I know I been runnin' my ass off makin' money that just seems to disappear right down the drain. I reckon not enough is goin' to runnin' the operation. It's goin' for fancy dinners in French restaurants and goddamn yachts and hunnerd dollar whores." He directed the final remark at Gillmore.

Gillmore smacked his hand on the table again and brought it up with a pointed finger. "This yacht was paid for through

WORLDWIDE. Which *I* own. *My* money. Which I can spend any fucking way I like."

DeLoop sucked a tooth. "Do you wanna know just how much dope I'm havin' to hustle these days? How much it's costin' me in cover and bribes? Hell, I'm damn near retired, and ever day I get a fax for more money, more cash, more this, more that. And a whole shitpot of those requests come from Europe. From here. Now, my understandin' of the agreement was a two-way thang. We sometimes help you, you sometimes help us. You are makin' plenty of money in arms, I know damn well you are, on account of the fact there are plenty of wars and gung-ho generals to sell 'em to."

"We did have a rather large shortfall last year," said Regis smoothly, "because an African sale fell through at the last moment. It was connected with the matter of the tapes..."

"If I hear another word about those tapes, I'm leaving the room," said Gillmore petulantly.

"Fuck the tapes," growled DeLoop. "You goddamn foreigners are bleedin' us dry."

Gillmore banged his chair away from the table and stood up. "That's it. I'm leaving. I told you, if you mentioned those tapes again..."

Dr Carlton Fine peered through his large round glasses at the Australian. "Sit down, Harvey." He turned to DeLoop. "I think it's time you shut up, Herk. Save it for later. We've got a lot to do, and you're not helping."

"I'm not here to help," said DeLoop. "I'm here to kick some ass about these goddamn millions and millions of dollars pourin' into the shithole of Europe..."

"You can be an embarrassing fool sometimes, Herk," Fine said evenly. There was something about the man which was solidly menacing. When he spoke, his authority seemed profound. "We'll proceed with the agenda as agreed. As Regis said, our most pressing business is the formation of a governing body. A head. A brain. It is time our movement became more formalised, and I have some proposals to make." He paused for a moment to check through his notes, then got up and went to the

170

head of the table. He was a commanding figure and moved as confidently as he talked.

"I'll tell you now *what* we need," he continued. "Later on we can decide how we arrive there. We need a council, and we need an executive. And it needs to be designed for speed and efficiency. We all know how important those factors are. For the executive, I prefer one man. One man to be advised by the council but who will have full powers of enforcement which are binding on members. Disagreement can come beforehand in the council, fighting it out with words, facts and figures. When decisions have been reached, the executive is advised, and he then takes action."

"Yeah?" scoffed DeLoop. "What happens if somebody don't like these orders? Like me, for instance. What if you say I gotta do this, and I say go fuck yourself?"

"I'd rather leave that question for the moment. But I will tell you now that I am also recommending our Direct Action units be upgraded and expanded to carry out internal security and punishment." He stopped DeLoop from interrupting again with the weight of his voice. "I insist, however, that the whole process be completely democratic. We must proceed on that principle, as we always have. The council will be freely elected from among our members, and the executive will be elected from the council."

"A splendid idea," Regis agreed.

"The council will be constituted," Fine continued, "by elected representatives of our membership. Each country will be allowed a number of representatives based on their population. If the figure is, say, 15 million, then Britain would have four reps and America would have 18. Approximately..."

"I'm not sure I agree with a strict population factor," Regis said.

Dr Carlton Fine turned to the Englishman. "This is an initial proposal, Michael. In fact there will probably be a number of factors, but population is a primary one. Others will be GNP, military strength, nuclear capability. So Britain shouldn't be *that* badly off." He stopped to clean his glasses with a handkerchief. "However, this is a good example of just the sort of provincial

171

behaviour which has constricted us in the past. Eventually we will sweep away national boundaries, except for administrative purposes. That is another cue we have taken from the former Communist Internationals." He smiled indulgently at his audience as he replaced his glasses.

"I'd rather not take anythang from the commies except their blood," DeLoop growled.

Alexander Hinkley became suddenly animated. "Oh, no, that's where you are wrong, I'm afraid."

"I don't like to be called wrong by small men," said DeLoop.

Hinkley laughed awkwardly as he continued. "There are many things we can learn from our more successful enemies. In this case the communists had a worldwide organisation, all cooperating together for a common goal and, most especially," he held one finger in the air, his eyes glittering. "Most especially, they had ideological commitment! *That* is our most important operational gain."

"Thank you, Dr Hinkley," said Dr Fine. "Except we, of course, are committed to freedom and democracy. The freedom of all men to choose their own lives, where they live, where they travel with the political freedom to vote for any political party of their choice. The freedom of managers to manage their businesses with the minimum of governmental interference. The freedom to trade in any part of the globe, to set up a business, to buy at the right prices and sell at the right prices. The companies they call transnational these days are, after all, merely companies. Doing business. Yet at every international border we have problems. While all we want to do is trade freely and do business."

"There have been spectacular advances here as well," Regis commented. "Due mostly to our coherent strategies the sting has been withdrawn from the unions..."

Dr Fine turned on him. "A good example of why we need a central executive, not just 'think tanks'. Dealing with the unions has been far too time consuming." He stopped and drummed his heavy fingers on the table before him. "Our organisation began in 1948. We grew slowly, even painfully. Made many mistakes. The *obvious* tactic in dealing with unions always eluded us.

172

There we were faced with these monolithic and barbaric collectives who undermined every company they ever infested. We tried the law but found unions had a great deal of money to spend in their own lobbies. Corruption and bribery and pressure were only partially successful. Media investigation, a little more so."

He paused again and looked at each man owlishly. "Even in the 60's and 70's we knew the real answer. Technology. With increasing technology, productivity went up, prices went down, sales went up...and employment went *down*. Employment went down," he murmured again significantly and smiled his first smile. "And continued downward, and continues even today. Creating a whole body of men who are broke and unemployed and who will work very, very hard for much less than their union friends. We could have and should have seen this many years ago."

Wren Olsen spoke for the first time. "I would point out, Carlton, we would not have had the political atmosphere at that moment in time to take advantage of the information, even if we knew its value. Particularly in the States. We *had* to rid ourselves of all that liberal garbage, the so-called Democratic Party. Nixon was a man we could do business with, but first we had Kennedy..."

"We took that son of a bitch out," said DeLoop.

Gillmore turned to look at the Texan. "We?"

There was an uncomfortable pause, then Dr Carlton Fine spoke quietly to the newspaper publisher. "Herk was part of the operational team which carried out several key assassinations, including the two Kennedys and Martin Luther King."

DeLoop leaned toward Gillmore. "And if you put that on a goddamn tape, and I find out, I'll stomp your ass into a mudpuddle."

"You'll be killed, Harvey, if you're taping this conversation," said Regis. "It's as simple as that. I checked this room over this morning, but I am no expert. And neither are you."

Gillmore seemed not to have heard Michael Regis. "So it's true, then? About Kennedy?"

Fine laughed. "Of course it's true. Nearly everyone knows it's true. But that's all they know. And it's all they will know. In a way, it is to our advantage because it gives us an image of invincibility and super efficiency. Brilliant operations. Brilliant."

"Well, thanks, Carlton," DeLoop smiled. "Never thought I'd hear a compliment from you."

The jowl around Wren Olsen's face trembled as he shook his head and continued. "We thought we could do better business with Johnson, but in fact it was worse as he got on his rabble-rousing high horse. Taking out the second Kennedy cleared the way for Nixon. Finally. And you all know what happened there. With Reagan, however, we made up for lost time."

Fine burst out laughing. "An absolute jackass."

They all laughed, except for Gillmore. Olsen continued. "But perfect. A dumb actor who could read lines. He stayed asleep most of the time, until someone woke him up to sign something or say something. Perfect."

"I hate to boast," said Regis, "but not as perfect as Holy Mother Margaret."

"Is she one of you...us?" Gillmore asked.

Regis crossed his legs. "It has been decided that actual leaders should not on the whole be members. We always prefer to simply have people we can do business with. Those are the ones we support. Thatcher and Reagan both allowed a real housecleaning, though. Many of our people are now in the mainstream civil service. And we now have two cabinet ministers, due to Thatcher's choice of the right ones to fast track. The BBC has been - how should I put this? – counter-infiltrated? The so-called National Health Service is being forced to account for itself financially, prior to its break up and sell off to private institutions. The nationalised industries are being broken up and privatised and all forced to sink or swim in the marketplace where they belong. Consequently taxes are being lowered, and money is flowing into the country. The City of London is throbbing very much as it was in the 19th century, free from the shackles of over fifty years."

Wren Olsen nodded. "Incidentally, did you know, Michael, that the International Monetary Fund was set up by liberals?" They all laughed. "Yet it has become for us the perfect instrument for international policy. We can reach any government on the planet, no matter how small, how insignificant. It's simple. Do it our way or no money. Many say no, of course. Until their currency becomes worthless and their people are rioting in the streets. Then they take their caps off and knock at our door. Ten years ago, no five years, could you imagine a major nuclear power like Russia, on its knees at our doormat, begging for a few billion? They'll get the kind of government we want them to have."

"Exactly," said Carlton Fine. "A free, democratically elected government. And thank God for that."

"Amen," said Gillmore. That reminded him of Christ and how he had doubted during this past year. After his heart attack he practically blamed God for all his troubles. WORLDWIDE was teetering on the brink of collapse, he was knocking at death's door and all his so-called friends were deserting him. And now WORLDWIDE was thriving. He had a new satellite channel. *The Johannesburg Star* was his. Along with the *New York News Reporter*. And now, this minute, he was moving even closer to the seat of ultimate power. Global power. It had to be because of the power of God and His only Son. There could be no other explanation. At that very moment, while the others were talking, he even thought this was a Message. Maybe even a Vision. God was telling him to return to his prayers or all these fruits may be taken away. The first time was a warning, and Gillmore could not ignore it now. That very evening he would get down on his knees and pray to God. To pray for the success of this wonderful new venture.

He knew they wanted him because he was important. He was the greatest newspaper publisher in the world. He could reach the mind of the common man. None of the others could do that. As Gillmore drifted back from his Vision, he realised that little twerp, Hinkley, was talking.

"...the problem exists, of course, of this necessary permanent body of unemployed workers, and Dr Fine and I have been exchanging papers over the past few years. They must remain a constant threat to the employed, so euthanasia was quickly dismissed. And of course it is morally questionable as well." He adjusted his polka dot bow tie which he wore even in the heat. "But we began looking at an updated version of the old workhouse. Whatever people may say, the workhouse arose during a period of our greatest economic success. There could be a connection here," he said, looking around the table significantly. "We believe an updated version could almost be like Butlins. Clean, decent but cheap accommodation where everyone would work for their food, heating, clothing and lodging. Privileges - for instance permits to leave the camps on visits - would be used as prizes for good behaviour. The camps themselves would be sealed off and policed by...those drawn from the unemployed, of course. For higher pay and better housing. Ultimately, you see, this would be the privatisation of unemployment benefits. In other words it would pay for itself, gentlemen. No money need be passed out at all, as all their needs are taken care of. And in return for that, they work. Clearing rubbish, cleaning the roads and pavements. Or - and this is under discussion at the moment - servants. In this age of technology they could help relieve the employed, particularly the middle classes, of time consuming duties like laundering, washing up, polishing, mowing...those sorts of things."

"Now *that* is a fucking good idea," said Gillmore enthusiastically.

Jeremy Evans looked at his mentor with eyes brimming with admiration. He had been lucky enough to study under Professor Hinkley, and now, here he was on the same team. The logic, the insight, all were still there, still luminous. He might be a small man, but his inner vision was grand and clear. He also knew of Dr Fine and had read his work avidly. These were the people at the cutting edge of the New Ideology. They were, he knew, the Wave of the Future.

* * *

Enrico Gomez put down the binoculars and slipped on his lightweight but wrinkled jacket to cover the small automatic he carried under his arm. There was no trouble getting through customs with the gun, unless he was unlucky enough to be searched. Because the pistol was made almost entirely of plastic, a new model made especially for airline hijackers. Or so he thought. What else was it for? Anyway, it was fucking useful to him. It bucked a little more in the hand when he fired it, but it made the same hole.

He looked out the window of his villa again at the motor launch moving toward the shore, still a speck to the naked eye. The broad was coming ashore. The DeLoop woman. He'd had a call from Mr DeLoop about an hour ago and had waited at the window with binoculars until he spotted her. Another broad was coming as well.

Gomez had not left his villa since his arrival, but this didn't bother him. He hated the sea. Hell, he had grown up with sea all around him. He'd seen enough ocean to last a lifetime. Instead he just rested in his room reading girlie magazines or drank crap beer in the tourist taverna nearby. He didn't like the look of Greeks he met anyway, and he had been really shocked when some of the waiters started dancing with each other. Now he was convinced they were all fags.

This was all going to be real easy money, this trip. Just follow the DeLoop broad around and make sure she didn't get a chance to screw any of the locals. Though he certainly wouldn't mind dipping into that honey pot himself. Just thinking about it made his dick grow hard, even though he had jacked off the night before, looking at that slinky blonde centrefold in Hustler. He remembered Mrs DeLoop tried to shake him in London, but he knew all the tricks. All of them. Stepping in one door of a taxi and out the other, waiting for a subway train and jumping through the sliding door at the last minute - or jumping back off using the same technique. He'd had *real* pros try to shake him.

The spot on the water was growing bigger, so Enrico Gomez got his hat and went downstairs.

The two women got into the Jag, and Gomez followed in his rental car. A piece of cake. The driver ahead took it nice and easy as they drove to Corfu Town, and he could see the women's heads in the back seat, yakking away to each other. The other broad was a knockout, too. Hadn't seen her before. She had dark hair and a real nice figure and was wearing shorts, a halter top and low heeled sandals. But Mrs DeLoop...wow, he thought. A tiny short pink skirt and a skin tight sleeveless top with no bra, low heeled sandals and toe nails painted like candy. Man, she could make the centre pages of Hustler any day. His dick started getting hard again. He would take either one of them. Or both of them, now that would be something.

After they got into Corfu Town the traffic was horrible. Finally he saw the Jag pull over to the curb and let the women off, obviously to do some shopping. Then the big sedan pulled away, leaving them on the sidewalk. Gomez found a space to park his rental and couldn't have cared two shits whether it was legal or not. The women were still standing on the sidewalk talking so he just leaned against a lamp post and watched them openly. Fucking broads were probably trying to plot some way of getting away from him. Why didn't they just take their medicine, relax and enjoy themselves?

Suddenly the DeLoop woman started signalling for a taxi, and one pulled up right beside them. With a nigger driver. Jesus, he thought to himself, that's disgusting. Niggers everywhere, even in fucking Greece. He turned around quickly to run back to the rental car and ran straight into a concrete pillar.

Or it felt like a concrete pillar. Later he vaguely recalled the image of a motorcyclist in a full-faced helmet. Something grabbed his neck so tightly he couldn't breathe, and that was all he remembered before waking up in the hospital emergency room with a fierce headache and a hairline fracture of the skull. His gun was gone, and so was his knife. But all his money was still there.

He was later told he had bumped into a motorcyclist who apparently thought he was under attack and grabbed Gomez by the neck, slamming him back into the lamp post. The

178

motorcyclist was very broad across the shoulders, but nobody could remember anything else. The police had taken his passport and wanted to know why he had attacked the motorcyclist in the first place. No mention was made of the gun or knife, so Gomez assumed the fucking cops stole them. Or the hospital orderlies. Thieving Greek fags. He had another knife but not another gun. Gomez looked at his watch. Two and a half hours had passed. Fuck knows where the broads would be. Then he started worrying about what he was going to say to DeLoop. If anything.

* * *

Haug and Sarah Courtney sat under the awning of a tiny taverna on a nearly vacant beach. Ralph Harrison had given them directions. Because it was a difficult place to find and a long way from the popular parts of the island, it was relatively unused. Though it would no doubt grow in the future as tourists found something else unspoilt to spoil. It was very quiet and you could hear the waves lapping into a jagged pile of rocks which looked like a ruined cathedral and broke the straight line of the shore. They had just arrived and were waiting for two beers from the owner/waiter. They were the only customers. One Time and Corky DeLoop had run off down toward the big pile of rocks hand in hand. He had to admit the Texas woman was one hell of a good looker. She had looked Haug up and down behind her sunglasses and said he was kinda ugly but would certainly do on a rainy day. Haug told her she was wasting a first class body on a third class Romeo like One Time. Corky DeLoop really sparkled. He liked women like that. Their personalities glittered like crystal, reflecting beautiful colours all around a room. Then One Time had grabbed her hand saying, later, man, later. Corky took off her sandals, and they both ran like kids to the cathedral of rocks.

"Would you mind giving me a ride on the motorcycle on the way back?" Sarah Courtney asked.

Haug had borrowed the Vincent from Ralph Harrison, promising to take very good care of it. In fact he had considered

179

poleaxing Gomez from the bike but decided there was too much risk to the machine. "I'd be very happy to give you a lift, Miss Courtney. A beautiful woman on a beautiful machine."

She laughed. "I'm not so sure I feel beautiful today, Mr O'Connell."

Haug had introduced himself using an old friend's name. "Just call me O'Connell."

"Only if you call me Sarah."

"You gotta deal."

The waiter brought two bottles of Mythos and two glasses. Haug took a drink from the bottle while Courtney poured hers carefully into the glass. He could tell the woman was tense and a little jumpy.

"So," he said finally, "how're you enjoyin' your visit on board the Matilda?"

She took a sip of beer and stared out at the sea for a few moments. Then she turned brightly toward him and smiled. "Oh, it's marvellous. Wonderful weather, gorgeous sea, fresh air. What more could you want?"

"Are you with anybody in particular, or..."

"I'm a guest of Harvey Gillmore's. Do you know him? Who he is?"

Haug took a long drink from the bottle. "Yeah. I know him. Slightly. I introduced myself once."

Sarah Courtney lowered her sunglasses and looked at him. "Do I detect disapproval from your tone of voice?"

"I personally think he is a low grade asshole and would do me and the rest of the world a big favour if he sat down real slow onto a roarin' chainsaw. I'm sorry if you like him and all, but I always find it best to say just what I think. That way we don't get all tangled up in misunderstandin's."

"Oh, he can be very nice," Sarah said, turning to look out at the sea.

"Well, you probably know him one hell of a lot better than I do. We only met briefly."

"What did you do to that man who was following us?" she asked, changing the subject.

180

"I introduced him to a lamp post. It was love at first sight."
He leaned over and pulled off his boots and socks. Then he
rolled up his jeans as far as he could. "Interested in doin' a little
beachcombin'?"

"I'd love to go for a walk, yes." She slipped off her sandals.

Haug signalled to the waiter, and with hands, fingers and
grunts asking if it was OK to leave their footwear there while
they walked on the beach. The Corfiot understood immediately
and kept nodding his head with a big smile, gesturing toward the
beach. Haug took another pull on his bottle of beer, then peeled
off his shirt, rolled it up and stuffed it in his back pocket.

The beach was smooth and sandy, and they walked silently
along the water's edge away from the cathedral of rocks. The
silence was a little uncomfortable for both of them.

"Look," Sarah Courtney said finally. "I don't want to be
impolite, O'Connell, but I'm only just with Corky today. I came
along because she wanted some company, and..."

Haug laughed. "Don't worry, Sarah. That's all I'm here for,
too. Just company for One Time. And your company is an
unexpected pleasure. I am not lurin' you down this beach to try
and fuck you."

"Oh, I didn't mean..."

"I know what you meant. I could feel it in the air. So let's
you and me just enjoy a little wet feet and a nice walk, take a
little pleasure from the sunshine and relax. We can talk about
anythang you want. Except Harvey Gillmore. Start talkin' about
him, and I might stomp a six foot hole in this beach."

She laughed shortly and folded her arms across her chest.
As they walked on silently, she looked down at her feet. She
could still see the marks from her high heels. "To be honest, I
don't like him either. In fact I loathe him."

"We definitely got somethin' in common then," Haug
replied. "How come you don't leave?"

She shrugged, looking a little more uncomfortable. "I came
down for a week or so, and it would be a little rude to turn right
around and go back home. Besides, I adore this part of the world
at this time of the year. Look at this place. Isn't it gorgeous?"
She was smiling, but the smile was not convincing. "So it's a

181

kind of holiday. *And,*" she turned to him with a raised finger. "*And* I know one of the other guests."

"Um-hmm," Haug nodded.

"And I'll bet you don't know this one," she said. "His name is Michael Regis."

Haug stopped dead in his tracks.

Sarah turned back to him. "You *do* know him?"

He stared at her through his sunglasses. Of course, he thought. That was why she was a guest of Gillmore's. The penny should have dropped a long time ago. One of Regis' girls.

"Do you know Jennifer Montgomery?" he asked.

Sarah Courtney paused for a moment, cocking her head. "Yes. I do, as a matter of fact. But how..." She suddenly clapped both hands to her mouth, squealing through them. "Oh, no! It can't be! It's impossible!" She dropped her hands and held one of them out toward Haug. "But it's got to be. I remember she said '..bald headed with a ponytail, built like a wrestler..'"She laughed and turned out toward the sea. "I don't believe this, but it's crazy enough to be true. You must be Jennifer's boyfriend."

Haug felt a stone with his big toe and leaned over to pick it up. It was smooth, worn down for many years as the sea tossed it back and forth across the seabed. He threw the stone, and it disappeared into a small cresting wave.

"I don't know whether this is a good or bad thang," he said finally. "You recognisin' me. The last thang I want is for somebody on that boat to know I'm here. I mentioned Jenny because I had a hunch about somethin'. I didn't imagine she woulda talked to you about me."

She shook her head. "You don't have to worry about my talking to anyone about you. Except Corky. She's the only one I talk to. Even Michael...he's usually so nice, but even he keeps his distance while I'm with..."

"You're one of Regis' girls, aren't you? Like Jenny?"

She was still staring out at the sea. After a moment she nodded her head reluctantly.

"And Gillmore's the client?"

182

Sarah Courtney couldn't bear it any longer and felt the tears coming. She took off her sunglasses and wiped her eyes. "I don't know what I would have done if it hadn't been for Corky. Do you know what she did? To get me away from that monster for four hours a day, she agreed to go with him on the last day herself." She was sobbing now and found it more difficult to speak. "I had to force it out of her. She didn't want to tell me. And she made him stop beating me...and...and..."

Haug stepped over and put his arms around the young woman. She drew her elbows inside his arms and lay her face against his chest, crying. He patted her head, stroking her hair gently. "Don't you worry about cryin'. Cryin's a good thang, not a bad thang. Next time I meet that good for nothin' son of a bitch, I'm gonna cloud up and rain all over him."

She banged one of her fists onto his chest. "I hope you hit him once for me."

"I'll put your name on it." He stroked her back. "That Corky must be some woman."

Sarah nodded, pulling away so she could see his face. "She is. I was going through hell. He makes me stand for hours and hours in these damned high heel shoes, and I didn't know if my feet were going to last. And sometimes he uses this gag, and I can't eat or drink because he says I'm too fat or something..."

"That man wouldn't know beauty if he had his face pushed in it to make a mess of it. Now, I tell you, you're one hell of a beautiful woman. And I'm a fuckin' expert. I got a black belt in beauty appreciation."

She tried to smile. "I can see why Jennifer likes you so much."

He grinned good naturedly. "She's just blinded by my overwhelmin' sex appeal."

"You're even making me laugh."

He let her go but kept an arm around her shoulders as they continued to walk slowly down the beach. "What else did Jenny tell you about me?"

"She said you saved her life. But she wouldn't explain. Said you had a pickup truck and a motorcycle. A *motorcycle*! Of course. That should have been a clue. I can't wait to tell her.

183

If I get back. God, how many days have I got left? Six, I think."
She laughed again, sniffling.

Haug pulled his shirt out of his back pocket. "Here. Wipe your face with this."

"Are you sure?" she asked, taking the shirt.

"Hell, it's been used for everthang else."

She wiped her eyes and gave it back with a smile. "When did you last talk to Jennifer?"

"Just before I left," said Haug. "She'd got back from a tour with the RSC."

"Oh. So you didn't have much time together."

"She's got a new boyfriend..."

Sarah Courtney stopped. "I'm sorry. I didn't know..."

Haug laughed, put his arm around her shoulder again, and they walked on. "Naw, it's a good thang. What Jenny and I've got together is special. It's more than boyfriend and girlfriend. It's possible we'll always love each other. Which is probably a hell of a lot better than movin' in with each other. 'Cause both of us need big bags of privacy, and both of us got strong opinions." He scratched his chin with his free hand. "Yeah, I guess I'm a little jealous, but I'm nearly twenty years older than her. She needs to see some sights, spring from rock to rock, make mistakes, laugh and get drunk and make a fool of herself, sleep with a few guys her own age.."

"That's very generous."

He shrugged. "Not tryin' to be generous. If we got any chance at all, I gotta risk lettin' the bird fly away. If I tie a piece of string around her leg, I'll damn sure lose her for good. And I'd hate to do that."

They walked on in silence for a few minutes before stopping to watch a small boat putter into the lone jetty.

Sarah Courtney put her head against Haug's shoulder. "It's not fair. Why don't I meet any men like you?"

"Hell, what do you mean? You just met me."

She poked him in the ribs. "You know what I mean."

"Mostly, I think it's because we look for the wrong thangs. We look for *excitin'* men or women. Dangerous ones. Know what I mean? They make the blood run a little hotter and the

184

heart beat a little faster. Maybe we tend to step over half a dozen good 'uns to get to the worst choice in the room. And spend the next few months or years regrettin' it. We think we know the direction of our lives, then the compass needle starts spinnin' around like crazy, and we find ourselves in bed with somebody who's half insane or hacksawin' on your nerves or borin' you to death. Anyway, that might be part of the problem."

"But you can't go for anyone if the zing isn't there," she said.

"Yeah, but sometimes you find the zing by fannin' a little flame first and not just jumpin' into the biggest fire and grabbin' at each other's crotch right away. Though I've done enough of that as well."

She grinned and hugged him. "I think Jennifer's got the most wonderful taste in men."

He smiled back at her. "Just about as good as her taste in friends."

She looked at her watch. "Maybe we should start back soon. Remember, I only had four hours, and it's a long drive back to Paleokastritsa."

They turned and moved slowly toward the rock cathedral, which was still in view. When they got back to the taverna, One Time and Corky had just arrived. Both of them had cat-and-canary smiles and were still touching each other fondly as they drank cold beer. Haug and Sarah joined them for a last drink before setting off.

Haug had thrown Harrison's helmet in the car after the incident with Gomez, as he wanted to take advantage of the Greek laws. It took three good cranks to start the big V-twin, and the sound reverberated down the deserted beach. Sarah Courtney got on the pillion seat behind him, holding onto him tightly, and they wound up the narrow road into the low hills with One Time following behind in the car. He didn't drive fast, only gunning it a few times to feel the incredible surge of the torque and hear the kind of sound which was so elemental it was part of his soul. A big British or American twin throbbing like kettle drums against the roaring orchestral wind. He could feel the woman behind him enjoying it, too, when she hugged tighter and pressed her head against his back. Somehow the big motorcycle provided a release for them both, a little discharge for the current which had built up between them. Thought was not coherent or even logical anymore as the road unfolded and then twisted tightly before him. It was instead a single continuous expression of emotion, one he could not duplicate even by standing before a beautiful painting or listening to a Bach cantata. The right motorcycle, unlike any car, becomes a *part* of the rider. You are not in it or even on it. Rider and bike form a single unit, the emotional flesh and the hard rationality of the machine joined inextricably and, it sometimes seems, almost timelessly.

He gunned the big Vincent once more, leaning into the bend, but the traffic had increased now, and the moment slowly dissolved back into the reality of the world he had forgotten during the ride.

CHAPTER ELEVEN

On Friday morning Sir Jonathan Mainwaring left the St James's Park Underground station after arriving from Waterloo and walked briskly toward Victoria Street. He then turned into Dacre Street wondering if the Minister would be on time for their meeting this morning. Ian Castleberry had been drinking a little more these days, and Mainwaring suspected the Minister was having difficulty getting up some mornings. His driver would arrive at Castleberry's house and have to wake him from the car telephone. And the Minister's mood was never good until he had cleared his head with a midday nip from the brandy bottle. Mainwaring had a tricky argument to present to his Minister and was going to assume a hangover, which would affect the way his cards were dealt. He would get his way as usual, but the Perm Sec had a busy day lying before him, and he wanted to get his way as quickly as possible.

The well dressed, fit looking man stepped out of the large black Rover just in front of him.

"Sir Jonathan Mainwaring?" the fit looking man asked in a neutral tone of voice.

Mainwaring was taller than the man blocking his path, and he looked down at him as if peering at dog dirt. "And who, may I ask, are you?"

With a single movement the man fetched an ID from an inside pocket and flicked it open.

Mainwaring snatched the ID from the man's hand and examined at it. "Special Branch?" He snapped it shut and handed it back to the fit looking man. "If you know who I am, you know where I can be found." He started to brush the man aside with his umbrella but found a hand on his chest, and his wrist was held in a vice-like grip.

"Take your hands off me!" Mainwaring said in a voice that would have blistered paint. With surprising force he smacked the side of the man's face with his umbrella.

Another man slid out of the Rover, and he heard the engine start up. At the same moment the first man did something very

187

quickly with the wrist he was holding. Sir Jonathan's briefcase clattered to the ground, and he was doubled over with pain as his arm was forced up his back. Pedestrians were turning to look but hardly slowed their pace as Mainwaring was bundled forcibly into the back of the black Rover. His briefcase, umbrella and bowler hat were thrown in after him, and the wheels of the big car squealed as they pulled sharply away from the kerb.

The Perm Sec was sitting between the two men who had thrown him into the car. The man who accosted him first was sitting on his right and spoke first.

"I am Detective Inspector Green, Sir Jonathan..."

"Well I suggest, Detective Inspector Green," Mainwaring interrupted him, "that you return me to the point where I was kidnapped and submit an apology both to me and the Department of Trade and Industry."

"Kidnapped, Sir Jonathan?" asked Green. "You are simply being taken for questioning." He introduced the man on his left. "This is Detective Sergeant Malley..."

"If this is an arrest," Mainwaring interrupted again, "then you must inform me of the grounds of the arrest and give me immediate access to my solicitors."

DI Green laughed. "I'll inform you of what I think you need to know. In the meantime..." He suddenly smacked Mainwaring across the face with the flat of his hand, which he immediately turned into a warning finger. "That is for hitting me with the umbrella *Sir* Jonathan..."

Without hesitation Mainwaring sank his teeth into the finger.

"Jesus Christ!" DI Green screamed. "Get him, Malley!"

Sergeant Malley hooked his right arm underneath Mainwaring's chin and began applying pressure. The Perm Sec had little experience of fighting, but he had known immediately where these men came from and why they picked him up. He also knew his best chance of escape was some time before they arrived at wherever he was being taken. Therefore, when he felt Malley's forearm against his neck, he drove his elbow with all his strength backward, still holding on fiercely to DI Green's finger. He was not all that strong, but his bony elbow must have

188

hit something because there was a great rush of breath past his ear and the arm across his throat loosened. He pushed across the screaming Detective Inspector and tried to open the door. He couldn't. It must be electronically controlled by the driver. He let go the finger and launched himself forward at the back of the driver, who was trying to look around and see what was going on.

Then suddenly there was nothing. When he regained consciousness he was only aware of how uncomfortable he was. His wrists were handcuffed behind him, he was lying on the seat and the two officers were sitting on top of him. He made no sound as he woke. The handcuffs were very tight, but he brushed the pain aside. Thinking was needed now. If they had taken him like this, his prospects were not good. For the arm of the law to reach directly into the heart of the establishment and brutally pluck out one of its most respected members meant but one thing. These were their opponents, and Sir Jonathan Mainwaring was unlikely ever to see the inside of a courtroom. And not very likely to even see his wife again. He had tried to escape once. He must look for every other opportunity.

He thought of Haug. What would *he* have done? Eaten the two thugs alive, probably, and left the bones clean picked. How could he get word to the others? He had read in stories that you must try to remember all the railway lines you cross and when there is a bridge or steam whistles blowing. Mainwaring quickly dismissed the thought as foolish. Instead he started to design his resistance on his own playing field. The playing field of the mind. That's all he had now. But it was quite a lot, really.

* * *

After lunch on Friday Haug was listening with One Time at the receiver. The group on the boat was having another long winded discussion on how they were going to rule the world. Both men had headphones on and didn't hear Raul Dominguez enter until he sat down.

"You were out late last night," Haug said, taking off the headphones.

189

"Yes, señor. And I slept far too long this morning. I have been listening to the tapes I made last night. The quality is not good, but I think there may be something which might interest you." He held up a microtape.

Haug took the tape. "I'm sure it'll be more interestin' than this crap. These guys are comic book characters, right outta Batman. Most of 'em are crippled where walkin' sticks won't help 'em." He stuck it on the recorder.

"I've left it in the right spot," Dominguez said. "Late last night one of them took a telephone call, I think. He must have moved out onto the deck to talk on the phone. Or perhaps he had a mobile unit. I think he wanted privacy for the call."

Haug pushed the play button, keeping his fingers on the volume control. There was a great deal of static mixed with noise of the wind and sea. Then he heard what he thought was a voice. Yes, it was a voice. But it was lost in the static and noise."

"I am sorry, señor, but it was the best I could do," the Cuban murmured.

Then Haug could hear the voice again. This time it was a bit clearer. Sounded a little like Regis, but he wasn't sure. Suddenly he stopped the tape and rewound it slightly. This time he turned up the volume. The crackle filled the room, and One Time took off his headphones to see what was going on. Haug held up his hand. He again played past the voice and again rewound the tape and played it again.

"Fuck it," Haug said, jumping up from his chair. He turned to One Time. "See if you can get anythang any better. I'm gonna find Harrison. I'll be goddamned if I don't think he said 'Mainwarin'' in there somewhere.

One Time indicated the larger recorder was already in operation, taping the proceedings of today's meeting. Haug was worried as he went quickly downstairs to find his host. Why the hell would they be talking about Jonathan? At that time of night on a telephone? Alarm bells were ringing all round his head, and he felt his stomach flutter. He found Harrison in his office looking at something unintelligible on the computer screen.

"Have you got any way of cleanin' up a tape, an audio tape, so you can hear it a little better?" he asked the mathematician. "I think it's important."

Harrison took his glasses off and thought for a moment. "I can try. I don't have a sound studio. That would be the best bet."

"No time," Haug said. "We gotta do somethin' with whatever we got here. As soon as possible."

Harrison stroked his short beard. "We will have to digitalize the sound. Now, I don't have any software for that particular operation. But I see no difficulty in writing a programme myself."

"Will it take long?"

"A maximum of two hours before I have something for you."

Haug ran back up the stairs. One Time was bent over the recorder. When he saw the American he held up his finger and pressed Play. Again there was static and wind noise and then the voice, this time a little clearer. It was Michael Regis.

Haug stared at One Time. "Did he say somethin' like '...and then kill him'"?

One Time nodded his head, and Dominguez turned to Haug. "It is what I thought when I played the tape today. Which is why I informed you."

Haug told One Time what Harrison was doing and asked him to look after things. He ran down the stairs and out to the car. He dare not risk a telephone call from the house. Not even from the village. He would have to drive into the town of Corfu and find a public telephone. As he got into the car he wondered if he was overreacting and allowing his imagination to frighten him. But Haug was simply trusting his intuition. The very little he managed to hear on the tape had hit him like a ram in the gut. Perhaps he heard more than he thought he did. Subliminally. Or maybe there was something in Regis' tone of voice. His certainty, though, was overwhelming his doubts.

It was not altogether wise to telephone from the island at all, even using a public telephone. He didn't understand telephone technology these days, but One Time tried to explain things to

191

him once. Computers and digitalization had changed things over the years. Telephone "taps" were now extremely simple, and you no longer heard ominous clicks or noises when a tap was engaged. Whole exchanges could be scanned easily for key words or phrases that would lock on a tap and record the message. He had no idea whether or not they would or could filter foreign exchanges. But he had to risk a call. He didn't understand most of what One Time told him. Except that telephones were the most insecure form of communications these days.

He found the biggest hotel he could remember seeing and pulled into the parking lot. Entering the lobby, he went straight to the Reception Desk and explained to the attendant what he wanted. The man spoke excellent English and assumed he was a resident at the hotel. Haug explained he wished to pay for the call in cash rather than have it added to his bill, managing to make it sound as if it were a secret call to his mistress in London, adding a wink and a smile for effect. The attendant returned his smile knowingly and asked for the number.

Haug was certain Friday afternoons were Louise Templer's regular surgery at the Red Rose Club, and he gave the man that number.

He went to the booth and waited while the attendant placed the call. Finally his phone rang. It was the secretary, and Haug asked for Louise. Told she was busy in surgery, Haug said it was extremely important. The next voice on the phone was her agent, Tom Howard, whom Haug knew of but had never met.

"I'm terribly sorry," Howard said. "Mrs Templer is very busy just now. Could I take your number and call you back?"

"Please interrupt her," Haug replied. "This is really, really important."

"May I ask who is calling?" Howard asked.

"You can, but I'm not tellin' you. Just inform Louise there is an urgent call from Corfu. Very urgent."

"I'm afraid I can't disturb her at this moment, but I will take your telephone number, and she will call you back as soon as she is free..."

192

Haug interrupted him. "Just tell her that one thang, Mr Howard. Tell her there is a very urgent call from Corfu. If she then says no, I'll try again. But she won't say no, because she'll be runnin' to the phone. If you *don't* tell her, she is goin' to be awfully mad at you when she finds out."

There was a pause, and he thought he heard Howard sigh. "Just a moment, please."

Haug had done his best to be nice and not explode at the agent and call him every name he could think of, but he realised the telephone receiver was cracking in his hand. So he took several deep breaths and waited.

Finally he heard her voice on the other end of the line. "Hello..is this..."

"It's me," he interrupted. "Just lissen. I want you to find a secure telephone and call me back. I'm not goin' to give you the telephone number. You will have to find it out for yourself. I don't know how you're gonna find a secure phone, but use your imagination. Go to the Prime Minister, if you have to, but only use one that scrambles the words, OK?"

"Is this about Sir Jonathan?" she asked.

"Is he alive? No, don't answer that. That's all I'm gonna say. Do you understand?"

"Yes. I'll do my best."

"Speak to you later." Haug hung up the phone and ground his teeth. He could tell from the tone of her voice. Something had happened. To Mainwaring. Haug had a feeling deep inside that his friend was dead, and Michael Regis had ordered his execution. He reminded himself that immediately attacking the Matilda and drowning those slimy sons of bitches was possibly the wrong thing to do in the circumstances. But it was what he wanted to do. Tie every one of the bastards to the anchor chain, drop it overboard and hope the water was shark infested.

"Are you alright, sir?" asked the Reception Desk attendant.

"She ran off with another man," Haug said darkly.

"Ah," he said with a sympathetic shrug. "Very sorry, sir."

"Could you connect me with the airport, please?" Haug said finally.

"Certainly, sir."

193

There was a flight at half past seven, but the only seats which were available were first class. He booked two. Hanging up the telephone, he asked for the bill and left a tip for the attendant. As he crossed the lobby to the door, he realised both his fists were clenched and other guests were moving cautiously out of his way.

On the drive back he tried talking to himself. First of all, he didn't *know* Jonathan was dead. He only felt it. He also did not know what was really on the tape, and he had only made inferences from Louise's tone of voice. And on the strength of all these *feelings* he had now completely changed his plans and had booked a flight to London that evening. Of course he could cancel. He took off his cap and wiped the top of his head with a handkerchief. Maybe it was the heat. Maybe the sun was driving him loco. But goddamn it, something was wrong. He'd bet his hat and ass and two cords of wood on that.

* * *

"How on earth did you find that gorgeous black man?" Sarah Courtney asked lazily. They were lying alone on the deck in the late afternoon. Both women had their tops off and were wearing only bikini bottoms. As usual the men were in the dining room, all turned toward the tables in the middle, all talking and arguing as if their lives depended on it. None of them showed the slightest interest in two nearly naked women lying forty feet away in the bright sunshine. And, as usual, the crew kept a discreet distance and did not come near, unless Corky called for the steward.

"Honey, I can find a man in the middle of a convent of Roman Catholic nuns and virgins with barbed wire on the walls. My stupid husband thinks he can keep me pure for his bed, but I got more ways of gettin' laid than he's got gangsters to catch me."

"So you're not going to tell me," said Sarah.

"Lissen, I just stand around, and they pop up." She laughed at her own joke. "And when I see a good 'un, I grab him by the dick and climb on. I had my eye on that cute little steward, but he runs like a rabbit ever time I lick my chops, 'cause ole Herk threatened him on the drive in from the airport. And I suppose Gillmore strikes the fear of the Lord into him. Anyway, he'd probably be so scared he couldn't get it up."

"Corky?" Sarah Courtney paused for a moment and bit her lip. "Why did you agree to spend an afternoon with him..."

"Now, how many times are you gonna ask that question? I told you. Look at those sexless bastards in there, a bunch of self-inflated rich men who think whatever they're doin' is important. I needed somebody sensible to talk to, if I can't have my little steward."

"You're always evading the question, Corky. That's why I keep asking. It's almost made the trip bearable having every afternoon off with you. And now there are only *four more days.*"

"I got that pervert figgered out anyway. Like a lot of men, he's scared of women. That's why they wanna control us, see? Look at those fools in there. Gimme five minutes with any one of 'em, and I'll have his eyes rollin' around in his head like pinballs. All that importance and rationality will be gone in a puff of lust, and they'll have their tongues hangin' out, pantin' and promisin' anything. They don't like that, lettin' themselves go, lettin' their emotions crash through and just roar on until they give out."

"Yes," said Sarah, "but Gillmore is different. He wants to take your soul away as well."

"He doesn't give a shit about your soul, honey. You know what he told me when we made the deal? He said he only got his rocks off when he fucks a woman who doesn't want him. The more she hates it, the better he likes it. The buzz is to *make* the woman do it anyway. Like he did to you. And me, for that matter."

"Yes. Exactly. He knows I loathe him, yet I have to pretend to want him and beg for him and jump around on the bed when he touches me. But the acting mustn't show or he immediately punishes me..."

Corky lifted her sunglasses and looked at the Englishwoman. "He hasn't beaten you again, has he?"

She shook her head. "I have you to thank for that. But he finds a way. Last night he tied my wrists to my ankles and made me stand in the corner like that. I started having cramps in my legs and felt like I was going to die. When he finally let me go, I felt something extraordinary. It's hard to explain. And a little embarrassing. Corky, I actually felt grateful. There was so much pain, here, in my thighs with cramps all down the front, that when he unlocked my wrists from my ankles, I actually fell in front of him in gratitude and kissed his feet. Can you believe that? I wasn't acting. *And* he knew it."

"What a shitass," Corky said with disgust. "Yeah, he's gone mental on control. He's crazy, you know that?"

"*That* is *very* clear," Sarah replied.

"He wants to be a kinda god where he can stand in front of the ocean and make the water come in and go out to please him. Like that ancient king. Because he's got a lot of loot, he reckons that entitles him to give orders to the universe."

"Well, he does it, doesn't he? Look at me. At six o'clock I'll go get my stockings on, and my shoes, paste on my smile and do anything he asks. Spread my legs, beg him for his limp cock, crawl on the floor, serve him his fucking Diet Pepsis. All because I want his money. And if I say no, there's always somebody else who'll do it. It's true. Money buys anything. I mean, even you. You're living with your husband because of...his money."

"There's certainly no other reason, honey. But what you've got to do is use your head. Look at that body you've got. Terrific. And you're still in your twenties. So think. Decide what you want. Work it out. If you want a lotta dough, a bunch of bucks, use what you've got to get what you want. But remember this: you *pay* for it. In this world, you pay for everthing you get. Now, I'm livin' a rich life and stand to be really, really rich when that old bastard dies. Meanwhile...*meanwhile*, I gotta live with the horse's ass and do a lotta things I don't like. That's what I worked out before I married him. But I wouldn't call myself *happy*."

Corky rolled over onto her belly and supported her chin with a cupped hand. "Now, you could be plumb lucky and find a

196

nice, rich stud who looks like a movie star - maybe is one - who treats you like a decent human bein', and you live happily ever after. I'm not sayin' that cain't happen. I just say I'll believe it when I see it. So. Either you gotta make some kinda choice like I made, or you save up from the shit you're doin' now and hope you got enough when gravity pulls your tits down to your belly button and your face slides half off. My point is, you cain't just drift. That is a recipe for disaster. You gotta choose your hell and hope you only get close enough for a good tan."

Sarah turned on her side, facing Corky. The sun was lower now and warmed her back. "A couple of years ago it all seemed so simple. Now does this make sense? All I want to do is just have a good time. Enjoy myself, enjoy life. Right? My parents have practically disowned me because I dropped out of university, took a few drugs, drank much too much, came in at all hours or not at all. But really, I don't *want* to do anything particularly important in life. Like, be a doctor or solicitor or power-dress for the City. And I don't particularly want to change the world. It's fine with me as it is. So I'm not interested in being a social worker or psychologist or even an artist or actress, like one of my friends. I just want to be useless. Sleep til midday every day, have a little breakfast in bed, spend a couple of hours in the toilet without pressure, go out to an interesting lunch in the West End, visit friends, maybe go to a show or nightclub and maybe even get laid by some nice hunk and fall into bed about three o'clock. Is that asking too much for a person who's decided she's absolutely useless?"

Corky laughed. "Well, there's nothin' wrong with that life. I mean I *do* wanna do somethin'. I don't know what. I really get a bang outta travel. You'll probably laugh at this, but I've got a secret desire to be a travel writer. Now wouldn't that be a great life? Rome, say, with all those nice young Eyetalians in tight pants? Germany, Africa, the Far East..."

"Have you tried writing?"

"A little bit. Hey, you know what? Tell you a secret. You know those shitty soft porn magazines men read that always make you feel lousy about your body? I got a story published in one of those..."

Sarah Courtney giggled. "You didn't!"

"Used the name Sherry Bourbonne - with an ne on the end. They liked it. Your guy yesterday, what's his name?"

"He's not my guy, though I wish in a way he was. I told you he was going with one of my best friends..."

"Ahh, what difference does that make, among friends..." They both laughed.

"His name is O'Connell."

"He sure gave Gomez a smack. That little weasel is a real killer, cut the balls off a sweet innocent man I had a little affair with..."

"Oh, my god."

"So, I was real glad to see the slimy bastard get his head cracked open. Looks like a real bull, O'Connell. Wonder if he's hung like one." They laughed again.

"But Corky, he was so sweet. He sort of understood I was feeling low, that my confidence was gone, and he just held me in his arms and comforted me. Just that bit of physical contact, that reassurance, was what I needed. After all this. I nearly melted with gratitude. I don't think I've ever met a man like him. Damn Jennifer Montgomery..."

"Who?"

"My friend, who, you know...right? Jennifer, now, she is a *real* knockout. Those girls in the soft porn mags would crawl off the page and hide if Jennifer was around."

"Sorry," said Corky. "Don't care to meet the lady."

"Oh, you'd love her. So long as there were no men around..."

"Exactly."

"Now Jennifer is more like you. She uses her head, knows what she wants to do. Very bright. She's an actress, but she used to do this as well. You know, work for Michael Regis. Want to know how much a pop? Fifteen hundred pounds. One night."

"Goddamn," said Corky. "I'd do it for *that*. Hell, two or three times a week with some old fart. You're talkin' about action money, there."

"*And* there was a long queue."

198

"Imagine somebody payin' fifteen hundred pounds for a piece of ass. Honey, I don't want that woman within a *mile* of me."

Sarah giggled. "Oh, you're completely different types. You'd probably split the men in the room right down the middle."

"Lissen, sweetheart, I want 'em all. I want my pick. Right? Keep her away from me."

Courtney looked at her watch, and her shoulders sagged. "Twenty to six. I've got to go get my kit on. Got to be standing at attention for him as the second hand sweeps the twelve. Or else." She got up and did not bother to put her top on as she turned away. "Thanks, Corky. Wonderful afternoon."

Corky turned to watch her new friend go. "Hang loose, baby. Four more days."

* * *

It was twenty minutes to six when Ralph Harrison's telephone rang. Haug was sitting beside the little wicker table, and it made him jump. He picked up the receiver before the first ring finished. It was Louise Templer.

"I finally found one of these damned phones," she said. "General Portland had to help me. So it's a military one."

"Great. Thanks," Haug replied quickly. "Now. What do you know of Mainwaring?"

"He disappeared this morning on the way to his office. The police have been informed. His wife has not heard from him. It's not at all like him..."

"There's no more news?" Haug interrupted. "Nothing else?"

"No. Nothing. We are all very worried."

Haug released a quick breath. "God, I thought you were gonna tell me he was dead."

Louise Templer paused for a moment. "Dead? Why?"

As quickly as he could Haug told her the story of the Cuban's tape. "My clever friend here managed to dilate the voice - or whatever he called it - on his computer. So we got most of Regis' end of the conversation. He was talkin' to

199

somebody called Gordon. Can you find out who that is? Anyway, I gather the last meeting you had was partially recorded by somebody, and they know Mainwaring is the head of things. At the end of the conversation Regis says..." Haug looked down at the piece of paper in front of him. "'Pick him up tomorrow and take him to Unit G3. Squeeze everything out of him. I mean *everything*. I want to know all details. Names, dates, times, everything. Then kill him. Make it seem an accident, yes, you know what I mean...'" Haug broke off for a minute. His heart was pounding again. "I'm comin' in on Flight 106 Heathrow with One Time at 11.30 pm your time. Get in touch with Keef and ask him to meet me with my pickup. I also want you to meet me, if you can, or somebody else, like Stuart, with the following thangs: an Ordinance Survey map showin' me where Unit G3 is..."

Templer interrupted him. "Just how am I going to find that out? I never heard of such a thing."

"I don't know," Haug replied. "But you're a bright lady. I suspect this is Special Branch or MI5. That's General Portland's area as well, so he might know somebody trustworthy who can tell you what their lingo means. Anyway, find Unit G3 for me. Please."

"What are you going to do?"

"Why, I'm gonna go get him and bring him back."

"How?"

"I don't know yet. Oh, yeah. Two thangs about Keef. Tell him to bring lots of tools. And Nightmare Andy, if he can find him."

"Nightmare Andy?"

"You wouldn't wanna meet him," Haug said. "I know all this is a lot to ask, honey, but I got to count on you and the rest to help me here."

"What about the operation in Corfu?" asked Louise.

"Covered by friends. I'll bring the tapes I've got and give them to you at the airport."

There was a silence on the other end of the line. "Do you think Sir Jonathan is alright?"

"Don't ask me a question like that, 'cause it's been goin' round and round in my mind for the last four hours. But Louise," he stopped and thought for a moment, and his voice softened. "Be careful. These are dangerous assholes. Now, One Time assures me these telephones are absolutely safe, cain't be cracked by the biggest computer in the world. But they'll have your name already, and you may be watched or followed. Take the greatest care. Please."

"Thank you, Haug. And I will echo the same to you. Please, please be careful."

"While you got that fancy telephone in your hand, use it to call and inform as many of the others as you can. Or get the general to do it. Watch what you say on any other phone."

"Haug?"

"Yeah?"

"I never knew it would get this deep this quickly. I mean, the idea of Sir Jonathan being...I mean, how could they? Oh dear, this is really rather serious..."

"Lissen, Louise, you're pretty smart, but I know what I'm sayin' here. At this point you gotta just forget about doubts or how serious thangs are or how dangerous. You plan ahead, and you move decisively. Don't look to the right or the left or stand aroun' with your finger up your ass. Just keep your eye on the prize...and go. Just think: Unit G3. That's all. Unit G3, Heathrow Airport, Keef. Think specifics, not abstracts. Death is abstract. So is fear. OK?"

"Sensible advice. I'll try, Haug," Louise said in a calmer voice.

"See you at 11.30. Take good care."

"And you."

Haug hung up and looked up at the three men who sat with him in the lounge. His holdall and One Time's cases stood in the middle of the floor.

Harrison smiled reassuringly. "We'll take good care of things here. Don't worry. And I will call your London number if there is an emergency."

"Thanks, Ralph," said Haug. He pulled Gomez's gun from his belt and slid it across the coffee table toward Raul

Dominguez. "You better take this. I cain't risk gettin' stopped by Customs tonight."

The Cuban picked up the weapon. "What is it?"

"Plastic gun. Doesn't show up on X-ray machines. Latest thang for the international jet set."

"Gomez?" he asked as he examined the piece.

"Yeah," said Haug. He pulled out the knife from a pocket and slid that across as well. "And here's his pig sticker. Sharp as a razor."

Dominguez shook his head. "No use for the knife, but the gun is very nice. It will save me much difficulty and time. Because I am going to London, too, señors. I will wait until the meeting on the Matilda is finished, and then I will follow. I will bring the rest of the tapes, and I thank you for allowing me copies."

Haug checked his watch and got up. One Time rose with him. They grabbed their gear and shook hands all round.

"Good hunting, señors," Dominguez said to them as the two men left through the open front door. "And be very careful. These are dangerous men."

* * *

It was nearly midnight on the Matilda, and Michael Regis had had a very busy and stressful evening. It was now nearly midnight, and he sat at the large table in the dining room drumming his fingers silently. Everyone was looking at him, and everyone was there, except for Sarah Courtney. Six pairs of eyes watched him drum his fingers on the top of the table. He was quietly and articulately telling them all a story. One of them, Jeremy Evans, already knew the ending, but the rest of them were riveted by his little tale.

It began with a fax he received from Gordon, from Special Branch in London. The fax was a transcript of a telephone conversation made from the Corfu Grand Hotel to the Red Rose Club in North London. The conversation was between an unknown party in Corfu and the Labour MP, Louise Templer. After reading and re-reading the fax Michael Regis had gone to his room to think. An hour later he picked up his phone and called Jeremy Evans' room, asking him to drop in for a moment. When Evans arrived, he handed him the fax. The Deputy Director of MI6 sat down in an armchair to read it.

"What the devil does this mean?" Evans asked when he finished reading.

"It infers two things," Regis replied. "Neither of which is very pleasant. One is a strong inference, the other a weak one. The strong one is as follows. We are being watched by at least one, probably more, on the island of Corfu."

Evans nodded and leaned forward on his elbows. His hair fell down over the top of his forehead. "Yes, that's clear. And very serious."

Regis was sitting in the other chair, a cushioned one but without arms. He was wearing slacks and a dark short-sleeved silk shirt, examining the fingernails of one hand. "The second one, the weaker, is even more sinister. Either there is an informer aboard the vessel or we have been bugged."

Evans pushed his quiff back in place and looked worried. "I don't understand. Both are impossible. We are all family, except for the prostitute, and neither she nor the crew are allowed near the dining room when we are talking. Nothing is said otherwise. As for bugging devices, well, that's a preposterous idea."

"It was not felt necessary to sweep the place or de-bug simply because it was unthinkable," Regis continued Evans' thought. "Few knew of our meeting in the first place. We came in at different times. Gillmore's crew is always heavily vetted, and besides, they live in constant fear of him. However, that is where my suspicions for the moment lie. Whoever it is must have some contact with the man or men ashore."

"That's clear," Evans nodded.

"I'm afraid we have shown the mark of arrogance in not ensuring our own security, Jeremy."

"It is hardly arrogance to assume we would be completely safe in the middle of the Ionian Sea."

"The arrogance, dear Watson, was in the underestimation of our enemies," Regis replied. "However, unlike the venerable

Holmes, I want to begin with elimination of the weakest inference. I only know a very little about bugging devices, but I do know what some of them look like and where they may be placed. I am aware you have little operational knowledge yourself, but nevertheless, you are the one to assist me."

"You want to search the place?"

"I do. We'll have to get the others off the boat somehow tonight. I'll get Carlton to suggest a meal ashore, and they'll all be shooed off for a couple of hours. You and I will make excuses about a telephone call from Gordon - which, incidentally, I am expecting."

Jeremy Evans sat up and looked at the darkness beyond the window. "How do you know...what makes you think someone was listening to us?"

Regis picked up the fax which Evans had laid on the table. "Yesterday evening I spoke with Gordon. He gave me information of this leftwing cabal which has apparently been organised to oppose us. They are much further advanced than we imagined, and we must have information about them quickly. I therefore ordered their leader to be picked up and questioned, then killed. Their leader's surname is Mainwaring."

"Good lord. Trade and Industry."

"Yes. Now look at this transcript. The male speaker from Corfu *knows* he may be dead. This is directly after lunch today. There is only one way he could have known. He heard it. Or someone else heard it and told him."

It took them over two hours to find it, and it was Jeremy Evans who made the discovery, standing on the same table Corky had used. When he separated the wires at the top of the chandelier, he saw something metallic, but he needed a table knife to get it out. He had waved excitedly to Regis because they had both agreed to hunt in silence in case there *was* a device and someone was listening.

Regis held it in the palm of his hand and nodded grimly.

The six pairs of eyes watched as he opened the fingers of the same hand, revealing the six inch device which looked very much like a nail. He carefully put the nail down and slid is

204

across the table top. It stopped directly in front of Corky DeLoop, and six pairs of eyes turned to look at her.

"What am I supposed to do with it?" she asked, picking it up and putting it back down again. And then fear constricted her heart as an identical nail slid across the table from Regis. It, too, stopped in front of her.

"We found this one in your make-up case," Regis said very quietly. "Do you mind telling us about it?"

CHAPTER TWELVE

Sir Jonathan Mainwaring lay naked on the floor of the padded room and thought he heard himself groan. Was that him? Had he made that sound? He began to lecture himself severely for the audible complaint. The fact that he could organise himself well enough to lecture suddenly struck him as odd. The drugs must be wearing off. So he tried opening his eyes. Everything was bright and white. The floor beneath him was some kind of canvas. Floor, walls and ceiling didn't seem to have joins. The lights were dazzling. He closed his eyes again. Indeed, his thoughts were becoming more ordered, but he felt nauseous and had a hammering headache. Hangover from the drugs, must be. And he hadn't eaten anything since breakfast. What time was it now? he asked himself. No way to tell, no way at all. So he didn't bother to try. Guessing time was a waste of time, and time must not be wasted, whatever it was.

The first thing to do was recap everything he could remember, try and recall what he said, what happened, the order of events. It was difficult. Thoughts and memories were like a series of parallel lines which had shattered, with jagged ends joining haphazardly to other fractures. A mess. A series of events takes place over time, and in order to determine time, you must have some references or coordinates. The car, yes he could remember the car alright and the long journey made painful by handcuffs.

When he was taken from the car, he was aware of a big house. A big brick house, yes. DI Green was growling at him and punching him in the kidneys because of his damaged finger. He was pushed, that's right, and dragged to the door. Then he was in a room. A grey haired man was peering at him through glasses, asking the officers about the bruises. DI Green blustered about his finger. Mainwaring had stood straight, towering over all three men. He wanted to know where he was and who the grey haired man was. He was ignored, so he kicked the grey haired man in the crotch to attract his attention. The line of memory was then shattered. Probably attacked again by the so-called policemen.

He found a jumble of other memories and tried to sort them through by logical order. He was strapped into a chair without his clothes. Hands strapped, legs as well. Yes, and head. He could not move his head. That annoyed him immensely, he recalled. Another image. Yes, that must come next because it is clear. An injection in his thigh by the grey haired man. The doctor? After that, images were difficult. But they must be sorted.

He was aware his body ached terribly but did not want to move because even now he was probably being watched. Let them think he was still unconscious. That would give him more time for thought. He was lying on his side and desperately wanted to roll over on his back to ease his joints. Suddenly he thought of Sarah, his wife, and a ball of anguish formed in his gut. He knew it was unlikely he would see her again or watch her from the window as she dug in her beloved garden with green wellies and those silly dungarees she wore. And of course the old straw hat. When had she bought that? He couldn't remember, but it must have been just after their marriage.

Yes. Some of the questions were about Sarah. They had been talking about Sarah to him, and maybe that was why he was so certain he would never see her again. Because they said so. And he had cried. The thought was completely humiliating to Mainwaring. Never in his life could he remember crying. For any reason. But he had cried when they told him he would never see Sarah again. Why were they doing that? For a few moments he could not understand. Finally he found an answer. Stirring up the emotions to weaken him, bending him back and forth like a piece of metal until he broke.

Memories of more pain came rasping through his consciousness like saws. Different kinds of pain. He tried to think. It was truly awful. The electrodes. Involuntarily Mainwaring drew his body into a foetal position, holding onto his genitals tenderly, because they were sore. They had forced something into his mouth and attached electrodes to his nipples, testicles and penis. The first dreadful shock must have come

208

close to breaking his spine. It was so unexpected. Then there was another. And another. And another. All unpredictable.

Mainwaring realised he was crying again, and with the greatest effort he forced back the tears, clenching his teeth, looking desperately for the mental tools which had never failed him before. The search became very nearly panic stricken as he fought to overpower the surges of fear and humiliation. Then he felt cooler air. Someone had opened a door.

"You can't fool us, you old dog," said DI Green. "We know you are awake."

They held him down easily as the doctor again plunged a hypodermic into his thigh. He was on his back, and when he opened his eyes to look up, he saw Green's grinning face above him. It seemed to Mainwaring as if it were under water or under water and drowning.

"I'm feeling good, my son," he heard Green say. "I've just come back from fucking your wife. Gave me a terrific blow job. For an old bag, that is."

The drug made Mainwaring's limbs nearly useless, but with monumental determination he focussed all his will into one act. He spat at Green's swimming face. Almost at once an overwhelmingly nauseous pain showered into his abdomen, and he realised distantly that Green had grabbed his testicles. Despite the pain, he was glad he spat. Keep spitting. Keep spitting. Keep spitting. He repeated the sentence like a mantra as they dragged him by the heels out of the white room and back into the lower depths of hell.

* * *

They were in a small meeting room at Heathrow Airport. Louise Templer had arranged with the airport management to rent the room, paying for it with a personal cheque. There were chairs around a table, a sofa and two armchairs, but everyone was standing. Except Haug who was half sitting on the table as he listened to Templer. Stuart Easton and Keef Sams were standing beside her. One Time stood with Haug and had taken off his beret to examine the lining.

"So far," she told them, "we have not been able to trace Unit G3. So there is no map as yet. Kenneth Cranshaw is being the most helpful. He is still at GCHQ hunting through computer files of the security services. That's the bad news, Haug. The good news is that he is certain he can find it. He is senior enough not to be questioned about what he is doing or why. I have brought a mobile telephone, and he will call us from a secure unit at GCHQ as soon as he has the information."

"Shit," Haug said, looking at the floor. "I was hopin' for a little luck. If we coulda found the joint tonight, we coulda hit 'em early in the mornin'. Early."

"Is that so important?" Louise asked.

"Damn right. Best time. That's why all the cops do it. 5.30 in the mornin', bang, bang, everbody's half asleep, undressed, not alert. Best time," he repeated. "Also, if this goes into tomorrow, then we're movin' onto thinner and thinner ice, particularly where Jonathan is concerned."

"What do you mean?" asked Stuart Easton.

Haug shook his head. "He won't hold."

"Oh, I don't know," Easton said. "He's a tough bastard."

Haug continued to shake his head. "No, he'll use the wrong way of dealin' with it. Now, there's no right way, but there is definitely a wrong way. He'll try to deal with it through reason. That's his biggest weapon, and that'll fail him right away."

"How do you know?" Louise asked him.

Haug caught her eyes. "'Cause I know these people. How they think. The way they operate. And what they'll do. It's emotion they'll use to break him down. Fear, despair, hopelessness, humiliation, self hatred. They'll hose out all his self confidence, and the rest is easy. Take away confidence and reason will turn against you and destroy you." Haug still held her gaze. "I know. I've used it on people, you see."

Louise Templer bit her lip and looked away. "I feel a little out of my depth here."

Haug held up a finger. "Don't say that. This is the depth you are at, so you just start swimmin'. Jonathan Mainwarin's life depends on it. 'Cause when he breaks, he's a dead man. I know that too, on account of the fact I shot 'em when I got the information outta them."

She turned back to him, angry. "You don't have to parade your brutality in front of me again and again. I'm quite aware of it by now."

"Don't accuse me of brutality when we all live in the same world. This shit goes on ever day in just about ever country in the world, and you folks who live in nice houses prefer to ignore it. Don't blame the hangman. Look at the system that hires him. If I'm brutal, so are you, because you condone it."

"I'm not going to stand here and listen to a lecture from a killer!" she said through her teeth.

Stuart Easton stepped forward. "Whatever the merits of this argument one way or the other - and I *do* have an opinion - I want to get this thing back on the rails. There are plenty of enemies to fight without turning on allies. You seem to know what you are doing in these situations, Haug. So tell us what you need in support when the information comes through."

"Well," Haug said. "The most important thing is this. If we had been able to find the place tonight, One Time coulda cut all the telephone wires just before we hit it and, I think, jammed the mobiles." He turned to One Time, who nodded. "If we go in daylight, we gotta stop the phones. Otherwise they can call down all kinds of heat. Obviously they cain't be cut, so it's gotta be the exchanges. Somebody who knows somebody, I don't know. It's gotta be done, though. Next is a place to take him when we get him out. Not his home. But I want a nice, calm, safe, quiet place, and I want his wife there. I know he really loves her. And if he's got one or two close friends. Support, he's gonna need a shitpot full of it. I want a good doctor and a really good head doctor. Not one of those rat torturers. A kind, sympathetic man."

Haug took his cap off and scratched the top of his head. "And somehow we gotta run interference in front of the police, 'cause as far as the police are concerned, these guys are right and we're wrong. If he's alive, we'll get him out. But there's no way we can hold off the whole police force, Special Branch,

MI5, MI6, the paratroopers and a division of tanks. I got my limitations."

Easton grinned. "A touch of modesty?"

"It doesn't become him," Louise Templer said with a little edge to her voice.

Haug turned to Keef. "Where's Nightmare Andy?"

Keef opened the palms of his hands. "Couldn't find him. His woman say he'll be back later tonight."

Easton raised an eyebrow. "Nightmare Andy?"

"You don't wanna meet him 'less you have to," Haug said. "But we need him, so we'll have to go find him now. We'll keep in touch by mobile, in as much code as we can manage. I got one in the pickup, so give that number to Cranshaw when he calls." He stopped and turned to Easton. "It would help, I think, if we had a kinda central command centre until this thing is over."

"General Portland's house in West London. I'll be there," he replied quickly.

"Will you stay with them?" Haug asked Louise.

"No," she replied. "I'm coming with you."

"Bullshit. You're stayin' with Stuart."

She shook a finger in his face angrily. "Don't you fucking tell me what to do, Haug, just because you're a typical swaggering male taking charge."

He stood and faced up to her. "Well, I'm tellin' you now, Louise Templer, you're *not* comin' with us! So get your ass in gear and try to help instead of hinder."

She didn't give an inch. "You've just accused me of being a middleclass snob not wanting to dirty my hands in the grinding wheels of our brutal society, and when I volunteer to join you, you say bullshit, go away and do womanly things like make telephone calls. Do you want me to sweep the floor and wash the dishes as well?"

For a moment Haug didn't reply as he glowered down at the diminutive MP who stared up at him with her chin thrust forward. Finally he turned to Easton. "Stuart?"

"Don't turn to me, comrade, you're on your own."

"I'll give you my mobile, and we'll use hers, then. Good thang the pickup's got an extended cab." With a smile he put an arm around Louise's shoulders. "Come on, Private Templer, we gotta haul ass." He grabbed his bag and nodded to Keef and One Time.

She grabbed his arm. "Thank you, Haug. That was very gallant."

Haug raised one eyebrow. "If you don't exactly love *my* methods, you're gonna *hate* Nightmare Andy."

* * *

Corky DeLoop stared down at the two electronic devices lying in front of her on the table. Then she looked up at Michael Regis with steady eyes. "What have they got to do with me?"

"I just said," Regis replied affably, "I found one of these little toys in your makeup case. We are waiting for *you* to tell *us* what they have got to do with you."

She picked up the first one. "Well, I think it would be obvious to any jackass that whoever put this one wherever you found it, also put this one.." She picked up the second bug. "...in my makeup case."

Michael Regis nodded, still affable. "That is, of course, one explanation, Corky. And we thought about that one at some length. Then we telephoned Mr Enrico Gomez at his hotel and had a little chat with him. Very interesting conversation, Corky. After some initial hesitation, the Cuban gentleman said he had been in the hospital. Apparently someone assaulted him just as you were getting into a taxi driven by a black driver. We subsequently found there were no black taxi drivers in Corfu. So. Who was he, Corky?"

She looked down at the nails and dropped them on the table, rolling them back and forth.

Hercules DeLoop smashed his heavy fist on the table. "Answer the man, you double crossin' little bitch!"

"Don't you call me a bitch, you big stupid horse's ass! I woulda thought you would be takin' my part and smackin' these bastards around the room for tryin' to say I woulda done

213

somethin' like this. But no, you jump right in with 'em, with your number fourteen boots on."

He smacked his fist on the table again. "Answer the goddamn question!"

Corky DeLoop took a deep breath. "I *thought* he was a taxi driver. But he was a tourist and didn't charge us a cent. Took us to a nice beach, Sarah and I had a swim and a good talk, and we got another taxi back to Corfu."

Michael Regis smiled and looked at his well manicured nails. "That is not what Sarah told us."

Corky smacked her own hand on the table. "Well, that's what happened! And I'm fed up with this third degree and wanna go to bed! Then all you men can sit around and hatch your plots til the cows come home for all I care.' Corky DeLoop felt her fuel gauge was resting on empty without a gas pump in sight. The sight of the two electronic bugs had floored her, but she had managed to brazen it out and was almost home free when Regis mentioned Sarah. She had forgotten about Sarah. Of course they would have questioned her. She did not come with them for the meal, as Gillmore would not hear of it. There was no way of knowing what she told them. Probably she tried to cover as well as she could, but obviously her lie was not the same as Corky's. All the faces were looking at her. Staring. She wanted to get up angrily and go to her room, but something within told her she shouldn't.

"I vote for killin' her," Hercules DeLoop growled from his chair.

"I'll second that," Dr Carlton Fine said in an even voice.

Corky stood up, her eyes blazing. "I don't want any of you bastards near me! I swear to god, I'll bust the balls of any man who gets within two feet of me! Now, you lissen for a minute. I have been accused, tried, judged and sentenced, and you haven't even lissened to a word I've said. You throw those nails on the table in front of me, and I don't even know what they are, what they're supposed to do or be. Then you say they're mine and I've done somethin' awful, but you don't tell me what it is. But whatever it is, you then say I'm guilty of it, shrug your fuckin' shoulders and say 'kill her', just like that! I am your *wife*, Herk!"

"Not anymore, you're not," said DeLoop without moving. "By tomorrow mornin' the sharks will have gobbled up all that beautiful body, and I'll have to go to the trouble of findin' myself another good lookin' woman."

Corky DeLoop grabbed a brass platter hanging on the wall and threw it as hard as she could at her husband. He did not quite manage to duck, and the platter glanced off the top of his head and crashed into the opposite wall. She looked for something else to throw. If she could get to the door, her best chance lay in diving overboard and swimming to shore. If she could. Probably she could find the raft, have a rest, then swim on towards the lights. Maybe she wouldn't make it, but she had realised there was no chance at all if she remained here any longer. The problem was that the men and the table were between her and the door.

As DeLoop got up from his chair and advanced on his wife, Regis turned to Harvey Gillmore, who had remained quiet and thoughtful during the interrogation. "I believe you have something, Harvey, which might be useful in holding this woman in one place."

Gillmore allowed himself a sneer. "If you catch her and hold her, I'll make sure she won't move until we've decided what to do with her." He got up and eased around the table using the advancing DeLoop as a shield.

Without a word, the rest of the men got up, except for Alexander Hinkley, who was nervously fiddling with his bow tie looking frightened and out of place. Fine and Regis went to the other side, and Wren Olsen followed DeLoop.

"Don't you bastards touch me!" Corky screamed. There was only one chance, and without a thought she took it. As the men closed in on her, no one was in the centre. Except for the table. She kicked off her shoes and made two long legged bounds to the table and leapt. One foot touched the table, turning it over, but now there was no one left between her and the door. She heard the scrambling behind her as she reached for the handle, turning it with one swift motion. The door was open, and she could smell the sea and freedom. Her heart pounded like a drum as she cleared the doorway.

Then suddenly she sprawled forward across the deck on her belly. What the fuck had happened? Immediately she tried struggling to her feet, but they were held by Michael Regis. With all her strength she simultaneously pulled one leg and pushed the other. It was free. She kicked at the head viciously, but there was another shape now, another man. She couldn't see who it was, but he grabbed her free leg. Corky DeLoop was fighting for her life now. She knew it and rained blows with her fists at anyone who moved or came near.

A large shadow fell over her from the spill of light from the dining room. It was Hercules DeLoop. Desperately she tried to hit him in the balls, but he grabbed her arm in one huge hand, and it was like a heavy vice. With the other hand he smacked her across the face before trapping the other arm.

Corky DeLoop bucked with her body, trying to kick, trying to free her arms. Then she filled her lungs. "Help me!" she screamed. "Help me! Please help me! Help! Help! Help!..."

Something was forced into her mouth, and she couldn't see what it was or who was doing it. A strap went behind her head and was brutally pulled tight as she tried to spit out the limp rubber balloon. Then it was being inflated, forcing open her jaws, filling her whole mouth. The only sound she could make was through her nose.

She lay on the sofa in the dining room facing the table where the men were talking. She wanted to cry, but she was damned if she would give them the satisfaction. It was such a stupid way to end her life, a life she had thrillingly enjoyed. Her ankles were shackled together and her wrists were held by handcuffs behind her. The shackles were leather and not metal, so they were not cutting into her flesh, despite the fact they were tight. Harvey Gillmore's bedroom toys. Now she was going to be thrown into the sea. How long would it take? One minute? Three minutes? Should she try and hold her breath or just gulp down the water right away? Goddamn it, what a stupid way to die! The men were talking now. What the fuck were they saying? Let them do it and get it over with. Every minute she waited now was going to make it more and more horrible.

DeLoop sucked through his teeth. "She ain't gonna tell you anythang, I can tell you that right now. Might as well get it over with and dump her.

Dr Carlton Fine shook his head. "We need to know why she did it, who she did it for, whether she is working for them and, if so, for how long."

"This is a stain on my reputation," DeLoop muttered.

"We *do* need the information," Regis said. "This snooping was totally unexpected, and we must know who it was. And whether they were connected to the English group we've winkled out or some other agency."

DeLoop banged his hand down again. "Well, I tell you, I know that woman. We can put her here on the table and pull little strips of skin off her all night, but she's as stubborn as a blue nose mule. You could build a fire under her, and she'd burn like a witch before she'd move."

Harvey Gillmore leaned forward and put his elbows on the table. "I have a suggestion which will give happy results all round."

"We are well aware what you would like to do with her, Harvey," Regis said with a slight smile.

Gillmore held up his hand. "Give me a doctor with the right drugs and a secure environment, and I'll do two things for you. I promise. First of all, I'll get every piece of information she's got in that head of hers and, secondly, I'll return an obedient woman to you, Herk."

DeLoop laughed. "You're as fulla shit as a Christmas turkey, Gillmore."

The Australian sat back in his chair. "Did any of you happen to see one of my favourite films made a few years ago? Called *The Stepford Wives*?"

All the men laughed together. Dr Carlton Fine waved his hand. "That would be the answer, wouldn't it? To all our problems with women."

"A heaven on earth," Olsen giggled.

Gillmore leaned forward again conspiratorilly. "Well, I can do it. I have done it before, and I can do it again. Look at Mary. You know my wife, Mary, don't you, Michael?"

"Not very well," said Regis. "She just appears, smiling, then vanishes."

"Exactly," said Gillmore. "Never gives me any problems. Ever. I give the orders, and she follows them. Dresses as I like, comes when I like, goes when I like, feeds me when I want, fucks on demand. I haven't had one complaint from her in over ten years." Fine started to interrupt, and Gillmore held up his hand. "It is the way I run my business as well. It is management policy. And, gentlemen, I learned it all from my father. The secret of human motivation."

Alexander Hinkley came alive for the first time. He rested his elbows on the table and tented his fingers. "WORLDWIDE is an extremely efficient business organisation built upon low wages, high productivity, rapid turnover *and*," he raised one finger from the tent. "Strong motivation. Consequently there is enough capital for major investment and expansion. It really is a model of a thoroughly modern company."

"What the fuck has this got to do with my fuckin' wife?" DeLoop growled.

Gillmore got up from the table. "I'll give you a demonstration."

He left the room and returned a few moments later followed by Sarah Courtney, who had been chained to his bed. She was naked except for stockings and high heels, and she had a troubled look on her face. When she saw Corky lying on the sofa she stopped in her tracks, and her hands went to her mouth. "Oh, my god. I'm so sorry, Corky. I don't know what to do."

Corky shook her head vigorously, trying to reassure her that it was not her fault.

Gillmore turned on Courtney, snarling. "That will be twelve hard ones, sheila. One more whimper, and you get twelve more. Now smile! A sexy smile, not that one! And come over here by my chair."

Gillmore sat down while Sarah Courtney smiled like a mannequin beside him. "Now this one's a whore, and I'm

218

paying her money, but it really is the same thing." He looked at the rest of the men. "There's no difference between this one and that one lying over there. They're both in it for the money. Herk's money or mine, what's the difference? They want the good life and are willing to pay for it. But most men don't have the gumption to *make* 'em pay." He reached over and grabbed Courtney's buttock with his hand and squeezed. "If I want it, I take it. She'll fuck anybody in this room if I tell her to, even your wife," he nodded to DeLoop. "Won't you, whore?"

"Yes, Mr Gillmore," Sarah said quickly. Her thoughts were tumbling in confusion. She desperately wanted to tell Gillmore to stuff his orders and his twisted mind, but she was in a room of staring, sweating men on a boat in the middle of the sea. If there was no one to help Corky DeLoop, there was certainly no one to help her. She did not really know what was going on, but she had heard Corky's screams for help from the other room. It must be about the two men they met on the beach, but why were they treating her like this? She had thought Michael Regis was a nice man, but here he was, not lifting a finger to protect her or Corky. What was she supposed to do? Fight and be beaten? And then she thought about that awful cane and the twelve dreaded strokes. Sarah Courtney very, very much wanted to leave the Matilda, money or no money. The atmosphere in the dining room was turgid and threatening and dangerous. Meanwhile, she simply withdrew inside herself defensively. It was her last barricade. Her only one.

"Get down on the floor, whore, and lick my feet," Gillmore ordered.

The others watched as the girl knelt down in front of the newspaperman's chair. Olsen actually rose up from his chair so he could see better. The fat man was sweating, though it was not a hot night.

Gillmore turned to DeLoop. "Now tell me. How would you like a wife like that?"

DeLoop eyed Courtney's bottom and screwed up his face. "I'd pay half a million bucks, cold cash. If you can do that with her over there, I'll give the money to you with a grin on my face, and I ain't never done that with nobody."

219

Gillmore turned to Regis. "Michael?"

"First of all," said Regis, "let's have a drink."

"Get up, woman," Gillmore barked at Sarah Courtney, "and fetch everyone a drink, a Diet Pepsi for me, lots of ice."

As the woman left the room to get the drinks, Michael Regis was thinking. Because he was worried. Harvey Gillmore nauseated him as a person, and he was uneasy about this particular aspect of sexual deviancy. It held no fascination for him. In fact he found it a little tiresome. Regis never had any difficulty in picking and choosing women he fancied. Most of them would step over a newly wed bridegroom to get to his bedroom. If anything, he had a contrary problem - that of too much choice and too fine a selection. Even before he accumulated his wealth there was a constant stream of beautifully turned out women to share his bed. Charm was the key, and animals like Gillmore - or DeLoop - didn't have the faintest idea what it was or how to use it well. Charm was a wonderful tool, and winkling open women's legs was simply charm.

On the other hand, Gillmore's suggestion had some merit. DeLoop's wife could be taken to one of the G-Units, and one of their doctors could extract the information. Normally a traitor would then be killed. Giving her to Gillmore might possibly be a worse punishment. Her mind might possibly be damaged after the interrogation anyway, but perhaps there would be enough left to torture her with regret for the rest of her life. Suitable justice under the circumstances.

While the drinks were served by Courtney everyone stopped to watch her breasts as they swung forward as she leaned over to give each man his glass. When she had finished, the Australian ordered her to return to the bedroom.

"Well, Michael?" Gillmore asked, as the door closed. "What do you say?"

"Alright, Harvey. She's yours."

Gillmore sat back in his seat and looked over at the prisoner. He caught her eyes as they slowly filled with terror and held them, enjoying the images flickering through his mind.

"How the hell we gonna get her back?" asked DeLoop. "There's no way we can carry that woman, buckin' like a bronco, onto an airplane."

"I will arrange a hospital flight for tomorrow," said Regis smoothly. "A doctor will give her an injection, and she will wake up in a G-Unit under the kind and sympathetic direction of our Australian newspaper proprietor..."

Corky DeLoop struggled with her bonds with all her strength and realised she was screaming through her nose. The men at the table were all looking at her and laughing, raising their glasses to her. She was trying to tell the monsters to throw her in the sea. What she had heard pushed her towards a nightmare. She didn't recognise her husband anymore. No, that wasn't right. She recognised her *real* husband far too late, and that was her fault. Yes, he was brutal, but she was always arrogant enough to think she could deal with it, manipulate it to her own advantage. She was more than naive. She was stupid. These men were ghouls and had sealed her fate in the most awful way possible. It would be kinder to throw her to the sharks than to feed her to that sick, ugly little man.

Was there any way out? she wondered desperately. Sarah would be too terrified to help. They were bound to threaten her, so she couldn't count on Sarah. What about the black man? And his friend? She was sure they would help her, if she could get word to them somehow. All they would know is that the devices were switched off. So maybe they would watch the flights. Seeing the hospital plane would give them some clue to what was happening, surely. So Corky wouldn't know until she woke up whether she had been rescued or not. She found herself praying the two strangers would come to her aid. It was her only hope.

"It will be necessary to continue our discussions in England," said Dr Carlton Fine. "We really must have draft agreements for the bulk of our agenda so the main project can go ahead. Namely the election of a Leader."

"A place will be found," Regis said. "Without difficulty. After all, there is no point now in travelling separately. Someone knows of our official existence. Moreover they know

221

far, far too much if they have recorded our conversations in here. And we must assume they have."

"Call in a Direct Action group from Rome to sweep the island," Fine replied.

Regis shrugged. "The moment their listening devices went dead, they were alerted. They will be packed and gone before the DA can get here. We should have had a unit stationed ashore during our visit. The Cuban, Gomez, was inadequate. Obviously. This is the second big failure of security we have had..."

"And who's fault is it this time?" Gillmore grumbled.

"...and I am determined to make it the last one."

"I hope so," Carlton Fine said ominously.

Regis smiled gently. "You've had a number of security failures in America, I believe."

Fine looked at the Englishman unblinking. "We've dealt with them, too."

"Indeed. As we are doing."

Alexander Hinkley squirmed in his seat, thinking it was a good idea to try and change the subject. "Dr Fine, I was absolutely fascinated with your paper today proposing new methods of dealing with the criminal community. You suggested neutering or the reduction of testosterone or the introduction of oestrogen. Have you thought about the relevance of genetic engineering?"

Gillmore sighed and wiped his eyes with his fingers. Regis leaned back in his chair, pretending to listen.

"Oh, yes," Fine said decisively. "There is a big future for genetics. A big future. Research is being carried out at this moment in time, and we are currently looking at developmental intelligence. If, through endocrine engineering, we could induce a certain docility, and, through *genetic* engineering, a lower intelligence with high manual dexterity - well, obviously we would be talking about the ideal workforce, wouldn't we? It would not even be necessary to surround a worker's village with something as crude as barbed wire. We could surround them with *technology*. A technology they would be incapable of understanding. Ideal."

222

"Hmmm." Hinkley re-tented his fingers. "Now take this unfortunate woman over there. Mrs DeLoop. If it is truly possible to alter her behaviour patterns so radically her personality is changed, why do we not consider experimenting upon our enemies? Perhaps a combination of endocrine and genetic engineering direct to human subjects could make research more cost effective. And shorten the time scale."

"Indeed," Fine grinned. "We have already instituted the use of this method. Unfortunately chemistry is inexact, and therefore mistakes are made. We experimented with a pesky Congressman who thought he had found an amazing series of connections during the Iran-Contra operation. In fact, he *had*." Fine smiled again. "We picked him up and tried an erasure procedure which we are at the moment attempting to perfect. A failure, I have to say. Instead it produced an advanced state of Alzheimer's. Pity. But at least it removed an obstruction."

He turned and stared clinically at Corky DeLoop. "It's very interesting to watch people change under the influence of powerful drugs. They think they won't break, but they always do. Because the inside of your mind is all you have for reference. So if you alter that, you lose all your normal reference points. I have seen some very interesting results." He shrugged his shoulders. "And some terrible failures, too."

He turned to Harvey Gillmore. "What you and the doctor must do is make certain she has no alternatives but one. Each time. You see, I have seen mice run through flames - or across electrical grids - if they are presented with no alternative. Of course in her case it won't matter if you kill her during the experiments."

"I won't kill her," Gillmore said evenly. "She'll just wish she was dead."

Michael Regis stood up. "I need to make a couple of telephone calls, so I'm going now to my bedroom." He turned to the Australian. "Have you got something to tether her in place so she can't flop about and throw herself into the sea?"

"I do, Michael," Gillmore replied. "But before we break up the meeting, I think it would be nice if we offered a little prayer to God..."

Regis looked uncomfortable. "Ur, Harvey..."

"I think it's a damn good idea," Dr Carlton Fine said. "We don't offer our thanks to the Almighty enough these days."

"Go ahead, Harvey," Wren Olsen said in a respectful voice.

Hinkley and Regis looked uneasy as Gillmore closed his eyes and turned his face to heaven. DeLoop, Fine and Olsen bowed their heads humbly.

"Oh, Lord, we are gathered on Your high seas this evening as we modestly try and carry out Your work here on earth. We ask for Your blessing as we go forth during troubled times to bring freedom and democracy to our fellow man. Guide our hands, O Lord, as we try and be Your willing servants and carry Your Word to the sheep and lambs of the earth. In the name of Christ the Son. Amen."

"Amen," said the three Americans at the table, as Gillmore got up.

The rest of the men rose from the table as the Australian left the room. They all looked down at Corky DeLoop as they left the room.

Hercules DeLoop was last to leave, a glass of bourbon still in his hand. He stood over his wife for a few moments. "You just had to be too smart, didn't you? I hope they roast your ass."

Gillmore returned as DeLoop left carrying a collar and chain. He leaned over and put the collar around Corky's neck. "Well, bitch, you're mine now. Feel like making another deal? Huh?"

He grabbed one of her breasts and squeezed until she closed her eyes in pain. "You are going to be crawling on the floor, begging me to fuck you." He squeezed harder. "Now I am going to go in and beat the shit out of that tart. And that's nothing to what you're going to get." He placed his face close to hers. "Nothing."

He released her breast and moved the sofa a couple of feet so the chain would reach a bracket fitted to the wall and locked the other end of the chain to it.

"Sweet dreams," he said as he turned out the light.

CHAPTER THIRTEEN

Dr Claude St John sat in a chair watching Sir Jonathan Mainwaring crawl slowly across the floor. The doctor had a clipboard on his knee and was taking notes. The disorientation was now nearly complete. The subject had little sense of balance, and sensory information would be distorted. The subject could still talk, though sometimes it was inaudible. The furniture in the room simply wouldn't make much sense to him.

There were two windows which had grills fitted over them, but today the curtains were drawn. Artificial light was much better for these purposes, preferably neon, and he had a private theory the pulsation of neon was subliminally effective under the influence of certain drugs. The subject was squinting, for instance, as if the light were painful to his retina. St John made another note.

White was an excellent colour. Or lack of colour. The only coloured item in the room was the long black table. The subject would not go near that table now. This was predictable, of course. In a few moments Green and Malley would return to pick up the subject and place him back on the table, and the electrotherapy would begin again. The drugs the subject had been given psychologically exaggerated the effect of electrical current, so the dosage could be kept within safe limits. After all, the subject was a man in late middle age. No heart attacks just yet. The heart attack would come later. After the man had talked. After he had been wrung completely dry.

He had already begun, of course. They all thought they could hold on, defeat the system. This was civilised treatment, not the barbarism of South American torturers, but for that reason it was more effective. Some held out longer than others, but it was useless in the end. Most of Claude St John's subjects were IRA terrorists, and this very room was where much was discovered of their operations. St John had wondered about the subject on the floor in front of him when he was first brought in. After all, he was knighted, a senior civil servant. But he was told the man was a traitor, deeply involved with the Provisional movement. So he had no sympathy, really, for his suffering. They were vermin, and this was his duty to his country. It was a job. A vital job. And somebody had to do it.

Green and Malley sat in the conservatory of the old country house. Green was looking out at the garden. It stretched for about eighty feet to a stone fence, beyond which he could see sheep grazing. The conservatory had a stone floor, a glass roof and large French doors. Two beautiful fig trees in large pots dominated the area. Both were almost twelve feet tall, and their branches nearly met in the centre of the room. It was south facing, an excellent place for plants, and a number of other pots held a variety of shrubs and flowers.

A china pot of tea sat in the middle of the round oak table next to a plate of biscuits. The sun was out, and the room was quite warm, so the French doors were open. The two policemen sat at the table with their tea. Their coats were hung on the backs of their chairs, and Malley munched a chocolate biscuit.

"Pity it doesn't take the doc longer. It's like being on holiday down here." Green propped his feet up in an empty chair. The forefinger of his right hand was still bandaged, and he noticed it as he picked up his cup. "That bastard bit through to the bone. Still throbs."

Malley laughed. "They're going to love the story back in London. Bureaucrat bites copper. Bureaucracy bites back." He laughed again.

"It wouldn't be so funny if it was your fucking finger."

"I hate this place," Malley said. "Can't wait to get back. Everybody's spooky here. And it's too quiet. Fucking sheep." Malley had grown up in Shepherd's Bush and hated going out of London.

Green pushed the teacup away. "What do you think of this operation?"

"Well," said Malley. "It's one of ours, isn't it? *Special* Special Branch. This fellow Mainwaring is a leftie, and from what Gordon says, he's the head of some group which is trying to take over the government. And undermine us."

"I think we ought to shoot every one of them. Drive up, pop 'em in the head. Gordon helped clean up the Specials. Now we need to finish MI5 and start on plod."

"Plod just does what plod is told." Malley pulled out a packet of Marlboros and lit one.

DI Green turned as Turner, Stimson and Henry came through the door with a tea tray. They were three Specials on rotating duty at Unit G3. Stewart Wilson was not with them, as at least two men should be on duty at all times. But it was quiet today, so only one had been left on the top floor. Green thought it was too many men for guard duty anyway. If there was ever any trouble, they could always call in plod. Gordon, however, had insisted they request two extras because of Mainwaring's status. There was no barbed wire fence around the place. No fence at all, actually. The whole point was to have a secure house which looked as normal as possible. This one was situated on the edge of a farm and had one dirt road running by the front. The garden was wired, and so were the doors and windows. And the roof. No way in without sound. And no way *out* for any of the poor bastards in the white rooms. Once they were doped up, they were helpless anyway. Didn't know their arses from their elbows. Green dropped his feet out of the chair so Henry could sit down.

Chris Henry was not a pleasant looking man. He was from South London, born into a family of villains. He disappointed his father by joining the police force, principally because he wanted into the Special Patrol Group. In the SPG he could practice legally what he best liked doing. Battering men to the ground and giving them a good stomping. He had big hands with scarred knuckles, and the tea cup looked tiny when he grabbed it.

"Why don't you learn some manners, Green. I've got to sit where you've had your feet."

Green shrugged. "Sit somewhere else." He watched with hostility as the bigger man lowered himself into the chair. Henry didn't scare him like he did some of the others. The only one who ever worried him was Martin Stimson, who had hooked a chair with his foot and sat down opposite. Stimson was short

227

and wiry but had large staring eyes. Stimson was a psycho. Being short, he used his head as a weapon. He called it the Liverpool kiss. Liverpudlians were crazy anyway. Green didn't trust anybody who wasn't from London. Ian Turner was looking out the open doorway. Turner was a good man, a real professional. Didn't talk too much. Just did his job. Green chose a biscuit and got up to join Turner.

"What do you think of all this fresh air?" he asked, biting into the biscuit.

"Too much for me, Inspector. Give me petrol fumes any day." Turner leaned one arm against the doorway. "When's the doc going to finish with the old bugger?"

"Can't be too long. Good to see one of those toffees slobbering around on the floor begging for help. Should have seen him when we picked him up. The bowler, the umbrella, the pinstripes and briefcase. Lord of the fucking universe." He heard the buzzer in the hallway. "Hello. Here we go again. I'd let one of you do this if I didn't enjoy it so much."

DS Malley joined him as he left the room and crossed the hall to the interrogation room.

The room swam in front of Mainwaring as he tried desperately to orientate himself. He could find a wall, but immediately wondered if it really was a wall. When he tried touching it, it would feel brittle. Or soft and furry. Or slimy and sloping. Was it an illusion or was it real? Real? What was that? Nothing was real anymore. There were only bright things and dark things. He tried to stay away from the dark things. He had to. Memories. He had no control anymore. Someone gave him a kitten when he was three or four years old, and somehow he strangled it. Or drowned it. Which was it? But he could see it happening. The poor little kitten. He really loved it, but wanted to see what would happen if he put it under water. His mother screamed and screamed at him later.

Another image. He adored his father, but his father never, ever touched him or held him. That made him want to cry. Why not? I am just a little boy, he thought. I haven't been bad. Touching. Oh, if he could only touch Sarah now. The memories were so confusing. Sarah had been here, he was sure of it.

When? And she had laughed at him. Laughed. Then she had made love to one of the policemen on the floor beside him as he watched and cried. Why would Sarah do that to him? Like his father, she no longer wanted to touch him. She recoiled when he reached for her.

What was happening now? Bits of the room were going faster than other bits, and that always made him feel like vomiting. He was rocking. Yes, and there were voices. The policemen again. Fear suddenly overcame him. Policemen. The dark table. Let it be anything but the dark table. The doctor's voice, too. He could still recognise voices, so his mind had not completely gone. It would soon, though. Or would it? Suddenly there was a rush of anger through his body as he felt the dark table under him. Anger. Anger was a good thing, yes. And he had to remember something. What was it? It was something...it was important, very important.

While he was trying to remember, the terrible thing happened. Every nerve in his body screamed in total panic. Pain began in his genitals and flowed through his body in vicious surges. He couldn't breathe. He couldn't get his breath for the fear. He had to spit. Yes, that was it! What he had to remember. Spit. Spit. Spit. When he heard a voice, he spat. Again there was the hellish pain, indescribable pain, pain which had its own colours and tints and bright flashes. Then the voice again.

"Tell us more about the United Opposition," the doctor asked. "Earlier today you said something about tapes. What kind of tapes? Whose are they? Where did you get them?"

Dr Claude St John frowned and turned to DI Green. "He's trying to spit again. That's what he is holding onto, you see. Very interesting. I haven't seen that one before." He leaned over close to the subject's face. "Your wife is here again, but she didn't come to see you." He paused as the subject looked hopelessly around the room muttering her name. "She came to see Inspector Green. They are kissing just over here..."

DI Green made smacking sounds, trying unsuccessfully not to laugh.

"You see," said Dr St John, "They are laughing at you. They think you are peculiar. Do you know what peculiar means? Odd. She doesn't want you anymore. Oh, dear, she is taking her clothes off and trying to get into Inspector Green's flies."

Green bent double with laughter. Malley joined him.

"Can you see, Mainwaring? Can you see her kneeling in front of Inspector Green and putting his member in her mouth?"

Malley slapped his thigh. "Member! Member! I can't stand it."

Mainwaring was looking toward the noise the two policemen were making with a look of abject and total despair. Tears filled his eyes quickly and ran down the sides of his face. Then the electrical current came again, shattering the horrible picture growing in his mind. It drove the pain he felt from his wife's heartlessness into his body like a vibrating nail. Then there was the voice again, this time soothing.

"You can change things, Sir Jonathan. You know that. You can stop the pain yourself. Easily. All you have to do is talk to me. We'll have a nice long talk, then your wife will return to you and stop fornicating with the policemen, and all the pain will go away. Isn't that reasonable? You are making your wife behave like that, you know. She is doing it because you are so stubborn. It is your fault. Look, she is turning to you. She has a poor dead kitten in her hand. Is it the one you murdered? I believe it is."

The doctor pressed the button again and watched with interest as the body jerked and bucked on the table, pulling against the straps holding it. This time he administered a second shock quite soon after the last one. And then another. And another. Then he waited.

"There, you see? Your father doesn't want you, nor does your mother. Your wife certainly doesn't. No one wants you anymore. You are alone. Only you can bring it all back. Or it will be gone forever. Gone, gone, gone..." he repeated softly and hypnotically.

Sir Jonathan Mainwaring's consciousness was disintegrating, but at this point he was not aware of it. Mainwaring played chess at a high club level, and his analysis of a board was phenomenal. So was his memory. He could hold a perfectly clear visual picture of a chess board with its assembled battle lines in his memory whilst trying a number of possible moves. He was very proud of his memory and felt it resembled a series of accessible compartments. Open one and there would be the whole of Byron's *Don Juan*. Open another and there was a list of his minister's every letter for the past three months. In another would be four Mozart operas, the melodies of all the arias in Italian or German. It was a facile mind - some said too facile. Above all Mainwaring was wholly confident of his mind in any company. Seldom, if ever, had it let him down.

Except now. The compartments were wrecked, smashed, with the neat little doors hanging on bent hinges. Great monsters with horrible faces rushed from one end of his universe to the other gobbling up words and ideas and memories and then spraying them out in unintelligible fragments. The real and the unreal, it seemed, had fornicated, and their offspring were something he could not recognise. It was one long, continuous nightmare. Something raw and savage had been let loose in his consciousness, and it was quite literally tearing him to pieces.

He would have held on, if he could have held on to the concept. But concepts had been dashed like china pots against the wall. Where concepts had once lived there was now a deep and bottomless hole with hellish blood red sides, stretching down to inner infinity.

* * *

It was just after ten o'clock the next morning when the call came through from Kenneth Cranshaw at GCHQ. He had worked through the night tracking down computers of the security services. It had taken him so long because the information was extremely well hidden. In fact it was in a code which he had to transcribe and use other facilities to break. He hadn't eaten, nor had he even stopped for a cup of tea.

The sun woke Haug before 7 am. He had fallen asleep on the floor in the front room of Louise Templer's house. Surprised he had fallen asleep, he looked around him. Louise was on the sofa. One Time looked elegant in an armchair, even when he was asleep. Keef was in the other chair, and Nightmare Andy snored on his back on the carpet.

They picked Andy up at his house at half past two that morning, and, as predicted, Louise Templer did not like him one bit. Nightmare Andy was elemental, a present reminder of what man had perhaps been like in earlier, maybe prehistoric, years. He was extremely large and throbbed with electrical savagery. His head was shaven, except for an scalplock in the back, and his eyes were piglike slits. His neck was piglike, too. On his chin hung a ragged and sinister goatee. Tattoos on his arms were lettered in Greek, because Andy was a Cypriot Greek, something of a legend in the London Greek community. Haug didn't know whether to believe all the stories he heard about the man, but he didn't doubt that they *could* be true. In his estimation Nightmare Andy was the best fighting man he had ever worked with - or the worst, depending on your viewpoint. He was certain it would take several guns of large calibres to stop Nightmare Andy once he was in motion and full cry. Faced with violence, Andy would go totally berserk in a very controlled fashion, extinguishing what irritated him in an economical way. His ferocity was ruthless, pitiless and relentless. And there were no rules. Hard men with strong wills broke and ran for their lives, throwing down their weapons in terror.

The trouble with using Nightmarc Andy, Haug knew, was the difficulty in varying the amount of damage. Because with Andy it was maximum or nothing. On or off. There was nothing delicate or intelligent about the attack. Haug only used him if they really needed his brand of ferocity or they were badly outnumbered. This time it was a guess, because he did not know what he was going to be up against. There was no time to reconnoitre Unit G3, wherever it was. They were going to have to hit it blind, so it was best to assume the worst. Go in as hard and heavy as if it were being defended by two platoons of battle hardened marines.

Haug didn't want any unnecessary killing, either. These men were likely to be policemen of one stripe or another, and there were too many unknowns about them. They could be ordinary plods who were just following orders, for instance. Which was the danger in taking along Andy. You could never tell Andy to go easy. He would just start gobbling when he encountered resistance, only stopping when all opponents were dead or disabled.

They were going to have to have a lot of luck. Even if they got the address in time, there was no assurance that Jonathan was still there. They may have moved him. He might be dead already. It could be the wrong address, and they would burst into the dining room of some middle class family sitting down to a joint of lamb.

He brushed the doubts aside. They were going to do it. They were going ahead, whatever happened. So long, that is, as Cranshaw came through with the address.

Later Haug was sitting in the kitchen alone, drinking a cup of black coffee. It was half past nine now, and he had the mobile phone beside him. Despair had begun to leak into his watertight joints. The day was overcast, but it wasn't raining. Would rain help or hinder them? He wasn't sure.

"Why didn't you wake me?" Louise Templer said as she came into the kitchen, tucking her blouse back into her jeans.

"Nothin' to wake you for," he said. "May as well sleep. Might need it."

She raised an eyebrow. "No call yet?"

Haug shook his head. "Not even a wrong number." He slid off the stool and grabbed a clean mug. "Water's just boiled. Want a cup of somethin'?"

"Made yourself at home, I see," she said with a half smile.

"Always do," he replied.

"Tea with milk, then. If you know where everything is."

"This guy Cranshaw, is he...you know, reliable?"

"As reliable as Sir Jonathan. And conscientious. And committed. And a good friend of Sir Jonathan's. He won't have slept like we did, I promise you."

Haug nodded and handed Louise her cup of tea. Then he went over and stood looking out the window. "Then we just gotta be patient. And patience is damn near impossible for those without wisdom, like me."

Templer sipped her tea. "You really like Mainwaring, don't you?"

"Yeah," he said finally. "Yeah, I do. Last summer he took me to Lord's. The Australians won by an innings, but I really enjoyed it. He was different. Relaxed, if you can imagine that. We went in his old Morgan. He's had it since he bought it new in the '60's. Wore a flat cap, and crew neck sweater and a scarf. His wife fixed a hamper of homemade pate, smoked salmon, cucumber sandwiches - and I ask you, how can you make a sandwich outta cucumbers?. And there was a bottle of the nicest wine I've ever tasted, and he said he had made it himself. A dandelion wine. It was a beautiful day. Sun shinin', no rain. We had a seat in one of those special boxes. Jonathan was smilin' and jokin' and laughin' at me and Americans. You know, he's really warm underneath all that gun metal severity. I don't believe there's a bad bone in his body."

Haug took a sip of his bitter black coffee. "That's why he started all this stuff. It wasn't right, it wasn't moral, it wasn't just. Someone had to stand up, and he stood. OK, he's kinda naive when it comes to politics. At least that's what I think. But he's a good man."

She came and stood beside him. "What are they doing to him?"

"Takin' his brain apart. They've probably advanced a lot since my day, but they do cocktails of drugs which completely disorient you. It's not just sodium pentathol anymore. It's uppers and downers and hallucinogens. Sometimes the hangover is as important as the high. And they'll probably be combinin' this with some kinda physical violence or threats."

"How can they do that to anybody?" Her voice was heavy with anger.

"Because they want somethin', that's why. In their world that's why anybody does anythang. They want it, so they take it. If it's important, they'll run over you with tank treads to get it..."

Haug stopped mid-sentence, and they looked at each other. The sound was startling. It was the telephone.

* * *

234

Harvey Gillmore sat on one side of the polished table with his granny glasses on reading the list of demands. He wasn't really reading them, though. He was too annoyed to read. Pissed off. Here he was in Manchester, a city he hated, in the editor's office of the *Manchester Echo*, talking to scum who had the arrogance to think he would be interested in their "demands" and "concessions". He didn't want to be in Manchester, not even if it was in a newspaper office. But he was buying the *Echo*, and he had received a call from Heathrow that the whole deal was falling through because the unions refused to work under the conditions he laid out for them.

The *Echo* had been part of his long range plans. He had a hugely successful national daily in *The News* and two national Sundays. Scotland was now covered with one paper in Edinburgh and one in Glasgow, both traditionally Scottish. Manchester was in the middle of the old Labour industrial heartland, and they must be re-educated in modern market and democratic processes. *The News* did not sell that well in this part of the country, and the strategy now was to buy up local papers so they could hammer home their message over and over again - until the population finally came to their senses and realised there was no alternative to the New Ideas. No one any longer got something for nothing. Welfare from cradle to grave had turned these people into a mass of lazy, union infested, workshy people who wanted to give two hours labour for eight hours pay.

And Gillmore was also pissed off because he had to change his plans. Since the night before he had been looking forward to dealing with the DeLoop woman. He had lain awake part of the night laying plans with relish. He couldn't remember ever breaking anyone like her, and he anticipated it like a child waiting for Santa Claus. Regis had called in a hospital plane, and the doctor arrived on the Matilda at midday. No questions were asked, of course. The doc simply popped an injection into her arse, right through her skirt. Eight seconds later she was out cold and was carried from the yacht on a stretcher. An ambulance met them at Heathrow and whisked her off to one of their Unit houses. Gillmore wanted to be on that ambulance. He wanted to be there when she woke up. But, no, there was an urgent telephone message for him in the VIP lounge, so he immediately booked a flight to Manchester.

After all, he was a businessman. Business came first. He glanced over his glasses at the men opposite him. There was the editor, Peter Winchurch, the so-called Father of Chapel of the NUJ, Joe Bedford and Adrian Finchley, a partner in Finger Platt, the firm of accountants brought in by Gillmore. Gillmore pushed the papers aside and took off his glasses.

"Tell me in your own words," he said to Bedford, "just what it is you think you want."

Joe Bedford was in his fifties, like Gillmore, but had acquired weight around his waist at the same rate he lost his hair. He was a highly respected feature journalist on the newspaper and had worked for *The Echo* for over eighteen years.

Bedford smiled at Gillmore. "When I spoke at our chapel meeting last night, I pointed out the difficulties *The Echo* faces, of rising costs and falling circulation. We also fully understand we are in the middle of a recession, and titles are being squeezed by a contracting market..."

The editor, Peter Winchurch, nodded. "And we have already made some fairly substantial changes in our operation. As you know, Mr Gillmore, the old systems have had to go in the onslaught of modern technology. For instance, we tried to keep on as many compositors as possible in the changeover. But many, unfortunately, had to go. It was a sad time. We were like a family here."

"So you are quite aware," Gillmore said in a soft voice, "that jobs are hard to come by these days."

"Oh, yes," Bedford replied with a laugh. "I don't know what I'd do if I had to go out into the marketplace today. Which is why we have offered to take a cut in wages and, if necessary, longer hours of work before overtime cuts in."

"There won't be any overtime," said Gillmore. "That's a thing of the past." He turned to his accountant. "Give them a copy of our conditions, Adrian." He turned back to the editor and FoC. "These conditions are final and non-negotiable. You either accept them or your don't."

236

Harvey Gillmore watched with a great deal of satisfaction as the two men read the papers handed to them. The blood drained slowly from the editor's face while the face of the union bastard turned bright red.

Joe Bedford was the first to react, smacking his hand across the paper he was reading. "You can't do this!"

"What do you mean, I can't do it?" asked Gillmore mildly. "I just did it."

"But it's insane," Bedford replied angrily. "Inhumane."

The editor, Peter Winchurch, was shaking his head sadly. "It looks like I don't have a job."

Gillmore turned to him. "Did you expect a job after your rotten performance? Anyhow I like to have my own nominee as editor."

"Do you know how long I've been with *The Echo*?" asked Winchurch.

"I don't care," replied Gillmore calmly. "I run newspapers, not almshouses."

Joe Bedford was really angry. "Peter's got a home here. Lived in Manchester all his life. And that life has been dedicated to *The Echo*. For Christ's sake, he won't find another job at his age. He's got a mortgage and three kids. OK, he knows he's not going to be editor anymore, but there are a dozen other positions on the paper, maybe a little less salary, but he's willing to talk about that."

"You're breaking my heart," Gillmore replied.

"From the look of this," Bedford smacked the papers again, "you don't have one to break." He looked down and adjusted his glasses. "'Fifty percent staff cuts. No overtime. Flexible hours commensurate with job.' And get this one. 'All staff on six month contracts, renewable on review.' Incredible, unbelievable. Unprecedented. 'No coffee or tea breaks, no talking on matters unrelated to business, two brief toilet breaks, maximum thirty minute lunch break, no paid holidays, one day at Christmas off, not paid by company, minimum legal pension scheme, paid sick days only if examined by company doctor, no one to leave the building without permission, expenses paid by editor's estimate.' Here's another one. 'Insolence and insubordination will result in instant dismissal.' Oh, yes, and this is not unexpected. 'Recognition of all trades unions will immediately be withdrawn. Former members must show their torn union cards to supervisor and swear company oath never to join one again.' Wonderful. Where does that leave me?"

"Out of a job," said Gillmore. "And out of the newspaper business."

Joe Bedford blew out his cheeks. "How the fuck can you manage that, Mr Gillmore? You don't own all the newspapers in Europe."

"I've given you an entry in White & Small," Gillmore smirked.

"Oh," said Bedford, "the blacklist. Those rightwing bastards who operate out of Chelmsford. There are some newspapers who don't use..."

"I entered you as a communist agitator who spends all his time stirring up trouble and none working. You won't work again on a newspaper. Trust me."

Bedford exploded. "A communist agitator! Me! I voted Liberal last election! Not the next one, though!"

Gillmore shrugged. "There you go. Labour Party, Communist Party. Same thing."

Peter Winchurch looked devastated. "Is there an alternative, Mr Gillmore. We've been talking amongst ourselves about a staff buyout..."

The Australian turned to his accountant. "Adrian?"

Adrian Finchley smiled briefly. He had very thin lips and watery eyes. "The financial position of *The Manchester Echo* is so poor the banks have now withdrawn their support completely. The publisher wants to sell to Mr Gillmore, and a price has been agreed. The banks are more than amenable. Neither the publisher nor the banks believes a cooperative scheme will in the circumstances be viable."

"I knew your reputation," said Joe Bedford through his teeth, "but I couldn't believe you were such a perfect shit. You think you can just push people around, pay them what you want, impose your will, cut people's wages, ruin their lives..."

"I don't think I can," said Gillmore. "I *know* I can."

238

Bedford stood up, glowing with anger. "Well, I'm going out there to tell my members just what you've said to me. You may produce a newspaper here, but you're going to have to print the fucker yourself!"

Gillmore turned toward the outer office door. "Boys!"

Two large men in suits entered. Both had close cropped hair. One of them had a scar across his cheek and the other one wore wrap-around sun glasses.

"Boys, I want you to take this man and drag him by the heels through the news room so everybody can see what you're doing. Then I want you to drag him down the front steps and leave him on the pavement. Throw his belongings out after him."

Joe Bedford was game and squared up to the bouncers. "The first one of your bastards to touch me loses his teeth."

Bedford managed to smack one of them on the jaw before they overpowered him. He was knocked off his feet, and the bouncers grabbed an ankle each.

"I'll get you, Gillmore," Bedford screamed as they dragged him away. "This won't be the last you see of me, you horrible little shit!"

The editor, Peter Winchurch, had his head in his hands. "I never thought I would witness something like this. Never. Not at *The Echo*." He looked up at Gillmore. "Don't you see? Don't you see this is...uncivilised?"

Gillmore shrugged. He could hear an uproar from the news room. "Go collect your things and piss off."

Winchurch had tears in his eyes. "Mr Gillmore. I'm already three payments behind on my mortgage because I took a wages cut to try and save the paper. That house is all I have got, and there's nearly ten more years to pay. My Visa is at the limit, and my car isn't paid for. It's a disaster. I suppose I have to ask: is there no job at all for me on your newspaper?"

Gillmore threw the papers given to him by Joe Bedford in the waste paper bin. "What would you do for a job, Winchurch?"

The editor's face brightened. "Well...just about anything. I started out as a copy runner, and I've done just about every job there is to do on a paper."

"Would you get down on your knees and apologise for the disrespectful and disgraceful way you have spoken to me today?"

"I beg your pardon?"

"You heard me."

Peter Winchurch looked confused. "Well, my goodness, I never heard such a..."

Gillmore smacked his palm on the desk. "Do you want a job or not? Don't waste my time."

The editor looked at the accountant in embarrassment, and the accountant looked back at him with his watery eyes. "I...well, I suppose, if it would help..."

"Either do it or get your arse out of this office," Gillmore barked.

Winchurch slid off his chair looking very uncomfortable. He knelt in front of Gillmore's desk. "I...sincerely apologise for speaking out of turn, for being disrespectful..."

"Get down on all fours and bark like a dog."

Winchurch seemed about to cry. "Really, Mr Gillmore..."

Gillmore leaned forward. "Do it or get out."

The older man dropped onto his hands. "Woof. Woof."

"Now come round here," said Gillmore. "On all fours. Come round to my side."

The editor crawled around the desk and stopped a few feet from the new owner of *The Echo*. His head was hanging low.

"Sit up and beg," said Gillmore. He watched as the man slowly raised up on his knees, made his hands into paws and panted with his tongue hanging out. "Roll over." He threw a pencil across the room. "Go fetch." When the man returned out of breath with the pencil between his teeth, Gillmore stared at him for a moment. "Now lick my shoes, you pommy scum."

Winchurch closed his eyes tightly against the surge of inner pain. He thought of his house and his wife, Martha. She loved that house, and he loved her. With the greatest revulsion he leaned over and put his tongue out tentatively, touching the expensive shoe with the tip.

"Lick!" said the voice from above.

He licked.

"Keep licking," Gillmore said. "You can have your job as copyboy back for the period of one month. You will listen to what every member of the staff has to say behind my new editor's back, and you will report every word to him. Every word. As a matter of fact, I think you better record it all on tape. If I like your work, and my new editor likes it, after one month I will make you his assistant. Play your cards right, and one day you might be editor of *The Echo* again. Now stop licking my fucking shoes and tell me if you agree to your new terms of employment."

Peter Winchurch rose to his knees, but he didn't look at Harvey Gillmore. Never in his life had he felt so wretched. He didn't know how he could do such a horrible thing to the staff of *The Echo*. He had known some of them for years. Many were friends of his, close friends. It just seemed too awful. He surely would die of shame if he did such things. It would be better to lose his job and probably his house and his peace of mind and maybe even his life.

"I agree," he heard himself say. "I agree."

"And remember," Gillmore said, glancing at Adrian Finchley, "We have entered into a *free* and *voluntary* agreement."

* * *

Corky DeLoop sat in the corner of the white room staring at a white wall. She woke up lying in the middle of the floor. Naked. It took her some time to remember what had happened, because so much of it seemed like a nightmare. She had no idea what time it was or where she was. Someone had given her an injection in her butt. Then the lights went out. And now, here she was in some kind of padded cell. It *was* a cell. There was an outline for a door, but there was no window and no door handle. There was, she noted, a spyhole, though. Where she could be looked at by...whom? Was she in Corfu? No, she had heard them talking about bringing her back to England in a hospital plane. Is that what happened? Was she in England? Or in hell for her sins?

241

When her head had cleared a little, she went to the door and tried to see out of the spyhole. Nope. Then she gave the door a kick. It was solid, like padded steel. She kicked the walls. All solid. She checked her wrists and ankles where she had been held by the shackles. They weren't too sore, and you could only see faint marks, so they must have been off for some time. The muscles in her jaw were a little sensitive from being forced open by that damn gag. Sarah Courtney was right. That thing sucked.

So she went and sat down in the corner. There was nothing else to do. At least whoever might look through the spyhole wouldn't see as much of her body that way. After sitting down, though, she began to slide slowly into what looked to be an Olympic-sized depression. Normally she would never call herself a depressive sort of person. But these circumstances did not look good. She drew up her knees, put her forearms on top and rested her chin on her forearms.

"You are in a fix," she muttered to herself. "A bad fix, honey."

Obviously there had been no rescue from the beautiful black spy, whoever he was. So. Either he hadn't heard in time or he didn't give a shit. No hope he would find her here, wherever *here* was. Thinking back to the night before, the beginning of the nightmare, she remembered the conversation at the table while she lay helpless on the sofa. Men talking about her like she was a dog. No, worse than a dog. Like a sack of potatoes. They decided this about her and that about her. They would do this or that to her. She had been "sold" to Gillmore, she recalled, and he had promised to be here when she opened her eyes. Well, he wasn't, was he? She had no doubt, however, that she would see him sooner or later, and that was a prospect she did not look forward to.

They meant to turn her into some kind of slave or automaton with drugs and violence. She honestly feared the drugs more than the violence because she knew they affected the mind. She didn't know how or to what degree, and that was the source of her fear.

With a struggle she put the fear aside and tried to think of her alternatives. She must try and decide if she would try to kill

242

herself or survive. If she wanted to survive, what must she do? Try and escape, obviously. Look for every opportunity. *Create* opportunities. If she faked compliance, those opportunities might be sooner rather than later. Boy, it was going to be hard, though. Harvey Gillmore. Serving him his fucking Diet Pepsis, begging him for sex. Ugh. She'd rather have sex with a giant toad.

She smacked her hand against her knee. It wasn't a question of suicide or survival. She knew she had to survive. *Had* to. For one reason. Revenge, by god. Whatever they did to her would be paid back with interest. Gillmore and Hercules DeLoop, her loyal, loving husband. That would be what she would hang onto, that one thought. Revenge.

CHAPTER FOURTEEN

"I'm afraid I must agree with Dr Fine," said Sir Samuel Goodman. "Potentially we have a situation which could spiral completely out of our control. With disastrous consequences. True, Michael, you have moved quickly and decisively, but conditions should never have been allowed to reach this point."

Sir Samuel Goodman was Cabinet Secretary, and he was sitting on the patio in the garden of Michael Regis' house near Chalfont St Giles. It was a large, well manicured garden, and the grounds of the manor house extended for nearly fifteen acres. It was a very beautiful patio. The small glazed tiles had been lifted with care from a Warwickshire Tudor mansion and placed down in the exact pattern of the original design. Most of the tiles were red, but the black and white ones formed a complex geometric puzzle in the centre and were also used in the border. A round, weathered oak table sat to one side of the central design surrounded by comfortable wooden armchairs. Dr Carlton Fine, Wren Olsen and Hercules DeLoop were staying as guests of Regis.

The Cabinet Secretary arrived earlier that morning in response to a telephone call from Regis. He was a tall, well-built man of 62 with a commanding presence. His white hair was plentiful but held firmly down to the outline of his head, with just a hint of an upward curl at the hatline. He had a large face dominated by a flared nose, and his eyes were considered by his enemies to be cold and calculating. This morning he was not at all happy.

"Conditions have reached this point, though," Regis replied almost languidly as he looked out over his extensive grounds. "And we have responded."

"It should never have happened in the first place," said Dr Fine. "You didn't even know of the *existence* of this group. What's it called? The United Opposition? I thought that was the name of the party out of power in your Parliament. Has it got anything to do with your socialist party?"

"Protective coloration, I assume," Regis responded in the same manner. "So they could talk about themselves openly. Nothing at all to do with the Labour Party. Except some of its members are drawn from it, of course."

"Security has been really slack here," Fine said. "Hell, we know the moment three people come together to talk about the weather in the States."

"Oh, really?" Regis replied. "According to my information this morning from the interrogation at G3, there is an American group at least as large as this one."

"What?" Fine roared. "No way. You're pumping water out of that guy, not blood."

"For the moment," said Sir Samuel in his patrician tones, "the highest priority is the recovery of the tapes made from your meetings aboard the Matilda. I need not draw your attention to their explosive nature."

Michael Regis smiled grimly. "I have instructed our operatives at G3 of this new priority and expect an answer today. Mr DeLoop's wife will also be providing information, though I am of the opinion she is only marginally involved. Someone talked her into planting the listening devices. Meanwhile I have alerted two of our Direct Action units to stand by. Hopefully the whole affair will be unravelled and dealt with before the weekend is over. Or early next week at the latest."

"When...and *if*...you recover the tapes and deal with the spies," Sir Samuel said, "I think it would be wise to consider the future of the doctors who are helping extract the information..."

"Terminate with extreme prejudice," Fine said.

"Ha," laughed DeLoop. "Like the pirate who shoots the crew after they bury the chest of gold coins."

Sir Samuel Goodman turned toward Hercules DeLoop, looking down his nose. "This is not the time for levity, DeLoop. Under the circumstances I believe it would be best for you to dwell in silence."

"Well, you lissen to me, Sir Lord God Almighty. I'll laugh at anythang I think is funny, and if you don't like it, you can kiss my ass."

Goodman ignored him. "Despite your assurances, Michael, I am worried. It is already messy and getting messier. My career is not the only one which depends on your efficiency. If the public have access to information regarding our existence, they would no doubt misinterpret our motives before we had a chance to explain it was in the best interests of democracy, that in fact if we had not developed from the early days just after the war, the world would now be under the heels of communist tyrants. Instead of sitting here today we would be labouring in the fields like oxen."

"I don't think it was quite that dangerous," said Fine loudly. "From the early days we have realised the importance of controlling information. We may have a fire, but it's not going to burn the house down. Even if they manage to keep the tapes somehow, nobody's going to believe them. Who's going to believe them? Tapes can be faked. We can simply deny it, even if they play them on loudspeakers on every corner of London."

"That's not what they would do with them," Regis said.

Fine turned in his chair. "You tell us, then. What?"

"If it were me," Regis replied. "I'd use them to recruit, gather in more membership and undermine the enemy. They are of more value that way. Make them public, and they are devalued. A year hence Sir Samuel might find himself eased out to pasture, and one of theirs would take his place. I might find it difficult to get export certificates. A crucial banker would shrug his shoulders helplessly when we needed funds. The Monopolies Commission could make Gillmore's news and TV acquisitions impossible or break them up completely. That is the real threat of the tapes. They would hobble us just at the point we need to gallop."

"Yeah," Fine nodded agreement. "That's how to play the cards, alright. Which means, we've got to find the goddamn tapes."

"At least Mainwaring is out of the picture," Sir Samuel said with pleasure. "That man was a real danger."

"How come?" DeLoop asked.

"Because his integrity is unchallenged in the whole of the civil service. He is known for his fairness to all parties, and his

247

presentation and preparation for ministers is legendary. In his whole career he has hardly put a foot wrong. I might add his name has been bandied amongst ministers as my successor. How he has got himself entangled with these rogues is quite beyond me."

"Yes," agreed Regis. "When I found out, I didn't hesitate, whatever the risk. I knew immediately he had to be picked up, questioned and killed."

* * *

Unit G3 was located near a tiny village outside Arundel, near the river, and the pickup moved slowly up the narrow road. According to the map Louise Temper provided the house would not be far. She sat in the back seat behind Haug, acting as navigator. One Time sat in the middle, and Nightmare Andy on the other side. Keef was in the front seat next to Haug.

"There should be a T-junction at the top of this little road," said Louise. "Turn right, and the house should be about a hundred yards down, on the left."

Haug checked his rearview and stopped the pickup. "Keef, how would you and Andy like to get out and climb under that tarpaulin in the back?"

Without answering, Keef opened his door and slid out. He carried a pickaxe handle. Nightmare Andy followed him through the door with his Louisville Slugger. He also had a machete stuck through his belt.

Haug got out his side with the two stick-on registration plates and went around to the rear.

"Legs and backs, Andy," Haug warned the Greek as he stepped into bed of the pickup. "Try to stay away from heads." He peeled away the back and carefully stuck the phony registration over the real one.

"No problem," Andy said with a grin as he held up the tarpaulin for Keef.

Haug went round to the front of the truck and covered the registration number the same way. One Time was moving into the front seat.

As he got back into the cab he turned to Louise Temper. "Now this is just advice. I know you're gonna do whatever you want to do in the end, no matter what I say. But my *advice* is the moment thangs start crackin', get down between the seats and stay there until we get back. I will not faint with surprise if these assholes are armed, so it's the safest place for you."

"Yes, Haug," she replied.

"In one ear and out the other." Haug put the pickup in gear and started up the hill.

Green and Malley stepped into the conservatory with cups of tea. This time they hadn't bothered with a teapot and used bags. It was quiet after all the screaming in the interrogation room.

Green yawned. "I don't know how the old bastard takes it. You have to squeeze it out of him a word at a time. What was he saying in there just now?"

Malley shrugged. "'How.' Just kept saying 'How.' The doc would ask him who had the tapes, and the old boy asked him 'How,' like he was barking. I think his mind's gone myself."

Green sucked on his tea and walked over to the open French doors. It was overcast now, but the weather was still warm. "The doc says the old fucker's got to rest a few minutes now. I think we need the rest more than he does with all this acting we've been doing. Fancy going on the stage, then?"

"What, a double act?" grinned Malley. "I suppose I'll have to be the straight man, and you..."

He was interrupted by the buzzer above the hallway door. It was the security alarm.

Green turned to look at the source of the sound. "Now who the hell has set that thing off now?" The noise of an engine drew his attention back through the French doors. Some bastard in a bloody huge pickup truck was travelling across the lawn.

"Hey!" shouted Green as he stepped through the door waving at the driver. "Hey! Get off the property! This is private property!"

An idiot in a baseball cap leaned out the window of the cab. "Is this the way to Buckin'ham Palace?" the man drawled.

A fucking American tourist, Green thought. That's all I need. "Go back to the road! You are on private property!" He pointed vigorously at the road. "That way!"

"Oh, sorry," said the American. "I'll just turn this thang around."

Green shook his head incredulously as the pickup truck started to reverse. It was reversing back toward them. And it wasn't stopping. It was picking up speed. Green stumbled back inside, and he and Malley started retreating to the hall doorway as the back of the pickup crashed through the French doors, overturning the two large fig trees and smashing the table and chairs underneath the rear wheels. Before it stopped something truly awful sprang up from under the tarpaulin. Green had never seen anything like it. It looked like a cartoon monster, huge and bald and screaming in a foreign language. There was a big black man as well. Green was transfixed for a moment before collecting himself and reaching for the pistol inside his jacket.

Keef's pickaxe handle broke DI Green's upper arm before he could withdraw the gun. Malley simply panicked and turned to the hallway door. Nightmare Andy' baseball bat caught him at the top of his legs, and the edges of both femurs tore through the front of his trousers. Keef and Andy thundered into the hallway, closely and silently followed by One Time, who carried only his garrotte with a wooden toggle at each end. Haug slammed into the groaning Detective Inspector and found the pistol. Shouting for Keef, he tossed him the gun and returned to the wounded Special.

He grabbed Green by the neck with one large hand and picked his head off the floor. "You only got one chance, bo, and it's a quick one. Where is he?"

Green was trying to speak, and Haug loosened his grip. "Who the fuck are you?"

Haug put his face close to the policeman's. "If I have to ask that question again, it'll be somebody else answerin', 'cause you'll be dead. Where?"

"Interrogation room," Green muttered.

"Where the fuck is that?"

"Across the hall..."

The blood had drained from the Special's face, and Haug saw the man had passed out from shock. He heard shots from the back of the house. Then there was screaming. He quickly stepped over to the other fallen Special and found his pistol. Then he spun around the doorway of the hall, ready to fire. No one. He crossed the hall to the big door and tried the handle. It was locked. More firing, from upstairs this time. Stepping back and to the side, Haug fired three times at the lock on the door, then kicked with all his strength. The splintered door sprung open.

Nightmare Andy had continued on down to the end of the hall while Keef followed One Time up the stairs. If he found a door, he kicked it open. The first one was a kitchen, and a cook was cowering underneath a table. Andy ignored him and surged back out of the room. A second room was empty. As he returned to the hall another door opened quickly and a man stepped out holding a pistol with both hands in front of him. He fired at what he at first thought was a wild animal charging toward him, head lowered and bellowing.

Nightmare Andy did not even feel either bullet. One passed through his left shoulder, and the other went through the flesh of his left arm. Then he had the man with the gun. He threw the ball bat aside and grabbed the face with both hands, digging his fingers into the flesh and pulling with all his strength. Ian Turner's mouth and nose were torn open exposing his teeth on one side. One of his eyes popped from the socket and bounced once before rolling back through the doorway leaving a bloody trail. Turner staggered backwards wailing, but Andy followed him after twisting the pistol from his grip. As he sagged to the floor the big Greek straddled the man and hammered the gun butt straight through his teeth, forcing the handle of the pistol back into his throat. As the policeman lost consciousness Andy snarled and spun on the body to retrieve his bat. His eyes glowed like coals heated by some inner hell. He kicked the remaining doors open praying he would find someone else behind them, even a cook. Then he ran toward the stairs. Gunfire from above. Good. There were some more left. He took the treads two at a time.

There were two flights of stairs. One Time reached the first landing just as Stewart Wilson came through holding a gun in front of him. Dodging to one side One Time grabbed the man by the belt, lifting and pushing. Wilson plummeted down the stairs, meeting Keef on the way up. Keef stopped his descent with the pickaxe handle. Using it like a staff in the cramped space, he whacked the man in the midriff. As he dropped, Keef caught his head with a knee, and Wilson's facial features were immediately scrambled into a kind of ratatouille of flesh, blood and splintered bone. As Keef raced up the stairs past the man, he was aware of a figure at the second landing, and he was showered by pieces of splintered wood as the man fired from above. Pulling the gun Haug gave him from his belt he fired two shots into the ceiling of the first landing but couldn't tell whether or not the bullets went through. But the man above stopped firing. Keef carefully started up the second flight.

One Time had stepped silently through the landing door on the first floor and stood quietly listening. He heard the firing outside, and Keef didn't say anything or scream, so he assumed he was alright. One Time moved nothing but his head and eyes. There was someone else there, he could sense it. When there was a brief moment of silence outside he heard some mechanical noise, and his eyes stopped moving. He knew the direction.

Moving slowly and carefully down the very edge of the hall, he paused briefly after every step. More gunfire, and then someone screamed horribly downstairs. During the scream he moved on quickly. A door was open at the end of the hall. He could just see it. Slowly and smoothly he moved towards the open door. The mechanical noise again, and then One Time knew what it was. He identified the sound. Three more steps took him to the door jamb, and he could hear a voice whispering.

"Mayday, mayday, Unit G3, request assistance immediately...mayday, mayday, mayday..."

To an observer it might have looked like One Time's eye developed a stalk which proceeded his face around the door. The eye watched for movement, any movement, and found it. A man was hunched over a radio transmitter which mostly emitted a low level of static when turned on receive. The static came from One Time's ghetto blaster in the back of Haug's pickup. One Time's face followed his eye into the room with his body close behind.

The black man was already half way across the room when Martin Stimson turned suddenly and looked at the apparition in the middle of the floor. Without hesitation the Liverpudlian launched himself at the black man. All he needed was a grip of the lapels, and he would rearrange his face for him. He was within a half inch of grabbing One Time when the black simply seemed to disappear from view. The only thing left was his leg, which caught both Stimson's feet in midair.

A moment after the Special hit the floor, One Time was on his back with both knees and slipped the garrotte swiftly around his neck. It was nearly half a minute before the policeman stopped struggling. The black man got up and, with a smooth movement, flipped the man on his back. Placing his own knee against the man's kneecap, he pulled smartly up on the ankle, dislocating the joint.

He got up and looked over the radio setup. Then he jerked the wires away and threw it toward the closed window. It went through with a crash, taking the frame with it as it plunged toward the ground.

Nightmare Andy burst through the door at the top landing. He saw Keef kneeling at the corner with a pistol in his hand. Keef waved him down.

"He's in the second room down with a gun," Keef said to Andy, then saw his arm. "You're bleeding. Hurt bad?"

"No problem," Andy muttered. "Cover me."

The Greek got into a crouch as Keef put his head around the corner and squeezed off a couple of shots. As he fired Andy sprang forward, crashing into the door of the first room. It was a big, old fashioned door, but it burst open from the force. The man down the hall fired, but it was too late. Andy was inside.

Keef watched, puzzled, as Andy jerked at the door from inside the room, smashing at it with the ball bat. Then he got his fingers in the crack between the door and the frame and literally wrenched it off its hinges and dragged it into the room with him.

Chris Henry heard the noise from the next room but was puzzled. There was no interconnecting door. What were they doing in there? Then he heard the pounding on the wall. The whole house seemed to shudder. Boom. Boom. Boom. It sounded like a battering ram. Were they trying to come through a brick wall? He looked up as plaster started falling from the cornice. Then the plaster on the wall began cracking and crazing. Boom. Boom. Boom. He put his head around the door to see if the black man was still there and a bullet thudded into the woodwork a few inches above his head. So how many men were in the next room? A dozen? With sledgehammers? Plaster was beginning to fall in sheets.

Henry thought he would be relatively safe. He was at the front and top of the house. No one could get to him except down the hall. He had been sure he could hold them off until help arrived. Looking back around at the wall, he could now see the brickwork. Boom. Boom. Boom. Boom. Bricks were coming loose. He couldn't believe it. The whole wall was shaking now with each blow, and the room was filling with plaster and mortar dust. There were guttural shouts coming from the other room, and they were getting louder.

Chris Henry's stomach began to knot in panic. He couldn't really leave the doorway, and he couldn't cover the collapsing wall without leaving the doorway. What the fuck to do? Backing off carefully, he glanced out both windows. No roof. Straight down, too far to jump. Or was it?

Suddenly a hole opened in the wall. Henry was backed up near the centre of the room, turning his pistol first toward the doorway, then toward the wall. The hole widened, but he couldn't see much, and he was beginning to cough. Should have opened the damn windows.

"Drop the gun!" a voice shouted from the doorway.

As Henry spun toward the doorway, something horrible, something from the stinking depths of hell burst through the wall. He glimpsed only a shadow in the clouds of dust. But it was a huge shadow, and he would always remember the crazed eyes in what seemed like a pig headed grizzly bear which engulfed him a moment before he lost consciousness. There was only a brief flash of pain as his nose was bitten off. Then nothing.

When Haug entered the Interrogation Room, he froze. There were two men in the room. One was cowering naked on the floor, and another recoiled to the other side of a black table. The one behind the table was fully dressed. Haug put the pistol under his belt and slowly advanced on the doctor.

"Are you..." Dr Claude St John stuttered. "...are you IRA?"

Haug's voice was low and menacing. "You gonna *wish* I was the IRA, bo. You gonna wish I was Himmler's SS. You gonna wish I was the devil."

Dr St John tried to back up, but there was no place to go. The big man was between him and the door. "What do you want with me? I'm only a doctor."

Haug stopped and pointed to Mainwaring, who was curled into a foetal ball and had his thumb in his mouth. "That man down there on the floor is a very, very close friend of mine."

The doctor stood up straight and tried to be firm. "He is a traitor. And I was just doing my job. You cannot accuse me..."

Haug moved like a big cat and grabbed the man. He wrenched his arm behind him, and with the other hand grabbed his hair, pulling his head back. "Now show me on that shelf behind you what it was you gave my friend."

Dr St John screamed. He had never felt pain like the pain now shooting through his arm and shoulder. "I'll tell you, I'll tell you, let me go!" He pointed wildly at a vial on the shelf.

Haug let go, and the man dropped to his knees, rubbing his shoulder. He picked up the vial and a hypodermic, filling it with the entire contents. Then he kicked the doctor in the back, flattening him on his stomach. With a smooth movement he jabbed the needle in his buttock to the hilt and squeezed the contents into his backside. Finally he snapped off the top of the syringe, leaving the needle inside the flesh.

There was a blanket on top of the black table, and Haug carefully covered Mainwaring's body with it, tucking the sides

255

gently underneath. Behind him he heard the doctor groaning and vomiting. As he picked up his friend, Mainwaring pulled his thumb out of his mouth.

"Sarah? Is that you, Sarah?" he murmured. "Oh, why, my darling? Why? I'm...I'm..."

Haug stood up. Mainwaring was not very heavy, despite his height. He looked down into the face as the civil servant looked up at him with a frightened, puzzled expression. "Who are you?"

Haug stared at his friend and, despite himself, he felt his eyes filling with tears. "I'm takin' you away, Jonathan. It's OK now. Hang in there, ole buddy. We're goin' some place where nobody can hurt you anymore. Some place nice and warm and heavenly. Sarah will be there. Sarah's waitin'..."

"Sarah?" Long, bony fingers grabbed his waistcoat. "Sarah? Sarah?"

Haug held the man close and instinctively kissed the top of his head. His insides were in turmoil as he walked slowly towards the doorway.

Louise Templer still stood beside the van of the pickup truck, frozen to the spot. The suddenness of the violence had shocked her into a kind of catatonia. She could not move. The men had acted so fast, and two human beings lay on the ground, both of them horribly wounded. They were moaning. There had been gunshots all over the house and screams like she had never before heard in her life. Now something was thundering somewhere above her head. Thoughts careered through her mind drunkenly. Were they all killed? What had she got herself into? Since before her teens she had always thought of herself as a decisive girl and woman. She could go into a room full of men and take charge. She could think on her feet. Should she help those two wounded men? Should she stick her head around the door to try and see what was happening? Or should she crawl back into the pickup like Haug advised? Like some *man* suggested?

Her eyes focused suddenly. Haug came through the doorway carrying someone in his arms, and she could see tears streaming down his face. He was crying. Her heart leapt as she rushed forward.

"Oh, no," she said, reaching out to touch the skull-like head protruding from the top of the blanket. Sir Jonathan's greying hair was in a tangle, and she smoothed it down. "Oh, no," she repeated. "Is he...Haug, is he alright?"

"No, he's not alright," Haug said venomously. "He's fucked up. Goddammit. Goddamn those sons of bitches." He shook his head to try and clear it. "Sorry, Louise. This feller means a lot to me."

He moved forward towards the passenger side, kicking aside one of the fig trees and sat down carefully on the seat of the pickup. Gently he rocked Mainwaring back and forth. The civil servant was holding on to Haug's neck with both arms.

Louise Templer stood beside them. "Is there anything I can do?"

"Not right now," Haug replied softly. "He's gonna need a lotta kindness, I think. And a lotta time."

Mainwaring raised his head drunkenly. His voice was a croak. "Father? Did you touch me, Father?"

"Oh, my god," she murmured, biting her lip.

Haug kissed the top of the man's head again and started singing off key as he rocked. "'Rockabye...and goodnight. With roses bedight...' It's OK, Jonathan, it's OK...".

* * *

One Time and Keef rode in the bed of the pickup. Louise Templer sat in the back seat with Mainwaring's head in her lap and his arm around her waist. Nightmare Andy was in the front seat. Haug had bandaged his arm and shoulder after cleaning the wounds. Luckily the bullets had exited from both wounds. The one through the arm looked superficial, but some muscle had been torn in the shoulder. Andy, however, ignored whatever pain he might have felt and ate two sandwiches while Haug drove. Fighting, he said, made him hungry. Haug was relieved no one else had been hurt. The gunfire he heard had worried him. But he could not leave the side of Sir Jonathan Mainwaring

257

to help his friends. It seemed none of the policemen had actually been killed, and that was a relief. A big relief. He had no idea whether they were part of the plot or not. For all they knew, they might have just been doing their duty, thinking they had been attacked by the IRA. There were a couple of them, though, who wouldn't be walking a beat for some time.

It was a little less than seventy miles to Sarah Mainwaring's cottage which was actually her mother's cottage, but her mother was currently recovering from an operation and staying with her sister in London. The sisters were in their eighties and as active as they were forty years ago. It was not a huge house, even though around the turn of the century it had been a mill . A small, crystal clear stream still ran underneath part of the house, though the actual mill had been rebuilt because it was crumbling when Sarah's family purchased the cottage. Sarah Mainwaring loved the house and had many happy memories of her childhood there.

They were all there to meet them as the pickup pulled through the gate and into the drive, and it had just begun to rain a little. Sarah had on a green cardigan which she held closed with both fists. Her white knuckles belied the calm expression on her face as she broke into a hurried walk toward them. Behind her were Matthew Tillson, the Tory MP, General Sir Timothy Portland and Stuart Easton. Further back, at the doorway, were two other men. One was Dr Raymond Sheppard, who was the family GP, and the other was Professor Simon Beauchamp, who held the chair at Guy's Medical School in psychology. Professor Beauchamp's speciality was psychological trauma.

Sarah Mainwaring looked into the cab of the truck as Haug carefully picked up her husband from the rear seat. "Is there anything I can do?" she asked him as she brushed tears from her cheek with one hand.

Haug lifted Mainwaring in his arms. The Perm Sec responded to Sarah's voice and began to moan. "The best thang you can do, ma'am, is just what you're doin'. Bein' here."

Haug followed her up the stairs and into a lovely, bright, warm room which had net curtains pulled back to reveal a view of the meadow. Haug placed him gently down on the bed and patted his shoulder.

"It was my room when I was a child," said Sarah Mainwaring softly as she sat on the edge of the bed and took her husband's hand from under the blanket which still covered him.

Haug nodded. "Which one of those guys is the head doctor?"

"His name is Professor Simon Beauchamp." She pronounced it "Beecham". Turning away from her husband for a moment, she looked up at the American. "I don't know how to thank you, Mr Haug. Because he means a great deal to me."

"He means a lot to me, too, Mrs Mainwarin'." He turned and left the room.

They were all downstairs in the sitting room, which was a large comfortable looking room with plenty of well worn soft armchairs and sofas. But no one was sitting except Nightmare Andy. Dr Sheppard was carefully re-dressing his wounds.

"Professor Beauchamp?" he enquired as he entered the room.

The distinguished man in his 50's stepped forward and extended his hand. He had very curly hair, receding and cut short. "I understand you're the hero, Mr Haug."

Haug shook the hand. "Professor, I think you and the doc should go up soon, but I just wanna say somethin' to you both. You may be scientists and medical people, but I know somethin' about what's happened to that man upstairs, so I'm gonna give you a little piece of my advice, for what it's worth. Whatever you do - and I'm sure it'll be the right thang - give him kindness and warmth. Lissen to any tale he wants to tell without givin' a lotta advice about it. And reassure the man. For one thang, he's gonna have no confidence left, and he's gonna think he's an asshole for bein' weak and givin' in. Well, he's not, because there's no man on earth can bear that kinda pressure. No, Professor, he's the hero, not me. Him and these guys with me. They took all the bullets while all I did was get Mainwarin' out."

Professor Beauchamp smiled benignly. "It sounds as if you could possibly do my job as well as you do your own." He moved past Haug and Dr Sheppard followed him. "I think we

259

better go up now. Lady Mainwaring made us promise to give her a few minutes alone with him."

Haug and Louise went with Keef, One Time and Andy back to the pickup. Haug told his friends he was going to stay on at the cottage for a while until he was sure Mainwaring was out of trouble. He asked Keef to drive the others back to London and keep the pickup for him until he returned. Then he peeled off the phony registration numbers and threw Keef the keys.

"Remember," he said to Keef. "That thang can push out seven hundred horsepower. It's not like these puny European cars."

"Yeah," Keef grinned. "I know."

"Also, it's got a busted rear light, so you better take it around to my garage tomorrow. I'll get the dents knocked out later."

They waved them off, and Haug winced as Keef spun the wheels, and the pickup fishtailed down the road.

Louise Temper turned to him. "Let's take a walk."

"Hell, it's rainin'."

"So what?" she asked, starting off toward the stream.

"Yeah, OK. Skin's waterproof," he replied, following her.

They walked to the stream and turned away from the house, following along the bank. It was not yet raining heavily, but the drops were getting heavier. There was a fence on the other side of the bank, but Haug could see no cattle and didn't know whether or not the land belonged to the old mill.

"Do you think he will recover?" Louise Templer asked. She was walking in front of him on the path.

"I don't know," Haug replied. "Somethin' like that affects people in different ways. He's under the influence of a strong drug right now. That's one of the reasons I wanted to wait around. To see how he comes out of it. The problem is, they were tryin' to get the information outta him as quickly as possible, so they were hammerin' at him day and night, usin' a lotta powerful stuff. That's my guess, anyway. Sometimes they go about it slower, and that can be worse in the long run." Haug walked on a few steps. "I'd say he had a good chance."

"How could anyone do something like that?" she asked bitterly.

260

Haug stopped her and turned her around. "You do it 'cause you think it's *right*, Louise. If you thought it was right, you'd do it yourself. Everybody's got to admit that in themselves."

"Bollocks. I'd *never* do that to another human being." She was getting wet and her hair was sticking to the sides of her face.

He pointed his index finger at her chest. "In there you got emotions in places you probably don't even know you got places. They work for you or against you. They don't come up by arithmetic or logic. They come up 'cause they feel you need 'em. Now you tell me the answer to this question: if one person knows where your only child is bein' held and raped, and he won't tell you, what the fuck are you gonna do? Reason with him? Beg him? And if he still won't tell? You start hackin' lumps offa the son of a bitch or runnin' hatpins through his balls. And your emotions will give you the strength to do all that because you know - not *think* - you *know* it's the right thang to do."

She spun away angrily and walked on, her head down. The rain was coming down harder now, and Haug could see the drops splattering on the water.

"And when they're against you?" he heard her say against the sound of the rain as she continued to walk with her head down.

"What?"

"Your emotions."

"They're always tryin' to help," he said, stumbling over a rock. His boots were not ideal for a slippery bank. "They're tryin' to help Jonathan right now. They're tryin' to take his mind somewhere safe, like in childhood. When I found him, he was curled into a ball on the floor. His emotions were doin' the best they could for him. Torturers know that, the good ones. That's what they use as a tool against you."

She stopped at a tree, turned and leaned her arm against it. "You still haven't told me what you do when emotions are against you. Why they're against you. How."

The bill of Haug's cap was dripping, and he stared at her for a moment. "They're old thangs, emotions. Been around in the race probably before it was even a race. And they're strong.

261

They need to be. And they don't lissen very well when you tell 'em you're married and don't want to betray your husband."

She held his eyes steadily. "You bastard. You know."

"'Course I know," he said quietly. "I knew since the first time we looked at each other."

She slapped Haug across his face as hard as she could, but he didn't move. He just stood and looked at her. Then she stepped over to him and put her arms around his chest, hugging him as hard as she could. He slowly put his arms around her and caressed the wetness of her head with a big hand. They swayed in the embrace for several minutes, and the sounds seemed to be amplified. The rain on the tree above, the water falling onto them from the leaves. The stream sounded like an ocean.

She pulled away from him slowly and touched his cheek. Then she reached up and kissed it. "I'm sorry, Haug. I didn't mean to hit you."

"That's emotion for you." He looked down in her face, now streaming with water. She wore no makeup, and the wetness, framed by damp hair pressed to her head made her absolutely beautiful. When he kissed her, he could taste the rain at first before he could taste her. The rain was cool, and the inside of her mouth was warm and tender. Her tongue sought out his, then ran along the roof of his mouth, behind his teeth. He felt her breathing heavily, and her body began moving against him. So small and compact but so strong, too, like a demon.

And the demons were invading Louise Temper's spiralling thoughts, the demon of guilt losing to the mighty demon of desire. She could never remember wanting a man like this before. Before today she could not even admit it to herself. The guilt demon screamed Why? as it retreated in panic before the awful, wonderful surge that roared in her ears, drowning even the rush of water behind her. She didn't know the answer. She didn't know why. He was not her "type", he was not this, he was not that, but, damn it, he was so *real*. When she felt his hand on her breast, gently stroking the nipple through her bra, she hardly knew what she was doing anymore. She realised almost with a blush that she was grappling hopelessly with his belt buckle, wanting to rip his jeans off, tear them off. He unbuttoned her blouse, and she suddenly pulled away from him to get the thing off. Her bra followed, then she struggled out of her own jeans. The man was already naked, and she did not bother with her socks but simply leapt at Haug as nimbly as a lemur. She landed with her arms around his neck and her legs locked on his hips. As they kissed again, she felt him lose his footing on the slippery bank, but at that point she didn't care. All she wanted was their skin touching. Terrifyingly she felt a sudden desire to tear him open and crawl inside, licking everything in a frenzy.

They slid down the bank into the water, which was cold, and she straddled him like a porpoise. Suddenly she could feel the mossy rocks beneath her feet and knees. It was not deep, and Haug was not completely under water. His hands seemed to be everywhere, and everywhere they touched left a burn in her flesh, contrasting with the freezing water of the stream. When she felt the hardness of his penis beneath her she instinctively reached around and grasped it like a handle before guiding it towards her vagina. It went in slowly, and she could feel it stretching her. Every nerve in her loins tingled. The rain was pelting down now, and Haug was laughing happily, rolling in the water beneath her. She realised she was laughing, too.

"Fuck you, Haug!" she screamed, pounding him on the chest with her fist. He was completely inside her now, and she sat up on him, waving her arms in the air like a mad woman. "Fuck you! Fuck you! You bastard!" She pounded him again with her fist. Again and again. Then he grabbed her wrists, and she swayed against him with all her strength. And then she was there. In the very middle of a holocaust. She heaved and screamed at the top of her lungs, wrenching her trapped arms with the weight of her whole body. She shook her breasts and felt their weight and the water flying from them. It was so overpowering she wondered for a moment if she was going to die. There. Then. Wave after wave hit her, rolling her up and then down, helplessly, like a cork in angry seas. Again and again she shook her breasts, loving the sinful feeling as the man below heaved beneath her. Her eyes were tightly closed, but she imagined a crowd, an audience watching her, men looking on in awe as she shamelessly exposed the wildness which had finally burst through. Laughing and screaming with glee, she dipped her head down to Haug's mouth. He let her wrists go, and she clung to his neck as her pelvis continued to move. He was coming, she knew that, and his arms were crushing her to him. Both of them rolled in the water, over to one bank, then back to the other. Mossy stones bruised her body, but she did not care any longer. Her nose and ears were full of water when she heard him bellowing like a water buffalo. The image struck her as hilarious. A *water* buffalo! She wanted to feel everything. The stones underneath her, the cold rushing water, the rain, the man's body and his penis still in spasm, his wonderful hands, his chest and shoulders.

They lay still in the stream for a few moments, clasping their bodies together almost in desperation, before awkwardly disengaging and crawling out slowly like weary amphibians, collapsing on the wet leaves of the bank. Gradually Louise Templer realised how cold she was.

With an effort she raised herself up on her elbows. "My god, Haug. I've never done that before in my life. I've never even made love out of doors." She was shivering, and Haug collected her in his arms again. His body seemed a lot warmer than hers.

"Well," he said. "You looked like you were enjoyin' yourself."

She pulled away slightly. "I wasn't ridiculous, was I?"

"You were fuckin' great. That's what sex is supposed to be like."

"Is it?" she asked, touching her cheek to his. "Oh, I feel so guilty now."

"About your husband?"

"Well, yes. But mostly about Sir Jonathan. While he's lying back there in some kind of hell, we're enjoying ourselves. Like animals."

"You're thinkin' logical again, aren't you? Life isn't arithmetic, like I said. Two and two don't always add up to four."

"I think it was the violence," she said softly. "I was frozen to the spot. Couldn't move. Yet I was fascinated. Like vertigo. And then, after all that, you were carrying out poor Sir Jonathan with tears streaming down your face. It moved me so much. The hideous brutality, then the gentleness and love."

They held on to each other underneath the dripping tree, cold and wet but reluctant to break the embrace.

CHAPTER FIFTEEN

"What the hell kind of organisation have you got over here, Regis? Are you telling me a safe house was attacked and seven armed men couldn't hold it? Right here in the middle of England?" Dr Carlton Fine was standing in the large lounge facing the patio terrace where they had been sitting that morning. It was now raining, and the French doors were closed. He turned back to Regis, who was still by the desk where he had put down the telephone a few moments before.

"I spoke to the Detective Inspector in charge, Carlton. It was a ferocious attack. DI Green has never seen anything like it before. Walls were battered down, and there must have been twenty attackers, all armed with machine guns and clubs. Green managed to get the registration number of the vehicle, but I already know the man who led the group."

Fine spun around sharply. "You *know* him?"

"Our paths crossed last year," Regis said. He appeared quite calm and unruffled, but beneath this carefully constructed exterior, he was seething with anger himself. "In fact he is one of your countrymen. An ex-Congressional Medal of Honour winner."

Carlton Fine laughed cynically. "Well, I guess that explains how the mission succeeded, if he was American. A CMH winner, you say?"

"Yes," Regis replied. "Apparently he returned the medal to the Congressional authorities when he became disillusioned with the Vietnam War where he won it. There were a number of other important decorations as well. Widely reported in the States at the time. His name is Joe Wayne Haug. A redneck from North Carolina."

"Sounds like he's one hell of a redneck," Fine said with ironical pride.

Regis drummed his fingers on the desk. "I'm going to have to do something about him."

"Police?" asked Fine.

"I think not," said Regis. "We don't want him broadcasting what he knows from a courtroom."

"Well, if it's going to be a wet job, you better make sure this time. Mainwaring escaping is bad enough. It looks like things are starting to unravel."

Regis leaned on the desk with both hands, looking down at the highly polished surface. "I have a suspicion this redneck is the key. He may be acting as their protection, he and his gang. When we sweep him out of the way, perhaps the others won't be much of a problem."

"I hope you have somebody in mind. Somebody good, Michael."

"In fact, I do. He knows Haug, so he won't underrate him. A straightforward hit. It shouldn't be too difficult." Regis looked at Carlton Fine and smiled grimly.

* * *

Corky DeLoop was lying on the floor of a funhouse room. Except it was not much of a funhouse, and she was crying. It was hard keeping her eyes open, because the rubbery, swaying walls, the long undulating desk and the wobbly chairs made her feel nauseous. There were two men in the room with her. One was sitting at the desk. That was Gillmore. She guessed the other one was a doctor. Both looked like they walked out of funhouse mirrors. She could hear what they said, but something was wrong with her vision.

Gillmore had arrived...she didn't know when he arrived. A long, long time ago, it seemed. She hadn't slept. They gave her drugs to keep her awake, but she was sure at least one night had passed. Time meant nothing with the white walls of her cell, and in this room, the funhouse room, the walls were white, too. There were windows high up, but curtains were drawn. Both rooms were drenched in the most awful white light.

At some point two orderlies in white uniforms came to her cell and held her down while the doctor gave her an injection. Whatever it was made her wobbly and weak. She could walk, but only with great concentration. She could talk, too, but only

268

slowly. They had dragged her into this room, put collars around her neck and wrists, which were pulled behind her and locked together. A chain from the collar on her neck was attached to her wrists, keeping them high behind her. Then they taped something to her nipples, pulled her legs open and attached something else down there. She had tried to fight, to kick, but it was hopeless, like moving in molasses.

When she received the first jolt, it was a kind of pain she had never before imagined. Much, much worse than a dentist drilling through a nerve in her tooth. It was biting, sharp, overpowering, terrible.

That is why she was crying. She simply could not bear the pain. Gillmore was doing it, pressing a button on the desk somewhere. She knew Gillmore, but something was wrong with her memory. She couldn't remember *how* she knew him. Did she *hate* him? She couldn't remember.

Harvey Gillmore looked over at Dr Horace Cranley. Cranley was a chubby little man, only a little taller than the newspaper publisher. Tufts of white hair circled his bald cranium, which was as ruddy as his face. His hands were chubby, too, and his fingers looked like little sausages.

"She's getting there," said Dr Cranley. "Oh, yes. She's getting there. By the end of the day we should be able to lower the concentration of drugs and look for a maintenance dosage." He turned to look at Gillmore. "That's what you want, isn't it?"

The Australian didn't answer. He was looking at the notes beside the tape recorder. "Do you think this is all she knows? A black man. Doesn't know his name. She met him as he tried to climb into the Matilda, took to him and they fucked. He talked her into putting the bug into the light fixture. They met once at a beach. Fucked again. The abo was with another white man, name may be O'Connell." He looked up at Dr Cranley. "Do you think that's it?"

Cranley nodded rapidly. "Oh, yes. I'm sure that's it. That's all she knows. I can tell, Mr Gillmore. I can tell when they reach the bottom."

"OK, doc, that's it. Leave her with me."

269

Cranley rubbed his chubby hands together as he moved towards the door, smiling nervously. "If you need anything, just call." He checked his watch. "You've about four hours before she's due for her next injection."

Gillmore watched the doctor close the door. From his briefcase he pulled out a plastic bag. He took a pair of red high heeled shoes from the plastic bag and set them on the edge of the desk. He chose them from a specialist shop in the south of London using a pair of Corky's own shoes to get the right size. The ones he bought had open toes. They also had six inch heels with ankle straps.

As he got up from the desk and walked over to the prone naked body of the DeLoop woman, Harvey Gillmore realised just how much he had been anticipating this. Corky DeLoop was one big, beautiful woman with an attitude problem he looked forward to correcting. He leaned down and grabbed a handful of tangled platinum hair and pulled. She started howling but finally came up on her knees. He held her head back and leaned close to her face.

"Remember me?" he asked.

She was thinking. "Harvey Gillmore," she said finally.

He smacked her across the cheek hard. "*Mr* Gillmore. Never Harvey. Who am I?"

Again she thought. Her eyes were glazed with fright. "Mr. Mr Gillmore."

Still holding her by the hair with one hand, he put the other one underneath her breast and jiggled it up and down. "Now I can do this anytime I want, can't I? Anytime."

Something was churning inside her, and Corky couldn't recognise the emotion. But she found some words. "Go fuck yourself, asshole."

Angrily Gillmore tugged her forward by her hair. She walked slowly, one knee at a time until she reached the desk. "Say that again, you bitch."

Corky tried to remember the words. "Asshole. Fuck yourself."

Instantly Gillmore pushed the button on the console, letting go of her hair. Her body arched backwards as she opened her mouth in a blood curdling scream. He held down the button for a full four seconds, the maximum, as she screamed and flailed her legs in the air. He felt himself becoming quite aroused as he watched the helpless woman writhe on the carpet. Her tits were jiggling like jelly and her legs flailed wildly. Releasing the button, he stepped over and grabbed her hair again, slowly pulling her back up on her knees. Again he put his face in hers.

"If you ever say anything like that again to me, you bitch, I'll give you a dose twice that long. Understand?"

She was convulsed with sobbing and did not answer him immediately. Gillmore dropped her head and went for the button. As Corky DeLoop realised what he was doing she panicked and pleaded for him not to, but almost at once the indescribable pain began again. It felt as if her nipples were being seared in hot boiling fat, and the pain shooting through her abdomen was utterly crippling. A fiery poker from a roaring forge couldn't have been worse. She had never coped with this kind of pain before. It was beyond the horizon of anything she had ever imagined.

The man had her hair again, and his undulating face was in front of hers. Fear of that face was beginning to possess her, and instinctively she recoiled from it this time. Her cheeks were wet with tears, and she could not stop crying.

"Now, we'll try again, sheila. *Understand?*"

"Yes!" she said as fast as she could say it. "Yes, yes, yes, yes, yes..."

He was pulling her hair out at the roots. "Yes, *what*, you cunt? It's always either 'sir' or 'Mr Gillmore', never anything else. Do you understand?"

"Yes, Mr Gillmore, yes, sir, yes, Mr Gillmore, yes, sir..." she said as fast as she could.

He was still holding her hair. "I'm your teacher, sheila. I'm going to teach you how to behave to me and to your husband. Do you understand?"

"Yes, sir. Yes, Mr Gillmore." What was he asking? Corky wasn't sure. Wanted her to behave. OK, OK, boss. No more, no more pain right now. I just can't take it. Make him happy, whatever it takes, keep him away from that button... He let go of her hair, and she started to collapse forward, she felt so weak. Then again he grabbed her hair, harder this time. It felt like he was scalping her and she screamed again.

"Up straight. With your head up, bitch, shoulders back," he snarled at her.

Fear coursed through her body, as she was certain he was going to reach for the button again. Fear gave her the strength to keep her body rigidly upright as she knelt on the floor in front of the big desk. His hand was hovering over the desk, and she heard herself praying, praying out loud.

"Please, please, please, Mr Gillmore. I will.." What was the word? What was the word? She couldn't think. "I will...behave."

The face leaned toward her again. "I *know* you're going to behave. You're going to do *more* than behave, sheila. I remember you out on the Matilda, prancing around like you were too good for me. The fact is, you're not good enough. So you've got to learn. And I am your teacher, bitch. Right now you are a filthy bitch. Filthy bitch. Say it!"

For an instant a horrible force rose in Corky, a rebellion so strong she very nearly did not contain it. Then that force crashed together with the awful fear and crumbled. Just crumbled. She started crying again. She couldn't help it.

"Say it! You're a filthy bitch!"

"I'm a filthy bitch, Mr Gillmore."

"A dirty slut. Tell me that, too," Gillmore said. "And this time say it like you mean it, or I'll turn this thing on and hold it down til my thumb gets cramps."

Fear rolled around inside her, recoiling and striking like a gigantic poisonous cobra. The great hooded head of the cobra struck absolute terror into her.

"I am a dirty slut," she said, then immediately tried again. "I am a dirty slut, Mr Gillmore, sir."

"That was a little better," the Australian said, relaxing. He patted the top of her head. "Good girl."

The fear receded, and immediately she felt better. Thank god she had done something right for him. She focused her eyes through her tears. He seemed to be letting down his trousers and taking them off. Carefully folding them, he placed the trousers on the desk. The desk! No! Fear gripped her for a moment. Then he took down his underpants and put them on top of the trousers. When he turned back around, Corky did her best to keep her body upright and her eyes forward. But she saw his prick from the corner of her eye, and it seemed to be nearly erect. It was a big one. Or was that her vision? The room wouldn't stay still. Now what was she just thinking? The man approached her, and the penis - yes, that's what she was thinking - the penis was a big one. It stopped about two inches from her nose. He was talking again.

"A few minutes ago, you dirty slut, you called me an arsehole. Or as you Yankees say, *ass*hole. So I'm going to let you kiss my arsehole. You're going to kiss my arsehole and tell me again you're a filthy slut. Now listen carefully to me." He grabbed her hair and pushed her head back. "When I bend over my hand will be near the button. You remember the button?"

Corky felt her eyes widen in fear. "No, no, no, please, please, Mr Gillmore..."

"Then do everything I tell you the instant I tell you to do it. Understand?"

"Yes, sir. Yes, Mr Gillmore." Her heart was thundering, and she was trying to clear her head so she could think clearly and remember. Must listen, must listen, must listen. Concentrate. The man was bending over in front of her, his bottom close to her face.

"I'm spreading my cheeks now, slut. Can you see it?"

Concentrating as hard as she could she looked at the little pink hole. "Yes, sir, I see it."

"Now kiss it."

Immediately Corky pressed her lips against the little pink hole and kissed. She kissed it again and again, hoping desperately he would not press that button again. Then she heard him speak again.

"Lick it. Lick it clean, and tell me what a dirty slut you are. And you better mean it."

Corky put out her tongue and licked the pink hole, licked it over and over, hoping it was good enough for him. There was a

273

faint taste which was unpleasant, but she ignored it. "I'm a dirty slut," she said. "I'm a dirty slut. I'm a dirty slut..." He stood up suddenly and turned around. The penis was more erect now and pointed directly at her.

"You certainly are," he said. "I bet you never thought you would say that to me, eh? Or lick my fucking arse. Remember that, you slut. You have licked my fucking arse. And I have recorded it on camera. You are an arse licker, aren't you?"

"Yes, Mr Gillmore, I'm an arse licker. And a dirty slut, sir," she added quickly, hoping to please him.

"Now," he said. "Put my prick in your mouth and suck it. Suck it like your life depends on it."

He pushed it toward her, and she opened her mouth to receive it. She felt his hand grab the back of her head, and he pushed it in brutally, so it went right to the back of her throat. She couldn't breathe, and then she started to gag before he pulled back and stabbed forward again. She opened her eyes as she heard him speak again.

"Keep telling me you're a dirty slut while you're sucking. Over and over, just keep saying it, even if it comes out as a mumble. Every time you say it I want you to see a picture of yourself. Dirty. Offering to give anybody a blow job, anybody. For a dollar. A dollar a blow job."

She tried to say it, but her tongue was depressed by his penis, but she tried, over and over. And the images came. She was ugly and toothless. Her breasts sagged, and her hair was unwashed. Her clothes were old and loose and didn't fit. Horrible, horrible. She was in a dirty toilet with some filthy bum, sucking his dick, and he gave her a dollar and laughed.

"Hey," said Gillmore, his voice light. "I'm coming! You're lucky. This is the first time in a long while. I want you to drink it all, you dirty slut, you lucky dirty slut..."

Corky felt the spasms as he came. He still had his hand behind her head and forced his large penis further down her throat before withdrawing and pushing forward again. It became quicker and quicker, and she tasted the sticky fluid which seemed to fill her mouth around his organ. Though she was trying to swallow, it was difficult with the movement. Then, suddenly, he was finished. He pulled out. She closed her eyes as he wiped his organ on her face. Finally, she swallowed the warm fluid in her mouth, again nearly gagging. He was still wiping himself back and forth across her cheeks and forehead, in her hair.

"Don't wipe that off," he said. "I want it to dry there to remind you who your boss is."

Her eyes were still closed, but she heard him getting into his trousers again. The images wouldn't stop, no matter how she tried. She felt so dirty. She remembered seeing a prostitute in Houston once. A woman in her mid-forties, she stood on the corner with torn fishnet hose and run down high heels, a tatty red dress and phony silver bracelets. Corky remembered laughing at the time, but now she realised it was her. The realisation revolted and frightened her, and she shook her head, trying to get away from the visualizations. She was worthless, he said so. For a moment another thought tried to shoulder its way in, a thought with "So What?" hung around its neck. She opened her eyes. He was doing something else to her. Oh, my god, he was releasing her arms. She gasped from the pain as her arms fell to her sides. Muscles which had been stretched and held in one way so long were now nearly limp and useless. Rubbing her elbows and shoulders they felt better, much better. He was talking, so she concentrated again. Must concentrate.

"There, you are, sheila. That's for giving me a real good blow job." He shook his finger in her face. "If you play your cards right, I might let you do it again sometime. I might even let you stand up one of these days. But right now, I want to see you crawling around. Like sluts. Sluts crawl. Now, follow me over to my desk like a doggie."

Her arms would barely support her, but she crawled after him as best she could, swaying from side to side as her hair fell into her face. He sat down in his chair, and she crawled up beside him. When she looked up he had a long cane in his hand.

"Remember, sheila, when you said you wouldn't take a beating? That's all changed now, isn't it? Every time you give me any trouble, you get six to twelve. Do you understand?"

275

"Yes, Mr Gillmore," she said as quickly as she could. Before she knew what was happening he suddenly leaned forward and whacked her across the bottom with it. The sting was shocking, and the inside of her whole head seemed momentarily to light up. She crouched down in terror.

"Back up on your hands and knees," she heard him hiss and struggled up. "Now beg me for another one, and push your arse around here so I can get a proper swing at it."

She looked up at the man imploringly and saw his hand hovering over the awful button. Again she panicked and scrabbled around so her bottom was towards him. Closing her eyes and clenching her fists she yelled. "Please, please, Mr Gillmore, hit me again! Please sir! I'm a dirty slut, sir! Please hit me again!"

"Alright. Since you really want it."

The pain again. The dreadful stinging pain. How much pain could she bear? No more, no more. Please.

"Now, stand up, whore, and sit on this desk in front of me. And listen carefully. You're excited, very excited. You want to have sex, but you can't. So sit here in front of me," he patted the desk. "Lean back on your arms, spread your legs with your knees up, and show me your pussy."

Slowly she struggled to her feet a little dizzily and caught the edge of the desk to steady herself. When she put her bottom on it, there was coldness and pain, but she moved awkwardly, trying to remember what he had said. She felt him tapping her with the cane to guide her into position. But she tried not to look at the black box with a red button on top which lurked near his hand. She was feeling giddy. Funny. Images returned, and she was in a whorehouse somewhere, on a bed. A man, a big man was fucking her. Why was she there? What made her think of that? Was she a whore? Yes, a dirty slut. The image changed to a street corner, and she had on a torn red dress, pulled up to her waist, and a man was sticking it in her....

Harvey Gillmore leaned back in his chair and contemplated the open legs and sex organs of the woman on his desk, allowing himself one of his rare smiles. Well, who would have thought it? The big tigress is just a little pussy. They can all be tamed, if you use the right methods. Mollycoddling, that was what was wrong with women today. He put his hand forward and spread her vagina with two fingers. As he suspected she was wet. There was a little wire protruding, the end of which was taped to her thigh. Plenty of room for fingers, though, so he pushed them in, and she moved her hips. The doc had told him this drug made her highly suggestible. They called it a chemical hypnotic. Well, he would have to order up a few cases of this stuff. He reached over and grabbed the shoes, holding them up for her to see.

"Look, whore," he said softly. "Aren't they beautiful? Aren't these the most beautiful shoes you have ever seen?"

Corky opened her eyes, and her mouth fell open. Where had he found such wonderful shoes? She would *die* for a pair like that. They were gorgeous. Putting her weight on one arm, she reached out for them.

Gillmore pulled them away. "Oh, no you don't. I *might* let you wear them, if you're good. But only if you're good. You'd be a pretty whore in these, instead of a sickening, ugly whore."

Gillmore laughed as he saw the disappointment on her face as he put the shoes back on the desk. The laugh made a strange sound in the room. Now for the coup de grace, he thought, the real whackeroo. He reached under the desk and pulled out a mirror which he placed in his lap, facing her.

"Look at the dirty slut. Look at the filthy whore. Look at her. Look at her saggy old tits and her gaping, poxy cunt, her fat ugly thighs and her fat ugly belly. Look at her. That's you."

The horror was nearly too much to bear as Corky DeLoop stared at herself in the mirror. Her face was grey and sagging and her hair sparse and white, sticking up in tufts. Dirty wrinkled flesh hung from her body in folds. Her breasts were rubbery sand filled socks rolling sideways into her armpits. Lumpy, veined legs spread away from an awful gaping ugly slash with something slimy crawling from the top of it.

"Oh, no," she murmured softly. "No..no, no, no. Please, no. Please, take her away."

"Keep looking," he said. "That's the *real* Corky DeLoop."

* * *

Professor Simon Beauchamp stood in the dining room facing the group who watched him expectantly. Sarah Mainwaring was standing in the doorway, and everyone else was sitting. Like many in his profession, his face gave nothing away. Carefully he rested his hands on the back of a straight chair, as if on a lectern.

"I'll begin in reverse," he said. "With the prognosis. I know this concerns you all. Sir Jonathan will recover, and the recovery should be complete, though it may take some time. The period varies with the individual. Theoretically it is possible he will be quite normal tomorrow. Perhaps he will, I can't say. I plan to visit him here once a day, until I am convinced he is well on the road to this recovery."

He stopped for a moment and rapped his fingers on the top of the chair as if searching for words. "During the course of my examination, I admit to becoming quite upset. Quite angry. Furious, in fact. The physical manifestations were few, but I was able to ascertain that some...objects had been attached to the areolae and nipples and to his genitalia, both penis and testicles. There are no burns to the areas.

"I have taken a sample of blood, which, I might add, was extremely difficult under the circumstances. Sir Jonathan is exceedingly sensitive to pain. I would not have persisted if it weren't necessary to confirm my own tentative diagnosis with laboratory analysis."

Again Professor Beauchamp paused, this time looking around the room. "I have not been told what has happened to Sir Jonathan beyond rather sketchy details, and, from the nature of the company gathered, I doubt I ever will know." Pausing again, he took off his spectacles and held them in one hand. "There are certain psychotropic drugs which are unavailable either on the market or the black market or even to professionals like myself. I do, however, know of their existence. Without reservation I condemn them. They have no known medical uses, nor am I convinced they have any value whatsoever in psychology. They have been developed for - and in some cases by - the security

278

services of the world. I am terribly sorry if I offend anyone present, but I have to say I condemn the usage of these drugs in *any* circumstances on my fellow human beings."

Again he paused as he put his glasses back on and looked severely around the room. "I won't trouble you with the name of the drug I suspect has been used on Sir Jonathan, but I will tell you something about it. It magnifies and enhances physical pain, which assists those who apply pain to human beings, for it leaves no traces. It also has the 'benefit' of not threatening other organs. Electricity, for instance, can be applied at lower voltage and wattage. On the one hand there are no indications of burns, on the other the heart is left undamaged. In other words, the pain is mostly psychological - which is not to say it is not 'real' to the subject. On the contrary, it is terrifyingly real. This drug is often used in conjunction with another one, closely related chemically, which heightens the subject's suggestibility, particularly when combined with sleep deprivation.

"As you know we all have doubts within. It's a part of the human condition. Magnify the doubts and suppress self esteem by constant feedback, and you begin the destruction of consciousness. This drug acts exactly that way. As a feedback. Initially it was thought it may have conventional psychiatric uses, for, of course, one can feed back self esteem as well. It was later discarded as far, far too dangerous.

"The effects of the drug are now wearing off, though its somewhat toxic nature will leave him with a hangover. I have given Sir Jonathan a muscle relaxant, and Dr Sheppard has prescribed some sleeping pills. At this time sleep is the best doctor in the house for him. I will return tomorrow morning to check on his progress." He turned, picked up his case and left the room.

"Hell," Haug said. "Sounded like he thought we did it to him." He was sitting on a sofa in a dressing gown which was too tight for him, and Louise Templer sat opposite him in one much too large. Their wet clothes had been put in the tumble dryer. He had given the others a brief description of the raid on Unit G3, including the estimated damage, before Professor Beauchamp had come downstairs.

279

"I also know of the existence of these drugs," said General Sir Timothy Portland, "and I share the Professor's distaste for them." The General was a tall, lean man in his early 60's but looked younger. His remaining hair was combed straight back on his head and was as neatly trimmed as his moustache. He was the only man in the room wearing a suit and sat in a straight-backed chair with his legs crossed and his hands folded on his lap.

"What will their reaction be, I wonder?" asked Stuart Easton, as much to himself as to the others. "Will the police be brought into it?"

"They may, but I doubt it," said General Portland. "I guarantee one thing, though. They will be duly impressed."

"Impressed enough to back off, I hope," said Louise Templer.

General Portland shook his head. "On the contrary, I'm afraid. They will be looking for retribution by striking again at Sir Jonathan or attacking one or more of us."

"Well, General," Haug said, "I got a somewhat limited army here. I cain't protect everbody all the time. Personally I think we gotta do somethin' ourselves instead of sittin' around waitin' to see what they're gonna do. That's always a good way to lose."

General Portland smiled. "There speaks a former army man. I was going to suggest one gambit here, but since it carries some degree of risk, I will have to confirm your agreement first. I would like to make an approach to Sir Gerald Humphries..."

"London Commissioner of Police," Stuart Easton snorted. "*Very* risky."

"Though his loyalties are unknown," Portland continued, "I have been making detailed enquiries. Know him slightly myself, actually. Member of my club. Put it this way: I do not think he is *un*sound."

"Would he not be obliged to present the matter to the Home Secretary?" asked Louise Templer.

"Who is *definitely* unsound," said Matthew Tillson. "I can assure you of that."

280

"That is the principal part of the risk we would have to take," Portland replied. "Because, without exception, everybody describes him as 'a good honest copper.' And all that means. Indeed he may feel it his duty to report the matter to the Home Secretary whatever the consequences. On the other hand, I may be able to present it to him in such a way that I enlist his support directly under the Crown."

"I'm against it, Timothy," Easton said decisively.

"Now lissen Stuart," Haug said. "This is gettin' to be a very risky business. I have already said I cain't cover all of you. If they made a *real* effort, maybe I couldn't even cover one of you. Bullets actually go through me just like everbody else. The cops would be very, very useful in dealin' with these Direct Action groups they got lurkin' around. I reckon they only use Special Branch - normally - for wire tappin' and surveillance. Now those Direct Action guys don't fuck around. They're killers and thugs. Right now they can roam all over London without worryin' about cops. If they're picked up with a wheelbarrow fulla machine guns, the Specials say, it's OK, we're dealin' with that, and the normal cops back off. But if this police chief knows what's goin' on, I guess he's gonna be mad enough to stomp a hole in a concrete floor. I tell you, I would. What he's not gonna like is havin' one police force against another one."

"That's precisely my point," said Easton. "Policemen are policemen. The first - or maybe second - thing Humphries will do is call in the head of Special Branch to get an explanation. He will be told we are a bunch of loonies plotting the overthrow of the State, and he will back it up with a call to MI5. You, Timothy, will be portrayed as an ex-Army officer whose judgment has been affected by drink..."

Haug held up a hand. "We hold one high card here, Stuart. I'd like Jonathan's opinion on whether or not to play it now, but he's sick. So we have to decide. We've got tapes. We got the ones from last year, and we've got the ones from Corfu. The ones from Corfu mention the head of Special Branch - Gordon somebody - and how he works with 'em. And we've got the voice of Jeremy Evans on the tape. Deputy Director of MI6."

"Where are the new tapes, incidentally?" Louise asked him.

"I gave them to Keef. As soon as he gets back to London, he's gonna have copies made. My secretary will send the sets of copies to the same people who hold copies of the first tapes. These are dispersed. One address is in America. Then I'll bury one set and we'll have another one to play with. If I die, the sets will be sent to heads of committees."

"We ought to have them transcribed as soon as possible," she said.

"Yeah," he said. "Lizzy'll be on to that today. Keef and One Time will keep guard while it's all bein' done, and that'll make her mad. She reckons she can handle herself and any ten good men. And she might be right, but I'm gonna be kinda nervous until they're safe. They've got no way of knowin' we've got 'em, but I'd rather be on the safe side. Act as though they do know, and you won't be surprised. I don't like a lotta surprises in my life."

"When will the transcripts be ready?" asked Easton.

Haug thought a minute. "I reckon it'll take her two days."

General Portland clasped his hands together. "As soon as the transcripts are ready, I propose an approach be made to Humphries."

Easton shook his head. "Too risky, Timothy. I think something as risky as this needs to be voted on by the membership."

"No time," said Haug. "We gotta use our best judgment now. They gonna be down our throats with both feet before we got time to spit. If the risk pans out, at least we got the police with us."

Easton finally agreed, and he, Matthew Tillson and General Portland left for London. Louise and Haug looked in on Mainwaring, but he was in a deep sleep, Sarah by his side. Later she made a small meal of cold cuts, bread and cheese, and the three of them talked quietly together before the two visitors said they were very tired and were shown their bedrooms upstairs on the second floor. Haug helped Mainwaring's wife move a folding bed into her husband's room so she could sleep at his side.

Haug couldn't sleep, although every muscle felt stretched, every joint twisted. He lay under the covers with the small bedside lamp on, staring at the ceiling. He had not told the others his real feelings about just how dangerous things were. They were all in danger now. Rank meant nothing. He wished Jonathan were well. He would know what to do. Or at least he would have a better idea than Haug. He hoped he had done the right thing downstairs, backing General Portland. They had to do something, to try and gain the initiative. Action was nearly always better than reaction. Any bar room fighter would tell you that. And Haug knew he was not much better than a bar room fighter thrown into a very complicated situation.

His thoughts were interrupted by a tiny tap at his door. Louise Templer put her head through.

"You asleep?"

"Come on in," he said. "Maybe you can help stop me worryin'."

She was barefoot and wore the same dressing gown. Clasping her arms together she sat on the foot of his bed.

"I nearly went back with the others," she said, looking down at the floor. "But I didn't think we should just leave it like that, after this afternoon. I don't know what I want to say to you, Haug, so forgive me if it all comes out wrong. I've never had an experience like this afternoon. I don't suppose I've ever looked for one, either. Though I don't think I was looking for that one. I know I wasn't. You disturb me and have done from the beginning. At first I thought you were just an American lout with tattoos on your arms with a lot of muscle and few brains. I was wrong about the brains and wrong about the American lout. Most of all, I've been wrong about myself. All my life I have tried to be one thing, a bright and committed woman. Against a sea of obstacles - and I can tell you they are legion for a woman - I put my nose on a chalk line and pushed. And now you lurch into my life, and everything seems meaningless. I want you. Badly. Insanely. Here we are in the middle of a nightmare social struggle we have to win, and I can't even think properly about it. Suddenly my nose is off the chalk line, and I don't know where the hell I am anymore."

283

"It's called passion," said Haug. "It happens between men and women, sometimes unexpectedly."

"Passion, is it?" snorted Louise Templer. "I haven't got time for passion."

Haug laughed. "It's not somethin' you make time for. It's like a bear trap. Or a pile of dog shit. You've already stepped in it before you realise it's there. One of those thangs you cain't plan for."

She turned and looked at him. "Since this afternoon, out there in the rain, I haven't been able to *think* of anything but you. That has *never* happened before in my life. Ever. I'm desperately worried about Sir Jonathan downstairs, and I'm outraged at what happened to him. And I want to smash this network which has insinuated itself into our political and economic lives. Yet...yet, this thing has shoved all that to one side. It's still there, but flooding into my immediate consciousness is this...river of desire. Sitting on top of you in the middle of that stream, I... Haug, I felt so *wanton*, so madly sexual. And I don't fucking understand it! I don't even *want* it!"

"Your body is as beautiful as your mind," Haug said quietly.

"What did you say?" she asked aggressively.

"Maybe you've never thought of that," he replied.

She stood up and jerked open the dressing gown. "This...is beautiful?"

Haug looked at her. She was a tiny woman and, standing there with her arms wide, she looked almost like a statue of delicate porcelain. "Yes," he said. "As beautiful as any woman I've ever seen."

She dropped her arms to her side, and as she looked up at the ceiling the dressing gown dropped to the floor. "I'll try and believe you for a moment or two, Haug." Slowly she lowered her head until she looked him directly in the eyes and walked deliberately to the side of the bed, raising her arms gracefully. "This? Is beautiful?"

Haug threw off the covers, exposing his own naked body. "It's what Mozart would have made if he'd been a sculptor, everything small and delicate and exquisite." He gently touched her breast. The nipple was already standing erect. "Your skin is like warm silk, Louise." His hand moved down to her abdomen. "And I've never in my life felt such a sexy tummy."

She grabbed his hand with both of hers, breathing heavily. "Oh, hell. I love it. I suppose that makes me no more than a stupid typical little girl."

"You know goddamn well you're not stupid or typical or a girl. Little, yeah." He drew her towards him.

Very slowly she closed her eyes and lay down on top of him, locking her thighs around his erect penis. The feeling was so grand that she shivered.

"Are you cold?" he murmured.

"No. Just feeling sexier than the slinkiest movie star who ever slunk into another movie star's bed. I think you're beautiful, too, Haug." She raised her head and kissed him deeply, putting her arms behind his neck and squeezing with all her strength. His hands were caressing her back and bottom, and she knew she wanted him.

She wanted him at that moment more than anything she had ever wanted in her life. In spite of everything. It was foolish. It was stupid. It was certainly inadvisable. It was wrong. It was the wrong time. It was the wrong place. Maybe it was even the wrong man. But Louise Templer no longer cared.

CHAPTER SIXTEEN

On Sunday morning the sun was shining through the window as Haug woke. Someone was tapping on his door, and for a moment he was disorientated. The room, the tapping reminded him of something. And someone was holding onto him from the back. Looking around he saw the small dark head of Louise Templer, and everything fell into place at once.

"Just a minute," he called out and felt Louise wake suddenly behind him. He put his finger to his lips, pointing at the door, then slid out of bed and grabbed his dressing gown. He opened the door, filling the gap with his body. It was Sarah Mainwaring.

She smiled. "Jonathan is awake and is anxious to see you."

"Will he mind if I'm dressed like this or should I get my jeans on?"

"No. Please come as you are." She put her hand on his arm. "I haven't had a chance to thank you privately for what you have done..."

He patted the hand on his arm. "Naw, now none of that. He's back, and he's alive. That's the main thing. Now we gotta get him on his feet and well again."

She squeezed his arm then leaned over and kissed his cheek quickly. "You're a good man, Mr Haug."

He held onto her hand. "How is he?"

She smiled. "A lot better. Not right by any means, but so much better. So much..." She pulled away her hand and turned to wipe tears from her cheek. "I'm sorry. I'm trying to be strong. I have loved him since we first met. Thank you so much...for bringing him home safely."

"I'll be right down," he said with a smile, closing the door.

Louise Temper was sitting up in the bed, and he grinned at her. "He's better," he whispered.

"I heard," she said, returning his smile. "That's wonderful." Then her smile faded, and she bit her lip. "Oh, god, what have I done? Haug, what have I done?"

He leaned over. "You've had two real good fucks, and you've got the rest of your life to work out the moral consequences." Caressing the back of her head, he kissed her softly, and their tongues met briefly.

"Oh," she said. "Oh, my god. Now I want to do it again. Out of here, so I can get back to my room and, I hope, to some sanity. I'll be down shortly." She wheeled out of bed and grabbed her dressing gown from the floor.

Haug blew a kiss as he left, and went down the stairs.

Sir Jonathan Mainwaring was propped up on a raft of pillows, and his pyjamas were buttoned right up to the top. His hair had been carefully combed, and he was very pale and sallow. But he held out his hand immediately when he caught sight of the American. Haug crossed over and grasped it carefully, and Mainwaring enclosed it with his other hand, holding him at his side.

"The no doubt modest hero," Mainwaring murmured. "Well, I'm going to have to bore you with my deepest gratitude." He shook his head to keep Haug from speaking while he caught his breath. "No, I am not in the mood for any of your bucolic witticisms or denials. What I want to hear is every detail - and I mean *every* detail - of the rescue. The bloodier, the better." He removed one of his hands and patted the side of the large bed. "Come. Sit here."

Haug sat, still gripping his friend's hand. "I'll tell you. Every detail. But first you gotta tell me how you feel."

"Not important," whispered Mainwaring. "If you must know, very much better in respect of the fact I can now distinguish between ceiling and floor. However, I feel as if I have consumed several bottles of the cheapest Spanish wine before being dragged between a team of horses over a very uneven landscape." He paused to get his breath again. "Now. Please. Begin. I am absolutely consumed by rage, and I want to try and dissipate it through your story. I am going to close my eyes, the better to see it more clearly. Lots of blood, please. Plenty of gore. I can't begin to describe my lust for revenge."

Haug did his best to tell the story accurately, though he had to describe the events upstairs through the eyes of One Time or

Keef or Andy. Mainwaring was absolutely delighted by Nightmare Andy and loved the name. He made Haug promise to introduce them. Several times he stopped Haug and made him repeat a scene, slower and in more detail, and Haug found himself exaggerating a little at times. Half way through the story Louise Templer came in on tiptoe, and Mainwaring waved to her with a big smile. She leaned over and gave the Permanent Secretary a kiss on his cheek, but he wouldn't let her interrupt the story, urging Haug on impatiently.

Mainwaring lay in silence after Haug finished the tale, his eyes closed with a smile on his face.

"You broke off the needle in his bottom, did you?" he asked finally.

"I know for a fact they're gonna have to cut that thang out, 'cause it was jammed right in there."

"I only regret you didn't plug him into the mains on your way out," Sir Jonathan replied.

"I would've, if I'd had the time. Or drug him behind the pickup for a mile or two."

"Excellent idea!" the Englishman exclaimed.

Louise pulled a chair near the other side of the bed and reached over to touch his shoulder. "You look so much better. We were so worried. Devastated. Now it's your turn. How are you? Really?"

He sighed heavily. "Your word. Devastated. Unlike Haug here, I was somewhat less than heroic. Cowardly, I believe is the honest word. I caved in like a house of cards. Easily." He turned away from them for a moment. "I'm afraid I have to confess I told them quite a lot. I'm not sure how much, but at the end there was nothing left at all. Nothing at all. Pretty much a paper tiger, at bottom."

Haug's voice was soft and caring. "I know that's the way it looks right now, and I know why, too. Sometimes when you look in a mirror you see a nice feller, and sometimes you see a horse's ass. But I wanna tell you somethin' honestly, too. You are the real hero - though I gotta admit I don't really believe in heroes at all. Lissen, you can ask a lot of a human bein', and you can get a hell of a lot. But, no matter what you do, you cain't get

289

one who can flap his arms and fly off a cliff. That's askin' the impossible. I know that stuff they gave you, and I don't know a man alive who could resist it. I bet one thang, though. I bet you lasted longer than anybody I ever met. I bet you flew about twenty feet from the cliff before droppin' like ever other person in a belly flop on the ground below. Whaddya wanna be? A god as well as a knight and top man at Westminster and the brainy leader of a big resistance movement? If you do, I think you're an arrogant son of a bitch."

"I'm an arrogant son of a bitch," he replied mildly. "Now, where is Sarah? I don't want her too far away from me at the moment."

Sarah Mainwaring had crept back into the room and was standing at the doorway. She came over to the bed beside Haug and leaned over to kiss her husband. She was slim and had her long greying hair pulled back in ponytail. It hung forward over her shoulder as she bent down, and he put his arms around her, holding her to him firmly.

"I can't tell you how happy I am to be back with you, Sarah. I missed you so much, and they...somehow made me doubt you."

"Well," she said, "that was silly, wasn't it?"

He looked over her shoulder at Haug. "Broke their bones, you said? Those two detectives?"

Haug nodded. "Yep. I doubt one of 'em will walk again for a long time, and they other one will have to abuse himself left-handed."

"Excellent," Mainwaring muttered. "Splendid. So pleased to hear it."

"Do you think you could face some breakfast?" she asked her husband as she pulled away.

He held up a bony finger. "Only on one condition. Only if it consists of kippers, properly jugged, fresh bread thickly cut and toasted lightly, unsalted butter and some of your orange marmalade."

She nodded with a smile. "Of course."

"I've been dreaming of it since I woke," he said warmly.

"Well, why didn't you say something?" she asked in mock anger.

290

"First of all I had to speak to my Yankee rescuer. I had to have my vicarious revenge."

Mainwaring looked after his wife longingly as she left the room, then suddenly sat up sharply before falling back on the pillows in pain. "I just thought of something. My memory is shaky, and I'm having a great deal of difficulty sorting out the real from the imaginary. But I think...no, I'm nearly certain...they know of the Corfu operation."

Haug and Louise Templer spoke together. "What?"

Mainwaring closed his eyes and, despite great self control, his features distorted with pain. "They were pounding at me, over and over, again and again. Tapes, tapes, tapes..."

"Are you sure they weren't talkin' about the other set, the ones last year?" Haug asked.

"No," said Mainwaring emphatically. "They mentioned the boat, the yacht. Wanted to know who was doing it, who was responsible. And...I may have given them your name, Haug." His voice trailed off as his features twisted in agony. "I may have. Please excuse me for a moment." The Perm Sec curled slowly into a ball as if drawn involuntarily by great pain. He groaned. "Oh, god. Oh, god. I can't...tell...you any...more. Just now. Please forgive."

Louise Templer sat on the other side of his bed and stroked the back of his head. "You don't have to. You don't have to say anything. Your friends are here, your wife is here. You're safe. We're just so happy to have you back with us."

"Are you?" He turned to face her, trying to straighten his legs. "Are you really? How extraordinary."

"You are very, very important," she replied. "Not just what you have done in forming together the United Opposition, but *you*. Sir Jonathan Mainwaring. A man who represents a vanishing breed. Perhaps it has already vanished, save for you. A good and brave man..."

He snatched excitedly at her wrist. His voice quivered. "Do you really believe that? Despite what has happened. Despite what I have done. Despite those I have betrayed."

"Who have you betrayed?" Haug asked levelly.

Mainwaring turned to the American. "You, for one."

Haug scratched his ear. "The way I understand it, betrayal is a kinda partnership or somethin'. You gotta have the agreement of both parties."

The Permanent Secretary narrowed his eyes. "You're not humouring me, are you? Saying things you think I want to hear?"

"The only time I can remember humourin' you, is when you took me for a ride in that Morgan, and I pretended you were a good driver."

Mainwaring relaxed back on the pillows and closed his eyes. "I think you may be a good medicine for me, Haug. Feeble attempts at humour are about all I can take at the moment, and at those you are a master."

"I figgered mosta my humour was too sophisticated for you."

Mainwaring held up a warning finger. "No, now don't make me laugh. Please. My diaphragm is aching for some reason. As far as sophistication goes, you are completely untainted and virginal. You are light years away from understanding sophistication even in its most primitive and prelingual forms."

Haug thought a moment. "Virginal, you say?"

Mainwaring nodded. "I'm quite sure that, too, is a relatively unfamiliar concept from the little I know of your lifestyle."

"Hold on there, Jonathan, you're blowing gas faster'n you can cap it. Don't wanna empty out your head all at once like that or you'll get the bends comin' back to normal."

Louise had been shaking her head and chuckling. "The two of you are absurd. Absolutely mad."

Mainwaring looked at Haug for a moment speculatively. "I've never in my life had a friend like you. Perhaps it could be said I've never had a friend, not really. No time. Too frightened. Oh, yes, frightened, that's the right word. Don't let anyone get too close." He turned and looked at Louise. "You see, I adored my father, really. But he never, ever let me touch him, except formally. As a child. Kept me at a distance. I don't know why I'm telling you this." He stopped and looked distressed. "But it's nice to hold onto both of you just now. I hope you don't mind. I'm really a bit of a mess, I'm afraid. Forgive me for being a little peculiar."

Haug grinned. "Why, that's only 'cause you're English. You cain't help that."

Mainwaring looked at Louise. "The usual envy of an inferior savage. Tiresome, isn't it?"

She smiled. "Perhaps we could teach him to speak the language while he's here."

Mainwaring lifted an eyebrow. "Hmmm. I doubt it."

His wife came through the door with a large wooden tray, and Mainwaring instantly became animated.

"My kippers! Silence, now, everyone while I enjoy these humble fish." Then he stopped and looked around. "But I can't eat alone. Don't you have anything for our guests?"

"Of course I do, Jonathan. It's in the kitchen on the table."

"Please, bring it in here. I want you all here with me so we can have breakfast together. I feel better already."

Sarah looked at Haug. "I wonder if you would mind bringing a table through." She turned to Louise. "And perhaps you wouldn't mind giving me a hand with the food." Then she shook her finger at her husband. "You're a lot of trouble, you know."

"Quality has its price, dear," he said, as he plunged a piece of fish into his mouth with his fork.

* * *

With great effort she concentrated on her balance, taking one careful step, shifting her weight, then bringing the other foot level. Take another step. Her arms were held out from her sides delicately, and she focused her eyes at a point on the wall. She mustn't let her head move, she knew that. Or the book would fall, and she would have to start all over again. She couldn't remember how many times it had already fallen. When the book fell, she had to bend at the knees, keeping her back straight and her eyes forward to pick it up again.

But this was the first time she had got over halfway across the room, and she was having to fight off her excitement because that spoiled her concentration. It was so difficult with the beautiful shoes he let her wear for the first time that day. The heels were so high it tilted her pelvis forward and made it awkward to keep the back absolutely straight. They made her feel a little sexy, and she was hoping it made Mr Gillmore think she was not quite so ugly.

Corky DeLoop was very, very tired and had no idea how long she had been at this place. She had seen no daylight and certainly no darkness. More or less, she assumed night was when the man went away for a long while. Or did he go away? She wasn't sure, and felt herself frowning, pausing a moment as she felt the book begin to slide a little. His voice was always there, wasn't it? Saying things over and over again. So he might be outside the room with a microphone. She didn't want to think of the words he said because she had to concentrate on her movement. Three quarters of the way across, now. Oh, my god, she thought. I'm going to make it! For the first time! He will be so pleased! Fiercely she drove the thoughts from her head and focused on the point of the approaching wall. One slow step, another one. Success! As gracefully as she could, she reached out and touched the point she had used for focus.

"OK, very good," Gillmore growled. "Now turn and walk over here to the front of my desk."

With a great deal of satisfaction he noted her intense concentration as she turned slowly towards him, her head hardly moving at all. He could not remember enjoying himself so much since he was a kid, he thought as his eyes crawled slowly over her body. What a body! That morning he had let her have the shoes, and he felt for a moment the stupid woman was going to cry with joy. He had thrown her some stockings and a red silk suspender belt, and that was all she now wore as she teetered slowly across the floor. And that was all she was going to wear. He never remembered seeing a woman look that good in his favourite gear. She must be about six foot four with those heels, maybe six foot five. A giant piece of pussy. He dearly wished he could bring the old Corky DeLoop back to look at herself now, placing one leg demurely in front of the other, her hands held femininely out for balance.

He had taken the advice of Doctor Cranley on the wording of the tapes he played in her cell all night long. Break down her self esteem and make her obsessively focused on him, that's what he told the doc he wanted. Sleep deprivation was very important, the doctor had advised. A little sleep, but not too much. Two hours, four maximum. So two hours it was. May as well be on the safe side. The tape played over and over again, all night. A large photograph of Gillmore had been placed high up on the wall so she would have to raise her eyes to see it. Yeah. All good stuff. She was coming round alright. Very little rebellion now, but they had to make sure the drug was continued on time.

He looked up. She had reached the edge of the desk and stood waiting for him to speak. Jesus, she was a big woman.

"Now curtsy," he barked. "Without dropping the book."

"Yes, Mr Gillmore," she said in a tiny voice. He had told her that her natural voice was too loud and horrible and sounded like the old whore. She must be quiet and feminine. He was trying to help her. She dropped one foot carefully behind the other and bent her knees, coming up very slowly. The book shifted a little, but she managed to re-balance it just in time.

"Take the book off your head, bitch, and put it on the desk. But stay straight. You look a lot better like that."

Her face brightened as she placed the book carefully on the desk. "Oh, thank you, Mr Gillmore."

"Now, sit down in the chair," he ordered. He had placed a hard, straight backed chair in front of the desk.

Keeping her back and head absolutely straight, Corky sat in the chair, still holding her hands carefully out at her sides. Crossing her legs and remembering to hold her tummy well in, she placed one hand on the top of her thigh and the other one on top of that hand. Finally she smiled as genuinely as she could with her mouth slightly open and held the smile in place as she looked at another spot she had picked out on the wall behind Mr Gillmore.

Gillmore couldn't resist a little smile. She was learning a little faster. He would be able to bring old DeLoop in before too long and get his half million bucks. But not, he thought too quickly, before he had damn near worn out this great big piece of prime Texas beef. He had been determined not to fuck her until she was completely broken down, and this could be the day. She was doing well so far, and it was the first day she had shown no sign of rebellion. He thought it was going to be harder than this, but then women never impressed him as having strong wills. Mostly bluff. The big Texan loudmouth had just been so much wind. He could see she was extremely pleased at having done so well and was now waiting politely for him to speak.

Gillmore picked up the book on the edge of the desk. "Do you know what this book is?"

"No, Mr Gillmore," she said in her tiny voice.

"This is the Bible. The holy book of God. And I have marked out several passages I want you to read each day when you are taken back to your room. I want you to read them carefully, because I will ask you questions about them, OK? You will find everything I have told you reflected here in the Bible."

"Yes, Mr Gillmore."

He replaced the Bible. "I want you to tell me what you look like. Tell me exactly."

The smile faded from her face, and she furrowed her brow. "I...I..." She stopped and had trouble going on, and her eyes seemed to lose their focus.

Gillmore brought a cane from underneath the desk and laid in front of him. "Do you want me to use this?"

"No, Mr Gillmore," she said quickly. "I'll tell you now." Her words began to tumble out. "I am very big and awkward and heavy. That's why I need to learn to walk and sit properly, and you're helpin' me, sir. And my face is very much like a horse's, with teeth like a horse. My neck is wrinkled, and my shoulders slump, and my tits sag down to my navel, and..." she was starting to cry. "And...my tummy is fat and lumpy and so are my hips and thighs. And my ankles are thick and ugly, and there are big veins on my lower legs."

"Do you want to see a mirror?" Gillmore asked.

"Oh, no. Please, Mr Gillmore..." she said, fighting back the tears. "No one wants me. No one wants me. No one wants me. No one..."

"Shut up." he barked abruptly. "I *might* want you."

Corky DeLoop brightened. "Could you really? Oh, Mr Gillmore...I'm too ugly for you!"

"Spread 'em," he said.

She uncrossed her legs and opened them as wide as she could and suddenly remembered her smile. She had been crying but dared not wipe her cheeks.

"Now look at me, you old whore. Look right in my eyes and play with yourself. I don't have to tell you how to do that, do I? That's it, get your fingers in there. Look at me and play with yourself. I *might* just fuck your arse. Think about that."

Corky DeLoop looked at the man behind the desk. For a moment or two it almost seemed he was black, a big, good looking black man. She could feel her face flush, and she was beginning to gasp in little shallow breaths as her fingers stroked the top and inside lips of her vagina. The awful sense of fatigue which had been making her lightheaded lifted, and the room was brighter, softer. It wasn't a black man. It was a white man, but his eyes were black. Deep and black. A handsome, mysterious, dangerous man. A man who had hurt her, but also a man who had helped her. Helped her so much. She was overwhelmed with a wave of desire for this man with the penetrating eyes. He could see right into her soul, and she felt for a moment like she could see into his. Her hips were beginning to move spontaneously, and her chest started to heave.

"Stop," Gillmore said suddenly. "I don't want you to come, you stupid bitch. First, Corky DeLoop, I want you to beg. Now listen to me carefully. I want you to beg like you've never begged before. I want you to beg me to stick my dick in your filthy pussy like it was a matter of life and death. If you convince me you really, really want it...well, I might just fuck you."

He got up and came around the desk and stood in front of her. She still held his eyes as he unzipped his trousers and took out his penis. Already it was nearly erect.

297

"Look at my cock now. That's what you want. You want it desperately. More than anything else in the world."

Her eyes widened as they fell on his penis. Had she seen it before? No? This was beautiful, the most gorgeous one she had ever seen in her life. She wanted, she wanted...what did she want? Memories tumbled over each other in rapid, confusing images. No poverty, she hated it. Money, wealth. Young men. Men's eyes on her. Why were men's eyes on *her*? With her body? Getting laid. This image dominated and grew, larger and larger. She wanted to get laid and could actually feel the longing in her loins. And she wanted to be wanted, wanted someone, this man, to want her. Please, please let him, please let him want her...

"Please want me," she finally screamed out in utter sincerity, as she felt her wits scatter completely like a burst light bulb. She felt herself sliding off the chair onto her knees, and she put her hands prayerfully in front of her, still looking at the trembling penis. Her loins were now on fire, raging. Throwing her arms wide she shook her breasts as lewdly as she could. Then she brought her hands back underneath them, pushing them up to him.

"Please take 'em, please have 'em. They're yours. Yours."

He didn't move. He didn't want them, and desperation was tearing at her insides, now raging alongside the desire. Falling onto her back, she spread her legs and inched toward him using her shoulders and buttocks. Her head was uncontrollable now and rolled from side to side, but her eyes remained on the now rigid cock. Cock. Cock. The word.

"I want your cock in me," she begged desperately. "Please, please, let me have it inside. I'm going to die. Oh, please, just touch me with it, please..."

She arched herself up into the air trying to touch him with her vagina. No. Her pussy. That's what he called it.

"Please, take my pussy. I want you. I want you. I want you. No one wants me. No one wants me. No one wants..."

"Shut up," he said viciously. "And stand up. Correctly."

With every ounce of self control, Corky tried to pull back and get her feet under her, but she could not tear her eyes away

298

from his cock. Shakily she hurried to her feet, straightened her back and neck and put her hands out daintily to her sides.

Gillmore was almost crazed with contempt and desire. The woman standing close to him towered a full twelve inches over him, yet she was *his*. *His*. Her tits were right in front of his mouth, and he licked one. The woman trembled as if he had struck her with the cane. With the other hand he reached up and grabbed the other one, squeezing, watching with great pleasure as her flesh oozed between his fingers. He continued squeezing the tit as his other hand felt her arse, that great arse. His, now. His arse. His tits. He dropped the hand holding the tit to her crotch and grabbed a handful of hair. She squealed, and for a moment he thought she was going to collapse. Her chest was heaving, and her hands were fluttering like leaves in the wind. His *pussy*. *His*. His dick was harder than he could remember it, even before that shit with what-her-name? Beth. It was as hard as the bone in his leg.

"Open," he said to her in a harsh whisper.

Immediately she stepped out with one foot, and he rubbed her pussy eagerly. Never could he remember being this worked up. Plunging his fingers into her, he heard her beginning to cry again. The sound came from above his head.

"Please fuck me," she said. "Please, please want me. Just once."

He almost chuckled to himself at what he felt was his complete mastery of her. "Lay your arse on that desk, and show me your ugly cunt."

She forgot her posture in her eagerness to please him and sat on the desk, leaning back on her elbows, opening her legs wide for him. He walked slowly over and used his hand to guide the head of his prick to her vulva, rubbing it back and forth, tauntingly. Her body was trembling, and those great tits were like big jellies wobbling on a platter.

"Please, please, please..." she begged plaintively. "Oh, god, oh, god..."

"Don't take the Lord's name in vain," he said sharply. "Keep begging."

"Oh, I'll do anything, anything. Please, sir...oh..."

299

Gillmore had pushed the head in sharply. That big Texas pussy was now on the end of his dick, and he was going to shove it all the way to Dallas. He suddenly pushed with all his strength, burying it inside her. She was his. Finally. All his.

Corky DeLoop screamed at the top of her lungs, and her body was simply no longer in control anymore. Her hips thrashed up and down on the desk, and her head shook from side to side. Abruptly she felt a stinging pain on her cheek and opened her eyes in shock. His face was glaring from between her breasts.

"You're not allowed to come, you bitch," he snarled at her, his eyes crazed.

She had difficulty understanding what he said, but slowly the fog cleared. She banged her fists on the table and squeezed her eyelids together, trying her best to hold back. She wanted to so badly. It would help her so much. But her hips moved anyway, with their own volition. She just could not help herself. Her cheek stung again, and her eyes flicked open.

"Lie still," he whispered savagely. "Or I'll show you the mirror. You want the mirror?"

A chill gripped her chest like a frozen hand, and she felt the heat draining from her, evaporating like steam.

"Now watch me come in you." His voice was almost demented. "Watch me. Watch me come inside you. Do you remember? Do you remember? Do you remember the other Corky sneering down like I was a piece of arse wipe?"

Gillmore no longer knew what he was saying because his world was spinning too fast. The woman was beginning to move again, move with him, her hips, her whole body. And he didn't want to smack her. No, he *wanted* her to come. Her wanted her to come with him. He found himself trying to scrabble onto the desk with his knees, wanting to lie on that body, touch it, touch himself to it. Gillmore was propelled by hidden and powerful hands, and as he lowered himself onto her, he felt her arms around him, holding him, caressing him, tearing at his clothes to get underneath to the skin. He suddenly ripped at his own shirt, desperate for her warmth. His hips were bucking uncontrollably, and he was kissing her breasts, her chest, her arms, her neck and then her lips. As he held her, she held him, her legs now around his hips, pushing him into her again and again. He felt her juddering, and it was like the beginning of a mighty earthquake. He was coming and she was coming, and - if he had been able to speak at that moment - he would have said it was the most powerful sensation he had experienced in his life. He wasn't able to speak, but he was shouting her name. Not cunt, not whore, not slut. He was shouting 'Corky.' And 'Corky, darling.' He was also seriously blaspheming.

Huge forces were also unleashed in her. They were powerful but much different. Like an electrical storm there were layers of superheated air colliding with a cold and freezing atmosphere. She wanted this man inside her with insane desire, but it was a wanting of something else, something more. Or was it someone else? But reason wasn't there to help her analyze. If she had known what the layer of frost was, she would have known it was hatred. A cold, hard, biting icicle deep down inside, at the centre, the core of her being. The desire unleashed the hatred and provided fuel for it as it threatened to consume her whole body. Perhaps at that moment she saw hatred as lust, because it was just as powerful. He had commanded her not to come, but she could no more stop now than she could have stopped the sun in the sky. He was on her, touching her, shouting and screaming like she was, and she clawed at him as the explosion came and grew and mushroomed until darkness fell in the room and in the world...

Harvey Gillmore finally slid down her body and collapsed on the floor at her feet. He was too weak to move and just lay there on his back, looking up at the motionless red high heel shoes above his head. There was much turbulent confusion inside, but the only thought he had at that moment was the absolute beauty of those shoes and the perfect curve of her calves. He had not kissed a woman in a long, long time - and *never* had he kissed one like that. Wonderingly he reached up and touched one of her calves, closing his eyes as his hand followed that beautiful curve down to her ankle. His touch was gentle, and - had it been anyone other than Harvey Gillmore - could have even been called loving.

He got to his knees, then slowly found the strength to stand as his eyes devoured the body lying lifelessly across the desk. It was beautiful. He had to admit it was the most beautiful thing he had ever known in his life. He put his hand carefully on her thigh. It was so long, so smooth, and, as he moved the hand slowly above the stocking, warm and wonderful. He moved to her belly, a perfect roundness, then on to her breast which he first traced with a finger before touching gently.

Drawn as if by magic his face bent slowly down to kiss her warm belly. He found himself covering it with kisses, little quick ones. The scent of her was almost toxic, yet he felt he wanted to draw her whole body up through his nose, inhale her like fleshy smoke.

Opening his eyes as he pulled away from her stomach, he caught her looking at him. But he was not angry. He held her eyes and said nothing. It seemed to him they were soft, luminously blue, like cobalt, and he could feel the beat of his heart in his ears. Neither blinked, but Gillmore felt drawn into those blue eyes set in a face beyond the ability of a Michaelangelo to paint or draw.

Something had happened to Harvey Gillmore, and he could no more say what it was than he could have named all the galaxies. Shakily he began to pull back, pull away from her, slowly and carefully as if retreating from a dangerous booby trap. He backed away from the desk and the beautiful goddess who still lay stretched motionless across it. His shirt was torn in shreds, and he realised she had clawed his back raw. He backed across the room to the door before remembering to re-zip his flies. He opened the door and slipped outside. He had to have some air. He had to think. He had to find out what had happened to him.

Corky DeLoop lay on the desk for a long time. She, too, was trying to think. Something had happened during the orgasm as memories soared around in the torrential winds. Memories and images. It was so important she was determined to try, step by step, to piece together her shattered consciousness. Just like learning to walk with a book on her head. At first it was difficult, and she had to stoop and pick it up dozens of times.

302

Something had happened, something had changed, she thought as she started yet again. What? What was it before? Change? From what to what? It was a drug, an injection that was keeping her from thinking straight. It made thoughts run together funny. The man. He had *wanted* her, and that made her feel warm. And she was not a bitch or whore because the man had called her Corky and because he had touched her like she was beautiful. She could see that in his eyes. Why had she thought she was ugly? Because he said so. Now he said she was beautiful. So confusing.

Start again. Something changed. The man had hurt her. Why did she want him? With a suddenness that made her jump she remembered the electrical shocks when he was grinning and laughing. Yes, yes, he did that. And the awful mirror. Maybe it was a trick mirror. She grappled for anything she could hold on to.

Start again. Something had changed. Be basic, she told herself. She could do it. She was intelligent, she could think. *He had changed*. Yes. But why? The thought was so rapid and ridiculous she almost rejected it. But wait. What was it? *She* had changed *him*. Was it possible? Of course it was possible. She was Corky DeLoop, she always changed men...

And more memories began to float to the surface like photographs in chemicals, the outlines gradually becoming faint, then stronger. Some would fade, and she couldn't remember what they were.

Start again. Something had changed. She was stronger now. She had more power. Power! Hold onto that word, that thought. Hold onto it. It was important, more important than food or air or anything. *He* wanted *her*. Yes. That was *power*. Currency. Money. She could use it. Why?

To...to get out! Out of here!

Oh, god, she thought, please, please let her hold onto this thought, this new freedom, this feeling of power. It was so much better than feeling weak. Let her hold on, please. Some sleep. Maybe then she could think better. Some sleep.

Harvey Gillmore sagged against the wall of the kitchen down the hall with a can of Diet Coke in his hand. It was night, and he stared blankly out the window. All he could think of was the sight of that naked woman lying on the desk in the Interrogation Room. The image was burned into his memory with a hot iron. Or painted by an angel. He felt his loins tingle and knew he wanted her again. But he dare not go into that room now. *Dare* not. Because he no longer trusted himself, not tonight. Never in his life had he stumbled across an experience like that. Corky. What a lovely name.

He shook his head angrily and took a drink of Pepsi. He was drinking it straight from the can, something he never did. She should be serving it to him by now. But how the hell was he going to keep his hands off her if she did? He wanted to touch her all over, again and again.

The Pepsi was trembling in his hand, and he smashed it down on the counter to make it stop. Fuck it. I am Harvey Gillmore, not some doe-eyed, greasy-haired young yob just out of adolescence! He knew he was going to have to get away from Unit G5 for a day or two. He had to leave that night. Get away. Get back to London and his newspapers. His stupid emotions had derailed his mind, and it was his mind which was valuable.

Before he left he changed his shirt and asked the doctor to let her sleep that night. Just one night. Wouldn't hurt.

The doctor looked at him with a raised eyebrow but said nothing. But he did think to himself that it certainly wasn't like Mr Gillmore to be kind...

CHAPTER SEVENTEEN

It was raining, and the windows of the Range Rover were fogged. The Range Rover sat in the parking lot at Hampstead Heath, and the man who just got in beside Michael Regis was Sam Bernstein. They had arranged to meet at the Heath and walk along the ponds, but the weather outsmarted them.

Regis was putting a CD disc back in the case, and he replaced the case in its little library shelf. "Haug," he said simply.

Sam Bernstein leaned back in the seat, stretching his leg. It still bothered him sometimes, especially in wet weather.

"Haug," he repeated. He knew the name, and he knew the man. He was the man who broke his leg in the first fight he had ever lost. He was also a man he respected, for that reason amongst others. As he had stared at the man across a dimly lit room that night, he saw in his eyes the look of the warrior. The man who was not going to give way, the man who would give his best until his last breath, and a man of cunning, watching and hearing everything, not given to panic like so many. If you made the slightest mistake with such a man, you were dead.

Sam Bernstein was not dead because in their duel Haug had recognised the same things in him. Seldom did two such men meet in these days of technology. Most who called themselves warriors or professional soldiers were either windbags and braggarts or men of uncontrolled violence, fuelled by rage or fear. Only in the very best did the head clear and the priorities fall into place as mind and body became an efficient fighting machine. Haug was good, and his men were good, too. Much better than the bunch he led that night. They deserved to win, and therefore Bernstein held nothing against his old foe.

Regis had been drumming his fingers on the steering wheel. "Haug has become an intolerable nuisance."

Bernstein chuckled. "I imagine he has," he agreed. "I would have told you that, if you had asked."

"I want you to kill him."

305

"Alright, Michael. I'll kill him," Bernstein said. "But after that, I don't want to work for you anymore."

Regis raised an eyebrow. "May I ask why?"

Bernstein thought for a moment, running his hand through his short, wiry hair, now flecked with grey. "I've been in this game for a long time, and I've done some things I'm not very proud of. Like peeling the skin off the soles of Arab feet to get a piece of worthless information for Shin Bet. I fought for my country in several wars when I thought Israel was a country for the wise. The wisdom bought and paid for through endless stacks of Jewish corpses in many countries over hundreds of years and ending in the obscenity of the Holocaust. Instead I fought for a country which has become just as ignorant and brutal as any other. Worse than many. Maybe not as bad as some..."

"What has this got to do with Haug?" Regis interrupted a little testily.

Bernstein turned and looked at the suave Englishman. He could smell his expensive aftershave. "Quite a lot, really. I don't know much about art. Painting, for instance. Maybe you do. For me, a photograph of a Rembrandt on the wall is just about as good as the real thing. But I do know something about fighting men. I know the difference between a phony and the real thing. Haug is kinda rare. He is a first class fighter and...not a bad man. If he was a bad man, I'd say, OK, fine, bang, bang, and go to a bar and have a beer, never think about it again."

Regis turned to the Jew, resting his arm on the back of his seat. "Haug is a bad man for me. For us."

Bernstein shrugged. "I don't make policy. I'm just a soldier, always have been. I carry it out. It's like a business. I do work, you pay me money. So I haven't gone into the ethics of your organisation or the one he works for. I suppose, when it comes down to it, I don't give a shit."

"Then why quit? You're the best operator we have in Europe."

Bernstein looked into Regis' dark eyes without blinking. "If you don't understand what I've just told you, Michael, I can't draw you a picture. Like I said, I'm no good at art."

Regis opened the glove compartment and handed him a plain manila envelope. "I hope you will change your mind, Sam. In the meanwhile, here are the details. Photographs, address, associates, all we know about him."

Bernstein sighed and took the envelope. "I'll need a partner. Of my choice."

"Choose anyone you need from the DA groups. You trained them, so they should be good."

"Yeah," said Bernstein ironically. "And there's not a single one of them who could take Haug alone."

Regis smiled and spread his hands. "Well, then, pick as many as you need. But we want him out."

Bernstein stuffed the envelope in his windbreaker and opened the door of the Range Rover. "He's a dead man."

He slammed the door of the car and walked off towards his own anonymous Escort, head down against the rain.

* * *

Sarah Courtney put down the phone in frustration. That was the third time she had got Jennifer Montgomery's answerphone, and there were already two messages from her on the tape. She had returned from Corfu on Saturday and immediately called to try and find how she could get in touch with O'Connell, the man she had met with Corky DeLoop. He was the only one she knew who might be able to help somehow. Even though he was probably still on the island. Or would he be? Surely they would know the thing they had planted had stopped working.

She was no good at this sort of analysis, but she knew she must try and do something after all the kindness and friendship the Texan woman had shown her. The morning following that horrible evening on the Matilda, Harvey Gillmore practically shoved her off the boat after throwing a cheque at her and accusing her of robbing him blind for the worst sex he had ever had. She tried to ask him what was happening to Corky, but he swore at her and ordered the crew to remove her. So she went, unhappy, crying and nose-diving to a low and dark plateau. The only thing she could think of was to hire a taxi to drive around the town of Corfu while she desperately looked for a big stylish black or a bald headed man on an old British motorcycle. Knowing it was hopeless before she started didn't help, and neither did the taxi driver who reckoned he had just the shoulder for her to cry on. His persistence finally provoked her to demand that he drive her to the airport where she waited four hours for the first available seat on a return flight to London. She had initially planned to stay at least a fortnight in Corfu relaxing in the sun and reading junk novels.

Instead she returned to two virtually sleepless nights wondering what had happened to her new friend. She had heard and experienced a barbarity in those men which stunned her. Not just the perverted Australian but in Michael Regis as well. Regis, for Sarah Courtney, had always been a benchmark of elegance and urbanity, the sort of man she was thrilled to be seen with. A good an experienced lover, too. Yet there he was at the head of the table, plotting with the rest of them while Corky was chained to the sofa like some animal. Is that what they really thought of women? Was it? Lumps of meat they could screw or send out of the room like children, patting them condescendingly on the bottoms? Or if you stood and fought like Corky, then you were wrestled down and caged? And how could the suave Michael Regis have allowed her to be used like a slave by Gillmore? Even for a lot of money?

These were questions Sarah Courtney had never asked herself before. Damn it, she was young, and there were so many exciting things to do. Parties, good-looking men, lots of money to spend, jolly nights at expensive restaurants. She had had a good time! And she never had any use at all for what she called the Lesbian's Movement - or Les Move, in her witty shorthand. All those ugly fat women in sandals made from Vietnamese rubber tyres. Well, they *were* a little bit ridiculous and much too far over the top. Boring, as well. But, damn it, it *hurt* being treated like that by the men on the Matilda.

Sarah Courtney had a nice flat in Kensington on the two top floors, and she was sitting downstairs in her kitchen on a stool. The window faced a school play area, and she looked down at the children. OK, she thought, Gillmore's a pervert, OTT like

308

the Les Move. But the humiliation she felt during her week on the Matilda was not that much different from some of the incidents in her past - and not just with clients, either. It was all a matter of degree. Maybe she wasn't the smartest person in the world, but men always treated her like...like...her brains weren't even wanted. Just the body, the right expressions, then fade away when the men start to talk. There was a Guards Captain she knew who treated her little better than Gillmore. He didn't beat her, of course. But the voice, the look, the exclusion, even the sex was humiliating.

Suddenly she slapped her hand on the white-topped counter. Yes. There was an actor's directory of some sort, wasn't there? Find out what it's called, and then she should be able to find Jennifer's agent. The agent *must* know where she is.

* * *

Gillmore arrived suddenly in the newsroom like an apparition. He seldom visited the offices at all, and when he did it was always in the company of Colin Greenaway, the editor. There was a brief, stunned moment when every journalist stopped working and stared. The moment was short, though. Because instantly every head was re-buried over the computer keyboards, eyes riveted to the video screens in front of them. Activity accelerated. Telephone calls became more intense. Those moving around increased tempo. It was as if an unpleasant electrical current had passed through the room.

The owner of WORLDWIDE, which included *The News*, stood at the doorway surveying the room gloomily. He did not speak, nor did he move, except for his head which swivelled slowly like a turret, stopping occasionally to glare before continuing its threatening survey.

Five minutes passed. Ten minutes passed. Each minute seemed an hour to employees desperate to avoid the gaze, hoping those awful eyes would not stop at his station or her desk. Then Gillmore began to move.

Stopping at one of the desks, he snatched open the top drawer, looked in it and turned his eyes to the middle-aged balding man who was cowering speechlessly behind his computer.

"Where is your Bible?" whispered Gillmore.

Clive Hurley lurched to the right and then to the left before finding the handle of the right drawer, a bigger one at the bottom. At first it wouldn't open, and Hurley tugged and rattled it, biting his tongue to keep from swearing. All the office equipment at *The News* was cheap and nasty. None of the old fashioned wooden desks they had in Fleet Street before the move. These were laminated blockboard which could be assembled or disassembled in twelve minutes. Finally the drawer sprung open, and Hurley dug like a badger in the papers which filled it. Then, triumphantly, his hand emerged with the Bible. He handed it to his boss. Behind Gillmore he could see a half dozen employees checking their left hand drawers.

Gillmore ignored the book for the moment. "It should be in your top left hand drawer. At the front. The first thing you see when you begin work in the morning."

"Well, it was there, sir. The last time I saw it, it was there, and..." Hurley's voice trailed off.

"Lying is a sin," Gillmore said simply, taking the Bible from the hapless man.

The publisher started to return the Bible to its rightful place, and then changed his mind. He flipped open the first page to the flyleaf. As he did so, all the blood drained from Clive Hurley's face.

For what seemed a very long time Gillmore studied the flyleaf. "Is this supposed to be funny?" he asked finally. "'This book belongs to God - and our souls belong to the Devil.' Is that a humorous comment?"

A pall of doom had settled on the face of Clive Hurley. "No, sir. It's not."

"Not what? Not humorous? Or not supposed to be humorous? What are you trying to say, man?"

"It's neither, Mr Gillmore," Hurley answered frankly.

The publisher looked at the ceiling speculatively. "And who, in this case, is the Devil?"

Hurley swallowed hard. "Satan, sir. The foe of God. In the Bible."

"I think you're lying again," Gillmore replied evenly. "I believe you mean me. You think I am the devil."

The man was shaking his head. "Oh, no, sir. No way." He laughed nervously. "How could anyone think of you as a devil? Sir?"

"Clear your desk, whatever-your-name-is, and get out of my office," Gillmore murmured as he moved on to the next desk.

"But I have a family," Hurley whimpered. "I...didn't do anything, just forgot to put my Bible..."

"Out," Gillmore said over his shoulder as he looked down at the red-haired woman.

As he was about to pull out her top drawer, the swinging doors at the other end of the office thundered open, and Colin Greenaway charged through, dipping his shoulders like a wide boy, his side-buckled shoes snapping on the tiles.

"Alright, you layabouts, do you know what time it is? Why haven't I got...?" He stopped mid-sentence and mid-thought and had the look of a man suddenly dropped into a barrel of hot tar. Before anyone could blink, his whole body language changed from strut to cringe. "Mr Gillmore. Mr Gillmore. Mr Gillmore," he repeated in an incantation as he rushed across the room with knees slightly bent, his side-buckled shoes no longer snapping on the tiles.

The Australian ignored his speedily approaching editor as he pulled open the drawer. A Bible was placed neatly in its place, and he closed the drawer. Behind him was the noise of Clive Hurley clearing his desk.

"And what do you do?" he asked Annabel Cunningham.

"I am an assistant sports editor," she said calmly.

"A woman sports editor? That's odd, isn't it?"

"Is it?"

"Gillmore!" a voice screamed behind the publisher. "Gillmore!"

Gillmore turned slowly just as Colin Greenaway skidded to a halt beside him. Clive Hurley stood holding a box. His face was beet red.

"You *are* the fucking devil, Gillmore! I hope you rot in fucking hell!" Hurley turned away in a rage and hurried towards the door.

Gillmore raised his arm and pointed at the back of the man. "I want him destroyed, Greenaway. Do you understand me? I want you to squeeze him until he crawls back into this office to apologise to me and my staff."

"Of course, Mr Gillmore," Greenaway said, wringing his hands. "I know just what to do. We've handled his type before. I, er, I'm sorry we didn't know you were..."

"Why do you have women working on the sports pages?" Gillmore interrupted.

"Her writing is as right as rain," the editor said. "Nothing to complain about. Almost as good as a man."

Gillmore held out his hand. "Let me see an example."

Like Hurley, the blood had drained from Annabel Cunningham's face. Though she maintained a superficial calm, her hands were trembling slightly as she fumbled through her copy. Finding a printout, she passed it to her boss.

Gillmore glanced through the copy. "This is crap." He threw the printout back to the red-haired woman and turned to the editor. "Give her a mop or a broom. Something she can handle. Have her clean this newsroom from top to bottom, and, if she does a good job, let her work on the fashion or gossip pages. Don't you know anything about women, Greenaway?"

As the two men moved away, Annabel Cunningham stared straight into space as tears of rage glazed her vision. She could feel her nails digging into her palms as she struggled to suppress the volcanic emotions threatening to erupt into an avalanche of invective. Exactly what was a job worth these days? She was ambitious, nothing wrong with that, and she loved journalism in general and sport in particular. And now she was working on a national with the highest circulation in the UK. If she exploded, if she rebelled, if she said what she wanted to say to that little shit, she knew she could forget about journalism in this country, except perhaps for one of the locals. And you couldn't make a living at that. Annabel Cunningham was bringing up two children on her own and had a whacking great mortgage to pay.

312

So one day she could have her own home. And until then she must stay in bondage to this little shit or be very nice to him so he would give her a strong recommendation for her next job. What other choice did she have? Answer? she thought. None. Unclenching her fists, she got up to look for the brooms and mops.

Colin Greenaway was flicking a piece of lint from the shoulder of Gillmore's suit jacket as he checked yet another drawer. "Most of the employees here are deeply religious," he said unctuously.

"This place is a shambles, Greenaway," Gillmore said mildly as he opened the flyleaf of the Bible.

The editor looked as if he had been smacked. "It was a shame you had to come in without warning, Mr Gillmore. At the end of the day..."

"At the end of the day you may not have a job," he said, peering into the computer screen to read copy. "More crap. These imbeciles don't know how to write, and you don't know how to edit. That's what's causing the fall in circulation."

By now Greenaway was dry washing his hands in agony. "It's only a slight..."

"Circulation drops are never slight." Gillmore pushed the editor out of his way and walked to another desk. "Not when you have to deal with advertisers paying top dollar. Don't you understand anything about newspapers, Greenaway?"

"I..."

"Shut up, Greenaway. I'm trying to read." He was leaning over scanning another terminal at Peter Hindmarsh's desk.

Peter Hindmarsh was in his mid-thirties, a good-looking man proud of his abundant hair which had been carefully combed with a frontal quiff. He was trying to maintain a jaunty air as the boss read his copy.

"Well, Mr Gillmore," he said with a bluff smile. "What do you think?"

Gillmore looked around at the man who had spoken and suddenly grabbed his ear. Hindmarsh came half way out of his seat with pain, but the publisher pulled him by the ear until his nose was touching the screen of his terminal.

"Nevermind what I think," said Gillmore. "What do *you* think?"

"Mr Gillmore, you're hurting me."

"I'm going to kick your arse if you don't answer my question."

"Well, like, I don't think it's too bad," Hindmarsh said in an anguished voice.

"It's crap," Gillmore replied, still holding on to the ear. "What is it?"

"Crap," Hindmars agreed.

"Thank you," his boss said, finally letting go of the ear. He turned to his editor. "Even they think their stuff is crap. Let's go into your office."

As they moved through the desks and into the central aisle, they met Annabel Cunningham vigorously mopping the floor. A bucket stood near the swinging doors.

"You're just making a mess," Gillmore said rudely as he grabbed the mop away from her. "The only way to do this job properly in on your hands and knees. Wash it down in sections, then dry it off with clean cloths. Am I the only one who knows how to do anything around here? Do I have to tell everybody how to do everything?"

Annabel Cunningham swallowed hard. "Mr Gillmore. I don't mind doing it that way, but I didn't bring any suitable clothes today." She was wearing a mid thigh skirt and a saffron blouse.

Gillmore stared at his employee with indifference. "Either get down on your hands and knees and clean the floor or clean out your desk. It's your choice."

They watched in silence as Cunningham went without another word to the bucket, took off her shoes and put them aside, found a cloth, dipped it into the water, wrung it out and got down on the floor to scrub the tiles. She wore tights and had to stop from time to time to pull down her skirt in the back. They waited until she had finished the section between them and the swinging doors before walking across the damp floor and out of the newsroom.

314

Gillmore studied the photographs laid out on the editor's desk. They were a series of shots of the Princess Royal taken from some distance with a telephoto lens as she emerged from her car with two friends. You could tell from the hair that it was a windy day, and in one photograph a gust had caught the hem of her dress, blowing it up one leg, just showing a faint suggestion of her pink knickers. In the next photograph the Princess had turned toward the camera with an awful expression on her face which made her look like a fishwife as she wagged her finger at the photographer.

"Great stuff," said Gillmore. "Print 'em both. One on page one, this one on page two."

Greenaway bobbed his head. "Yeah, uh, yessir. But, uh, all things being equal, you see, the thing is..."

"What the devil are you trying to say, man?"

Greenaway smiled oleaginously. "It's the Palace, sir. As you can see, the Princess was aware of the photographer. I believe one of her friends pointed him out. And the Queen's chief arse kisser called me personally to forbid..."

"Forbid?" It was a strange word in Harvey Gillmore's mouth, or at least that is how it sounded. A foreign word, exotic and unsavoury. He repeated it again, as if trying to expel it, along with the distasteful thought. "Forbid? Some layabout old bag who wears a crown she doesn't even own, living in a palace she hasn't paid a cent for, is telling *me* what I can print and what I can't print?"

"Well, basically speaking..."

"Some unelected, untalented, overpaid family has *this* kind of power in a democracy?"

"Yessir. I thought I would lay my cards on the table, and..."

"And you let them get away with it, Greenaway?"

"Well, yessir. No sir. What I mean to say is, at the end of the day..."

Gillmore filled his chest. "We print a newspaper for the people. *The News* is for the *people*. Kings and Queens can't tell *us* what to do. I am Harvey Gillmore. I am WORLDWIDE. And," he approached Greenaway and grabbed his lapel, causing the editor to buckle downward to his employer's height. "And I

315

am the servant of Almighty God." He let go of his editor and grabbed the picture of the Princess showing her leg. "This is important news. This tells a whole story, you stupid idiot. The haughty bitch shows her snatch in this one, and in the other one we see the *real* royal, right? *That* is what the people need to know. The people of this country. The ignorant people of this country who keep an expensive millstone like this hanging around their necks. We are trying to educate and improve their intelligence, Greenaway, and *this* is the way to do it. *And* it will sell newspapers. *And* it will get the circulation back up. We are talking hard-hitting journalism here, Greenaway, and you are trying to tell me you were going to back off because of a phone call from some arsehole with a double-barrelled name and poofy accent? Is that what you are trying to tell me, Greenaway?"

The editor knew he was caught between a rock and a hard place. "At the end of the day we do sometimes need the cooperation of the Palace and the Queen..."

"Fuck the Palace. Fuck the Queen. Print it. The people need to know. And give the photographer a big bonus. That's the stuff we like. And if there's any bad news about the Government, like unemployment being up, trade being down, bad opinion polls, bye election losses, NHS queues - then print a small column beside the photograph with an upbeat header. That way no one can say we don't frontpage bad news. But the *real* story will be this expensive whore with her dress over her head. Basic journalism. Do I have to teach you everything? Every time I come here?"

Greenaway's head was bobbing like a cork in bathwater. "Well, yessir, I was going to ask you personally, of course before..."

"Take your trousers down, Greenaway, and bend over that desk. Put those photographs right in front of you so you don't make any mistake about why you're getting the dozen."

Colin Greenaway's shoulders slumped. He knew there was absolutely no point in objecting or arguing. It would just mean more strokes in the end. He tried to look at it philosophically. This was part of his job, and his job was editor of *The News*, owned by a crazy Aussie cunt. A crazy *rich* Aussie cunt, he corrected himself. He unbuckled his belt and pushed his trousers and underpants down to his ankles. Then he lay across his own desk, staring stoically at the two photographs. He knew instinctively it was going to hurt like hell this time. Gillmore was in a funny mood.

Gillmore *was* in a funny mood. He had to take sleeping pills the previous night as he tossed and turned in bed, unable even to shut his eyes. And today he was still full of stress, like an overstrung bow. He had never known himself to be so irritable and unsettled. Yes, and he damn well knew why, too. That woman. Until he walked into the newsroom this morning he had thought of nothing else but her. Disciplining his employees had taken his mind off her momentarily, and he was grateful for that, grateful for his business, anything to turn his mind away from that recurring image of Corky DeLoop lying across his desk after the most powerful orgasm he ever experienced in his life. For hours afterwards he felt as if his guts, his *self*, had spurted into her. As he started to enter her, he was in command. She was *his*, a toy. A big, beautiful toy which he was finally possessing. But afterwards.. Afterwards something happened, something fateful, something truly awful.

He raised the cane and slashed down on the pair of white pimply buttocks in front of him, ignoring the muffled nasal moan from the editor. There was a word he was avoiding. He struck again, harder. And that word was *love*. The cane swished down again. Love. He remembered sitting on the floor and looking up at that lovely leg, that was when the word first came to him. And it scared hell out of him. He *loved* her. And that was not fucking possible. He struck the white buttocks again and again with all his strength. He was trying his best to keep away from her for a day or two so he could return to normal.

Greenaway slid off the desk onto the floor, crying. "That's twelve. That's twelve, Mr Gillmore." Curling up with his bottom turned away, he tried to get his trousers back up ineffectually.

Harvey Gillmore ignored the man and turned away to the window to look out on the decaying housing estates in the distance. Most of all he wanted to test her. Let her come off the drug. Then he would see her again. Instinct told him she would be spitting like a cat with its tail on fire, and maybe that's what he needed to destroy the thousand-headed hydra laying waste to his consciousness. Let her come off the drug. It was a good idea anyway, as the training games had been too easy. He would be able to show her the videos recorded by the two cameras. Gag her. Tape her eyelids open. Make her watch herself as she gladly licked his arse then begged to be fucked. Show her what she would be doing for the rest of her life. Serving and servicing him. And DeLoop. DeLoop! He had forgotten about the husband and the wager. How *could* he forget? Fuck. There was no way. He could not let her go. Not now.

Love. This was an unusual word for Gillmore, like "forbid". It had odd angles and tumbled about awkwardly in his head, refusing to come to rest, and it made him uncomfortably angry. Women were...well, *women*. They had something he wanted. And whenever he wanted something in life, he either bought it or took it. If, for some reason, neither was possible, he simply destroyed it. If he couldn't have it, no one else would, either. It was the way he did business, and look at him! He straddled the world like a colossus and no longer had to care whether people liked or disliked him. What difference did that make? Love or loathe him, they still crawled to his office to beg for his political support or his money or his influence or his time. Whenever he spoke in a crowded room, everyone stopped to listen and then immediately agreed with whatever he said. He recalled a group of scientists who agreed polar bears came from equatorial Africa because they wanted his patronage.

Women. Women had never been a problem, either. He'd broken dozens of them on the rack of his will. He was totally convinced most of them craved "mistreatment" anyway, and why should he waste his time being nice to them just so he could fuck them? Long ago he found the secret of women. The bitches flaunted themselves with tight jumpers or plunging necklines, short little dresses and high heel shoes - pretending innocence all the while . Their real message was the same as any stall holder displaying goods. Pay the right price, and you get to squeeze the fruit. So he paid, usually, and squeezed until all the juice was gone and there was nothing left but the peel. He didn't have anything in particular against women. He did the same thing to competitors, socialist politicians, trade unions, corrupt government officials, incompetent managers, dishonest bankers and lawyers, inept employees and public sector layabouts. Hell, to the little men of the world he was a hero, a fearless campaigner, one against millions.

He smacked the cane against his leg and heard Greenaway jump behind him. But what was he going to do about Corky DeLoop? The very name made his stomach churn with desire. Well. The answer was clear. One way or the other, she was going to be *his*. He would do whatever needed to be done. He would have it. And if he could not have it, he would destroy it.

* * *

Sir Gerald Humphries put down the last page of the transcripts, took off his reading glasses, carefully folded them and placed them back in their black leather case. Then he switched off the anglepoise reading lamp. Finally he turned to General Sir Timothy Portland, who sat in a vast armchair near the window with a glass of whiskey and ice in one hand and a Havana cigar in the other. Physically the two men were superficially similar. Humphries was tall, lean and angular and had a long bony face with prominent nose and cheekbones. General Portland, on the other hand, was a little shorter with a round face and heavy shoulders. The General was nearly ten years older than the Commissioner of Police, but both were fit men for their age. There were also other similarities. Both spoke in declarative sentences which invited little argument, and both were sparing with their smiles.

"I want a copy of this," Humphries said suddenly. "Together with the tapes."

"Not possible, I'm afraid," said the General, taking a sip of whiskey.

"Do you realise whom you are speaking to?"

Portland swivelled the armchair so he was face to face with the Commissioner. "At least it is not possible at the moment,

319

Gerald. And I think you very well understand why. This is not a simple police matter, after all. It is complex. I have come tonight to discuss this matter with you in complete confidence, something to which you agreed, albeit grudgingly."

"Confidence is one thing, Timothy. If these represent accurate transcripts taken from genuine recordings, then we are speaking of treason on a rather grand scale."

"Exactly," Portland agreed.

"And I can only guarantee confidentiality so long as it affects only me and my office. Something of this nature must be directed instantly to my superior. The Home Office Minister."

"Adrian Chesterman."

"Yes."

Portland took another sip of whiskey and put the glass on the side table. "Yet you read something about Adrian Chesterman just now in the transcripts."

"That is neither here nor there. It has to go to him. You must know something about the chain of command, Timothy."

"Even when your superior officer is under suspicion of corruption, disloyalty and - your word - treason? No, I'm afraid in my case I would use my judgment to bypass that officer in such unusual circumstances."

"The Prime Minister, then."

Portland took a puff of his cigar. "Gerald, you're being very unhelpful tonight. Else you're being intentionally obtuse. Our first objective is discussion. Do you understand that? What we have here is not just an indication of *illegal* activity but of actual and relentless penetration of our government and our economy by a transnational organisation. And it is nothing at all like membership of the Masons..."

Humphries snapped a pencil down on the desk. "I am *not* a Mason."

Portland waved the hand holding the cigar. "I didn't imply that you were. I merely constructed an analogy to convey a thought. In other words, this is not simply a loose international organisation whose members share a particular interest or ideology. It may well have begun that way and grown over a period of years. No. It is quite frankly a subversive organisation

320

made up of members who serve interests alien to HM Government. As far as we can ascertain, these members are sprinkled through key positions of power - political, economic and legal."

Humphries looked over the General's head at the row of bookcases on the far wall. "You say 'we'. Who, exactly, are 'we'?"

Portland pulled an envelope from his inside jacket pocket. "We call ourselves the United Opposition, and I have here a membership list which I may or may not give to you at the end of the evening."

"You mean," asked Humphries sarcastically, "that you won't give it to me if I refuse to join your little group?"

"Not at all," the General replied as he replaced the envelope in his pocket. "I won't give it to you if I have any lingering suspicion that you may be one of them."

Sir Gerald opened his mouth to speak, then snapped it shut again.

Portland went on. "You see, we are in a difficult and dangerous position. We know of them, and they know of us. And the battle is beginning to erupt in the streets."

"If that's so, why have I not been informed?"

"Because, as you may have deduced from the transcript, Gordon Hastings and the Specials are blocking you from that information. In other words, the chain of command has already been broken. On Friday morning a highly respected secretary of state was assaulted in the streets, bundled into a motor car and taken to a secret address called Unit G3 where he was beaten, tortured with electrical current and saturated with psychotropic drugs prior to being executed."

Humphries stared directly across his desk. "If true, it is an outrage. But is it true?"

Portland studied the policeman for a moment. "We rescued him in an attack on Unit G3, and a number of Specials were injured..."

The policeman was livid with anger. "You are trying to tell me a paramilitary attack was made on members of the Special Branch, and I'm sitting here none the wiser?"

"Why weren't you told, Gerald? Why didn't Gordon Hastings inform you? Why did the Specials not call for police assistance? You'd think it would be the first thing they would do in order to easily catch the culprits, wouldn't you? You have been left out, Gerald. Detached from the circuit. Listen to me carefully now. From time to time there are teams of armed groups, referred to in the transcripts as DA's or Direct Action Groups, who roam British streets with a licence to intimidate or liquidate." He held up his hand as the policeman came half way off his chair. "No, let me finish. I am *not* exaggerating. I have documentary proof I can lay before you." He slapped his inside pocket. "And on this list you will find names of highly respected members of our community - in Parliament, in Westminster and elsewhere - whose lives are now very, very much at risk. And above all, Gerald, note *which* side came to the police. Note *which* side reported the matter."

The Commissioner was not satisfied. "Why did you not come directly to me when the distinguished but unnamed permanent secretary was abducted?"

Portland sighed. "Surely I don't have to explain basic tactical operations to a police chief. It had to be secret and sudden and - most importantly - unexpected to succeed. Informing you would have been a breach of security..."

"...a breach of security!"

"...because, for all we knew, you could have been a partner in the illegal operations, and it would have taken too long to convince you if you were not. Witness my present efforts. We had no time. The permanent secretary is our able spokesman, and he would have lost his life."

Sir Gerald Humphries could not contain himself any longer and rose from his chair, coming around to the front of his desk to confront the General. "Let me be abundantly clear on this matter. You and your group unilaterally decided to take legal and police matters into your own hands, excluding me because I might be a security risk? Is that what you're trying to say to me?"

Portland rubbed the ash from his cigar into an ashtray. "That's correct."

"Then I find I must caution you that what you say may be used in evidence as I bear witness to what you are telling me. Legally this transcript and even the tape supporting it are hearsay. What you are doing is legally untenable in a democratic state."

"We no longer live in a democratic state, Gerald."

"I see no option here except for the prosecution of you and the group you represent. Then you may have the privilege of explaining this entire conspiracy to a high court judge."

The General took another puff from the Havana. "I feel a great deal of sympathy for you, Gerald. I have dealt you something of a Hobson's choice."

Humphries was puzzled. "*You* feel sympathy for *me*?"

"Indeed. I am now convinced you are not one of them, and that will make your life much more complicated and unpleasant. Therefore, if you are ill-advised enough to try and make public allegations against us, you will – ironically - be removed by them. Probably killed, as the last thing the other side want is public exposure, which your hidebound morality would press you to do even if sacked from your position. Your choices are therefore very limited. You can arrest us all and call the press tomorrow and die shortly thereafter. Or you can keep the whole matter to yourself. Or you can listen to what we have to say, especially regarding the tactics to return this country to its former democratic state. However miserable and inefficient a backwater it had become, it was still ours. We were not a first rate power, possibly not even a second rate one. But now, Gerald, we are nothing more than a corporate satellite, in bondage to decisions taken elsewhere by people elected by no one. Pressure is daily and corruptly applied to our government, either directly or indirectly, by a large international organisation allied to transnational corporations with an executive funded by the sale of drugs and arms."

Portland paused for a moment, but the policeman had nothing to say as he stared intently out the window. "I apologise for making the choice necessary, Gerald, but what you must choose now is them or us. There is no longer any neutrality. I sympathise because I faced the same choice myself." He again pulled the envelope from his inside pocket. "Look at the list of these names. Then there will only be one choice, I'm afraid."

Humphries stared at General Portland for a full minute before taking the envelope and returning to his seat behind the desk. He turned on the anglepoise and again took his reading glasses from the leather case, placing them carefully on his large nose. Then he slowly and cautiously opened the envelope.

CHAPTER EIGHTEEN

The man placed the plastic bowl and spoon inside the door, had a good look at her and left. The door itself was virtually noiseless, but her headache amplified the sound and caused her to squeeze her eyes shut for a moment. It was one of those headaches which began at the root of the neck, radiated up into the temples and coiled around behind the eyeballs. It throbbed with the beat of her heart and was beginning to triumph over the awful feeling of nausea in the pit of her stomach. She woke up with both. Headache and nausea. But she knew she had slept for a long time, and if the hangover hadn't been so awesome she would be able to think properly.

Corky DeLoop looked at the food the orderly had placed inside the door. Yeah, she was hungry alright. But could she keep anything down? Assuming of course it wasn't pig slops. She couldn't remember eating since she arrived - whenever *that* was. Days? Weeks? Months? Lurching onto all fours, she slowly crawled over to the plastic bowl and prised up the lid with trembling hands. Then she stopped. Yes, she had eaten. Like this. On all fours. Gillmore. She closed her eyes and her head sagged to the floor. Gillmore. Yeah. The son of a bitch. Memories flickered briefly in her mind like fragments of old film, but they had no order at all. There was no beginning, middle and end. Walking around in red shoes, very high, very difficult. The thought of the shoes gave her a feeling of some pleasure. Might be worth getting some like that, if she ever got out of here.

If? What did she mean by "if"? Goddamn it, she was *going* to get out, one way or the other But she couldn't do it if she had the drug. It was a drug alright, something that screwed up her head, screwed up her memory. The images flickering inside were like a dream sequence, though. Like they weren't real and maybe hadn't happened. Or maybe some happened and others hadn't. Damn it, that was cruel, not even knowing whether something happened to you or not. Her head felt like it was caving in from the back and sides.

She could smell the food and knew she was desperately hungry. Concentrate on that, she thought. Concentrate on getting the food down and keeping it there. Hunger was probably half her problem. Pulling off the lid, she peered in. Stew of some sort, didn't smell bad. She felt for the spoon and put it inside, tipping one edge to fill it with liquid. Her hair was falling forward, and she looked at it. Straggly and matted. No longer a beautiful babe, she thought. And then she froze. Not beautiful. Ugly. Breasts sagging down to her waist, folds of pasty flesh, legs with varicose veins. She sat up so quickly her head began to thud, but she ignored that as she looked at herself, checking everything she could see. The sense of relief was palpable. It was a mirror of some sort. A trick mirror? What a terrible thing to do to a woman, now that was *really* nasty. Take everything away, even her body.

No, Corky, she told herself. Stop thinking and eat. Eat first, think second. She picked up the spoon again and tried a sip. Delicious. Wonderful. Another bite, this time a potato. Then a carrot. Finally a piece of meat. Yes, yes. It was staying down. But take it slow. Don't eat too fast.

When she finished she rolled onto her back, exhausted, and put her arm over her eyes to shut out the white light. As they said in Texas, her stomach had thought her throat was cut.

Cut her throat? Could she do that? Would she have to? If the memories fitting together in her mind were real, she might have to. How did they manage to twist her like that? And then she recalled the pain. It caused her to curl slowly into a foetal ball. Oh, yes, the pain. It was impossible. Her mind would not accept the memory, but they had put things on her breasts and something else up her. Pushing it out of her mind, she turned again on her back. She was completely nude now, but she had been wearing red shoes. And hose. Stockings. Walking around, crawling around trying to please Gillmore. Angrily she thought, yeah, if that's the way it's going to be, yeah, I *will* cut my throat. No way am I going to be some man's servant, serving Pepsi Cola, flipping on my back any time he wants it or wearing gags.

Gags. Sarah. Sarah Courtney. That was maybe a hope. The girl on the yacht. Now, unless she was a real lousy judge of character, she bet Sarah was trying to do something, trying to find her. But how? These were powerful men. Up to now she didn't realise how much power powerful men had. In the past she thought it was just money, but no, these people could kidnap, drug, rape, kill, whatever they liked. It was more than money could buy. It was one powerful man linked to another and another and another - like a series of batteries, to boost the voltage. When one worked against you, they all did. It was combined power focused on one small point. Her. At first she was arrogant enough to think she could resist by willpower alone. She couldn't. So. Admit it. They *could* make a slave of you. They could do it. For Gillmore. Or Herk. God, what a thought. She knew Herk's taste. He'd want her in some little dainty garbage dress with frills and lace and crinolines. The thought revolted her, and she began to slip slowly downwards. Impossible to do, impossible to avoid. They have the power, and I don't...

Power. Something funny about that word. It shook a memory somewhere. Power. *Hold on to the power.* What power? Why had that thought been reverberating around her mind like a nursery rhyme? She had nothing, not even a stitch of clothes. They had taken everything that was hers. Her will, her joy, her love of life. Her body. And her mind. It was like returning to your house to find a burglar had turned out all the drawers, ripped clothes from the closet, torn up old photographs, poured salt and sugar and syrup over everything, stolen the hi-fi, the TV, the jewellery. Everything personal had been touched and handled and twisted. That's how she felt inside, and there was no one to help. No one. Just her. And what was she? Nothing. Soon they would come again to give her the injection, and she would be doing...whatever it was she had been doing. Whatever they wanted. The headache pounded like kettle drums to a funeral march, and again she rolled onto her side and curled into a ball. She fought it hard, but the tears came, rolling down her cheeks, and she tasted the saltiness in her mouth.

Oh, let them come with the needle soon, she thought in desperation. At least I'll be *something*. Not *nothing*. I'm nothing now. Nothing. They've taken it all. Everything. Bring back Mr Gillmore. Sir. She moved her hand to her bottom and felt the small weals. So he had got his way. He got everything he promised, no doubt. A sudden memory flashed. Sitting in a chair, her legs wide open in front of his desk. The memory was strangely arousing, and that completely surprised her. She was looking at him, and he seemed much handsomer, not like a little shit at all. The memory flashed away. But for just a moment she had captured the feeling the drug had given her, a kind of dreaminess. A dreamy weakness. Strangely, the feeling was almost nice, like being a little girl again and having a parent. If you were good, you would be rewarded. If you were bad...

She tried to think, but the headache was still hurting her. Thankfully, the nausea had receded. The food made her feel better. Or less bad. She still didn't trust herself to stand up. Or even sit up. But she had to think. They had given her mind back, so she mustn't waste time. It was a small hope, like the hope of help from Sarah Courtney. It was a simple and alien world these men wanted. A world they controlled. Control, yeah. The ultimate control. Come here, do this, do that or bad pain, little girl. No complications for them. You don't cause them any trouble. They wanted their power to soak into the bones of those they controlled. Power. *Hang on to the power.* What did that mean? What did she have that was powerful?

She took her arm away from her face in despair and opened her eyes. And she saw the photograph. She hadn't noticed it before. Gillmore. In some kind of Napoleonic pose, looking grave and important. For an instant she was aware the picture filled her with awe and a hint of desire. The Great Man who created an empire with a few simple rules. When he was away, his voice would come out of the picture. Yeah, sure. Recordings. While he was asleep, she got his voice over and over again. They were fucking up her mind, goddamn it! She beat the sides of her fists against her temples and immediately regretted it. The pain made her want to vomit, and at the same time it reminded her of the pain Gillmore caused.

Again she started sliding downward, her spirits plummeting like a stone. Oh, to hell with it, she thought. Make a deal with the son of a bitch. She would do what he wanted, if they wouldn't give her more drugs. OK. OK. Who knows, there might be a chance sometime to escape. Give in to the bastard. A chorus of voices inside her were chanting "Yes! Yes! Yes!", and she visualised herself with a dainty walk, a sweet smile and a tiny little voice. Making up beds, cleaning floors, serving drinks, being fondled and fucked whenever, wherever. In a twisted way the vision was alluring. In a way she almost *wanted* it. Be somebody else *for* somebody else. Give it all up. Surrender. "I surrender, Mr Gillmore, sir". Do what you're told and nothing else. No need to think or worry. A memory flickered again, and she recalled him grabbing her pubic hair, licking her breast. Again, there was a momentary surge of erotic desire. She had trembled. She wanted it.

Looking again at the picture on the wall, she felt totally divided. On the one hand she was repelled by the sight of the reptilian little creep. On the other, goddamn it, she wanted him. Wanted to hear his voice, even wanted his cock.

Oh. Yes. He had a big thing. A little man with a big thing. Another memory. She was on the desk on her back, and Gillmore was entering her. Oh, hell, that was great. Yet the thought made her almost throw up. She was caught between two rivers, but she also knew this was important. OK, they had fucked, and - admit it - it was fantastic. She stared up at the face intently. Something about the face. As he backed away from her. Yes, and he'd called her Corky! She remembered his face looking down at her, it was coming back. It was in agony. *His* face, not hers. Then he backed away like...like he was afraid. The memory faded.

Hold on to the power. She rolled over, turning her back on the photograph. OK, it's a penknife against a row of machine guns, but it was something. She almost chuckled. Would you believe it? The old Corky magic had worked even on Gillmore. She closed her eyes tightly and bit her lip. Hold on to that. Hold on. Build on it. Get your feet back under you. Corky is beautiful. Corky can't be beat. Corky feels great. It's great to be alive. Sick to my stomach, my head thundering, naked as a jaybird, dragged across the coals of hell backwards, hair in a mess. Get those feet with the pretty toes back under you, girl, because you got a lot of thinking to do. A *lot* of thinking.

* * *

The Dirty Duck was not full because it was half past two. Jennifer Montgomery was late, but found Sarah sitting alone at a table in the corner near a window. She explained to her friend that they had worked past lunch hour because there were no more rehearsals that day. She was off. Free. When Sarah Courtney first called, she thought she would only have the hour to see her. But the director had to have talks with the designer that afternoon, so plans were changed. She was playing Cordelia in the new *Lear*. Not the biggest part in the world, but not bad, either. Noticeable. And that would do her just fine.

She returned to the table with the drinks. Sarah was having a white wine, and she bought herself a bitter lemon. Alcohol in the middle of the day always made her sleepy.

"Is this your first time in Stratford?" she asked as she sat down.

Sarah Courtney sipped her wine. "I'll have to apologise, but I don't have much time for pleasantries today. I'm worried sick about a friend of mine and need to find your boyfriend."

"My boyfriend?"

"I would have asked you on the telephone, but I needed someone to talk to about this problem. And I think I need your boyfriend's help."

Jennifer was puzzled. "You want Adrian to help you?"

"I met him in Corfu..."

"You did? I was with him, why didn't he tell me you were there?"

Sarah looked at her friend curiously. "I don't know. You were there? Really? I *am* confused. He had a black friend and said his name was O'Connell, a big fellow with a bald head..."

Jennifer Montgomery threw back her head and laughed. "Haug! You met Haug! Now I know. He went out after I returned. Haug's not my boyfriend. He's the man I love."

"Ahhh, I think I see," she said. "Though I'm not too sure. So his name is not O'Connell?"

"He was probably doing some job and didn't want to give his real name. He is Haug. A fabulous man. You better not tell me you got your hands in his jeans or that'll be the end of our friendship, Sarah."

She shook her head. "No. No. I'm afraid I wasn't in any mood for that sort of thing after a week with Harvey Gillmore."

"A week?" Jennifer said with a shudder. "I couldn't even last a night with him. You must have the all-time record."

"I wish I didn't. I really mean that." She told Jennifer Montgomery the story of her time in Corfu, the awful sessions with Gillmore and her rescue by Corky DeLoop. Then hesitantly, almost with tears, she told her what happened to Corky and how the whole "holiday" was aborted. "I know I've got to help her, Jennifer. I've got to. And the only thing I can think of is O'Connell...Haug. But I don't know how to find him."

Jennifer Montgomery finished her bitter lemon. "Haug is your man, alright. We're going back to London right now."

"We?"

"I've got the rest of the afternoon off, and I'm not rehearsing tomorrow. Stratford and the Royal Shakespeare Company can do without me for a day and a half. Are you driving, or did you come by train?"

"Train."

"Great. We'll use my car."

* * *

"What if the Labour Party win the next election here?" Dr Carlton Fine asked a little truculently.

Professor Alexander Hinkley spread his hands then shook them dismissively. "Doesn't matter. Of course it would be regrettable because it slows down the momentum of change. But it would not - could not - alter the direction. You know of course we have colleagues within the Labour Party, and they are now very much in the ascendant..."

331

"It's the same as the States, Carlton," Wren Olsen interrupted. "Though more so. This is a little country..."

"A squirt of mustard on the hotdog," growled Hercules DeLoop.

"...and if someone, say the Prime Minister, starts to get bright ideas, he is taken off to a quiet corner to be talked to rationally." Olsen stopped for a moment to adjust his belt over his stomach. He had eaten too much at lunch. "First of all, they'll find it hard to get credit - certainly with the IMF. They'll have to have credit if they want industrial investment. And you know the primary thing we insist on: cut back on public spending, right?"

"So they raise fuckin' taxes," said DeLoop.

"If they raise taxes," Olsen continued, "they become electorially vulnerable..."

"They'll raise them anyway," Regis observed. "They're bastards for taxes."

Olsen waved him away with a smile. "Our associated firms, many of them financial institutions, threaten to re-locate in Frankfurt or Paris or Rome or Madrid. The British actually have very little actual control..."

"Just a moment," said Hinkley. "Let us get this into perspective. The British people are a part of something, a great movement. Of peoples. Economies. Towards an omega point of confluence in the future. We are the engine of a democracy so vast it covers the face of the industrialised world. It is misleading to think of the British as 'a squirt of mustard' or having 'very little control'. We have a control commensurate with our contribution to the Community of Association.."

"...which ain't jack shit," said DeLoop.

Alexander Hinkley turned on the Texan as he adjusted his polka dot bow tie. "I would point out that without the theoretical forge of the Thatcher years our Association would be more than a decade in arrears. Britain was the cradle of the Industrial Revolution and the New Capitalist Revolution, a revolution which has reverberated across Europe and torn out communism by its roots." He raised his small forefinger. "And I would also point out we provided the Americans for years with a

332

springboard into Europe, a springboard which proved vital with the development of the EEC."

DeLoop laughed. "The Brits didn't have any choice in the matter. They did what they were told and still do."

"That's enough, Herk," said Dr Carlton Fine. "Personally I'd like to return to the main agenda for this meeting. What we have today is a Technology Revolution, nevermind all the others. In my opinion the collapse of the USSR opens a lot of doors for us, and not just the obvious ones. The USSR is attached to Europe. Our main strategy up to now is to move all heavy industry to selected areas of Africa, South America and the Far East where wages are a fraction of what they are here or in the States. But look at what's happening in the Far East right now. A repetition of a pattern we all know. Invest in the country, and the country becomes richer, right? Living standards go up, and so do expectations. Soon you have unions creeping in, driving wages and running costs up. India, for instance. Now they've passed a goddamn law about rigorous safety measures in foreign owned factories. Again, costs go up. You get countries that 'wear out', the way I see it. Taiwan, South Korea, India. Finally it may not be worth re-locating any more industry to those places. OK, so far we've used Africa and South America mostly for raw materials and reasonably priced food. Now we're bringing Mexico on line in industry. Then maybe in a few years, Mexico will 'wear out'."

Fine stopped for a moment for emphasis. "Now let's think radically about Russia. It's a lot closer, so we've got lower transport costs. Also, and quite importantly, they have abundant raw materials to be exploited at bargain prices. The question I want to put to you is this. How can we create a constant source of industrial supply at a constant low cost without the risk of that country 'wearing out' - at least for a commercially viable period? Say, fifty years?"

"I'm glad you mentioned this, Carlton," Hinkley replied quickly, making little birdlike movements of excitement. "An enormous amount of land is virtually up for grabs in Russia and the other republics at real bargains. Once we have a stable government there - and let's face it, the Slavs are, on the whole, not a very bright race and are used to an autocratic government. Perhaps," he said with an element of inspiration, "Perhaps an autocratic government is their democratic choice! After all, if the people want to be ruled by an absolute monarch, they should certainly be free to do so."

"Of course they should," agreed Wren Olsen.

"The country is huge," Hinkley continued. "We would have virtually unlimited expansion. A place to make all the motor cars, lorries, aeroplanes, heavy plant and equipment, high quality steel - as well as top grade consumer durables like TV's, video and hi-fi equipment, washing machines, refrigerators, vacuum cleaners, computers, etc, etc. And as you say, Carlton, all the raw materials we need are right there. In the same land mass."

Alexander Hinkley was really excited now. He was sitting on the edge of Regis' desk, and he slid forward, tucking one foot under the other leg. "One could liken the development of the world to the human body. Here in Europe, America - Japan, even - we are the head, the intelligence. The head has the vision, the plans and directs the rest of the body. For mutual benefit, of course," he added hastily. "Here in the West - and possibly Japan - we will simply have people at computer consoles. Some will be simply directing traffic, as it were. Others are creating software and new computer designs. Physicists are working to further reduce chip size while increasing capacity. Philosophers are refining theory, as are economists. Some of the former working class will be drafted into this hotbed of intellectual activity. The rest, perhaps, will be trained to do the day-to-day manual labour necessary to free our computer and technology operators from the humdrum problems of child care, washing, cleaning, etc...."

Carlton Fine interrupted abruptly. "When it is possible, the manual workers - the drones - could be relieved of worry or even envy caused by the higher centres of human judgment. In fact I believe it will soon be possible for them to be *engineered* to like and expect their kind of life. After all, gentlemen, we are all pulling for the same things, aren't we? A better, more efficient, freer, more democratic way of life. If we were able to relieve them of their anxieties, would that not be kindness?"

334

"This is absolutely fabulous," Jeremy Evans gushed. He was sitting on the edge of his chair near the French doors and had been watching the debate between Fine and Hinkley like a tennis addict at Wimbledon. "I wish I could take it all in, all at once."

Dr Carlton Fine smiled grandly, adjusting his glasses. "Capitalism and democracy are triumphant. Ideological twins." He held up two fingers pressed together. "Our task now is to plan forward, as we have been doing for years, but this time to bring under our wing all of humanity. It is now finally possible. Politically and technologically. Because," he dropped one of the two fingers. "After Russia there is China! Also in the same land mass. But with billions more people. Numerically speaking what we are talking about here is almost unlimited expansion. Centuries, perhaps."

"Excuse me, Dr Fine," said Jeremy Evans. "Just how are we moving into Russia?

"The bandits, of course," Fine said with emphasis. Everyone laughed. "Yes. These are the real entrepreneurs. The ones who really understand power at the street level, building up bases, building up capital. They will be the men we will be dealing with in the future. So we support them now. Give them bankers. Give them encouragement. Go get it, we tell them. It's there for the taking. In a couple of generations, they will be the old rich, you see."

"It links in, doesn't it?" said Wren Olsen, nodding his head so the fat under his chin wrinkled and compressed. "Though the situation is still a little unclear, we offer reward for what we want and pain for what we dislike. Simple, really. An old concept, the carrot and stick, but it makes the donkey go. On TV they constantly expose the old communists as corrupt and evil and selfish and dictatorial to the core. Hammer it day and night. The press as well. Harvey's already bought into two newspapers over there, haven't you, Harvey?"

Harvey Gillmore was slumped into the leather armchair and wasn't really listening to this dull conversation of these dorks repeating what had been obvious to him for years. His mind was somewhere else. With a woman. With *the* woman. He tried desperately not to think about her. Every time he did, he got a hard on and had to cross his legs. Damn it to hell. Damn her. The same vision returned to him. The huge, beautiful woman lying on the desk, her head in a pool of gossamer platinum hair, the skin glowing lustrously, the large pale nipples still erect on tits which trembled every time he touched her, the waist spreading voluptuously into perfect hips, and from those hips glided the longest legs he had ever seen. He never made love to any woman without stockings on, never. And no woman he had known looked better than this one with them on. And her pussy... Gillmore's eyelids fluttered involuntarily, and he crossed his legs again.

What the fuck had come over him? All he wanted was to get the fuck out of this place and return to Unit G5. DeLoop had asked him how he was getting on, and it caught him off guard. He kept forgetting she belonged to him. Correction. *Had* belonged to him. Things had changed now. Now she belonged to Gillmore. Gillmore always got everything he wanted in life, except maybe peace of mind. He saw no reason he could not have Corky. Even if he had to kill DeLoop. Even if she didn't want to - hell, that never had anything to do with it anyway. Women could be bent or broken. All women. He recalled his first secretary. It was in Sydney, and he wasn't even twenty years old. She was thirty and married and had refused him a number of times. Yet he had her. Up against the office wall with her skirt pulled up and her knickers around her ankles. He had looked in her face, enjoying her embarrassment and humiliation as her tits hung out of her blouse.

But, damn it, this one was different. This was something he hadn't dealt with before, because what he wanted most was for *her* to want *him*. Why? Why should that make any fucking difference?

His mind turned again to the desk and the beautiful woman who lay there. That's where his mind returned dozens of times every hour. When he rammed himself into her something happened. She had put her arms around him, and her legs, and pulled him to her. Her mouth had sought his. Her face was full of joy, and her body was like a wild animal. Enjoying *him*. And he liked it. The room changed. The whole world changed...

336

"Harvey. Are you with us?" Regis asked. Everyone was staring at him.

Gillmore glanced at his watch. "Is that the time? Christ, I've got to go."

"The meeting isn't over, Harvey," said Fine quietly.

"I'm not a fucking philosopher," Gillmore said venomously. "I've got a business to run. You big thinkers just tell me what you want printed and where, and I'll print it. Tell me what to buy, and I'll buy it, if it'll turn a dollar. Meanwhile I've got newspapers coming out all over the world and thick editors to tell how to do their business. I'm a worker, not a fucking thinker." He got up and went to get his briefcase. He had to get out of there. He had to see Corky.

"Take some time off and see to that goddamn wife of mine," shouted DeLoop as he left the room.

* * *

Sir Jonathan Mainwaring walked slowly along the little stream eating an apple. He was wearing a crew neck jumper with patches on the elbows. It was the first time he had tried to walk out of doors, and Haug stayed close to his side, ready to catch him if he staggered.

"You don't have to hover," Mainwaring said. "I can usually tell when I'm about to have a weak moment."

"Is that why you didn't say a word before you fell over in the kitchen this morning?" Haug replied, spitting a stream of tobacco juice into the water.

"I'm sure that's poisonous," the Perm Sec sniffed. "And I enjoy fishing in this river."

"River?" Haug laughed. "It's just a trickle o' water over a few rocks. Even a flounder couldn't keep but one set of gills under water."

"I know. Everything is bigger in America. The biggest trees, the biggest rivers, the biggest fools." He took another bite of apple and stopped for a moment to fill his lungs with fresh air. "I need to talk to you but have to admit I don't know how to do it. It's not really in my nature."

337

"My personal opinion," Haug said as they continued walking, "is that folks don't have natures. They do have habits, though."

"Ah. But you're an American, you see. You have no idea of the English public school system. The products of this system have *natures*. We are plucked from our homes at a very early age to be regimented like daleks. There are parental pressures, social and peer pressures. Relentless pressures. Thus we all speak the same and wear the same masks, having been forced through the same sieve with extremely close tolerances."

Mainwaring held onto a tree while stepping down a small incline. "Sarah and I have always been very, very close, Haug. But even with her, I cannot unmask myself. Nor can she with me. Much of our love and respect is subtextual. Unspoken. Perhaps, however, I can speak with you. Because I need to speak. Desperately. And I have to admit I don't know how."

Haug stopped for a moment and took off his dozer cap. It was not far from where he and Louise made love in the rain. "I got to admit when I first met you, I was real impressed. Now, I can go into a bar room brawl and stand a good chance of bein' the last one standin'. You're able to do that socially, if you see what I mean. Doesn't matter about rank or what kinda verbal aggravation you are gettin'. You're like Cyrano de Bergerac, usin' your tongue as a sword. All your thoughts are there, marchin' out in the right order. The infantry, the artillery, close air support, armour."

He put his hat back on and leaned on a tree, looking out across the opposite field. "Now I know you a little better, though, and I feel thangs, despite the mask you wear. I know you got fucked over, and I know how you got fucked over. And I got some idea of what's goin' on inside you now. There are thangs I don't wanna talk about in my past. Correction. Thangs I don't know *how* to talk about. Probably do me a lot of good to try some day."

Mainwaring fastidiously brushed the leaves from a flat stone and sat on the edge. "We seem to have developed a strange friendship, you and I, and I would be flattered if at some time you felt safe enough to confide some of your own experiences."

338

Haug laughed. "It would probably be you rather than anybody else I know, Jonathan. But this is your turn. You're the one who's hurtin' now."

The Permanent Secretary sat very straight on the flat rock, the same way he sat on a park bench, with legs crossed. "Everything in me resists mentioning even a word of complaint."

He paused for a long while, and there was nothing but the sound of the stream. "Everything has collapsed, Haug. Everything. Such substance as I can manage is freefloating, built upon shifting sands. Where I once looked upon certainties, now there is only doubt. Where there was granite and marble there is a bog of sucking mud, threatening every moment to engulf me in darkness. I have to confess I no longer feel capable of occupying the Chair of the United Opposition, and I intend to resign."

Haug nodded. "Your vision hasn't cleared up yet, and you cain't see your friends standin' around you in a circle. I know it's a kinda invisible circle, but we're circlin' you for protection and support. You got as much time as you need to get well. In other words, we don't accept your resignation. Would you like to know somethin'? Easton, General Portland, even that Tory MP, Tillson, all wanted to go on the raid. Louise did come. The reason is, you're a good man. A warm man. It's not because you're intelligent. It's not even because we need you, though we do."

Mainwaring held up his hand in protest. "You don't see what I see in myself. A selfish, weak and petty man. A man without courage. A bundle of dark desires which have no way of expressing themselves except by silent and relentless screaming. Yes, I realise the abuse I received brought all this to the surface, but it would not have floated up if it were not already there, would it? I'm afraid it has overpowered the solidity - the appearance of solidity - and the masquerade of certainties..." His voice trailed off with a slight tremor.

Haug went over and squatted down beside his friend. "You are human, Jonathan, that's all. Ever one of us - at least everbody I ever met - is a kinda mirage, you know. It looks clear in the distance, but you walk up on it, and it just disappears into nothin'. Or into a lotta fragments. What you thought was solid in the past was just a mirage."

Mainwaring grabbed his arm in a surprisingly strong grip. "If that's the truth, Haug, how the devil do you live with it?"

"Well...I'm no expert. But you kinda got to accept the lack of permanence. This tree here seems solid, but even it is changin' slowly, and one day it'll fall down into that river of yours and rot. Your mind is never solid in the first place, and that's the only way you got of seein' yourself. A lotta people wind up seein' what they wanna see. Jack the Ripper might well have been a good family man, givin' a lotta money to the poor. Wouldn't surprise me. So maybe he wanted to see himself like that and didn't wanna see he was fucked up about women. I tend to look at it this way: There are cruel parts of me, selfish parts, cowardly parts, good parts, maybe even a touch of finery here and there. It's all part of the stew which has a particular taste of its own that makes you an individual. OK, maybe that's all not so profound, because the hard bit is knowin' where you go from there."

Mainwaring let go his arm and held up a bony finger. "Exactly. Precisely. Where do I go now with my bundle of fears, my debilitating lack of self esteem, my psychological liquidity? I don't have the faintest idea."

Haug pointed his forefinger at his friend. "I see in front of me a man who is at a fork in the road. Well...you think you're in a fork. Do I go this way? Do I go that way? Do I stand still? That way is the right way, I know it, but I don't have the guts for it. Because of the demons ragin' inside you, you cain't move. They're hollerin' at you. Mainwarin's a coward, Mainwarin's no good, not worth a shit, a farce, laughable..."

"All those things and many more..."

"Well," Haug said, standing up, "there's no good way outta this kinda mess, but I tell you what I'll do. Gimme your hand."

Mainwaring extended his right hand, and Haug pulled him gently to his feet and steadied him. "I want you to cross that little...river, as you call it, and I want you to do it without me touchin' you. OK? There are a couple o' rocks there, and one of 'em's flat, so you shouldn't have a problem."

340

Sir Jonathan Mainwaring frowned and started to refuse. Then he slowly eased himself down the bank, holding onto a tree. Putting one foot out carefully, he stepped on the flat rock, regained his balance, tested the next rock for stability, transferred his weight and used his other foot to step onto the opposite bank.

Mainwaring looked across at the American. "Now. What did I achieve? Besides wet feet?"

Haug scratched his chin. "On the way over were you thinkin' about your problems? Did you see any demons?"

"Well...I suppose not. At least not for the few seconds it took me to cross."

"So, you can do little thangs. And you can succeed. That's what you wanna do right now. Little thangs. You been thinkin' about a heap o' big thangs. The United Opposition, love, right and wrong, whether you're good or bad. And it's too much for the wirin' right now. Concentrate on puttin' one foot in front of the other, then pat yourself on the back when you do it. Try fryin' yourself an egg, maybe, or readin' a little William Blake, lissen to a little Mozart. It's a little like liftin' weights. You start with somethin' you can lift, then build up, addin' a little more when you get stronger."

"That sounds very time consuming," said Mainwaring.

"We'll wait. Some thangs are worth waitin' for. You take all the time you need."

Mainwaring stared at the rocks in the stream and then stepped quickly across to join Haug.

"You're right," Mainwaring said as he put a hand on Haug's shoulder to steady himself. "I'll try your little backwoods remedy. Meanwhile it seems you have taken on some of my responsibilities."

"Oh, not really. Just splittin' some logs and carryin' the firewood, nothin' important. I cain't really do much. Hell, I don't even know how to open a briefcase."

"That is an operation which calls for deep intelligence. And years of training."

"Oh, I know that," Haug replied. "Must make a man feel real important, too, totin' one o' those thangs around. I tell you

341

what, Jonathan. I just made myself a decision. I'm gonna bring the Harley down here and take you for a ride on it."

Mainwaring held up his hand. "You won't catch me near one of those horrible machines."

They continued walking on the path. "You got any honky tonks in this neighbourhood?" Haug asked.

"What the devil is a honky tonk?"

"Get you on the back of the Harley, and we'll go find a honky tonk somewhere. An old cinder block dance hall with one naked light bulb hangin' in the middle and a good bluegrass band playin'. I'll get you a nice pair o' cowboy boots and a decent hat, instead o' that bedpan you wear on your head, and we'll go in and kick shit outta some of these country boys around here, grab a couple a women with tight skirts wearin' too much lipstick and a quart bottle of Old Crow and have ourselves a good time in some cheap hotel somewhere."

Mainwaring stopped and looked back at Haug. "Have you actually done something like that in your life?"

Haug grinned. "More times than I can remember."

"Is it fun?"

"Well, while it's happenin' it is. Next mornin' when you wake up with her panties around your neck, wonderin' how they got there, the bed soaked with whiskey and the bottle smashed on the floor, and the sun comin' in and the flies startin' to swarm, and your head feels like somebody's been drivin' nails in it, and the woman on the bed crawls over and vomits in your boots...well, I don't know whether the trade off is worth it anymore."

"Thank you for that piece of realism, Haug," Mainwaring said as he continued the walk. "You very nearly enticed me with your little portrait of hillbilly romanticism. You see, I have never allowed myself to have that kind of fun. I knew it existed. I have even been envious from time to time. To be truthful, I am envious right now. Before the kidnap I don't think I would have even admitted that to anyone. Perhaps not even to myself."

"Well, there you are, Jonathan. There are good demons and bad demons crawlin' around in there. May as well have a good look at all of 'em while they're on swarm. But I'll make a deal

342

with you. Jump on the Harley one day, and let me show you my kind of good time, and, shit, I'll put on a suit and tie, grab one o' your spare briefcases, and we'll go to a restaurant in Mayfair or somethin'."

Mainwaring stopped dead in the path. "The thought of you in a suit is so anomalous that it is beyond my ability to imagine it. No. No, I can't do it. Yet I must see it. I must. It would be a visual treat, like seeing a chimpanzee in a tuxedo..."

Haug shook his head. "I said a suit, not a tuxedo. I got my principles."

Mainwaring held out his hand. "You have got yourself a deal, partner," he said in a very bad Southern American accent.

Involuntarily Haug started laughing at the accent and couldn't stop himself. He shook the hand, trying to speak, then gave up and pounded his hand on a nearby tree, tears rolling down his cheeks.

Mainwaring joined him, at first with a chuckle. Then he, too, laughed out loud. He thought it was an odd sound at first because he had not laughed like that for a very long time. Finally he threw his head back and barked up at the sky. The two of them would have appeared insane to an onlooker. A very tall, bony English country gentleman with his head thrown back, and a heavy-set powerful American redneck pounding helplessly on a tree trunk.

CHAPTER NINETEEN

Enrico Gomez sat with his feet propped on the table flipping through a copy of Penthouse. He was very tired of the DeLoop woman detail. It was boring. Gomez was a thoroughly urban person and hated the countryside. Countrysides were confusing places. They were empty except for hayseeds, animals, plants and shit. There was shit everywhere you tried to walk. Sheep shit, cow shit, duck shit and dog shit on the ground and bird shit coming from the air. He had been out of doors twice since he arrived at Unit G5. Once he sunk up to his ankles in soft ground and the next time he stepped in a pile of shit. His black and white loafers were almost ruined. *And* he was running out of hair gel. He only washed his hair about once or twice a month, and if he didn't have the gel it wouldn't lay down properly. He asked one of the cops to get some for him, but the asshole said he couldn't find any.

He hated cops. Any kind of cops, even this kind, who wore sports jackets or windbreakers. Cops were always the same. In Cuba, in America and here in England. No class. The limeys had a funny accent, and at first he couldn't understand their lingo. But finally he had introduced them to Miami poker and consequently had his wallet stuffed with pounds he couldn't go out and spend. They wouldn't play with him any more, and one of them, some kind of sergeant, accused him of cheating. If he still had his gun, he would have drilled him in the middle of the head for that. Of course he was cheating, but they couldn't catch him at it. Until they caught him, any accusation demanded satisfaction. So he said the sergeant would walk over the bodies of a hundred whores to fuck his own mother, and he thought the limey's head was going to pop like a red balloon. There was almost a fight. That was the last time he had played cards. Now he just read fuck books and jacked off. They had given him a bedroom of his own, but he could only sleep so much of the day and night. If Mrs DeLoop hadn't been receiving some kind of medical treatment, he would have tried to slip in one night to try his chances. He had never done it because old DeLoop paid so good, and he didn't want to kill the golden goose. But he was dying for a woman. He even found himself looking at the sheep outside the window. Hell, they were soft and warm and might even be good pussy for all he knew. They didn't have sheep in Cuba when he was young. He had screwed a burro and a pig, but you needed help to screw a pig.

He looked up from his magazine as he saw Gillmore enter with a holdall. His guess was that Gillmore was some kind of doctor, as he spent a lot of time with the lady. Except for the last day or two, when he hadn't seen him. He yawned and turned a page, not even bothering to nod to the little Australian.

"If I open this door, will you behave yourself?" Gillmore's voice came through speakers which must have been hidden in one of the white walls.

Corky DeLoop was sitting in the corner of the room, her head resting on her arms. It was the moment she had been waiting and preparing herself for. She raised her head.

"Yes," she said. "Yeah, I will."

"If you don't behave yourself, I have a buzzer in my hand. The orderlies are just outside, and they will come in and put you in restraint. Then they will give you an injection. But I want to talk to you as you are now."

She stood up, putting her shoulders back, then ran her fingers through her hair, fluffing it. "I'll behave, 'cause I wanna talk to you, too. And I really don't want any more handcuffs and drugs. OK? I promise."

A few moments later the door swung open, but Gillmore did not enter. So she walked over, adjusting her hair as much as she could manage without a comb. Then, taking a deep breath, she walked outside into the Interrogation Room. Harvey Gillmore was leaning against the desk staring at her. She caught his eyes with her own and held them as she walked slowly, almost languidly, across the room toward him. Still naked, she held herself erect. Not like she had been "taught" during the drug sessions, but her own way. Her chin was dipped slightly so she could look from beneath her eyebrows. Her weight was kept on the balls of her feet, and she carefully placed one foot down in front of the other. Not too much. Not in a posey way or

346

artificially. She tried to make her movement as natural as possible and - just slightly - suggestive.

Corky DeLoop stopped in front of the publisher and gave a half smile. "Hello."

Gillmore was clenching his jaw. The sight of the woman who had been on his mind constantly jarred loose emotions from unopened cupboards. Without a doubt she was the most beautiful and sexiest female he had ever seen in his life. He never even noticed she was not walking as he had trained her. And no one had ever been allowed to look into his eyes like that. But he didn't say anything. He couldn't. His jaw was held tightly in a form of muscle spasm.

"You're gorgeous," he croaked finally.

Her smile spread wider, and she almost shyly turned her head away. "Not my fault. I was born that way, I guess."

He sighed and looked away. "Do you remember what happened?"

"Some of it," she said, looking back at him.

"How much?"

"Quite a bit."

"And you're not pissed off?"

She looked down at her feet for a moment. "Well...yeah, a little bit. More than a little bit. You hurt me a lot. I guess I would've really hated you if it hadn't been for..."

He jumped. "Hadn't been for what?"

She glanced up at him, coy but sincere. "You know."

She waited for him to answer, but he didn't. "I've been doin' a lotta thinkin'. When I first woke up I was real sick and real angry. Depressed, too. Like I wanted to commit suicide if there was somethin' to cut my wrists with. But there's nothin' else to do in that white room except think. I couldn't remember anything at first, nothin' at all. Then it started comin' back in little pieces, and I sorta fitted the pieces together until I got a kinda cracked picture."

Gillmore had a wild look in his eyes. "I want to touch you now. I've got to touch you."

Corky smiled very naturally and moved to him, putting her hands gently on his shoulders. "Well...touch me, then."

He started to grab her breasts. He wanted to grab them and squeeze them and tear them off and stuff them into his mouth like food. Instead, something came over him, and he touched her shoulders instead. Her skin was incredibly smooth. His hands slid underneath to her armpits, which were warm and soft. Then, noticing he was actually trembling, he touched her breasts, amazed at their shape, their design, their firmness. The nipples hardened as he stroked them. He put his palms underneath and weighed them. Then his hands drifted down to her waist and hips. The smell of her was taking his breath away. Surprisingly, her body responded to his touch. Not too much, just a little. But he knew she responded. With a great deal of self discipline, he pulled away and took her hands from his shoulders.

Harvey Gillmore got up and walked across the room and stared at the wall. Somehow he had to escape from her eyes, just to think. His thoughts were reeling drunkenly, almost meaninglessly, through his mind.

"That was real nice," she said behind him. "Real nice. That's what I remembered, and when I remembered that, I wasn't so mad any more."

"Look, er...Corky. I got a little problem here. Everything in my life, I've always been certain about, and now I'm not certain. It makes me feel a little sick inside. It's not like me, I tell you that. I don't understand a fucking thing about women, except that I sometimes need them. What I need, I take. It's as simple as that. I can do it. Always have. This thing looks dangerous to me, and I don't like it. I only like things I can control, and this is wild and dangerous, a place full of deadly animals peering out from behind the leaves."

"I think..."

"Don't interrupt me," he said venomously. Then he softened a little but still did not turn around. "The problem is this: I have got to have you. Not just sexually right now on the floor, like I wanted the moment you walked in. I want you full stop. I want you. Therefore I'm going to have you. There's DeLoop, he's a problem, but I can see one or two ways around that. Then there's you. And that has fucking stumped me so far. But I'm going to go against habits of a lifetime and lay my cards out right

348

on the table. I'll provide you with a flat, a house maybe, somewhere nice. A car, credit cards, that sort of crap. But, like I say, I don't understand women. That is why I train them to do as they are told. So I won't have to bother with arguments or headaches or temper tantrums. Just the same as my employees. They all know the contract, the name of the game. They take the money, and they do as they're told. If they don't, I fire them or punish them. Yesterday I gave my own editor twelve strokes of the cane with him across his own desk for being a prick and for not doing his job."

He turned but did not look at her. Instead he paced back and forth in front of the wall. "So, there's nothing personal when I have to punish people, men or women. It doesn't mean I don't...I don't...care for them. So. What I'm saying is there might be times in our relationship that I have to smack your arse. I can't have you mouthing at me or arguing or that kind of shit. And the only thing that really seems to work is physical punishment. So, that's number one." He held up a finger.

"Number two is that I am a hard worker and make a lot of money. While you'll be doing fuck all. So I want service when I'm around, OK? When I push a bell, you come running. Much of the time I won't be there, and you can sit on your fucking arse, but when I'm there, you're busy. OK?"

"That's two." He held up three fingers. "The third is this: I like women dressed a certain way when they're with me. So I want you to wear what I choose for you to wear, and I don't want any arguments about it. On the contrary, I want you to *enjoy* wearing the clothes I like and be sexy in them."

He smacked his hands together decisively. "Finally, this is the way things are going to be, Corky. I have decided that. I would much prefer to do it the easy way, but I am prepared to do it the hard way. So, you have got to tell me now. Today. Are you willing to stay with me on these terms, or do I have to use the drugs and a couple of minders?"

"May I call you Harvey?" she asked simply.

"No," he said sharply. "I *hate* people calling me Harvey, particularly women. I don't even allow my wife to call me Harvey. Or honey or any of that shit." He paused a moment, thinking, pursing his lips. "You don't have to be so heavy on the 'yes sir' or 'Mr Gillmore', especially when we're alone. But around other people, I don't know. It shows respect."

He took a deep breath and turned to face her. "So. What's your answer?"

She sat on the desk carefully, tossing her hair back from her face. "Well, it's an awful lot to take in at once. I know one thing. I don't want those drugs anymore. I still have the hangover. My temples are crushin' in at the sides, and my stomach is still heavin' from time to time."

Extending one leg, she stroked it slowly with her hand. Her voice was low and modulated. "I don't mind wearin' any kinda clothes that turns my man on. That's always kinda fun. But it's kind of against my nature to be some kinda maid. And I really seriously object to punishment, unless it's playful, leadin' to a good fuck."

"I'm not interested in what you think about the proposal," Gillmore said through his teeth. "Just yes or no. If it's no, I'll call in the quack."

She held up her hand with a smile and drew her outstretched leg up onto the desk as she half turned to him. "Please. I think it's important you know my reasons, just so you can trust me, if nothing else. I mean, I, too, think we really got somethin' between us, somethin' special." Her smile widened. "You're one hell of a lover, and I've never been fucked like *that* in my life."

Gillmore coughed nervously. The way she was sitting made his eyes drift to her genitals, and it felt as if his heart was in his throat. For the moment he couldn't speak.

"So I *want* to continue, whether you force me or not. I *want* it. I want *you*. Have you got somethin' you want me to wear now? Would you like me to wear somethin' for you while we're talkin' about all this?"

"Yes, I would," Gillmore said quickly, trying to regain the initiative. He went to the leather holdall he had brought in with him. "I bought you some things, and I want you to put them on now."

350

She put her hand on his arm and he stopped mid-zip. "And I think," she said, "we'd both feel better if I had a comb and a mirror and a little make-up."

"I've got make-up for you in here," Gillmore said harshly as he continued to unzip the bag. "I'll buzz for a comb and brush for you."

She examined the clothes while he spoke to an orderly who brought what she wanted. There was a red silk dress with tiny shoulder straps. It was a little tacky but very expensive looking. There was a matching little bolero jacket. Well...it wouldn't be her choice, but it wasn't bad. The skirt was flared and looked fairly short. There was no bra. Good. She didn't want one. Her stomach turned over as she saw the red shoes with the extremely high heels, and she found herself trembling. Because a number of memories fluttered to the surface, memories she wanted for the moment to keep locked deep in the cellar. But she sort of liked the shoes themselves. There were times in her life where she could certainly use that kind of effect. She almost laughed when she saw the panties. They were high class, yeah, but in real bad taste. They, too, were red silk. Bikini style, they were so sheer everything could be seen through them. They were like gauze. And they were open crotch. What the hell. Why not?

The door opened and the doctor looked in. Gillmore asked him for a brush and comb. Then the door closed again.

She put on the garter belt and sat on the edge of the desk to pull on the stockings. Knowing Gillmore was watching her with burning eyes, she took her time.

She glanced up at him as he stood staring with his hands in his pockets. "What I was tryin' to let you know is that not all of your demands are objectionable. I like wearin' stockin's. They make me feel sexy, and I know they turn men on. Which makes me like 'em even more. The same goes for high heels, except they tend to kill your feet if you keep 'em on for too long." She took the other stocking and inserted her foot carefully. "Anyway, I'm gonna agree to your terms, but I want you to remember I'm not gonna be in a very good mood if you hurt me."

"You'll get over it," he whispered. "You'll get over it," he repeated, louder, in an uneven voice. His heart was thudding, and he hoped his by-pass operation was going to hold out under the strain. "There's one other thing. Until I can trust you, and until this blows over with DeLoop and the rest, you're going to have to wear an electronic tag..."

The door opened again, and Dr Cranley handed over a brush and comb. Gillmore put them on the desk.

She looked up from hooking on the garters. "A what?"

"It can go around your ankle like an ankle chain, but it'll be locked. If you go outside, it will be logged and an alarm will ring in my office. I don't want you going out. It's too dangerous, and I don't really trust you yet. If you *do* go out - or break the chain - while I'm away, the deal's off. No money, no property, nothing. And I will hunt you down, Corky. This is a foreign country for you. You can't go back to DeLoop. He will kill you. So will Regis or any of the rest of them if you're caught. And you will be caught. You will have credit cards and a telephone to order anything you need."

She slowly pulled on the panties. "Well, I hope it's a better prison than this one."

He turned away and paced again, unable to watch any more. "I have a flat in Eaton Square..."

"Eaton Square?" She put on the shoes.

"That's in Belgravia, the most expensive residential part of London, Corky. I use this flat for visiting VIPs, mostly from Australia or America. It has two large bedrooms, a reception room, dining and sitting room. Air conditioned and centrally heated, all mod cons. The others don't know about this place, so you should be safe enough. But if you pass through any outside door or any window, I'll know. I'll have you tracked down. I'll bring you back here, and I promise to take your mind away from you. Do you understand?"

She had the mirror propped up on the desk and was brushing her hair. Her face, she thought, looked fucking awful. Bloodshot, sunken eyes, rimmed with grey around the sockets. Pallid cheeks. She put down the brush and grabbed some base, rubbing it in carefully. "I understand. I cain't say I'm overjoyed about this deal, but I'm not in a position to argue. I want *away* from this place as soon as possible, and this flat - as you call it - sounds perfect. Sounds like heaven. Maybe after a while you can trust me and take the tracker thing off..."

"We'll have to see about that. But I want you to know something right now. I have made a hell of a lot of concessions here. I have gone to the trouble of explaining everything to you when I didn't have to. Anybody else, I tell you what I would have done. I would have walked into that room where they were keeping you and dragged her out here by the hair and given her a good hiding to get her attention. Then I would have *told* her what I wanted and how she was going to do it. I'm trying to be nice with you, and I'll probably fucking regret it the rest of my life."

She finished putting on the bright red lipstick and blotted it on a tissue. She got up and walked slowly over to Harvey Gillmore. With the red shoes, she really towered over him. His eyes were level with the nipples on her breasts, and she noticed he opened his mouth to breathe better as she knelt down in front of him.

"You see," she said, looking up. "You don't have to beat me or threaten me to get me on my knees. I'll do it 'cause I want to, you know." Her hands touched his hips and slowly circled to massage his bottom. His hands tentatively touched her hair, stroking it, as she nuzzled his trousers. "You got somethin' *I* want as well, you know. Somethin' in here..." She brought her hands around and rubbed him through the material. He was already hard, and she found the top of the zip and slowly slid it down. With a very light touch she began to get him out.

"Goddamn, Mr Gillmore, you've got a *very* big dick. A real beautiful piece." She put the head into her mouth and used her tongue carefully underneath the glans before taking it to the back of her throat in several rhythmical strokes.

She pulled her head back, and his penis slid out of her mouth. She looked up. His eyes were crazed, and his neck muscles stood out like steel tapes. "And I'll be right happy to suck your cock any time you want. Mr Gillmore, sir. It's somethin' I just *love* to do." She looked back down and guided it once again into her mouth, knowing this man was turning into a puddle of warm molasses.

"I can't...I can't...." he stuttered above her.

Corky DeLoop again pulled slowly away from the trembling penis. "Oh, yes, you can," she said, her voice husky with desire. She gracefully slid her legs around and lay on her back in front of him. With her stomach heaving slowly, she opened her legs and her mouth, as she massaged her own breasts. Her eyes were locked on his.

"I want you inside me," she said in a hoarse whisper. "Please, Mr Gillmore."

He dropped on his knees like a marionette, reaching for her vagina, pushing aside the thin sheets of silk before touching her. The moment his fingers were on her, she gasped as her body arched involuntarily into the air. Gillmore felt he must be very close to the edge of insanity. The white walls around him glowed in shades of pink and light green as they appeared to undulate. The head of his cock was drawn by forces too strong to understand or resist, and when it touched her, she grabbed at his body as he grabbed at hers. Groping, kissing, sucking, licking. And down below he felt his shaft sink slowly and inevitably, deeper and deeper into a woman who seemed to radiate an electrical sexual energy he had never before experienced. It was overpowering and overwhelming. His voice was somewhere distant, but he heard it howling like a wolf silhouetted before a full moon. Her thighs gripped him as he found her mouth with his. The smell of her filled his lungs with rushes of lust and pleasure beyond his power to grasp. His reason had long departed as he tasted the inside of her mouth with his tongue, his hunger growing stronger and stronger as he felt the volcanic surges grip his belly.

As he started to come, he flopped around as helplessly as a cod on the deck of a fishing boat, and inarticulate sounds poured from deep in his throat. The emotion was so deep he felt he was going to die, there, that moment. And he didn't fucking care. It was a death he welcomed as he flopped from side to side as the woman held him, bucking underneath, thrusting her hips, clawing at his back, holding his bottom and pushing him into

354

her. She was screaming and swearing as well as they rolled on the floor like wild animals.

And then, slowly, gradually, it was over. They lay on their sides, holding each other closely. When a fraction of his reason began to return, Gillmore realised he had never wanted to touch a woman tenderly as he was touching Corky now, caressing her softly, his arms wrapped around her, his head against her breasts.

"Hell's teeth," he muttered. "What the devil has happened to me?"

She held his head against her bosom. "We got somethin' goin' for us, that's what."

"Going for us? What the fuck are you talking about?"

"Now don't tell me you're a virgin," she said as she stroked his head, feeling a sense of victory which was very sweet. "That this is the first time this has happened to you."

"I must be a fucking virgin, then," he whispered.

"Not any more," she said, a big smile spreading secretly on her face.

* * *

As the house came in sight again, Haug stopped dead in his tracks, holding up his hand.

"What's the matter?" asked Mainwaring.

"Car in the drive. New car. Ford. The police have new cars. Police car. You stay here and keep outta sight, 'cause this looks like real bad news. I'll go check it out."

"Nonsense," said Mainwaring. "If they are policemen, I know how to deal with them better than you. Remember what I told you about public schools." He strode forward, pushing past the American.

"Yeah, like you dealt with those who picked you up in Westminster," Haug said as he caught up with his friend.

Mainwaring's shoulders were square, and his head was held high as he strode across the grass. "Well, you're here, aren't you? If they assault me, I want you to swat them down like flies. And if they have touched Sarah, I want you to kill them."

"Anythang you say, boss. But I'll need a telephone booth to change into my bulletproof costume."

"Our policemen don't carry guns."

"Yeah, and they help old ladies across the street, too, and give candy to kids and tell you the time of day...before they kick the livin' shit outta you and stuff the muzzle of the gun they don't carry down your throat."

Sarah Mainwaring met them at the door, and she was smiling pleasantly. "Two gentlemen have been waiting to see you, Jonathan."

Mainwaring stepped past his wife and into the sitting room as Haug tried to keep up with him. Two men were sitting on the sofa together and both rose as the Perm Sec walked in.

"Sir Jonathan Mainwaring?" one of the men asked.

"And who, may I ask, are you?" Mainwaring's voice had an edge like a hacksaw.

The man smiled. "Sir, I am Detective Sergeant Golding, and this is Detective Constable Simpson..."

Mainwaring cut him off abruptly. "And what is your business here?"

"We are from the Metropolitan Police..."

"This is Hampshire, Sergeant, not the City of London. By whose authority are you here?"

DS Golding held up his hands in a placating gesture. "Please rest assured, Sir Jonathan..."

"I am neither resting nor assured, Sergeant, and I am annoyed you are not answering my questions directly but hedging about furtively like a thief. I want to know on whose authority you are in the Hampshire Police area, and, secondly, why you are here."

Again Golding held up his hands while Detective Constable Simpson examined the polish of his shoes. "I am here on the authority and express orders of the London Metropolitan Commissioner of Police, Sir Gerald Humphries, to protect you and your family, sir. We have been asked by Sir Gerald to provide you with round-the-clock protection, and I must advise you, sir, that we are armed."

Sir Jonathan half turned as Haug noisily cleared his throat behind him. "You have been ordered to 'protect' me, have you? I'm afraid I have recently undergone the agony of police protection, which almost cost me my life."

"So I understand, sir," Golding said comfortingly. "I think you will find Detective Constable Simpson and myself quite a different kettle of fish. We have acted until today as personal bodyguards of Sir Gerald himself. Unlike those officers of another department you met recently, we are at your complete service, sir."

Mainwaring stared at the two policemen with less hostility, then turned toward the kitchen. "Sarah, would you be kind enough to bring tea for these gentlemen?"

Before he was finished speaking Sarah Mainwaring walked through with a tray holding a large pot of tea covered by a cosy. A plate held a number of very thin biscuits. She smiled at her husband as she made her way back to the kitchen. "I'll bring through a cup for you and Mr Haug, shall I?"

Mainwaring looked speculatively at the two men. "How much do you know about this business, Sergeant?"

"Officially or unofficially, sir?"

"Both."

"Officially I only know what Sir Gerald told us. That you are Category B which is the highest priority protection, the same afforded to the Prime Minister and visiting Heads of State."

"What's Category A?" Haug asked from behind the Permanent Secretary.

"The Queen and Royal Family, sir."

"His further instructions," the Detective Sergeant continued, "were that we take orders directly from him. Even other members of the Forces are not to be allowed to approach, sir."

"And unofficially?" Mainwaring enquired.

Golding exchanged glances with his constable. "Like many other organisations we have a grapevine. Would it be the Special Branch who have given you trouble, sir?"

As his wife came through with the additional tea cups, Mainwaring suggested they all sit down. He took the cosy from the teapot and poured, then added milk. Both policemen used sugar, but Haug and Mainwaring took theirs without.

The Perm Sec sat in an armchair, took a sip of tea, then put cup and saucer on a side table. "Do you know what happened?"

"I believe you were kidnapped and illegally interrogated, sir," the policeman answered, then bit into a biscuit. He turned and looked at Haug. "Would you be the gentleman who helped to rescue Sir Jonathan?"

Haug grinned. "I might incriminate myself here, officer."

"All I can say, sir, is well done." The Sergeant replaced his cup in the saucer.

"How do you know these things?" Mainwaring demanded.

"As I say, sir, there's a grapevine. Some of us have been aware over the years that some foolishness has been going on. We have reports of certain incidents from the public, reports which die in Special Branch. And as this...er, secret organisation expanded, there are those who can't keep their mouths shut. This happens in any big group of people, and the police are no exception, sir. A number of us have wondered for some time when something would be done about it."

"Why wasn't it reported, if it was known?"

A smile grew on the Sergeant's face. "I think you know the answer to that, sir. Who should we report it to? And who is he? One of them or one of us? We have our jobs and our families, like everyone else. One could say we were waiting for the likes of you, sir."

"I see," Mainwaring said, almost abashed. "I apologise for my unpleasant tone in the beginning, but I think you understand the reasons for my suspicions..."

Golding waved his hand and shook his head. "No need at all for apologies, sir. If I had gone through your experiences, I'm afraid I would have added some unprintable street slang, myself." He reached into his jacket pocket and pulled out his identification and warrant. Constable Simpson followed suit, and Golding took both and handed them to Mainwaring. "Please have a careful look at these, sir. I want you to be absolutely confident we are who we say we are."

As Mainwaring studied the cards Haug was studying the two policemen, and he liked what he saw. The sergeant talked smoothly, but he had the neck and shoulders of a wrestler. The constable was taller but had a whippy look about him, a man with tendons like piano wire. Nothing was hidden in either set of eyes. Haug could tell a hard man from a jack-off any day of the week, and these two looked hard. He certainly wouldn't fancy his chances against both of them, particularly as they seemed to work well together. They were the business, alright. He was sure of it.

The front door opened suddenly, and everyone turned together to watch Louise Templer come in. She was wearing a floppy hat borrowed from Sarah Mainwaring.

Sir Jonathan Mainwaring rose from his chair, as did both policemen. He handed them their identification. "Ah, Louise. These are two gentlemen sent by the Metropolitan Police to nursemaid me while I recover. They are quite genuine, I believe."

Louise Templer stared at the two policemen suspiciously. "Are you sure?"

The two men introduced themselves to the woman. "I believe you are Mrs Templer, MP for Islington," said Sergeant Golding. "The Commissioner of the Metropolitan Police has, I believe, spoken to General Sir Timothy Portland at length over these matters, and we would both be greatly relieved if you called General Portland or Sir Gerald to further verify our credentials."

"I'll call," Louise said. She took the walking stick she had been carrying with her to the other room.

Golding turned to Haug. "You are American, I believe, sir?"

"I'm impressed at your powers of detection, Sergeant Golding," Haug said. "What was it gave you the first clue?"

Golding laughed. "I must say you have been acquiring quite a reputation amongst my colleagues."

"I would like to point out," said Mainwaring quickly, "that Mr Haug has acted solely under the direction of our own opposition group, and I would draw your attention to the fact that this gentleman has placed himself in great danger on our behalf at a time when we were uncertain of the loyalty of the police. We had no other recourse, Sergeant. I would go so far as to say that, if it hadn't been for Haug, this conspiracy of traitors would have scattered or killed us all."

"I cain't stand this," Haug said as he sat down again in the armchair and grabbed his teacup. "All I did was slap a few guys around."

Golding was laughing again as he spoke. "You must have an awfully powerful slap, sir. I presume you remember a certain house in Haringey some time last year? It was declared structurally unsound by the local Council after you slapped a group of thugs from a Direct Action gang. And I have received word recently that one of the Special's Unit houses where Sir Jonathan was held is now unfit for human habitation." Detective Constable Simpson joined in the laughter.

"It was unfit for that before I ever did a thang," Haug said.

Mainwaring took his seat again, and the two policemen sat back on the sofa. "You appear to know quite a bit about what has been going on."

"As I say, sir, we do have a grapevine. I know our public image is sometimes one of bumbling incompetence. Rightly so, perhaps, in some instances. But, while we are not all saints, neither are we all sinners. In fact, sir, there is an unofficial group of us at the Met and at New Scotland Yard, who know quite a bit more about what has been going on than anyone, even Sir Gerald. We thought it best to keep a very low profile for the time being, sir. We have, however, accumulated a journal of incidents, either witnessed or reported. But, quite frankly, sir, we have not known which foot to put forward. Under the circumstances. We have, of course, known of you and your group, the United Opposition, and have given help where we could, principally by putting obstacles in the way of the Specials and increased harassment of the so-called Direct Action groups."

"I see," Mainwaring said with a great sense of relief.

"For instance, the East Sussex Police did indeed receive a distress call from Unit G3, despite the enthusiastic interference from Mr Haug. They were advised, however, to hold back until your operation was complete. And they provided cover for your escape. I might add, sir, this was done with considerable risk to the careers of the officers involved."

Haug was nodding. "I thought thangs were goin' too smoothly for it just to be luck. It was the cops I was most worried about gettin' outta that place. I thought they'd be on the swarm, and I'd have to outrun 'em."

Louise Templer returned and placed her stick in the umbrella stand. Then she turned and smiled.

"They are genuine, Sir Jonathan. Apparently the two best men available at the Met," she said.

Haug grinned as he looked at the two policemen. "It's your turn to blush now."

Lady Mainwaring came through the doorway. "Telephone for you, Mr Haug."

When Haug returned from the call, his face was dangerous and dark. He paused for a moment until the room was quiet. "They got somebody else they're twistin' on the end of a hook, and it's beholdin' on me to find her, if she's still alive. She gave us invaluable help in Corfu, riskin' her life to put the bugs in place in the yacht. Her name is Corky DeLoop, the wife of one of the American hotshots. A really nice woman. I'll be damned if I know how they caught her, but they did."

Mainwaring turned to Golding. "Do you know anything about this, Sergeant?"

Golding's face was grim. "No, sir. But I may be able to find out something for you." He pulled a cellular telephone from his pocket and got up. "If you don't mind, I could use your kitchen." Mainwaring nodded, and the Sergeant left the room.

"Are they sure she's in England?" Louise Templer asked.

"Apparently," Haug replied. "And *they're* here. My guess is that she's bein' held at some place like Jonathan was in."

Mainwaring's face was drained of colour, and his fingers gripped the ends of the armchair. "She couldn't have lasted, then," he whispered. "She couldn't have...the poor woman. My god, the poor woman." He turned to Haug. "Find her if you can, Haug. Help her. Bring her here, if she is alive. Sarah and I will look after her. I promise you that." He stared out in space unseeingly. "I promise you that," he repeated softly.

361

"I gotta get back to London, then, 'cause I'm gonna need some help. They'll know about the first hit, so this one'll be more dangerous."

Mainwaring pounded his hand on the arm of the chair. "She *must* be set free. There is no alternative."

"She will be so long as I got any life in my body," Haug replied. "Trouble is, I got this deep feelin' she's not alive anymore. They woulda squeezed all the information outta her days ago. But I tell you one thang. If she is dead, some asshole is gonna pay. Like Regis."

Sergeant Golding returned to the room briskly. He had not taken long. "A woman with American nationality passed through Heathrow on a medical trolley with doctors in attendance. She was with the party who returned from Corfu. It is believed, though this is not yet confirmed, that she was taken to one of the Unit houses. She has certainly not yet left the UK. I should have further information available shortly."

"I gotta get back to London as soon as possible," Haug said, turning to Louise Templer. "You comin' or stayin'?"

"Coming," she said as she got up. "In fact I'm ready to go now."

Haug turned to Golding. "Sergeant, could I ask you to break police regulations and get one of you to drop us at the railroad station?"

Golding smiled. "I can do better than that, Mr Haug. I will get a car from the Hampshire Police to drive you to London. But," he held up his hand. "I think we are now able to deal with this matter ourselves. It will be a lot quicker, more efficient - and of course more lawful. In addition," he added with a raised eyebrow, "we have no need to demolish the house during our inquiries."

Haug looked at Mainwaring. "I'd rather do this myself, to be honest. But it's up to you."

Mainwaring looked away for a moment, thinking. Then he turned to Golding. "How quickly can it be accomplished?"

"Very quickly, once we have the address."

"And would you promise to bring the young lady back here?"

Golding thought for a minute. "A little irregular, sir, but I think that can be managed under the circumstances."

Mainwaring turned to Haug. "We must be as lawful as we can. I insist upon that. Let's trust the police on this one, though I appreciate how you feel."

Haug still stood in the doorway and hadn't moved a muscle during the exchange. "You're the boss. But I still want to go to London, now that you're in good care."

Golding was using his cellular phone to dial the Hampshire Police as Mainwaring stared at his American friend. "Haug?" he called with a soft voice. "Haug? We've got to move as one on this. I know how you feel. I feel even more strongly about it than you do. Haug? You know I'm right."

"It's OK, Jonathan, I'm gonna let the cops handle it. But *I've* gotta go now and explain to my friend, One Time, just why we're not goin' in. And somehow I gotta stop *him* from goin'."

"One Time?" Mainwaring asked with a puzzled expression on his face.

Haug didn't know how to say it. "One Time and the woman...you see, they kinda were close for a short time, and..."

"Ah," said Mainwaring. "I see. Well, you'll have to explain to him we believe this is the quickest way, the best way."

"If they get her back here, you don't mind if he comes down to stay for a while, do you?"

"He can have your room and stay as long as he likes."

Golding snapped the phone closed and replaced it in his pocket. "Five minutes, sir."

363

CHAPTER TWENTY

Enrico Gomez sat in his car watching the rain on the windshield wondering what the fuck to do now. His boss had not given him any telephone number but a hotel, and DeLoop checked out several days before. He told Gomez he would be in touch at what they called Unit G5. But what if they stayed here, wherever the fuck he was? Eaton Square. Maybe the short Australian had taken her to see another doctor or something. Or maybe some party was going on. She looked like she was dressed for a party, wearing a short red dress and red high heels, looking good enough to eat.

At first, when they left the building, Gomez was confused. His orders were to shadow the broad. And they were leaving Unit G5. Were they coming back? What was going on? The kangaroo runt should have said something to him about where they were going. The two of them got into the back of the Rolls, and he watched the car glide out of the driveway before running to his rented Volvo to get on their tail. They were easy to follow as the Rolls wasn't hauling ass, and the license plate was AUS 1. It was a queer country, he thought as he drove along. A real queer country. It was bad enough driving on the left hand side of the road, but the other drivers drove like they were loaded to the eyeballs with drugs. They drove crazy. On the freeway they were going more than a hundred, with another car following three feet behind, trying to get around. People pulled out in front of him or slashed across, trying to get in a fast lane. It was much worse than Miami, and he thought Miami was the worst in the world. It was particularly bad when they got into London. A shithole. Everybody in the whole country must have been out in their cars. He'd never seen so many cars in such a small space. It would be quicker to walk. And all the cars were so close together. Once, while they were waiting in traffic he buzzed the window down and blew his nose out the window. Some of it got on the car in the next lane, and the asshole rolled his own window down and started to give him a lot of shit. Hell, the rain was going to wash it off. Anyway, he got tired of the man swearing at him, so he hawked up a wadge of snot from the back of his throat and spat it right in the asshole's face. The guy was so stunned he was just sitting there staring at him with a great big oyster sliding down the side of his nose. Gomez moved off with the traffic, and everybody was honking at the guy with snot on his face.

Gomez stared at the big black door across the road. The lights had gone on when they entered, so nobody must have been at home. Then the thought struck him. Maybe the short Aussie was fucking her. Now that is something DeLoop would want to know. It would be no trouble to cut his balls off, but how the fuck was he going to get in touch with his boss?

It was a large, magnificent flat. Why did the English call apartments "flats"? she wondered. There was an entrance hall with a living room off to one side and what he called a reception room on the other. Further down the hall was a small toilet with a shower stall. The large bedroom was wonderful. There was a king-sized bed, marble topped washstands, and a makeup table with a huge mirror in a gold frame. A double door opened into almost a Texas style bathroom. A big bath with shower attachments in gold, a toilet, a bidet, another makeup table and mirrors, a beautiful inlaid wood floor with flokati rugs. There had only been enough time for a quick wash at her old prison, and she longed for a soak. Maybe she would stay in the bath for a whole week.

She watched Gillmore putting the electronic tag on her wrist. He decided putting it on her ankle would interfere with the stockings he loved for her to wear. It was made out of tough-looking plastic and had a kind of ratchet effect, like a handcuff. You could pull it tighter, but you could not get it off unless you cut it. It held a small round hard case about the size of a wristwatch. She wondered if it would work under water in the bath. They were sitting on a gorgeous cream leather sofa that must have been twelve feet long, and she was looking out the huge bay window at the dark sky and the rain.

After he finished, Gillmore got up and pressed a button at the side of the bay window, and the curtains slowly closed. "I'd like a drink, Corky."

She bounced up. "Okeydoke. What would you like? Diet Pepsi?"

He nodded as he watched the hem of the red dress swirl when she turned to walk to the door. When she was gone, he felt a sudden emptiness inside. The room felt hollow and cold, and he began to fidget with the pens on the inside pocket of his suit jacket. He sat back down on the sofa, then got up again. Harvey Gillmore knew he was going to have to get hold of himself or he would be completely out of control, something alien to his nature. It was as if he were going down a steep slope, and he had to run faster and faster to keep from falling. He knew he couldn't stop. Not now. Not yet. Sitting back down on the sofa, he wanted Corky back in the room. He didn't even want her to leave to fetch for him, and that was just crazy. He smacked his fist into his palm. Damn it, he was Harvey Gillmore! She was a fucking beautiful woman, but she was still just a woman. He had to get hold of himself, get back on top, back in control.

Corky DeLoop re-entered the room with an ice filled glass and Diet Pepsi on a silver tray. She placed the tray on the table beside Gillmore and turned to him brightly. "Anything else, sir?"

"Yes," Gillmore said darkly. "Get down on the floor in front of me. On all fours." He poured the Pepsi onto the ice as he watched her gracefully get on her knees and lean forward on her hands. "I've got to make something clear to you. Right now. And that's the order of things. I want you to get that tongue out and lick my shoe." He grabbed the Pepsi and took a sip.

He expected her to rebel, to give him something to strike out against. But she completely surprised him. She cradled his foot in her hands and bent forward, licking and kissing as well. Her hands were on his ankles, and then they followed the ankles up the socks until they found the flesh of his calves. The electrical charge almost made him spill the Pepsi in his lap. He put the glass back on the tray and reached out to touch her luminous hair.

"I like to do it," she said as she looked up at him sincerely. "I just love the smell of you, even what you're wearin'." Then she hugged his leg.

It wasn't working. He knew it wasn't working. It was like trying to change the flow of an ocean current. "Get up," he said. It came out in a squeak. "Get up, Corky, and sit beside me here."

She got up slowly, rising like a goddess before him. As she sat down she reached for his hand and put it underneath her dress and against her sex as he came forward almost helplessly to kiss her. Holding his hand between her legs, she opened her mouth and gently guided his head toward her with her other hand.

Warning bells were ringing inside Gillmore's consciousness, but they were easily drowned out by the roar of lust and desire as he stroked her vulva which was already slippery. It seemed to move in his hand, almost like a separate being, ready, eager to take him inside.

* * *

Gordon Hastings was a fit man with his thinning hair clipped short. Every morning he took a two mile run, and every evening he was in the gym on the Nautilus machines. He was forty six years old but thought he could easily pass for thirty five. At least he still pulled the women, just like he always had. Of course Jilly didn't know - or he didn't think she knew. Jilly was forty four now, and frankly he didn't find her attractive anymore. She was getting a little fat and wrinkly.

He was sitting in the anteroom of Sir Gerald Humphries' office thinking about women. He supposed old Sir Gerald was going to bore his arse off about some bureaucratic detail he had forgotten, like a memo in triplicate. Or some sort of acid comments about his expenses. He looked at his watch. It was getting late, and he had promised Sondra he would meet her at seven. He hoped this wasn't going to take long.

Humphries appeared in the doorway suddenly. He was dressed in full uniform, which was unusual. "Come in, Gordon," he said, leading the way.

368

Hastings sat in the leather upholstered armchair on the other side of the Metropolitan Police Commissioner's desk as the Commissioner seated himself behind it.

"It seems I am the last one to know of you and your Branch's involvement in illegal and treasonous activities," Sir Gerald said bluntly, "But now that I know, I intend to do something about it."

Gordon Hastings felt his body tense, like a coiled spring. "What in God's name are you talking about?"

"You know what I'm talking about, and I have no intention of wasting my breath telling you what you already well know. So let's drop the pretence and talk instead of what we are going to do about it." He held up his hand as Hastings started to interrupt. "I would dearly love to sack you, charge you, prosecute you and, if at all legally possible, have you shot at dawn. However, we don't yet live in that kind of state - no thanks to you and your friends. And you well know there are political reasons why I can't just sack you. That will come later, I promise you."

"Sir Gerald..."

Humphries leaned across his desk, his eyes flashing dangerously. "Let me explain to you that I am so furious I'm having to use a great deal of self restraint to keep myself from throwing you bodily from the window. Let me tell you something, Gordon. I would never claim to be the most honest policeman who has ever lived. Yes, I have on occasion fudged evidence - when I was totally convinced the accused was guilty. I have verbally covered for colleagues, and I have on occasion lied to my superiors. However, I have never taken money, and I have never, ever, betrayed the police nor the Crown. Do you understand me!" he shouted, slapping the flat of his hand on the desk.

Gordon Hasting's fingers had grown cold. "Frankly, no, Sir Gerald. So far I have not understood one word."

The Commissioner pointed his large index finger at the head of Special Branch. It looked like a pistol. "You are an abominable liar. I tell you, Gordon, I *know*. I have evidence. Proof."

"Show it to me, then," Hastings said through his teeth.

"I have no need to show it to you because this is not a court of law. I dearly wish it were. I advise you to drop the pretençe, Gordon, so we can negotiate our way out of this minefield. I know all about the Community of Association, and I also know you are an associate..."

Hastings laughed. "Oh. Is *that* what you're talking about."

"Yes! It is!"

The head of Special Branch clasped his hands together, trying to look casual. "Sir Gerald, the Community of Association is merely a group of like-minded people who occasionally meet for political and economic discussions. That hardly constitutes a criminal offence."

Humphries' face looked like thunder. "Are you seriously going to try and convince me the Mafia are really just Boy Scouts trading stories around the campfire?"

Hastings pushed his palms at the Commissioner. "Calm down, Sir Gerald." Then he chuckled. "This has absolutely nothing to do with the Mafia or any criminal organisation whatsoever."

"It *is* a criminal organisation," Humphries exclaimed, slapping his hand on his desk again. "Fact!"

"Someone has been telling you tall tales, Sir Gerald. Everything about the CA is legal and above board, and I would be perfectly willing for you to examine any..."

"Kidnapping and torturing a highly respected Secretary of State for the Department of Trade and Industry. Allowing, even escorting, armed gangs of men, most of them foreign nationals, to assault, to threaten, to plunder, to rape and to murder. Illegally intercepting telephone calls of members of our elected government, moderate trade union officials, journalists, the judiciary. Using this information for blackmail and extortion. Illegally altering records to cover up this criminal activity. Acting as a private police force for an extra-national group of unknown provenance..."

Hastings laughed as he shook his head. "I'm afraid someone has been filling your head with..."

"Facts! Facts, Gordon. Your evasions make me angrier by the second." Humphries sat sharply back in his chair. "I will therefore assume that you are going to load lie upon lie, denying everything. So listen to me carefully. I am unable to report this outrage to my superior because the Home Office Minister, Adrian Chesterman, is one of you. No doubt you will report it to him yourself. When you do, however, please also report the following. If he tries to stop me in my relentless pursuit of what has become a lawless band at Special Branch, I will go direct to the Prime Minister and, if necessary, the Queen, to lay the evidence before them. I, like your Associates, would rather this not become a public matter for the most obvious of reasons: it is not unlikely that such disclosures could unravel our entire political fabric. I am determined to put my own house in order, even though I am quite aware that several chief constables are involved with your Association. My advice to you is the following. If I were you, I would now make a complete and full disclosure of my activities and commit these to paper in detail. If you now choose this sane alternative, I will keep the confession in my own safe and will personally intervene on your behalf when your Association is finally brought before the law. This will save neither your job nor your pension, but it may keep you out of prison. If you actively help us, perhaps your pension will be restored."

Hastings leaned forward on his elbows. "I actually feel sorry for you, Humphries..."

"Sir Gerald to you, Hastings!"

"You are standing in the path of a mighty wave, one which has already swept many better and more powerful men aside. On my part, I would like to invite you to one of our meetings. You would recognise many people there. Men you respect in this society."

"I'll come to one of your meetings," Humphries replied coldly, "if you'll tell me how many are to be in attendance. Then I shall know how many pairs of handcuffs to bring along."

Hastings shook his head sadly. "We are not that far apart politically. I'm sure you vote Conservative. Any sensible person does. And we are all *conservative*. Nothing we are doing

371

is treasonous, for god's sake. I would never do anything against the interests of the Crown, of this country. There's no one more patriotic than I am, not even you."

"I'll be the judge of that."

Hastings held his hands a foot apart, as if measuring something. "What we have here is inevitability. Look at the EEC. Countries join together for common interests. People join together for the same reason. That's all we have done, nothing else, nothing sinister. Or it is sinister only to the Left, which has used similar methods in the past. The difference is that *we support the conservative interests in each and every single State.* Do you see that difference clearly? So how could it be treason? There are transnational companies which now circle the globe creating employment and generating capital. The power of these companies when banded together in shared interests is phenomenal, greater even than the might of the USA. Indeed, they are a *part* of this might, this power. Our purpose now, today, is to see where we are going tomorrow, smooth the way for growth. That, Sir Gerald, is in *everyone's* interest."

Humphries did not immediately reply, so Hastings sat back in his chair, more comfortable in his exposition. "There are certain other groups which share other interests which are not compatible with ours, and these must either be controlled or rendered powerless. Do you not see how it all interlocks so beautifully? And do you not see how futile resistance is? Look at the fate of the former Soviet Union. Not long ago it was a superpower. What crushed them was this tidal wave of the future. It will crush anyone in its path, Sir Gerald. Including you."

"I've never heard such a load of rubbish in my life," Humphries said finally. "And I admit I find it difficult to sit here and listen to such bollocks from a man so recently involved in kidnapping, torture and contemplated murder." He leaned forward, placing his elbows on his desk. "If this Association of Maniacs is so inevitable, why on earth do you have to help it along with lawless and murderous behaviour? Let it go its own way inevitably, and you get back to your job of policing the streets of England which are now beginning to look like a war zone."

"Ah," Hastings said, raising his chin, "there is a war going on. Of course there is. It is between the Left and Right..."

It was his fist which banged the desk this time. "Then get out there and arrest them both when they break the law, man! Can't you even see your duty? I do not ask a man his politics when he carries a prohibited firearm. I take him into custody and prosecute him for the offence."

"It's not so clearcut as all that, Sir Gerald. If the Prime Minister was caught stealing or the Prince of Wales raping a young girl, the lines of the law become blurred..."

Again the fist came down. "Not with me, they don't!"

"Then you're a fool."

"I may be a fool, but I am also a policeman. I will do my duty and arrest the Prime Minister *or* the Prince of Wales. Others then may step in or intercede on their behalf, appealing well over my head beyond my authority or my remit. A simple matter you seem incapable to grasping, Hastings, is *the law* is *the law*. If you and your treasonous group want armed terrorist gangs on the street, then go first to parliament and make it into law. Then - and only then - will I defend them with my life. *Whatever* my personal opinion might be." He spaced out his final words carefully. "Do you get this very, very essential, very, very simple point, Hastings? You are a policeman. Not a philosopher. Nor a politician. Nor anything else under the sun as far as I'm concerned."

Gordon Hastings got up from his chair. "I can see there's no point..."

The big forefinger shot out again. "Sit down, Hastings. I am not yet finished with you."

"Well, that's too bad, Humphries, because I'm late for an appointment. Maybe you can send me a memo in triplicate." He walked towards the door.

The Commissioner's voice was low and dangerous. "Every Special found breaking the law will be arrested. And you, yourself, will be brought down and brought before the Bench. Or I'll die trying to do it."

Gordon Hastings turned back to smile at Humphries smugly before he opened the door and left without a further word.

* * *

Haug stood and looked at the people in his office who were silently staring at him, even Lizzy. He had just finished telling them that the police were going into the Unit holding Corky DeLoop, and they were going to wait to hear the results.

"So you're not going to do anything?" asked Jennifer Montgomery.

He turned to her. "Like what?"

"Well," she said dismissively, "you know the police, what they're like. 'Leave it with us.' And you never hear from them again."

"I'll hear tonight," Haug said. "If I don't, I'll call. If I can't get through or am fobbed off, I'll go in myself. I promised."

One Time was leaning carefully against Haug's desk. "Promise for me, too?"

"Yep. Sure did."

One Time was nodding his head, then shaking it. "You don't know, man. The police. You don't go to the police, not for this. That lady, man. She's hurtin'. And me? Here I am. Sittin'."

"Well," said Haug. "You're all lookin' at me like I should feel guilty about somethin', but I'm gonna tell you right now that I don't. I made the best decision I could make under the circumstances. Sure, I wanna go. I wanna go right now. But we're workin' with other people here, goddammit. And if we cain't work together, we're all gonna be picked off like flies. I can tell you that for sure. Now, these cops seemed OK, a different sort. I woulda bet my ass they were gonna do somethin'. Lissen. They've even been lookin' after us, some of 'em, runnin' interference for us while we been playin' cowboys and Indians."

Sarah Courtney was sitting in one of the two chairs, next to Jennifer. "What do you think they've done to her? Will she be alright?"

374

"You want an honest answer, lady?" He watched Courtney nod reluctantly. Haug examined the toe of his boot for a minute. "She's probably dead. You gotta face that probability..."

The telephone rang, and Haug bounded over to the desk to answer it as the others watched.

"Yeah," he said. "This is Haug." He listened and nodded as the voice spoke to him without interruption for almost two minutes. The room was as silent as a tomb. Finally, Haug hung up the phone and looked at them with half a smile.

"Well, for the thousandth time in my life I was wrong. She's still alive."

One Time punched the air as if he had just scored a goal. "Right now! One time!"

"But," he went on, "she's not at the Unit. She left this afternoon. With Harvey Gillmore."

"Oh, Christ," said Jennifer. "That's a bit like leaving with the Yorkshire Ripper."

"Tell me about it," added Sarah Courtney.

"This guy, Sergeant Golding, said there wasn't a lot they could do now, except question Gillmore, who they're tryin' to get in touch with. But she apparently left under her own steam in some kinda party dress..."

"In high heels, I bet," Courtney said. "I'm sure he must be holding something over her, some kind of threat. That's the way he thinks."

"Anyway," Haug said, "now we can move. I gave no promises about Gillmore. He's probably got her at his flat in Fleet Street, but we'll take the yellow van in case we have to sleep there. I wouldn't think he'd take her to his house in the country, as that's where his wife lives." He turned to One Time. "I'm supposin' you're goin' with me."

"Righteous. Van's at my place." Without a nod to the others, One Time moved quickly and silently to the door.

Jennifer got up and walked to the window, looking out at the rain and traffic on Junction Road. She was wearing jeans and sweatshirt. "I'm really angry, Haug. Someone must do something about that man. What he does to women is worse than rape, and he just continues to get away with it because he's wealthy and because he's Gillmore."

"I'm gonna pull his fuckin' balls off when I catch him," Haug muttered. "Ever time I hear his name I wanna throw up. What he does to women is worse, but he rapes the public with his newspapers. Keyhole journalism at its worst. Speakin' o' keyholes, where are my picks, Lizzy?"

Lizzy was sitting in the only comfortable chair behind his desk. "Would that be for locks or your teeth?"

"You know what I'm after, you stupid ole Irish peasant. Or are you still jealous I *got* all my teeth?"

"You could use a brush and toothpaste to get those tobacco stains off," she said, opening a drawer and bringing out a little metal chest. "These are your lock picks. Right where you left 'em, on top of my Tampax."

"I put 'em there to stop me reachin' in and smokin' one of 'em," he replied as he picked up the little chest and checked inside it.

"Be better for you than that horrible stuff you chew." She made a face and got up from the desk. "Anyway, I guess you don't need me anymore, so I better go over and look after my other two children."

He gave her a kiss on the cheek as she passed by on the way to the door. "Thanks for mannin' the phone for me, darlin'."

"I'll put it on the bill," she grinned and opened the door of the office. "Anything you need, just give me a call."

"I might be wantin' a blow job when I get back."

She slammed the door so hard the glass rattled, then opened it again and poked her head back in. "If you spit in that waste paper bin, I'm going to dump it all over your bed." She slammed the door again.

Sarah Courtney was amused. "Do you two go on like that all the time?"

"Most of it," said Jennifer Montgomery. "It's a good double act, could go into the Edinburgh fringe during the Festival."

Haug went behind the desk, rolled the comfortable chair out and sat down. "Well, how're rehearsals?" he asked Jennifer.

"Fine," she said, still at the window. "Who was that woman with you in the car? The one you kissed goodbye?"

"That was Louise Templer," he replied mildly. "She's the Labour MP for this borough."

"Does she kiss all her constituents like that?"

Haug shrugged. "I guess it's your turn to be jealous. I had my turn when you told me about this new dude of yours."

Sarah Courtney looked uncomfortable. "Uh, I wonder if I might..."

"Relax," said Haug with a smile. "Jenny knows she's the one I love."

Sarah laughed. "That's exactly what she said about you."

"Did she now?"

"Well," said Sarah, "If that's the case, you both love each other, then why on earth don't you live together?"

Jennifer Montgomery turned to look back out the window. "So we don't spoil it, I suppose."

"She's young," said Haug. "She's got a career that takes her here, there and yonder, and so have I. In the next six or eight years, she's gonna change her mind more times than I change my drawers, and she's got a right to do that. Good for her."

"Don't be patronising, Haug," Jennifer said sharply.

"See what I mean?" he asked, turning to Courtney. "We'd be arguin' and spittin' at each other. This way we stay in love."

Jennifer Montgomery crossed from the window and leaned over behind Haug with her arms around his neck, biting his ear. Her blond hair fell forward. "I nearly came downstairs, Haug, to show you that I can fight, too. I would have kicked that bloody Labour MP all the way to Tufnell Park."

"If you put your tongue in my ear again," Haug murmured, "we might embarrass Miss Courtney, unless she thinks she might enjoy watchin' two animals fuckin' in the middle of this floor."

Sarah started to get up again. "Are you quite sure that I'm not..."

"Don't pay any attention," Jennifer laughed. "He's all talk."

"Or maybe she'd like to join in," Haug suggested lewdly.

She slapped him on the top of his bald head in mock anger. "You filthy bastard! When I climb out of your bed, I *guarantee* you will not be capable of doing anything more dramatic than turning out the lights."

Sarah Courtney was laughing and shaking her head when they heard the horn blow outside.

"That'll be One Time," Haug said, getting up and grabbing the pick chest. "Why don't you two use my flat upstairs? I'll let you know what's happenin' just after it happens."

"My house isn't far," Jennifer said. "I think we'll stay there for the night. It's bigger." She turned around to face Haug, putting her arms around his neck. "And nicer."

They kissed, touching tongues quickly. "Take care, Haug," she said as she pulled away. "I don't want to lose you, you old bugger."

"You'll have to do a lotta shakin' to shake me off," he said.

The horn blew again, more insistently. Haug waited for the women to pass through the door before he turned out the lights and locked the office.

* * *

It was nearly midnight, and Haug finally got the desk open. One Time was behind him, still with his ear to the safe, slowly turning the dial. They had a great deal of trouble getting into Harvey Gillmore's flat. The locks were sophisticated, and so was the alarm system. At one point Haug felt he was going to have to give up the idea and just wait for the little Australian bastard to arrive. But he figured that if Gillmore was not here, he had taken Corky DeLoop somewhere else. That wouldn't be his home, either. Hell, someone that rich must have houses and flats all over London. He didn't think it would be a hotel, though. Not with Gillmore. So they decided to try and crack the flat. The alarm system was a fucking nightmare for One Time. The electrics could not be interfered with, and there were a series of invisible beams crossing the room. One Time had one pair of special optics which could make these beams visible, but it meant one of them had to crawl through the tangle, then throw the glasses back for his partner without breaking one of the beams. Haug was very tired and glad he got a good night's sleep

378

the night before. Going from the front door to the desk and safe required a lot of concentration and muscle control and accuracy. The locks were tough, too, and he was a little worried he might have damaged the one on the flat door.

However, he forced himself to think about what he was doing. They were looking for an address. Or list of addresses, something that looked right. He glanced over his shoulder at One Time, who was spinning the dial yet again for another try. He was sure his new friends in the police force wouldn't approve of what he was doing. The middle drawer had a file in it, some doodling, scratched telephone numbers, names to call, pencils and pens. He checked the file. Financial crap he didn't understand, pages of it. He pulled the drawer right out, making sure he checked every piece of paper. Nothing. He pulled out the first drawer on the right. There was a ream of printout, more financial stuff. A couple of seashells, a paperweight, paper clips, stapler. The second drawer looked more hopeful. There was a card index. As he went through it, he realised they were probably employees' names and addresses. Gillmore had comments on most of the cards, some of them very interesting. Names of mistresses, notes of indiscretions, salaries and other personal details, some of them quite embarrassing. He blew through his teeth as he closed the file box.

The bottom drawer was the largest, and when he opened it he felt a rush of blood to his head. Handcuffs, gags, women's panties, a paddle, ropes and one or two things that looked nasty, but he had no idea what they were for. Beneath the gear there was a long black address book. He pulled it out. All the names in the book were women's, and most of them were annotated. Some had red stars, others large black dots. Some comments were personal and fairly brutal. "Ugly. Too fat. Too old. Small tits. Short legs..." Others were sinister. "Bankrupted. Loony - hospitalised. Use the child. Jailed for theft. Give car." Then immediately under the last entry, "Take car away." Some had sums of money carefully entered. "£250 - too, too much. Agreed £150. Paid £50. Ha, ha." With a little imagination Haug could guess what the book was and why it was there. He closed it with extreme distaste and placed it back where he found it.

"One time," whispered One Time behind him. There was a dull thunk as he opened the handle of the safe door.

Haug moved carefully out of his chair and joined his friend. He knew there were no beams between the desk and the safe, but anything invisible worried him. As the safe door swung open, Haug played the light of his flashlight inside. It was a good sized safe with a number of inner drawers and a smaller interior safe with another dial. The drawers, however, were unlocked. A collection of whipping canes stood in one corner, and he heard One Time spit angrily as he saw them.

"I think you and me're gonna have to flip a coin for that son of a bitch," he muttered.

"No way, man," said One Time. "He *mine*."

Haug pulled open a drawer. "Always thinkin' of yourself."

"It's her I'm thinking about," he replied. "She did us good."

Haug opened another drawer and handed the contents to One Time. "Anything with an address on it, unless it's in Australia. You can have the little asshole when I finish with him."

One Time took the bundle. "Uh-uh. *You* have him after *me*. Or you have me first."

Haug pawed through the papers. "You're more talkative than anytime I've known you. I think I prefer you the other way." He put the stack of papers back and opened another drawer. There were several items with pink ribbon around them. He untied the ribbons and started searching. Court cases, mainly, the first one. He re-tied that and opened the second bundle.

"I think we've struck oil here, you ugly bastard. While you talk, I do all the work." They were deeds, some freehold, some leasehold. He found his pen and a piece of paper in his waistcoat pocket. "You call 'em out to me, and I'll write 'em down."

There were four addresses in London, including the flat they were burgling. One in Birmingham, one in Manchester, two in Edinburgh, one which was obviously his house in the country, one near Brighton, a hotel in Cornwall. Haug asked for the three London addresses first, then listed the other ones.

After replacing the deeds, Haug and One Time decided to check the London addresses that night - or morning, as it now was. The traffic would be lighter, and it wouldn't take long. After, Haug thought with a sigh, they managed to negotiate the invisible beams again. *If* they managed it.

* * *

It was late, too, when Professor Ewan Thomas pulled into his driveway. He had just returned from Hampshire where he was visiting Sir Jonathan Mainwaring that evening. Thomas had been very disturbed by the escalating events but was glad to see his friend on his feet. He had still looked quite ill, but obviously Sarah was taking extremely good care of him. General Portland arrived a little later, and he discovered the results of Portland's meeting with the Metropolitan Police Commissioner, Sir Gerald Humphries. Humphries had been convinced finally but had flatly refused to join the United Opposition. Instead, he had offered them support *so long as they stayed within the law.* That's the way policemen thought, the good ones anyway. However, Humphries had immediately sent down his own personal bodyguards on indefinite loan. That was a relief at least.

As a historian, Thomas knew the forces building up in conflict were now inevitably set in motion, and this was what was particularly worrying him. Before, there was mostly talk. Now the sides were drawn, and so were the swords. They were therefore entering an unstable period. Unstable and unpredictable.

He was too tired to be bothered with the garage and was about to turn off the ignition when he was aware another vehicle leapt from the ranks of parked cars on the street with its headlights off. This car swerved straight into his driveway, blocking him from reversing out. It happened quickly, so quickly Thomas hardly had time to think. If he had not just been musing on their tactical problems, he would certainly have been trapped. He might be trapped anyway, but he was damned if he was not going to try *something*.

381

He snapped the Rover's automatic gearbox into reverse and gave it plenty of throttle. The impact snapped his head back sharply into the headrest, but his fear concentrated him. He quickly swung the car out through the front garden and straight at the garden wall, a low one of about five courses. He hardly heard the bang as he steered down the pavement looking for a hole between the parked cars. Out through the gap, and he was on the tarmac, steering back to the left suddenly to avoid a collision with another parked car.

Finally he checked his rearview mirror, and his stomach turned over. The car he smashed was reversing into the road, and he saw one headlight come on. Headlights. Yes. He turned his own on. Both still worked, but he was aware of something wrong with the steering, and there was a scraping noise somewhere in front. Going through the low brick wall might not have been the best idea, but it was the only one he had at that time. He remembered talking with the American, Haug, and he had told him that was all a man could do when he was under pressure. First of all, act. Any action, but move. Let your onboard computer take over and make the decisions for you.

Well, that's what he had done, he thought as he drove recklessly to the bottom of the road and turned left, flooring the throttle. His Rover was not a particularly fast one, a 1.8 litre, but he did know the streets well in Richmond. Ewan Thomas was 54 years old, but he was extremely fit. The one thing he always loved doing was running. He was raised in the country, near Aberystwyth, and he loved running the hills in his youth. Most mornings he rose early for an eight to ten mile trot. It was so refreshing and cleared his head for the day. Running suited him. He lived alone now, separated for eleven years from his wife, though they were still friendly. Still colleagues, he should say. She, too, was a historian, and quite often they worked together on projects.

The car behind him was still there and getting closer. His Rover must be a wreck. There was little other traffic on the roads, and he wondered whether he should trust a police station. Normally, of course, that is what he would have done. But this was not the Met out here. Who was the Chief Constable? One of theirs?

He made a decision. The Old Deer Park and golf course. The wheels were pulling to the left, and he was glad he had power steering. The noise was coming from one of the wheel arches, and he thought it was getting louder. Looking at the car behind him, he wondered whether he was going to make it to the park. What would they do when they caught up with him? Shoot? Ram him? Wouldn't that make a scene? Did they care? Well, he didn't know the answers to any of those questions and decided he didn't want to find out, if he could possibly help it.

He was surprised his hands weren't trembling on the wheel. Maybe it was because of his anger, now that he could identify it. These people represented something he viscerally loathed. Autocratic reaction in the guise of saviour, an old story. The wolf kills the sheep to wear its skin.

It was almost two o'clock in the morning and traffic was thin, luckily. Or unluckily, depending on your point of view. When he approached traffic lights, he simply slowed down enough to check, then went through, green or red. So did the following car, except they did not slow down. Maybe that's why they were gaining. But he was near the park now. He had a chance. He knew that park like the back of his hand, even in the dark.

When he saw the edge of the green, he ran the Rover straight on it before braking. He slid into a slow spin before coming to a stop. With a single movement he opened the door and began to run without even looking behind him. But he heard the other car, and he heard the doors slam. He heard something else, too. A popping sound. Knowing nothing better, he began to zigzag, realising his mind was wheeling, close to panic. His legs stretched out. He remembered his youth. The young man with long legs and big lungs, hair bouncing in the wind. This gave his panic an earth wire. He was still alive but thought he heard them running behind him. Well...let's see if they can catch me, he said grimly to himself, and increased his speed, concentrating on his breathing.

Professor Ewan Thomas loped into the park like a deer. Behind him four men struggled even to keep him in sight.

CHAPTER TWENTY ONE

They went to an address in Hampstead first. It was a small terraced house in Perrins Lane, between Hampstead High Street and Heath Street. Haug parked the van further down the High Street, and they walked back. The windows were dark when they arrived. There was no garage, but a Mercedes was parked just outside the door. Haug walked straight up to check the door. He was on the point of ringing the bell when he was startled by a voice from the shadows.

"Could I ask your business here, sir?" a uniformed policeman asked as he stepped forward.

"Oh, hi, officer," Haug replied with a big smile. "I'm tryin' to find my brother-in-law, and I cain't remember all of the address. You see, I'm only visitin' here for a week before we go off to Paris and then on to Rome. Now I don't particularly like this guy, but I told my wife I'd sure look him up while I was in London. Trouble is, I cain't remember whether it's Perrins Lane or Street or Road or what, so I'm havin' to check 'em all."

"I see, sir. A tourist, then?"

"More business than pleasure, I'm afraid," Haug replied in a friendly tone.

The bobby nodded. "Could I have the name of the party you are looking for, sir?"

"Harv Gillmore. A little biddy Australian guy about so high." Haug positioned his hand about five and a half feet from the ground.

The policeman squared his shoulders in surprise. "You are Mr Gillmore's brother-in-law?"

Haug leaned toward the bobby conspiratorially. "His sister, my wife, is a fine woman. A *fine* woman. But between you and me, her brother is nothin' but a horse's ass. He'll never get bowlegged from totin' his brains."

The policeman smiled. "I believe this house does indeed belong to Mr Gillmore, sir, but it is occupied now by a family."

"You mean, he's not there?" Haug asked.

"That is correct, sir."

Haug took his cap off with a big smile. "Now that is the best news I've had tonight, officer. You're a witness, right? I *tried*. I tried to see the man and failed. And that's what I'm gonna tell my wife."

"Glad to be of assistance, sir," the bobby smiled. Then he pointed to One Time who had been standing quite still and almost invisible near the corner of the house. "Is this gentleman with you, sir?"

"Who, him?" Haug asked, glancing at One Time. "Yessir. That's my *boy*. Brought him over with me from Mississippi. Now, his family has worked my family's land for years and years and years, officer. He totes my bags and runs errands for me."

"I see, sir. Well, I hope I have been of some assistance and you enjoy your stay in London."

"Thank you very much, officer," Haug said as he turned down the lane. "Come on, boy," he hollered at One Time.

"Yassuh, boss," said One Time, falling in behind him in a little trot.

After they got in the van, One Time was laughing and snapping his fingers and pounding his thigh. "What was that again, man? My family has worked for your family...in Mississippi!"

"Hell," Haug said, "I oughta been an actor. He was almost feelin' sorry for you, and that'd be the first time a white cop ever felt sorry for anybody black." He started the ignition and pulled out. "Next stop, Eaton Square. Then Kew. Gotta be careful in these wealthy parts of London this late at night, on account of the fact that's where all the police are. All hell's probably breakin' loose in the East End and south of the river, people bein' pounded with hammers and bricks, women bein' raped and murdered, cars bein' burned, houses burgled, old folks thrown outta winders - and not a cop in sight. In Hampstead or Belgravia you got about two or three to the square foot, day and night.

Eaton Square lay on both sides of the King's Road and had confusing numbers which sometimes wrapped around into an adjoining street. The houses were solid and large and wealthy

386

looking. There was more activity near the King's Road at that time of night, so they were not as obvious in the little yellow van as they were in Hampstead.

Haug was wondering whether to risk ringing the doorbell at this address as they passed slowly in front of No 52 when One Time punched him in the ribs.

"Yes, man. Right now. One time," he said excitedly.

"This is it?" Haug asked. "Did you spot his Roller?"

"The rat man," said One Time. "Back there. Black Volvo. He be, she be."

"Okeydoke. And looky here, a nice empty parking space." He pulled the van in between a large BMW and a Porsche, switching off the lights. "Why do all these rich bastards buy German crap?"

One Time had his door half open, and Haug grabbed his arm. "Where the hell are you goin'?"

"Rat man."

"Now, hold on just a minute. We gotta think what we're gonna do with him first. Cain't kill him, at least not here. Come on, One Time. Close the door and think. You get eager, and you start makin' mistakes, OK?"

Enrico Gomez woke with a start, wondering where the fuck he was. He looked through the windshield into an alien world of yellow lights and darkness. Then he remembered. He had been really pissed off, as it looked like he was going to be here all night. He had found a restaurant nearby, and they made him some sandwiches. The wrappings were on the floor of the Volvo, together with an empty Coke can. He must have fallen asleep.

There was a scratching sound underneath his feet. That must be what woke him. What the fuck was it?

"Meaow...meaow...meaow..."

A goddamn cat. He stomped his foot on the floor a couple of times, but that seemed to make the thing scratch more.

"Meaow...meaow."

A fucking cat. That was all he needed after about the worst eight hours he could remember. Was it eight hours? He looked at his watch. Nine. Trapped outside this fucking house, unable to leave, unable to get comfortable. He was fed up. He had enough. Next morning, whether the short Aussie left or not, he was going to get the DeLoop woman and take her to his boss, wherever he was. OK, so he might have to shake that information out of the Aussie. Yeah, so he would wait until daylight and there were a few people out on the street again. Then knock on the door, get inside, hold a blade against the Aussie's throat until he spilled. He screwed the cap off the half bottle of scotch he had bought and took a swig.

"Meaow...meaow."

First of all, though, he was going to have to kill that goddamn cat. The scratching was really getting on his nerves. He reached over to the glove compartment and got out a flashlight, then opened the door. He looked around to see if anybody was watching. The thing to do was grab the animal by the tail, smack it against a post and sling it over the railings into the little park. He got down on his hands and knees and turned on the flashlight.

"Kitty, kitty, kitty..." He looked under the car and almost dropped the flashlight when the beam caught the face of a bald headed man squeezed underneath.

"Surprise, greaseball," Haug said with a big smile.

Enrico Gomez was *so* surprised he didn't even feel the thin rope pass over his head. And then he did drop the flashlight as he realised he couldn't breathe and couldn't speak. The world turned red. And then completely dark.

When Haug returned from delivering Gomez to Keef's house, he moved the Volvo onto a single yellow line in the King's Road and slipped the van into its place, just opposite Gillmore's house. It was now quite late, past four o'clock. There was no activity at all at No 52. One Time had insisted on staying on watch while Haug was gone, just on the off chance someone moved. The Cuban had been no problem. He had locked his head to the floor of the van with a motorcycle shackle lock, and when the man woke up cursing and kicking, Haug banged him with a lump of wood. When he emptied his pockets, he found the knife and a few hundred pounds wadded into a roll. The guy smelled like a stale can of sardines left out too long in the sun, and Haug wondered if he was going to have to hose out the van.

He had to lean on the doorbell to wake Keef up, and that didn't succeed. It was his wife, Wendy, who woke and called out the window in an angry voice. When Keef came down, he had to repeat everything two or three times to make sure the sleepy man understood. It was really the smell of Gomez that finally woke him, when Haug dragged him into the kitchen and bolted him to the plumbing. Keef got some disinfectant from the cupboard and poured it all over the limp body, saying the neighbours would complain to the council if he stayed there too long. Haug gave him Mainwaring's telephone number and told him to speak to Detective Sergeant Golding, who would have him collected.

One Time was too excited to sleep and wanted to take the first watch, and, despite the oily stench in the back of the van, Haug went straight to sleep when his head hit the little foam mattress.

* * *

They came quietly through Louise Templer's back door at 5.00 am. They had on balaclavas and surgical gloves. The sky was already light, so they had no need of torches. They knew Alan Templer was not at home, and they knew the MP was alone in the house. Creeping through the kitchen silently, they began to open doors carefully. One of the men touched the other on the shoulder and pointed up the stairs. Slowly they began the ascent, one slightly behind the other.

Louise Templer woke from a deep sleep suddenly and violently and completely. The curtains were drawn, and the room was nearly dark so she remembered seeing only briefly a dark shape looming over her. At the same time she screamed, she kicked and swung her arms at the dark shape. Then she felt her legs trapped. There were two of them, she thought just before she nearly lost consciousness. It was moments before she

389

realised she had been struck on the head and was now on her stomach. One of the men was wrapping tape around her ankles and legs while the other one had her arms forced behind her doing the same thing.

"Do you realise who I am?" she managed to shout.

"We know who you are, darling," one of the men said. "And you know who we are, don't you?"

The man who taped her wrists grabbed the back of her hair and jerked her head up sharply. She felt and smelled the sticky plastic tape cover her mouth before she was flipped over on her back.

One of them leaned over close to her face as he pushed her nightdress up and forced his hand between her legs. She felt his fingers thrusting at her brutally.

"We haven't got time to do you the big favour right now. Later, maybe. Give you something to look forward to." He chuckled and so did his partner as he jerked his hand out.

One man picked her up while another held open a mailbag, then she was lowered into it and pushed down into a cramped crouch as they tied the top. She felt herself being lifted up and slung over a shoulder before being carried downstairs and out the front door. A car door was opened, and she was dumped into what she quickly realised was the boot. The lid slammed shut, other doors were opened and closed, an engine started and they were moving as she bounced along on the floor of the boot.

For the first time since she was a small girl, Louise Templer was completely terrified. She realised the whole operation must have taken less than five minutes, but it seemed like five hours. Fighting panic desperately, she tried to rein in her emotions as reason fragmented and scattered. She wanted out. Out, out, out. Out of the mess, out of the United Opposition, out of the boot, out of all of it. Go back, go back, take it all back, reverse the reel. Louise Templer would be a good little girl, live a conventional life, be a housewife, have kids, shop at the supermarket. She promised, she promised over and over again if only...if only she could be out of this mess. Why had she fought and studied hard to achieve against all the obstacles? Why had she cared a fuck about the fucking community or the working

390

class or justice? Let someone else do it. Yes, please. I'll resign as MP! I'll do anything!

Slowly, though, her senses returned, and so did her will. She might be small. She might be a woman. But she still had her wits. Perhaps she would die. If so, so be it. Many others, many better people had died before her in the fight for a world that was better than a jungle of greed. South Americans shot against walls. Africans raped and disembowelled, Vietnamese napalmed. In her own country there was Peterloo, Newport, Tonypandy, the 1984 Miners' Strike...why should she have special privileges when her time had come? Fight them, she thought to herself firmly and sadly, die if you must. There will be others behind me, hundreds and thousands and millions yet unborn.

Through the tape sealing her lips she started humming the *International* as loud as she could. She hoped they heard her.

* * *

General Sir Timothy Portland had just woken up when he heard them downstairs. He always woke at 5.00am, even without an alarm clock from years and years of habit. It was also his favourite part of the day, particularly in the summer. Light and quiet, except for birdsong. Normally he would have got out of bed quickly, pulled on his corduroys, shoes and jumper for a brisk walk before breakfast. Even when it was raining. It always set him up for the day, almost making him feel young again. Young again! Those days as an ambitious officer with a difficult command, the Royal Marines. No, not a Guards Regiment that all the officers fought for. A tough one. But, while the Marines and Paras were the hooligan regiments, they were also the best for a quick rise to the top if there was military action.

When the man in a balaclava entered General Portland's bedroom, the first thing he saw was the barrel of a pistol steadied on the General's knees as he lay in bed. It was also the last thing he saw. The .44 calibre bullet entered his forehead and exited in the back of his head, taking a large portion of his skull and almost a quarter of his brains. These bloody fragments, closely and more slowly followed by the rising body of the dead man, slammed into his partner behind him. The partner, also in a balaclava didn't at first realise what had happened, so quick had the action been. The moment he did realise, two things happened. His anal sphincter loosened, and his bowels emptied into his underwear. Simultaneously, he stepped over his dead mate and ran like hell, sick about the awful dampness in his trousers, sick about his friend and filled completely with panic.

The second bullet from General Sir Timothy Portland's revolver caught the running man in the centre of the back as he took the first step down the stairs. Before he died, he was dimly aware of a powerful blow between his shoulders and a mass of red flesh billowing out like an umbrella in front of him. The force of the gunshot propelled the man off the top of the stairs. His head struck the lintel, redundantly breaking his neck, before he crashed to the bottom of the stairwell.

General Portland walked to the top of the stairs and looked down, listening. The house was quiet, very quiet. Slowly he descended the stairs, stepping over the body of the man sprawled at the bottom. Again he stopped and listened. It was darker in the interior of the house, but the door to the reception room stood half open, and the General moved through the doorway, then swiftly crossed the room to the hallway door. It, too, was open, and he could see the hallway was very light. The front door must be standing open.

Portland was in his bare feet, and in a moment of decisiveness, he stepped into the light, raising his pistol. Another man, also in balaclava, stood on the front porch, his own pistol raised and steadied in both hands. He fired once as soon as he saw the General suddenly appear.

The shot caught Portland in the upper part of his left shoulder and moved his body back with the impact. Without too much haste, Portland took careful aim as the man fired a second shot which ripped off his ear lobe. Then he squeezed the trigger and watched the man lurch backward, throwing his automatic in the air. He never had thought much of the new, two handed grip for a pistol. Hearing a car start up in the driveway, the General stepped out on the porch, strangely aware how cold the tiles felt on his feet.

A black Ford was backing swiftly out of the drive, and again Portland took careful aim. With the roar of the revolver a small hole appeared in a crazed windscreen. The Ford reached the road, stopped, then leapt forward, the wheels spinning on the tarmac. Another roar, and a hole appeared in the side window. The Ford spun out of control, veered over a kerb, back out into the street, over the opposite kerb, and the right wing smashed into one of General Portland's favourite birches.

Portland walked over to the car and opened the door a little painfully with his left hand. The driver was slumped over the steering wheel, and blood was splashed over the dashboard and passenger seat. He felt for the carotid pulse. There was none. Closing the door, he walked back to his house, after first picking up the automatic from the lawn.

After collecting a first aid kit from the bathroom, the General went into his kitchen where the natural light was better. There he first cut off his nightshirt with scissors before examining the wound with a hand mirror. Good. There was entry and exit. He went to the kitchen sink and turned on the tap, holding his shoulder under the water to wash the wound. It was still bleeding, but he doused it with disinfectant, wincing at the sharp pain, before making a bandage pad, taping it down firmly, then wrapping the wound with gauze, over and over again under his arm and over his shoulder. His ear was also bleeding, and it looked like he might have lost all of the lobe. After holding his head under the tap for a few moments, he bandaged this small wound as well.

With difficulty he dressed himself. Casual clothes were all he could manage with the damned wound. Then he went to his study and found his address book in the top drawer. Picking up the phone he started to dial.

Louise Templer did not answer, and he wrote her name in one column with a query at the top. Neither did Professor Ewan Thomas, nor Stuart Easton, nor Matthew Tillson, nor Haug. He left warnings on their answerphones before getting through to Justin Lyndhurst and Kenneth Cranshaw, telling them briefly what happened and advising them to leave their homes immediately, without delay, taking great care. If there was any doubt or suspicion, they should barricade themselves inside and call him back. They were to call Mainwaring's number in Hampshire before noon, letting him know where they could be reached.

Then he called Mainwaring and got Detective Sergeant Golding on the telephone. After being informed all was well at the house, Portland re-told his story, advising Golding to be extra vigilant. The Sergeant thanked him and promised nothing would happen to Mainwaring and his wife.

He then telephoned Sir Gerald Humphries. It rang for a long time before his wife, Helen, answered sleepily. She told him, no, Sir Gerald had not come home the night before. She was surprised to find he was not in bed when the phone woke her up. This worried Portland, and he thought for a moment before asking her to check and see if his car was there.

He faintly heard the scream from the receiver, and his shoulders slumped. When Helen managed to get back to the phone, she was crying and hysterical. Slowly and patiently he tried to calm her, as, through her tears, she told him she found his Jaguar in the garage, the engine still running. Her husband was slumped over behind the steering wheel, and a hose was running from the exhaust to a rear window of the car. He told her to call Humphries' deputy immediately and ask him to come over. He called the hospital himself.

He phoned Detective Sergeant Golding again and told him the news of the death of the Metropolitan Police Commissioner and the circumstances. There was silence at the end of the phone, but Portland waited patiently for his reply.

"We'll stay, sir," Golding said finally in a hard voice. "No one but the Commissioner knows we are here." He paused again. "I *do* hope some attempt is made to attack Sir Jonathan's house, sir. I would look forward to it very much, sir."

Portland thanked him and wished them well before hanging up. His shoulder was beginning to throb, but he had no time to bother with doctors. Instead, he painfully opened his safe and removed the box of tapes and transcripts. Then he reloaded his nearly empty pistol. Putting the revolver in his belt and the automatic in his tweed jacket pocket, he left the house with the evidence and got his car out of the garage.

General Sir Timothy Portland had an idea it was going to be very rough going from now on.

* * *

One Time shook Haug awake about half past eight in the morning. He immediately looked at his watch and swore in a whisper at the black man. "What the fuck? Why didn't you wake me to take a watch? You lovesick bastard, now you're gonna be tired all day."

Haug put his eye to the disguised hole in the side of the van. Gillmore's Rolls Royce was double parked outside, the engine running. The chauffeur sat at the wheel in a peaked cap. One Time pulled him away from the hole and pressed his own eye against the hole, like a horizontal sub captain. He even had his cap turned around on his head so the peak wouldn't interfere.

"Goddammit, man, you only need to ask, and I'll move," Haug grumbled.

"He's coming out," said One Time as he sat up and started towards the back door of the van.

"By himself?"

"Righteous." One Time took hold of the handle, ready to jump out.

Haug grabbed him. "Uh-uh. Not yet. Think. Let Gillmore go, then we'll go in and wait for him to come back. Right? Alright?"

One Time stopped, waited a moment, then nodded in agreement.

Haug pointed at what his friend called his "ghetto blaster", a high tech electronic sweeper. "We take that with us. You know what these people are like."

One Time had his eye in the hole again. "In the back of the Rolls. Now, gone, man."

Haug heard the Roller whoosh away and watched through the windshield as it quickly turned the corner at the end of the square. One Time was up again, reaching for the door handle.

"Settle down. Take it easy, hambone. Have I gotta teach you everthang all over again? He mighta forgot his watch."

They waited for ten minutes from the front seats of the van, and they watched the well-dressed men and women leave and get into expensive cars. Dog walkers were out, too. One old gent stood patiently while his cairn terrier left a deposit of what looked like butterscotch pudding in the middle of the pavement. Haug checked his watch and nodded. They got out together.

One Time rang the doorbell and Haug braced himself a few paces back, ready to hit the door at a run when it opened. He had expected to see a burly man. Or a doctor in a white coat. The last thing he expected was Corky DeLoop fully made up in a short red dress with no shoes on.

Her eyes widened with surprise and glee, and she opened her mouth to welcome them Texas-style with open arms when she saw both men suddenly put their forefingers to their lips and wave their free hands. So she let them inside quietly and closed the door. Then she threw herself around One Time. Literally. Both arms were wrapped around his neck and both legs around his waist. Haug discreetly took the bag One Time was holding and waited patiently for the end of their embrace.

"Scan for bugs first," One Time whispered in her ear.

She whispered in his. "Gotcha, beautiful! What took ya so long?"

One Time held up one finger and nodded his head rhythmically as she disentangled herself. He then took out his ghetto blaster, turned it on, made some adjustments and began his sweep. The hall was OK. There was one in each of the rooms, though, except for the kitchen and bath. They went into the kitchen and closed all the doors. The black man took out a red box and put it on the table. He turned it on and fiddled with the dials as Haug and Corky waited.

Finally he stopped, satisfied. "Right now," he said out loud. "One time."

Corky spread her hands, shaking her head. "How?"

"Hell, we only heard about it yesterday from your friend, Sarah Courtney. We were told you just left that Unit place by some cops who're helpin' us, so we busted into Gillmore's flat, found some deeds, found this place and then got rid of the smelly spic outside. We waited til Gillmore left, and here we are. Is he leavin' you here alone?"

Corky showed them the tag on her wrist. One Time examined it carefully. "Cain't leave through the door or window. But that's alright, 'cause I don't want to."

Haug frowned, and he and One Time exchanged puzzled looks. "How come?" he asked.

She smiled. "Would you two guys like some coffee or somethin'? We better sit down and get comfortable with a hot drink, 'cause I gotta story to tell you two."

Haug and One Time both called for tea, and when Haug saw she was having trouble using an electric kettle, he took over.

"You go sit down and talk to lover boy, there," he said. "He's been as nervous as a longtailed cat in room fulla rockin' chairs since he heard you were taken." He looked over as he shook some instant coffee into a cup. Corky had just sat on One Time's lap, and they were kissing deeply. "And as far as I'm concerned you can fuck in the middle of the floor while I drink my tea and watch. Hell, I might learn somethin', you never know." He found a carton of longlife milk in the fridge, and opened it. When the water boiled, he filled the three cups, left Corky's coffee black and tipped some milk into the two teas, which he stirred.

Corky pulled away, still looking into One Time's eyes. "We might just do that, big feller, if you're sure it won't bother you."

Haug brought the cups over to the table. "Hell no," he said as he sat down in one of the chairs, "I've seen just about everthang there is to see at least twice, and watchin' somebody as goodlookin' as you fuck would not be a chore."

One Time searched for words as she laughed. "Ummm...ummm...ummm."

"I do believe my friend is embarrassed," Haug said as he took a sip of tea.

Corky kissed One Time again before she got up from his lap. "Now don't you go anywhere, you big, beautiful, black hunk of beef. I got *plans* for you." She sat in a chair beside One Time and picked up the cup of coffee, turning to Haug. "Did you say your name was O'Connell?"

"I lied to you. It's Haug."

"Haug? What kinda name is that? Sounds like a fruit bat or somethin'."

"You're right," Haug said. "It's far too sophisticated for Texas where most of 'em don't even have last names, since they never knew their daddies."

She whooped. "Where the hell you from?"

"North Carolina."

"They got indoor flush toilets there yet?"

"Yeah, 'cause we couldn't stand the smell o' Texas everwhere we went."

She laughed again. "You're OK, big feller. I like you." She took another sip of coffee. "Now. First of all, it's *great* seein' you two guys. You might have to excuse me, 'cause I've forgotten what normal people are like. You wanna know why I'm gonna stay here, right? Well, I'll tell you somethin'. I got some accountin' to do with Mr Harvey Gillmore Sir. You get my drift? I've been through nine grades of hell on account of that son of a bitch, and where I come from in Texas, if you buy in dollars, you pay in dollars. He's got a whole lot comin' to him, and I'm just about to start dishin' it out. I just cain't tell you how much I been lookin' forward to this. More'n I was lookin' forward to ridin' my first pony at twelve years old. Harvey Gillmore's ass is grass."

Haug leaned forward. "Now, lissen, Corky. I know that slimy little piece of possum shit real well. He may be little, but so are coral snakes and black widow spiders. What there is of him is full o' poison. He's *dangerous*. Now, my advice is to come with us. I gotta friend in Hampstead, and you can stay at her house. Or stay with One Time if you like loud crap music all night. Or there's my place, though havin' you around there would be like puttin' a chocolate covered banana split in front of a hungry food hog."

"Thanks for the compliment and the offers, but I *know* what I want. There is somethin' you can do for me, though. I'd like you to bring me a few things." She told them what they were, counting them off on her fingers.

One Time was grinning, and Haug laughed as he shook his head. "Yeah, I see what you're up to. Do you reckon you can do it?"

"I don't reckon, Haug," she said with a big smile. "I *know* I can do it."

"Well," he said, "it's gonna be a big pain in the ass, 'cause it means breakin' into his flat again, and that's one hell of a job."

"I'll do it, man. Today," One Time blurted, then turned to Corky. "Before I go, I put up a nail. You have trouble with the little man, I'm outside. Just call. One time. Right now."

She looked at him with her head lowered, a sexy smile on her face. "You're gettin' awful talkative all of a sudden."

"He's a real windbag sometimes," Haug said to her. "It's a deviant personality trait." He finished his tea and stood up, throwing the keys to the van on the table. "I'm gonna assume you know what you're doin' with that little poison dwarf, lady. I'll catch a taxi back to my place, and meanwhile I hope you two make a real mess of this kitchen floor."

She grabbed him and pulled his head down to plant a kiss on his cheek. "You know just how to treat a lady, don't you?"

Haug looked up from the embrace at One Time. "I never in my life thought I would be jealous of a sorry bastard like you." He stood up with a smile and looked down at Corky DeLoop. "You one hell of a woman."

One Time held up one finger and flashed a mouthful of teeth as Haug opened the door and tiptoed through the hall.

* * *

"Where in the name of Jesus have *you* been?" Lizzy asked as he entered the office, looking bone tired. "I won't say I was actually *worried* about you, but all hell has been breaking loose today. The telephone rings every five minutes, and there's a man upstairs in your bed. And you look like what's left of the dog's dinner, Haug."

"We found the DeLoop woman. She's OK," he said as he flopped down on the greasy sofa near the window.

"Don't sit down," she said. "There's no time to sit down. You found one and lost a half a dozen others."

He opened one eye and looked at her. "What?"

"Early this morning. Raids all over the place. The Metropolitan Police Commissioner's dead, and half your friends have disappeared..."

Haug sat up with a start. "Who? Louise?..."

"Yes, Louise Templer's gone. That Tillson fellow. Mr Easton..."

"Mainwaring?" Haug interrupted her.

"He's OK. So far. The General has killed several men, and he's OK. Professor Thomas is upstairs in your bed..."

"Goddamn, what the hell is goin' on?"

"I'm a secretary, not an oracle," she said. "Oracles get enough wages to live on."

Haug got up from the sofa. "I already pay you twice what you're worth. Is Thomas asleep?"

"He was waiting at the door when I arrived, and I haven't heard anything since he went up."

Haug pounded his fist into the back of the sofa. "Fuck." He turned to her. "What'd they say about Louise?"

"It was the General who left the message. Just said she wasn't there, suspected taken." She watched him go to the telephone. "The General said he'd call later. He's not at home. Apparently there's a lot of dead men all over his house. He was worried about you, but I told him you were out on a job."

Haug was dialling a number on the telephone. "It's Haug, Louise," he said to the answerphone. "Call me. Urgent."

"Ah," said Lizzy when he put down the phone.

"What do you mean by 'ah'?" Haug asked.

"It's just that I see something I didn't see before. I'm Irish, you know. A little thick."

"What the hell are you talking about?"

Lizzy pressed a couple of buttons on the wordprocessor. "Mrs Templer. Guess I'll have to paint another pair of open legs on the fuselage. You must be an ace by now."

Haug grabbed the phone again. "This is no time for jokes in poor taste." He dialled and waited until Detective Sergeant Golding answered. "Haug here," he said.

"Oh, well done. And how many did you slaughter, sir?" Golding asked.

"I was on surveillance all night," he said. "Found what I was lookin' for but missed all the action."

"How disappointing," Golding said.

"But I'm just about to get started again. Can I speak to Jonathan?"

"I'm sure he'd want to talk to you," Golding replied. "Just a moment, sir."

Haug waited only a few moments before he heard Mainwaring's voice.

"Thank god they haven't taken you," he said.

"Well, the Vietnamese Army couldn't do it, and I don't expect these bastards can, either. I found the party we were lookin' for, and she's OK. Now tell me somethin' about this goddamn disaster..."

"Thirty minutes ago I spoke with Michael Regis," Mainwaring said. "They want to talk with me. Us."

"When?"

"Day after tomorrow..."

"Too goddamn late, Jonathan. Let me take care of it. I'll grab the chicken by the neck and squeeze it till it squawks. I'll find out where they are. And they better not have been touched, I can tell you that."

"Now calm down, Haug. And a little thinking wouldn't be amiss here. While you're creating mayhem and rendering yet another of our houses unfit to live in, what is going to be happening to the hostages? For that is what they are. He even used that word. He promised me they would be well treated unless we tried to find the hostages or attacked members of their committee..."

"Which face did he promise out of?" Haug asked.

401

"Will you please let me finish, Haug? I'm quite aware of his shifty nature. I made this meeting dependent upon receiving two telephone calls each day and hearing the voice of each captive."

"Hmmm," Haug mused. "Are you thinkin' what I'm thinkin'?"

"I'm sorry, Haug. Tracing the calls are out of the question. I gave my word."

"Right. That's it, then." Haug knew when Sir Jonathan Mainwaring gave his word to anyone it was as inviolable as the Law of Gravity. It was more likely the sun would fall out of the sky like an apple than the Permanent Secretary would break his word, once he gave it.

"Besides," Mainwaring continued. "There is much for you to do in the meanwhile. Try and get in touch with Timothy Portland..."

"Sounds like the old boy handled himself pretty well. They grabbed a cat by the tail and found out it was an alligator."

"I have to say I'm rather pleased with Timothy myself under the circumstances. I spoke with him earlier and told him so. I believe Ewan Thomas is with you, is that right?"

"Upstairs asleep in my bed," Haug said. "Where I'd like to be if I wasn't trapped in the middle of a limey civil war. Lissen, Jonathan, I'm awful worried about Louise. These assholes don't have a fine reputation with women, and I'd like you to tell your Mr Regis that if they fuck around with her, they're gonna have to fuck around with me. I swear to you I mean that. There won't be enough of 'em left to be worth wrappin' in bandages. I don't like this way of goin' about thangs, 'cause I don't trust those people. You go around givin' your *word* to folks I wouldn't trust if they promised to breathe regular."

"I will pass on your remarks to Michael Regis," Mainwaring replied. "I have already given him my own warning regarding the safety of the hostages, and it was as acid as yours, even if not quite so earthy. To some extent our hands are tied at the moment, so we must negotiate with them."

"The only negotiation they understand is violent negotiation."

402

"I'll be in my own element, Haug. I would like Ewan to come along as well, if he will. Just you, Ewan and myself."

"I'll go wake him up and tell him."

"Haug?"   There was a few moments' silence before Mainwaring continued. "I'm awfully pleased you are well."

"Well thank you, Jonathan. Got to admit I was relieved to hear your voice."

"Yes. Well. I'll speak to you later."

Haug hung up the telephone and leaned forward on the desk.

"This thang's gettin' outta hand," he said to no one in particular.

CHAPTER TWENTY TWO

Haug sat at his kitchen table having filtered coffee with Professor Ewan Thomas who was scratching his shaggy, iron grey hair and trying to wake up. Thomas was tall and lean, but his lantern jaw and large hands suggested more of a dock worker than a history professor. He had not put his shoes on, and one of his socks had a hole in the toe. He contemplated the hole gravely.

"It surprises me you like Bach," he said.

Haug had put on a CD of the *B Minor Mass* while Thomas was in the toilet. "If I don't hear this Mass at least once a month, I feel like I've missed somethin'," he said. "I guess it doesn't fit in with my carefully manicured image of a slob."

Thomas laughed. "Much of what we know of any subject is supposition. Yes, I imagined you to be a Country and Western man. I'm not sure classical music is the usual fashion accessory of the action man."

"More like an inaction man right now. So I'm a little irritable. My instinct right now is to go out and find those people and to get 'em back here. But Jonathan had to give his word that I wouldn't, to folks who'd promise anythang to win a game they're cheatin' at anyway."

The professor sat back in his chair. "I certainly wish you had been there last night. It's strange, but I remembered what you told me once about action. It seemed to help."

"I think you did real well. Couldn't have done better if I'd been there. The key is, you have to play with the hand you've got. It's no use wishin' you had a full house or four of a kind when you got a pair of deuces. Just play the goddamn deuces the best you can. A fool can win a hand of poker with four of a kind. Takes some thinkin' to win with a pair of two's. Which is what you did. Wrecked your car and outran 'em. It worked."

"It was the one physical thing I was always good at," Thomas mused. "Running."

"And it's a good 'un. It's surprisin' just how many people cain't run worth a fuck. Like me. I can cover maybe 30 yards

405

like a sprinter. After 30 yards I need a wheelchair." Haug got up and opened the fridge. "Hey, I'm not bein' much of a host. Lemme see what I got here. You must be hungry as hell. I sure am." He pulled out a covered casserole. "Got a pot of black-eyed peas floatin' around a boiled ham and some cornbread I can heat up in the microwave."

"Sounds wonderful," said Thomas. "Even though I don't know what cornbread is."

"It's white trash food," Haug replied as he put the pot on the hob and turned on the gas. "'Bout the cheapest thang you can eat where I come from. If you got a big pot, you can feed a coupla adults and a bunch o' young 'uns under five dollars. When I was growin' up, you could do it under a dollar."

Haug returned to the table. "Jonathan says he wants you to come day after tomorrow. To the big meetin'. You and me and him."

Thomas rubbed his eyes. "I have no idea why he wants me along."

"A second barrel of intellectual buckshot, I reckon. I lissened to some of that crap we recorded from the Matilda. They know how to shove statistics around the board to make the comin' of the master race seem inevitable."

"Inevitable is a dangerous word to use about human affairs," he said and then chuckled. "And I say that as a Marxist. Of a sort, I hasten to add. 'Inevitable' is a word mostly useful for propaganda. A bit like the word 'democracy', really. These people want their system to prevail and encourage everyone, including themselves, to view it as inevitable. The right word for them is 'dangerous'. It is because they are so dangerous that I oppose them, and I will continue to oppose them until I die."

Haug swirled his coffee around the mug. "How come you say 'democracy' is a propaganda word?"

"Because it's a system much talked about, little understood and never really tried. A bit like socialism, but more acceptable as a word. The so-called democracies of the world are in fact forms of autocracy, sometimes with checks and balances of varying degrees of success or failure. What many people fail to realise is the checks and balances themselves are usually influenced by the autocratic power behind the government."

Thomas folded his hand behind his head and stretched his legs. "What makes these people, this Community of Association, so dangerous, is its devious extension of this system from a national to global entity, following on the coattails of economic capitalist expansion. Successful companies have grown larger. And larger. And larger. These companies have grown so large they share more interests with their competitors than they share either with the workers they employ or their nation of origin. The Community of Association is merely following a form of political logic dictated by this expansion. But it is in fact a fascist logic, not democratic at all. They want to take all the chocks away and let it all rip, and, except for one thing, they might even be successful."

"One thang?" Haug asked when Thomas paused.

"It's not going to work. Propaganda - called 'news' in the West - has repeated over and over that socialism is in crisis, so that it has become the received wisdom of the man in the street. There is a crisis, but it is not in socialism - which has never existed and possibly will not exist for some considerable time. The crisis," Thomas said, looking at Haug from under his eyebrows, "is in capitalism. It is difficult for anyone to tell what depth of crisis it is in, but it is deep. So deep that change is being forced on virtually every government on earth. There is a fascinating logic to it. Individual companies have grown so large and so powerful - and almost so irresistible - they are out of control.

"Growth is a strange phenomenon, Haug. In early stages it is difficult and can easily be stopped by lack of success. The chances for success are slim. But if food is plentiful, animals will continue to grow, some of them very large, either in physical size or in size of communities. However, at some point not easily determined, the system teeters on chaos, sometimes imploding, threatening to destroy itself. I believe that is the kind of crisis we have today.

"Things don't arise from nothing. They tend to evolve, using many of the instruments which worked in a past model.

407

America, for instance, believes it has a democratic system of government. So does Britain. Yet in the financial engine room of the economy, it is anything but democratic. The structure of a company still retains what is really a medieval concept of autocracy. The Elder - or group of Elders - rules as absolutely as the ducal landlord in the middle ages."

Haug got up to check the stew. Then he fetched the cornbread from the fridge and stuck it in the microwave while Thomas talked.

"This structure was useful for some time in modern capitalism," the professor went on. "That's why they kept it. For its utility. The Community of Association wants to take that old structure, streamline it, call it democratic of course, and use it as a solution to the structural problem, not realising they are hastening its death or ensuring radical change."

The bell on the microwave rang, and Haug began putting the food on the table. "Personally, I'd like to see the end of this rickety system, so why the hell don't we help 'em, then? Help 'em push?"

Thomas opened the pot and served some of the steaming food onto his plate. "Because of the human cost. I have a feeling it's going to be expensive enough without their meddling. With it, holocausts may become commonplace." He put some food in his mouth.

"Well, Ewan, you managed to bring me to life again. I could sit and lissen to you for hours if I weren't so hungry."

"This is delicious," Thomas said. "You must stop me when I start rambling on. I think that's why my wife and I separated. She is an historian as well, and we would talk and argue all day. Nothing ever got done. How do you eat this cornbread?"

"You slice it in the middle, put some butter inside, stuff it into your mouth and chew."

* * *

Jim Harper had been Harvey Gillmore's chauffeur for almost a year now, and he already hated the job. In fact he hated the job shortly after he got it. The Governor treated him like dirt and didn't even pay all that well, considering he was an important man. Harper was a good chauffeur and prided himself on being smooth and discreet. A good chauffeur was hardly noticed by an employer. That is what made them good. A bad chauffeur was always noticed. Jim Harper knew his job and had no complaints in the past, but Harvey Gillmore noticed him. Went out of his way to notice him. Went out of his way to make life miserable for him. It took him a while to realise he was just that kind of man.

He had finished washing the Roller, drying it off and cleaning the interior. The only other duty he had at the Fleet Street office was to watch the Governor's private entrance and make sure no unauthorised entry was made. Mr Gillmore used the private lift which had only one stop at the top flat. Another door opened onto the emergency stairs, but they were only occasionally used by the maintenance personnel. There were eight flights of them from the underground car park. From where he was standing, Harper could just see the pavement outside, and it was nice to watch women's legs, especially on a warm summer day.

That's what he was watching when he spotted the ten pound note which blew from behind a pillar and swept toward the far wall. Harper frowned and walked toward the moving note, checking first to see if anyone was watching.

As he leaned over to pick up the note, One Time slipped silently through the stairwell door with a long parcel wrapped with paper and string and an armful of evening newspapers. Taking the stairs two at the time, he didn't stop to catch his breath until he reached the top. Then he unwrapped the long parcel.

Harvey Gillmore was annoyed to hear his doorbell. That idiot Harper had not phoned to tell him someone was on the way up. The doorbell rang again, and Gillmore pushed back his chair and threw down his pen and glasses. He walked out of his office and into the hall before checking the video security camera. Then he stopped and frowned. No one was there. Then he saw the newspapers lying in front of the door and relaxed. Maybe Harper was improving after all. Obviously he had gone out and collected the evening papers for him instead of waiting on the delivery.

Gillmore opened the flat door and leaned over to pick up the papers when his eye was drawn to a gorgeous woman's leg in a stocking and high heeled shoe thrusting provocatively from the recess near the cleaner's cupboard. He picked the papers up and slowly approached the leg. Some lady was showing considerable initiative, he thought, and might be needing a reward for her efforts.

He was half way to the leg when he heard his flat door snap shut and for a moment he stopped in indecisive anger and curiosity before rushing back to the door. It was closed alright, and his keys were in his jacket pocket. He thumped on the door with frustration before staring at the leg again. It had not moved.

He narrowed his eyes as he approached the woman's leg. When he turned the corner, he saw it was a mannequin's leg propped against a cleaning trolley. He picked up the leg and threw it down the hall. A joke? Or was it something a little more sinister? He ran to the lift and pounded on the button. There was another set of keys in the Rolls glove compartment, and he felt a compelling urge to get back as quickly as possible.

One Time went straight to the safe, and his memory of the sequence was accurate. It opened on first try. Everything was going fine for him today. This was *his* day. He had the Texas woman back again, a woman like he had never met before. He could not believe some woman could enjoy sex more than he did, but he had to admit that one was just about more than he could handle. Beautiful. Demanding. Creative. Creative? She was a Miles Davis of the sexual act, an improviser, full of inner music. When they finally parted that morning, One Time was as spent and as weak as a discarded snake skin...and she had wanted more! Man! That woman!

He found what he was looking for quickly, put everything back where it had been, closed the safe door and spun the dial. Then he moved swiftly to the flat door, checked the security camera, opened it, closed it again and ran to the emergency stairs, glancing at the lift lights as he passed. It was on its way up again. Timing, man! One time! Right now!

At the bottom of the stairs he could just see the chauffeur staring up at the lift light, glancing around nervously. Opening the door gradually and silently, he waited patiently until the driver looked in the opposite direction, out towards the pavement, before he slipped out the door and walked toward the chauffeur.

Jim Harper jumped and felt what hair he had left stand on end as the black man in the gas board overalls with a clip board spoke behind him.

"Hey man," said One Time with a friendly smile. "You seen one of our vans around here?"

"Christ!" Harper said. "You scared the piss out of me. Where did you come from?"

One Time held out his hands and punched a thumb over his shoulder. "Back there, man. Looking for the van. So. Have you seen one?"

"What?" Harper was still unsettled. He had not heard a thing before the black man spoke.

One Time sighed heavily. "One of our vans. Gas van. Man supposed to pick me up an hour ago outside. Thought he might be parked in here."

"No," Harper said, trying to regain some authority. "No vans. Time you left now, if you don't have business here. Private parking only. Off with you now."

"Yes *sir*, General," One Time said with a salute as he grinned at the chauffeur's uniform. He moved quickly toward the entrance and then vanished.

Gillmore checked his office carefully, but nothing seemed to be disturbed. His pen was where he threw it, and his granny glasses lay undisturbed half balanced on the file. He checked his drawers, then went to the safe. Still locked. He frankly found the whole thing bizarre. Harper had denied delivering the newspapers at first, and it was only when he swore at the man that he finally admitted putting them there, though he still had a stupid, puzzled look on his face. He was going to have to replace that halfwit. A chauffeur who didn't even know what day it was most of the time.

The Australian suspected someone somehow had slipped into his flat. When he first opened the door, he was wary, looking around, checking every room. Nothing. Nobody. And nothing was disturbed, apparently nothing taken.

Was he going mad? Was this another manifestation of his obsession, the one which appeared to be taking over his life? He couldn't concentrate on his work, and the whole universe seemed to be falling apart. Like the peculiar events just now. Things like that didn't used to happen to him. Accidentally letting the flat door close, newspapers delivered by a dimwitted chauffeur who didn't even remember doing it. And what was that leg doing there, for fuck's sake?

Gillmore took a deep breath. It was all obviously logical, and it was just his state of mind which was playing tricks on him. The leg could have been...anything. Left over from a party downstairs, someone's private kink picked up by the cleaner, anything. Obviously the feeling someone had slipped into his flat came from the same source. Corky DeLoop.

As if on cue, the telephone rang. Somehow he knew who it was even before he spoke.

"Where the hell's my wife, Gillmore?" Hercules DeLoop bellowed down the line.

"She's left you, Herk. Decided to stay with me. Sorry about that."

"Lissen, you little Aussie scumsucker, if you don't get that woman back to me, I'm gonna come over there, tear off your head, scoop out the two ounces of brains and pack the hole with pig shit. You hear me?"

"Bad luck, Herk," Gillmore said calmly. "She fell in love with me, and I can't do anything about that, can I?"

"I wanna hear that from her," DeLoop howled. "Just before I punt her ass into the middle of the Atlantic."

"I'm afraid she's not available," Gillmore replied. "I'll get her to telephone you. Are you still staying with Regis?"

"Don't hand me that crap, you two-faced, yellow-belly weasel. I know what you done to her, and you've goddamn well made a fool outta me."

"That's impossible, Herk. You're a self-made man."

"You lissen to me and lissen to me good. You got two fuckin' days to get her back to me, and I might decide not to kill you. What have you done with Gomez?"

Gillmore frowned. "Gomez? Do you mean that smelly Cuban? Haven't seen him."

"If you've fucked her, you perverted little runt, I'm gonna have Gomez hack off your balls."

Gillmore knew how to handle people like Hercules DeLoop. "Oh, I've fucked her, alright. She begged me for it. Nice piece of ass. Mine now."

The silence on the other end of the line was ominous. "We're gonna meet soon, shorty. And when we meet, you gonna wish you'd been trampled by a herd o' buffaloes. Ain't nobody does this kinda shit to me." The line went dead.

Gillmore replaced the receiver and shrugged. He enjoyed that more than he thought he would. The big Texan was on his patch, and on his patch he called the tune and beat the time. It might be necessary to get a couple of bodyguards, but that was no trouble. Make sure they give DeLoop a real good kicking so he could walk over and spit on him. The Texan was a coarse bastard who had money but no power. Worse, he still confused the two things. It took money to gain power. Money was only the fuel which made the complex engine turn. It was nothing more than the coal which fired the stations where the turbines created that invisible and irresistible force which drove the world. Because power was immediately translatable into control. Control was necessary for people. To make more money, to make more fuel. And to direct them. Not one, not two, but thousands, even millions. Direct them so everyone danced to *your* tune and mesmerically watched your baton for the beat.

With newspapers in eighteen different countries all pounding the theme, it was impossible for his power not to grow. And now there was satellite TV. Technologically he would cover the

413

globe. Pounding them, over and over, tuning them and turning them so they said "yes" and "no" on cue. That's why all the politicians scampered and scraped for his attention, even the bloody socialist ones. One thing led to another. Perhaps he could become closer to God by being His representative on earth, His image, His mouthpiece. The power of God wielded by the hand of Gillmore.

The reverie shattered as he unexpectedly visualised the nude figure of Corky DeLoop cheekily sitting on the edge of the bed, beckoning to him with her finger. Was she doing it to *him*? No. That couldn't happen. He was in control, and he had always been in control. It was his flat, and she couldn't leave it. There was no where to go, and DeLoop would kill her if he found her. She was trapped. She was his.

But why, then, was he so obsessed? Why was the touch of her so electric? Right at that moment he craved her desperately. He wanted to be with her. That morning he forced himself to call the car and came in to work when all he wanted to do was stay in her arms, molded to her body, feeling the softness and warmth. It was so unusual, though. It had never occurred to him that he needed such things, yet now he felt he needed nothing else.

Forcing himself to pick up his glasses, he put them on and tried to concentrate on the figures in front of him. Then he laughed dryly to himself. After all, he almost said out loud, he broke her, didn't he? That's why she was so alluring, of course it was. He created her for his needs, that's all.

And she would certainly fulfil them.

* * *

Commandant General Robert Sessions, commander of the Royal Marines, leaned back in his chair and returned the transcripts to the folder. He was quite young for his command at 46 years old, and only his short sideboards were glazed with grey. The rest of his hair was almost jet black and, while not curly, had a natural wave. General Sessions was, in fact, a good-looking man and had been compared to the younger Sean

414

Connery. Tall, well-built, with a deep, modulated voice. He looked across at the man who had been his mentor, General Sir Timothy Portland.

"Nasty can of worms," he said. "Foolish men who should know better."

"Those foolish men are now creating a dangerous crisis in this country," Portland said. They were sitting in General Sessions study, and the windows were open onto a wide front lawn. Being Commandant of the Marines, a unit posted to Northern Ireland, the house was guarded, and Portland could just see one man standing at the far end of the drive.

"Now the question arises," said Sessions, "of the reasons you have shown me this material..."

A car pulled up in the driveway outside, and a man stepped out from the rear door. General Sessions turned to look out the window.

"It's the doctor. He is under my command, and I know him well, so no questions will be asked of how you received gunshot wounds at your home."

The doctor, Lt Colonel Harborough, was a lean man with glasses who entered with a bag. After introductions, General Portland removed his shirt. The Colonel cut through the bandages quickly and proceeded to examine the wound. He also looked closely at the ear. He returned to the shoulder, pressing on the clavicle, shoulder blade and socket, asking the patient to comment on the degree of pain. Portland never cried out, only once hissing air through his teeth. He was asked to accompany the doctor to the lavatory where both wounds were thoroughly washed and dried. Oddly, it was the ear which was still bleeding, and not the shoulder.

After medication and bandaging, a sling was offered to Portland, who at first refused to wear one. The Colonel insisted, pointing out that excess movement would only prolong the healing process. He told Portland mostly what he already knew. The bullet had gone through the muscle and some connecting tissue - though he couldn't tell the degree of damage without X-rays - and he was lucky the bone had not been hit. As for the ear, it would probably be painful for a few days, but basically the damage was cosmetic. Not once did the doctor comment on the fact they were bullet wounds, nor did he ask any questions about how he received them. He simply did his job as a professional and then, after nearly an hour, took his leave.

General Portland stared out the window as the car carrying Lt Colonel Harborough left the drive. "To answer your question," he said, continuing their earlier conversation, "I am bringing it to your attention because I instinctively feel their penetration of the Services is probably small or nonexistent. And because I have known you since you were a schoolboy. Finally, I think someone at your rank in the Services should know what a potential powder keg we have here. Potential may be too mild a word. The fuse is already lit, but its length hasn't yet been determined. Hence the Forces may be directly involved sooner rather than later."

"Good," said Sessions. "I'm glad you haven't asked for direct intervention at this point, Timothy. You know the problems with that as well as I do. The only thing I *can* do is clear up the mess at your home. I have no idea whether they are Specials or this - what's it called? - one of these Action groups. My report will be that they are in fact IRA, and that will automatically bring the shutters down on the press for the time being. I'm sure the Specials won't want to admit they are theirs. As it's an IRA matter, you will automatically have a guard, and I think I can provide that, at least at your home. Though," he laughed shortly, "you seem to do well enough without a guard. Four men? At your age? Well done, old boy. They don't make them like you anymore, do they?"

Portland turned down the corners of his mouth and shrugged. "Amateurish. The man who fired at me should have had me. No backbone. Damned fellow was holding his weapon with both hands, presenting me with the width of his body as target. They watch too many cops and robber films."

General Sessions got up from his chair and folded his arms across his chest as he studied the ceiling. "I have to admit to you that I am not that unsympathetic with some of their objectives, this group. Some of their ideas, rather. It provokes thought..."

"Robert..."

416

Sessions held up his hand. "No, don't worry. I'm not about to join any such thing as a Community of Association, nor am I interested in treasonable means to achieve these objectives. And these are treasonable, no doubt about that, if these tapes are anything to go by. And I damned well don't like the idea of armed bands of marauders swaying through the streets of England in speeding automobiles. On the other hand I am certainly not comfortable with so many left wingers associated with the United Opposition. Damn it, there's who? Easton, Templer, and Ewan Thomas..."

"Whatever you may say about them, Robert, they are patriots. I assure you we will continue the fight amongst ourselves when this particular enemy is defeated. Same as Hitler. We unite against the invader."

"Yes, yes, of course," Sessions murmured, clasping his hands behind him and walking toward the window. "Why hasn't the Prime Minister been approached?"

"We may have to shortly," Portland replied. "Unfortunately, he is a weak man and it is feared he is manipulated by the two or three cabinet ministers who are implicated in the treason. I can't really see him standing up to them. He will turn to the cabinet secretary of course who will deride the whole thing. Then he will call in Home and the Exchequer who will point the finger at us. None of the cabinet has any spine. It's this vacuum of power at the top which is hobbling us and helping them. This is our biggest problem. One of the reasons for coming to you and to the Commissioner, Sir Gerald. Dead for his efforts on our behalf."

"Are you certain it wasn't suicide?"

General Portland looked at Sessions from under his brows, saying nothing.

"Alright, alright. Highly bloody unlikely in the circumstances." The Royal Marine Commandant unclasped his hands and folded them again on his chest. "I will have one battalion placed on alert. It cannot be official, but we'll make it a practice of some sort. Leave it with me. But," he turned and pointed an index finger at Portland, "I am *not* going to place myself or the RM on the spot here. If the PM is not approached,

417

then it has to be Defence. That's my boss. I suggest Sir Jonathan Mainwaring approaches Norman Stone."

Portland nodded in agreement, and Sessions suddenly clapped his hands together. "Now. I'm going to insist you join us for lunch, Timothy."

Portland stood up a little painfully. His shoulder was now quite stiff. "Thank you, Robert. I accept."

* * *

Stuart Easton leaned back in his cane-bottomed chair and hooked the heel of one shoe on the rung. The side of his face was swollen where one of the thugs hit him with the butt of a pistol, and he suspected his cheekbone was chipped or broken. But he wasn't going to give these bastards satisfaction by complaining. He had been dragged from his bed by his feet and only fully woke up as his head hit the floor. He was pulled down the hall and then down the stairs. That's where he found the leverage to free one foot and kick the man pulling him right in the balls. When he doubled over, releasing his other foot, he regained his balance and kicked him in the head, which was the wrong thing to do barefoot. He almost made it to the garden door before one of the others jumped on his back and dragged him to the floor. Easton fought hard. His hands were still miner's hands, big and strong. He had loosened his attacker's grip and was just staggering to his feet when the third man hit him with the pistol. It hurt. Easton couldn't remember anything which hurt more, and tears filled his eyes - not because he was crying, but as a reaction to the blow. The three men stuffed him into a bag, and he was driven for miles in the boot of a car. He was brought to this house, dumped into this room and had a handful of clothes thrown at him.

There were bars on the window, the door was heavy, and the room had a disused clinical atmosphere. Two-toned green paint was peeling from the walls and ceiling. The table was institutional and so was the bed, which was hooked to the wall. Easton's guess was that the building was a disused mental home, one of the many closed down by the government, whose occupants were turned into the streets to save money.

The room was not, however, soundproof. Easton knew there were a few others who had been taken along with him. He heard Louise Templer's voice shouting, and when he heard it, he shouted, too, calling her name. The guard outside his door had entered. He carried a submachine gun hung from his shoulders. Easton shouted louder when the door opened, and the guard threatened him with the gun.

"Go on, shoot me," he said. "If you've got the guts. But you haven't, have you? Louise! I'm here!"

The guard was short and burly-looking with swarthy receding hair. "Fucking shut up," he said as he advanced on Easton. "I've had enough of you."

"You can't shoot me because you haven't got orders to shoot me, have you?" Easton taunted him. "You need orders for everything. Even to have a wank."

As the thug advanced, Easton moved back, trying to find a good place to give the man a kick. He heard Louise screaming again, and he made a lunge for the open door, trying to get past the guard. And then, suddenly, he was on his knees gasping for breath, desperately trying to suck in some air. The guard had moved fast, and the punch caught him directly in the solar plexus. Then the door had closed.

It stayed closed, except for once when a tray of rubbish food was pushed through. Easton knew they were hostages, and, on the whole, he didn't think their chances of leaving there alive were very high.

By the time Louise Templer was dumped on the floor of her room, she was in a state of raging fury. The three men in the room did not have on their balaclavas. One sat on the bed and was going through a pile of clothes they must have taken from her house. There were several pairs of underwear, and he was holding up a pair of knickers Alan had given her years ago as a jokey present. She had never worn them. They were black and lacy and minimal.

"These are my favourite, eh lads?" he asked.

419

The other two grunted their approval, and the man on the bed picked out the matching bra.

"Hey, you'd never have thought a commie MP would wear this kind of stuff." He laid out the black lingerie and then found a short black skirt and a small tight, red jumper. "There you are, love. Something for you to wear." He put the remaining clothes in the plastic bag used to carry them. "OK, cut her loose."

One of the other two men produced a small pen knife and slit the tape around her legs. Then she felt her hands were free. Without hesitation, she stripped off the tape from her mouth and unsteadily got to her feet, pulling her nightdress down. Her voice was abnormally low at first.

"I want to know the meaning of this," she said slowly. "I want to know why I am being held and where I'm being held."

"As for us," said the man on the bed, "we only want to know what you look like under that nightie."

The back of Louise Templer's hand caught the man unawares and spun his head to the left. "Don't you dare talk to me that way, you pig!"

"Hold her!" shouted the man on the bed.

It was a little more difficult than they imagined. Louise Templer was a short woman, but her strength now came from an inner rage. The man who grabbed her left arm was punched straight on the nose so hard he let go. The other man put his arm around her from behind, and Louise quickly selected a place on his forearm and bit into it like a Sunday joint. The man yelped in pain and withdrew his arm. As he did so Louise made a quick dash for the door, which had remained ajar. She fell full length as someone grabbed her ankles in a rugby tackle and immediately tried to fight off the two men who were making an effort to trap her flailing arms. She felt her nails engage briefly with a face before her wrist was slammed brutally onto the floor. The other arm was trapped by the third man. That's when she first screamed, because one of the men commenced to slap her face back and forth, first one way, then the other. The man holding her feet reached up with a free hand and grasped the neck of her nightdress and, in one fierce movement, tore it open all the way to the bottom. Hands were on her breasts immediately, rubbing them, pulling at the nipples. Another hand was on her belly, then pushing between her legs.

As she gathered her breath, she thought she heard Stuart Easton's voice calling her name. "Stuart! Stuart!" she screamed. "They are trying to rape me, Stuart!" Though she had her eyes closed, she heard their voices.

"Who's going to be first?"

"Look what she did to my fucking arm."

"It's going to take two of us to hold her legs. Think you can manage both her arms?"

"I ought to break her fucking neck."

"Well, break it after we fucking fuck her, OK? That's all these women understand."

Suddenly there was another voice from the doorway. "What the fuck do you think you lot are doing?" the voice shouted. "Let her go! Let her go before I kick holes in your heads!"

The men let go, and Louise quickly turned over and, clutching the two sides of her nightdress, got to her feet. An older man in a suit stood in the doorway. His hair was grey and trimmed short, and he wore a pair of horn-rimmed glasses.

"Are you in charge here?" Templer screamed at him.

"Nevermind what I am or who I am, Mrs Templer. You are our prisoner. Temporarily, I hope. But meanwhile I'm responsible for your safety," he said, turning to the three men who stood a little sheepishly, looking down at their feet. "And I won't have her harmed, unless she tries to escape. Or raped. We are trying to clean up Direct Action, and look at you. Three of you holding down a woman half the size of one of you. Use your pay to buy a whore, if you have to put it in something. But you're not putting it into the prisoner. Understood?"

"Look what the slut did to my arm." One of them held out his arm which had two elliptical bite marks and was bleeding from six of the separate tooth holes.

"I worry more about her being poisoned than your bloody arm. Out. All three of you."

"Just a moment," said Louise Templer, walking over to the bed where the clothes had been laid out, holding her nightdress together with one hand. She picked them up, wadded them into a ball with her free hand and threw them at the man who had sat on the bed. "Now give me the rest of my clothes, you pig. *I'll* choose what I wear. Not you or any other bloody man!"

The older man snapped his fingers impatiently, and the plastic bag was thrown to Louise Templer. It landed at her feet. The three men left the room, single file.

"If you're waiting for gratitude," Templer said to the older man, "you may have to stand there until you rot."

"I'm not looking for thanks," he said without humour. "For what its worth, I apologise."

"I will accept your apology when I am assured those three have been disciplined to my satisfaction. Short of hanging them, which I don't approve of, I can't think of anything suitable. Perhaps the surgical removal of their testicles. Their frontal lobes have obviously been removed already."

He shrugged. "You can go fuck yourself, lady. I've done my bit." He started to back out the door.

"You could tell me how long you plan to keep us here."

"I could, but I won't."

"Who else are you holding? Besides Stuart Easton? Where is this place? Who are you?..."

He held up his hand. "You are a prisoner and are entitled to know nothing. All I will do is promise you won't be raped. Not while I'm in charge, anyway." He slammed the door.

Louise Templer turned away from the closed door sharply and picked up the plastic carrier bag, dumping it onto the bed. She wanted jeans, but of course they hadn't brought any of those. So she chose a cotton skirt with a floral pattern, Marks and Sparks cotton briefs and bra and a long-sleeved shirt. As she dressed she realised her whole body was trembling. So were her lips. But she was determined not to cry. No one was going to make her cry, not now, not ever. She felt like it, though, as she finally sat down on the edge of the bed and looked at the spare, unfriendly room. Barefoot, she got up and went to the window to look out through the bars. A large garden and a high wall. Beyond the wall she could see a few houses and a road with cars speeding along in both directions. The normal world. The world you don't appreciate until you are forced into something bizarre and obscene. She longed to be in one of those cars travelling back to London. To her home. To her constituency. To the Houses of Parliament. To the routine she knew before and didn't fully appreciate.

Her thoughts turned to Haug. Would he find them? Would he come? Would he burst through her door, a gun in each hand? The Princess rescued by the Prince? Would he take her from this tower down to those trees, and would he hold her in his arms and let her cry and not tell anyone?

With those thoughts she suddenly realised how much of the little girl had stayed within the woman. Emotionally anyway. She thought of Haug first, not Alan. She and Alan made love occasionally, but it was never explosive, like it was with Haug. Alan was very like her. Haug was not. Alan was really a social partner while Haug was the forbidden fruit. If she ever behaved with Alan like she behaved with the American, her husband would be shocked because he had never known that side of her. *She* had never known it, either, damn it! Making love in the ice cold water of a stream in the driving rain, feeling wanton, an exhibitionist, wishing for other eyes to see her shaking her breasts, out of her mind with the roaring storms in her belly, willing to do anything to make it continue forever.

Louise Templer finally relaxed the tense muscles in her neck and shoulders and smiled as she looked out the window.

What fun it had been. What fun...

CHAPTER TWENTY THREE

If it had been that kind of neighbourhood net curtains would have been in motion all day as eyes peered at a certain address in Eaton Square. Vans appeared and men carried in large parcels, sometimes accompanied by other men dressed in suits. The names on the vans were either famous - Harrods, Liberty's, Fortnum & Mason - or a little sinister, like Zeitgeist, Fetters and House of Rubber. The door to the flat seemed to open and close with the regularity of a cuckoo clock as some arrived and others left. One Time, watching from the old yellow van, found it as interesting as a street scene in Barbados - always something new to watch. Though he managed to get a few hours' sleep, the noise and excitement kept his eye at the spyhole most of the time. That woman must be spending more money than he had ever seen in the course of his life. And she was spending it with speed. One Time knew his affair with Corky DeLoop was a rollercoaster ride, and he hoped he had the good sense to know when to get off the rollercoaster. Before it stopped suddenly leaving him doing cartwheels across the landscape with his dick in his hands. Never in his life had he met such a woman. And he had met a lot of women. It wasn't so much that she loved sex. Lots of women love sex. But this one wasn't *afraid* of sex, man. And it radiated from her like plutonium. You always felt the danger, just like the danger of an explosion a split second before it happened. When you touched her, she always reacted *totally*, with heart and soul and humour and confidence. Christ, One Time thought, as he felt his loins come to life once more, it is going to be hard as hell stepping off this rollercoaster. One Time decided to roll himself a small joint and try to relax.

Corky DeLoop stood in front of the bedroom mirror, finally pleased with herself. She had changed her makeup a number of times, darkening her eyes and eyebrows, matching the red of the lipstick to the red of her dress.

It was not the red dress Gillmore had bought for her. This one was an inspiration. While she had gone through hundreds of clothes from Harrods and Liberty's, looking for something just right, one of the salesmen helpfully gave her the names of specialist firms who might have something more to her taste. And he was right. This red dress was made of rubber and was bright and shiny and caught the light. It molded her body like a second skin. The top was cut very, very low and square in the middle, just barely covering her nipples and giving her a long and deep cleavage. A lace-up matching red mini corset underneath pushed them up and very nearly out. But the rubber clung and moved with her body. Wide straps at the sides went over her shoulders and crossed in the back. The dress came to mid-thigh, just covering the tops of very sheer black stockings with seams at the back. Although she had bought fourteen pairs of shoes and boots, she decided to stick with Gillmore's choice for high heels.

Just after her long bath that morning, the hairdressers arrived, touching up the platinum at the roots, combing and cutting and shaping so her hair now hung down to her shoulders, curling in at the bottom. It was soft and nice to touch for a change, and she swung it from side to side in front of the mirror, looking at herself in profile, leaning over to see if there was a danger of her tits falling out.

"Well," she said to herself out loud, "If I was a man, I'd go stark ravin' mad. You are one sexy motherfucker." She ran her hands down the dress. It was an new experience wearing a rubber dress. She had heard of them, of course, and had been curious. It felt luscious. Tight and supple and warm and naughty. If Gillmore hadn't been due soon, she would have called One Time in for a little fun. To break in the dress, so to speak. Instead, she kicked off the shoes and turned around to look at the heaps of boxes and stacks of clothes and shoes and boots and underwear. A beautiful mahogany chest now stood in the corner with a padlock on it. That was her toy chest. She picked up the parcel Haug had brought her earlier on from the top of the dressing table and thought for a moment before putting it in the bottom drawer at the back. Then she began moving all the empty boxes and packaging and great wads of tissue paper to the spare bedroom. An observer would certainly have noticed the spring in her step as she moved from one room to the other with armfuls of rubbish.

When Gillmore let himself in, it was almost half past five. Normally he stopped work only at seven or eight at night. Sometimes he even worked longer. Because he liked work. If more people worked like he did, it would be the richest country in the world. Richer than Japan. Today, however, his mind was never really on his work. It had been here, in this flat, looking desperately for Corky DeLoop, and, when it found her, desperately dressing and undressing her. Fuck it, he thought. Let his employees earn their money for a few days. He had a fax at this address and a telephone. He could be reached here by one or two who had the numbers. No one else really knew about the place. Gillmore was a secretive man and believed in not letting one hand know what the other was doing - unless it needed to know.

The moment he opened the door he could smell her presence. Not her perfume, her *presence*. He had been a little uneasy, a little worried that maybe she would not be here when he returned. It was unlike him not at least to hire a watcher, someone to keep an eye on his prey. He smelled her, and it was as sweet as anything he could imagine. But it was a few seconds before he actually saw her. She was standing at the far end of the room in the shadows, her head slightly lowered, her lips slightly open, her legs apart, her hands on her hips. Absent mindedly he closed the door and dropped his briefcase on his foot. His knees were trembling. What in God's name was she *wearing*?

With one hand Corky reached out and turned on the spotlight which flooded the corner and reflected on the shiny rubber dress. "Surprise, loverboy," she said in a husky voice. "Welcome home."

Gillmore's knees were shaking so badly he dropped to the floor. He was aware his mouth was open and moving, but no sound came from it. Slowly, more like a dream than anything else, Corky DeLoop moved toward him until she stood right in front of him, and again she moved her legs apart so the rubber dressed stretched, sharply outlining her thighs and buttocks.

427

Gillmore's eyes were on the same level as the hem of the dress, and he was very aware of the dark shadows underneath the shiny red rubber, secret shadows leading upward to mystery.

Gillmore's trembling hands touched her legs. The smooth nylon was electric and tingled through the tips of his fingers. One of his hands drifted to the inside of her thigh, seeking the warmth further up, a warmth he could already feel on his face.

Corky gently took that hand by the wrist and moved it to her hip. "Later," she whispered. "Let's wait til later. Feel the dress."

It startled him. What was it? It was slippery, like flesh, and warm. He reached further, touching the rubbery laces of the little corset, then further still toward those incredible mounds above the corset.

Again Corky clasped his wrist, moving his hand to her waist. "Later. Let's make it slow. Let's make it last. I want this one to last forever."

A low moan emerged from the Australian's throat. "I can't wait, Corky. I've been dreaming of you all day," he stuttered. "I...I...what is this dress? Where did you get it?"

"You left your credit card, silly," she murmured. "You said I could use it."

"But...but. It's beautiful. You're beautiful. Why can't we do it now? I've got to do it now," he choked. "Or I'll die." His hands were desperately feeling her buttocks through the thin rubber material. "It's mine. If I want it, I can have it."

"Of course you can," she agreed in her low husky voice. "But I've been dreamin', too. Of you. All day long. I want you in me. Now. But it's best to wait. To play a little while." Her sentences were short, like panting breaths. "I've bought lots of toys. To play with. To make it last. I want it to last. Between us."

It never entered Gillmore's head that he was on his knees in front of a woman. It just seemed natural to be so close to what he wanted most. She wanted to wait, to play. He wanted it now, here, in the front room, on the carpet. Anywhere. His whole body was trembling with desire.

428

"Listen, Corky..." It didn't come out right and was more like a squeak. He cleared his throat, gripping the back of her buttocks firmly, looking up at her with as much malevolence as he could manage. "Listen, Corky. I'm not in the mood to fuck around. I want you to get your big arse down on the floor right now. I'm telling you, I've *got* to have you..."

She took his hands away from her bottom and moved away toward the door swaying her hips. "Come on. Come with me. I've got something to show you."

"Damn it, woman!" His eyes widened with anger.

She turned languidly and slowly slid the rubber dress up her legs, exposing her thighs above the stockings and then her pubis which she touched softly with her fingers. "Aw, come on. Don't spoil it for us, now. Don't you want some of this?"

Gillmore's eyes immediately changed from anger to demented desire. He scrambled to his feet to follow her. She didn't bother to pull her dress back down as she walked in front of him like some carnal goddess, her buttocks smooth and round and trembling as she walked.

The curtains were drawn in the bedroom, and he could hardly see. She was sitting on the edge of the bed, but when he leapt beside her, she was gone. Looking up, he saw her leaning over the bed, her cleavage expanding and contracting like bellows. He reached for her, and as he reached, he felt something cold and hard on his wrists. There were clicking noises. What the hell was this? Handcuffs? Corky quickly ran to the other end of the bed, drawing a chain from underneath which held a pair of leg irons. Grabbing first one foot and then struggling with the other as the man resisted, she snapped them closed around his ankles. He was stretched sideways across the big bed. The chain ran underneath the bed from his handcuffs to his leg shackles. Harvey Gillmore found himself face down on his belly hardly able to move his body.

"What the fuck do you think you're doing?" he shouted as she turned up the lights.

Her voice remained low and sexy. "I *know* what I'm doin' Harv..."

429

"Don't call me that! Don't call me Harv! It's Mr Gillmore, you hear?"

She pulled the brocade armchair from in front of the dressing table to the end of the bed facing Gillmore's head. Then she crossed her legs and leaned toward him. "Now, I may be wrong, short stuff, but it's my opinion that the power situation has changed around here. I have been assured by an expert that that is a very strong chain, and weightlifters have been unable to break those shackles. Do you get my drift?"

He changed his tone hopefully. "Is this the game? Is it a game?"

"Sure it's a game, Harv."

"Don't fucking call me Harv! I *told* you!"

She leaned over and picked up something from just under the bed. "Do you know what this is, Harv?" She waved the balloon gag harness in front of his face. "Now I want you to put it on, like a good boy."

Gillmore started to struggle desperately with his bonds. "Fuck you. Fuck you, you fucking whore. You fucking slut. You wait. You wait til I get out of this, and I'll wreck your life. Remember that! Remember it!"

"Oh, I remember everything, Harvey boy. *Everything.*" She got up and kneeled on the bed beside his body, then straddled him and sat on his back. "Now open up your big mouth so I can push the little toy inside, OK?"

He was spluttering and swearing, hiding his face and clenching his teeth so she could not get the gag on. Putting it to one side, she reached underneath him and unbuckled his belt.

"What are you doing?" he shouted. "What the fuck do you think you're doing?"

After unzipping his trousers, she got to her feet and yanked them down to his ankles. Then she went to the new toy chest and unlocked it. Looking inside, she selected a nice whippy cane. She stood up and turned to the man on the bed.

"Words just fail me now, Harv," she said, tapping the cane on the palm of her hand. "I've been lookin' forward to this for so long, I'd need a famous poet to reel off the words describing the emotions that I'm feelin' right now." He was beginning to shout and protest, and she raised her voice. "First of all, I want you to tell me when you'll open your mouth like a nice boy and let me stick that gag inside. OK?"

She brought the cane down hard on his bottom, and he roared with pain. Again she hit him and again and again.

"Stop! Stop!" he said before she struck him the fifth time. "For God's sake, stop!"

She brought the cane down again, harder this time. "Stop, *what?*" she shouted over his scream.

"*Please!* Please, please, stop! OK, I'll do it. OK..."

Again the cane came down. Harder. "Please *what?* Please, Mrs DeLoop!"

"OK, OK, OK. Please, please, Mrs DeLoop, please stop."

It sounded as if he was sobbing. His bottom had angry red stripes across it, and the last stoke seemed to have drawn a little blood. Corky DeLoop didn't care because she was angry. She put the cane on the dressing table and picked up the gag. Well, well, he had been crying, she thought, as she pushed the deflated gag into his open mouth. She pulled the harness over his head, buckled it and snapped the small lock closed. It was now impossible to pull off. Slowly she pumped the attached bulb, watching his tear stained face as she did it. His jaw was forced open as the air entered, and his cheeks bulged slightly. Then she disconnected the bulb and hose, threw them on the dresser and picked up the cane again.

"Now I want you to do some heavy thinkin', Harvey," she said slowly. "Some real heavy thinkin'. You are now in deep shit, and you got nothin' to blame but your own black heart. Have you noticed what that felt like, Harv? One of these nasty canes across your ass? Well, Harv, that's what I felt, too. I felt just like you. It hurt like hell. Now, I don't know how many women you've done this to, but I'm gonna pay you back for me and at least for some of them. Do you understand, you stupid little shit?"

Slowly and deliberately she beat him on the bottom and the tops of his legs. Watching him tremble and writhe and hearing him whine through his nose, she felt no sympathy at all.

Harvey Gillmore was viewing the landscape of an unknown world. When he realised what she had done, the overwhelming feeling was one of betrayal. She had trapped him. Lured him like a sucker and trapped him. Then anger rolled out of his consciousness like black storm clouds. He would pay her back, the bitch. At some point she would have to let him go, and he would flay the skin off her bones.

That was before the first blow landed on his bare bottom. The anger rolled back, and terror rolled in, along with yelping devils of fear and pain. Not since his father had beaten him when he was a boy had he felt pain like that. His father insisted he take down his trousers and bend over his desk, taking the strokes without a sound. This pain brought the memories flooding back in little pieces carried overhead by the mad devils dancing through the red haemorrhage of pain.

The gag was nearly as bad as the pain. He couldn't answer back. He couldn't threaten any longer. He could say nothing. And it was uncomfortable with his tongue pressed onto the floor of his mouth, but there was nothing he could do. When she started hitting him again, again he felt betrayed. Hadn't she promised to stop? He couldn't take it. Even his father hadn't gone on this long. It was too much. He was collapsing inside, everything was giving way, the whole structure of his world was shattering. His head was bowed back, and he was maniacally trying to spit out the gag, to scream, to make noise. He couldn't beat it. It was too much. Too much.

And then she stopped.

"Had enough, Harv?" she asked mildly as she tossed the cane back on the dressing table. "I want to remind you that is what you're gonna get ever time you even look cross-eyed at me." Corky fetched a pair of scissors from the dresser and cut his trousers off, then pulled off his shoes and socks. She went to the bottom of the bed and hooked another chain through a shackle on one leg. She threw the end of the chain to the top and brought it underneath the bed to the end. Then she unlocked the shackle, immediately stretching his leg out. He didn't even resist. The fight had gone out of him. Using the other end of the chain, she pulled his other leg apart and attached it so that his legs now formed a V. She went to the toy box and returned with a smaller insulated cable connected to a tiny collar around a flexible metal mesh cage. Reaching between his legs, she grabbed his balls. Gillmore immediately started panicking, trying to roll from side to side. Though she had some difficulty at first, she finally managed to snap the ring closed around the top of his scrotum with his testicles enclosed in the mesh. She had been assured by the salesman that the only way of removing it was with a hacksaw or boltcutters.

The cable was quite long, over 60 feet, and the other end was connected to a battery box with a lever. Pushing the lever, she was told, would gradually release a flow of electrical current to the testicles. She was cautioned that pushing the lever all the way would cause total agony.

She sat down in the chair next to his head and showed him the box. "Know what this is, Harv? It's your new leash. I can use it like this..." She pulled it sharply and watched him arch up on the bed. "...or like this." Slowly she pushed the lever to halfway, watching him struggle and writhe. "And that's only half strength."

Corky snapped off the battery cassette, went to the dressing table and opened the bottom drawer. She pulled out the parcel Haug had delivered. "So now we're about ready for our injection, aren't we? You remember the injections, Harv?"

His eyes were huge as he watched her measure the drug as she filled the hypodermic.

"Don't worry, Harv," she said as she leaned over him. "I'll stick it *between* the red stripes so it won't hurt so much, OK?" She forced the needle into his left buttock and pressed down the plunger. "You're just gonna *love* this, honey, I can promise you that."

She knew from her own experience he would be weak as water, so she unlocked his wrists and ankles, and then took off the gag, before sitting back down in her chair. Gillmore remained in the same position on the bed and did not try to move. Keeping the battery box in one hand, she pulled a plastic carrier bag from underneath the dresser. Turning it upside down, she emptied the contents on the bed.

"Looky here, Harv. Look what I bought for you. A nice pair of high heeled shoes and some stockin's. You like 'em so much, I just couldn't resist." She put the shoes next to his nose. "See 'em, Harv. Red. Your favourite colour. In your size, too."

"Go fuck yourself, you bitch," he muttered.

She pushed the lever to halfway, and suddenly the bed became alive. Gillmore made horrible guttural noises as he juddered and flopped around, tearing at the bedclothes feebly. The guttural noises slowly became a howl, and she saw his eyes rolling up into his head. She pushed the lever off and turned her head away. It was too close. It reminded her so immediately of what she had felt, how horrible the pain was. She just couldn't do it. The poor bastard looked like he was dying.

She smacked her fist on the arm of the chair. Goddamn it, she just wasn't hard enough, and it wasn't quite as much fun as she thought. Except for the beating. By god, that felt good. That got a lot out of her system. She heard him trying to speak.

"I'm sorry," he simpered. "I'm sorry. Please don't do that any more."

Corky took a deep breath. "I'm tryin' to teach you somethin', Harvey Gillmore, somethin' you oughta learned a long time ago. Now, I don't wanna do that again to you. You just do what you're told, and I won't. You understand?"

There was a long silence. "I understand," he said softly. He had curled his body into a ball, and his head was nodding like a baby's.

"Now sit yourself up and put on your stuff. Take off your shirt and tie first."

She watched him as he tried to sit up, groaning with pain as his bottom touched the bed. But he managed to get his shirt off and threw it on the floor. He fumbled around with the stockings, not knowing what to do, but finally managed to pull them on before he realised he hadn't put on the suspender belt. Watching him struggle with the belt, Corky finally got up and hooked it for him. Then she snapped the suspenders to the stockings. As she was doing this, she felt his hand on her back. His other hand was trying to get underneath her dress. Corky straightened up and slapped him across the face.

434

"That is what happens when you touch a woman who doesn't want to be touched, Harv. You get smacked. You don't just grab at women, Harv. Now put your new shoes on, and let's see how you walk."

It made her laugh and improved her mood watching Harvey Gillmore stagger around in high heels. They were about three and a half inch ones, as she didn't think he could handle the really high jobs he made her wear. The drug made him appear slightly drunk, and several times he nearly tripped over the thin cable attached to his testicles. His head was low, and he only caught her eyes once or twice. She noticed with interest that his penis had grown and was half erect.

She pulled the chair back to the dressing table and got out the documents brought to her by One Time and Haug. "You just keep walkin' back and forth, there, Harv, up and down, while I get some stuff ready for you to sign here."

Harvey Gillmore was seriously confused. He never had women's clothes on in his life, but it wasn't an unpleasant feeling. Except for the shoes. The shoes fucking hurt. However, it wasn't the erotic nature of the underwear that was confusing Gillmore. There were two walls of emotion which seemed to tower over him, threatening to collapse any moment. On the one hand there was visceral outrage at being trapped and betrayed. This anger was alternately mixed with fear, a fear so deep and profound it reminded him of the night of his heart attack the previous year. He looked down at his genitals and felt round the restraint. She literally had him by the bollocks. The pain from the electrical voltage had been sickening. Awful. Nauseous. The trembling waves of electricity had gripped his testicles and travelled to his belly like punches from a boxer.

The opposing wall of emotion was his refracting desire for her. Like anger and fear in the other wall, this was composed of lust and hatred. He wanted her. He wanted to touch her. Yet he couldn't. She slapped him. Why couldn't he have what he wanted? He hated her for slapping him, almost as much as he feared her for the pain she caused him.

The drug was slowing him down. He couldn't think. He was confused. Thoughts would evaporate quicker than he could

435

record them. He felt a tug on his balls and looked up. The beautiful, gorgeous woman was sitting at the dressing table. Her tits were pushed up like perfect melons, and the dress rode up to reveal the flesh of her thigh. And she was reeling him in now, like a marlin.

"Got somethin' for you to sign, Harv," she said, handing him a pen. "You are givin' me a nice present for all the shit you've dished out. Just sign right here. It's called a transfer, and all it needs is your signature. I already have the land certificate and lease. Sign the transfer, Harvey."

The transfer swam into focus, and he took the pen, signing between the two little crosses. But something was wrong. Bad wrong. The pen fell from his hand and he looked at the two legal documents. They were his. From his safe. They were the title documents for this flat. *His* flat. She was stealing from him.

Between the two walls of emotion something erupted, something dark and black and powerful, spewing from the murky depths of his soul like hot acid lava. The lava swilled around inside his brain dissolving emotion and reason alike. It squeezed out behind his eyeballs, and the whole room seemed to darken. There was only one devil now, and that devil spotted something from the peripheral rim of vision. A pair of scissors.

The devil looked round to the other peripheral side like a primaeval carnivore. Her platinum hair was falling forward as she examined the paper he just signed. She collected the land certificate and lease to slip them into a manila envelope. The red straps of her rubber dress formed an X in the middle of her back. It was a Sign. The target was there. The means were there. The devil inside grinned, showing sharp ivory teeth and malignant, vengeful slits for eyes. Harvey Gillmore himself began to grin. This was why he *was* Harvey Gillmore. He could see things others could not see and strike where others had faint hearts. His left hand moved slowly toward the scissors. She was so pleased with herself she didn't even see him as he grasped them in his hand.

She would have seen nothing at all, if she had not accidentally glanced into the mirror as she licked the manila

436

envelope. There was Gillmore, stretched with his arm high in the air. And in his hand...

She lunged sideways, rolling with the armchair, the same moment the scissors plunged downwards. Everything seemed to slow down, and she was aware of tiny little details she would never have noticed in other circumstances. The look on Gillmore's face was as dark and twisted and frightening as anything she could recall seeing, and the face was illuminated and shadowed by the chandelier hanging over the large bed. She also noticed one of his suspenders came away from a stocking, snapping up in a slow arc as the scissors descended.

At the last moment Corky was certain the scissors were going into her side or hip, and she prepared herself for the pain at the same time she reached for the battery cassette at the end of the cable.

The scissors stuck like a spear in the side of the armchair as Corky DeLoop hit the floor and pushed the lever all the way over to maximum.

Harvey Gillmore seemed to explode backward and upward, hitting the side of the bed and bouncing onto the floor. The scream was that of an animal, and he began pinwheeling around the axis of his abdomen propelled by his legs as he pounded himself with his fists.

Corky was trembling as she reduced the power to half, but Gillmore did not seem to notice. Round and round he went in a circle on the carpet, pounding his guts with his fists, alternately growling and screeching with occasional babbled words like "please", "oh, please". She snapped off the power, and slowly his cries dropped to mumblings, and his body stopped pinwheeling on the floor. Instead he held his testicles and rocked back and forth, shaking his head from side to side. His eyes showed only the white sclera, as the irises had disappeared behind the lids.

She walked over and grabbed a handful of his thinning hair, pinning his head back on the carpet. Then she sat down firmly on his chest, trapping his arms with her thighs. Corky DeLoop was shaking with anger and relief at the narrow escape. She banged his head on the floor and slapped his face two or three times.

"You little son of a bitch," she spat at him. "As soon as I start feelin' sorry for you, you jump on me with a pair of scissors. "Look at me! I'm talkin' to you!"

His eyelids snapped open revealing eyes which appeared absolutely crazed. She held up the battery cassette. "You want more of this? Huh?" He shook his head insanely. "Then lissen to what I got to say to you. If you had played your cards right, you little prick, you probably coulda sneaked outta here by tomorrow or the next day. I'm so softhearted, I might even have given you a good screwin'. But now you have shown me exactly what you are. A murderous, scumsuckin' pig fucker..."

Corky stopped speaking because she felt his hands stroking her bottom. "I don't believe this. Get your hands off my ass! You just tried to kill me, you motherfucker, and two minutes later you're feelin' me up!"

"I'm sorry," he muttered. "Didn't mean to kill you. Just want you. Want you to marry me..."

She exploded into a huge laugh. "You're already married, you stupid fool. And anyway I'd rather marry a five and a half foot rattlesnake with a snappin' head at each end. The only thing worth a shit about you is your dick. Maybe I'll cut that off and stuff it for the mantelpiece."

Suddenly Gillmore went berserk, trying to buck her off. But Corky DeLoop was not a weak woman. She held him easily. The look in his eyes was even more demented. "Hit a sore spot, have I?" she asked. "Afraid of losin' that ole prick of yours?" Again he panicked, trying desperately to get out from under her. "Well, I tell you one thing, hot shot. You try somethin' like attackin' me with scissors again, and I promise I'll cut it off with a hacksaw, real slow."

She reached around behind her and grabbed his penis, which was now flaccid. "This what you so worried about? I mean it, Harv. I'll hack the son of a bitch off at the root."

Corky could see the abject terror in his face. He was trying to speak but couldn't. His mouth was moving, and she thought he looked like a demented goldfish. The blood seemed to have

438

drained out of his head. Certainly it had drained from his penis. She let go of it and got up, standing over him. He backed up, still white as a sheet, until he hit the wall with his head. Then he pushed himself up the wall until he was seated. His flesh was white and mottled and hung in folds at his waist. One of his high heels had come off.

"Please, please, Corky. Please don't even mention that again. I apologise to you. For the scissors. For everything. Keep the flat. OK, it's yours. OK, OK. It just made me mad. I can't explain. I'll...try and do what you want. I know...what you want to do to me. OK, do it. Fine. But just let me tell you this. I'm going crazy. Don't know what's inside me or why. But I want you so powerfully, I can't help myself. That's why I pushed myself over here to the wall. So I wouldn't try to touch you anymore. OK? OK?"

His words began to spill out faster and faster, and Corky listened in amazement. "I know you gotta have revenge," he said. "You're doing what I'd do. Maybe that's what I like about you. You're like me. But you've already had your revenge. You get it? Huh? Because you've made me crazy about you. I can't think of anything but you, your body, your tits, your cunt. Look at me. Look at my hand. Shaking like a leaf. OK, I'll ask you, Corky, I'll ask you, even beg you. Please let me touch you." He got on his knees and folded his hands together. "Please. Look. Harvey Gillmore on his knees, and you didn't even ask me to. I'm here. Please..."

"Harvey!" she stopped the torrent of words. "Harvey, you just tried to *kill* me!"

He bent forward and banged his fists on the floor. "Don't you bloody understand? That was because you were stealing from me! You betrayed me! You tricked me! So I tried to kill you! But that doesn't mean I don't still love you! Love you! Love you!"

Corky DeLoop sighed, wondering just what kind of dark crypt she had opened here. "You're crazy, and you're an evil man, Gillmore. To be absolutely honest, I don't want your slimy hands anywhere near me. But I *am* gonna show you what the flip side of power is like. What it feels like to be on the receivin'

439

end. I'm also gonna get Sarah Courtney over here so you can apologise to her. Meanwhile you can learn to be a houseboy. Cookin', cleanin', sweepin', servin'. Now, get up off that floor! Stand up!"

Gillmore slowly got to his feet and noticed one shoe was off. Clumsily he put it back on. Then, while Corky glared at him, he re-attached the loose suspender after several tries.

She went back to the dressing table and set the chair on its feet. She was not confident enough yet to completely turn her back on him. With a big effort, she pulled out the scissors, staring at Gillmore as she held them in her hand. Then she threw them into the toy chest and picked up the cane.

"Put your feet together, Harv," she said as she walked over and stood directly in front of him. "That's how we ladies are told we should stand. Feet together. And keep those rovin' hands at your side. Now look at me, Harv. Look at my tits. Here, smell them," she said as she thrust them toward his face. "Nice, isn't it? Well, if you were a normal man and approached me in the normal way, we could maybe have ourselves a hell of a time. But no, you gotta *force* me, right? You gotta beat me, right?"

His eyes were wide. "I've got to have you, Corky. I'm sorry about forcing you. I didn't know..."

"You're *not* sorry, Harv. You're just sayin' that to get around me. You'd say anything to touch my tits, wouldn't you?"

His face was only a few inches away from her chest, and he surprised her with his speed. Suddenly he was licking her, slobbering like a dog, and his hand grabbed her bottom again, rubbing, trying to get underneath her dress. She whacked him with the cane on the legs once, twice, three times, until finally he broke away yelping and dancing, trying to fend off the blows with his hands.

"Stand still, Harv. Now. We try it again. Until you learn: not to touch." She moved close again and could see his mouth trembling. "Go on. Try it, Harv. Try it again."

"I can't bear it," he squeaked as a couple of tears rolled down his cheeks. "I can't bear it..."

"Yes, you can," she said. "It's called self-control. You don't go through life grabbin' everthing you want. At least, not now you don't. 'Cause I got this cane in one hand and this battery box in the other. That's somethin' you understand, isn't it? Pain?"

After standing in front of Gillmore for a full minute, she walked over and sat on the edge of the bed. "Now come over here, kneel down and take off my shoes. They're the ones you gave me, and I kinda like 'em, but they hurt my feet after a while."

She crossed her legs and watched as he knelt down with trembling hands to take off her shoe. He pulled at the back of it, slipped it forward then slid it off, putting it carefully under the bed. She re-crossed her legs so he could remove her other shoe. And he almost finished before being overcome with his internal urges. Suddenly he grasped her foot, rubbing it, rubbing her leg. She brought the cane sharply down on his back twice before he stopped, and he fought with himself before clenching his fists and holding them down beside him. Then he took that shoe and put it alongside the other one.

Corky uncrossed her legs and put both feet side by side. "Now get down and kiss my feet, Harv. One kiss each. Just like I kissed yours."

He was hanging his head when he sat back on his ankles, and she noticed his erection had grown.

She touched his stiff penis with the end of the cane. "Well, well, Harv. Looks like you might just like this kinda thing. Is that right?"

"I don't know," he croaked miserably, shaking his head. "I don't know, Corky."

"Mrs DeLoop."

"Mrs DeLoop."

"It's Mrs DeLoop and ma'am from now on, you understand? And you know why?"

"Yes, Mrs DeLoop. I don't care. I just want to be close to you, even if I can't touch you." He started to move toward her, but she raised the cane, and he retreated, sitting on his ankles.

441

"And listen...Mrs DeLoop. If...if I try to do these things you want, will you maybe let me touch you again sometimes?"

Corky snorted, then laughed. "Boy, you keep tryin', don't you?" She thought for a moment. "I *might*. Then again, I might not. You will have to impress me with your behaviour, Harv. At nights or when I go out, I'm gonna chain you up like a dog because I don't trust you *at all*. Now you might feel a little different when you come off that drug, but things are not gonna change. You're still gonna be the houseboy, and you're gonna learn some manners if I have to beat the hide off you. Now tomorrow I want you to clean this fuckin' flat from top to bottom. Dust it, vacuum the rug, scrub the toilets, everthing. You are gonna work your ass off for me, you hear?"

Gillmore nodded. "I hear, Mrs DeLoop."

"And I tell you what you're also gonna do, Harv. And you better learn this real quick. You're gonna dress me and undress me, comb my hair, and I may even teach you how to put my makeup on for me if you can stop your hands from shakin' long enough." She threw her head back and laughed. "It might be real nice havin' a little dwarf servant in stockin's and high heels walkin' around me with a great big hard-on all the time."

Gillmore suddenly looked up at her with an inspiration. "Look, Cor...Mrs DeLoop. What do you think of this? Look, it's...this...I don't want to...what would you say to a deal? Huh? Alright, listen to this..."

"Ma'am."

"Yes, listen to this, ma'am. You've got the flat. I don't mind. OK. On top of the flat I'll pay you...fifteen hundred pounds a week...that's over seventy-five thousand pounds a year. Pay you, guaranteed. OK, I know you want your revenge. Today...tonight...do whatever you want. Get your own back. And tomorrow...we go back...no, to another stage, Cor...Mrs DeLoop. I can touch you. I can sleep with you. We can go out. Be together. I'll change. I promise. So you'll like me. But...it's...you see, I have a business I got to run. I'll pay you the money. We'll make it legal, put it in writing, anything you say...."

She was shaking her head as she interrupted him. "Harv. *I* make the terms now. Do you understand that? I make 'em because I got the power now. Like you used to. *Used to.* You don't have it any more. *I'll* tell you what deal we're gonna cut and when and how. You got that?"

"But.."

Corky whacked him hard with the cane. "All I want to hear is 'yes, Mrs DeLoop.'"

"Yes...Mrs DeLoop."

"Now get up, Harvey, and remember to stand with your feet together," she said as she rose from the bed and returned to the dressing table. Opening a drawer, she picked up a Bible. "Remember what this is, Harv? Remember? Now I'm gonna teach you how to walk."

She handed him the book and reclined on the bed with a mound of pillows. "Put it on your head, start at one wall and walk to the other one. Every time you drop it, I'll give you a little jolt in your balls. That's it, Harv, book on your head, arms out to the side, wrists bent, very feminine. Oh, you do look sweet! Walk by puttin' one leg in front of the other. Harv! You already know how to do this, don't you?"

She shook her head and laughed. "I gotta say you look awful peculiar with that hard-on bouncin' up and down in front of you....oh, Harv, you dropped the book. Now bend at the knees to pick it up. Next time you get a little tickle of electricity."

CHAPTER TWENTY FOUR

It was after midnight when Haug returned home, and he was tired. He pulled the pickup around the corner into Pemberton Gardens and switched off the ignition. Professor Ewan Thomas had loved his truck and confessed he'd never ridden in an American pickup before. After dropping off the gear to Corky DeLoop, Haug took Thomas to General Portland's house, which was about forty miles off the M25, and demonstrated the power of the beast. Some dingbat in a hot hatchback cut them up on the sliproad into the M25, and Haug blew his horn angrily as he swerved to avoid hitting the zippy little car. He was answered by two fingers pumping from the driver's window, so he grinned and told Professor Thomas to hold on. The Chevvy had a 454 cubic inch V-8 which had been heavily breathed on by an American firm which tuned engines for stock car racing, and it developed just over 700 horsepower. Haug had once induced wheelspin at 140 mph before backing off because of the instability of pickup trucks at those speeds.

As they joined the motorway, Haug glanced in the rearview and saw the two inner lanes were fairly clear of traffic, so he dropped the gearbox into second and floored the throttle. At first Thomas was panic stricken when the rear of the truck slewed from side to side as the rear wheels spun and screamed on the tarmac. The fellow in the hatchback had overtaken a car on the inside and was cutting across all the lanes to get into the outside fast one. Haug stuck to the centre lane and overtook the hatchback at 100 mph and shifted into third gear. The wheels squealed again as he accelerated away from the hatchback like a rocket. Then he slowed down and let the hatchback pass him. When he did, Haug shot him a finger. Professor Thomas was bracing himself against the door and was laughing uncontrollably, shaking his head from side to side. Through his laughter he told Haug he was nothing but an overgrown adolescent and ought to be ashamed of himself.

The four bodies had been removed by the time Haug arrived at Portland's house, and the pickup was stopped by a soldier in beret and battledress cradling a Koch and Heckler. They were ordered out of the truck while it was checked by another soldier, and by that time Portland was waving from the doorstep.

It had been late afternoon when they arrived, and the General prepared dinner himself, served with a really nice wine. He did not hide his admiration of Portland for his exploits. It had been decisive and final. Haug joked that he would have to revise his opinion of officers as men who direct the traffic but have no stomach for the driving. During his time in the army, Haug never met any officer he respected. They could talk tough, but when hell broke loose, they invariably turned to the NCO's for leadership. The only time officers rushed to the front was when the medals were being handed out. Portland agreed with him completely, to his surprise. The backbone of any unit was determined by the quality of its NCO's, he said.

Portland reported the conversation with General Sessions. Professor Thomas was very interested, pointing out the crisis was creating some interesting fissures in the surface of the power structure. He agreed it was vital now to approach the Defence Minister. That was obviously the next step, though it was clearly a dangerous one. The Minister, Norman Stone, had a reputation for being the ultimate political manoeuvrer in the Tory Party. He had no friends whose backs couldn't be used to stand upon if it meant reaching a higher rung of the ladder. Enemies were defined simply. Enemies were those who stood between him and the office of prime minister. With any luck at all, Norman Stone could have been prime minister, but the Defence Secretary had a well earned reputation for shooting himself in the foot - or kicking himself in the mouth - at the wrong time or the wrong place. Norman Stone would be a tricky man to approach, but he stood in a vital position. Certainly a job for Sir Jonathan Mainwaring.

The late edition of the morning papers and the evening news had led with the Metropolitan Commissioner's apparent suicide, but speculation was beginning to trickle out about some nefarious organisations. It was in everyone's interest, they all agreed, that the crisis should be contained. If the knowledge became public the whole situation could become quickly

446

unstable. If that happened, the weight of the media became vitally important. What information was the public to receive? It was unlikely to be the truth in any case. The truth would be a very difficult thing for the government to admit, and the Conservative government now controlled the bulk of the media. The few small independent organs would be swept away. It was quite possible the whole of the United Opposition could be rounded up and charged with treason. Or sedition. Or murder. At the moment everything was finely balanced on the razor's edge.

Portland felt the meeting with the Community of Association would be critical to their chances. Professor Thomas disagreed. They were holding hostages and wanted to dismantle the United Opposition by threats.

It was at this point Haug intervened, differing with both men. He was worried about the meeting for different reasons. They wanted Mainwaring. They wanted him out, and it could be a trap. Though not entirely true, they considered Mainwaring the head. Cut off the head and the body will die. That's the way those people thought.

They argued until late. Thomas was staying with the General for safety until the meeting, and Haug finally left after the Professor insisted on telling Portland all about his pickup truck, how it represented the best and worst of American culture.

Haug walked around the corner and found the key in his pocket as he approached his front door. He put the key into the lock and, for one split second, he was puzzled why it wouldn't go in - but only for a split second. Throwing his keys on the pavement, he dropped into a linebacker crouch and ran. Two bullets hit the door as he ducked, and he felt the wind of another at the back of his head as he charged toward the hoardings of the building site at the corner.

He hit the hoarding with his shoulder and every ounce of power in his body. The three-quarter inch plywood split, but held. However it moved back just enough to create a gap with the next piece, and he felt a sting across his back when he plunged through the gap into darkness. As he threw his body to the ground, he heard several more bullets ripping through the plywood. They were using silencers, and he could hear the thuks, so they must be close.

It was too dark to see much of the site, so he rolled his body downward into the basement which was being excavated. Feeling around with his hands, he found a lump of wood, a two-by-four. Then he remained absolutely still, thinking quickly. He would have to assume they had night vision, so he tried to plaster himself against the small rampart. Not much of a chance, he thought, but a better one than he had outside. He was sure there was more than one, and if they were pros, they would separate when they came through the gap.

And they did. He could hear them above his head but didn't want to risk an attack, fighting uphill against two guns. No, he thought. Stay quiet, and let them come to you. That was the only chance. Get one, get his gun, and then it was a different ballgame.

"Well, Haug, we meet again," said a voice he recognised. "You didn't disappoint me at the door and moved faster than I thought possible. It's an old trick. Superglue in the keyhole, walk up for a head shot while the man fumbles trying to get his key in. Right?"

It was Sam Bernstein. Fuck. A damn good agent. Haug knew immediately he should have killed the man last year when he had a chance. He listened. Yes, there were two, alright. They were moving slowly and quietly, one to one side, one to the other.

"I know you're good, Haug, and I honestly hate to kill you. I hope you understand that it's just business."

Bernstein had moved to the inside, the other man to the outside, near the road. They would now start forward. Haug knew he was going to have to act, because Bernstein was not to be fucked with. Go for the man on the outside and hope he can't shoot straight. Of course Bernstein will assume the same thing and will be ready for it. Haug didn't have the time, but even if he did, he would not have liked to calculate his chances. Fucking remote. Especially if they had night vision. They would see him in a moment. He drew his legs underneath him

448

and slowly lowered his shoulders. Well, goddamn it, he thought. This might be it. Finally. An absurd end to his life. Yeah, well, any kind of end was absurd. If this was it, it was it. I'll get that one son of a bitch, no matter how many bullets he's got left. Give me a little opening, and I'll get Bernstein as well.

He heard two muffled shots and flinched. But they came from above his head, and he heard a curse and cough from the man on the outside. A friend? Who? Keef? What the hell, any friend with a gun was welcome. He slowly turned back toward the inner wall. Bernstein. There was no sound from Bernstein now. No movement. He, too, was waiting. Haug could see nothing at all as he narrowed his eyes. Then he thought of something really corny, something he had done, but not in Vietnam. Something he had done as a kid fighting with BB rifles. Something you only saw in old cowboy films. He put his dozer cap on top of the two by four and moved it slowly, slowly out and up and forward. As he moved the dummy out, he carefully raised his head, keeping it very near the excavated wall.

He saw the barely visible muzzle flash and felt the two by four move sharply in his hand. His cap flew off into the rubble. His friend saw the muzzle flash as well and could hear two thuks above his head. And he saw Bernstein fire back. That is when he threw the two by four. He threw it end over end with both hands as hard as he could and immediately ducked down again.

"Shit!" he heard Bernstein say from the darkness. "Haug, you're harder to kill than a Louisiana cockroach."

"You're an ornery critter yourself, Sam. You walked right into my trap, and you're still alive."

"Trap?" Bernstein asked. "You knew we were coming?"

"Sure," Haug lied. "Message on my answerphone. Somebody tryin' to disguise his voice, but I reckon it was Regis."

There was no answer from Bernstein, so Haug continued. "I got a suggestion to make, Sam. You lissenin'?"

"I got one hand on my pistol," Sam replied, "and the other arm you hit with a plank. So I can't put my fingers in my ears."

"What I think is this," Haug replied. "I think we oughta call a truce, put your dead pal in the trunk of your car and go up to my flat and have a drink. That's what I think."

For a few moments there was silence. Then Bernstein spoke again. "Impossible. I've got a gun. Your friend has a gun, and for all I know you have one, too. If I throw you mine, I get a hole in the head. If you throw me yours, you might get the same. I think we'll just have to settle this, one way or the other."

There was another silence as Haug thought. "Tell me somethin', Sam. Do you believe in *honour*?"

The following silence was very long indeed, but Haug just waited, still with his eyes steady, turned toward the sound of Bernstein's voice, ready if the Israeli suddenly attacked.

Finally Bernstein laughed cynically. "I used to. A long time ago. I had to think for a while to remember what it meant."

"It's somethin' I had to come back to. I forgot for a while, too. In 'Nam." Haug laughed almost as cynically as Bernstein. "When I forgot what honour meant, they gave me a badge for it. That's why I sent it back."

"Yeah," Bernstein said with a twist in his voice. "And they probably didn't understand why you did it. Because most of those bastards have never been near a battlefield, and the only thing they ever killed was time."

"Señors," said a voice above Haug's head. "Please. I am lying on wet ground, and it is getting cold. Could you please decide whether to kill each other or have philosophy over a drink where it is warm."

It was Dominguez! Haug was dumbstruck for a moment. Dominguez? How the hell did he get here? "Just a minute, Raul," he said as if he'd known it all along. "Well, what do you say, Sam? Put the guns up, and we just trust each other not to pull 'em out again? If you say 'yes', I'll stand up right now. And you can decide whether to carry out Regis' contract or try to find out again what honour is."

Again there was a silence. "OK, Haug," Bernstein sighed finally. "I'm sure this is going to cost me. I haven't had any principles for years."

450

Haug stood up. He wasn't afraid, because he knew if he died from Bernstein's bullet, the Israeli was himself a dead man, even if he lived. Because he would be dead inside. He waited. His eyes had adjusted to the gloom inside the building site, and he could just see Bernstein sitting with both hands on his knees. They were empty. He turned to Dominguez above him.

"Raul," he said. "That is not how you play the game." The Cuban was standing but held his pistol down at his side, out of Bernstein's sightline.

"Honour is all very well between two white gentlemen," said Raul. "I remain still a little bit suspicious because of old memories. I am sorry."

"Put it up," Haug said as he climbed out of the basement. "Let's go have a fuckin' drink."

They sat around the kitchen table. Bernstein had bourbon and ice, Haug and Dominguez drank scotch.

The Israeli ran a hand through his wiry hair. "So you lied to me about the trap? About Regis?"

"If it hadn't been for the auspicious arrival of my friend here, I reckon I'd be lyin' down there fulla holes right now."

"I did not *arrive*," the Cuban said, taking a sip of scotch. "I was already here, waiting for you. And I see this car with two men. So I decide to wait for you and also to watch them. There is a block of apartments opposite the pub, and I went up the stairs and watched from the top landing. A little bit of a mistake, maybe, because when I saw you arrive it took me too long to get down to the bottom, and already you could have been killed, señor."

"Ah, these Heebs cain't shoot straight," Haug said.

"Yeah," Bernstein replied. "We're just not used to killing pigs."

Haug laughed and took a drink. "How's the arm?"

"Painful but not broken like the leg." He turned to Dominguez. "Did he tell you he busted my leg last year? Picked me up like a rag doll and busted it like a piece of kindling across his knee."

"Si, yes, señor. He almost broke mine as well. But no, he didn't tell me. A very strong man when he is angry. I think if it

451

had been me who had to kill him, I would have used a large calibre rifle from the top of the apartments. That way he cannot grab me if I miss."

Bernstein shook his head. "I'm not an assassin. I'm a soldier. I believe in head shots, close range. That way you make sure."

"Si. Yes. So sometimes you break your leg." Dominguez turned to Haug. "You, too, have a wound, señor. In the back."

"Yeah, I know," said Haug. "I looked at it in the mirror. Looks like about an eight inch graze. Plowed up a little skin, that's all."

Bernstein put his left elbow painfully on the table. "OK, Haug, what's all this shit about honour? You almost had me thinking out there, crying my heart out."

Haug took a long pull on his scotch. "You know damn well what I was talkin' about."

"You mean you weren't just trying to make me dishonour my contract with Regis? You meant all that crap?"

"Course I did, Sam. You know that as well. And you also know you cain't dishonour a contract with a liar, a man who lies to himself and everone else he thinks he can use. Honour's a social thang. Greed's an individual thang. If it's ever man for himself, there's no such thang as honour. Honour says somethin' about hope for humanity, that's what I reckon."

Bernstein laughed. "Then I guess I don't have any now, probably never did. And never will."

Dominguez cleared his throat. "You have it, I think. You just do not *believe* you have it."

Bernstein shrugged. "Bullshit."

"Despite my own cynical comment about white men, señor, and of course my damp belly, I was very interested in your little conversation in the dark. A man with no honour at all would never take the risk. He took it. And you took it. I remained a little sceptical, maybe, because I don't understand the language so well, the nuances, the little tones of voices. A little joke, maybe, about the white men..."

Haug snorted. "It's no joke. I'll never know why any black man believes anythang a white man says. Or a red man or any

452

other colour. If they go by the past, the best thang to do when a white feller comes up with some big deal or another is bury an axe in the back of his head when he walks away."

"Of course, not all whites are bad," Dominguez said with a smile.

"Yeah, and there are plenty of black assholes - maybe the same ratio of assholes there is in the white race. Trouble is, the white assholes run the place and give everbody else a bad name." Haug turned to the Israeli. "I'd like you to join us, Sam."

Bernstein slid his drink across the table and got up. "Ah, shit. Now I've heard everything. I louse up a hit - and that's the second one involving you - welsh on a contract, have a long talk about honour...what the hell is my life coming to, I ask you?" He walked to the window and moved the red curtains aside to look out at the yellow street lamps and light traffic. "Your outfit is bound to lose, Haug. Do you have any fucking idea what kind of personnel they got stacked up against you?" He turned back to the table. "There's Direct Action, right? You know about them. They got the Special Branch and some of the regular police. They got the secret service. They got the politicians. Now you're asking me, already a three time loser, to join a little fucking Robin Hood band of merry men who are going to lose their *asses*. Haug, for chrissake, you don't think you're going to *win*, do you? You're a *soldier*, man! Wars are won by organisation, material and personnel! You got - *maybe* - organisation. You got shit for material and shit for personnel."

Haug spun his drink on the table. "You think winnin's the important thang, do you?"

"Well, what the hell else is there?"

"You got a dozen armed hoods comin' at you and your wife or girlfriend or daughter or son," Haug said. "You know you cain't win, but you do what? Run off and leave 'em?"

Bernstein leaned against the washing machine and looked at his feet. "Probably join the hoods."

"Bat crap."

"You don't know how far down the road I've gone, Haug. After tonight, there's not much more to do than stick this gun in my mouth and pull the trigger. It's got where I can't even finish a fucking contract properly. You should all be wiped out by now anyhow." He turned to Dominguez. "You a real Cuban or a Miami Cuban?"

"A real one, señor."

Bernstein was shaking his head. "Well, now, you two make a fine pair of no-hopers. So you work for Castro?"

"No, señor," Dominguez said with a shrug. "I work for the Cuban people. And myself, of course."

"Well," Bernstein replied, looking from under his eyebrows, "take it from me, Raul, they are beginning to play taps for Cuba. A tiny little country is just about to be squeezed dry, like a lemon. In two years we'll have Havana full of casinos and whores."

Dominguez shrugged again. "Maybe. Maybe not. Nothing is certain. America makes it so we cannot trade simply because it does not like our government. If we cannot trade, we cannot eat. We are a little country and no threat to America."

"You're wrong there," Haug said. "Cuba's a big threat to America. If a socialist experiment is seen to *work*, that gives a lot of other people hope. So we gotta help make it not work."

Bernstein poured himself another drink from the bottle of Wild Turkey. "America doesn't like it because it's a dictatorship, right? That's what they say anyway."

Haug and Dominguez both laughed. Haug got the bottle of scotch and filled both their glasses, adding some ice from the bowl.

"Señor," the Cuban said, still laughing. "South and Central America are full of dictatorships and always have been. Surely America loses no important sleep over dictatorships. On the contrary, it seems to sleep better with them. You see, many of the people in Cuba call our country a democracy. Every street has an elected committee, and from this committee is elected an official who represents that street at the village. Or a part of the city. You don't have that in a dictatorship. People who work in a business decide how the business is run and any profits go to central funds which are then given back to the people in services."

"Yeah," said Bernstein ironically, "I bet *that* works."

454

"Of course in many cases it doesn't," Dominguez replied. "We have corruption, much of it. We have lazy people, greedy people, people who lie...what's the word? Hypocrites. There are also weak people. There are those who would like the old days to return because they profited individually from them. There are many sorts there, as there are here and America and Israel. America elects plenty of corrupt governments. Johnson and Vietnam. Nixon and Watergate. Reagan and Iran-Contra. Corruption is not singular to Cuba, señor. But we have very few homeless, very few who cannot receive the best of health care at no cost to them, very few who cannot have a good education, very few who cannot retire in old age with a pension."

He took a drink of scotch. "You see, I remember the old days under Batista. America never worried about the dictator Batista, eh? OK, I was young, but I remember the streets of Havana. My older sister, Maria, was a whore. At fifteen she was a whore, because the family needed money. I stole in the streets, a pickpocket. So we survived. But it is no way to survive. Then Castro came, and many things changed like we had never seen before. My sister was cured of venereal disease. Later she returned to school, and today she works as a manager in the public transport system in Havana. I went to college, not to jail where I would have gone eventually. And, well, here I am. Maybe not so much better, perhaps. But I think I would rather be doing this than serving in jail."

Bernstein took a gulp of whisky. "I don't really give a shit. Socialism, fascism, democracy, dictatorship, what the hell, it's all the same. I used to be political years ago when it looked like Israel could give people a little hope, but not now. I don't trust any of the bastards there or here or in the States. Or Cuba. Fuck 'em."

"To say you're not political," Haug muttered, "is one of the most political thangs you can say. That means you get pushed along this way or that way by whatever tide happens to be in or out. Germany was fulla non-political folks when the Heebs were gettin' fried by the million. The non-politicals were as responsible for the killin' as the people turnin' on the gas and all those showin' their armpits at the rallies. You oughta know that,

Sam. You cain't choose to be non-political, just like you cain't choose your dick to be longer. It's one of those thangs you are if you're alive and around other people. You're political, whether you like it or not."

Bernstein gulped down the remainder of his drink and turned to the window again, parting the curtains to stare out blankly. "Goddamn you, Haug, you're fucking up my life. Opening up all those old dusty, rusty trunks full of kids' toys and honour and decency and hope. No doubt Santa Claus and the tooth fairy are also there." He spun around suddenly and pulled out his pistol from his shoulder holster, holding it up by the side of his head, pointing at the ceiling.

Haug could feel Dominguez tense, but he caught Bernstein's eyes and held them. He was wary, but not tense or afraid.

"I'm a soldier, Haug," he said quietly. "I can shoot you now and probably get Raul before he gets to his gun. Then I can go to Regis and collect £15,000, maybe £20,000 for both of you. Because if I take you out, I take a lot of his troubles away. With the money I can drift somewhere else. South Africa. Lot of action there, and I know people in South Africa. Nice climate. Good beaches, plenty of women. Or Eastern Europe, though it's kinda messy there, but the money's good. Then there's always South America, as you said. Let the top dollar tell me which way to point my weapon."

Slowly he lowered the gun and levelled it at the centre of Haug's forehead. Haug could feel Raul ready to move, and he put his hand over and laid it on the Cuban's forearm.

"What do you think, Haug?" said Bernstein in a low voice.

"I think you already know what you're gonna do," Haug replied evenly. He reached for the scotch bottle and refilled his glass, then he refreshed Raul's glass. Taking a sip, he looked over the edge of the glass at the pointed gun. "And you're pissed off at me and you're pissed off at yourself, because reclaimin' yourself can be painful to you, soldier or not. Welcome aboard, Sam."

Bernstein stared at the centre of the bald head down the barrel of the pistol, noticing his hand was trembling slightly.

Haug's hand, the one holding the glass of scotch, was steady. Slowly he dropped the gun to his side, shaking his head.

"You've got more guts, my friend, than any man I've ever met. There was a half second there when I just about pulled the trigger, you know."

"Yep," Haug said, taking another sip of whiskey. "Nothin' I could do about it, though, was there? It was up to you, not me. I'm not particularly ready to die, but I know I'm gonna, and I'm not gonna be ready then, either. And I reckon death while fightin' for your soul might be marginally nobler than suckin' down some vomit in my sleep when I'm eighty three."

"My soul, eh? Is that what you're after?" Bernstein said with a nasty laugh.

"A figger of speech," Haug said, getting up and setting his drink on the table. "I think we need a little music to celebrate. How about some Mozart? Everbody like *Exsultate Jubilate?*"

The Israeli put his pistol back in the holster. "You're nuts, you fucker. You got a communist nigger sitting at your kitchen table, a Jewboy who just about ended your worthless life, and now you want to listen to Mozart. You can't be a self-respecting redneck and carry on like that. They'll take your white sheet away from you when you get back to the Deep South and won't let you handle snakes any more at church meetings."

Haug grabbed his cap off the hook in the hall and slung it back toward Bernstein. "Look what you did to my best dozer cap, you goddamn antichrist. That is a genuine Harley hat, there. Came from Milwaukee, and I hold you responsible for puttin' a hole right through the precious American eagle."

Bernstein picked up the cap from the floor and shouted at Haug in the other room. "I do not believe you used that trick. The last time I saw that was in a Hopalong Cassidy movie."

"You were outmanoeuvred by superior intelligence and technology," Haug said from his bedroom as he put on the CD in his disc player.

When Haug came back through the kitchen door, Bernstein smiled. "Shit, I'm glad I didn't kill you. I haven't met anybody I liked in a long time." He listened for a moment to the joyous opening of the music. "My father wanted me to be a violinist.

That was in New York. He played a little 'cello, and he was always trying to get together a string quartet. I did play the violin for a while. Liked it."

"Wish I could play some kinda instrument," Haug said, picking up his drink. "Or sing. I couldn't carry a tune in a wheelbarrow. Imagine doin' what that lady's doin' with her voice."

"Maybe I'm a little drunk," Bernstein replied, "but I haven't felt like this in years. Been able to talk. Been able to feel something. Been able to relax a little. After being kicked out of Shin Bet I decided to just be a loner. No more marriage, no more friends, no entanglements, no loyalties, no home. Then at some point, when I got a little older and a little slower, somebody would finally put a bullet through my head. It seemed logical. It seemed right. Appropriate."

Both Haug and Dominguez nodded. They knew what he meant, and Bernstein knew they knew.

"Women?" the Israeli went on. "Women? Well, when I found one who wanted to, we fucked. The moment she started getting close or trying to get close, I left. I've been what they call self-sufficient for almost ten years now. I've asked nothing from anybody, and I've given nothing. Aw, shit!"

Bernstein turned away toward the window again but didn't open the curtains to look out. Instead he realised he was crying. Or trying to cry as he desperately held himself back. A few tears squeezed out, though, and he reached for the tea towel to wipe his eyes.

"Too much liquor," he murmured, "and the brave warrior cries like a sissy. Another half hour of this shit, and you'll have me wearing a pair of diapers, Haug."

"You're a real arrogant son of a bitch, Sam. You know that? You're another one of these guys who thinks he's superman or some super hero. Sure, you can kill a man, squeeze off a head shot and then finish the sandwich you were eatin'. You got a lotta guts. You got a lotta brains. You've also got a lot of feelin's. You got needs. You'd like the company of other folks. You'd like warmth. You'd like to be held close and loved..."

458

Bernstein turned around. "Stop it, Haug. That's enough. Don't say any more." He was serious.

Haug smacked his hand on the table. "Now, goddammit, Sam, do you think you're somethin' so special you can swing through the trees of the world like Tarzan without ever touchin' your feet on the ground? You're a human bein', and human bein's are social animals, so most of your toolbox is fulla thangs to deal with social situations. If you were built to be a single individual, you wouldn't need emotion. Or not very much of it. An individual is like a robot, maybe. You're tryin' to live a life with half your head tied behind your back. That's why I called you arrogant. You think you can still whip the world like that."

"Listen, Haug. I just cried. I can't remember when I last cried. Thirty years ago?"

"Yeah. And when you cried, you went up about ten degrees in my regard."

"Up?" Bernstein asked, incredulous. "Up?"

"It's 'cause you're feelin' somethin' strong, and it cain't come out any other way. Lissen to the Mozart. That's strong. How come you cain't feel strong thangs?"

The Israeli was quiet for a moment, thinking. "Because...I get let down," he said finally. "And I always regret it. Someone takes advantage."

"You mean like Raul and me are gonna make fun of you or somethin'? That we're gonna tell everbody you're a crybaby?"

Bernstein seemed not to hear him. "Women let you down. Parents let you down. Friends let you down. Israel lets you down."

"Am I gonna let you down?" Haug asked.

Bernstein laughed shortly and swung his head. "Probably not. That's an irony, isn't it? The man you want to kill is the only one who won't let you down."

"Well, let me tell you somethin'," Haug said. "You're only partly right. I don't think I'll let you down. But I know I'm human, and there might be a time when I'm not thinkin' or I'm in a funny mood or havin' too good a time with a woman or my mind is somewhere else. And at those times I might just let you down, I don't know. One person cannot guarantee anythang one

459

hundred percent to any other person. That *other* person has to realise that, too. You're lookin' for too many perfect thangs. A perfect woman, perfect parents, a perfect country. You may as well look for a pot of gold at the end of the rainbow, 'cause you're not gonna find any of 'em. They're all gonna let you down."

Haug topped up his drink again and put a couple of fresh cubes of ice in it, then he poured more for Dominguez. "Now take this little group of ours, the United Opposition. They'll let you down, too. When we win - if we win - thangs'll just bust away, and the sense of purpose will be lost. They'll forget the idealism, time will pass, and thangs'll start gettin' rotten again. One way or the other."

Bernstein pointed his finger at Haug. "Exactly. My point. So tell me, redneck. Why bother in the first place? Let the CA have it. Give it to them. It's all going to end up in a heap of shit."

"For one reason," Haug said. "To try to keep it from gettin' worse and reversin' ourselves through the evolutionary process so all of us wind up bein' slugs and bugs."

"So fucking what?"

Haug scratched his eyebrow. "Take the Holocaust. Quite a few so-called Aryan Germans did resist, did help. Probably nobody even knows their names now. Hid a few Jews, gave 'em a lift to the border in the trunk of the car, covered for them in one way or another. Maybe even a milkman gave a few extra pints through a hole in the wall. It *slows 'em up*, that's what it does. It doesn't *help* 'em. If you're non-political, you *help* 'em. If they didn't have some kinda help, not a single Jew would've escaped."

"Here we go again," said Bernstein. "The fucking Holocaust."

"You'd think after that the Jews would be the kindest folks on earth to the dispossessed, but, no, the first thang they do is pull down their pants and shit all over the Arabs."

"That's because we're scared. We don't want it to happen again..."

460

"Yeah, you're so goddamned scared of it happenin' again, you go and do it to somebody else."

Bernstein sighed and took a drink. "Fear blinded us. It is hard to see when you are blind."

Haug studied the Israeli for a moment. "You're lonely, aren't you, Sam?"

With a sudden fury Bernstein threw the remainder of his drink in Haug's face and almost threw the glass.

"If you'd warned me about that," Haug observed, "I woulda opened my mouth."

Bernstein threw him the tea towel. "Sorry. I got a bad temper. It was a lousy thing to do to a guy who might be a friend."

Haug turned to Dominguez as he wiped his face. "You're awful quiet, there, feller."

The Cuban shook his head and finished his scotch. "Oh, no, no, señor. It is fascinating. And there is good music, good drink. An interesting... unusual... conversation. It is also late, I think. Perhaps I should be going. Though I did wish to talk to you when you have some time." He started to get up from the table.

Haug stopped him. "Look here. I got a spare room. There's a sofa bed, and I got an air mattress in the closet. Both of you can stay here, and I'll make you a real nice breakfast in the mornin'. How's that?"

"Well," said Bernstein, "I'm too drunk to drive, and the cops pull everybody at this time of night. Be kind of difficult explaining Heinrik's body in the trunk. So I guess I'm stuck here."

"Anybody want another drink?" Haug offered the nearly empty bottle.

Bernstein took a deep breath. "I know where your friends are being held."

Haug turned, the bottle in midair. "You do?"

"I do. I also know about how many men are guarding them and about what it would take to get in. There are a few other things I know as well. Like how many DA groups there are and where they are based, and I've got some idea of the

461

communication and support system. Like I say, I don't think we have a chance in hell. But I'm getting a little older and a little slower already, so it doesn't much matter whose bullet it is. It may as well be one of theirs."

"Well, peel me a grape," Haug said. "You've just stopped bein' non-political."

"Don't worry, Haug. It's just another mistake in a life full of mistakes. At least I'll be killing people I don't like. Most of 'em are scum."

"I would be glad to help, señors. Illegal, of course. But what they are doing to my country is also illegal. I wish only that you share some information with me."

"That's up to Mainwarin' and the committee," Haug said. "But I'll put in a real firm word for you, Raul."

Dominguez studied his empty glass. "Of course I, too, have some information to share, because already I know how many drugs come into this country. And it is not smugglers in fishing boats."

Haug turned to Bernstein. "Well, there you are, you drunken, cynical Heeb bastard. They may have the quantity, but look at us. We got the *quality*."

The Israeli sighed. "Hmm. Yeah. But we haven't got enough of it. We need a quantity of quality. You better get that air mattress out right now before I fall on the kitchen floor. A windbag like you shouldn't have any problem blowing it up."

Haug got up and stretched. "We're talkin' technology here. It goes up in six seconds. Compressed air."

"Hissing right through that thick red neck..."

CHAPTER TWENTY FIVE

Harvey Gillmore was on his hands and knees scrubbing the kitchen floor, and the little insulated cable stretched out behind him. It went out the kitchen door and down the hallway before snaking through the bedroom doorway. He could not see into the bedroom, but he would very much have liked to. He wondered what she was doing. His work was clumsy because he was unused to menial labour. In fact he had never done it in his life. Except, of course, when he was a child. His father made him tidy his room every day, and once a week he had been required to dust and wax the furniture. His clothes had to be neatly stacked into their respective drawers, the socks folded a certain way. No untidiness had been allowed at any time. The maid cleaned the rest of the house, but Gillmore always had to take care of his own room. He remembered the maid. She was an Italian immigrant of thirty who spoke broken English. A dark woman who carried a little too much weight around her hips, Louisa was made to work hard for her Australian dollars. His father roared at her when he found a little dust on a window sill or a badly washed plate. Gillmore remembered her on hands and knees scrubbing floors, and occasionally he got a look up her dress. She had plump thighs at the top of her stockings, and Gillmore became obsessed about her as he passed into adolescence.

Louisa was his first woman. She didn't want him and cried, but he forced her by promising to report her to his father if she didn't. So he had her, on her hands and knees. On the kitchen floor, her drawers around her knees.

On the kitchen floor. He broke out of his reverie and rung out the dirty cloth into the bucket. Looking at his fingers, he saw they were turning red from the hot water and detergent. Why was he doing this? After all, he was Harvey Gillmore. He concentrated hard, his sour features dragging downward with the effort. He was doing it because she would beat the shit out of him if he refused. Why did he let her beat him? Why? He wiped the sweat from his forehead nervously, using his forearm. Because she forced him, that's why.

But there was another reason, and when he momentarily captured that reason, trapped it for questioning, he quickly released it. The reason was that he wanted her. The fact he was Harvey Gillmore, the greatest newspaper publisher in the world, suddenly meant nothing to him anymore. That's as far as he could get before he began thinking about something else.

That morning he woke in a foul mood. He didn't want any more. He wanted out of it all. He wanted somehow to escape back to a world of sanity, one he recognised and controlled. She had locked him in the spare bedroom with an iron collar around his neck, chained to the heavy bed. A bedpan had been left in case he needed it in the night. She told him to sleep with his shoes and stockings on, but he finally kicked off the shoes because his feet were cramped and uncomfortable. He still slept poorly. What he wanted to do most was masturbate, but Corky had locked him into some sort of penis restrainer which had taken him a long while to get on properly. She had sat in the chair giggling at his efforts to make sense of the contraption. His flaccid penis was squeezed inside, and there was no room for an erection. That is what kept him awake. He dreamed of her and could not dissolve her image. The fact he could not get an erection increased the intensity of his sexual frustration. He chewed on the pillow. He pounded the mattress with his fists. He tried to winkle himself out of the restraining device.

He must have dozed in the early morning hours, though, because she woke him up with the cane across his bottom. He screamed and flopped onto his back, struggling desperately to understand what was happening or where he was. And she stood there, holding the cane in both hands and smiling. He didn't have his shoes on, she told him, and that wasn't allowed. He was transfixed, though, and could not move. Because Corky DeLoop was standing at the foot of his bed completely nude. She struck him again across the tops of his thighs, and he scrambled down on the floor, looking for the shoes. Confusion, anger and fear rumbled through him in equal proportions. He found the shoes and sat on the floor to put them on, and Corky unlocked his collar, telling him to fetch her a bowl of cereal, some toast, butter and jelly.

His feet were really aching in the shoes, but he clattered into the kitchen and finally managed to find everything. He, too, was hungry. All he had the night before was a bowl of soup, and she made him lap it up from a bowl on the floor. The kitchen and a small dining room were formed from an L shaped space. Corky DeLoop came through, still naked, carrying a paperback book she had been reading the night before. Gillmore carried the breakfast through on a tray while she ignored him. She ignored him, too, while she ate her cereal. He could not ignore her, though. His eyes followed every tiny movement of her breasts, and at one point he actually felt his mouth watering. Not for the food she was eating but for those gorgeous tits. Once he had been able to grab them whenever he wanted. It seemed so long ago somehow, but it wasn't. Was it only two days? He couldn't follow a thought properly because she kept moving.

When she finished her cereal, she leaned back in her chair, buttering her toast. She told him she wanted some head. He didn't know what she meant at first and hesitated. She grabbed the cane and smacked him, then told him to get down on his knees between her legs. She wanted some head while she finished the chapter she was reading because "it was kinda sexy..."

Never in his life had Gillmore performed cunnilingus. He thought it was demeaning for a man to do that to a woman.

The water in the bucket was overflowing as he stared out the window at the large hedge in the garden. Quickly he turned off the tap and dumped out some of the water. The bucket was heavy as he lifted it down to the floor. It was what he always demanded from his cleaners. First you scrub the floor - on your hands and knees. Then you rinsed it with fresh warm water. Finally you dried it off with clean towels. That is the way to clean a floor. He got down on his hands and knees and started at one end of the kitchen.

But as his knees touched the floor, his mind returned to the morning. On all fours he had crawled underneath the table. Her legs were open, and she sat on the edge of the chair. The soft brown hair was curly, and as he moved his face toward her he could smell her body. Not the sexual smell, not yet. But the odour of the skin, of her legs. He wedged his face closer, his cheeks touching her thighs, but he did not know what to do. Tentatively he put his tongue out and touched the outer lips, feeling himself trying to become erect again.

Finally Corky grabbed him by the hair, told him to keep his tongue out, then guided him to the right places, moving him into the right rhythms. Above his head he heard her eating toast while he went up and down with his tongue, in and out, up and down. Occasionally she grabbed him again and redirected his efforts.

It was an extraordinary experience, Gillmore had to admit that. On the one hand he felt like a dog on all fours, licking a bitch in heat. On the other, he had to admit he liked it. At least he was touching her, and with his nose and tongue he was actually inside her. After a few minutes Corky began moving her hips sensuously. When he touched her legs with his hands, she hit him again with the cane. That is when something very strange happened to him. Previously he detested the pain from the cane, and sometimes it made him angry. This time, though, he was unprepared. Because he *liked* it. Was *"like"* the right word? No. It *stimulated* him. He had her smell and her wetness on his face and could taste the slight saltiness of her fluid. It must have been the mixture of sensations which did it. The smell, the taste, the feel of her - then the burning pain on his hip. It heightened everything, making his humiliation seem almost enjoyable. This caught him completely unawares, something which was horrible and foreign suddenly entrapping him. His discomfort, his lack of sleep, his frustration fell away. He increased his efforts, doing his best to stimulate her, trying to be as good as he could at this new technique.

When she came, she gripped his head with her thighs and held it into her with both hands. He could not breathe. He could hear nothing but the drumming of his heart, and for a moment he thought he was going to die from asphyxiation. Finally she released him, and he dropped to the floor, gasping for breath. As

466

he lay there he realised from the sound that she was buttering another piece of toast. Her bare foot was inches from his eyes, and he stared longingly at the perfect toes with their painted pink nails. Quite spontaneously he found himself kissing her feet gently, warmly, even worshipfully. She did not stop him, and Harvey Gillmore realised with great astonishment that for those few moments he was happy. Content. He did not question it then, but it worried him later.

He dressed her soon afterwards, his first time. It was not easy. For one thing, he was clumsy. For another, his hands were trembling too much. The stockings were the most difficult of all and took him a while. Getting them straight, hooking them properly. Then there were the silk ivory French knickers, so light and thin he could see the outline of her pubic hair through them. She wanted to try on a number of dresses and different pairs of shoes. He hung up each one she rejected and fetched out something else. She finally settled on a luminous white sun dress with a halter top and white sandals with a two-inch heel. He was hoping she would wear the red rubber dress again, but no, he hung that up in her closet and put the beautiful red shoes in the shoe rack, now completely full.

He had combed her hair. No, that wasn't right. He tried, he began to learn how to comb it. You didn't just rake the comb through it. You had to hold onto the roots with one hand so it would not pull, and any little tangle had to be teased out carefully. It took him a while. Then he painted her fingernails in her favourite shade of pink. In fact he painted them twice. The first time he got varnish all over the cuticle. Meanwhile she read her story, sitting in the chair and propping her feet up on the bed. She made him watch carefully as she applied her lipstick and told him he could try it next time. He watched her use the eye liner and brush as she gave her eyebrows a little colour. It was quite fascinating, and he was surprised at the level of his concentration. She chatted to him a little, too, telling him the treatment he was getting was deserved because of the way he treated women. She asked him if he remembered beating the shit out of her. Did he remember the mirror? Holding the mirror in front of her, telling her how ugly she was? Making her kneel and worship him and his lousy dick? Did he not think women were human beings?

Well, no. He didn't. He still didn't. Harvey Gillmore never in his life knew what to make of women. They could have dropped in bean pods from outer space for all he knew. They did, however, always have a profound effect on him. He would spot one and want her, right then, right there, immediately. His instinct was to walk over and pull up the skirt and push his hand straight into the woman he wanted. After all, it wasn't *his* fault his guts turned over and his prong got hard. It wasn't hard before some woman walked into the room, was it? Logically, it was *her* fault, all of it.

For Gillmore, women were another species. He never even considered they thought rationally or had feelings or worries or hopes and failures, just like men. No, they spitefully carried a pussy between their legs to distract and taunt him. He punished them simply because they held power over him. A secretary bending over while he was on the telephone could make him forget what he was saying, destroying a train of thought, maybe even losing him millions of pounds. By degrading women, he degraded their power over him. *He* was in control. As he always had been.

Something snapped inside him about Corky DeLoop, though, something vital. There were dead notes on the old keyboard. Yet he wasn't entirely certain he missed the old tunes, and that was another thing which worried him. Apart from his rude awakening that morning, he occasionally found himself contented in the role he was playing. The shoes hurt his feet, and his walk was still unsteady, but he gradually found the look of his legs very interesting. They almost looked like a woman's legs. While he was alone in the kitchen he occasionally reached down and touched the material of the stockings. It felt nearly the same as a real female leg. Is that what women felt when they were touched? If they did, he was a little envious. How grand if he could have all his power and that power as well!

As Gillmore stood up to survey the sparkling floor, he felt a sharp tug at his balls. Quickly drying his hands on a tea towel he hurriedly tick-tacked out of the kitchen and down the hall. And

468

he *remembered* this time. He knocked lightly on her door and waited for her to call him in.

Corky DeLoop was lying propped up on the bed. Her book was turned face down beside her. He stood beside the dressing table waiting for her to speak.

"I've just been talkin' to a friend of mine on the phone, Harv. Friend of yours, too. Remember Sarah Courtney? Well, she's on her way over for lunch. Now, I don't trust your cookin' for anything much more than toast at the moment, so I ordered a hamper from Fortnams. Don't worry. I'll answer the door, 'cause I know your ugly face is recognisable. But when Sarah gets here, I want you to be on your best behaviour. Open up the hamper, chill the wine, lay out the knives and forks and plates, serve the food. Got it?"

Gillmore looked down at the floor and frowned.

"Now don't tell me you're gonna give me a heap of trouble, Harv," she said forcefully. "You got this comin'. I *promised* this to myself, and to her."

Gillmore cleared his throat and looked at her beautiful crossed ankles. "Mrs DeLoop..." he began hesitantly. "I've been thinking a lot, and I'm not sure I know what I've been thinking. What I'm trying to say is that I don't mind...so much mind...what I'm doing. At times I suppose I almost like it, some of it. I don't know why, but I do. OK, I can be around you. That's really all I want. But I don't want anybody else here. To see me, you know..."

"Frankly, I don't give a holy shit what you want, Harvey Gillmore. I'm just tellin' you what *I* want. And I can get what I want, OK?"

Gillmore was becoming mesmerised as he stared at her ankles and feet, so close to him on the bed. Her toes were just peeping from the front of her sandals. He suddenly fell to his knees at the foot of the bed.

"Don't you dare touch, Harv!" She held the battery cassette menacingly in her hand.

"May I just kiss them, please," he whimpered. He held his arms at his sides with great determination.

Corky DeLoop smiled. Then she swung her legs over the edge of the bed away from him, and put her feet on the floor. Her dress rode up to the tops of her thighs, but she did not pull it down. "I'll tell you what, Harv, old boy. You go back to that bedroom door and get down on your belly. You remember that? Huh? Then you crawl on your belly over to my feet, tellin' me you'll do anything I ask you to without any more of this bullshit. That includes servin' Sarah and me lunch and doin' what Sarah wants while she's here. Anything she wants. You readin' me, Harv? You got a lot of doin' to do before I ever turn you loose."

She watched with amusement as Gillmore first buried his head at the foot of the bed then got wearily to his feet. "Stand up straight, Harv. Remember where you are. Chin up. One leg in front of the other, not too big a steps and remember to hold your arms out at your sides, wrists upward like a little fairy."

When he got to the door he turned back to her, trying his best, putting one foot at an angle to the other, holding his arms out and his wrists up. "May I ask you one more question, Mrs DeLoop, please?" He paused for a moment. "When will you take this thing off my...dick?"

Corky smiled sweetly. "When I feel like it, Harv. Maybe when you start behavin' yourself properly like a nice, feminine little maid."

She watched with a glow of pleasure as he knelt on the carpet and got on his stomach, commencing to crawl slowly towards her feet. As he crawled, he begged and promised. It sounded as if it was being drawn out of him with fish hooks. Today she was quite enjoying herself goading the filthy little man coming across the carpet at her. It was interesting that the more she goaded, the more he seemed to respond. Originally her intention was to put him through hell then cut him loose dressed in women's underwear in the middle of Trafalgar Square. On the other hand, she could use a household servant. Particularly a servant with such a nice stack of unlimited cash credit cards. She would be able to carry on any interesting affairs without worrying about a homicidal husband now. Including the gorgeous black man. Last night she had gone to the yellow van and thanked One Time, telling him everything was under

470

control. She promised she would telephone him soon, and they kissed deeply before she ducked back from the window and looked at his big grin. He held up one finger, started the van and drove off with a squeal of the tyres.

Looking down at the back of his head as he kissed her feet, she realised just what an unattractive little mouse he was. His hair was unwashed and oily and showed a bald patch at the back. His skin was sallow and pimply, and a tuft of hair grew out of a mole at the base of his neck. His legs were without ample flesh, and he looked utterly ridiculous in stockings. The ones he had on were already laddered. The thought that such an inconsequential man had such enormous power revolted her.

But what the hell. She was having fun now. "Don't get greedy, Harv, and lissen to me, you hear? I want you to roll over on your back, put your arms by yours sides and lay absolutely still. If you move a muscle, I'll stomp on your dick. Do not move until I tell you to."

She stood up and placed one foot on either side of his head so he could look directly up her dress. She could see herself in the wardrobe mirror. The dress was nice and flattered her waist and legs. A good length. Looking down she saw the bottom of Gillmore's torso and looked at the penis restrainer. It was bulging as his body fought hopelessly against the leather for an erection. He was trembling, and she noticed his fingers digging into the thick carpet. Blue veins stood out on his spindly forearms.

"Talk to me, Harv. Tell me what you see. Tell me what you feel."

"Ohhhh..." The exhalation sounded as if he had been wounded. "I can't stand it. I can't stand it. Want to shut my eyes, but can't."

"No, keep 'em open, Harv. And keep talkin'."

"I love you, Cor...Mrs DeLoop. I never loved anybody before.."

"Bullshit. You don't love me, Harv. You just love what you see. What you cain't touch. What you cain't have. That's all you love. Except for yourself, of course."

"No, I'm telling you, Mrs DeLoop, it's so powerful it's overwhelming me. I don't know how long I can keep from touching...from..."

"You touch me just once," she said, dangling the battery cassette, "and I'll make you jump around like a wet fish on a pier."

He groaned. "Please, please tell me something. If I'm really good, if I really change and do everything you ask, is there some chance you might...that sometime we might, you know, fuck?"

"You ought to wash your mouth out, Harvey Gillmore, usin' words like that." She thought for a moment. "I might. Then again, I might not. You never know. I got different moods."

"I've got no idea what's happening to me," he said weakly. "I'm sliding down a hill, and I don't care. I just want you. Want you. Desperately...and..."

The doorbell rang.

"Oh, dear," she said, stepping over his body. "That must be our hamper, boy. You can come and fetch it when the door's closed. Then I want you to try on your new apron. I've got a nice, feminine one for you in tacky pink nylon." She walked gaily to the door before turning back to the man who still lay prone on the floor. "You'll just *love* it, Harv."

When Corky DeLoop opened the door Sarah Courtney's face expressed a number of emotions. First she reached over and hugged her, then, with her eyes wide, she looked over Corky's shoulder.

"Is it OK?" she whispered. "He's not here? You're OK?"

Corky dragged her into the flat. "Sure, I'm OK. Come on in. Close the door. How do you like my new apartment?"

"Yours?" Sarah asked in astonishment.

"Yeah, mine. This is the livin' room, where all the livin' takes place, so get the weight off 'em and pick a chair. I'll show you around in a minute or two. First of all, would you like some coffee or tea. I hear you limeys drink tea all the time."

"I'll have a tea, thank you," Courtney said as she sat in a comfortable looking leather armchair.

"One tea, one coffee, boy!" Corky shouted down the hall as she tugged on a cord held in her left hand.

"Golly," whispered Courtney. "You have servants?"

"I got one servant, but I'm thinkin' about cuttin' his salary." Corky sat near the window on a chaise longue and put her feet up. She kept the little box attached to the cord in her hand.

"You're looking great. Fabulous. I can't wait to hear all the stories, Corky. Haug told us you had everything in control. Then he said something else I can't repeat."

"Go on, repeat it," Corky said with an impish smile.

"He said if he was ever locked in a room with you, only one of you would come out alive."

She laughed. "He's right, the bald-headed bastard. I've been thinkin' about gettin' my hand down his trousers."

"Well, beware his girl friend. She's mega beautiful..."

"Oh, yeah, I remember. Afraid I never wanna meet the bitch..."

They were interrupted by an apparition at the door. Gillmore appeared with a nylon apron around his neck and tied at the waist. It was very frilly and cheap-looking and fell just below his stocking tops. The Australian was staring stoically at the ceiling.

Sarah Courtney clasped her hands over her mouth, her eyes wide in astonishment, and dropped backward into the large chair. She was speechless. She was also terrified.

"Meet Harv, my new houseboy," Corky gloated. "Harv, this is Miss Courtney. She is havin' the tea."

Courtney had not moved a muscle and seemed to be in a catatonic state with her hands still over her mouth and her knees drawn up defensively.

Harvey Gillmore teetered over to her chair and bent from the waist, offering the tray to her. She still did not move.

"I don't believe it!" she whispered dramatically.

"Miss Courtney. Your tea, ma'am," Gillmore said hoarsely.

"Go on, Sarah. He's not gonna bite. Not any more."

She poured the tea from a small pot with trembling hands, glancing up nervously several times, added some milk and retreated with cup and saucer back into the chair.

"Harv!" Corky barked.

Gillmore cleared his throat and looked again at the ceiling. "I would like to apologise to you, Miss Courtney, for my filthy behaviour..." He trailed off.

Corky snapped her fingers and Gillmore hastened to her side with the mug of coffee. She took it and turned to him. "Put the tray down on the table, boy."

"Yes, Mrs DeLoop."

Sarah Courtney was steadying her cup and saucer on the arm of the chair. "I don't believe this. I simply can't believe it. I must be dreaming."

"Hands and knees, boy. Crawl over to Miss Courtney and tell her what a shit you are."

Gillmore crawled to Sarah Courtney's feet and hung his head. "I'm a shit, ma'am. A dirty little shit, and I apologise again for harming you. I think you were quite a person to put up with it, and I would like to offer you compensation of fifteen thousand pounds as a part-payment for the indignities you suffered."

Courtney opened her mouth wide and turned to her friend. Then she closed it. "Well, Mr Gill..."

"His name is Harv, but he answers to 'boy'."

"Well, er, Harv..." She turned to Corky with her lower lip between her teeth. "Golly, I don't know what to say."

Corky swung her legs off the chaise and got up. "What you say is, 'That's not enough, Harv. Swing your ass around here so I can get a crack at it.'" She took a cane from behind the chaise and handed it to Sarah Courtney. "Here you are. You can see I've already done my bit from the stripes across his ass. Don't bother tryin' to hit between them."

She took the cane almost reluctantly, as she was repelled by it. Gillmore turned obligingly with his bottom towards her, his head still hanging down.

"Go on, Sarah. Just remember what he did to you with one of those after you pleaded with him not to leave any marks. He didn't care, did he? He didn't give a shit if he left marks. No. He *wanted* to leave them, Sarah, to prove he was king of the earth. To prove you were garbage. Now, you don't have to do

474

it. But I'm offerin' you the chance. OK? Remember who he is. Remember what he did."

Sarah Courtney sat in silence for a few moments, and as she thought, her knuckles grew white on the cane. She suddenly lashed out at the scrawny little bottom. Then she hit him again. She stood up, knocking over the cup of tea, which broke on the saucer. The cane came down again and again as Gillmore squirmed and tried to hold still for the thrashing. Finally she threw the cane away, sat back in the chair and put her face into her hands.

"I don't like doing things like that," she muttered.

"Yeah, I felt a little sorry for him at first," Corky said as she sat back down on the chaise. "Then I kinda got mad at myself. He was never sorry for me. That wasn't why he stopped makin' me crawl around to lick his ass, or whippin' me with one of those things. It's because he wanted somethin' else outta me. He wanted my *love*. But he wants it like he wants another newspaper as a trophy to hang on his wall. He wants a love robot."

Sarah shook her head incredulously. "But how did it happen? How did the tables turn? Why? It's astonishing."

"'Cause the little man met his fuckin' match, honey! He's desperate for me, for my body. He wants to possess me now, and I won't even let him touch me. That makes it worse. The more he cain't have it, the more he wants it. Come here, boy, I want to put my feet up."

Gillmore obediently crawled over and turned sideways to the chaise. She swung her legs to the top of his back. "Look at him. He's tryin' to look up my dress." She threw her head back and laughed.

Sarah Courtney joined her on the chaise, shaking her head. "You are an original, Corky. But tell me, what are those things, there, that he has on. Down there." She pointed.

Corky told her briefly about her experiences in the Interrogation Room and the horror of the electrical devices. Then she explained the cage around his testicles and the restrainer. "I also thought I'd give him a taste of wearin' high heels around all day, since he loves 'em so much."

475

Her friend nodded briskly. "Now that, *that* I can completely agree with." She spotted the cup and saucer on the floor and leapt up. "Oh, I completely forgot. I've made a mess here."

"Siddown, sister." Corky swung her legs back onto the chaise. "Clean it up, Harv. You can scrub the carpet later. We'll want to have lunch soon, so call us when it's ready."

Gillmore picked up the fragments and left the room quietly.

Sarah Courtney fanned herself with her hand, rolling her eyes at the ceiling. "Wow. What a change. The last time I saw you, you were chained to the sofa on the Matilda, tied and gagged. I was sure something dreadful was going to happen to you, and when I got back to London I managed to find the two men we met there. They went charging off to rescue you." She laughed. "Obviously it was Gillmore who needed rescuing."

Corky shook her head. "Goddammit, there were times I felt I wasn't gonna make it. I crawled around in this padded cell lookin' for somethin' sharp to kill myself with. I was most near turned inside out, honey. There are things," she waved her hand as if fending away a thought, "there are things you just don't wanna see, except maybe once in a lifetime. That's enough. What surprised me was the realisation that the bad is so close to the good, the clean to the dirty, the warm to the cold. Even life to death. All so close, so near. The hag sits on the same throne as the goddess. I never knew that stuff before, and I reckon I could do without knowin' it now, seein' what I had to go through to learn it."

Courtney pointed her finger at the doorway. "But look at him now. You won the battle of wills. You broke him."

"To be absolutely honest, it wasn't a battle of wills. If it was, I wouldn't have won it." She held up her hand. "No. No, I mean it. One thing about Harvey Gillmore is he's got a will of iron. He's completely *obsessive*. And *that* was where I won, honey. Yeah. I tapped into that obsession. I diverted the river, and he just flooded all over me." She leaned forward with a slight smile and raised eyebrow. "He cain't think of anything but screwin' me, and I won't let him, so he just keeps chasin' his tail, round and round in circles. If you want the absolute truth, Harvey Gillmore's brain is wrapped loose."

476

"I beg your pardon?"

"He's a half bubble out of plumb. Crazy. Yet he's the billionaire, while normal people like us scratch for chickenfeed in front of somebody else's henhouse. Now, I don't know a thing about psychology, and don't want to, but it's a screwy world that puts the lunatic in charge of the insane asylum. Which is what we got here. Look at all those men back on that fuckin' boat. Not one of 'em comes within eight grades of bein' normal. Yet between 'em they probably got enough money to pay off the debts of a couple of good-sized countries. You got Harv here with a roof that isn't nailed on tight. There's ole Hercules, my dearest, who basically made his dough by accident, buyin' and sellin' at the right time and place. Otherwise he's just a simple-minded redneck who would be better off pushin' wheelbarrows of dirt back and forth for a landfill company. Even that guy Regis isn't smart..."

Sarah shook her head. "Now I think you're wrong there..."

"...no, I'm not wrong. He's got the same mentality as a Southern evangelist who doesn't believe a thing he's sayin' about God and the Bible, but says it so convincingly he's got everybody with their hands in the air sayin' 'hallelujah' while he's got *his* hands in the pockets of the men and the panties of the women. He gets richer and he gets laid while they get poorer and pregnant. He cain't fool me with that fancy accent, honey. I've seen his type before. I may not know much, but one thing I *do* know, is men. There have been those who've fooled me, but not for more'n about ten minutes, max. I don't know the rest of those guys on the boat very well, but let me tell you, there's not one of 'em I'd trust to run a bath, never mind a company or a country."

"Well, they're clever enough to fool me."

Corky held up a finger. "Only if you don't look at 'em closely. Now you got some experience in this. You tell me if any of 'em ever let you get that close. Close enough to look. Really look."

She thought for a moment. "Certainly not Michael. I doubt anyone has got close to him..."

"And why? Why? *Because there's nothing there to see.* That's why. He's like a ball with a clever design to make it look solid. But when you let the air out of it, it just lays on the ground like a cow pat. They look important, they dress important, they talk important. So folks think they *are* important. I'll tell you, the only men who impress me are the ones who are easy in themselves, relaxed enough to show you anything you wanna see, and I'll tell you, honey, the ones like that I've met I can count without usin' all the fingers of one hand."

She leaned forward on her elbows. "But Corky, don't you think that destroys a little of the mystery about men? About people?"

"Hell no. There's plenty of natural mystery there, if they're normal and not tryin' desperately to hide it. Little funny surprisin' bits. Odd bits. Contradictory bits. There's acres there."

"Tell me about the ones you have met. The men who are relaxed in their mystery."

"Come to think of it, I don't even need any fingers. Cain't think of one. So if I cain't find the right one, I might as well use men to please me. 'Cause they have it the other way around most of the time, right?"

"Well, all the time, as far as I'm concerned."

"I gotta watch myself with Harv, though. Got a lotta poison in him. The water's not deep, but there are some tricky currents."

She laughed suddenly. "I just remembered somethin' back at school. I was kinda precocious in the upper storey. You know, my tits started to grow big kinda early, and this huge boy who used to terrify everybody on the playground sneaked up behind me and grabbed 'em. Two big handfuls. I didn't slap him when I turned around. Instead, I grabbed *his* – his balls. And held on. I could feel in my hand that I had the whole shootin' match there. He screamed, and he threatened and he hauled off as to hit me, but I kept a good hold. I made the bastard apologise to me right there in front of all the kids gathered around, and then I made him apologise to all the other girls he had been grabbin'. And I tell you, honey, that was the

478

end of him. He was no more problem at all. The *problem* was that none of the other boys would come near me after that. So I developed the habit of goin' for them. I'd pick me one out to go to the prom or the football game, and then he'd be as surprised as hell when I drug him into the back seat of the car after the game and screwed his handsome ass off."

"Oh, I was nothing like that," Sarah Courtney said. "I like a good time, and I just drifted. My family does have some money, but I had a great row with them because I didn't want to be a doctor or solicitor or accountant - or at least to marry someone who was. I wanted to do something on my own alright, but I could never find anything I wanted to do. You understand? I was drawn to the bright lights and the bright sparks, anything to lower the boredom threshold. But when you look behind all the glitter you find little nuggets like Gillmore. Or Regis, for that matter."

"Come in, boy!" Corky shouted at him.

Gillmore entered. The apron was a little crooked, and there were a few stains on it already. His stockings sagged at the knees. He looked up at the ceiling. "Would the ladies like another tea or coffee?"

CHAPTER TWENTY SIX

Sam Bernstein sat at the wheel of his car in a layby, staring out the windshield. He could just see the old asylum surrounded by a crumbling wall on the hilltop and looked again at his watch. Another half hour to wait, but it was better arriving early and waiting than arriving late and rushing things. Raul Dominguez sat beside him in the passenger seat. The Cuban did not talk much, and that suited Bernstein. He was glad finally to have a good man with him, though. A man he could brief, a man who listened carefully and asked the right questions, a man who could act on his own without supervision and not make a fool or a corpse of himself. Bernstein had been involved in the early recruitment of Direct Action, and most of the recruits were flotsam washed to him from other armies, principally from Israel and South Africa. There were also British, Dutch, Belgium and French mercenaries. Of the lot, the Israelis and the Brits were the best, but that wasn't saying a lot. None of them were real quality. Most were thugs or goons looking for a chance of a little violence. There were plenty of violent people in the world but few who could focus it to a pinpoint for the instant it was needed. Those ruled by violent emotions were simply useless. And most of the DAs were useless, he had to admit that. It was Bernstein who organised this flotsam into three and four man teams with the best man leading. Three or four represented a good number for kidnap, hits and intimidation. Three teams together, and you were up to squad strength, usually enough for anything they were likely to encounter. He had meant to build up a flexible force, able to react quickly and efficiently, yet not too large to attract attention. Three or four men could move from country to country a lot more easily than larger units.

Bernstein sucked a tooth and looked up at the sky. Overcast, but no rain. Warm, though. He rolled his window down and rested his elbow on the door. Well, he had done his best with what material he had been able to recruit. They were successful enough until they hit real opposition. And opposition was growing in several countries, not just the UK, as people became slowly aware of the nature of the forces against them. The development of the DA groups was a final stage of the plans, as he understood them. First there was economic pressure, built up through alliances with transnational companies. This economic pressure found an ideology which naturally expressed its interests, and then political alliances were made in country after country. It proceeded like an infection. Beginning in America it spread first to Britain and from Britain to the continent - and of course to many of the former colonies scattered around the world. It was a bit like AIDS, Bernstein thought. The disease was passed from one person, one country, to another but then spent a dormant phase as it slowly undermined the natural defence systems of governments. It was funny how something in the microcosm of nature often reflected the macrocosm of society. Ah, well, that stuff was too deep for him anyway.

Haug thoroughly unsettled him. Last year Haug and his men had defeated a whole squad of DAs. Fairly and squarely. Bernstein's men had been out-manoeuvred, out-thought and out-fought. And Bernstein spent a month in hospital with a badly broken leg. But it wasn't that defeat so much as the recent encounter. *Honour*, for chrissake! He was almost embarrassed, but he knew the American really meant it. It was partly the mention of the Holocaust which really shook his columns. Because, what the hell was he doing with his life but helping to set up a newer and bigger and more efficient system for the same kinds of madmen. What was the result going to be? He was not so stupid he couldn't think it out, look at the logic of it. A systematic creation of two or three tiers of human beings. So who was going to draw the short straw this time? The Jews again? The blacks? The poor? All of them? Did it matter? Well, it didn't matter until he started thinking about it. Since his early idealism, since all that was shattered, he considered himself firmly non-political. Fuck all the systems, and fuck the people who run them. Make himself a few bucks here and there by using the only skills he had, and, if he made it to old age, buy a house somewhere away from all other human beings so he could stare out at the ocean. Or the desert. He hadn't decided which yet.

And here he was, switching sides. In an instant. For less money and certainly for a less sure thing. It became clear to him when he was pointing the pistol at Haug's head, the night before last. In an instant. OK, if it was impossible to be non-political, then why should he help build the ovens again, whoever was going to be shoved inside this time?

Ever since he had moved to Israel from New York when he was a teenager, all he could remember was fighting. Training and fighting. From a starry-eyed idealist he slowly descended into the sewer, finally reaching his nadir as an Arab hunter for Shin Bet, renowned for peeling the skin from the soles of Arab feet to extract confessions from screaming men and women whom he later shot. Whether they confessed or not. Bernstein clearly remembered the sensations. The more vicious he became, the easier it was to be cruel - a never ending spiral. For years he was quite unaware of his conscience, if he had one at all.

Then there was the battle with Haug in Cornwall last year. That's when it all began, wasn't it? The two of them had faced off without weapons, two warriors, both of them past their best days. At that moment, he recognised in Haug something of himself. He looked into the man's eyes and saw a fighter, a man who would stand and defend until he died. There weren't many people like that. Bernstein had only met a few in his life. Most "hard" men played games, put up fronts, then ran like hell when faced with real danger. He had hit Haug with his best shots, only to discover it made his enemy stronger. That's what it was. Both men carried a furnace of anger deep inside, an anger emerging from some unmentionable hell.

Despite the breeze through the window, Bernstein realised he was sweating and got out his handkerchief. Raul Dominguez hardly moved a muscle and seemed relaxed and calm. "How come you're in this shitty business? What demons are you carrying around?"

The Cuban turned and looked at him. "Only the demons of failure, señor."

Bernstein laughed shortly and looked out the window at the road. There were not many cars passing. Local traffic, he assumed. "Yeah. Couldn't put it better myself."

"I think," said Dominguez, "that we are nearly the same age, and both of us may have seen many things. I failed as a person to be what I wanted, and many things I believed in have failed. When I was young, most things seemed possible. Now most seems impossible. Also when I was a boy I thought I could make things happen. Now I realise I am a straw in the wind."

"A fine way to express it. Yeah. Yeah. A straw in the wind. The mighty forces around us bang together, and the dead fall out like dust. Nobody gives a shit. The mighty forces just keep moving on relentlessly. I thought you were certain of things, like Haug."

"I am certain of very little, señor. Haug is not so certain, either. Big emotions burn inside him, though, and all the heat makes him seem certain."

"Why are you doing the job, then? If you're not certain."

Dominguez smiled. "If I had to wait for certainty, I would sit like a stone without even eating, señor. So I move towards what seems best. Cuba also. We tried to move for something better than what we had, tried to make a path through the wilderness where there was no path before. At first we had friends. Now we have no friends, only enemies."

"That's what I used to think about Israel. It's funny. It seemed new and real, and everybody's shoulder was against the wheel, pushing. Then the wheel began to move out of control and crushed everything out of us."

"Hope is new, experience is old, maybe. But I still have hope, señor. I have hope some day so many will not have to be poor in order that so few are rich. Perhaps we do not have exactly the right way in Cuba, but we try."

Bernstein shrugged. "When dog eats dog, some dogs are eaten, and some are fat."

"A sad way to live, though. There are better ways, if we want to find them. The more we try, though, the harder it is to win. The fat dogs don't want to lose weight."

Bernstein glanced at his watch again. It was nearly time. "So, tell me something, Raul. Why the hell did I change sides when the fat dogs are clearly going to win?"

"I don't know you well, señor. In many ways you are like Haug, but it is difficult to see you at times. I think often the romantic wears the mask of the cynic to disguise himself from himself. Sometimes it is difficult to admit you are tender and feel pain."

Bernstein started the car, looked back to see a clear road and pulled out of the layby. "Tender, eh? Tender?" He laughed out loud.

* * *

To Haug, Regis' house looked like a mansion. There were three floors and two wings. The circular drive outlined a reflection pool with a fountain in the middle. The pickup was stopped at the gates by a heavyset man in a suit. Two others stood at the sides, alert. After taking their names, the heavyset man used his mobile phone to talk to the house. There was a brief conversation, and Haug was asked his name again. The heavyset man was unsmiling behind his dark glasses.

"You want me to spell if for you, bo? Or rap it out on top of your head with my knuckles?"

The man moved closer to the window, a sneer developing on his lips. "You say your name is Haug? That right?"

Haug suddenly grabbed the man's dark tie and yanked his head inside the cab. He pulled down sharply so the door caught his windpipe. Then he pushed up hard, and the back of the man's head banged on the top of the open window. With his other hand he pulled off the man's dark glasses and placed his own nose directly in front of the dazed man's face.

"That's right, bo. Haug. Remember it." He let go the tie and, as the man sagged away from the pickup door, he crushed the sunglasses in his hand, tossing the fragments out the window. "Only Americans can wear shades on cloudy days, and you don't qualify." Letting out the clutch, Haug went through the open gate, spraying gravel backwards towards the three guards.

485

Sir Jonathan Mainwaring cleared his throat. "Was that absolutely necessary?"

"Bet your ass it was," Haug said. "It gives him some necessary information about us. I was usin' a form of communication you might not understand. But he did."

"It did have a kind of rudimentary jungle logic to it," said Ewan Thomas from the back seat.

"It's not that I felt any sympathy for the man," Mainwaring replied. "It just does not seem the right way to begin what are certain to be rather difficult negotiations."

Haug was looking at the cars parked beside the house. There was a Range Rover, and a Bentley peeped from the portico. Parked well away from the drive were two large vans with windows. There were two more guards standing by the doorway. These, too, were dressed in dark suits.

"I wonder where he got the money to buy all this?" Haug asked sarcastically.

"Various Middle Eastern and South American despots, I should think," Mainwaring murmured as they got out of the pickup.

Michael Regis was standing in the doorway looking immaculate with his hands clasped in front of him, a half smile on his otherwise immobile face.

"Surprised to see me, Regis?" Haug shouted to him as the three of them walked towards the door.

"Should I be?" Regis replied, raising one eyebrow.

"Well, I would be if I were you," Haug said. "If I'd paid a lotta money to have a man killed, I wouldn't want his ghost showin' up on my doorstep a couple of days later."

Regis looked past Haug to the other two guests. "I don't have the slightest idea what you're talking about. Hello, Sir Jonathan. Professor Thomas. I was expecting to see General Portland as well."

Mainwaring's face was set in granite. "I am not in the mood for idle pleasantries, Regis. Nor do I care for any pretences of civility. Will you be good enough to show us in?"

"I'm afraid I am going to have to ask you to open your briefcases for Peter and William." Regis glanced at the one in

486

Haug's hand. "A little out of place as a fashion accessory for a thug, I should think."

Peter and William moved forward. They were near clones of the heavyset man at the gate, except both had closely-cropped hair.

Haug was shaking his head. "We're not openin' our briefcases, Regis. Not for you or for Peter or William."

Michael Regis shrugged. "I'm afraid I'm going to have to insist."

Peter and William moved to each side of Haug. Peter reached for the briefcase. As he reached, Haug brought the case up with great force. It smashed directly into Peter's face, and the man dropped to his knees, holding both hands over his wrecked features. William backed off slowly, his hand snaking inside his jacket.

Haug advanced on the retreating guard. "If he pulls a gun outta there, Regis, I'm gonna kill him. Up to you."

"It's alright, William," Regis said, turning to Haug. "Why do you object to opening your briefcases, Mr Haug? Is it because you have brought weapons? Or perhaps a bomb?"

Haug took a step towards Regis. "It's none of your goddamn business whether we're armed or not."

"We have no bombs," Mainwaring said. "And to my knowledge we are not armed."

Regis smiled pleasantly. "Then why not open your cases?"

"We will be happy to open our briefcases, Regis," Mainwaring replied, "if you are prepared to let us examine the contents of your office and browse through your files."

Regis turned to William, who still stood with his hand inside his jacket. "Peter seems to be bleeding badly. Help him to the kitchen and, if necessary, call a doctor. If you gentlemen will follow me." He moved smoothly towards the door, and the three men followed him into the house.

As William helped, Peter staggered to his feet. His nose was completely demolished, and a row of shattered teeth protruded from his nearly severed bottom lip.

Haug studied the layout of the room carefully before selecting a seat. It was very elegant-looking, and he was unsure

487

whether to call it a living or reception room. Or maybe even a library. Half of one wall was lined with bookshelves filled with leather-bound books. Two of the other walls and the other half of the library wall were covered with gilt-framed oil paintings. Haug was uncertain of the provenance of the paintings but guessed they were early 18th century. Three large floor-to-ceiling windows were spaced along the outer wall, which looked out on the reflection pool. Royal blue curtains hung to the sides of the windows. The room was longer than it was wide with high ceilings trimmed with gilt mouldings. The furniture varied, but all of it looked extremely expensive and old. A long teak table had been placed in the centre of the room, and it was surrounded with chairs. The five places at one end already had neat piles of paper and files. There were only three places at the other end, and two decanters of water had been put out for the opposing sides, surrounded by crystal glasses.

Haug considered a number of alternatives. There were two double doors opening into the room at each end. For a moment he was tempted to push a heavy armchair against one of them and sit in it so any entry would have to be made from the other end. Then he dismissed that as being too obvious - and too aggressive at this stage.

"I reckon I'll take General Portland's chair, bo," he said to Regis, "since you didn't seem to expect me."

Regis turned to him and smiled. "Please. Choose any chair you wish, Mr Haug."

He walked to the other end of the room and opened the door. A moment later Dr Carlton Fine entered, followed by Hercules DeLoop, Alexander Hinkley and Wren Olsen. The two sides stared at each other expressionlessly until Regis introduced everyone. Finally they all sat, the two groups facing each other.

Haug dragged over a more comfortable-looking easy chair. He sat back from the table facing the windows in a position where he could cover both doors. The others were already seated. He was not happy with the position, but he didn't expect any trouble during the opening session. He had noted a security camera above the rows of books and assumed the place was wired for sound as well. He placed his briefcase beside his right foot.

"Well," Regis said, spreading his hands, "at last we meet, though..."

"I find being in the same room with you distasteful," Mainwaring interrupted him. "Hence we will come directly to the point, shall we? In the first instance, I want your immediate assurance that our three associates are safe and have not been physically nor mentally abused."

Regis nodded as he poured himself a glass of water from the carafe. "All three are well, though Mr Tillson was slightly injured whilst resisting arrest."

Mainwaring raised an eyebrow. "Arrest? Surely the word you want is 'abduction', or perhaps 'kidnap'. Arrest implies *legal* restraint."

"Indeed," Regis replied. "Which is why I used it."

Sir Jonathan Mainwaring sat upright and still. His long bony hands gripped the arms of his chair. He was still pale, but his eyes were piercing and unblinking. "Your choice of words is as loose as your reasoning. And you have not yet answered my question fully. Are they now or have they been mistreated at the hands of morally depraved doctors and hoodlums?"

Regis took a sip of water. "I think you'll find my answer was complete. I said they were well. They have suffered no ill-treatment and are being held in comfortable cells."

"And does that include Mrs Templer?" Haug asked abruptly.

"Of course." Regis turned back to Mainwaring as he glanced at his watch. "This meeting should be quite short and straightforward, really. What we require from you is this. The so-called UnitedOpposition must be immediately disbanded." He accepted a file handed to him by Dr Fine. "I have a statement here which must be signed by you before you leave this house. Another copy will be immediately taken to all members of the United Opposition, not just the committee heads, to be endorsed by them as well. Then, and only then, will your associates be released unharmed. The statement is a confession of all conspiracies to date with a codicil list of crimes committed by members of your illegal group. The codicil will be kept as a secret protocol unless further attempts are made against us or against the State, at which point you will be hunted down, arrested, charged with the crimes and conspiracies and brought to trial. It is, I am afraid, a simple choice, Sir Jonathan. Negotiation is useless and a waste of time."

Mainwaring rested his elbows on the arms of his chair and tented his fingers. "And what are you threatening, legally or otherwise, if we refuse to comply?"

"Your three colleagues will be destroyed," Regis replied evenly. "Slowly destroyed, I might add. I'm sure from your own experiences you may be able to extrapolate from that. In addition, the three of you will be restrained and eventually taken to join them. Are you familiar with a medical operation known as lobotomy?"

"Yes, indeed," said Mainwaring. "I also know the meaning of criminal insanity and find myself in the outrageous position of having to negotiate with psychopaths."

Regis smiled thinly. "As I believe I said before, negotiation is neither necessary nor possible."

Mainwaring remained still as a statue. "Let me be absolutely clear on these issues which have been inadequately presented by you. Having kidnapped three of our colleagues whilst making failed attempts against two others, you now presume to hold them to ransom for this country."

Regis, Fine and Hinkley all started to speak at once, but Mainwaring overrode them. "Do allow me to finish. I note that two of your colleagues are Americans..."

"...and so, indeed, is one of yours," Regis managed to squeeze in.

"He is an American resident of this country and subject to the laws of parliament, unlike Dr Fine, Mr Olsen and Mr DeLoop, who are only visitors. You, Michael Regis and Alexander Hinkley, are traitors to the Crown who conspire with foreign nationals to subvert the interests of this country and the sovereignty of parliament through bribery, menaces, economic and physical threat, blackmail and the organisation of private armies, funded primarily through illegal arms trade and profits earned through the illicit sale of opiate drugs. It takes my breath

490

away to be accused of crime by such moral filth as you. And, in answer to your 'simple' question, I would draw your attention to the even simpler fact that I have no authority either to sign or negotiate any petition for the release of the hostages on behalf of my country. You will have to approach the prime minister, perhaps through the foreign minister, or the Queen for that."

"In the circumstances, your signature will be quite adequate." Regis drank a little more water from his glass.

Alexander Hinkley was fidgeting, and his face was blotted in places with colour. "One moment, Michael. I'm afraid I am simply not accustomed to being called a traitor by a bureaucratic civil servant obviously on the make for political power..."

Mainwaring turned his unblinking eyes toward the man. "Surely something else I said upset you as well, Professor Hinkley. Do you or do you not obtain funds from the illicit sale of arms and drugs?"

Hinkley threw his head back and adjusted his glasses. "We obtain our funds from many sources, and I understand donations are..."

"If you deny it," said Mainwaring, "then you are a practiced liar as well as a traitor."

Dr Carlton Fine slammed his hand on the table. "Look here, Mainwaring. Your insults don't mean a damn thing. You're washed up, and you know it. Your back's to the wall, and you don't have any options anymore. I advise you to sign the paper and shut up."

"I presume I am now addressing the organ grinder and not his monkeys," Mainwaring said evenly. "So that is some progress. Have you already nominated yourself as Fuhrer of the comically named Community of Association? And have you told the English traitors who are your fawning admirers that they will simply be following orders as they goose step to the tune you are whistling?"

"Is this asshole callin' us Nazis?" DeLoop rumbled.

Fine's voice was strong and emphatic. "Our organisation is *completely* democratic, Mainwaring. If time permitted, I would explain the whole thing to you in words you could understand. This is nearly the twenty first century now, and economics is the

491

dominant force in the world today. Any fool can see that. Your old-fashioned ideas don't apply anymore. It is now necessary to have all countries - all major countries - economically coordinated in order that growth can continue. Transnational companies have grown across borders, reaching out branches to drop their fruit for millions of citizens of the world. We - the political structure - must be the democratic instrument of this economic growth..."

Professor Ewan Thomas leaned forward on his elbows. "Are you saying economics determine the nature of a democracy?"

Hinkley smiled smugly. "Of course we are. And in that, we are surely not far off the Marx, you know." He laughed alone at what he thought was a joke.

"Oh, you're nearly as far from Marx as you are from democracy," Thomas assured him quietly. "Democracy is a complex idea, and certainly one worth trying."

"Come to America, then," DeLoop growled, "and you'll see what it looks like."

Ewan Thomas smiled benignly. "In America you have virtually the same structural system as we have here. The differences are basically in terms of land, population and natural resources. Both governments serve the interests of one group of people at the expense of others, thus neither are democracies."

Hinkley laughed again, this time patronisingly. "Professor Thomas, I will draw your attention to the simple fact that all citizens in both countries are franchised for the vote and completely free to vote for any party or any individual they choose. Evidently you are unfamiliar with that definition of democracy."

Thomas spread his hands. "Who can they vote for? Only the major parties, otherwise a vote is wasted. What is the fundamental ingredient of a major party? Finance. The finance is provided by whom? Largely it is provided by the only institutions capable of long term support: large companies. Are large companies going to contemplate support of parties which have policies contrary to their interests? Well, no, obviously."

"Oh, come on," Fine said contemptuously. "You got the Labour Party here, and that's supported by the big unions."

"There is the Labour Party," admitted Thomas with a shrug. "They continue to survive with financial support from union contributions. I will point out two things here. It is much, much less in total than business support for the Conservatives - or the Republicans in America. In fact it is, by comparison, minuscule. But it is enough to scare hell out of the business community and their politicians. Which is why there has been a general attack upon the unions both here and in the States. To weaken the support. To return to the old system of two virtually identical parties, both supported by financial institutions, which is to say, in effect, one party and one party only. A *democratic* system would, by definition, have to be one where the pressure came from the grassroots, the people. Not from the top. Or the middle."

Michael Regis sighed. "I believe we are drifting from the point of this meeting..."

"Just a moment, Michael," Hinkley said, agitated. "This is important. Professor Thomas, please understand that *economics* affects *all* the people..."

"...but only some of the people benefit from the economic system..."

"...and the economy must be directed towards fulfilling the hopes and aspirations of all the people. *That* is the purpose of our Community of Association. Only by the growth of business and technology can millions upon millions of people hope to be free from the economic shackles binding them to poverty. The only way to raise the standard of living is through economic growth."

"Of course that is your point of view, Professor Hinkley, but please do not call it democratic. Combined with your supranationalistic genetic ideas, it is more akin to what used to be known as National Socialism, commonly called fascism. In other words, the financial institutions and economic interests install an executive to ensure the bonding of the large body of people necessary to enforce expansion."

"I really must interrupt this absorbing conversation," Regis said with considerable determination. "We are some distance from our agenda..."

493

"I gotta question for you, bo," Haug said. Everyone turned to look at him as he leaned back in his chair and crossed his legs. "You say that if we sign that piece of paper, you're gonna let us all go back home, and you're gonna release the hostages, right?" He stopped for a moment as Regis nodded. "Well, what I'm wonderin', is why would you do that? You see, I've been thinkin'. You got us trapped in here with I don't know how many goons outside, and the gates are shut, and there's a wall around the place. Now, it appears to me that it would be a lot easier for you guys to just do what you threatened to do if we *don't* sign. That is, haul us up to wherever you're holdin' our friends, then get your doctor friends to saw through our brains. You could then show those papers to anybody who's interested and say we're basically crazy anyway, so you had our brains sawed apart and put us away for our own protection. You might even do it through some court, so it would seem legal to anybody who didn't look too close. Tie it up with pink ribbons, that sort of thang."

Regis smiled pleasantly. "You are very distrustful, aren't you, Mr Haug?"

"Comes from a lifetime of dealin' with bandits."

"Well," said Regis evenly, "I don't even think it deserves a reply."

"I do," Mainwaring said quickly. "His reasoning is sounder than your rejection of it. After all, you lured us here under false pretences, assuring me that you wished to negotiate the release of the hostages. Then virtually the first thing you say is there is to be no negotiation. Instead, you present your terms and demands and insist they be implemented. I therefore demand an answer to Haug's question before we proceed any further."

Regis turned his head to look out the window. "And I have a question for you, Sir Jonathan. You advised me General Portland would attend this meeting, yet he is not here. Instead he is now meeting with the Defence Minister. Exactly what is the topic of their discussion?"

* * *

494

General Sir Timothy Portland watched Norman Stone writhe uncomfortably in the chair behind his desk. He did not think he was suitable to deal with such a man. Mainwaring would have been so much better. But it was impossible to obtain an appointment yesterday. It was nearly impossible today or any day for the next six months. A government minister's diary is usually completely filled, and it was only because of the pressure brought by Mainwaring that an hour was found somewhere in the day. That somewhere was exactly the same time as he should have been taking part in the negotiations with Michael Regis. Those negotiations worried him. His advice had been to seek a neutral ground for the meeting, but Regis carried the whip in this one. He had the hostages. So they had reluctantly agreed the venue.

He was considerably relieved Haug was able to go along in his place. A fine man to have around in an emergency, even if he was American. Obviously the American Forces were capable of producing at least one good soldier who depended more on his wits and initiative than on firepower and technology. Ideally such men should be officers, but the demands of class dictated their highest rank as NCOs. Well, as he had said many times before, it was NCOs who ran the army. Without them, the best general in the world might as well retreat or surrender.

"This is...very interesting material," Stone said uncertainly. He had a fine head of hair, now going white and cut unfashionably long and brushed back. It was cut long because of Stone's vanity. He was a good-looking man, even in late middle age. His body was trim and fit, and he was tall and seemed robust. His body belied his mind, however. Though he was a quick thinker, his only attraction to a principle of any sort was how useful it might be to him, personally or politically.

Stone laid his half-glasses aside and rubbed his eyes. "To whom have you shown this material?"

Portland told him. "Because of the increasing violence of attacks," he continued, "we are now forced to reveal the nature of the conspiracy to a wider body."

Stone held up his hand as he spun his large leather chair to the side so Portland could appreciate his profile. "Obviously it

495

must be kept under wraps, Timothy. We wouldn't want this splashed all over the tabloids one morning, would we? Unknown consequences."

"Oh, I agree, Norman. Yet that is exactly what is beginning to happen, isn't it? The chaos is spreading, and soon it will be out of control. If we act sharply, however, the genie may yet remain in the bottle. From my own perspective, it would be a mistake for you now to introduce this evidence at a Cabinet meeting. Firstly because we know for certain that two of their ilk are directly involved - in the Exchequer and Home. Secondly because it increases the likelihood of leaks."

"Well, I must inform James," Stone said, still gazing out the window. James Wharton was the Prime Minister. "That is obvious."

"I will have to leave that to your discretion," Portland replied. "It does, however, deserve some thought. I've met the PM but do not know him personally. He does have a reputation for weakness and indecision, though."

The Defence Minister spun his chair back to face the General, looking at him from under his bushy eyebrows. "What would *you* suggest I do, Timothy?"

Portland got up from his chair and walked over to the window. "I realise you will be looking at this from a political point of view. Taken from a logical viewpoint, however, what must be done is this. Presuming you agree this corruption and betrayal must be opposed, we cannot simply try and suppress it by brute force. That would threaten to tear the fabric of our society apart. On the other hand, they cannot be allowed enough growth to sweep our whole system of government into the dustbin. This is the conundrum. Therefore the only alternative is to seek a kind of truce, pushing the whole problem over to you politicians. Now that we know they exist and know their motives and most of their principal recruits, it should be theoretically possible to contain them - and perhaps even seal them off hermetically, I don't know. I would think even their side might see a standoff to be the optimum compromise under the circumstances." He turned around to look at the Minister.

496

Stone spun his chair to the window so he was facing Portland. "In the meanwhile...?"

"In the meanwhile we need intervention, Norman. Adrian Chesterman at the Home Office, perhaps, that's up to you. A very quiet word in his ear explaining carefully the issues at stake here. We are convinced that Dr Carlton Fine is the real authority in the group. He remains in the shadows, but it is his decisions which seem to be implemented. If you approached Chesterman, Chesterman would go to Fine."

"Not Regis?"

Portland shook his head. "Regis is an apparatchik. A functionary. A salesman." He walked to the edge of Stone's desk and looked directly into his eyes. "We need something else as well. We need physical protection during the interval. I approached Commandant General Sessions, who rightly directed me to you."

The Defence Minister held up his hand again and swung back toward his desk. He was shaking his head. "I cannot allow that, and you know it, Timothy. Can you imagine the consequences? How could I possibly mobilise, say, a battalion of the Royal Marines to protect you from elements of the British police? Impossible. Unthinkable."

Portland walked back to his chair and sat down. "I am not so politically naive that I would suggest such a thing. However, the discreet presence of a few Marines here and there would surely make them take a step backward. Sessions would be certain to agree with that himself."

Stone was still shaking his head. "No. No, I don't think that is possible. No." Then he began nodding his head. "Yes, by all means I will approach Adrian. Not only will I approach him, but I will ensure that he knows this monstrous business must be brought to an immediate end. I am absolutely appalled by what has been happening, Timothy. Appalled!"

The General leaned forward, placing his hands on Stone's desk. "Perhaps you don't yet understand the danger we are in, Norman. I killed four men the other day, either Special Branch or members of their private army. They attacked me in my home. Three of our members - all of them MP's, one of them in

497

your own party - are being held, possibly being tortured, as hostages. Sir Jonathan Mainwaring, one of our most respected civil servants, was tortured and almost killed by them. They are vicious, unscrupulous pirates, and we are about to be overwhelmed. All I am asking is for two Royal Marine sentries at each household until you have talked some sense into Adrian Chesterman and he calls his hounds off."

But the Defence Minister was already shaking his head again. "Can't be done. I'm sorry, Timothy. It is political gelignite to set the unheard of political precedent of dispatching HM's Forces to settle a domestic problem."

"What about Northern Ireland?"

"That's different. Altogether different. If you need protection on the mainland, the police are the proper authority..."

"We don't want police protection," said Portland angrily. "Not now. Not since Humphries was murdered."

Norman Stone raised his eyebrows. "A suicide, I believe."

"No, he was murdered because he supplied bodyguards for Mainwaring. And because he gave Gordon Hastings a rocket."

"I see," Stone said moodily. He paused for a moment. "If you do not require police protection, then I'm afraid I can't help you. But then I wouldn't really worry." He smiled reassuringly. "I will speak to Adrian at my first opportunity. This evening, I hope. Surely you can all hold on until then?"

The Defence Minister got up briskly from his desk. The interview was over. He put his arm around General Portland's shoulders as he ushered him to the door. "We will have to talk further on this bizarre matter soon, Timothy. The PM will have to be told sooner or later, and so will Cabinet. That is the way a democracy works, eh?" He stopped and frowned suddenly. "But under no circumstances must this affair be allowed to leak out to the public. No telling *what* the consequences would be. God knows. So." He extended his hand at the door. "No word to anyone else, Timothy. Let's keep it contained, shall we? So glad you brought it to my attention."

As General Portland left the Defence Ministry he was thinking that at least he had been half successful. That is, if Norman Stone could be trusted. It was probably because he was

498

so preoccupied he didn't see the black Ford pull away from the kerb. In fact he only saw it at the last moment, just before it hit him. It was time enough to jump back - but not far enough. The left wing caught him on the hip, throwing him into the air. He landed on his shoulder and rolled with the force of impact as the Ford accelerated and disappeared into the traffic.

CHAPTER TWENTY SEVEN

"Why don't you like to be called Harv, Harv?" Corky asked as she stepped out of the bath. Gillmore was waiting with a large mustard-yellow bath sheet and began drying her body, beginning with neck and shoulders.

"I don't like Harvey, either. So it stands to reason I especially don't like the diminutive, ma'am."

She held her arms up so he could get the towel around them. "Why don't you like Harvey, Harv?"

"Because," he said finally, "my mother gave me the name. It was her idea, not my father's. Ma'am." His hands were trembling. He knew her breasts were next, but he tried not to rush drying the arms, the armpits and her back.

"You don't like women, do you?" Corky asked. She looked at their reflection in the big bathroom mirror. Gillmore had on his pink nylon apron. He was getting better moving about in his high heels, though. She had to lock them on with straps around his ankles, as he kept kicking them off when he was asleep.

He touched one breast with the towel and watched with fascination as it trembled. "I love..." He cleared his throat and tried to dry the slippery breast. "I love women. I just don't understand them, that's all."

"What's to understand, Harv? We're just like you. Stop shakin', will you? And don't linger so long on my tits. Just dry 'em off."

"Yes, ma'am." He finished the other one quickly, then moved the towel down to her belly. "Women aren't like men, not to me they're not. We're not built like this."

"No, you're built to fit, just like we are, stupid. I'm talkin' about minds, personalities." She put one foot up on the side of the bath so he could get between her legs.

He dried the thigh of her leg on the bath. "I'm sorry, Mrs DeLoop, but how can I think about minds and personalities when I'm doing this? It's crazy. It's crazy. It's crazy..."

Harvey Gillmore couldn't bear it any longer. Something snapped, and he dropped the towel and put his hand between her legs, feeling for a moment the softness and warmth and wetness from the bath water. Then something happened. He was suddenly sitting on the bathroom floor at least a yard from her feet. He shook his head to try and clear it before he realised she had slugged him on the jaw with her fist. A woman had knocked him down with her fist. Anger surged through his body, overpowering his reason. No one had hit him with their fists since he was an adolescent, and he had never been knocked down by a woman, ever. In a rage, he struggled to his feet and launched himself at the beautiful body in front of him, flailing his arms, trying to get to her.

She hit him in the stomach, and he sagged miserably to the floor gasping for breath.

"I don't need electricity," Corky snorted. "I can whip you with my bare hands, Harv."

"Damn you," he muttered, holding his stomach. "Damn you. You can't hit me like that and get away with it..."

"Cain't I?" she asked, then reached down and grasped a handful of hair, tugging upward. "You've been abusin' women all your life, haven't you, Harv? Talk to me, you little bastard."

"Let go my fucking hair!" he screamed. "I want out of this. I don't want to do it anymore. I want to go back to my office. Let go of me."

She slapped his face so hard it stung the palm of her hand. Harvey Gillmore spun around and draped over the side of the bath. He shook his head to try and clear it again, then, without warning he rose and swung a haymaker which glanced off the side of Corky's head.

Her eyes blazed with anger, and her lips drew back across her teeth as she cracked a fairly good straight left jab to his jaw. She followed him as he staggered backwards, clumsy in his heels, and connected with a right hook. Gillmore skidded down to the floor on his hands and knees. A kick to his ribs turned him over on his back, and Corky leapt on him, straddling his body. He was semi-conscious and moaning, so she reached over into the bath, uncradling the shower attachment and turned on the

502

cold water tap. She directed the cold water into his face and
watched him splutter back to life. When he started hitting out
with his arms, she threw the shower back into the bath before
trapping his arms and leaning into his face.

She could see swelling under his left eye. "Don't you
understand, you little weasel? I don't care what you want! It's
not a game, Harv! Now answer my question. You have been
abusin' women all your life, right? Right?"

"I don't know what you mean," he cried. "What the fuck is
abuse?"

She freed one of his arms and immediately trapped it with
her knee so her hand was free. Then she slapped him hard on the
face. "This is abuse, Harv. That's what it's called. Only this
time, it's the other way around. And you don't like it, do you?
Do you?"

"No!" he squealed.

"Do you think *we* like it? Huh?"

"Yes! No! I don't fucking know!"

She put her face right in front of his. "Then take a fuckin'
guess, Harv!"

"You're hurting my arm with your leg."

She followed his face with her own as he squirmed. "So
what, you son of a bitch? I'm gonna hurt you a lot more before
I'm finished. I'm gonna break you. Ever heard that one before,
Harv?"

He started to cry softly, squeezing his eyes together.

Corky pulled back a little but still held onto his arms. He
was actually a weak little man, and she found it easy. "Now you
were gettin' along fine, Harv, and I even took you off your nice
drugs. And here you are rebellin' and tryin' to hit me."

"I didn't want to hit you," he blubbered. "I mean it. I didn't
really. I'm so fucking miserable, because I want you so much. I
really, really do, Cor...Mrs DeLoop. And you made me so mad
by hitting me. You beat me up."

"That's because I'm stronger than you are, you little twerp.
And why did you beat women up? Huh? Because you were
stronger, right? You had more money, more power. You forced
them. Force, that's what you're all about, isn't it? So you

503

understand what we're into here, right? You tried to force me, and you failed. We had a battle, and you lost."

He was still crying. "It was the first time...I ever lost. Ever."

"I didn't even have to use the electric box, Harv. I beat you physically. And mentally. Ever which way."

She stood up and placed one bare foot on his face. Pressing down with increasing force, she looked down at him. "Are you ever gonna try and hit me again?"

"No ma'am," he murmured from underneath her foot.

"Are you ever gonna touch me when I don't wanna be touched?"

His voice increased with alarm as the pressure increased. "No, ma'am."

Corky stopped the pressure but kept her foot in place. "You like bein' beaten, don't you? You like bein' helpless."

Harvey Gillmore didn't answer, and she took her foot away and looked at him, a smile spreading across her face.

"I know your secret," she said. "You *like* it."

She walked slowly and gracefully over to the chair in front of the makeup mirror. Turning it around, she sat down facing the wet and blubbering man on the floor and opened her legs wide.

"Look at me, Harv. This is what you wanted women to do, isn't it? Except this time you cain't touch, 'cause *I'm* in charge. I'm the engine, and you're the caboose. You follow where *I* go." She put the fingers of her right hand on her vagina and carefully parted the lips, stroking herself gently. "I'm gonna bring a black man in here soon, Harv." She watched his eyes widen in disbelief and horror. "Maybe tomorrow night or the next night. Whenever I want. He's gonna sleep with me, Harv. He's gonna play with this and my tits, and I'm gonna play with his dick. Then we're gonna fuck. I've already fucked him here, the first day. When you went to work. We did it on the kitchen floor."

As the images flickered through her head, her fingers moved faster and she felt the first wave coming. Throwing back her head, her left hand moved to her nipple, gently pinching and massaging. "Ah...ah..ah...ahhhhh. Oh, Harv, it was so *good*

504

havin' him inside me." Again she felt herself coming. "Ohhhh, ohhhhhh, ahhhh...Harv! Don't you wish...don't you wish you could fuck me like that? Huh?"

Looking over at the little man, she saw he was mesmerised like a rabbit caught in the headlights of a car. His eyes were wide and his mouth was open and dribbling saliva. Unconsciously his hands drifted down to his restraining harness, and he began to tug at the belt around his hips and then at the leather thongs trapping his penis.

"Get on your hands and knees, Harv, then crawl over here and give me some good head."

Gillmore was writhing on the bathroom floor when he heard the command, and immediately he struggled up on all fours. Not once had he taken his eyes off her. He was as riveted to the centre of her body as a demented miser ogling his carefully hidden hoard of gold.

"Tongue out, teeth in, like I've taught you, Harv," she said as his head approached and slid between her thighs. "Learn to do it right, and I might let you do it often, who knows?" She felt his tongue flicking inside her lips. "But it's when *I* want it, not when you demand it, right? With the black man, it's when *we* want it. That's how some normal people are, Harv. They do it when they *both* want it. You never learned to do it that way, so you have to do it this way. When *I* want it."

Her breath was coming in short gasps, and she stopped talking to enjoy the head. Gillmore's tongue still wasn't perfect. He was no artist, not yet, but he would do. She grabbed a handful of his hair again and began using his face and nose, up and down, as she ground her hips on the chair, clenching and unclenching his head with her thighs.

He continued to lick her after she came again, and she pushed his face away, staring down at him, trapping his eyes.

"You do like it, don't you?" she asked, her voice low. "You like bein' my slave, don't you, you little asshole?"

For a long time he didn't answer as she held his eyes mercilessly. Then his lips began to move. "It makes me feel...alive. Pain, frustration, hate, love, life. I'd never seen it like that...Mrs DeLoop."

"Are you going to be a good boy from now on? Not give me any trouble? Learn your role and live it? Do your best?"

"I'll try, ma'am," he muttered, finally dropping his eyes.

She got up and walked towards the door. "Clean up this mess, then. And do somethin' about your appearance. You look like a little sewer rat," she said as she left the bathroom.

Harvey Gillmore put his bruised cheek against the warm seat of her chair. He felt crushed.

* * *

Sam Bernstein stopped the car in front of the gate and waited for the guard to approach. It was one of his recruits, but he couldn't remember his name. The guard recognised him and smiled as he leaned forward with a kind of salute.

"Didn't know your were coming, Mr Bernstein."

"Open the gate," Bernstein ordered. "There's been a change in plans, and I'm in a hurry."

"Yes, sir," the guard replied as he walked towards the gatehouse. "But I'll have to call ahead and let them know who it is."

"Fine," Bernstein replied as he let off the handbrake and drove slowly through. He saw the guard using his telephone through the rearview mirror and turned his eyes to the building. Another two guards stood at the door, and they were armed with Koch and Heckler submachine guns slung across their chests. When he pulled up and stopped, he and Dominguez got out together, and he saw Harold Gassman coming through the front door as he retrieved his holdall from the back seat.

Gassman had his hand out and was smiling. "This is a pleasant surprise, Sam. What are you doing up here?"

Bernstein shook the hand and turned toward the Cuban. "This is Luis, head of Spanish operations. Good man."

Gassman shook hands with Dominguez and turned back to Bernstein. "Well, what can we do for you, Sam?"

"We've got a problem down south," he said as he walked towards the door of the asylum, "and we've come up in a rush. There's some information we need to squeeze out of these

506

bastards, and it's got to be done quickly while the negotiations are still going on. I don't think there'll be any problem, if you give me a hand."

Harold Gassman ran to keep up with the Israeli. "Sure, Sam. What do you need?"

Bernstein stopped inside the doors and looked at the two sets of stairs, thinking. Then he spoke decisively. "I want you to cuff the MP's and get them down here. The best thing would be for me to interrogate them on our way south. Luis could drive, if you've got a van..."

Gassman was holding up his hands and shaking his head. "Now that..I'm sorry, Sam, but I would have to hear from Regis on that one. That is a direct order. No release unless he calls and gives a code word. I'm sorry..."

Bernstein waved his hand dismissively. "It doesn't matter. In that case, herd them all into your most secure room, one with two outside walls, if possible. Regis is in the middle of the negotiations and can't be reached. I'll try and get the information here and phone through."

Gassman smiled. "Now, that we can do." He walked over to an internal phone and punched three numbers. He spoke softly into the phone and then hung up. "Won't be long. They're all on the same floor, and the guards are moving them now."

Bernstein fetched a cigarette packet out of his shirt pocket and shook one out. "Have you got sound and video?"

Gassman shrugged. "We've literally only just moved in here. We haven't even had time to give it a coat of paint. So, no, is the answer to your question. Afraid not."

"That's alright," Bernstein replied, lighting the cigarette and inhaling. He only allowed himself six a day now, down from a couple of packs. "I've got a recorder with me."

Gassman looked at the holdall. "And the kitchen sink from the size of the bag you're carrying."

"You know me, Harold. I carry my office with me. I'm not the sedentary type."

The older man sighed and ran his hand through thick hair. "Well, maybe you have time to talk to some of these men here,

507

the guards. You may not believe this, but I had to stop a couple of them from raping the lady MP."

Bernstein smiled grimly. "I believe it. I do my best, but you can't make silk purses out of sows' ears."

The internal phone buzzed, and Gassman picked it up and listened, then replaced it. "I'll show you up. Top floor."

Bernstein stubbed out his half-smoked cigarette into a plant pot before he realised it was plastic, and he and Dominguez followed Harold Gassman up the stairs.

The Israeli asked the guard for a duplicate key as he led them to the corner room at the end of the building. He pocketed the key and turned to Harold Gassman. "How do I get hold of you if I need something?"

"Bang on the door for the guard..." Gassman replied.

Bernstein waved his hand. "I don't want a guard. What I'm doing is highly confidential."

"...or there's a phone just there." He pointed to a recess at the end of the hall. "The number to push is double one. Anything you want, just ask. I may not have it, but I'll try and get it for you. OK?"

Gassman turned and retraced his steps back up the hallway followed by the guard. Bernstein got the key out of his pocket, listened for a moment for movement in the room, put the key in the lock and opened the door. He and Dominguez stepped quickly inside.

Matthew Tillson sat on a wooden chair. His left arm was in a splint and hung below his chest in a clean sling. Louise Templer and Stuart Easton were together at one of the windows, standing nearly shoulder to shoulder. All three stared at the two strangers with unsmiling faces.

Bernstein re-locked the door from the inside and put his holdall on the old chipped enamel table near the wash basin. Then he sat down in a bent chrome chair with an odd tilt to it, and, after a moment's hesitation, flicked out another cigarette.

"Smoking's bad for your health," said Easton.

Bernstein ignored him. After lighting up, he leaned forward on his elbows and took a long drag. Glancing around he saw Dominguez still standing near the door, quiet as usual.

508

"Well," said Louise, "you look important, if not intelligent. What's it to be this time? A kicking or an execution? Or a rape?"

"I answer to either Sam or Bernstein, take your pick. This is Raul Dominguez. I know who you are, so that's the introductions over with."

"How civilised," Tillson said sarcastically.

"Shut up and listen to me as carefully as you can. You are in big trouble here, and you won't be allowed to leave - at least not with your heads intact. I don't know personally whether they mean to snuff you or wheel you into the operating theatre to seriously re-wire your brains, but it will be one or the other." He stopped and took another drag on the cigarette.

They all started to speak at once, but Matthew Tillson jumped up from his chair. "You are threatening members of parliament..."

Louise Templer advanced on Bernstein, her forefinger out. "This has gone quite far enough, Sam or Bernstein. If anything happens to us, your whole organisation will be dismantled."

Stuart Easton hadn't moved from the window. "If you start murdering us, you will be risking what amounts to a civil war."

Bernstein laughed ironically. "Oh, no, they won't. You forget, Mr Easton, the degree of control they have over the apparatus of the State and the media. It may create a little stir, but it will all be swiftly swept into a corner while the TV plays soap operas and sport, and the newspapers report new sexual deviations of the Royal Family. You don't realise how easy all that is, and that was part of your problem all along."

Louise Templer folded her arms on her chest, a troubled look on her face. "Just a minute. You're saying 'they'. Not 'we'."

"That's right, Mrs Templer," the Israeli replied, blowing smoke away from her. "An asylum is an appropriate place for me right now, because I need my fucking head examined. Night before last I tried to assassinate Haug..."

They all moved forward in alarm as he stopped them with his hand. "It was the second time I've tried to kill him, and I've *never* been unsuccessful twice. To make a long story short, we declared a truce and bullshitted the rest of the night, drinking too much liquor. In your Christian terminology I had a kind of resurrection. Somewhere among the ashes inside I discovered an old piece of garbage that used to be a conscience. I guess you'd call it that, a conscience. Anyway, I never wanted to see it again, but there it was, still intact. More or less."

He got up and went to the basin, ran the tap and doused the stub of his cigarette. "So I was one of *them* but now, for my sins, I'm one of *you*. Dominguez here dropped from nowhere on the night I was trying to kill Haug and helped foul up my plans. And he helped give me my dose of ethics - and, believe me, I'd rather have a dose of the clap - which led to me offering my services."

Matthew Tillson sat back down in his chair. "It's impossible to believe, so it must be real."

Stuart Easton walked straight over from the window and offered his hand to Bernstein. "I'm afraid we're a little short of Christians here, but you're resurrection is welcome nonetheless."

Bernstein shook his hand then took Louise Templer's. "The bad news is that I don't give the whole operation a hell of a lot of hope. They've got more than twenty men here, and even if they're lousy fighters, they shouldn't have any problem taking out four men, one with a broken wing, and a woman."

"Are you planning on fighting your way out?" Easton asked.

"No. It all depends a lot on timing. Haug will be fighting his way *in*, and we'll be trying to hold this room until he gets here. *If* he manages to fight his way *out* of the place he's at now. He's a lucky son of a bitch, and he's going to need all that luck, plus some, today."

"Can't we try and break our way out, or talk our way out?" asked Matthew Tillson.

"Nope. Well, let's say we have even less chance, OK? Regis has a code word for your release, and Gassman won't let us get very far without it. They've got machine guns, and even if we get to the car, we'd never make it to the gate. It's about sixty or seventy metres. One or two of us might get through, but no more. The car would be like Swiss cheese, caught in a crossfire."

"Just a minute," said Easton. "Why will Haug have to fight his way out? Where is he?"

Bernstein told him about the negotiations and their suspicion of the assurances given by Regis. "We think their plans are to bring Haug and his people up here to join you, then have a general roundup of the whole group. Damn near fill up the asylum, wouldn't it?"

Louise Templer sat on the edge of the bed looking worried. "My god, they're monsters, Stuart." She turned to Bernstein. "How on earth are you going to hold this little room?"

The Israeli went to the table and opened his holdall. "Not with sticks and stones, lady. I've got two Uzi's here for Raul and me and a shitpot full of ammo." He pulled out a pistol and laid it besides the machine guns. "This is for which ever one of you has a good aim. A real cannon, a 44 magnum, go through eight men and a brick wall. A sawn-off shotgun and grenades to keep 'em out of the hall. And both Raul and I have pistols. Could have done with a rifle for window work, but this will have to do."

"I don't know how much help we can be," said Stuart Easton. "We're politicians, not soldiers."

Bernstein put the equipment back in his bag. "Well, I'll give you a little tip, Stuart. We'll try to put off the action as long as possible, right? I'm supposed to be in here interrogating you. As far as they're concerned at the moment, I'm still on their side. But I can't know when Regis might call. When he does, they'll know, right? That's when the shooting starts. The main thing is to get your mind around what is going to happen. The tip is this: Everybody has fear. That includes me and Raul, who are used to this stuff. But, to keep it from taking over and freezing you, take one thing at a time and don't let your imagination run away with you. There will be noise and the smell of cordite, but they don't have weapons heavy enough to pierce these walls. So you're safe if you're on the floor. Which is concrete, by the way."

There was a silence, then Louise smiled at him. "I'd like to say it's a very brave thing you're doing, Mr Bernstein."

"It's not brave. It's fucking stupid. I could be on my way to a nice sunny beach in Spain or somewhere if I'd managed to shoot that goddamn redneck. Yet here I am joining the Don Quixote squad, swapping my good sense for fucking ethics. If Haug does manage to get through, I might shoot him yet, the bastard."

Louise Templer stood up and looked out the window. "He is an interesting man."

"He's more than that, Mrs Templer. If you want my opinion, he's the guy holding your whole operation together. Regis is too stupid to know that, but if I'd managed to take Haug out, you'd have been fucked. I promise you that."

"I believe you, Mr Bernstein," said Stuart Easton. "I've been thinking about it myself from time to time. In every revolution a single man seems invariably to emerge. Napoleon and Lenin spring to mind. Though very different men, they did the right things, made the right moves at the right time. And those moves electrified those around him. They seemed to give purpose - no, purpose is the wrong word. Purpose was already there. They gave a polarisation to extremely large bodies of people, enough to overwhelm other bodies which were more indecisive. Now, this may not be a revolution, but it's strange to see someone like Haug emerge from virtual obscurity to polarise us. I would say he is a kind of mechanic. Does that sound right? A mechanic knows how things work. He may not know all the theories, but he knows how objects and people fit together."

"If you will excuse me señors and señora," said Dominguez. "I believe it is because of this." He pointed at his eye. "He sees. And he translates a good image to his head without too much prejudice. It is a simple thing, yet it is very, very difficult and rare. Castro has it also..."

"Castro?" asked Louise Templer suddenly. "You must be the Cuban Haug spoke of, the one he met in Corfu."

Dominguez smiled. "I am he. Him? Is that right? My English is rusty."

"Well, it's better than mine," said Bernstein. "Yeah, we got all sorts here. We got left wing MP's and a right wing MP and a Cuban communist and a fucked up Jew - all waiting for a crazy redneck from Carolina in a pickup truck. Right in the middle of England, for chrissake. When I was young I dreamed of a life of

512

drama, and here I am playing in a cheap farce waiting to be hooked off stage by the management."

Louise Templer smiled at him warmly. "Are you really that cynical, Sam? Or is it an act?"

Bernstein walked over to the back window and looked outside, ostensibly to check angles of fire. "To be honest, I have no idea. Which is a little frightening, I think. You change from a safe course to a deadly one for no reason at all. No, I don't think it's cynicism. A lot of anger, maybe."

"Yes," said Easton, "but you have reasons, don't you? It sounds to me like you may have drifted away from the ideals you had when you were young and found yourself doing a lot of rotten things. Now you're a little embarrassed to realise you cared after all."

Bernstein moved to the side window and looked out. "They haven't got a flat enough angle to hit anything but the ceiling if they fire into the room from outside, but they may do it anyway just to terrify the meek. So try and keep your heads turned away in case of flying glass. Could be some ricochet off the bars as well. Probably be best for the non-combatants to stay under the mattresses. You can use the two beds and table to make a kind of shelter in the far corner."

He turned and faced the three MP's. "Now, don't get me wrong. I don't *regret* changing sides. I'm just...pissed off with myself. It's all so meaningless."

"It is only meaningless if you do nothing, señor," said Dominguez.

Matthew Tillson hadn't spoken much, but he had been thinking. "We had to choose, just like you. I didn't want to either. It would have been so easy simply to ignore it all, let it all happen and pretend nothing has changed when it's over. I have a reasonably safe seat and could expect to hold it for the rest of my life. Or manoeuvre myself into the Lords, perhaps. I felt like you at first, angry and full of doubt, resentful for spoiling the even passage of my life. Yet I have discovered friends like Stuart and Louise, who sit opposite me in the House, and I feel more alive than I can remember feeling. More real."

Tillson moved his broken arm into a more comfortable position, wincing slightly with pain. "In the name of democracy we have slowly become less and less democratic, that's what I have seen. And I have no desire at all to see our country - and other countries - ruled from the boardrooms of gigantic international companies. They are, after all, looking after their interests and those of their shareholders. But the shareholders of democracy need looking after, too."

Stuart Easton snorted. "We don't have democracy here in the UK. Never have. Not even close."

Tillson held up his good hand. "Perhaps not, Stuart. Maybe you're right. But the Community of Association is taking away even that. Whatever we had. So I had to choose."

Bernstein pulled himself up on the window ledge. "Well, I don't feel more alive. I've been dead for almost twenty years. Maybe now I've chosen my own funeral."

Raul Dominguez cleared his throat. "You see, I know of Sam Bernstein. I first heard of him when I was in Angola, and he was working as an advisor with the South African Army."

Bernstein raised both hands. "Yeah, I admit it. Sure, I was there. I worked with BOSS, too - the Bureau of State Security. Teaching white bigots how to interrogate, terrorise and terminate blacks more efficiently. Before that I was with Shin Bet running electricity through Arabs so they glowed in the dark. Yet, when I was a boy..."

He broke off and unconsciously reached for his cigarettes again. His hands were shaking as he put one in his mouth and lit it. "When I was a boy I was full of anger and indignation because others had done such things to us for so long. The Jews must fight. That was my cry. They must not let it happen again. But whose side was I fighting on? Eh? In the end, even Shin Bet didn't want me."

He lit his cigarette and took a long drag on it. "As a boy I knew there were things like good and evil. And love. I wanted to fight for good and found myself a soldier for evil. And I don't see where it happened. I can't find the join."

There was a long silence. Louise joined him at the window, looking out. "It's called corruption, Sam. It happens to

514

everybody, it seems, who is really concerned. It just happened more dramatically to you because you were a fighter. It happened to me as well, all of us, I suppose. Well, maybe not Stuart."

"Don't make a saint of me, Louise," Easton said tartly. "I'm not. I've fought hard but not enough and never effectively. Westminster is corrupting. That is a fact. It corrupts everyone, and that includes me. In Westminster I'm a hollow drum because I've never been allowed near power and never will be. For Labour as well as the Tories, I fulfil the role of clown. Clown to the circus of Westminster. Meanwhile real miners are suffering as their jobs go and the safety regulations we fought so hard for are dismantled. Mines are being abandoned, and the union has been rendered powerless by relentless Tory revenge. Yet my seat is safe because they trust me to do something for them. And I can't deliver. Not even one mine. Not even one job in one mine. I stand by impotently as I watch their communities destroyed, families being turned out of homes they bought and can't sell, their pension funds being robbed and their hopes turned to coal dust."

Stuart Easton stood up straight and pointed his arm out the side window, his grey eyes passionate. "For all that, I know if word spread among the miners that I was being held here, the roads would be jammed with cars and vans and lorries and coaches. Soon the whole countryside would be dark with miners marching on this place. They would keep coming, even as the ones in front fell from the gunfire, and they would tear down the doors and carry us away on their shoulders."

"You must be much loved, señor," said Raul Dominguez softly.

Easton let his arm fall. "And I've betrayed them. Those men I love so much. I should have stayed in the mines. That is where I came from, and it's where I belong."

Bernstein shook his head. "Goddamn you people. Talking about *ideas* when you're going to die."

Easton spun on the Israeli, and one finger shot up like a weapon. "That's what people *are*! *Ideas!*"

515

Bernstein opened his mouth and then closed it again. "I was going to say something sarcastic, then changed my mind. I was going to say 'bullets always put an end to ideas' and realised something."

"Nobody's asked Mr Dominguez why he's here," said Matthew Tillson quietly.

The Cuban shrugged and smiled slightly. "It is easy for me, señor. I am only doing my job."

Louise Templer moved away from the window and sat on the bed. "Your job could hardly include protecting three corrupt MP's and an Israeli searching for his soul."

Dominguez waved a wiry arm. "Oh, we are corrupt only if we compare ourselves with unlikely models, and the truly corrupt never know their corruption. My fight is not so important as yours. Drugs and the money from drugs are doing much damage to my country. Following the drugs led me here. And here I am. I have some information Señor Haug passed to me, and I hope you will be kind enough to hear my plea for more of it. Then I would guess my own government would place this evidence before the United Nations - or perhaps they would approach some people in the United States directly, I have no idea. As I say, I am only doing my job, and if I can provide any assistance to you in the meantime, I am happy to do so."

"Even though you might be killed?" asked Easton.

Again Dominguez shrugged. "I did not choose to be a bank clerk, señor. I will try not to be killed, of course, but if I am, my last moments will not be full of surprise. In which case, it would be a kindness if you passed what information you could to my embassy."

Matthew Tillson chuckled. "Two years ago I would never have believed I could be instantly agreeing to the sharing of secret information with the Cuban government, but should any of us survive, then we will see it is done."

"Thank you, señor."

There was a muffled knock at the door and everyone froze except Bernstein. First he went to his holdall and stuffed something into his jacket pockets. Then he picked up an Uzi, checked the clip and jacked the top bullet into the chamber.

Again there was a knock, this time louder. "Sam! I want to have a word with you. Can you open?"

It was the voice of Harold Gassman. As Bernstein went to the door, Dominguez grabbed the other Uzi from the table and moved against the wall near the door. Bernstein got the key out of his pocket.

"Wait a minute, Gassman. Gotta unlock the door." He turned the key, leaving it in the lock, hid the Uzi at his side and, putting the butt of his still glowing cigarette in his mouth, opened the door with his left hand.

He smiled at Gassman. "What can I do for you?"

There was an armed guard standing beside Harold Gassman who cradled his Koch and Heckler in his arm, a finger lightly touching the trigger.

Gassman had a worried expression on his face. "I've just spoken to Michael Regis, Sam." He tried to look into the room, but Bernstein filled the doorway. "Can I speak to you out here?"

"Sure." Bernstein seemed relaxed as he opened the door slightly. Just enough to bring up the Uzi. The first shot went through the centre of Harold Gassman's head and blew out the back of his cranium, splattering the opposite wall with blood and bone. The second shot went into exactly the same place in the guard's forehead but strangely didn't make an exit at the back. As the guard went down, the Israeli glanced down the hall, noticing that it was filled with guards. Some were aiming their guns, while others were in a state of confusion about shooting the man who had formerly trained them. Meanwhile Bernstein leaned over and rolled a hand grenade towards them. He watched long enough to see his hastily trained soldiers become a tangle of panic stricken arms and legs squirming back towards the stairs.

Bernstein ducked into the room, and the explosion was absolutely deafening. Then he stepped into the hall again and sprayed the remainder of the clip on automatic.

He took the cigarette from his mouth and threw it on the floor, then ejected the spent clip and inserted another. "I always was a classy man in a bowling alley."

517

Stepping over the two corpses in front of the door he went slowly down the hall. Raul Dominguez immediately dropped behind him to cover. The double doors near the stairs were propped open by legs and bodies at strange angles. Someone moved slowly in the pile, and Bernstein quickly popped a round into the top of his head. Then he stepped over the remaining bodies and looked down the stairwell cautiously. On the ground floor pandemonium had broken out. Men were shouting at each other, and the doors opened and closed as more men poured in trying to find out what was going on. Just exactly as Bernstein had taught them *not* to do. Now he was going to teach them why.

He pulled the pin on the second grenade and aimed it carefully down the shaft between the stairs like a bomb. Then he let it go and aimed another one quickly, dropping it and stepping back towards the double doors. One thunderous blast followed closely on another. The violence of the twin explosions would have been followed by silence if it hadn't been for the screaming at the foot of the stairs.

Bernstein and Dominguez, without a word, quickly began checking all the rooms in the other wing. They smashed or shot open every door, and all were empty. They then checked the rooms on their own wing. They, too, were empty. Two doors away from the end room they found a modern operating theatre fully equipped and apparently ready for use. They collected the unused weapons from the five dead guards and carried them back.

When they entered the room was foggy with cordite and plaster dust. Stuart Easton stood by the doorway with the .44 magnum in his hand looking a little stunned. Louise Templer was still on the bed, and she was holding her head in her hands, rocking backwards and forwards. Matthew Tillson sat beside her, his good arm around her shoulders.

"Well, a little bit of luck, there," Bernstein said, as he dropped the guns into a corner. "Due to the fact they were a bunch of ignorant bastards, we got at least five of them, plus the boss. Add to that figure whatever we got with the two grenades downstairs. That should give Haug an almost even chance of getting in."

He looked around at the three shocked and mute MP's. "*If* he manages to get out of his own difficulties, that is."

"When would he get here?" asked Louise Templer.

"Afternoon," Bernstein replied as he looked out the window towards the gates. "Late afternoon, if he's still lucky. Never, if his luck's run out."

CHAPTER TWENTY EIGHT

"Socialism is dead!" Dr Alexander Hinkley screamed as he leaned across the table. "Dead, dead, dead!"

Ewan Thomas shrugged his shoulders and smiled. "Is the unicorn dead? Can something be dead when it never in fact existed? How can you say socialism is dead when we have never had socialism?"

Hinkley was very angry. "What do you call that evil empire, the former USSR? A former communist country, a socialist country. And it's dead! We defeated it!"

"Calm down, Hinkley. Your face is going blotchy," Thomas said.

"Nevermind my face."

"The Soviet Union technically applied a form of capitalism imposed within the structure of a command economy. Trade was still carried on and profit was still made within its economic structure, but theoretically this profit was plowed back into social benefits for the citizens. If 'socialist' in the name is confusing you, that is because it was founded as a country aiming to tread a path to socialism in the future. The *idea* of socialism is no more dead now than it was five, ten or a hundred years ago."

Hinkley smacked both hands on the table. "You cannot deny that the *idea* of capitalism is triumphant over the *idea* of socialism. It is impossible and illogical."

Thomas leaned back in his chair and ran his hand through his shaggy hair. "Your organs of propaganda in the west have said this over and over again as if it were true. Socialism's collapse. The crisis in socialism. There can be no crisis in a nonexistent economy. The crisis is in capitalism, which is groaning perilously under the weight of its own geometric expansion."

"There is no reason at all," Hinkley replied, "that capitalism cannot go on expanding indefinitely..."

"Oh, yes, there is."

"...All mankind wants capitalism and its benefits because it brings the opportunity for each individual to make something of

521

himself. It's a creative, wonderful, beautiful economic system, expressive of the best of mankind."

"In fact," Thomas said, "I wouldn't disagree that capitalism contains elements of beauty and creativity, particularly as it flourished in the nineteenth century, and, to some extent, in the twentieth. Its attempts now to form a global, rather than a national, structure through the cartels of the transnationals, represent an enormous and dangerous transfer of power, including the power to deal with domestic social problems. This power transfer is directionless at the moment, but there is strong evidence that the international cartels are being forced into the very structure they so recently and rabidly attacked. The command economy. The planned economy. The economic highs and lows have become too giddy and devastating, respectively - and too frequent. It will inevitably lead to instability - unless a planned economy is enforced. Enforced is the word, not democratically decided by the people of the world - if that is indeed possible. Your Community of Association is a political manifestation of this enforcement."

Michael Regis had returned to the room during Thomas' speech and took his chair with a worried look developing into a frown. He was trying to assess the information he had just received from Harold Gassman. Professor Hinkley was ready to reply with one forefinger in the air when Regis held up his hand.

"This issue must be decided now. Time is short." He turned to Sir Jonathan Mainwaring. "I'm afraid your signature is a necessity, so be kind enough to sign the declarations."

"Oh, it has become a necessity now, has it?" Mainwaring had been listening to Thomas and Hinkley with great interest, allowing his mind to drift. "I wonder what has caused this dramatic change of emphasis."

"Because," Regis replied testily, "this meeting is in danger of becoming a debating society."

"And it appears you have been losing the debate," Mainwaring replied.

Regis shrugged. "That doesn't concern me. Signatures do. Sign."

"I have already stated my position, Regis. It is impossible, if not illegal, for me to sign on behalf of the country. However, I would like to issue a warning should anything at all befall the hostages. If they are harmed in any respect, I shall not rest until each one of you, together with all involved in holding the hostages, is brought to justice. If, on the other hand, you now wish to negotiate, then..."

Dr Carlton Fine smashed his fist on the table. "Sign!" He smashed it on the table again. "Sign or die!"

Sir Jonathan Mainwaring looked at him evenly. "No."

Haug was watching closely. When he saw Michael Regis slip his hand into his pocket, he leapt from his chair and smoothly stepped toward Regis . Dr Fine rose from his own chair, and as he rose Haug turned back and grabbed him from behind, his forearm across his throat. Fine was the man he really wanted. Fine was the important figure. His movement was so quick and decisive it took everyone by surprise, even Mainwaring and Thomas.

At the same moment, the doors at both ends of the room opened. Four guards appeared at each door.

"Tell 'em to get out and close those doors, Regis, or I'll break his fuckin' neck." With his free hand, Haug fumbled in his waistcoat pocket and pressed a buzzer no doubt similar to the one pressed by Regis a moment before.

DeLoop was on his feet, towering over the men at the table. "He'll chicken out, Mike. If we all rush him, he won't have a chance."

"You don't know *me*, Tex, but Regis does." Fine was struggling, and Haug increased the pressure, now using his other hand as well. "He knows I'll break it."

"He's strong as an ox," Fine gasped. "Tell 'em to go back."

Regis shrugged and motioned the guards away. When they closed the doors, he sat back down in his chair, composed and steady. "There's no chance of you escaping. There are twelve armed men out there."

Haug released Fine's throat, then reached down and pulled his feet from under him. Fine fell heavily on his stomach but managed to catch himself with his arms and elbows. Haug planted a knee in his back, forcing him all the way down, then grabbed his briefcase, knocked it open and pulled out his Streetsweeper.

Before he could unfold the stock, which needed two hands, DeLoop launched himself at Haug. DeLoop was in his sixties, but he weighed well over three hundred pounds, and his sheer mass knocked Haug backwards and off Carlton Fine's back. The Texan grappled around trying to gather Haug into a bear hug, holding him on the floor with his sheer weight.

Immediately Regis sprang from his seat and helped Fine to his feet. "Come on," he said as he turned to Hinkley and Olsen. "Out. Move. Now. Quickly!" Regis led the confused, frightened men towards the door.

Sir Jonathan Mainwaring threw himself on DeLoop's back, trying to get his thin arm under the big Texan's neck.

DeLoop's weight was oppressive, but the need to move quickly gave Haug the strength and anger he needed. He brought the heel of his palm underneath the Texan's chin and pushed with all his might. The big head slowly went back and with it the big body.

Haug kicked himself free just as Regis threw the doors open and ushered his three associates through. He snapped the folding stock into place and quickly jacked a shell into the chamber. The Streetsweeper was a special American weapon becoming popular with drug gangs. It was a twelve-gauge shotgun with an eighteen inch barrel holding a drum of twelve shells. It looked a little like the old tommy guns made famous in the Prohibition days of the 1920's and even had a pistol grip in front of the drum. Instead of .45 calibre bullets, it fired double-ought buck, spreading as it travelled. At close range a more lethal weapon did not exist.

"Get down!" he shouted over his shoulder as he rolled away from DeLoop and his two friends.

Three of the guards were on their way through the door, guns drawn and held with two hands as Haug fired four rounds in quick succession. All three men were simply picked up and thrown through the doorway and against the facing wall. In fact the three men had become eight separate pieces before they hit the wall and fell into a red foaming mass. Two geysers of blood rose from severed arteries.

Haug got to one knee and whirled towards the other door, which had been partially opened to accommodate the barrel of an automatic pistol which was firing in the general direction of his position. Haug brought the Streetsweeper around and fired in an arc across the big double oak doors which splintered and shattered as if hit by cannon fire. The pistol dropped into the room attached to a hand.

He stood and turned towards the windows. Two men were running from the side of the house, and Haug moved toward the inner window, firing. The glass and frames blew away from the house almost as far as the two men, who were caught in an expanding pattern of heavy buckshot. They fell, writhing, on the ground.

He quickly turned and kicked over the big oak table before noticing that Mainwaring's body was trapped underneath the bulk of Hercules DeLoop, who was bleeding from a hole in the side of his neck. Haug pulled the big Texan off and knelt down beside his friend.

"Jonathan. Are you alright?"

Mainwaring opened his eyes. "Of course I'm alright. Except for general physical compression and ruptured eardrums."

Ewan Thomas had already crawled behind the table and gave Haug a thumb's up sign. "Just like in the movies," he said weakly, attempting a smile.

Haug grabbed his briefcase and extracted another drum, ejecting the empty one. "One of you can reload that drum for me," he said, as he attached the fresh one to the shotgun. "I'm sure you're smart enough to figure it out."

They could hear gunfire from the rear of the house, and Haug listened carefully. "Well, I took half of 'em out. Keef and the boys should be able to handle the rest."

There was a sudden roar of a car engine from the front of the house, and Haug got up quickly and went to the window. He fired four times as the accelerating Range Rover hurtled towards the gates. The gatehouse was unmanned, and the gates sprung open violently when the Range Rover hit them.

"Well," he said, "there go *our* hostages, so there's gonna be no easy swap. Have to apologise about that fuckup. The Texan was as heavy as a buffalo."

"Now I know how much a buffalo weighs," Mainwaring said. He was studying the drum like an archaeologist with an Egyptian artefact.

Haug knelt down and felt DeLoop's carotid artery. "He's dead as a doornail. How did you manage to get underneath him?"

Professor Thomas had joined Mainwaring in attempting to figure out the shotgun drum and was trying to get it out of the Perm Sec's hands. "Just a moment, Ewan. I'm perfectly competent to understand a simple mechanical design." He turned back to Haug. "I jumped on his back and tried to use that wrestler's hold you used on Fine."

Haug laughed as he kept his eyes on both doors. "He must have thought he was bein' raped by a stick insect. Looks like he may have saved your life, though. No bullet would go through that much fat." He glanced around at the two men who were still fumbling with the drum. "What *are* you two high class intellectuals doin' with my shotgun drum? You push 'em through the hole. Just like sex..."

He broke off as he heard noises in the hall and levelled the Streetsweeper at the right hand doorway. A white handkerchief appeared and waved slowly back and forth. It was held by a black hand.

"We give up," said Keef. "We've had enough." He walked through the doorway with a big smile on his face. Nightmare Andy followed him, carrying a baseball bat which had blood and matted hair on the end of it.

Haug didn't hear One Time ease his big body through the left hand doorway. Suddenly he was just there.

Keef looked at the pile of bloody body pieces against the wall, and the corners of his mouth turned down. "You had all the fun up here. We only had two, and Andy got both of them.

And two got away. One of the ones Andy got ran right into his bat."

Haug bit off another piece of tobacco from his pouch. "We gotta haul ass now. Regis and his gang managed to slither away, which complicates thangs. Bernstein and Dominguez should be inside the asylum now, and we gotta get up there. I got a feelin' Regis is on his way to the asylum as well."

Mainwaring stood up behind the table. "Exactly what is going on? Do you mind explaining things to me?"

"I'll have to apologise, Jonathan, for makin' a few decisions myself here, but I knew you had to keep your word so your honour would stay virginal. I'll explain everything on the way up."

"Up where?"

"To the asylum where Louise, Stuart and Matthew are bein' held. In Essex."

Mainwaring paused for a moment. "Do you know where they're being held?"

"'Course I do. I'm a sleuth." He spat a mouthful of tobacco juice in the middle of the expensive carpet and picked up the Streetsweeper and briefcase. They followed him out through the rubble to the pickup.

* * *

Sam Bernstein sat in the window watching the gate, the Uzi in his lap. Raul Dominguez was taking his turn guarding the top of the stairs. It had been very quiet since the earlier action. He assumed the casualties at the bottom of the stairs had been dragged off and were being attended by doctors. Now all they had to do was wait for Haug. Bernstein was feeling a little more optimistic now, due to the fact he had been a lousy trainer of fighting men. No, that wasn't really true. He had trained some very good men in Israel. And in South Africa. He never liked the recruiting system they chose. Regis used his contacts to draft in skinheads, here and on the continent. Skinheads with tattoos and big boots who got their courage from glasses of beer and large numbers. They had secret talks with the National Front, and there were no end of volunteers. Of course Bernstein had a visceral dislike of the NF and any of the scum associated with them. Which is why he had tried to bring in ex-Israeli soldiers or South Africans. He laughed wryly to himself. Imagine a Jew training cadres of fascists who might tomorrow be torching Jewish houses. It was ironical just how far he had drifted. Drifted, yeah, that was the word. He drifted because he had been brain dead. What was it Tillson said? He felt more alive now?

Well, Bernstein admitted he felt more alive now than at any time he could remember. He wanted to win for a *reason*, not just because it was a job. He hadn't spoken to the others since he pulled himself up on the window sill because there was something inside he had to look at carefully. It was a small glow, a little warmth. Now he could identify it. It was pride. Yeah, pride. He liked these people. He liked Haug. OK, maybe he didn't believe what they believed in, but there was a kind of strength in their belief which he had begun to suckle like a parasite.

He swung down from the window sill and went to the table, digging in the holdall to pull out a plastic bag. "Here's some sandwiches. I'd forgotten. They're kind of squashed. Haug made them last night.." He stopped and snapped his fingers.

"Oh, yeah," he said turning to Louise Templer. "He had a message for you. Said he didn't have any limey marmite, but he would send you a piece of cornbread he made. It's in here someplace."

Louise frowned. "Cornbread?"

"It's a redneck hick food they eat down in the South. Probably something they fed to the pigs at one time. That would account for its popularity with white trash. Here it is." He handed it to her. "There's ham and cheese, lettuce and tomato, some pickles which he guaranteed were not kosher. Pimento cheese, and I think this is a pork chop sandwich which he made specially for me, but if anybody else wants it, I'll take something else. There's also some biscuits - which you call scones over here - filled with Grandma's molasses and butter. No wonder the South is full of fat slobs. Anyway, take your pick. There's also some Coke for those who like warm soda pop." He took the pork chop sandwich back to his window, put the Uzi on the sill and bit into it.

"It's quite good," said Louise, holding a hand underneath her chin to catch the crumbs.

"It was thoughtful of him," Matthew Tillson said as he bit into a pickle.

Stuart Easton picked up a second sandwich. "I'll take one to Raul."

"You know," Bernstein said around a mouthful of pork chop, "I don't think most people want democracy. Maybe they want to think they've got it, but they really want something else."

"Cynicism again, Sam," said Louise. "People have always wanted freedom. There has always been a movement from below, a pressure, an upward pressure for a more equal share of the fruits of labour. Historically, every society we know of had a vision of what we now call socialism. Many times it took religious forms, but it has always been there. And it always will, so long as there is abuse of power at the top and grossly unequal distribution of wealth."

"Yeah, maybe," Bernstein replied and took another bite. He chewed for a moment, thinking. "Personally, from my own observations, I think people are just greedy. That includes those at the bottom of the heap. If the Arabs were suddenly given power and wealth in Israel, they would treat us just as bad as we treat them. Or worse. Everybody without power is greedy for power. Give it to them, and they use it the same way those they took it from did."

Stuart Easton had returned while Bernstein was speaking. "Strangely enough, I agree with you. But we have to begin somewhere. We have to find some social and economic mechanism that will work, or we're lost."

Bernstein used the rest of his sandwich to poke the air. "I'll tell you something else. And this is why I don't think democracy will work at all. A hell of a lot of people *enjoy* control, you know what I mean? Not just the controllers, but those *being controlled.* They want to be told or forbidden or allowed to do things. You can do this, you can't do that or you'll be punished, right? There's a kind of *pleasure* going on in this exchange of power and control. I don't know any other word for it. So why should we bother? Correction. Why should *you* bother?"

Matthew Tillson finished the first half of his ham and cheese sandwich. "It's my view that change occurs slowly and naturally, and government should only steer a steadying course. Yes, many - if not most - people actually want someone to choose for them, tell them what to do and punish them if they don't do it."

"Whilst diverting the wealth created by working people into the pockets of your class," Templer said contemptuously.

Bernstein took another bite of his pork chop sandwich. "No, now don't drag the soapboxes out. I'm just trying to tell you what I've seen in life, OK? And this is kind of strange. Strange to me, anyway. You got a huge body of people who say they are free and live in democracies, right? But they're about as free as shit. They got a mortgage, car payments, maybe health insurance payments and all kinds of other insurance. Then they got credit cards, bundles of credit cards. Hell, they're not even free to quit their goddamn jobs. They're like slaves in the old days. Chained to their houses, chained to their jobs, chained to their kids and credit cards. What can they do? Very little they're not allowed to do, right?"

He put the last piece of sandwich in his mouth, wiped his hands on his trousers and turned to face them. "Now the interesting thing to me is this. They *like* it that way. They *want* it that way. Offer most of these millions or billions of people real freedom, and they'd start crying. No shit. Now I have done a lot of things in my life, and I tell you. You could drop me in the middle of China in a parachute without a dime in my pocket, and I'd survive, even though I don't speak Chinese. I would walk out of China with money in my pocket. The prospect doesn't scare me at all. In fact, it kind of interests me. But these millions and millions of free democrats couldn't wipe their own asses without toilet paper. Now you tell me why they can enjoy a life like that."

Matthew Tillson smiled. "Do you enjoy your life?"

Bernstein shrugged. "Touché."

"Of course it's a modern form of slavery," Stuart Easton noted. "From the time we are children we have a deluge of propaganda in the form of news - and news is only gossip - convincing us that it is really information. What chance does a child have? He's told numerous times every day at home and at school that he or she is in a free country with a democratic government. The child may rebel, but economic levers of punishment force him or her down certain corridors like rats in a maze. For many the *illusion* of choice is all they want. That is enough. As for enjoyment, what else can they do but try to enjoy their predicament?"

Bernstein smacked the palm of his hand on the window sill. "So why the hell are you fighting? Let Regis and his crowd of halfwits have it. Nothing much will change. Probably nobody'll notice anything anyway."

Louise Templer brushed the crumbs from the buttered cornbread off the sill at the rear window and pulled herself up on it. "For the same reason all our ancestors fought, Sam. So that *our* offspring - some day - will have realisation and enjoyment in their lives. If we don't keep up the pressure constantly, the Regises of the world *will* have it. Without the pressure - the revolutions, the revolts, the fighting - we will have their kind of world. A world of two or three classes. Just like the army you must know as a soldier. The general staff at the top, the officers and NCO's in the middle and the poor privates who do what they're told."

Again Bernstein shrugged. "So what?"

Her voice raised a level. "So the human race never has a chance to be what it could be. And because ultimately their way leads to sure destruction. Which means the end of us all."

The Israeli turned back to the window. "Are those really the answers?"

"No one has the real answers," Stuart Easton said in an uncharacteristically soft voice. "But we'll never find out what they are if Regis and Fine are in charge."

"Well," Bernstein replied ironically, "it looks like they're going to be in charge for some time yet."

Templer frowned. "Why is that?"

"Because, right now, coming through the gate are four armoured vans. Look like police vehicles of some sort. They are full of armed men. My word for them is reinforcements."

Easton and Templer moved quickly to his side. Tillson got up painfully to join them and looked out the window. The vans pulled up in a line at the front of the asylum and opened their doors. Men in riot gear with rifles and submachine guns moved toward the building.

"Oh, shit," Easton muttered. "Is there some way..."

Bernstein held up his hand for silence. After a few moments he turned back to the others. "I was counting them. Forty-four men. Forty-four trained, well armed men. No way is Haug going to get through them, and, conversely, no way are we going to get out. In short, we are fucked. One hundred percent fucked. I hope nobody here is too squeamish about dying."

* * *

The pickup truck raced around the M25. The asylum was located near Colchester, and the A12 was on the other side of the London ring road. Behind them was the black Ford carrying Mainwaring's bodyguards, Golding and Simpson. They had been waiting outside, parked on the soft shoulder of the tarmac. After debating their loyalties, they decided to follow Mainwaring to the Regis residence. They arrived just as the Range Rover was careering out the smashed gates and swerved to avoid it. Haug had stopped the pickup, and Mainwaring gave them potted details of what was happening. The two police officers decided to follow them to Essex.

Mainwaring, though, wanted to ride in the pickup with Haug. He sat in the front, while One Time, Thomas and Keef sat in the back seat. Nightmare Andy refused to be cramped and was riding in the rear, his scalplock blowing in the wind. He seemed to deter objections from any drivers Haug was overtaking at high speeds, sitting like a warrior from a time warp of the thirteenth century, an eater of babies from the East, a heathen sucked off the plains of Kazakhstan and blown by a very ill wind to the back of an American pickup truck on the English M25.

The black Ford carrying the two policemen had difficulty at times keeping up with the flying pickup, even though the car was police issue and more powerful than civilian versions. Particularly when accelerating. The pickup simply left them for dead. They wouldn't have had any chance at all if it hadn't been for the normal clumps of traffic on the motorway which slowed Haug down. They had already attracted the attention of the traffic police, but Golding used his radio to explain it was an emergency.

"What would you do," DC Simpson asked at one point, "if you had to arrest that gent in the back of the truck?"

Golding grunted with amusement. "Call in the SPG, let them do it. They're all animals anyway, just like him."

Simpson shook his head. "That crazy American. Look, he's overtaking that Porsche who must be doing better than 140."

"Which is about our limit, too. Just try and keep him in sight..."

"You just overtook a Porsche," Mainwaring said with a slight edge of awe in his voice.

"One time," said One Time from the back.

"Crummy German engineerin'," Haug muttered. "They don't have the intelligence to make anythang but crap cars in that country."

"He did look rather stunned," Ewan Thomas commented. "I have to admit I'm very impressed by this unusual vehicle."

"Oh, come on, Ewan," Mainwaring said acidly. "Just look at the thing. Like a dance hall on wheels. The ultimate in poor taste. Over-the-top, overpowered and over here."

"Just like us Americans," Haug said.

"Exactly." Mainwaring tightened his seat belt. "The wastefulness is breathtaking. The engine would be better utilised pulling a train. Or powering an aeroplane. You can see the petrol gauge fall every time you put your heavy boot down. Americans never seem to understand what *enough* is."

"Well, to paraphrase Blake, you cain't find out what enough is til you've had too much."

"I forbid your using English poets to support spurious arguments of Yankee overindulgence."

"I can spot jealousy there, Jonathan. The English are never happy til they're really uncomfortable. That's why they wear tweed, live in unheated castles and love dogs that shit all over their lawns. Bein' comfortable is not a mortal sin, you know. You won't go to hell for it."

Mainwaring raised an eyebrow. "I thought for a moment I heard you use the word 'jealousy', but I must have misheard you because of the atrocious butchery of your accent to the natural beauty of the English language. Jealousy of an American would be a serious sign of mental illness..."

"Well, from what I've observed, Jonathan, mental illness is kind of an epidemic in this little backwater country. Maybe it comes from too much intermarriage or spendin' your lives bein' uncomfortable. I kinda feel sorry for you people."

Mainwaring snorted. "Why should one be jealous of the intellectually lame, the culturally unstable or the sheer poverty of imagination which makes your country such a desert of chrome and neon and polystyrene wrapped fast food? An enormous country blighted and offered to the gods in return for something soft to sit on or lie upon whilst the mind is polluted by sixty-seven channels of relentless advertising. You are asking me to be jealous of hell itself..."

Ewan Thomas listened to the badinage with a smile. He realised it was an antidote to nervousness and anxiety and frustration. He was unsure just why he was going on this trip to Essex. He was an academic and writer, not a soldier of fortune. Yet he had been swept along by events like a paper boat in a fast moving stream. There was a bonding between them now, all of them. He didn't really know the two black men sitting beside him very well, but they were all like relatives. It was a very strong force, he realised, maybe one of the basic human forces. Men aboard ships felt it, men in army units, orchestras, stage plays. The force could extend historically to include whole nations of people. He knew the force began to fragment when it grew too large, but during emergencies it would hold many millions together. The Soviet Union contained many varied republics, but they all rose as one angry hoard to crush the invading German armies in the last war. It was the same in the UK on a smaller scale. Whatever the differences between Scotland, Ireland, Wales and England, they put those differences aside to fight almost as one man against the Germans. Indeed, in each country there were classes at war as well. These, too, were held in abeyance for an emergency.

After an emergency the force was still there, but weaker. Politicians recognised it, of course. And used it heartlessly. Universal literacy was at first feared by leaders until they realised its potential value to them. Thus they were ready for the advent of radio and television, using them unscrupulously to manipulate opinion and taste, and so ensure their hold on power.

He looked at the extraordinarily broad shoulders of the American driving the pickup, the bald top of his head, the tiny ponytail made with the remainder of his hair. For most of his life he had felt an uneasy contempt for this kind of man, the so-called man of action. He believed those men who rose to power gained their power from the body of people surrounding them, not from anything innate within the single person. He still believed that, but now he had seen action from close up, he knew there was something else.

In Regis' house, he and Mainwaring had been prepared for the intellectual grappling necessary to try and wrest the hostages from them, but Haug had prepared himself in a different way. He had seen the logic of it better than Thomas or Mainwaring, in other words. Looking at it now in retrospect Thomas could see it was unlikely Regis would let them escape from his house. They were to be taken prisoner as well. Obviously it was clear to Haug from the beginning, so he spent his energy making provision for it.

He was not certain what it was that caused the American to act, but when he *did* act, it was with total commitment and professionalism. He grabbed Fine, not Regis. Fine was the most important. Then he remembered that awful weapon he had brought with him, a rapid-firing shotgun. There was no hesitation when he used it, and the result was bloody and deadly.

In a wink of time he and Mainwaring were peripheral. They were peripheral now, really just along for the ride. Yet during the negotiations, *Haug* was peripheral. In an instant it all changed. If there was a leader of the United Opposition, it must be Mainwaring. But Haug was clearly the leader now. Somehow he had found out about the location of the hostages, and they were thundering to the rescue. Thomas had no idea what would happen when they got there, but he was certain Haug did. In effect, he had *given his trust to this man he hardly knew*, a remarkable phenomenon. He had given his trust because he knew Haug represented their only realistic chance of success.

Is this what happened in revolutions? Were there special kinds of people who remain dormant until faced with...what? Chaos, that was the word, wasn't it? Faced with chaos, perhaps these dormant personalities flowered. Not often. But when they did, it was spectacular. His action at Regis' house had been like that. Thomas himself had been shaking inside like a leaf, his eyes wide open, riveted by the slow motion horror and beauty of it all. Beauty? Yes. It had been like a ballet, almost an orchestrated pantomime of chaos. He remembered the guards trying to enter the door, and they had fear in their eyes. They were menacing but uncertain, they hesitated for an instant. And in that instant they died. Haug seemed to act as a kind of lightening rod to chaos, a central pull of order at the edge of a world which was crumbling.

It was a door to power the man driving simply did not recognise. He was sure of that.

They took the A12 exit from the M25 and were just past Chelmsford when they spotted the Range Rover ahead. It was barrelling along at over 100 mph in the fast lane. The A12 had patches of three lanes which occasionally narrowed to two. Haug closed the gap between them, even as the Range Rover increased its speed. The rear window was fractured with small pellet holes, and so was the bodywork. Keef hammered on the rear pickup window to catch Nightmare Andy's attention, then

536

pointed at the vehicle in front. Andy picked up his baseball bat and leaned across the top of the cab, waiting.

"What I got to do here," Haug said, as much to himself as anyone else, "is get 'em into the inside lane. Damn near impossible while there're three lanes. Have to wait til it narrows down again, if it does."

Mainwaring stared at the Range Rover. "What do you plan to do?"

"Why, kill 'em, if that's alright with you."

"Why the inside lane?" asked Ewan Thomas.

"If I bump 'em into the central reservation, they might go skiddin' into the oncoming traffic. Be safer if I find 'em a nice hard shoulder with maybe a bridge support to run 'em into."

In front of them Regis was beginning to take risks with the other traffic, overtaking on the inside, whizzing between two cars, cutting up other drivers. Horns began to honk and two finger salutes appeared from drivers' windows. Haug did his best to be polite but looked down once to see another driver making the wrist movement that told him he was a wanker. It was the middle of the afternoon, so the bulk of the traffic was made up of travelling salesmen and lorries.

Haug checked his rearview mirror. The black Ford was just managing to keep up, and he watched as DC Simpson placed a magnetic blue flashing light on top of his car. That seemed to calm the angry drivers, who made the assumption the pickup and Range Rover were being chased by the police.

It was another ten minutes before a stretch of dual carriageway appeared, and the road narrowed from the left. Haug waited for a gap in the traffic, dropped into the nearside lane and accelerated sharply. As he overtook the Range Rover from the inside, he could see Regis behind the wheel and Carlton Fine in the front passenger seat shouting at him. Andy was leaning over the side of the pickup with his baseball bat, but Haug didn't come close enough for him to have a swing.

After overtaking Regis, Haug quickly pulled back into the fast lane. Then he began slowing down. He thought for a moment the Range Rover was going to try and ram him, but Andy moved to the back of the pickup with his bat, and Regis dropped back out of range. The Range Rover was now closely sandwiched between the pickup and the police car behind them. Haug continued to drop his speed, keeping one eye on the road in front and one eye in the rearview. They were at 50 mph, then 40, then 30. Traffic built up behind them, afraid to pass a police vehicle on the inside. Much argument was going on inside the car behind them.

Suddenly the Range Rover swerved out into the nearside lane, accelerating rapidly, trying to get in front of the pickup. Haug easily matched speeds and began edging closer to the racing vehicle. Andy had moved to the left side of the truck bed and was glaring balefully at Regis, waiting, the bat in his right hand. As Haug moved left, so did the Range Rover, just remaining on the tarmac.

"Hold on," Haug said. "We might bang him here."

He swung the steering wheel suddenly, coming within inches of the Rover. There was a heavy bang, but it was not the two vehicles colliding. It was Andy's bat. A huge dent had appeared over the driver's head, and the glass had shattered in the window.

Haug rolled down his own window. "Pull over you son of a bitch!" he shouted at Regis, whose tanned features now looked quite bleached.

"I'll get you, Haug! I'll chase your ass to the ends of the earth!" Fine screamed at him above the roar of the two big engines.

Haug swung in again, and the back window of the Range Rover disappeared in a shower of glass. Then Andy began hammering on the top again, one mighty blow following the other. The Range Rover was literally driven onto the soft shoulder, and he could see Regis struggling for control at the steering wheel. Ahead he could see an deep embankment and pushed even closer. He watched as the embankment moved closer and closer, finally accelerating just a little ahead of the Rover.

"OK, Andy!" he shouted. "Hit him!"

The words weren't out of his mouth before the windscreen of the Range Rover was blasted apart by the bat. Haug veered

538

away as the other vehicle slewed out of control, sliding sideways towards the embankment. Haug slowed down the pickup to watch as the other car went over the lip of the precipice backwards before beginning to tumble end over end to the bottom of a deep excavation. Haug put his foot down and moved back into the fast lane.

"Not much of an off-the-road car, was it?" he asked Mainwaring casually.

"Are they dead?" the Perm Sec asked, trying to see the wreck behind them.

"I haven't got time to stop and check their pulses right now, but we can hope. To kill 'em properly you probably have to drive silver stakes through their hearts and chant the Lord's Prayer backwards."

"Nice driving, Haug," Keef said from the back. "Couldn't have done much better myself."

"Right now," said One Time.

Haug turned half around to Keef. "Ever time I let you drive it, I gotta get new rear tyres. And you *never* fill up the gas tank."

"Well, I'm glad to have them out of the game," Mainwaring sighed. "Even if it's only for the time being.

During the final leg of the journey Haug told them about Sam Bernstein and Raul Dominguez and the outline of his plans for the rescue. Sir Jonathan Mainwaring did not grumble too much at Haug's initiative once it was pointed out the alternatives were impracticable.

Professor Ewan Thomas did not talk much from the rear seat. Instead, he listened carefully to the exchange between the two men in the front. Now he was delighted he had joined the group. He was able to watch in close detail a phenomenon which had puzzled him for many years - the nature of leadership and what it really meant to those who led and those who followed.

CHAPTER TWENTY NINE

The asylum was about twenty-eight miles north of Colchester. Mainwaring had been navigating by an Ordnance Survey map of the area Haug bought the day before. It was a relatively narrow "B" road and a combination of long straight stretches with elbows and corkscrews at inconvenient intervals. It was a road used mostly for farm vehicles and local traffic. His mind was already at the asylum, leafing through a number of scenarios depending on the layout, when he rounded a tight bend to encounter a huge ready mix concrete lorry which was reversing up the road. He had to twist the wheel sharply to avoid the monster and skidded to a halt on the soft shoulder. The driver of the concrete lorry was shouting at him, and Haug grabbed the map from Mainwaring and got out of the pickup.

"Sorry," the driver was saying. "Are you alright?"

As Haug walked over, waving that he was OK, the man got out of the cab. "You can't get through on this road," he said, seeing the map in Haug's hand. "Police got everything blocked off."

Haug looked worried. "The police?"

"Yeah. They got the road blocked off," he repeated. "Can't get through. Roadblocks near the asylum. Some kind of emergency. There's some shooting going on, either that or fireworks. You lost?"

Haug became intense, thinking. "Do you know these roads around here?"

The man nodded and grinned. He had one front tooth missing. "Lived around here all me life."

Haug punched the map anxiously. "Do you know if this road's closed?"

The man studied the map carefully. "Oh, no, don't think so. Well, it won't be closed until you turn back towards the asylum, which it does, so you'll just have to reverse back again."

"How close is it to the wall?"

"Runs right by the wall, four, five foot away."

Haug scratched his nail on the map. "And this is a hill, where the road comes down to the wall?"

"Oh, it's a little hill alright. Don't get many hills in these parts, but it's a little hill. Are you American?"

"Hang on just a minute," Haug said, then turned and trotted back to the pickup, asked Mainwaring to join him and walked back to the black Ford. He explained the situation as quickly as he could, impressing the two policemen with the urgency. The cops got out of their car and the four men approached the lorry driver.

Golding reached for his warrant card and held it open as he confronted the driver. "I am Detective Sergeant Golding, this is Detective Constable Simpson." He held his arm toward Mainwaring. "Permanent Secretary of State at the Department of Trade and Industry, Sir Jonathan Mainwaring..."

The driver whipped off his hat and held it with both hands, his eyes wide. "Oh, I've never met a real knight of the realm, sir..."

"We are going to requisition your cement lorry, sir, for emergency police and government work. Sir Jonathan will give you a signed piece of paper which you or the lorry's owner may present to the Department of Trade and Industry to reclaim any costs for damage to lorry or goods carried."

The driver scratched his head. "Oh, well, I don't know what the governor would think about that, sir, I don't..."

Haug interrupted. "Is that thang fulla concrete?"

"It is, sir. I was taking a load to the asylum, where they're doing some work. But the workmen aren't there today. Just police everywhere..."

Haug turned and was trotting to the pickup. He told Keef to drive and follow him in the lorry. Pointing to the map, he showed Keef where to park when they got there. He asked Ewan Thomas to move to the police car, picked up the briefcase holding the Streetsweeper, then trotted back to the group near the concrete lorry. Mainwaring was writing out his "requisition" on PC Simpson's back. Haug clambered into the cab and threw the briefcase on the seat beside him. He opened it, unfolded the

542

handle, stuffed his pockets full of the remaining shells and put the spare drum down his belt.

"Do you want me to show you how to drive her, sir?" the man asked, looking up at him, cap still in his hands.

"I can drive anythang that's got wheels," Haug replied, starting the engine and putting it into gear. As the vehicle moved slowly forward he felt the weight. It was an older version and was therefore made of heavier gauge steel with a huge bumper at the front. Then he began scrutinizing the inside of the cab, estimating how much room he would have to manoeuvre. The righthand turning was not far ahead. Keef, One Time and Andy followed in the pickup while the police car went forward towards the road block. Now that the Community of Association was headless for the time being, they might be able to rattle the local constabulary with knighthoods and Metropolitan Police officers.

The old engine in the lorry wheezed and complained as it climbed the hill. It was steeper than the driver led him to believe, and that was a relief. He double-clutched and dropped to a lower axle ratio as he tried to estimate the weight of the lorry and the load it carried but got lost in the arithmetic. Heavy enough, he hoped. Heavy enough.

* * *

Surprisingly, they still held the stairs. The hallway was just clearing from the tear gas canisters fired into the end windows. Bernstein had anticipated the gas attack and raided the surgery for surgical masks and goggles, distributing them to the MP's and explaining quickly what to expect. They were to lie flat on the floor underneath a little barricade of beds and mattresses and cover all skin surfaces. The smell of the gas would be terrifying at first, but he told them to breathe little shallow breaths as close to the floor as possible. Meanwhile he broke out all the windows in the room for ventilation. Then he opened doors to empty rooms and shot out as many panes of glass he could before the first canister arrived. He skidded back to the top of the stairs on

543

his belly, coughing violently. Raul defended one side of the double stairs, he took the other.

Lying there, he knew it would be only a few moments, and he was right. He heard the boots thundering on the stairs below as the reinforcements charged from the ground floor and the remaining guards on the first floor attacked the final flight.

Bernstein waited until the guards were around the newel post, knowing they would be partially hampered by gasmasks. The first two guards' heads were just rising past floor level when Bernstein and Dominguez opened fire with the Uzis. The men fell backwards, and the Israeli got up to his knees, coughing and spluttering, as he raked the whole stairwell, ejected the spent clip and banged in a fresh one. There was not much return fire, but he could see the reinforcements pouring onto the first floor, so he started down the stairs, jumping two steps at a time over the bodies. On the landing he could see better and sprayed the Uzi back and forth at the hurtling bodies searching for cover, some returning fire.

He saw - or rather heard - Dominguez on the other landing, and between them the automatics trapped the guards and policemen in a withering crossfire. Again Bernstein ejected a spent clip and snapped in a full one. Listening during a lull in the din, he realised men were again mustering in the entrance hall downstairs.

"Dumb assholes," he muttered, reaching for one of his remaining grenades. He quickly pulled the pin and aimed before dropping it, then waved to Dominguez to retreat back up the stairs.

He was breathing heavily as he shouted to the Cuban after the blast. "I counted eight bodies on the floor downstairs, and there are four I've been stepping over. How many up your side?"

"Only three, señor. Sorry."

"That's fifteen, plus whatever we got with the last grenade. Not fucking bad for two old men. But still not good enough. Still too many of them."

"Si. You are right, señor. Too many."

"They should stay quiet until they think of some other tactic. Give 'em long enough, and they might find the right one. Meanwhile, I better check on the hostages. Shout or fire if there's a problem." He backed away around the corner and stood up again, realising his knee joints were complaining.

"I shouldn't be doing this at my age," he thought as he walked back down the hall. Most of the gas had cleared, and he pushed the goggles up on his forehead and raked down the surgical mask so it hung from his neck. As he suspected, they had used the hallway windows for the gas canisters because there were no bars. But there was a nice strong wind blowing through now. Bad luck for them.

Louise Templer was crawling out from the little refuge coughing and cursing as Bernstein entered and went to the wash basin. He filled it up with water and splashed it over his burning skin, using the soap to wash off the stinging gas.

"This is what you do, lady," he said. "There's a nice little breeze blowing through here now, so most of the shit is gone." He dried his face on the inside of a towel.

Templer staggered over to the basin and began washing as the others crawled out.

"I can see why they call it teargas," said Matthew Tillson. "I can't see a thing."

Stuart Easton rolled out. "What happened downstairs? Sounded like a war."

"The score is fifteen nil," Bernstein replied as he faced the breeze coming in from the broken window.

"That sounds pretty good," Louise commented as she turned, wiping her face with the towel.

"They were real stupid, Mrs Templer, but I expect them to wise up soon. If they had somebody battle experienced, getting us out would be a simple matter."

Easton turned to him. "What would you do, if you were in their position?"

Bernstein shrugged. "I would have used grenade launchers, both ends, then the gas, then rush by twos. Once they're on this floor and in the hall, it's simple. Or should be. Another route is the roof. Which is probably the one they'll think of next, if they can't get hold of grenade launchers."

"They must be stunned by their losses on the stairs," said Easton. He was helping Matthew Tillson wash his face and hands.

The Israeli shrugged. "That kind of assault is OK against civilians, but not well-armed soldiers. And I got 'em with another sucker grenade. They must be really green. Which is why I enjoyed fighting the redneck, because it gives the mind..." He stopped and focused on the little hill at the side of the asylum. There was a huge concrete lorry, and behind it was the pickup truck.

"Well, kiss my ass and call me Suzie," he muttered. "When you speak of the devil...will you look at that crazy son of a bitch!" He pointed out the window at the lorry, and the rest of them rushed over to watch.

"What's he going to do?" Templer asked in a frightened voice.

Bernstein turned and raced out of the room to warn Dominguez, who was still guarding the stairs. Then he dashed into the surgery and found a large sheet, which he tucked under his arm. Banging into one of the other rooms, he spotted a can of paint and a brush left by workmen. He grabbed them and raced back to the end room. Haug was still at the top of the hill. Bernstein threw the sheet on the floor and tore off the lid on the paint, calling for two people to hold it while he painted a huge arrow on the sheet. Then he ran and tied the sheet to the frame of the window at the end of the hall. The arrow pointed to the end room.

Haug was just beginning to move when he saw the sheet go up. He knew what it meant and floored the throttle of the old concrete lorry. The engine groaned at first with the weight, but then the big truck started picking up speed, moving faster and faster. Haug braced himself against the steering wheel.

"What is he *going to do*?" Louise Templer almost screamed as she repeated her question.

Bernstein was excited. "He's trying the only fucking chance he's got. I love that bastard, Jesus. Between the two of us, we could have whipped the whole PLO!"

"That's not very politically correct," Easton muttered darkly.

"Like I said, fuck politics."

Louise was frantic. "Will you *please* tell me what he's going to do?"

"Just watch," Bernstein replied, glowing with exhilaration.

The lorry must have been doing almost seventy when it hit the wall surrounding the asylum and not much slower after it went through it, scattering pieces of brick and masonry up to forty yards away. They could hear bricks hitting the asylum as if they were parts of the sonic wave from the thunderous explosive crash. Immediately behind the lorry they saw three figures, two black, one white and carrying a baseball bat. They were running hard.

"Better hold on to something!" Bernstein shouted as he spun and gathered two Koch and Hecklers after jamming the Uzi in his pocket. He was just going out the door of the room at a run when the lorry hit the building.

It was like an earthquake. It was worse than an earthquake. The floors seemed to tilt and judder. Plaster tumbled from the ceiling and walls. Door and window frames cracked and sagged. Crazy patterns appeared in the concrete floors. Great palls of dust rose from the stairwells, one of them in the shape of a mushroom. Suddenly in a huge roar, the front of the building collapsed, the first floor and then the second.

The noise and dust were hellish. In a panic the three MP's threw themselves to the floor and crawled back toward the mattresses for some kind of cover. It sounded as if the entire building was coming down - not just the front corner but the centre as well, and maybe even the other wing. It seemed like the asylum had been hit by rockets from a fighter squadron.

Sir Jonathan Mainwaring, Professor Ewan Thomas and the two London policemen had the best view. They had very much impressed the chief constable, who was himself leading the constabulary in the cordon thrown around the gates to the asylum, and he had allowed them forward with six of his men to speak to the leader of the Specials inside the building. In fact they had just passed through the gate when the lorry hit the outside wall and roared onward into the front side of the building, and the effect reminded Ewan Thomas of an old 3-D movie. It was as if a giant had thrown a bowling ball the size of a boulder down the front of the asylum. The facade sagged and crumpled, then came down in sheets of masonry and bricks, finally exposing part of the stairway and inner rooms of the upper floors.

Thomas realised his mouth had dropped open as the spectacle unfolded before him. As the noise of the collapsing building died away, they could hear screams of men in agony. A few Specials and asylum guards wandered around in a daze, failing to believe what had happened to them.

What *had* happened to them was a little freakish. When Haug's lorry hit the solidity of the asylum, breaking through the outer wall as it slowly ground to a halt, the big drum on the back carrying the concrete detached itself and continued on through the building at a velocity slowly diminishing from nearly sixty miles per hour. The drum gradually tore itself open against the walls and supports and girders, scattering cubic yards of ready mix concrete into the far wing of the building.

Sir Jonathan Mainwaring stood frozen to the ground, very erect, despite the flying pieces of plaster, brick dust and glass.

"I don't believe this," he muttered, almost inaudibly. "He must have killed everyone inside the building, including himself..."

"It's rather impressive," Thomas commented. "You have to admit that. Reminds me of London during the blitz. I remember a bit of it as a child."

"Awesome," Detective Sergeant Golding murmured behind them. "Fucking awesome."

Keef and One Time helped pull Haug from the smashed cab of the lorry. He was unconscious, and his face was covered in blood. They carefully carried his body behind the mass of tangled wheels and twisted chassis. Nightmare Andy grabbed the Streetsweeper and stood guard.

"He's breathing," Keef said as he checked the arms and legs for broken bones.

One Time stood up and looked around. A geyser of water was pumping from a broken mains supply. He found a pan and some sheets and filled the pan with water. Returning to the unconscious American, he carefully lifted his head into his lap and began gently washing away the blood.

Keef was watching. "I think it looks worse than it is. At least I hope it does."

Haug opened one eye and looked up into One Time's concerned face. "I hope the hell you washed your crotch last night," he said and realised he had a broken tooth.

One Time grinned. "Can't kill the *man*."

"Not yet anyway," Haug said as he rolled over painfully. "What's the damage to my beautiful face?"

"Broken nose," One Time replied. "Maybe the cheek, too."

"I think we better get our asses in gear before they jump on us with both feet. Anythang movin', Andy?"

"No problem yet," Andy said as he looked down the front of the devastated building.

Haug got to his feet and shook his head to try and clear it. There seemed to be a growing roar in his ears. Andy gave him the Streetsweeper, and they began to move forward cautiously.

Haug shook his head again. The roar was getting louder. One Time and Keef looked up at the sky as Haug suddenly identified the sound.

"Hit the ground!" he yelled. "Helicopters!" It was a sound he knew well, one that immediately churned his guts as he slid between a twisted steel support and brought the Streetsweeper around, resting it on what remained of a wall.

The two camouflaged Army helicopters came in very low and very fast, setting down quickly - one to the left and one to the right of the asylum. The instant the wheels touched down, the troops jumped out one behind the other and dived to the ground, forming perimeters. A machine gun from each squad instantly raked the building across the middle as the blades of the helicopters slowed when the engines shut down.

549

Bernstein was on the point of leading his group down the stairs when the helicopters arrived. The moment he heard them he and Dominguez shooed the MP's back up the stairs to the top. He pounded the top of the newel post in frustrated anger.

"Fuck! The fucking bastards! We had *made* it. Against any kinds of odds, we *made* it. The redneck tore the fucking building apart for us, and now the fucking Army fucking arrives just in fucking time to fucking finish the fucking job..."

He heard the machine gun fire and immediately threw himself on Easton and Templer. Dominguez shielded Matthew Tillson. Bernstein was still pounding his fist on the floor when he heard the bullhorn.

Following the rake of machinegun fire, a tall officer in battle fatigues and wearing a beret ducked out of the helicopter near the wreckage of the lorry with the bullhorn. He stood upright with one hand holding his gloves behind his back and spoke in a clear Sandhurst accent which was commanding and chilling.

"All people in this area - whether police or civilian, men or women - will throw down their weapons, raise their hands over their heads and gather in a group between the two helicopters. Failure to do so or any sign of armed resistance will be rewarded by decisive action by my men." He paused for a moment as a few of the guards and Specials threw down their rifles and submachine guns and did as they were told. Then he continued.

"I believe there may be some hostages amongst you, and if any remain alive, I want them to form a separate group just in front of this perimeter. I must insist the hostages also disarm themselves and keep their hands in the air." He turned to the group of civilians and policemen crowded at the gate, including Mainwaring and Thomas, who had not moved.

"I am not indulging in idle chatter. Corporal!"

The Corporal fired a burst over the heads of the group at the gate who immediately raised their hands and moved to the centre to join the clumps of defenders. The officer waited a few moments before speaking again.

"No hostages alive?"

All heads turned to watch the figure of Louise Templer come carefully down the stairs with her hands up at her shoulders.

Alone, she picked her way through the rubble, occasionally having to drop her hands to move a shattered door or step round a lintel. It took her several minutes to negotiate the debris, avoiding dangerous or unstable areas, and when she finally stepped out onto the grass, her shoes were covered in wet concrete. But she continued straight across to the tall officer with the bullhorn.

"Mrs Templer, I presume," he said, not unkindly. "Are you the only hostage left alive?"

She put her hands down. "No. The others are there, along with their defenders. I and they refuse to leave the building until we have assurances regarding our safety..."

"I will remind you, Mrs Templer, that you are in no position to make any demands. I want everyone who is alive out here at once. Do you understand?"

She shook her finger in his face. "Do you understand that we are prepared to die here with some honour rather than face death or medical experimentation at some other time and place?"

"I insist you do as you are told, Mrs Templer. I will clarify everything the moment your people present themselves unarmed, not an unreasonable request. Now..." He gently but firmly pinned Templer's arms to her side and began to move her to the front of the perimeter.

"Take your goddamn hands off that woman, bo, or you're gonna look like a wrung out sponge!"

The officer stopped and dropped his hands, heaving a big sigh. The corporal spun around with his machine gun to face the ruined corner of the building.

"Hold your fire, Corporal," he barked and put the bullhorn down on the ground before walking toward the building, both hands behind his back grasping his gloves. He walked directly toward the broken piece of wall where he could now see the menacing barrel of a shotgun protruding a few inches from the rubble.

"You can stop right there, bo."

The officer ignored the warning and continued to walk purposefully forward, and the American sat up, holding the shotgun ready to fire but moved the barrel away from the

551

advancing man. A little further back the officer saw two black men with pistols and what he thought at first was a hulking gargoyle which may have dropped from the roof ornaments. Then he realised it was a man holding a baseball bat in one hand and a machete in the other.

The officer stopped and peered down at Haug, who had blood smeared across his face and looked like he might have a smashed nose. "I gather you are Mr Haug, and I assume it was you who caused all this damage."

"Well, I hoped it wasn't a property protected by English Heritage," Haug said.

"I would like to try and convince you, Mr Haug, that the most sensible course of action is for you and your brave friends to lay down your arms and join Mrs Templer over there. Personally I would detest ordering my troops to fire on you, but make no mistake about it. I will."

Haug was studying the officers uniform. "I cain't remember foreign insignia too well, but you're a general, aren't you?"

"Well spotted. General Robert Sessions, Royal Marines."

Haug's shoulders relaxed. "General Portland's friend, right?"

"My former colleague and mentor," Sessions said. "Will you now do as you are told, Mr Haug, so we can quickly wrap all this up and attend to the wounded?"

Haug stood up. "If you give me your word of honour as an officer that the three hostages in our group and Sir Jonathan Mainwarin' and Professor Ewan Thomas will be returned unharmed to London or wherever they want to go, we'll come out unarmed, General Sessions, but not with our goddamn hands over our heads. I have never surrendered in my life, and I ain't startin' now."

Sessions smiled thinly. "I give you my word they will be freed unharmed after questioning. Now, follow me, please." He turned and walked back to the perimeter with Haug, One Time, Keef and Andy in single file behind him.

Haug leaned over and picked up the bullhorn. "OK, Sam, Raul. These are actually the guys with the white hats who're just a little late with their rescue. Lead Stuart and Matthew out but

552

leave your guns and stuff inside. You are not surrenderin', so you don't have to put your hands over your heads." He turned to the group of people from the gate. "That includes Mainwarin', Thomas, Golding and Simpson. Put your hands down. We don't surrender."

Apparently exasperated, General Sessions took the bullhorn from him, and Haug walked over to Louise Templer, who seemed to have tears in her eyes.

"Hello gorgeous. Miss me?"

She grabbed him and hugged as hard as she could, and he wrapped his arms around her, rocking back and forth.

"I'm so glad to see you," she whispered. "Thought you must be dead. So glad."

Sam Bernstein led the group down the stairs and through the rubble as Raul and Stuart Easton helped Matthew Tillson.

"Corporal," said General Sessions, "Two men to guard prisoners, the rest to find and assist the wounded."

"Sir!" said the Corporal as he got to his feet..

"And Corporal," said Sessions, stopping the squaddie in his tracks.

"Sir!"

"These people here are the hostages, not prisoners."

"Sir!" The Corporal began shouting orders to the two squads.

Haug and Louise Templer walked over to meet the group coming from the ruined asylum as soldiers rushed around them, calling to the wounded. Haug shook hands first with Bernstein, then Dominguez as Louise Templer and Stuart Easton helped find a place for Matthew Tillson to sit.

Bernstein grinned. "So you were going to take on the army as well, eh, Reb?"

"They weren't army, asshole. Marines. So it was an even fight. One paratrooper and five men who can count to ten without usin' their fingers against two squads of marines. No sweat."

Bernstein turned and looked at the building, shaking his head. "You leave an awful messy battlefield. How the hell did you do that?"

Mainwaring's group was approaching, and everyone turned to greet them. Haug waved over Keef, One Time and Andy, introducing them to Bernstein and Raul as Mainwaring spoke to the MPs before coming over to take Haug aside.

"Thank you," he said to Haug softly as he guided him a few feet away. "I've never seen anything so spectacular in my life." He gave the American a genuine smile before continuing. "General Sessions spoke to me and said Timothy Portland is badly hurt and was taken to the Charing Cross Hospital with suspected spinal and pelvic injuries."

"Shit," Haug muttered. "How'd it happen?"

"I don't know yet, but several military vehicles have arrived in front, and they will accompany us to Colchester where he wants to speak to us."

The house was not actually in the city but in the nearby town of Wivenhoe. It was owned by an ex-Conservative MP, and the driveway of the detached house was filled with two long black limousines, several Royal Marine vehicles, the black Ford and Haug's pickup truck. Royal Marines guarded the driveway and the door to the house, and six of them stood around the perimeter of the rear garden where the meeting took place. The sun had broken through the clouds, and chairs were arranged on the lawn. One table at the side was filled with refreshments, including soft drinks, wine, small sandwiches, chicken wings, biscuits and cheese.

After attending to Matthew Tillson, a Royal Marine surgeon set Haug's nose, advising him to have the cheek X-rayed as soon as possible. He also suggested he see a dentist about the tooth, which had broken clean at the gum. The surgeon left him a bottle of pain killers which Haug stuffed in his pocket after taking two.

The man with the long, swept back hair and expensive suit spoke.

"For those who may not know me," he said, "let me introduce myself. My name is Norman Stone, and I am defence minister in the current government. I have asked everyone involved in the atrocities this afternoon to attend. The prime minister himself would have come if he had been able. He sent me in his place. I must advise you at this point that today's unfortunate events and everything which is said here is covered by the Official Secrets Acts and nothing may be divulged to any outside source either in whole or in part. Copies of the relevant clauses of the Act are available for those unfamiliar with its provisions."

Norman Stone waved his arm dramatically around the garden. "I have decided to hold this meeting *al fresco*, as we have a marvellous garden and a warm summer afternoon, and please avail yourselves of the refreshments." He cleared his throat and examined his scrupulously manicured fingernails. "I decided upon intervention after being advised of the outrageous and cowardly attack upon General Sir Timothy Portland in Whitehall today. His condition, incidentally, is said to be stable, though I am advised he may never walk again."

He turned into the slight breeze and looked out at the beautiful rows of trees and shrubs shielding the garden from overview. "I need not point out to you that we have here an exceedingly difficult political problem. A problem which will take much time and thought to unravel. I do not yet have full knowledge of the horizons of the problem myself, but I am aware of the potentially explosive nature of the events, should they come into the public view. At this very moment, the airlocks of the ship, so to speak, are being screwed down. Watertight doors are being closed and locked. Once security is complete, then we shall begin to solve the conundrum, not before. I would like to reassure those who may have doubts, that we are determined to bring this potential chaos to an orderly close."

"And what about those who have flouted the law of the land with intimidation and murder and conspiracy?" asked Stuart Easton in a sharp voice.

Norman Stone held up the palms of his hands. "I believe both sides have taken the laws into their own hands. However much I may sympathise with your intentions and your good will, it is a fact that you have proceeded outside judicial and

555

parliamentary law. You should have approached me or the prime minister in the first place with your initial suspicions..."

"Bollocks," shouted Louise Templer. "We would have been individually killed or intimidated, which is their way."

"Please," said Stone. "I am not here to argue the details of every nail and screw in the edifice. That will come later, but I can assure you that justice will be done and the will of the people carried out."

"You just said you were going to exclude the people in the debate," said Easton. "By battening down the hatches and retreating to smoke-filled rooms. I suggest we forget about the Official Secrets Act and present the facts on a specially advertised television programme. Tell the people of this country that their sovereignty has been usurped by a huge international cartel of transnational companies acting in the interests of their owners and shareholders and that this new order is being enforced by gangs of paramilitary and political thugs who use kidnap, extortion, bribery, rape and murder to lobby for their interests in a country which used to pride itself on parliamentary democracy."

Norman Stone smiled benignly. "We are all aware of your political position, Stuart..."

Matthew Tillson struggled to his feet. "Actually, Norman, I second that proposal. What do we have to fear? Have we come so far from our ideals that we are actually frightened to tell people the truth, believing we have the right to strain and sieve and weigh each particle of evidence to ensure it has the correct political spin? That is what *they* are doing through the newspapers of Gillmore and the BBC and other media outlets where they have control or influence. I am a member of your party, Norman. I am a Conservative. But I have seen what twisted truth and twisted information can do. I have seen the danger of it. I think the whole matter should be thoroughly ventilated before the people of the country. If they then wish to ignore it, they will have no one else to blame but themselves for our future."

The Defence Secretary nodded. "I certainly agree with what you are saying as well. In principle. However, it is not my decision, as you well know. It is the decision of the prime minister and the cabinet. I shall put your views to them as forcefully as I know how. In the meanwhile, I'm afraid these events must fall under the Official Secrets Act..."

Sir Jonathan Mainwaring sat with his chin on his chest, staring at his long, folded arms, listening to what they were saying with only one ear. Haug was sitting beside him, and he knew the American expected him to leap to his feet and attack with a rapier. But he could not move because he was lost in a labyrinth of thought. He knew better than Haug what was happening because he had spent a lifetime advising government ministers. He had spent a lot of his time thinking since his ordeal in the White Room and the "interrogation". Most of his life had been spent learning and then practising the art of illusion. He well knew the most likely outcome of events now was...nothing. They were being presented with an elaborate illusion that it was *something*. But it would be nothing. They would be allowed the *illusion* that they had won the battle. Mainwaring could accurately predict the entire scenario. The two cabinet ministers directly involved with the Community of Association would be allowed to resign "for personal reasons". The Special Branch would undergo an internal investigation, and a few policemen would lose their jobs. There would be a few further cosmetic changes, and then Mainwaring and his group would be informed justice had been done and democracy restored - so there was no longer any reason to have a United Opposition.

And in fact nothing would happen. No significant legislation would be drafted to limit the powerful thrusts of transnationals into domestic politics. Their leverage, unblunted, would continue to force fiscal, social and political acts which supported their expansion. Britain, in fact, would continue to do what it was told to do. If the country could not provide cheap labour, they would move elsewhere - and to create cheap labour, the trades unions had to be emasculated. They demanded low taxation and free movement of money. Low taxation meant severe cuts to social programmes, and greater fiscal freedom meant yet more leverage against financial institutions which

557

could be affected by huge inflows and outflows of cash and credit.

Technology was rampant, and the ever increasing speed of the rollercoaster was making even the wealthy who climbed aboard giddy. There was of course nothing wrong with technology itself. But the transnationals were feeding on it like carrion. If the direction remained unchanged, real power would rest with a few information centres in the world. Where they were located wouldn't really matter because it would be parasitical upon any host. They were in grave danger of reversing a natural order. Instead of using technology for the greater benefit of mankind, people were being used by the huge lakes and mountains of profit made through the creation and usage of technology. The tail would truly wag the dog.

Yes, they had, against all odds, won this little battle against the enemy. Mainwaring simply hadn't realised how large the battlefield really was. So what could they do? Give in? Smile and nod when reassured that all was now well? Agree to disband the United Opposition? And then go gratefully to sleep at nights content that the really savage events would most probably occur after his death?

Sir Jonathan Mainwaring raised his head, realising he had not really been listening, even with one ear. He knew what was being said anyway. From the corner of his eye he saw Haug look at him again, so he turned and gave the man who was fast becoming his closest friend a warm smile. Then he patted him on the shoulder.

"Now," said Norman Stone with what he hoped was a reassuring smile, "General Sessions would like a quick word with you before our departure to London." He stepped and turned towards the refreshment table.

The General got up from his seat and moved easily to the front of the small group. He still had his gloves in one hand.

"I haven't anything to add to the minister's remarks, actually. I simply wanted to advise the company that I propose recommending Mr Joe Wayne Haug to Her Majesty for receipt of the George Medal..."

He was interrupted by spontaneous applause as everyone turned to look at the American whose colour was changing to a bright, luminous red.

"As you know," the General continued, "this is the highest civilian award our country has to offer, though in fact it was a military feat of the highest gallantry and bravado. In my own experience I've never heard or seen anything quite like it." He held up a hand as Haug got to his feet and started to speak. "Just a moment, Mr Haug. I've not quite finished. I understand you have been the recipient of the American Congressional Medal of Honour, amongst other high awards for bravery. I also understand you returned these awards because they conflicted with your own sense of integrity. However, under the circumstances, I hope you will allow me to put forward your name for this honour as a small token of our gratitude."

Haug started to say something from where he was, then decided to step to the front. He smiled and offered his hand to General Sessions.

"Well, thank you, General. That was a mighty kind thang for you to do, and you're the first marine who ever took me completely by surprise." Sessions laughed as Haug continued. "But I gotta tell you right now that I don't believe in medals, and I'd be lyin' if I said I did. I was with a group of people who all cooperated and helped, so why should I get some kinda medal? Mrs Templer, Mr Easton and Mr Tillson held on and didn't give way an inch. Jonathan Mainwarin' and Ewan Thomas whipped 'em with words and dazzled the police and locals. General Portland almost got killed talkin' to Mr Stone. Golding and Simpson risked their jobs to clear our way along the highway. Sam Bernstein and Raul Dominguez, who have not been allowed out here 'cause they're foreigners, did more than I ever could to protect the hostages, buyin' us some time. And by my side, I had three good friends and fighters I could trust. One Time, Keef and Andy. On top of that, General, you came in with a couple of helicopters, and I thought we were gonna have to whip you as well. Sorry. Thanks very much for the thought and the honour, but I just cain't accept it."

Again there was applause. General Sessions' face was expressionless. "Perhaps, then, Mr Haug, you would allow me to make you an honorary Royal Marine. Unofficially, of course."

Haug grinned. "I tell you what, General. As an ex-paratrooper, I'm just gonna swallow my natural pride and accept. In return I make you an honorary North Carolina colonel."

General Sessions smiled as a couple of people laughed. "I shall swallow *my* pride and accept as well."

Sir Jonathan Mainwaring was smiling, too. Genuinely. But behind the smile his thoughts were leading to other thoughts, and those thoughts were leading to doubt. Doubt of himself. And doubt of the only world he knew.

CHAPTER THIRTY

Corky DeLoop opened the door of her Eaton Square flat and looked at Haug for a full ten seconds before she spoke.

"Well," she said finally, "you look a mess. Have you got kicked in the face by a horse?"

"Hiya, Tex," he said and grinned, showing her he'd lost a tooth as well. "You gonna invite me in or embarrass me by just standin' there lustin' after my body?"

She threw back her head and laughed, opening the door wide. "Come on in, hillbilly."

Haug stepped inside and followed her into the sitting room. He took off his dozer cap, threw it on the table and fell into a deep armchair. Corky excused herself for a minute and left the room. He was still tired, even after a night's sleep, mostly because his injuries prevented him from getting comfortable. And Louise Templer stayed until past midnight. They hadn't talked much. She just wanted to lie on the bed with him, cuddling up close while he drank a big glass of Jameson and listened to the Rachmaninov *Vespers*. He had taken a shower and was in his terrytowel robe and, despite himself, became aroused by the closeness of her body. When she realised it, they began to make love. She just took off her jeans, not the top, and straddled him. His nose and mouth hurt too much for anything wild, so he had just laid there moving his hips, touching her with his hands, enjoying the slow, gradual rhythm.

It wasn't the most powerful lovemaking he'd ever experienced, but it wasn't that kind of sex. Really, it was intimate touching between two lonely and temporarily inarticulate human beings. They both came, but it was a clinging and holding orgasm, and afterwards they simply lay together until he fell out of her. They didn't talk much, just held and rocked and murmured. Then she took a shower, called a taxi and kissed him gently on the cheek before leaving.

Corky returned with Harvey Gillmore trotting behind her. He was now wearing a little maid's costume in black nylon with little frilly cuffs, black seamed stockings, high heeled black court shoes and a little white hat. He carried a tray and stared down at it balefully.

Haug took one look and started laughing until his nose bled. "I wouldn't have believed it if I hadn't seen it," he said when he caught his breath.

"Fetch Mr Haug a tissue for his nose, Harv," Corky said sweetly.

Gillmore went to a side table, opened a drawer and put a box of tissues on the tray. Then he walked to Haug and stood there rigidly staring at the wall.

"Why, thank you, missy," he said as he took the box, pulled off a tissue and wiped his nose.

"Would you like a drink, sir?" Gillmore asked in a neutral voice.

"Bring me a beer, boy. Just the can, no glass."

"Yes, sir,"

Haug continued to laugh as the newspaper magnate left the room, walking quite well in his heels now, and a pile of red spotted tissues began to form on the coffee table. He looked over at Corky DeLoop who was wearing a beautiful pink summer dress cut very low between her breasts. She also wore a pair of sandals which displayed her carefully painted toenails.

"Well, ma'am," he said. "I just don't know what to say for once in my life. You gotta tell me how you did it."

"We had a battle, and I won," she said with a big smile as Gillmore returned with one can of beer in the centre of the tray. "Harv just adores my body, don't you, Harv?"

"Yes, Mrs DeLoop," he replied as he placed the can on the coffee table.

"Now run along and continue with your housework while my guest is here."

Haug watched Gillmore walk to the door, then back out with a slight bow before closing it. "I reckon you're just one hell of a woman," he said as he turned back to her. "That bastard has more poison in him than a wheelbarrow fulla water moccasins."

She shook her head. "He's still fulla poison, Haug. Ole Harv and I are playin' a dangerous game together. A game I plan to win. Hell, he signed over this apartment to me. I own it

562

now. All of it. No mortgage. Now I got a place to hide til Herk gets lonesome for Texas..."

"That's what I've come to talk to you about, Corky. Your husband. He's dead." He paused for a moment as Corky opened her eyes wide. He picked up the box of tissues. "You can have one of these, if you're gonna bust into tears."

She put her pink lower lip into her mouth and bit it softly. "You're not bullshittin' me, are you, Haug? Herk is dead?"

"Yep, that's right." He took a big sip of his beer.

"Eeeeeeee...hawwwwwww!" she yelled, bouncing up from the sofa and doing a little miniature square dance while she sang the first four lines of *The Eyes of Texas Are Upon You*. Then she bent down and gave him a big kiss right in the middle of his forehead. "Haug...that is the *best* news I ever had in my life. Here I was thinkin' I'd have to rebuild everything after sacrificin' some of my best years with that fat slob. Now I get his money as well as a fine little shack in London. Hell, we oughta go gamblin'. I'm on a roll!"

He nodded his head sadly. "It's just like I thought. I knew you were gonna be awful torn up about it. I always hate to be the one who tells the relatives. It's a mournful task."

Corky grabbed the door and opened it. "Harv! Bring *me* a beer, too. No, wait a minute. Bring me a glass of Wild Turkey and lots of ice." She turned back to Haug. "I cain't believe it. Ole Herk dead! Let the party begin! Did you kill him?"

Haug ran his tongue across the painful root of his tooth and winced. "I was about to when a stray bullet caught him in the neck. Last time I saw him he was bleedin' on a rug that looked like it cost over a half a million."

She stopped dancing suddenly and looked worried. "You sure he's dead?"

"Well, I didn't have time to do an autopsy, but he didn't have any more throb at his neck arteries. Which means he didn't have any blood for his brain."

"Oh, hell, he never had enough brain to need any blood," she said, still a little worried.

Gillmore re-entered after a little knock on the door, came in and placed the drink on a small table nearest Corky DeLoop. On

563

second thought, he picked up the drink and put a folded napkin underneath before replacing it on the table.

Haug watched the Australian closely. The hooded eyes were set in the sullen face like two black olive stones.

"Just a minute, boy," Haug growled at him as he started to leave again. Gillmore stopped. "You remember me?"

"Yes," the publisher said after a pause.

"You remember Beth Howell?" Haug asked. Beth had been the wife of Gillmore's chauffeur.

"Yes," Gillmore's voice was low, almost dangerous.

"Well," Haug said, "I'm gonna tell this lady all about Beth, and I just hope she beats the holy shit outta you for what you did. And you're lucky she found you before I did, 'cause your ass wouldn't make good fish bait after I finished with you." He waited a minute, and Gillmore remained were he was, trembling either with fear or rage. "You can go now, boy."

"Who is this?" Corky asked as Gillmore closed the door. "Beth who?"

Haug told her the story. The Australian terrorised the chauffeur's wife, estranging her from her husband, and, after torturing her with guilt, used her as a sexual doormat. The woman finally reached the end of her psychological tether and threw herself into the Thames after Gillmore colluded in her husband's death.

DeLoop's face clouded with disgust. "I guess he's spent his whole life snarin' women and fuckin' 'em up. I kinda got an insight into the little bastard now, though, and I'd almost feel sorry for him if I wasn't so hell bent on revenge."

Haug took another pull from his can of beer. "There's a lot of thangs not very nice about revenge, but I tell you somethin'. It sure does make you feel a lot better."

Corky leaned forward, and Haug couldn't resist looking right down her cleavage. She used her fingers to count. "He's got money, and he's got power. And with these he traps women in this web of his to control them."

"Power means control," he added. "The more power you have, the more control over other people. For my money, Gillmore is a perfect livin' individual example of the political values of today. His newspapers profess a phony moral tone while feedin' his readers gobs of sleazy sex and glamourous violence."

She reached over and took a long sip of the Wild Turkey. "You know somethin'? He's never loved anybody. Not even himself. For him, sex is love. Somethin' you can buy or force somebody to do. But the sex doesn't satisfy him, so he punishes the woman! But I found out somethin' funny. *He* likes punishment, too. There's so much guilt inside that little creep sloppin' around like thick vomit."

"How did you do it?" He was really puzzled.

"He flipped out about my body," she said with a coy smile. "Some wires came loose somewhere. So now I just dangle it in front of him like a piece of candy he cain't have."

"I imagine you're pretty used to men flippin' out about your body," he said, still gazing at the valley between her breasts.

She leaned back on the sofa and did a kind of waggle with her chest. "Well, I *got* it. So why not use it while I can? You gotta remember, when women reach your age, their value starts dropping like shares in a depression. Men don't have that problem, honey, so they don't understand. I got maybe ten years - maybe a little more if I find a good doctor. And now that I got lots of money, I am gonna have myself one fine time. And you know what?" She paused for a moment before answering her own question. "I don't even feel bad about it. Naw. I feel great."

"Well, one day, Tex, when you're tired of prancing' around on pretty horses and wanna get your legs around an ole mangy Brahma bull that'll give you a real good buckin', I'll invite you to my rodeo."

She threw her head back and laughed again, shaking her soft platinum hair. "Honey, after I ride you, you won't be fit for anything but munchin' grass in a pasture."

He roared, making his nose bleed again. "And your ass'll be so sore you'll walk bowlegged."

Corky took another drink of Wild Turkey. "Well, why don't we find out right now whether your dick is as big as your mouth?"

565

"Any musician'll tell you it's not the size of the instrument that counts. It's the way you play it."

"I'll be the judge of that," she said with a wicked smile as she smacked the seat beside her on the sofa. "Why don't you bring your fiddle over here and let me tune it for you."

Haug looked at the Texan, as gorgeous and as lush as the Mekong Delta. He realised the blood was pounding in his temples, and his loins were tingling. "We gotta raincheck this thang, honey. You're more temptin' than a gold plated Harley, and I'm already startin' to sweat. But I only came today 'cause One Time is no good at words, and you had to be told about your husband. But right now he's goin' through his whole wardrobe to find just the right mix of fancy threads so he can high step over here in style."

She raised an eyebrow. "You turnin' me down, big feller?"

"One Time's a friend of mine," he said simply.

Again she laughed and clapped her hands together. "Well, there's a first time for everything," she said as she got up from the sofa and grabbed her drink. She stood up, legs apart, and held out her glass towards him. "To the Carolina hillbilly who turned down the finest piece of ass that walks the face of the earth."

Haug got up and held out his can to touch her glass. He had a big grin on his face. "I said *raincheck*, didn't I? I definitely wanna come to another game on another day. I'm sure it'll be just as good then as it would be now."

She put her arms around his neck, holding her glass behind his head. She was as tall as he was, and their eyes were locked together. "I am no man's property, you know. That goes for Harvey Gillmore and One Time and you."

He put his hands around her waist. "One thang about me, Corky. I don't sneak on friends. That goes for One Time, and I reckon it goes for you, too. What I do behind your back is nothin' I wouldn't do in front of your face. That's the way *I* like to live."

"Nobel sentiments." She kissed him on the cheek and took her arms away. "I lived a different kinda life, Haug. Everybody expects a woman to do everything for somebody else, and I just kicked like a mule at that little idea. Know what I mean? I wanna live for *myself*, right?"

"That's what Gillmore wants, too."

She shook her head violently. "Hell, I'm not talkin' about walkin' all over everybody else, but I am talkin' about walkin' tall without steppin' aside for every dude in the road. I got a right to my piece of the sidewalk. And I like sex. So if you want it with me, you gotta take it on *my* terms."

"If I say the same thang, that'll mean we don't fuck."

She nodded in agreement. "That might be true, and it might just be a pity if it *is* true."

"There might just be another way to do it, Tex."

"Well, I'm willin' to try anything, honey, if it's likely to be a lotta fun." She finished her drink and put the empty glass back on the table. "Meanwhile, since I am now loaded - and I mean *loaded* - why don't I take you all to some fancy restaurant. We'll rent the whole place for the night and have a real blowout. You and One Time and...who's the other feller?"

"Keef. And Nightmare Andy. Sam Bernstein and Raul Dominguez."

"And Sarah Courtney. And...yeah. That's a good idea. Bring that real good lookin' girlfriend of yours, and let me see what kinda competition I got in front of me. And that is a real generous offer," she added, "as I *hate* serious competition."

"Well," he said, picking up his dozer cap, "you tell me the night and the place, and we'll be there. I could do with a little fun myself." He walked toward the door, then turned back to her. "And you be careful of that little shit. Any problem, call me or One Time."

* * *

Louise Templer stood in her kitchen door with a mug of tea in her hand watching a squirrel lope towards the big tree in the back of her garden. She sat down carefully on the door ledge and stretched her feet out in front of her. She was wearing a pair of shorts and plimsolls, and the sun was warm on her bare legs. Last night, after she left Haug's flat, she spoke to her husband on

567

the telephone. He was still in Oxford and had no idea what had happened to her, so she left the explaining for another time in order not to worry him.

She had slept late that morning but didn't really feel rested. She recalled traces of disturbing dreams but couldn't remember many details. During a brief period of time her life had changed, she knew that. That was the easy bit of assessment. Weighing the change and assimilating it was more complex. After her harrowing experiences she now felt she had been playing at politics, observing the rules, going through the motions, swimming with the current. It was like tennis. Or cards. Gains and losses were minimal so long as you played cautiously - by the rules. And by the rules was the only way you could play. Any unsportmanlike behaviour would not be tolerated. Talk about *real* problems, respond fully and emotionally and she would be ostracized first from the front bench, then the House, then her constituency. The game must be played in a certain way or you were not allowed to play anymore.

It wasn't so much her abduction and captivity and the terror and killing which slid open these doors for her. It had much to do with her sexual experiences with Haug. She realised there were floodgates within - floodgates she had pretended to ignore all her life. In fact she had been holding them closed with an iron will. For fear of the unknown. For fear of chaos. It was the lovemaking in the rain which finally blasted open the steel doors. That day was still so real to her she could feel the cold water of the stream on her body and that glorious feeling of wanting to show her tingling naked body to all the world. No, Louise Templer did not feel any guilt at all. It was wonder she felt, overpowering wonder. That day, that moment had given her a wholly new view of her life and the world around her. Politics. What was that? Yes, she always felt passionate about politics. But it was a cold intellectual passion, the passion of a mathematician peering at a tricky problem. Now she could see a different linkage she had spent much of her life denying. And the reason was she had been trying to compete with men, beat them at their own games, out-think them, out manoeuvre them, outwit them, prove that *this* woman was different. That she was as good as they were at *their game*.

How, though, could you separate reason from emotion? More importantly, *why* should you? She had not bottled up her emotions because of being frigid or afraid of sex, no that was the wrong angle entirely. She froze them out because that was one of the rules of the game, wasn't it? Margaret Thatcher leapt into her mind like the witch of the western world. It now seemed clear to her that Thatcher's success was based on the power of her emotion which swept all before her. It was venomous, deadly emotion, oozing from a deep suppurating cancer and sprayed out with killer jets. Everything it touched withered and died, and it very nearly killed the country itself.

There must be some way, she thought, to bring together emotion and spirit with the intellect. Not to kill, but to bring forth life. Perhaps there was such a thing as good and evil after all. Thatcher and the dark, stifling world which gave birth to the twisted and criminally insane seemed to her so satanic as to personify evil. When the darkness fell over the land, the foul mushrooms like Regis and Fine and Gillmore grew on the potent stalks of power, sucking out strength until they grew bigger and fatter and their moldy spores stuck wetly to all life forms, bringing more sickness and darkness.

Trying to defeat such a Terror with reason was doomed to failure. Louise Templer knew she must learn how to bring the two mighty potions together. Like Margaret Thatcher did. Unlike her, however, she would try to bring clean air fit to breathe, enough food so no one starved, affordable housing for all, the best medical care for every citizen. At the same time and with the same passion she could turn to British industry. Restore what had been throttled and strangled and cheapened and sold off and closed down. Maybe another Jeanne D'Arc was needed, this time an English one, to raise aloft a shining sword for Good. Maybe that was the meaning of good and evil, really. Maybe it was embedded in folk tales for a purpose. The Reason of life and death recharged with Emotion in the realm of Spirit.

Louise Templer took another sip of her tea, now gone tepid. Looking up, she thought even her garden looked different.

569

The weather on the weekend remained warm and bright and sunny, and the big Harley Electro Glide throbbed its big double heartbeat on the A road as they made their way leisurely to Brighton. The road was rolling and snaky in the Sussex Downs, and the trees almost met overhead, dappling the tarmac with diamond bright patches of sunlight. Haug wasn't going fast, just over fifty miles an hour. That was the best way to ride a Harley. Majestically. Cars overtook him, but with caution, the occupants looking at them with curiosity or envy or admiration or distaste. But they all looked. They couldn't help themselves. A full dress Harley in the English countryside is as out of place and out of time as a tricerotops loping down the road. Haug thought about taking the Triumph T160, a lean British machine made for roads like this. But on second thoughts he decided on the Harley. Besides, he wanted to give Jonathan a treat, a taste of pure Americana undiluted by any cultural ambiguities.

He almost burst out laughing when he saw Mainwaring emerge from his house that morning dressed in an expensive herringbone sports jacket, tartan scarf, a pair of old goggles he used when driving the Morgan, a flat tweed cap and knee-length handmade hunting boots. His first comment was that his friend looked like a joke Englishman. Mainwaring tartly observed he was a perfect complement, then, for a joke American.

Haug wore a sleeveless Harley T-shirt with a big American bald eagle on the front grasping the logo in its claws. He had half a cigar stuffed in his mouth underneath the Hi-way Patrol sunglasses. The gloves were thin leather fingerless, and the cuffs of his jeans were turned up over engineering boots. Mainwaring mounted gingerly after much difficulty putting on the helmet and sat with the knees of his long thin legs as high as Haug's shoulders. Leaning on the backrest he felt quite comfortable, despite his awkward-looking position. As they burbled down the driveway, Sarah stood at the door with arms folded looking quite dubious.

Haug had promised him a ride on the Harley and finally talked him into it. A trip to Brighton was agreed, though they knew it would probably be crowded on a warm weekend. There was still a little bruising and swelling around his nose, but Haug didn't notice it much anymore. His cheek was X-rayed and a small piece of bone was mobile, but he thought he could probably live with it. His dentist had done well, and a new front tooth had been glued into place only the day before. He couldn't honestly tell the difference. It felt like his old tooth.

But he had been thinking of the dinner party Corky had thrown at a posh SW1 Chinese restaurant. She booked the whole place for the evening, courtesy of Harvey Gillmore's gold Amex. Haug hadn't eaten so much good food for years, platters and platters of it in the most exotic presentations. Jennifer Montgomery had come with him, and he would always remember Corky DeLoop's face when she met her. It actually drained of blood as she looked the English woman up and down. Haug had warned Jennifer beforehand, so she was delighted to dress for the occasion in a knee length gossamer white silk dress that followed every line and crevasse of her body, yet moved freely when she walked. She wore white stockings and little delicate silver sandals with a moderate heel. She was in complete contrast with Corky who had decided to wear her red shiny rubber number with the outrageous high heels, making her the tallest person in the room. Her platinum hair was light and frothy, haloed in the lights. When Corky entered the restaurant, one of the Chinese waiters was so stunned he looked like an oriental pillar of salt. Hor d'oeuvres slid slowly off the end of his tray and the noise of their crash onto the floor woke him from his trance.

If Jennifer Montgomery was a beautifully cut diamond, Corky DeLoop was an outrageously large, light-refracting ruby. As the Texan surveyed the beautiful English woman, she muttered that she could understand now why she had been turned down. In the end the two women got along famously. At first Jennifer was quite frosty, but soon she warmed to Corky's mighty humour and extravagant sexuality. One Time was dressed immaculately in dinner jacket and bow tie. Everybody wore a coat and tie but Haug, even Nightmare Andy. It was the only time Andy ever looked comical. Sam Bernstein got drunk and was a surprisingly good raconteur. Keef brought his wife, Wendy, who watched the battle between Corky and Jennifer with great delight, sometimes laughing too much to eat. Raul Dominguez seemed relaxed for the first time Haug had known him. He and Bernstein appeared to be developing a professional friendship.

Haug and Jennifer caught a taxi back to her house at two o'clock in the morning. They began screwing, standing in the hall the moment she closed the door. Both were fully clothed, but they had been touching in the taxi. Just touching gently and electrically. The charges built up to dangerous proportions, and neither she nor Haug could wait any longer. He unzipped his jeans and entered from underneath her French knickers. It was an explosion, a discharge of passion that could not wait a moment longer. Then he carried her up the stairs to the bedroom, stopping several times so they could kiss and whisper to each other. When they finally reached the bed, they undressed and got under the covers, holding on, fondling and caressing until the electrical charges built up again. It was longer that time, beginning gently and slowly but ending in a wild, tearing, thunderous, exhausting, thrashing tangle of limbs. The sounds of their voices built into a crescendo, cursing and swearing, guttural and screaming - the unmistakable sounds of two lovers desperate for the moment and desperate to prolong it forever.

One of the most attractive features of motorcycles is how easy they are to park, and Haug found a place quite near the pier. He held the bike while Mainwaring dismounted, then opened the top box and dropped their two helmets inside after removing his dozer cap and Mainwaring's tweed cap. After locking the machine, they walked slowly toward the pier. It was not yet noon, but the pier and beaches were already swarming with tourists.

Sir Jonathan Mainwaring clasped his hands behind his back. "It's not a proper motorcycle, you know. Nevertheless, the journey was comfortable, so I shan't complain."

"Well, that is a surprise, Jonathan. I suppose if I'd had an old Norton Dominator wideline with a seat like a board, you'd have felt more at home." Then he grinned. "But I got to admit those featherbed frames still cain't be beat. They go around curves damn near horizontal. If the limeys had a mind to do it, they could still build the best motorsickles in the world."

Mainwaring didn't answer at once. He looked at the crowds, then removed his jacket and scarf. It was quite warm. "I'm sorry, Haug. I've been preoccupied since the recent traumatic events ended, appropriately, at an asylum. Beginning with my incarceration. Even Brighton looks alien. Still vulgar and faintly attractive. But now the people seem more tense, less relaxed, more compelled. Perhaps it is because I am now an adult and see it through different eyes, but I don't think so. There have been external changes. And recently, inner ones as well."

They were walking through the arcades, moving down the pier towards the end. Even the sea breeze was warm. Hundreds of kids punched buttons on electronic machines, begged for sweets or money or cheap trinkets, queued with parents for rides or T-shirts or teddies.

"I knew somethin' had happened," Haug replied. "I could see you kinda withdraw from thangs, but I was only partly surprised, seein' what you went through."

"I'm not a little Englander," Mainwaring continued. "Nor do I consider myself chauvinist. Nor do I think Britain is the greatest country the world has ever known. Far from it. But some kind of balance must be struck, Haug, mustn't it? Obviously we are part of a world community, a community beginning to search for mechanisms of economic balance where everyone everywhere has opportunity for fulfilment. I think it would be ruinous if it were all the same. Or if one or two cultures were overly dominant. Those who live on this little island - and those islands elsewhere - must be allowed their uniqueness or living would be hellish."

They were reaching the end of the pier, and both men leaned their elbows on the railings and looked across the sea at the horizon.

"I'm not sure I am capable of framing my new ideas just yet, Haug. Which is why I wanted to talk to you. We are obviously quite different people, yet there is an underlying sympathy and compassion in you which is refreshing. Besides, you are a good listener."

"I'm a good listener only to good talkers," Haug replied, still looking out at the sun reflecting off the ocean.

"Britain is being swept up in change. By 'swept up' I mean the residents have little to say about the course or the speed or even the conditions on board. We have been swept into the EEC because there is apparently no alternative as large alliances form in both East and West. Our industry was undermined because they had to compete with rebuilt countries after the war, and we had no money to invest in rebuilding. Rather we had the money, but it inevitably followed easier and quicker returns elsewhere. Now we have an army and air force and navy with virtually no interests or empire to defend. And who could we fight? Modern components must be purchased from Japan or America. Therefore we have little control, even of our armed forces."

He removed his tweed cap and held it in his free hand. "I know that feeling from my so-called interrogation. Loss of control. The darkness inside covered everything that was bright and free. I had no hope, no self-esteem, no confidence, no wish for anything but for the pain to stop when I was lying naked on the floor. That feeling is still with me, Haug, and it undermines my entire being."

Haug took off his own cap before the wind blew it off. "Well, Jonathan, there are millions of folks who live with that feelin' all their lives. I hate that you had to see it like you did. Some people go from cradle to grave feelin' little else. And most of the people who have the power, the control, don't give a shit. They use these people to make fortunes for themselves and to gain more power. It comes out in violence against their families or neighbours or in drinkin' and self destruction. And it's a waste. We waste all those millions and millions of people who have the same equipment we have. But all they are used for is to labour when there is work to do and to be thrown in the garbage when the work runs out. Disposable people. It's like

Coca Cola. Suck out the drink and throw the empty bottle in the ocean, like those floatin' down there."

Mainwaring paused for a few moments. "These were alien thoughts at one time in my life, and I still feel what you say is a little simplistic. What concerns me, I suppose, concerns me because it has always been my job. Try and see the entire chess board, the strategy. But I believe your analogy is sound. These huge economic entities, the transnational companies, the gigantic economic groupings forming East and West - I can well see they are using us, the British, as a disposable country. Indeed. We are helpless without basic industry, Haug. Others can come and go with their money and factories, whilst we bob around like corks. As for democracy, we have little say in the matter."

"Oh, you got somethin' to say alright. 'Yassuh, boss - and nosuh, boss,' just like the slaves in the old South. Or the Indians and Chinese and blacks durin' the high tide of the British Empire."

Mainwaring slapped his cap against the railing. "Damn it, man, I didn't come to the seashore to stand at the end of the pier. We must roll up our trousers. Get our feet wet."

"Tell me somethin'," Haug said as they turned away and started back. "How come your hair always stays in place, even in a strong wind?"

"Because I was trained as a child how it should be groomed, and it has always been combed just that way. And to be completely honest, I use a dab of what they now call gel on it."

When they returned to the Harley, Mainwaring and Haug took off their boots and put them in one of the panniers, rolled up their trousers and tenderly stepped off towards the beach. The pebbles were hot and uncomfortable to tender feet, and they walked as quickly as they could down to the water. Haug pulled off his T-shirt and stuffed the end of it into his back pocket. The water was icy cold.

"Jesus Christ," Haug said. "I keep forgettin' this water comes from the North Pole."

"It's not cold," Mainwaring replied. "It would be if it weren't for the Gulf Stream. Americans are such sissies. It's perfect for swimming, save for the effluent from the sewers, of course."

Haug was distracted by two girls lying near the water's edge, one in a tiny bikini with the top off, the other in a very high cut one piece. They had a portable stereo between them. He stopped and stared.

"It's like a barbecue all laid out on the table ready for eatin'. I bet they are lip-smackin', finger-lickin' good."

The girl in the one piece, aware she had attracted the eyes of a male, turned and looked briefly at Haug before turning away again with a look of bored disgust on her face.

He chuckled and walked on. "I guess she doesn't know a real high class man when she sees one."

Mainwaring made a small noise of distaste. "How did you get that big, Haug?" He rolled up the sleeve of his shirt and placed his arm next to the American's. "Look at the difference in the size. It's obscene. Your wrist must be larger than my ankle."

"I'm just an advanced model, Jonathan. Don't feel bad about it."

"More like a simian throwback than an advanced model, surely," Mainwaring murmured as he bent down to pick up a stone. He examined the stone carefully, lost in thought. "Decadence," he said finally. "Decadence."

"Who? Me or you?"

"Look around you. Here on the beach or in London. No one genuinely seems to be enjoying themselves, but everyone is in hot pursuit of enjoyment, of pleasure. Children screeching for another ice cream, families loaded down with junk they've struggled to bring to the beach. Umbrellas, audio systems, hampers of food, folding chairs, coolers for drink - all packed into the family automobile to move in slow traffic queues to the seaside. Then unloaded and dragged two hundred yards with the children and dogs. And still they are not happy. All that work, all that trouble, with happiness still a remote horizon. Why do they do it? It is decadence. Each individual desperate to find the right palliative, and all that is achieved is greater depths of desperation."

After a long pause Haug nodded. "Yeah. It's the wrong translation of democracy, isn't it? Freedom of each individual to do whatever he wants so long as he's got the money to do it. Nevermind that it might foul the water or the air - hell, I don't wanna lissen to that crap music those two broads were playin'. Every one of em's sayin' 'what I want is important,' 'cause that's what they've been taught. That's what they read in the papers and see on TV. That's what they get from their parents, each one wantin' this or that and doin' it whatever the cost. Keepin' folks unhappy must be part of the market economy. 'Buy this trinket, and you'll be happier.' You buy it and are happy for two seconds before you throw it away and buy somethin' else..."

Mainwaring had stopped and was looking out to sea. "By instinct they know this is - or was - a beautiful place. Yet the water is syrupy with rubbish and chemicals and human excrement. And even here, with the breeze, your lungs fill up with carbon expelled from the obligatory automobile each family must now have. Natural vegetation has been felled for roads to carry them and concrete to park them on. They come to what was once a beautiful place, carried perhaps in folk memory, to confront the same stressful world they left behind in London or Birmingham."

Haug took off his Harley dozer cap. "I was brought up in this so-called democratic world of individualism. I'm a foreigner here in this country. I ride Harleys and drive pickups...to be an individual. But what I feel most lonesome for is a real community, even a real family. Where everybody's workin' for somethin' decent. I probably won't have a family and won't find a community."

Mainwaring raised a bony finger. "Yet where is the political apparatus for a community-based democracy which allows for individual differences? The Nazis presented one argument, didn't they? A few narrow-minded individuals decided what kind of ideal community they wanted and slaughtered all those who did not step through the template. However, they were briefly successful. The communist countries, on the other hand, were very tolerant of some differences, intolerant of others."

577

"Well," said Haug, "I fought against a so-called communist country, and the most powerful nation in the world got their asses whipped. A skinny bunch of rice farmers and fishermen beat Japan, then France, then America. Because they all had one purpose, and they were passionate about that purpose. America has great weapons for fightin' at a distance, so the Cong fought up close. They called this 'huggin' the belt.' We had choppers to carry us places, and they walked. They ate a tenth of what we ate, less than that. But the main thang is, they had a purpose and we didn't. What you see layin' around here are people without any purpose at all. Except maybe readin' *The News*, watchin' a soap, buyin' a new car, eatin' an ice cream, gettin' laid. Yeah, I guess you could call that decadent."

Mainwaring was still staring out at the sea, motionless. "Is that why we gave it all up? Aimlessness?"

Haug scratched his bald head and put his cap back on. "I think what would surprise a lotta these people in the West, here, Germany, France, America, is that they live in a totalitarian society, not a democratic one. That's what it is, if you look at the thang. Big business has to make a profit and satisfy shareholders, not the citizens of the country. They have one purpose, and the people have another. The businesses lean on governments, and they lean on the people. Advertisements are everywhere. Buy this, easy terms. When that's worn out, buy somethin' else. Movies are censored by market forces. So is TV, even books to some extent. But nobody reads books anymore anyway, so they don't matter. When it comes time to put your vote in the ballot box, people vote to cut their own throats 'cause that's what they have drummed into their ears ever minute of the day. We cain't have a real alternative party, 'cause political parties cost dough. Socialist parties don't own newspapers or TV stations, 'cause who's gonna advertise in 'em? Individuals? That's a big laugh. They're just a herd of sheep, munchin' away on the grass, waitin' to be fleeced or eaten one at a time."

Mainwaring turned and continued to walk, dodging a frolicking dog. "I'm not a socialist, Haug, nor will I ever be. The arguments sound fine, but corruption always filters in, doesn't it? I do value the merits of democracy, whatever the economic system. The people in control. If, that is, they know what they want any longer. That is all I am fighting for with the United Opposition. That is my remit. This is my country and, because of accident of birth, I rather like it."

He stopped again and turned back out to the sea. "If you look far enough towards the horizon, it is still beautiful, much like my distant ancestors must have viewed Brighton from the beaches. Just raise your eyes and don't turn back and look too closely at what is behind you. Close your ears to the pop music, and perhaps even hold your breath for a moment. I personally believe I was lucky to have such a majestic inheritance, and I refuse to let it be squandered without a fight."

Mainwaring sighed briefly and began to walk slowly again, enjoying the feel of wet sand between his toes and the cold hardness of the pebbles. "I shall be returning to Westminster next week..."

"Hell," Haug said suddenly as he threw a stone out to sea. "I brought you down here to have a good time, and here we are talkin' about thangs we can talk about any time in London. Let's go get a big greasy bag of fish and chips and eat 'em while we're tryin' to find a decent pub with a good pint of Guinness and a dart board. Just for your sake, I'll be an Englishman for a day."

Mainwaring laughed out loud. "You couldn't possibly be an Englishman, even if you spent the rest of your life in deep study. But, yes. Fish and chips and a good pint. Splendid idea."

They turned away from the sea and walked tenderly back towards the concrete pavement and the slow moving tangle of cars.

SPLIT INFINITIES

ABOUT THE AUTHOR

Born in a small rural town in North Carolina, Bill Bailey began his itinerant life after graduating from university with a degree in philosophy. Subsequently ejected by the US Army, he found work as a prison guard in Canada before briefly prospecting for gold in British Columbia. Having meanwhile accidentally married a Texan heiress, he moved to Houston, Texas where he managed a ranch, scrambled motorbikes, rallied sports cars, worked as a bouncer, taught English and French, cut wheat and organised the first white collar union in the US meat-packing industry. Backing quickly away from Texas after stumbling into the acting profession he moved to London. Within a year of his arrival he became the first full-frontal male nude on the British stage. In the course of his acting career he has worked extensively in film – in Hollywood and Europe – television and London's West End. He now lives with a foul-mouthed parrot called Dizzy.

Printed in the United Kingdom
by Lightning Source UK Ltd.
9843400001B/2